The Indian War Novels

The Indian War Novels

The Horsemen of the Plains
★
The Last of the Chiefs

Joseph A. Altsheler

LEONAUR

The Indian War Novels: The Horsemen of the Plains
& The Last of the Chiefs
by Joseph A. Altsheler

Leonaur is an imprint of Oakpast Ltd

Material original to this edition, this editorial selection and
presentation of text in this form copyright © 2011 Oakpast Ltd

ISBN: 978-0-85706-693-0 (hardcover)
ISBN: 978-0-85706-694-7 (softcover)

http://www.leonaur.com

Publisher's Notes

The views expressed in this book are not necessarily
those of the publisher.

Contents

The Horsemen of the Plains   7

The Last of the Chiefs   231

The Horsemen
of the Plains

CHAPTER 1

Friends in Need

A boy sat in a little room in the frontier town of Omaha. It was a poor and cheap place. A flimsy table stood in one corner, an equally flimsy bed in another, and one or two pictures from newspapers were tacked on the bare, pine walls. There was no carpet on the floor. Nothing showed quality, except a rifle that lay across the foot of the bed.

The weapon was a fine breech-loader, advanced in type for the time, and a skilful hand had carved initials and several graceful little decorations on the stock. Anyone would surmise that it was highly prized by its owner.

The boy himself was a match for his rifle, a stalwart youth, seventeen years old, with the stature and strength of a man. His brown hair, cut short, curled just a little, and his blue eyes were set wide apart, as they usually are in those of large minds. His face was brown with tan, but, at the edge of the collar, his fair white skin showed.

A comely boy, and a strong and brave one, as the most casual observer would have inferred. But he was dressed poorly, and the look upon his face, just now, was not cheerful, although his was a nature disposed to see the better side of things, and he had all the flush of early youth. The window was open, and he gazed out of it, but saw little, because his thoughts, for the moment, were turned elsewhere.

What the blue eyes did not see was an expanse of new wooden houses, built hastily for shelter, and not for beauty, unpaved streets, with sidewalks of boards, and, beyond them, the circling eddies of a great brown river that flowed from regions yet largely unknown.

But a sky of an extraordinary, brilliant blue curved over the new town. The same intense vivid light that showed all the crudeness of the houses and streets, surcharged the air with buoyancy and hope, and made the world itself seem very beautiful.

The wind was blowing steadily out of the west, and it was a remarkable wind. It swept over two thousand miles of clean land, as pure as the sea, but it was touched with a faint odour of coming spring, of the young grass beginning to appear on the boundless plains, and of the buds breaking forth in the mountain forests.

The note of the wind at last reached the boy. He raised his head a little, and the indefinable perfume, faint in fact but powerful in fancy, entered his nostrils, and all his senses were keenly stirred. The blue eyes turned toward the west, and they began to see at last. But they did not see the rough wooden houses and the muddy streets. They saw the vast west, that lay beyond the white man's plough, the land of the unknown, of mystery, of the shaggy buffalo herd, and the pitiless Indian. It was an enchanted region, none the less so because of its dangers, and just now it was calling to the boy in a voice that he must hear.

He bent his head a little toward the wind, and gradually the gloom went from his face. The blue eyes grew bright as became his years and his mind roamed far in pleasant lands, through great adventures.

He left the window presently, and, going to the bed, took up the rifle, which he handled with affection. It had belonged to his father who fell three years before, in the great Civil War, at the Battle of the Wilderness, and he had left little but this fine weapon and his memory, to his son.

The war was over a year and Robert Norton, without either father or mother or any near relative, had wandered into this frontier town, not knowing what he was going to do. He had no plan. He had spent a little time with an emigrant train; he had helped farmers to break horses, but, passing from one task to another, he had been moving steadily westward.

He did not realize until now the direction in which his course had taken him, but when he saw it he also understood it. It was the great west, the mighty west, the west of mystery and romance that always beckoned him. Since he could remember he had heard of it, the wonderful tales of the Forty-Niners, the plains, the mountains, the wild animals, the wild Indians, the gold, the furs and the danger.

Now, with the feel of the rifle in his hands, he took his resolution. He would go into this vast and yet wild west, and fend for himself. One could not go alone, but he might find comrades, and there was no better place than this town of Omaha, the point of departure for the plains, in which to look for them.

All his confidence returned. The tide of early youth was at the full, and, rifle on shoulder, he left the house, going into the fresh, perfumed air, which still blew strongly from the great regions of mystery. Many people were in the unpaved streets, and, like himself, they were occupied with thoughts of the west. Their faces were seldom turned eastward.

The fact that a boy was carrying a rifle attracted no attention. Nearly everybody carried either rifles or pistols and often both, and there was abundant need of them. Before a man went many miles west of Omaha his life depended solely upon his own skill and courage.

The crowd in the street interested the boy greatly. It was a cheerful throng, thinking little of the dangers it was about to face. An emigrant train would start for California by the Santa Fe route in the morning, some gold-seekers would leave a few hours later for the mountains of the far north-west, and a pony express was just going.

Robert looked at both the emigrant train and the gold-seekers, but he decided that he would not apply for membership in either party.

His walk took him toward the river, and he stood looking at the brown stream, his face turned towards its source. His feeling of mystery and fascination was deepened by the Missouri, which was not in itself a beautiful object. But it came from the unknown, the lands that he longed to enter.

While he looked, a half dozen boats, flat and broad, manned by perhaps thirty men, appeared, floating on the muddy current. The men were clothed partly in white garb and partly in skins. Their faces were almost as brown as those of Indians, and their hair grew long. Everyone was well armed, and the boats were filled with large bales.

The boy knew that they were fur hunters, returning from a successful expedition, probably lasting two or three years, into the Rocky Mountains. They appealed to him more than either the emigrants or the gold-seekers, and he regarded them eagerly. What wonders they must have seen and what deeds they must have done!

"Looks as ef they had been somewhere, don't they?" said a cheery voice beside him.

The boy turned abruptly. He had not noticed the approach of anyone, but the voice was so deep, it had such a round, full and hearty tone, that he knew an honest heart must have inspired the speech.

He beheld a man of middle height, but uncommonly big of bone and very powerful. He had thick curly hair, rosy cheeks and a magnificent set of large, white teeth. All of his dress was civilized but a raccoon skin cap, with the short tail hanging down behind. He was fully armed, carrying a fine rifle on his shoulder and a revolver and knife at his belt. But he had a wonderfully ingratiating smile, and the heart of the lonely boy warmed to him at once.

"Trappers comin' back," said the stranger, nodding toward the men in the boat, "an' they've been in luck. They've got somethin' worth sellin'. Took a long time though."

"Wish I was with a party like that, going instead of coming," said the boy. "I'd like to be a fur hunter."

"Good trade," said the man, "an' it ain't dead yet, by no means. Has its dangers, though. Injuns, lots of 'em. Look out for 'em. But do not be a pessimist, my boy. It's a habit."

Robert stared and the man smiled back at him in a gratified way.

"I'm always hopin' for the best. It's comforting" he said. "My name is Sam Strong an' I come from Kentucky, but I've been a hunter an' trapper more than ten years. What's your name?"

"Robert Norton," replied the boy, not at all offended by the question, which was natural on the border.

"Robert, h—m! That's long for Bob. Bob's better, and Bob it will be."

"As you like," said Bob smiling.

"Now, Bob," said Sam Strong, "I saw you standin' here lookin' at them fur boats, an' I knew what you was thinkin'. You was wantin' to be out in the wilderness yourself takin' furs."

"That is so," said Bob frankly, "you read me right."

"An' you was lookin' tre-men-je-ous lonesome, but there's a good time comin' for you. Now Bob, you want to go fur-huntin', an' fur-huntin' you shall go."

"What do you mean?" asked Bob, his whole face beaming. Sam Strong of the twinkling eyes already inspired confidence in him.

"Didn't I just tell you I was a trapper an' hunter? I'm one of a little band that's just startin' out, an' we need another. You want to go, an' we take you. So we kill one bird with two stones."

Bob smiled at his mixture of the proverb, but he was happy. His heart had cried for a friend, and he was finding one.

"I'll go with you," he cried, "I'll go anywhere with you, and I'll do my part of the work."

"An' your part of the fightin' too, I take it, if any is to be done. Well, variety is the salt an' pepper of life, an' you an' me, an' the rest of the fellers ought to see some lively times together, Bob. I'm takin' you on faith, an' you're takin' me the same way. Come along."

They left the river, and went back toward the centre of the town, the minds of both intent upon the business ahead. The crowd was still lively, and, in one or two places, it had become turbulent. The cause of the turbulence was obvious. The trapper looked at the offenders in disgust.

The eyes of Sam Strong, usually so benevolent, snapped with disapproval. "Fools! Little children!" he said. "Seems strange to me, Bob, that anybody should want to get that way with bad liquor, when this air itself just fills him up with wine."

He too lifted his head, and inhaled the perfumed wind that blew from the great clean west.

"I reckon I'm a good deal of a wild man, Bob," he continued. "I like to come into a town now and then, to see the sights and have a good time, but for a reg'lar life give me the wilderness. Now this party of ours ain't a big one, an' we don't go by water. We ride across the plains."

"I haven't any horse," said Bob, with a sudden sinking of the heart, "and I haven't money enough to buy one."

"Ain't that too bad!" said Sam Strong. "He ain't got any horse an' he ain't got money 'nough to buy one. Now he's invited to join a trappin' outfit, everybody expectin' him to do his share of the work, an' his share of the fightin' if need be, an' he thinks nobody will grubstake him."

His playful little satire was so obvious that the boy blushed. It was a long time since he had met so much kindness, and his heart warmed more than ever toward stalwart Sam Strong.'

"I'll pay you back out of the very first money I earn," he said earnestly.

"Don't I know that?" said Sam. "Did you think I'd take you, if I didn't know you was the right stuff? Here's our shanty. I'll introduce you to the boys, an' make you one of the gang."

He led the way into a large wooden house that served as a hotel. The lobby was crowded with all the types of the border, and the air was thick with smoke, but Sam did not stop there. He ascended the narrow staircase that led to the second floor, Bob by his side. Two men, to whom he had given glances that Bob did not notice, detached themselves from the crowd and followed.

Sam Strong went down a narrow hall, opened a door and entered a large room. The two men who had followed came in also, and then he closed the door. Three others who were already in the room rose to their feet and one of them said:

"Hello, Cap, what's this critter that you've brought us?"

Bob blushed again, knowing that five pairs of inquiring eyes were upon him, but Sam Strong laughed.

"This," he replied, "is the camp baby; that is, he's goin' to be. We thought we needed one more feller for our trip, an' a likely chap like this can be a lot of use. Boys make things lively around a camp, an' he can wait on us, when he ain't got anythin' else to do. I ketched him down by the river, an' brought him in."

All the men laughed and Bob was embarrassed. But he knew that word and laugh were kindly. While Sam Strong was giving his name and pedigree, and introducing him in his easy western fashion, he looked carefully at them all, one by one.

They were a marked lot. Second to Sam Strong was a tall, lank Missourian with a scarred and weather-beaten face, called Bill Cole. Then came two younger men, Tom Harris and Porter Evans. Harris was from Michigan and Evans from Tennessee. They had fought on different sides in the Civil War, and that fact now made them the closest of friends, although they never agreed in anything about the late great strife. Then there was Louis Perolet, a little French-Canadian, compact and strong like a coil of woven steel wire, and Obadiah Pirtle, a slow spoken man from Maine, completed the list.

All were dressed in a mixture of wild and civilized garb, and their faces showed many signs of life, far beyond the fences that the white man builds. Everyone seemed to the boy to speak, by his very appearance, of the mountains and the plains. Their rifles leaned against the wall, their pistols were at their belts, but their voices were gentle, and no hostility was in the glance of anyone of them.

Bob was seized with a mighty sense of intoxicating joy. He had found suddenly, and, without the least hope, that for which he longed most. He, an inexperienced boy, was going to be admitted to a most glorious company. No young squire, about to become a knight, was ever more enthralled. He resolved, if he passed the ordeal of trial successfully, to devote his last breath to the common good, if need be.

"Well boys," said Sam Strong, "havin' looked him up an' down an' studied his p'ints, what do you think of the colt?"

"Strappin' big youngster," said Porter Evans. "We had a lot like him at Shiloh when we give the Yankees such a terrible beatin."

"Give us a beating did you?" exclaimed Tom Harris. "I could live and grow fat on such beatin's as that. Why, we chased your whole army right into the middle of the Tennessee River, an' for all I know it's there yet."

"That'll do for you two," said Sam genially. "If you are bound to fight the war over again, go out an' do it in the hall. Now, Louis, what do you say?"

"Heem all right," said the shrewd little Frenchman. "He look all of us ver straight in the eye, an' that enough. He one of us, he help me wiz ze cooking."

"An' you, Bill Cole?"

"Looks smart to me."

"An' you, Obe?"

"I reckon he'll do."

"Then it's settled," said Sam Strong, clapping a heavy hand upon the boy's shoulder. "You're chose, Bob. You're a member of this here band. Our secrets are your secrets, an' we stand together, every man for the lot. Shake hands with your new pards."

Bob shook hands, taking them in turn, and his feelings almost overpowered him. But he was duly silent, as became a tyro, and, taking a chair, he listened, with consuming attention, to their talk. It was all of the wild places where they had been, and to which they expected to return. The six were veterans. Both Harris and Evans had been on the plains, when they were boys, before the war, and as soon as the struggle ceased, they had returned to their old life.

It surprised and delighted the lad to find himself fully accepted into fellowship. Now that he had been made a member of the band they kept nothing from him, but discussed their past lives and their plans, with the utmost freedom, in his presence.

After an hour he went with Porter Evans, the Tennessean, to his boarding house to pay his bill, and to obtain his few belongings. The afternoon was well advanced when they stepped out, and the western wind was growing colder. Bob shivered, just a little bit, but would not let the Tennessean see it. He would have been deeply shamed to show lack of endurance at the very beginning of his career. But the thoughts of Evans were elsewhere.

"I was right, Bob," he said, somewhat anxiously, "when I told Tom Harris that we beat the Tanks at Shiloh. We had 'em well thrashed when Buell came up. What happened after that don't count. Tom was there on the other side, an' he knows, but he won't admit it."

Bob laughed from sheer exuberance of spirit.

"You are surely right, Mr. Evans," he said, seeing that his comrade wished to be confirmed by his opinion.

But Evans suddenly stopped and faced him.

"What did you call me?" he asked.

"Why, Mr. Evans, of course."

"Now, see here, I'm Mr. Evans only to them that don't like me, an' that I don't like. To them that run with me I'm Porter, or Port. Which do you mean to be, a friend or an enemy?"

"A friend, surely, Porter."

"That's all right. Now we'll go on an' get them things of yours."

Bob had little to take back with him—merely a large old-fashioned valise, filled with clothing and, in a half hour, he was at the hotel again with his new comrades. The big room, in which they were staying, had several beds, and he was to sleep there with the others. When he put his valise down by the wall Harris drew him to one side, and said in a whisper:

"I know Port told you again about the Battle of Shiloh an' claimed that they licked us, but don't you believe a word of it, Bob. We drove 'em right into the Tennessee."

"Of course, of course, Tom," said the boy.

He meant to be no arbiter of history, nor did he make the mistake of calling Harris "Mister." He began in this case with "Tom." The cold was increasing as the prairie night drew down, and a negro brought in logs for the big fireplace, at one end of the room. Soon a fine blaze was crackling and roaring, and they sat in their cane chairs in a loose circle about it. Bob had little to say, but he still listened, all ears, although a pleasant, drowsy warmth was creeping over him.

They went down to the main dining-room presently, and ate supper together. Then they returned to the rear room, lighted by the fire, and the men brought forth their pipes. The smoke rose, and deep content permeated the air. Outside a chill wind screamed over the prairie.

"Them ham an' eggs was mighty good," said Bill Cole, "an' they've filled up a big hollow right in the inside of me, but I've knowed buffalo steak to taste better, 'specially when Louis here cooked it."

"Have you really lived on buffalo steak, Mr. Bill?" asked Bob eagerly.

Bill Cole took his pipe out of his mouth, and blew a beautiful ring of smoke to the ceiling, where it broke.

"Have I lived on buffalo steak?" he replied in tones of deep satisfaction. "Well, I should say! For whole months at a time, an' I lived tre-men-je-ous well. You just wait till Louis there cooks one for you. You could live on them kind for a whole year, an' then ask for another year of the same."

"We'll have 'em soon," said Obadiah Pirtle.

Bob's eyes glowed with admiration.

"We've got to advance the boy enough money to buy a pony," said Sam Strong. "'Twon't take much, an' I reckon we can clear out of here in about another day. They say that the battle ain't to the swift nor the strong, but I reckon that it often is. I mean, Bob, that some places in the Rockies are much better for trappin' than some other places, an' we want to get to the best first."

Then they began to run over the tally of their resources, the rifles, the pistols, the ponies, the steel traps and the provisions. Bob gathered from their talk that they were well supplied with money, and that they had obtained the best of everything. As he listened his eyelids grew heavier, and the lids pulled down hard. The warmth made him dreadfully sleepy. He tried to hide it, but Sam Strong caught him at last.

"Don't be ashamed, boy," he said. "Tumble over into bed there at once. The wisest thing that a man can do is to go to sleep when he is sleepy, if the place allows."

Bob obeyed without demur. For a few minutes he saw the fire and the men smoking their pipes, and then he was dreaming a mighty dream, in which single-handed he was slaying buffalo herds, and fighting Indian tribes.

CHAPTER 2

In the Wilderness

When Bob awoke, dawn was coming in at the uncurtained windows. All his comrades were up but the two young soldiers of the great war. Not willing to be last, the boy sprang out of bed, and began to hurry on his clothes.

"That's right, Bob," said Sam Strong cheerily. "You've beat both them lazy generals the very first mornin'. Good start for you."

Harris and Evans opened their eyes at the same time, and, at the same time, both sat up.

"What kept me asleep," said Harris, "was dreamin' about that time we whipped the Johnny Rebs so bad at Chickamauga. I was just helpin' chase 'em into Chattanooga, when I heard your disturbin' voice, Sam."

"You beat us at Chickamauga!" exclaimed Porter Evans. "Why, we give you the worst lickin' of the whole war then, an' when you woke up we were chasin' you, not you chasin' us."

"Shut up," said Sam Strong. "The war has done been dead an' buried a whole year, an' I guess we'll go down to breakfast. We'd better post Bob here, an' tell him not to say anything about our plans."

While the laggard two were dressing, Strong told the boy that it was necessary for them to keep their expedition and all its plans secret. The only good trapping grounds left were deep in the Rocky Mountains, and trappers would stalk one another in order to discover a choice reserve. Men in Omaha now were watching Strong and his comrades, believing that they might follow them and profit by it.

"If anybody asks you questions, Bob," said Strong, "just tell him you don't know anything, an' you'll be tellin' the truth, too."

Bob promised, and nothing could have made him break the promise. They ate breakfast and dispersed about their errands, having agreed to meet again at the hotel late in the afternoon. Bob's business was to buy a pony with money loaned him by Sam Strong out of the common fund. He was a good judge of horses, and, as they were for sale everywhere, he soon selected a strong young animal from a group in a corral at the edge of the town. Several spectators stood by, as the boy bought his horse, and one of them, a tall man of strong build and dark skin, said in the most casual manner:

"You seem to have a good eye for a horse, my lad. That's a fine one you bought just then, and you didn't let them make you pay too much."

Bob flushed with appreciation at these chance words of praise, evidently so sincere, and replied:

"I hope you're right, sir. I've need of a good mount."

"Going across the plains, I presume," said the man in the same casual tone. "It's dangerous, but it's a great thing for a youngster like you."

Bob was about to reply, but checked himself suddenly, remembering the warning that Strong had given. However, there was nothing in this man's appearance to cause apprehension. His smooth, slightly foreign face was well cut, and his eyes had the look of benevolence. His English was modulated correctly, and without accent. His manner was decidedly attractive, but Bob was already devotedly loyal to his comrades, and he was resolved to be on the cautious side, even at the risk of seeming churlish.

"It's a long ride to California," continued the man, "unless you're stopping somewhere in the Rockies, and one has to be a member of a strong party, too, as the Cheyennes, both northern and southern, are out, and are taking scalps."

"So I've heard," said Bob vaguely, and mounting his new pony he rode away. He found the others already at the primitive hotel, making all their things into packs for the start. He thought at first that he would not say anything about the stranger, but the manner in which the man had continued his inquiries, or rather suggestions, caused him to be suspicious as he thought it over. So he told Strong of the circumstance. The leader was at once alert.

"Now I always think the best is goin' to happen," he said, "but it won't happen unless you help it to happen, an' it seems to me somebody else wants to put a finger in our pie. What kind of lookin' feller was he, Bob?"

"Tall, strong, smooth face, dark skin, hair and eyes."

"Look like a preacher?"

"Yes, he did, and there was something foreign about him, too. It showed mostly in his voice."

"Hear that, Obe?" said Strong. "I'm always hopin' for the best, but who do you think that fellow was?"

"Juan Carver."

"An' you, Bill? You ain't a bad hand at guessin'."

"Juan Carver, an' it ain't no guess, neither."

"An' our two generals here, an' Louis, think the same way," said Sam Strong. "Still hopin' for the best, I know it's Carver, an' he means to follow us. He was tryin' to pump you about us, Bob."

"Who is Juan Carver?" asked the boy, his nerves tingling with curiosity.

"Juan Carver is a bad man," replied Sam Strong. "I like to think the best of everybody, but there ain't a doubt of it. He's the son of an American father an' a Mexican mother—that's where he gets that touch of the foreigner—and they do say that he ain't got the virtues of either, though full of knowledge an' cunnin'. He's a trapper with a band of his own. Some say he's independent, an' some say he represents the Hudson Bay. If a few fellers like ourselves were to find rich trappin' grounds an' streams he'd foller along, drive us away, an' take 'em himself. Like jumpin' a claim, don't you see?"

Bob saw very well, and he was glad that he had not let the man draw him on in regard to their plans. His news stirred his comrades greatly, and they held a council in their own room. It was agreed that they should make a night start as soon as the moon rose. Their horses and supplies were on the other side of the town. Bill Cole was to slip away first and have everything ready. Then the others would come.

"We want to shake Juan and his crowd clean off," said Sam Strong, "an' if we get a good start they'll never find us."

"We can be forty miles from here by dawn," said Obadiah Pirtle.

Bill Cole left at eight o'clock, and then the others followed about nine, everyone armed with a rifle and revolver and knife. Bob's revolver and knife, like his pony, were bought from the common fund. The night was dark, which favoured their wishes, and it was but ill lighted by a few flaring gas lamps.

People, mostly men, were still in the streets, but so far as they could see, no notice was taken of the comrades, and they sped to the other side of the town, where at one of the corrals, used by outfitting expeditions, Bill Cole was waiting for them.

"Haven't seen anybody watchin' us," said Bill, tersely. "B'lieve they think we're not going for several days yet."

"Hope you're right, an' it's good always to hope for the best," said Sam Strong.

Besides their own mounts they had fifteen pack horses, all trained to follow without being led, which was a valuable quality, when their owners wished to be free for action. These horses were well loaded with supplies besides carrying a number of extra rifles and revolvers, several fine breech-loading shotguns, and great quantities of ammunition.

Bob mounted his horse and they rode out. Every nerve in the boy thrilled with a vast and vivid delight. Here he was, embarked upon his great adventure, and, from the first moment, they were in the thick of it. He sat his saddle firmly. His rifle was strapped across his back and he looked straight ahead at their leader, Sam Strong, whose figure had become dim, as the dark deepened.

They passed, with the rhythmic sound of hoofs, out upon the prairie into the land which belonged to him who could take it. Bob looked back. The light of the last flaring street lamp was gone, and the night had blotted out everything. Overhead, the stars were hidden by drifting clouds.

A horse and rider rose out of the prairie.

"Which way, friends?" asked a voice, and it was that of the man who had accosted Bob when he bought his pony.

"None of your business, Juan Carver," cried Sam Strong.

Bob was startled by the change in his leader. All the gentleness was gone from his voice which had the sharp, fierce crack of a pistol-shot. Without an instant's hesitation Strong rode his horse directly at Carver, whose own horse went down under the impact, carrying with him his rider who uttered an angry cry, as he fell.

Strong's horse leaped clear and his rider called out: "Come on, boys!" as he swung away at a swift gallop. The six followed at the same pace, Bob's heart beating loud and fast, as he galloped over the swells. They heard the faint sound of a shot behind them, but Sam only laughed.

"That's Juan," he said, "but he's only wastin' a good bullet. His horse will walk lame for some days, an' the rest of his band are too far back to catch us. I'm always hopin' for the best, an' I don't think Juan Carver will have the chance to raid our fur village."

They galloped on over the low swells, and the supply horses in a close group thundered after them. Bob kept his place next to Sam Strong, riding with an easy but firm seat. His heart was not beating so loud and fast now, and pride began to take the place of excitement. He had been under fire! That shot might as well have been aimed at him as at anybody else.

Sam let their pace sink to a hand gallop, but, even then, they ate up space at a great rate, never veering from a course that led due west. Bob trusted everything to his pony, knowing that he was keen of sight and sure of foot. The night darkened further, but he could see that the country was free from obstructions, just the low swells, succeeding one another, at almost regular intervals.

He felt once more that singular penetrating thrill, giving a pleasure so keen that it was almost a pain. He was now well into his magic world, and the first of his wishes had come true. About midnight they stopped and Strong and Cole, taking the boy with them, rode back a hundred yards or so.

There they listened intently, but could hear nothing, not a single sound of pursuit. Bob heard instead a low moaning, but he knew it to be the wind sweeping over the swells. Sam Strong dismounted at last and put his ear to the earth.

"Nothing Captain!" said Bill Cole after a wait of two minutes.

"Nothing" replied Strong with conviction. "We've shook 'em off. There can't be a doubt of it an' Juan, whether he stands for himself or Hudson Bay, will have a hard time in findin' us."

They rejoined their comrades, and rode at a walk about three hours longer. The sky was then beginning to lighten, the clouds having gone away. The great stars were coming out, and they danced in the blue in what seemed to Bob a friendly way.

They came to a dip, deeper than the rest, at the bottom of which flowed a shallow creek, and Sam Strong gave the word to dismount. "It's a sheltered place, as good as any we can find," he said, "an' we'll camp here, but there are to be no lights. We'll just roll up in our blankets and go to sleep."

Bob, stiff from the long, hard riding, was glad enough to dismount, and he did not delay about following the second part of Sam's directions. After the horses were tethered he picked out the softest spot on the ground that he could find, folded his warm blanket about him, and in five minutes was sleeping soundly.

He awoke when the first bar of grey was just appearing in the east. He saw, with sleepy eyes, that Strong and Cole were on watch at the edge of their little camp. Most of the horses had lain down, and all were still. Three recumbent forms near him showed that the others were yet asleep.

Bob himself was only half awake. He was in the dreamy, delightful state when one neither remembers nor plans. He lay there, still looking toward the east. He saw through filmy eyes the great red rim of the rising sun that seemed to come bodily out of the earth, pouring a brilliant light over the grey prairies. He saw one of the sentinels moving on noiseless feet, and, although he knew the day was at hand, he fell asleep again.

When he opened his eyes once more it was to awake completely, and to find that all the others were up and moving. He threw off the blanket and sprang to his feet, ashamed of himself, but he was greeted only with laughter, full of good nature.

The sun was a full three hours high, and over a fire of sticks some broiling birds gave out a fine odour.

"Yes, you've slept late," said Sam Strong. "I believe in takin' rest when you need it, an' can get it, without payin' too high a price, so, as last night was most likely the first of the kind you ever had, we let you snooze on so sound that you didn't wake, while Tom and Porter were fighting the battle of Gettysburg over again for a full hour. Ain't that so, generals?"

The two young soldiers grinned and nodded. The broiling birds were prairie chickens that Bill Cole, an uncommonly good marksman and hunter, had shot. Bob was invited to help himself, and, broiling one on a sharpened twig, he ate the whole of it. The morning air, with the wind blowing, as it usually does on the prairies, was sharp and crisp, and he could never remember to have had such an appetite before.

After breakfast he went down to the shallow stream and drank. The water was not very clear, and it had a slightly bitter taste, but he did not mind it. Again that wonderful air made everything seem good. Then he began to work with the horses and the packs, and to look after as many details of the camp as he could, resolved that he should justify the confidence that had been placed in him.

Sam Strong watched Bob out of those benevolent blue eyes of his— eyes that were shrewd, eyes that could become as cold as steel—and he was pleased. The lonely boy by the river had appealed to him, but he never would have chosen him for their party had he not judged him the possessor of qualities that would prove valuable. Now he was justified, and he turned to Bill Cole.

"He's the right stuff, ain't he?" he said, nodding toward the lad.

"True blue, all wool and a yard wide," replied Bill, sententiously.

Then they held a brief conference. They were about thirty miles from Omaha, and already in No Man's Land, but they knew the locality well. Nevertheless they must choose their route, and proceed with great caution. Both the northern and southern Cheyennes were raiding the plains, and many terrible tales, most of them true, had come into Omaha.

"We've got to watch sharp for warriors," said Sam Strong. "If they're only a few when we see 'em we'll stand 'em off; if they're a lot we'll run."

It was now past eleven o'clock, and they rode away again, the mustangs proceeding at a long, easy walk that they seemed able to keep up forever. Bob rode now by the side of Obadiah Pirtle, who pointed out to him how spring was approaching. He called his attention to the tiny shoots of green, almost hidden under the dry grass of last year. They saw here and there also a modest little flower just raising its head.

"Spring will come runnin' now," said Obe. "She'll just bust out. This ain't like the country in which I was born. Up in Maine there are big forests, an' heaps of rocks, an' lots of clear water tumblin' down the hills. Here there ain't any forests, nor rocks, an' mighty little runnin' water, but I love it all the same."

"So do I," said Bob with so much earnestness and emphasis that the down easter smiled.

That night they reached another shallow creek, and encamped in the fringe of cottonwoods on its banks. Strong permitted them to build a fire, as he believed that they had thrown Carver off their track, and that no Cheyennes were near. It was still cold at night, and the blaze was grateful. Several of the prairie chickens were left, and they ate them, preferring to save their stores.

That night Bob at his own request helped with the watch. He was to keep the first half and Porter Evans the second, and he felt the weight of his responsibility. But he was proud of it also. He saw the men lie down in their blankets, and then become still. The wind moaned across the swells and a restless horse moved now and then, but the boy was not lonely.

The darkness thinned away, as his eyes grew used to it. He saw the cottonwoods, not yet in spring foliage, swaying back and forth in the wind, and he clearly saw the outlines of the horses tethered near. He walked for a long time in a half circle about the camp, the creek forming the segment. He trod softly lest he awake any of his comrades, and he never ceased to watch. Doubtless no camp on all the plains that night had a more vigilant sentinel.

It was about midnight, when he heard a low wailing cry, far off on the prairie, and it made a little shiver run through his flesh. He thought at first that it might be a Cheyenne signal, but it was only the howl of a coyote, scavenger of the plains. He shook his rifle a little scornfully, and walked on. He would not let wolves annoy him.

But, as the moon faded and the night grew colder, and the wind stronger, Bob was glad to keep a little closer to his comrades, his half circle narrowing perceptibly. He felt now the full immensity of the wilderness and its desolation. The coyote howled again, a dismal weird howl, full of ghostly suggestion, and Bob came a little closer to the fire, glad to see that some coals were left yet, sparks of living red in the grass.

Despite his occasional attacks of goose-flesh, the boy never shirked his task. He made it a test for himself, subjecting his own body and mind to stern discipline. He was to go off duty about one in the morning, but he purposely waited an hour later before he awakened Evans.

The Tennessean yawned prodigiously, as he came from his blanket.

"One o'clock, is it, Bob?" he said.

"Yes," replied the boy.

But Evans had a watch and there was light enough for him to see its face.

"Why, it's two o'clock," he said, "an' you've watched an hour over time! What did you do it for?"

"I forgot," said the boy in some confusion.

Evans eyed him keenly and with suspicion.

"You didn't do anything of the kind," he said. "You gave me an extra hour on purpose. I won't forget it, Bob."

They rode on two more days without event. They saw antelope in the distance, several times, but they did not turn aside for a shot, and once Bob beheld on a distant slope huge, shaggy forms that he knew to be those of the buffalo. They were all sorely tempted to try for such big game, but the leader finally ruled to the contrary.

"What we want to do," he said, "is to cover ground, not to shoot buffaloes."

But, as they continued their journey and saw no signs of Indians, they turned aside for buffalo and antelope, the game still being plentiful. Both Sam Strong and Bill Cole argued from its abundance and comparative tameness that neither white men nor red had passed recently through that region. Bob helped at the killing of a fat cow and they enjoyed a great feast, Louis Perolet cooking the steaks with the skill and delight which perhaps only a Frenchman knows in such pursuits.

"Eet ees good," he said, "this buffalo steak, an' eet belongs to America. The Old World have hees triumphs, an' the New World have hees too."

The next day they saw a long blue line under the horizon which Bob mistook for a haze. But he was soon set right by Sam Strong.

"That's a range of hills or buttes," he said, "an' they're a good place to stay away from. The Sioux an' the Cheyennes keep lookouts, posted on the highest summits, an' when they see an emigrant train or any other white party passin' they signal to the warriors on horseback below. We'll sheer off."

They turned from the blue haze, but Bob saw the low line for a long time. The air was so wonderfully clear that it refused to disappear in the plain, and the faint blur did not go until sunset came.

That night it was again Bob's turn to keep the first half of the watch and, for precaution, Sam Strong was sentinel with him. The night was light, with a good moon and plenty of bright stars, and the boy found himself looking, nearly all the time, toward that point on the horizon, where the unseen line of buttes lay. His eyes were drawn in that direction by a sort of terrible fascination. The idea of the savage warriors, watching on the crest of the buttes to signal an ambush, made his flesh creep once more.

"When he had been on watch about two hours, and, while his eyes were turned toward the haunted horizon, he saw a light, faint and very far. He thought at first that it was some star hanging low, but its motion and radiance were unlike those of a star, and, when he saw it swing slowly from side to side, he knew that it was a signal. He touched Sam Strong on the arm and pointed to the light.

"It's a Cheyenne talkin' from the top of one of the buttes," said the leader. "Now I wonder what he's sayin', but anyway some friend of his will be answerin' him soon. There, look! See the other fellow talkin' back?"

A second light appeared on the horizon to the right of the first, and it too swung slowly back and forth. It ceased and the first took up the talk again. The second made a vigorous rejoinder and then both disappeared like the blowing out of a candle.

"What do you make of it?" asked the boy.

Sam Strong shook his head in doubt.

"Nothin'," he replied, "except that there was never a better time for us to be watchin'. The Cheyennes are full of tre-men-jeous-ly bad medicine, an' they've got two chiefs, Roman Nose an' Black Kettle, as bold an' cunnin' as they ever make 'em. I'm goin' to wake up the rest of the boys, Bob, an' we'll move on in the night."

He shook the sleeping men one by one, and they sat up.

"I know you both were dreamin' that you won Antietam, or some other of them big battles," he said to Evans and Harris, "but if we don't look out we may have a battle of our own not so big, but jest as dangerous to us. Me an' Bob have seen Cheyennes talkin' to each other, a long way off, it's true, but it's time for us to scoot."

The men asked no questions, knowing that Sam Strong would not act without good cause, and in fifteen minutes they moved away with their horses in the dark, advancing at a rapid gait, but as before into the west.

The country was now slightly more broken. At intervals, they skirted shallow oblong depressions, which Bill Cole told Bob were buffalo wallows. Some of these basins still held water from melting snows, and twice they stopped for their horses to drink from them. Once they heard a snort, and the hasty tramping of heavy feet. Bob saw dusky forms disappearing, and he knew that they had disturbed resting buffaloes.

They did not stop until nearly daylight, camping in a little grove of cottonwoods that grew between two high swells. Strong and Cole watched and awakened the others at the first upshot of the dawn. The day came on, grey and lowering, and everyone scanned the entire circle of the horizon with anxious eyes. No fire was lighted, the breakfast being of cold food, and Bill Cole, who went on scout around the grove of cottonwoods, returned with the report that he had seen the hoofprints of unshod ponies.

"'Bout a day old, near as I can guess," he said, "an' Cheyennes were ridin' them ponies. There can't be a doubt of it."

"Which means that Cheyennes are somewhere near us, may be to the right, may be to the left," said Sam Strong. "I am always hopin' for the best, which I believe a man should never fail to do, but jest now I think we ought to get ready for the worst."

CHAPTER 3

The Shadow in the Dusk

All their journey hitherto had been made in fair weather, but now was a promise of foul. The wind that nearly always blew across the plains, shifted to the northwest, with great rapidity, and its touch made Bob shiver, with sudden cold, clear to the very marrow. The horses seemed to feel apprehension, and all of them—whether for packs or for riding—crowded close together.

"Looks like a blow," said Obadiah Pirtle, "and maybe rain or hail with it, too."

"I'm always hopin' for the best," said Sam Strong, "but I think you're right. After all it may not be a bad thing for us, as a storm may hide us from the Cheyennes."

They decided to move at once from the cotton-woods, as a fierce wind might send the trees crashing upon them, and they advanced into the open plain, here rising and falling in gentle swells. The whole sky was now leaden, and the whistling wind, out of the northwest, steadily grew colder. Even the horses shivered, and, when they reached the deepest dip that they could find, the riders dismounted and arranged them in a ring, some tethered and others held by their lariats. The men stood in the centre of the ring.

Before these brief preparations were completed, solemn thunder began to growl on the horizon, and lightning flared in the same direction. Then both thunder and lightning ceased, and the wind died. After two or three minutes of intense stillness, both lightning and thunder began again, but in a wholly different way. There was a crash, so tremendous, that it made the boy jump a foot into the air, and then came the stroke of lightning, cutting the heavens across with a dazzling flash and blinding everyone, for a moment or two.

As soon as Bob recovered from the glare, lightning and thunder came again, surpassing anything that he had ever heard or seen further east, and frightening him, despite every effort of the will to control himself. It was, perhaps, fortunate for him that he, as well as the others, soon had occupation. Some of the horses, terrified by the storm, were pulling at their lariats, and it was hard work to hold them all. Yet this must be done. Their horses were like boats to sailors, and they did not wish to lose a single one.

The men, knowing what was to come, had wrapped blankets about themselves, and Bob did likewise. Soon the thunder sank, and the lightning faded. Then the cold wind from the northwest sprang up again, and with it came the rain in slanting sheets, that soon deluged the earth. But in ten minutes the rain changed to driven hail, and then they were glad enough to have the ring of horses about them as shelter.

Bob wore a cap, the brim of which he pulled down to protect his eyes, and cowered against his pony. But the hail beat upon his blanketed back and shoulders like bird-shot. He was cold, partly wet, miserable physically, but he would not complain, although several of the men whose characters as plainsmen were already established, did not hesitate to grumble.

While the hail was still falling, they heard a rumble, and saw a dark, moving mass to the right of them, but several hundred yards away. It was a buffalo herd stampeded by the storm and fleeing before it. Bob was glad they were not in the path of the mighty beasts, whose numbers ran into the scores of thousands. They were over an hour in passing, and their line extended further than he could see. For the full hour their hoofs kept up a steady rolling thunder.

When they were gone Sam Strong looked significantly at Bill Cole, and Bill Cole gave back the same significant look.

"Frightened by the storm," said Sam, "but something else may have been after them, too."

"Cheyennes been huntin' them most likely."

"I'm hopin' for the best, but I guess you're right. The hail is about stopping an' we'll move on again."

The hail ceased entirely in five minutes, the clouds marched away in battalions, and a brilliant sun began to pour down warmth. All the hail quickly melted, and the earth would soon be drying. The men threw off their blankets, saddled their horses anew, and once more sped into the west. It was Strong's idea to travel in a course exactly opposite to that taken by the buffalo herd, in order that the distance between them might widen as fast as possible.

The day seemed bent on atoning for the storm in its early hours. Not a single cloud was left in the sky. It was a vast arch of blue, shot with the gold of the sun, and the wind, which now came from the south, was laden with warmth. The earth, drying fast, showed new green where the bunch grass was appearing.

All of them recovered their spirits, and the two soldiers, in the utmost friendliness, began to whistle *Dixie* together. Several of the horses raised their heads and neighed, showing that they, too, appreciated the change.

"Here we are, all right and not a Cheyenne in sight," said Louis Perolet. "Our General Sam Strong ees like ze great Napoleon. He lead us out of danger every time."

"Don't you bank too much on that, Frenchy," said Sam. "The time may come when you'll have to fight your way out of danger, or stay in it."

Beyond a doubt Strong was still anxious, and his apprehension was reflected in the face of Bill Cole, the next best plainsman, and second in command. Both of them looked anxiously for hilly country in which they could escape observation, but there was no promise of it. In fact, it could not be expected, unless they cut across the course of some considerable stream.

"I'm hopin' for the best," said Sam Strong, "but the bands of Cheyennes are certainly somewhere about, an' maybe old Roman Nose himself is near. I think we'd better torn south. I know of a stream that we'll strike ten or fifteen miles from here, an' we can travel in its bed where we won't be seen."

"Like ze great Napoleon who use everything, the earth eetself, to help him," said Louis Perolet, admiringly.

They rode rapidly on their new course, and, in a half hour, they saw far to the north of them a thin column of smoke, rising into the heavens like a spire. Presently another rose to the same height, but several miles to the eastward.

"Cheyennes talkin' again, an' now they are talkin' in the daytime," said Sam Strong. "The sooner we hit that creek bottom the better."

They reached it in about an hour, a wide, sandy bed with a depth of about five feet or so and a width of thirty or forty feet, a narrow stream of cold water flowing down the centre.

They led the horses into the channel, although they were reluctant, having some fear of the sand, and then all dismounted.

"We're hidden here from anybody at a distance," said Sam Strong, "an' now we'll go downstream, leadin' our horses, an' lookin' out for quicksands."

It was not the best method of travelling, but it was the safest, and they trudged along in the shadow of the banks until nightfall, several times narrowly escaping the quicksands.

Sam Strong breathed a mighty sigh of relief when the darkness came, and then everyone in his turn breathed a similar sigh. They emerged from the shelter of the stream into a pleasant little valley, where oaks as well as cottonwoods grew. They secured their horses with lariats to the trees and bushes, not hobbling any of them, as they might wish, at any moment, to make a speedy flight.

They ate cold food in the dark, and Bob slept through the first watch. He was awakened about one in the morning to relieve Perolet, and had as his comrade Bill Cole, who had relieved Sam Strong.

Bill took the northern side of the camp, and most of the time walked back and forth in a semicircle. Bob had the semicircle on the south, and they met at each side of the circle which the two made complete. Then they would exchange a word or two in a whisper and pass on.

Bob felt his responsibility, and he appreciated to the full the great trust that these men put in him. Throughout their journey and flight he had watched the plainsmen, studying their craft and precaution, and now he imitated them. He felt the fine rifle that he had inherited from his father, and saw that the cartridges were slipped in just right. He loosened the pistol in his belt that it, too, might be ready on instant call. And he was careful as he stepped to make no noise whatever. It had become a matter of pride with him that no footfall should be audible, and that no one should hear him brushing against the bushes.

The night was peaceful. The wind did not keep up its usual moaning across the swells, and the branches of the oaks and cottonwoods were still. The horses seemed to be at rest. Bob apprehended no danger, but he was glad whenever he and Bill Cole met. The gaunt but friendly face of the trapper cheered him, and the few words that he spoke were a comfort to him in his loneliness.

Two hours passed and it seemed to Bob that the watch might well be relaxed. The stars twinkled and danced in the most friendly fashion, and the wind was yet still. He met Bill Cole, they exchanged the usual friendly word or two and the boy passed on, describing the southern arc of the circle. His path led through the thickest clump of oaks, and just beyond them in a close group were the horses.

Bob's eyes, good at any time, had become used to the darkness, and he could see very well. He saw clearly the outlines of the horses, nearly all of them lying down, but two standing on the side nearest to him. A peculiar spell or intuition caused him to remain there, well hidden in the clump of trees, and look at the horses, especially the two that were standing.

One of the horses raised his head with a quick, jerking motion, and at the same time the other stamped with restless foot. Both motions seemed unusual to the boy, and he leaned a little forward, staring with all the power of his eyes. Was it a shadow that he saw just beyond the first horse? and if a shadow, was it caused by a bough or trunk of a tree?

Bob's heart rose up in his throat. The feeling assailed him with overwhelming power that here was an alien presence. His hands clasped his rifle lightly, and it was cold to his touch. He trembled ever so slightly, and then was quite still. He knew his responsibility and accepted it. He must save his comrades as well as himself. The danger was here on his side of the circle, and he would detect it.

The boy took a step forward, holding his rifle in front of him, but he was yet hidden in the cluster of oaks. There had been no sound since the stamping of the uneasy hoof, but now one of the horses moved again, and Bob believed that he heard a soft hiss, so very soft that it was scarcely more than the whisper of the wind in the grass.

But he knew. He had heard it. It was not fancy. He sprang forward and a shadow appeared from behind the horse, the shadow of an Indian, fully armed and in all the panoply of war-paint. The warrior with a sweep of his knife cut the lariat of the horse, struck him on the side, and uttered a loud, thrilling shout. Bob fired at the same instant and cried, "Up! up! the Cheyennes have come!"

Bill Cole rushed down from the northern segment of the circle, Sam Strong was on his feet in a moment, thoroughly alive and awake, and the others were but little behind. The centre of the trouble was obvious at once.

"Look out for the horses!" cried Strong and Cole together. "They are tryin' to stampede 'em."

Bob sprang forward, seized a flying lariat and checked the impending flight of a pony. The two soldiers hurled themselves into the group, and they seemed to be all hands, grasping at least a half dozen ropes. Louis Perolet was just behind them, calling upon the name of the great Napoleon as his patron in war, and, at the same time, acting with speed and decision.

Strong and Cole ran toward the edge of the grove and fired twice each. Scattering shots came in reply, and then the long, fierce yell of the Cheyennes, which the plain beyond took up, and then sent back in a quavering under note, like the savage whine of some wild beast.

But the cry was not repeated, and there was no other sound in the grove just then but that of the struggling horses. These, too, were soon reduced to silence, and, although they stood quivering, they made no further effort to get away. Not one had escaped, so quick and resourceful had been the trappers, although the lariats of half of them had been cut. Across the shoulder of one of them was a long, red streak, where the Cheyenne had drawn his knife in order to add pain to fright. Sam Strong growled deep when he saw it.

"I try to think the best of people," he said, "but I'd like to get hold of the Cheyenne who did that." He walked to the edge of the grove, took a long look, came back and said: "You saved us, Bob, my boy, an' we didn't make any mistake when we picked you up. The Cheyennes, the ugly snakes, came on your side and you saw 'em in time. If they'd stampeded the horses we wouldn't have been much better off than sailors in a sea without a boat."

Bob flushed in the darkness with pride. It was, as Louis Perolet would have said, like having the approval of the great Napoleon, and he was ready, at that very minute, to lay down his life for his leader, Sam Strong. But he said nothing, as Strong was already in conference with Bill Cole. Instead he stood guard by the horses, holding three lariats in one hand, and his rifle in the other.

Strong and Cole, masters of all the wiles and arts of the plains, considered their situation extremely dangerous. So far, only one Cheyenne had been seen clearly, but many more were probably near. Strong had no mind to be besieged in the grove. They were largely hidden by the trees at night, but by day it would be a different matter when the Cheyenne sharpshooters swarmed on every side of it. They must steal away now, not so difficult, perhaps, for the men to do. but the horses would make noise.

"It's got to be tried, though," said Strong, in a grim whisper, "an' Tom, maybe you an' Porter will have a chance to be in a better fight than the one at Gettysburg you talk so much about."

"Suppose we go back into the creek bed," said Obadiah Pirtle.

"We might be penned up there."

"If we were we could shoot from the shelter of the banks, an' if they ain't watchin' close on that side, it'll give us the better chance to get away unseen."

The plan carried and they began to move, leading the horses slowly and very cautiously. Fortunately it had turned a little darker, the moon being gone, and many of the stars ceasing to twinkle, and there was a chance that their movements would be completely hidden by the oaks and cottonwoods.

Strong and Cole stayed fifteen or twenty yards in the rear, and Bob was at the head of the troop, by the side of the Maine man. It was a hundred yards to the bed of the creek, but it seemed a mile to the boy. His head was throbbing with excitement, and the soft footfall of the horses fell on his ears like thunder. He heard a rifle-shot behind him, and the horses jerked on the lariats. A second shot followed and then several more.

"Keep movin," whispered Obadiah Pirtle. "They've sent scouts forward, an' Sam an' Bill are drivin' 'em back. It's all right. It'll make them Cheyennes think we're still stayin' in the grove. There's the creek bank."

They led the horses down with the greatest caution, and luckily none of them slipped. Then they paused, huddled close together in the thick shadow of the bank, and Strong and Cole leaped lightly down beside them.

"I think I nicked the shoulder of a warrior," whispered Strong, "an' they are likely to be cautious. They won't find out that we've gone for a half hour yet, an' that half hour will be worth an ordinary year to us."

They advanced southward, the soft sand drowning the tread of the horses. Ten minutes passed and they heard no alarm. Fifteen minutes and yet there was none. Twenty came, and Strong led them out of the sand upon the hard plain.

"We can mount an' gallop for it now," he said. "Of course, when daylight comes they'll find our tracks in the sand, but we'll have a good start then, an' we may stave 'em off."

Bob, his heart exulting, sprang into the saddle. It seemed to him that they had already made their escape complete, and he settled himself firmly, while he waited for Sam Strong to give the word of command. In the few seconds of pause a long cry, piercing and full of anger, came from the grove that they had left.

"They've stalked the place, found out that we've gone and they're mad about it," said the leader. "Now boys, hold firm to the lariats of your led horses, and away we go."

All swung into a gallop, and in a group they swept toward the southwest. Bob felt the cold night air rushing past him, and before him he saw only a misty, undulating world. He did not know where he was going, but all the little pulses in his head were throbbing with excitement, and he had unbounded confidence in these brave comrades of his. The men seldom spoke. The wiry mustangs seemed to show no weariness, and mile after mile fell behind them.

Just before day they stopped, changed the packs on seven of the horses, and took fresh mounts. Then they increased their speed somewhat, but soon the great red sun sailed out of the east, and the dazzling morning came. They stopped their flight and looked back. The keenest eye could discern nothing on the plain. It merely rolled away, in swell after swell, touched lightly with the green of early spring.

"We've shaken 'em off," said Bob, triumphantly, "Those Cheyennes will never find us."

But Sam Strong shook his head.

"I'm always hopin' for the best," he said, "but when Indian warriors want your scalp, an' want it real bad, you don't shake 'em off so easy. I'm jest tellin' you this, so you won't be disappointed if somethin' happens."

It did not seem possible to Bob, The plain was so empty; and surely the warriors could not trail them fast enough to overtake them. Strong announced that they must rest a while, whether or not the Indians still pursued. It would not do for them to be overtaken when their horses were broken down, and all dismounting, they sat upon the ground. The horses began to nibble the young grass, and they, at least, were content.

"What do you think of it, Bill?" asked Strong.

"Six of one an' a half dozen of the other," replied Cole. "They may ketch us, or they may not, but, if they do ketch us, I'm thinkin' that they'll have a hard time to hold us."

"We have come for the trappin', but, eef we must, we'll do the fightin', too," said the valiant Louis Perolet. "The great Napoleon not fight until the time come, but then he fight most terrible."

"Seven Napoleons, like ourselves, can make things hum," said Obadiah Pirtle, dryly.

They rested about three quarters of an hour, and Bob noted that the day was going to be one of the most brilliant that he had ever seen. The air was absolutely transparent, and distant objects came very near. It was this effect that caused Sam Strong, just as they remounted, to notice dim, moving specks under the horizon. He took a second glance in order to be sure, and then he announced quite calmly:

"Boys, the Cheyennes have followed our trail. See 'em comin'."

His long forefinger pointed them out.

"Louis," he said, "I think you can soon prove that you're another Napoleon, an' Tom, you an' Porter can fight Gettysburg all over again, but you've got to be on the same side now."

CHAPTER 4

The Dog Soldiers

Strong, like a good general, sought a field of battle to his liking, and he observed a slight, sandy elevation in the plain, a few hundred yards further on. The sandy nature of the hill caused him to hope for something else, and, when they reached it, his hopes were fulfilled.

The hill had a slight crater, and in this crater were a dozen deep buffalo wallows, where the herds had rolled and scratched themselves for generations against the grateful sand.

"It's a fort! A real fort!" exclaimed Strong, joyfully. "We'll stand 'em off here!"

"He ees the great Napoleon," said Perolet, admiringly. "He has found the best place to fight."

They rode the horses into the buffalo wallows, tethered them together, and then took their own position in the deepest of all the depressions. They were so well protected that only the head of an animal showed now and then over the hill.

"Makes me think of Little Round Top at Gettysburg," said Tom Harris.

"If it hadn't been for that blamed hill we'd have beat you," said Porter Evans.

"See how fast they come!" said Strong, pointing toward the eastern horizon, "an' there's a lot of 'em, too."

Bob was by the leader, and he was tall enough, standing at his full height, to see over the crest of the hill. Now the wild horsemen of the plains were in full sight, fifty or sixty strong, galloping straight toward the hill.

"They make a fine sight," said Sam Strong, impartially. "Them must be the Dog Soldiers!"

"Dog Soldiers!" said Bob, "what does that mean?"

"The Cheyenne warriors are divided into bands like societies, and the band that comes first is the Dog Soldiers—Hotamitaneo is their Indian name. They generally lead the battle, and they are most to be dreaded. They picked up our trail somehow, an' I reckon they think our goose is cooked."

Strong pressed his lips tightly together, and his blue eyes were full of resolute fire. It was evident that if the Cheyennes thought their "goose was cooked," he did not.

The approach of the warriors on their trained mustangs was spirited, and not without poetry. They were still far away. Only the extreme purity and thinness of the air made them seem near. But Bob saw the feathers in their hair waving, and the short rifles in their hands. They rode without reins, letting them fall free if they had them, and urged on their horses with a pressure of the knee.

They formed a line, curving slightly outward, and the horses were eight or ten feet apart. They were coming at a full gallop, but, when they were within a third of a mile, every man raised his rifle in his right hand above his head, as if by signal, and altogether uttered their war-whoop, a long thrilling cry that was repeated in echoes across the plain. Then they filed suddenly to the right like cavalry men, trained at drill, each horse keeping his regular place, and they galloped about the hill, at a uniform distance of a third of a mile.

"It's the Dog Soldiers sure enough," said Sam Strong, "an' maybe old Roman Nose himself is there. How do you feel Bob?"

"I feel that we can beat 'em," replied the boy with spirit.

"That's the way to talk," said Sam Strong. "Still I wish that this hill which ain't much of a hill after all, was higher an' that these wallows were deeper. But I'm hopin' for the best."

Bob, in spite of the fact that they sought his life, had admiration for the Cheyennes, who rode about them with savage grace, their sinuous brown forms shining in the crystal air. They stopped presently, and, some of them dismounting, walked near their horses, seeming to ignore the presence of any enemy.

"They're tryin' to show us how little they think of us," said Sam Strong. "They're pretendin' that they've nothin' to do when they get good an' ready, but ride right over us. It's an Indian's way. He wants to rub it in before he sends you to the happy huntin' grounds."

The Cheyennes took no action for at least half an hour, sitting their horses or walking about the plain as if they had all the time in the world. It was Bob's guess that they wished to worry the besieged, and make their nerves unsteady, and probably he was right. But he was soon to see the methods of Indian warfare, as usually practised on the plains.

"They'll be feelin' for us in a few more minutes," said Sam Strong.

A dozen warriors, mounted on fine ponies, rode out a little distance from the group and began to gallop up and down, and these men carried lances, as well as rifles, which they shook in a threatening way at the little white band. They began to shout also—cries of many kinds.

"Do you know what they're saying?" asked Bob of the leader.

"I can understand some Cheyenne," replied the leader, "an' I ketch a word here an' there, enough to tell me what they mean, an' they're sayin' to us, Bob, that we're mean, low down, cowardly white people, that we're thieves, robbers, skunks, coyotes, that our grandmothers an' grandfathers ain't what they ought to be, an' that our grandsons an' granddaughters, if we should live to have any, which we won't, would be worse, an' they say that we've lived as long as we ought to, or are goin' to, an' they're promisin' to dissect us most beautiful, an' then to have the precious remnants scattered wide among the tribes. These are a few of the things they're sayin' about us, but don't you be scared, Bob; most of them descriptions ain't true, an' not many of them promises will come to pass."

"I'm not scared," replied Bob, stoutly.

He told the truth. The situation had not yet impressed him with the full sense of danger. It was too unreal, too much like a play, a great spectacle of the open air. The gentle wind of the morning was merely the breath of peace. The brandishing of the lances added colour and life to the scene, and while the shouts of the warriors might contain taunts, they came musically at the distance.

The galloping warriors presently cast their lances from them, and came closer. The speed of their horses increased, and the riders lay flat upon the backs and necks of their mounts.

"Keep close all!" suddenly shouted Strong in sharp warning. Even as he spoke he pulled Bob down, and the others ducked.

Four Cheyennes had suddenly dropped down on the far side of their horses, and fired under the necks, leaving only a clinging hand and foot exposed, targets too small for the distance. Two bullets sang over the heads of the crouching trappers, and two more buried themselves, with a nasty little spit, in the sand bank.

The prologue was over. The play had begun in real and deadly earnest. Bob saw it and knew it. Sam Strong's eyes narrowed.

"That's an old trick of theirs," he said, "to shoot from the other side of the horse, an' under his neck, an' it's worked often with greenhorns, but we know a trick or two ourselves, don't we, Bill?"

"Beckon we do," answered the saturnine Missourian.

More bullets made the sand fly up about them.

"Take the first horse, Bill," said Sam.

"I hate to do it, but I'll get him," said the Missourian.

The shouting warriors swung a few yards nearer. The Missourian rested the barrel of his rifle on the sandy bank, aimed with great care, and pulled the trigger. The sharp report, and the rising puff of white smoke followed. The foremost pony made a half leap in the air, and then

ploughed forward, falling upon his side. The Indian, who had been hanging to his far side, sprang clear, alighting on agile feet, but at that instant
Sam Strong, too, pulled the trigger.

The deadly bullet sped, and the warrior, his protection of the living
pony taken from him, fell prone upon the plain and lay still. A shout of
rage came from the other Cheyennes, but now they galloped away from
the hill instead of toward it.

"People have got to pay for their fun," said Sam Strong, as he reloaded.
"I think that a lot of foolishness is over. At least I'm hopin' for the best."

The retiring Cheyennes fired several shots, but all of them fell short,
and then two, riding with their ponies between them and the hill, began
to approach the dead warrior.

"They come for their slain comrade," said Perolet.

"That's so, Frenchy," said Strong, "an' while they're doin' it we won't
fire on 'em."

The two warriors cautiously approached the fallen figure, but as no
bullet came, they seemed to feel that they were safe in their task. They
leaped down, quickly lifted the body across one of the ponies, remounted
as quickly and galloped away.

"I wonder if they feel any gratitude because we didn't shoot at them,"
said Bob.

"'Tain't likely that we'll ever know," replied Strong.

The Cheyennes, now out of rifle range, gathered in a group, and
seemed to take counsel. Meanwhile, the defenders waited patiently.

"Makes me think of the time when we stood on the ridge at Gettysburg, while Pickett and his men were gettin' ready to charge," said
Harris.

"I saw 'em go," rejoined Porter Evans, "an' if there had been more of
them Virginians you wouldn't be here, Tom Harris."

"Thought that war was finished," said Obadiah Pirtle. "Seems it's
ragin' 'bout as bad as our own with the Cheyennes."

Sam Strong took food out of their packs, jerked buffalo meat principally, and gave a share to everyone. Then he showed his method and his
coolness under fire. Buffalo "chips" were lying about near the wallows,
and, throwing several of them together, he lighted a fire on which Perolet
boiled coffee.

"Tastes good, Bob, my boy, don't it?" he said.

"Fine," replied the boy, drinking two cups.

"The great Napoleon say that an army crawl on ets stomach," said
Perolet, "an' he ees right, as always. It fight on ets stomach, too."

A long time passed without any further hostilities from the Cheyennes, and it was very trying. Spring seemed to have melted suddenly

into summer, and a great sun, poised in the centre of the heavens, poured down millions of fiery rays. It grew extremely hot in the shallow depressions, and they felt the want of water. The horses, too, moved restlessly, and had to be quieted now and then. Bob's lips became parched and his tongue lay hot and dry in his mouth.

"What do you think will be their next move, Sam?" asked Porter Evans.

"Hard to say," replied Strong, "but most likely a charge. There are no clouds, and no promise of a dark night, so they can't creep up on us without our seein' 'em. My eyes, but it's hot!"

They had water in canteens, and every man took a sip, but there was none for the horses. Bob being so young, and not yet toughened by experience, suffered the most. But he refused to complain. It seemed to him that the hot air was burning into his brain, but he lay with his face pressed against the sandy bank, and said never a word.

The boy held his rifle in both hands, and the barrel of it was hot to his touch. All the time he was staring out upon the plain at the group of Cheyenne warriors. The heat rose in waves and shimmered before his eyes. By and by the figures of the Cheyennes, some on horse and some on foot, moved further away, and became unreal. Millions of black specks danced before his eyes, and the tint of the air was blood red.

"Here, boy, take a drink of this!" exclaimed Sam Strong.

The sharp voice of the leader called the boy back to earth, and he drank mechanically from a little flask that Strong held to his mouth. It was unpleasant, burning stuff, but his mind and brain cleared instantly.

"Too much strain an' too much sun," said Sam. "Shake yourself up a bit, Bob! Roll around in that wallow, if you want to, while the rest of us watch."

The boy did rise and walk about a little, shaking his head, as if he would clear away the mists and vapours, and flexing his muscles. In a few minutes he felt much better.

"It's pretty hard on a new hand," said Porter Evans. "The terriblest thing about the Civil War was always the long waiting lyin' on the ground, before we marched up an' whipped the Yankees."

"You never—" began Harris, indignantly, but Sam Strong raised his hand warningly.

"Stop that old, dead war, boys," he said. "Here's our live one. The Cheyennes are about to move, I think. See 'em spreadin' out."

Bob ran back to the bank. He could look now with clear eyes and a clear head, and once more the figures of the warriors were sharp, distinct and real. They were dividing into three bands. One remained where it was, and the others filed to right and left.

"They mean to charge from all sides," muttered Sam Strong, "an' with this poor place to fight behind, it's only a matter of how much they'll stand."

He posted his men in a thin circle about the hill, cautioning them all to lie deep in the wallows. He divided their little territory into two half circles, with himself in command of the northern half, and Bill Cole in charge of the southern. He had Bob and Obadiah Pirtle with him and Bill took the other three.

"Now, Bob," he said, "you've heard Porter an' Tom talkin' about all them big fights east of the Missip, in the Civil War, but this is our own special scrap, an' you want to take partic'lar notice of the order of battle which will be somethin' like this: they'll come on in three bands, jumpin' their ponies from side to side, screechin' an' yellin' somethin' terrible. But don't you be flustered, an' don't you fire too soon. They'll be dodgin' behind the necks an' sides of their horses an' plunkin' bullets into our hill here, but jest you wait, an' when you get a good thing to aim at, hit it."

The three bands of Cheyennes hovered a while just out of range. The sun was growing more intense than ever, and the heat floated in waves across the plains.

Bob heard a Cheyenne who wore a great feather headdress, a magnificent war-bonnet, utter a long, thrilling whoop, which was taken up, before it died, by the others. Then the three bands charged their horses at the hill. But they did not come on straight and direct, like white men. Instead, they made their ponies career from side to side. They never ceased to shout their war-cries, and often beat with lances upon the heavy buffalo skin shields that many of them carried.

Some of the exhibitions of horsemanship were splendid. A warrior, hanging it seemed by his foot only, would fire under his horse's neck, and the bullet always struck near the defenders. The blood began to surge to Bob's head, and his finger crept down toward the trigger of his rifle. The Cheyennes were yet at long range, but the temptation to fire was overwhelming. A bullet sang a little song within two inches of his nose. The blood flew to his head, and his finger touched the trigger. But the firm hand of Sam Strong pulled it away.

"Jest a little longer, Bob," he said; "I know it's hard to wait, but we can't waste lead. They'll be near enough mighty soon now."

The weird shouting grew louder, and the rifles of the Cheyennes began to crack fast. Gusts of smoke rose and floated about the plain, and Bob distinctly heard the trampling hoofs as the Cheyennes drew nearer. It was well now that they had the buffalo wallows in which to crouch. A bullet grazed Bill Cole's head and another nipped Porter Evans's arm. But neither man made any outcry.

The shouting of the Cheyennes ceased quite suddenly, and then a single cry arose. It was the signal of the chief who wore the great feather head-dress, and, when they heard it, the warriors of all three divisions ceased their gyrations, and made straight at the little white band, every man bent down almost flat upon the neck of his horse.

"Now, Bob," exclaimed Sam Strong, "pick your man an' let him have it!"

The boy saw through a red mist, but he aimed at a coppery face, just showing over the head of a mustang, and pulled the trigger. Then he saw the mustang galloping away riderless, and he felt, with a kind of a shuddering horror, that he had not missed. But that feeling quickly passed, and was succeeded by another. The desire of combat took hold of him. He lifted his rifle and fired again and then again.

All around the circle the rifles of his comrades were flashing, and they were fired by men who knew how to aim true. The Dog Soldiers, most valiant of the Cheyennes, faced a rain of bullets. Both men and ponies were down, and confusion seized them. They had not expected a fire so fast and deadly, and the rising cloud of smoke caused them to gallop into each other, adding to the confusion.

Ponies, wounded or frightened, reared, threw their riders and galloped over the plain. Others, made riderless by bullets, followed them, and then, above the sound of the shots and the shouting, rose the clear, high-pitched cry of the chief. He was calling his men away when they were yet thirty yards from the wallows, and the Cheyennes were admitting repulse.

The warriors, lifting their dead upon the ponies, fled across the plain, and out of rifle-shot. The defenders turned to their own wounds or needs, all except the valiant little Frenchman, Louis Perolet, who stepped out of his wallow and called after them:

"Ah, you red Indian! You have start to us. Then why you not come? We have the banquet ready. But you stop when you half way an' go back. Then we invite you the second time. We treat you most hospeetable. Or ees eet that you have enough already?"

He waited for an answer, and, as none came, he grew more bitterly sarcastic.

"Ees it that the famous Dog Soldiers of the Cheyennes, of whom the whole world has heard, are afraid of our guns? Do you retreat when the battle has just begun? It was not the way of the great Napoleon. He would go to the feenish, an' the feenish with him was victory."

"Set down there, Frenchy," called Sam Strong. "One of them fellers might reach you yet with a bullet."

"Then I die in a grand cause," rejoined Perolet.

But he came back to the wallow and at once began a congenial task.

"I still remember the saying of the great Napoleon that an army fights on eets stomach," he said, "an' now I feex the stomach while we rest between the mighty battles."

Several buffalo chips were left. In five minutes they were lighted and the coffee was boiling over them. Bob could not eat much, but he found the coffee soothing, and he was very grateful that they had escaped so well. Nobody on their side was killed. Three had received slight wounds to which, after the manner of veteran plainsmen, they paid no further attention when they had been bandaged. But several of the choice Dog Soldiers of the Cheyennes had been slain, others were severely wounded, and the first combat had been clearly in favour of the little band in the buffalo wallows.

"What do you make of it, Bill?" asked Sam Strong, looking attentively at the Cheyennes.

"Nothin'," replied Cole, "'cept that they've had enough of rushin' us for the time, an' mean to wait."

"I size it up the same way. Wish we had a stream of nice fresh water runnin' at our feet, Bill."

Strong looked uneasily at the horses, which were shuffling about restlessly. Only the fact that they were roped together had held them during the firing.

"It's so," said Bill Cole. "They'll want water tre-men-jeous bad before long. We've got enough to last ourselves three or four days, but none for them."

Sam Strong did not answer, but looked up at the blue sky, in which some great, black birds were now wheeling on slow wing. Staunch hunter and borderer though he was, he hated the sight of those birds, and they gave him a little shudder. But he would not let the feeling go far. He summoned up all the courage of his brave hearty and, in his own language, resolutely hoped for the best.

"Think you could sleep a while, Bob?" he said in his most kindly tone to the boy.

"Sleep!" exclaimed the boy, "why how could I at such a time?"

"Sleep, of course you can!" exclaimed Tom Harris. "Why, I slept a full hour at Antietam, jest before we made the last charge that licked the rebels, an' I was right in front of that charge, too."

"You didn't lick us at Antietam," exclaimed Porter Evans, indignantly. "We licked you till we got tired, an' then we walked away, leavin' to you the ground that we didn't want any longer."

"Never you mind these two bull dogs, Bob," said Sam Strong. "They make me think of a fat fellow in a play by Shakespeare that I saw in St. Louis once, though I admit that Tom and Porter here are good men in a scrap when it comes off. Now, Bob, you just try to sleep. You'll be surprised how easy it'll come, an' it'll do you a lot of good. If the Cheyennes come up here an' have an engagement with us we'll wake you up, don't worry."

Bob concluded to try it. It seemed to him the part of a veteran campaigner, and he wanted to do the proper thing. He lay down in one of the wallows, put his folded blanket under his head, and then his cap over his eyes to shade them from the light.

It was a little after noon, and the sun was amazingly bright and hot. From under the edge of his cap brim the boy saw the heat waves rolling up again. He also saw wheeling in the heavens the same great, black birds that Sam Strong had noticed, but he did not draw the same inference from them. They were birds to him, and nothing more.

Bob, still resolute to do what a veteran should do, exerted all the power of his will over his muscles and senses. He lay perfectly still, and tried to imagine that he was in a bed, and that no danger was near. Circumstances helped him. The camp grew quite quiet. The horses ceased their restless shuffle, the men sat quite still. Three of them had lighted pipes and were smoking. Bob, remembering his earlier youth, began to say the multiplication table to himself. It seemed so amusing to him that he should do such a thing, at such a time and place, that he laughed under his breath.

The laugh was soothing. Gradually his pulses ceased to beat so strongly. The fever went from his brain, his whole figure relaxed and Sam Strong's words were coming true. It was easier to sleep than he had thought.

The wheeling birds became dim and were lost in the sky. The figures of his comrades sitting near him, and of the horses, floated off into space. His eyelids drooped, shut entirely, and there upon the great plain, fresh from the battle, with the Dog Soldiers of the Cheyennes yet about him, the overtaxed boy slept. His regular breathing soon rose, and was noticed by the men. Sam Strong walked to him and pulled the brim of his cap a little further over his eyes.

"Good stuff, ain't he?" he whispered, with something of a father's tenderness in his tone. "We made no mistake when we picked up that Bob boy, did we?"

"Not by a long sight," replied Bill Cole. "But he's got baptized mighty early. He's come right into the middle of a terrible hot thing."

Bob slept soundly a long time, and he would have slept longer, but the hand of Sam Strong was on his arm, and a voice said in his ear:

"Wake up, Bob, somethin's goin' to happen."

The boy sat up instantly, wide awake and grasping his rifle with his hands.

"Are the Cheyennes about to charge again?" he asked.

"No," replied Strong, "they're not. Somethin' else is comin' into this little affair of ours. Look there, Bob. Look out into the east!"

The boy followed the long pointing finger, and beheld an immense dark cloud that came on fast. But this cloud, although it banked against the horizon, was not of the air. It clung close to the earth, and it filled the entire east.

"It's a buffalo herd," said Sam Strong, "an' most likely it's the same one that we had the run in with the other day. It's been wanderin' aroun' in search of grass, an' two to one its been scared ag'in by the Indian hunters. But, boys, whatever the cause, an' whatever be runnin' through them there heads of theirs, that buffalo herd, a million strong, has come just in time."

"Why, how can it help us?" asked Bob.

"It ain't meanin' to help us, but it will, an' it will help us a heap. Just you wait a few minutes, an' you will see."

But by waiting Sam did not mean that the time should be spent in inactivity. He issued short, swift orders, and they were obeyed with the same speed.

"Untie the horses!" he said. "Fix the packs! Look to your arms! Have everything ready to march at an instant's notice."

Bob sprang to the work with the others. He led his own pony from one of the wallows, and he held the lariats of two more. Meanwhile, the mighty buffalo herd was still rapidly approaching. Sam was probably right in his surmise that it was the same herd that they had seen a few days before, but it seemed to have increased in numbers, perhaps others had joined it, and they could not see anywhere a break in the dark line that spread from the northern horizon to the southern.

"It will carry everything before it," said Sam Strong. "While I was hopin' for the best, the buffaloes have come an' saved us. Look, the Dog Soldiers are tryin' to shoot a way through them."

The Cheyennes, all mounted now and in solid mass, were firing into the herd with the evident purpose of making it break in half, and pass to right or left. Usually such an effort would have been a success, but this herd was so immense, and it was driven on by such a powerful impulse, that the dark line remained unbroken, others closing up where their brethren had fallen.

"They'll have to run for it," said Bill Cole. "an' so will we."

"But we run willingly," said Sam Strong. "There, look! the Dog Soldiers have broke, an' see that long tongue of buffaloes streamin' by the side of 'em on the south. They've got to gallop to the north, an', boys, we'll gallop to the south, while a million buffaloes come in between. To your saddles!"

Everyone sprang upon his horse, holding firmly to the lariats of the led animals, and with Sam Strong at their head they galloped out of the wallows, turning due south.

Behind them the whole plain shook with the tread of the mightiest herd that Sam Strong had ever seen, pushing forward in irresistible columns between the Cheyennes and the little white band that they had regarded as their sure prey. Wider and wider grew the separating current, until a full five miles of buffaloes flowed between.

Southward rode the comrades at a good pace, and they were joyous now. They knew it would be long before the Cheyennes could pick up their trail again, probably never, and they might regard themselves safe, at least for the time. Moreover, the sun was setting, the pleasant coolness of the twilight was coming, and the brisk air gave new life.

Porter Evans suddenly began to laugh.

"Now, what under the sun is the matter with you, you Johnny Reb?" asked Tom Harris.

"I was just thinking Tom, that while you an' me don't agree much about the Civil War, you claimin' that you whipped us, an' we knowin' that we jest eternally wore ourselves out whippin' you, that none of them big battles, in which you an' me was such important figgers, was ever stopped by a herd of wild cattle buttin' in between the two armies."

"That's mighty true, even if it is the first true word that you've ever spoke about the Civil War, Port," said Harris.

The sun went down like a plummet behind the hills, the twilight turned into the night, clear and cold, and Strong checked their speed. From the north came the faint rumble of the marching million.

"The Cheyennes might as well try to ride their ponies across the Missouri in flood as get through that herd," said Obadiah Pirtle.

"Well spoke, Obe," said Strong, "an' bein' as the best that we've been hopin' for has come to pass, we might walk our horses a while. 'Pears to me what we need most now is water for our animals, an' we must keep on until we find it. Scratch your head, Bill, an' see if you can rec'lect any spot on this piece of land where it can be found."

Bill Cole took the suggestion literally. He removed his cap and ran his finger nails thoughtfully across his head. "I've hunted buffalo 'roun' here more 'n once," he said, "an' there is a sunk place where the water oozes out of the ground and makes a big pool that drains away into the plain, an' then is lost farther on. But it is tre-men-je-ously hard for me to locate it as there ain't no sign posts that I can see, an' I don't see no guide comin'."

"Rub your head real hard, Monsieur Bill," said Louis Perolet, entreatingly. "It is massage. It make the brain act queeck, an' maybe it bring you the intelligence you need."

"All right, Mossoo Looey," said Bill, good-naturedly. "I'll do it. I guess it's what the great Napoleon always did when he wasn't sure about things."

He rubbed his head with great vigour, and then spoke up triumphantly.

"It does work, Frenchy," he said. "Now I remember. As certain as I'm sittin' here on top of this horse, that spring lies off there, the way my finger's p'intin'."

They rode without hesitation toward the southwest, where his finger pointed, and the further they went the more confident Bill became. In an hour the horse that he rode threw up his head and uttered a whinney of pleasure.

"That settles it," said Bill. "He smells water. Don't I know this horse of mine? Don't I know every neigh of his? He's got one for water, one for grass, one for feelin' good, another for feelin' bad, and so on. This is his water neigh, an' it's comin' straight from his heart."

The other horses pricked up their heads also, and without urging increased their speed. Before long the ground softened a little, they saw ahead of them a thin fringe of trees, and then, shining between the trunks, a blessed silvery surface that they knew to be water.

They rode straight into the pool, and every horse, standing with the water to his knees, drank deeply.

CHAPTER 5

The Snowy Pass

Bob had never before in his life felt so deep a thrill of happiness. They had escaped from a great danger. He knew now how providential was the intervention of the buffalo herd, and they had found the water, without which they could not live, even after slipping from the grasp of the Cheyennes. He sat on his pony, and listened to its gurgling as the good beast drank. The same gurgling sound was all around him.

"I guess these horses of ours are plum glad," said Obadiah Pirtle, "an' it makes me glad to see 'em glad."

"Same here," said Sam Strong, "but we mustn't let 'em drink too much right at the start. Lead 'em out of the pool, and we'll let 'em have another try at it in half an hour."

The horses were ridden out of the water, although they required much urging, and then they sought a likely spot for a camp. The pool, which was on the southern side of a swell, steeper than usual in that region, was forty or fifty yards in diameter with an average depth of about three feet. At the southern edge was the outlet, a tiny brook that soon lost itself on the plain. To the right of the pool was a hollow, dry and well enclosed with cotton-woods.

"Of course the Indians come here at times to drink and to water their horses," said Sam Strong, "but we've got to risk that chance, an' camp here tonight, an' what's more, after all we've been through have warm food and warm coffee. What say you, Louis? Are you ready to fix them for us?"

"Eef you keep off the rascally Cheyennes an' don't let them fire any bullets into my camp-kettle or coffee pot, I give you food and coffee that warm not only your body, but your soul," replied Perolet. "I am the great culinary arteest, an' it is at such times that I shine. The cook is greater when he cook under fire. What a great arteest the cook of the great Napoleon must have been!"

Strong knew that the fire might serve as a guiding hand to the Indians, but he knew also the great value of warmth and comfort to his band. Moreover, the danger could be minimized. They dug out a place in the soft side of the hill with one of the shovels that they carried in their packs, and then they filled in the space with dry fallen wood which they coaxed into a fire. The hole was like an oven and no breeze arose, but a great heat was thrown out. Soon a mass of coals was formed, and Perolet cooked food, and boiled coffee in abundance for them all.

Bob felt an immense relief. The night was chill, but he had drawn a blanket about his shoulders, and sat with his face to the coals. He was very tired, but it was a happy weariness, and he thought that God had been very good to them. It seemed to him that, the buffalo herd had been sent to save them.

"Sam," he asked, "do you think the Cheyennes will try to follow us again?"

"Not that crowd, anyway. It will be too hard for them to pick up our trail a second time, an' bein' at war with our people, they've got more important work to the eastward. Now, boys, we'll just smother up the rest of this fire, and most of us will go to sleep."

They threw earth on the coals, and, after securing the horses, all lay down to sleep except Sam Strong and Louis Perolet. Bob secured a promise that he would be awakened for the second watch, saying that he ought to stand sentinel as he was the only one who had slept in the afternoon.

The difference was very great, as he sought slumber for the second time in twelve hours. Then the hot sun was burning down upon him; now it was dark night, and the cold had come. But the heavy blanket, wrapped around him, fended off the chill, and made him feel all the snugger because of it.

He did not linger long at the border of sleep, but the events of the day passed rapidly before him. Most vivid of all was the charge of the Cheyennes, and its confused and terrible medley of men and horses, of fire and shots and shouts. He saw the whole red picture before him again, then it passed like a shadow on a screen, and he fell quietly to sleep.

But Bob did not stand sentinel any part of that night. About one o'clock in the morning, when the watch of Sam Strong and Louis Perolet was finished, Sam looked down at the sleeping boy. There was not much light, but the eyes of the two were trained to darkness, and they could see Bob very well. Although breathing regularly and steadily, his face was quite white. He showed plainly to the experienced men the terrible strain through which he had passed.

"Am I going to wake him, Frenchy, for his turn of the watch?" asked Sam Strong in a low, almost solemn voice.

"No, Meester Strong," replied Louis Perolet, "you are like the great

Napoleon, who, finding the exhausted sentinel asleep, took the rifle from his unknowing hands, an' did the watching heemself."

"Sometimes I think you're a great man, Louis," said Sam Strong. "You've read my mind most terrible exact. Now you wake up Obe, there, an' in an hour or two I'll make Bill take my place."

When Bob awoke, the coffee was boiling again for breakfast, and they only laughed when he asked, with some indignation, why they had not awakened him.

"Why didn't we wake you up?" replied Perolet at last. "Why, we couldn't. First Sam shake you until he get tired, then I shake you until my two arms ache. Then we wake up the others an' all together shake you, but you just snore on. Then we think of bringing up the strongest horse an' let heem keeck you, but Sam Strong say no. We cannot afford to have our best horse lamed."

They laughed again, and Bob, seeing that he could get no satisfaction out of them, turned to his breakfast, which he ate with the keenest appetite.

"Aha, Meester Bob is heemself again," said Perolet, contemplating him with satisfaction. "Like the great Napoleon, he is nearly ready now for another battle with the Cheyennes."

Bob laughed.

"I think I'd rather wait a day or two for that," he said.

After he had eaten, Sam, Bill and the boy ascended the hill, from the base of which the water trickled, and studied the entire circumference of the plain. They could see nothing but a few scattered buffaloes, grazing at a distance of a mile or so, although the eye ranged many miles in the thin, clear air.

"It's pretty sure that the Cheyennes either lost the trail or did not hunt for it again," said Strong. "At any rate I'm hopin' for the best, so we ought to stop a day at the pool, and renew our supplies for the long march that's ahead of us."

The suggestion seemed good to all, and they spent some busy hours. Sam and Bill rode out, shot a buffalo cow, and brought in fresh meat. Tom Harris and Porter Evans, both capital men with horses, looked after bruised shoulders or sore feet among the ponies. Now and then sounds of wordy strife over some battle in the Civil War arose, but they worked on in the utmost harmony and good comradeship.

"Funny," said Louis Perolet, "two men shoot at each odder for four years, an' then be such friends' that each would die for the odder."

Obadiah Pirtle was working among the stores. He had all a Yankee's cleverness and ingenuity, and he was reducing the size of the packs without throwing anything away. Bob helped Perolet with the cleaning and cooking of the buffalo meat.

"Eet ees one great science," said Perolet, "an' we French who have ceevilized the whole world, an' paid for it, teach it. Many a man has starved to death on the plains and in the mountains with food at hees hands."

Bob also took turns at the watch on the hill, but the day passed on, and they saw nothing hostile on the horizon. It was brilliant and hot, like the one just before it, and Bob felt as if the pool with the cottonwoods about it was an island, and that, when they left it, they were about to venture upon a trackless sea.

Everything was ready, and they departed just after nightfall, both Strong and Cole feeling that it would be safer for the present to travel in the darkness. But as there was no sign of danger that night, nor any the following day, they soon resumed the natural mode of progress, the night for sleep and rest, and the day for riding.

Now ensued a most wonderful journey. They were marching straight into the golden west, although their gold was to be taken in traps, and was not to be dug from the ground. Every hour of it was full of variety and delight for Bob. He saw spring, with magic touch, transform the plains. He saw the young grass springing up everywhere, and many a shy little wild flower almost hidden in its roots. Now and then, they saw far blue hills but they always kept away from them. Buffalo and antelope were abundant, and the prairie chickens whirred near the camp. Water was more plentiful than usual. Many pools were standing from the spring rains, and they crossed two or three shallow rivers, clear cold streams, flowing in wide sandy beds.

Gradually the picture of the fierce Dog Soldiers and the charge, when white and red came face to face, faded from Bob's mind. Again it had become a peaceful world through which he was travelling.

As they advanced far into the west the grass became thinner and the game scarcer. Now and then they crossed stretches of country which were desert, but always the air was pure, and had a snap to it It rained only once or twice, and, although they had two tents with them, they always slept in the open. Bob thrived wonderfully in this wild life. Already a strong, dexterous boy, the men could almost see him growing, and no one was handier with the horses, or at any kind of work. One evening in a wrestling match he threw both Porter Evans and Tom Harris, and pinned their shoulders squarely against the ground.

"You're comin' on, Bob," said Sam Strong, as he puffed at his pipe. "To down General Grant and General Lee in the same evenin' is a pretty big thing."

"It was more trick than anything else," said Bob, modestly.

"Good trick to know," said Obadiah Pirtle. "May need it some day."

More days of peace and easy marching followed. The great plains fell behind them, and one afternoon a dim blue line showed along the entire horizon in front of them.

"The Rockies!" exclaimed Bob.

"That's right." said Sam Strong. "We've been climbin' the slopes of the Rockies a long time, slopes so gentle that you don't notice it, but them's peaks you see there."

But to Bob it was his first view of the Rockies, of those famous Rocky Mountains of which he had been hearing all his life, mountains filled with danger, mystery and treasure.

"Our trapping grounds are in there somewhere, are they not?" he asked of Sam Strong.

Sam pointed vaguely toward the southwest.

"Down there," he replied, "among the high ranges, but we've got a good deal of rough travellin' yet."

"All right, we can stand it," exclaimed Bob, joyously. "We're to have a little experience with the Rockies."

Sam Strong smiled. He knew the value of enthusiasm, and he would never discourage it.

"That's the right spirit, boy," he said. "I've always tried to hope for the best, an' I'm glad to see that you're doin' it, too. It helps a heap. There'll be work an' danger in them mountains, but well do the one, an' conquer the other, won't we, Bob, my boy?"

"We will," said Bob, stauncher than ever in the respect and admiration that he felt for his leader.

There were yet four hours of daylight after the first sight of the mountains, and they rode until nightfall, but the ranges did not seem to come any nearer. Sam told the boy that they were yet a great distance away. They had seen them because they were so high, and the air was so clear. They would be riding all the next day, and the mountains would yet be a mere blue bank on the horizon.

The country, after a stretch of almost desert, began to improve again. The buffalo grass was abundant, and the horses throve on it wonderfully. Nor had Strong and Cole allowed them to be pushed, knowing how necessary to them these animals were. So it was a fat and sleek expedition that encamped that night on the plain. No longer having fear of the Cheyennes, they built a fine fire of buffalo chips, and ate plentifully of game that they had killed by the way.

Bob walked out a little distance from the camp later in the evening. There was a good moonlight, but he could see the mountains only in his fancy. Nevertheless, to see them thus impressed his imagination as much as the reality. He was eager to be up there among the peaks and ridges, where their work lay. He had seen enough of the plains for a while, and he longed for the crests, white with snow, the slopes and the valleys, green with great forests, and the rushing torrents of ice cold water of which his comrades had talked so much to him. They would find there the beaver, their special treasure, the elk, the bear, and the wolf and the mighty grizzly would not be absent. It appealed powerfully to him, and once more he vowed that he would never spare any effort or any risk to help these comrades who had been so good to him.

When he came back to the campfire, Louis Perolet looked at him quizzically.

"You have been staring at the mountains that you cannot see, Meester Bob," he said. "That ees right. The mountains have the majesty, the grandeur. Wait until you see them closer, with the white snow on their heads. They seem to reach up to the great God, and to be silent and awful like Heem."

The Frenchman had begun in a light vein, but he ended with the greatest gravity, and as Bob nodded, he added:

"You can never make fun of the mountains."

Bob watched the blue line all the next day, as they rode toward it, but when night came it was still a blue line, though heavier and darker than before.

"If we start bright an' early we'll strike the first slopes about tomorrow night," said Sam Strong, "an', if I ain't greatly fooled, we'll pitch our camp in the first belt of pines. It will feel good to me to smell the pines again."

They were on the march at the first start of dawn, and now when Bob saw white crests soaring far up into the air, he felt all the emotions that Louis Perolet had predicted. Sometimes clouds or mists hid the lower slopes, and then the snowy heads seemed to float in the air, adding to the sense of mystery and solemnity.

When the clouds and vapours floated away, the ridges and peaks began to take shape. Irregular lines were disclosed, and here and there appeared openings which, at the distance, looked as narrow as knife blades. As they rode on Bob also saw the green tint made by the evergreens.

The plain, watered all the year around by the melting snows, was now high in grass, and big game was plentiful. They could have shot enough in a day or two to feed a regiment. But a herd of wild horses, the first that he had seen, interested Bob the most. They were at least a hundred in number, fine, clean animals, and from a distance of only three or four hundred yards they watched the trappers riding past. Presently they threw up their heads and galloped off in a file toward the south.

"Happy critters," said Porter Evans. "Nothin' to do but eat an' see the world."

They rode rather faster than usual that day, and as Sam Strong had foretold, they reached the first gentle slope, where the pine was mingled with the ash and the oak. Here was a creek taking it somewhat easier after its rush down the slopes, but ice cold, as Bob's comrades had told him it would be. In fact, everything they had said was coming true. There was the keen balsamic odour of the pines which Bob inhaled gratefully, and the wind that blew now did not come over empty space. It whistled down through great forests.

The wind was cold, too, and Bob found his blanket very welcome. So was the fire built from fallen boughs of oak and ash, and as they sat around it they discussed the second stage of their great campaign. Bob learned that they were now at one of the high passes of the highest Rockies, known only to Indians and wandering trappers, and that their march through it would be slow and risky.

"Will there be any danger from Indians?" he asked Sam Strong.

"Not from Cheyennes, but some wandering Utes might take pot shots at us. That's a chance that we must risk."

They rested three days before undertaking the arduous passage of the vast ranges. The horses, already in good condition, cropped the rich grass and grew fatter.

Bill Cole shot a splendid elk, Porter Evans and Tom Harris caught trout in the creek, and they had a great feast. The remainder of the meat, according to their custom, they packed, ready to be carried on the horses.

There was another overhauling of clothing. Sam Strong told Bob to wrap himself up as warmly as possible.

"Maybe you won't think it's going to be very cold," he said, "but you'll find it out by the time we rise a mile or two. It ain't yet full summer on the mountains, an' there's snow an' ice in plenty."

The third day being completed they packed their horses and began the ascent of the pass. The trail was narrow, but for a long time it was good, though it rose rapidly. Before noon the men dismounted and led all the horses. Bob was near the end of the file, and it seemed to him that he had come into another world. Vast forests were about him. He looked down into a deep chasm on one side, and up to a mighty peak on the other. He saw great fields of ice and snow, and he heard the sound of rushing waters. Once a bear crawled through the underbrush, and again the elk were whistling on the slopes.

The wind grew keener and colder. Coming down from the snow-fields it had an edge of ice, and Bob was thankful for Sam Strong's advice about the clothes. But he was vastly interested, enjoying every moment of the march. He wished to see everything, to note every kind of tree, and to remember the slopes of the ridges and peaks, as far as his eye could reach.

They stopped about the middle of the afternoon and took a rest of an hour, much needed by men and horses. Bob looked back, and he was surprised to see that the plains were yet so near. There they were, rolling away in faint green swells toward the east, and the distance between him and that waving expanse did not seem to be more than a few hundred yards. They had been travelling at such an angle that they had not achieved distance as much as height. Obadiah Pirtle saw him looking back and he remarked tersely:

"It's goin' to be a tre-men-jeous climb, but we'll make it all right."

At three o'clock they began to ascend again. The ponies now proved troublesome. The steepness of the climb, the increasing thinness of the air and the cold seemed to terrify them. Four of the party now went before, holding the lariats, and three came behind armed with stout sticks, ready to beat the stubborn, or the sluggish, back into the path of duty.

They talked for a while, but after the first hour fell into complete silence. The steepness was telling on both man and brute, and the wind from the peaks was blowing with increasing strength and coldness. Already they had reached the region of snow, and Bob saw ravines and chasms in which it lay many feet deep. But the white heads seemed to tower as far above as ever.

His own riding pony, which he led with two others, stopped suddenly, made a desperate effort to catch the stony soil with his front hoofs, and, failing, was about to plunge downward five hundred feet, but Bob, with great presence of mind, released the other two, and pulled with all his might on the single lariat.

The descent of the pony, sustained a little also by his own efforts, was checked, but Bob could not hold him long.

"Help!" he cried loudly. "Quick! quick!"

The two soldiers, who were nearest, releasing their own horses, sprang forward and seized the lariat. The three pulled together with a mighty jerk, and the pony helping, he was drawn back into the path, where he stood weak and shivering, just like a human being saved from imminent death.

The other ponies had been thrown into fright by the plight of their comrade, and might have stampeded down the pass, but the three men behind them closed up and restored order. It was at least a quarter of an hour, however, before the animals were soothed sufficiently to go on without resistance or trembling.

Night came early on these eastern slopes of the heights. The sun was soon gone beyond the high peaks, and cold darkness advanced. Strong and Cole conferred anxiously, and it was evident to Bob, who saw them looking about, that they sought a place for a camp. They found it at last in a comparatively level spot, of half an acre or so, studded about with dwarf pines. Near the centre of it was a lakelet perhaps twenty yards across, but apparently deep, and they tethered all the horses near its edge. Brute beasts though they were, they neighed their gladness, and when the men built a fire of unusual size from the fallen timber, they drew as near to it as their lariats allowed.

It was their first mountain camp, and for a while all felt the cold and desolation. Having no fear of Indians here, they threw on wood until the fire fairly roared, but it was yet desolate and chill beyond the circle of the firelight. Bob, from where he sat, saw to the right and above him a vast field of ice and snow, glittering and unearthly in the moonlight.

Before their supper was over snow began to fall in huge flakes, whirled lazily here and there by the wind. They unpacked their two canvas tents and raised them as a protection, but it was not the whirling flakes, at this stage of the ascent, that worried Sam Strong. It was the omen of what might be when they approached the crest of the pass.

"It looks bad," he said to Bill Cole. "We've got to expect wind an' snow, an' lots of both."

Bill Cole nodded. But Bob, with his heavy blanket wrapped about his shoulders, was not feeling any apprehensions. He had an abiding faith that they would triumph over everything. He walked to the edge of the pine grove with Louis Perolet, and stood there looking out at the cold world. The plains could not be seen now in the grey of the night, and apparently there was a bottomless gulf at their feet But above them, just where the moon hung over the highest crest, it was brighter. Directly between him and the moon, Bob saw the outline of some animal, thickset, and with horns. The intense moonlight made it stand out sharply and seem very near. It was perched on a rock, gazing downward at the light in the pine grove.

"A mountain sheep," said Louis Perolet, "but too far away for a shot."

"I shouldn't want to shoot at him, even if he were near enough," said the boy. "We do not need him."

"You are right," said Perolet. "Why should we keel the monarch of the cliffs when he does not hurt us an' we do not wish to eat heem?"

The animal turned back from the projecting rock and disappeared. Presently a low sound, distant and rhythmical, came to Bob's ears.

"Do you hear that, Louis?" he asked. "What is it?"

"Eet ees a snow-slide," replied Perolet, "an' eet ees maybe a mile away. The snow has been loosened by the warmer air of spring an' eet plunges down the mountain in mighty masses. Eet ees lucky that we are not in the path of any snow-field here."

"It is so," said Bob. "It would be a pity, wouldn't it, if our great expedition were suddenly blotted out here by a hundred thousand tons of snow?"

Perolet nodded, and the two walked back to the fire.

CHAPTER 6

The Precipice

When Bob and Louis Perolet were in the full blaze of the firelight, Sam Strong signed to them to sit down, and they did so, warming their hands at the welcome blaze. It was evident to Bob that the others had been talking about a matter of gravity, and he waited for Sam to speak.

"We've been turnin' things over a bit," said the leader, "an' we want the whole gang to agree, so if things go wrong nobody can say 'I told you so.' I'm always hopin' for the best, but there's no use tryin' to hide from ourselves the fact that the weather is goin' to be bad, mighty bad, while we're travellin' across the mountains. It ain't goin' to be no summer picnic. Do any of you want to turn back an' wait until the warm weather has melted the snow more? If so, let him speak up."

He waited and there was a dead silence. Bob, watching him closely by the firelight, saw a faint smile flicker for a moment in the eyes of the plainsman.

"I don't hear anybody shoutin'," said Sam. "Now, whoever is in favour of goin' on, snow or no snow, ice or no ice, storm or no storm, let him say 'I'." .

"I!" shouted six voices together.

"An' I'll add another 'I'," said Sam Strong.

"Of course we'll go on," said Porter Evans. "The Yankee army would have turned back at these mountains, but the Confederate army would have gone straight ahead, hittin' only the high places."

"You got used to hittin' the high places, when we were after you," rejoined Tom Harris.

Bob kept the first watch with the leader, and as the night deepened and the fire died down, he felt to its full extent the mighty desolation of the cold wilderness. The settled east seemed inexpressibly far, so remote that it never could be reached again, and he was glad enough to have Sam walking beside him. Twice more they heard the sound of snow slides, and once the long, whining cry of a wolf.

"That's the mountain kind," said Sam. "Big, grey fellows. I've seen 'em six feet long, an' I wouldn't want to meet one, I can tell you, unless I had a gun along with me."

Bob watched only until midnight, and then he made his preparations for bed very carefully. He crawled into the tent, already occupied by Harris and Evans, spread one blanket carefully on some leaves that they had gathered, wrapped another around him from his neck to his toes, lay down on the first blanket, and composed himself for slumber, although he was situated so he could see through the open flap of the tent. He awoke at some hour of the night and saw that it was snowing, not a snow driven by the wind, but heavy flakes dropping straight down. They were so thick that he could not see the surface of the lakelet, but in his half dreamy state he was not disturbed. The warmth and comfort of his blankets only soothed him soon to deeper slumber.

They found the pass the next morning more formidable than before. The snow had ceased to fall, but it lay a foot deep on the ground, hiding the bad places of the pass and making the good ones slippery. Every man drew the flaps of his fur cap about his ears, tied a woollen comforter about his neck, and put on buckskin gloves. Strong led the way, and all the morning they climbed, choosing the trail with infinite care, and proceeding very slowly. Once they heard the roar of a coming snow-slide, and uncertain whether to go forward or turn back they stood still, all except the horses which shivered with fright, although they did not try to break from the hold of the men.

The avalanche passed two or three hundred yards to the right of them, bearing trees and bushes upon its crest. It made a tremendous, crashing roar, but in a few moments it was gone, and they could hear it thundering far down the mountainside.

"Feels just as if you were at Gettysburg an' a hundred pound cannon-shot had whizzed by your head, just tippin' your left ear, to let you know that it was passing" said Porter Evans.

The wind did not blow until nearly noon, and then it cut deep. Bob's hands grew cold, despite his buckskin gloves, and he was forced to take them out two or three times and rub them with snow to drive away the numbness. But the fine particles of snow, driven into their eyes by the wind, troubled them most. It was like hail, and it became so strong at last that they were forced to stop and turn their backs to it.

"We're goin' to have a blizzard, an' there's no use denyin' it, even if one does hope for the best," said Sam Strong, "an' what we want is shelter."

"An' we want it terrible queeck," said Louis Perolet. "It's a time when the great Napoleon himself would stop."

Strong and Cole, being the strongest, went on ahead a little distance to look for a camp, while the others held the horses. They returned presently, giving a shout of triumph as they approached. They had found a big hollow or cave-like opening in the rocks, three or four hundred yards ahead, where they would be protected from snow and wind alike.

They urged the horses forward anew, but they were a long time in travelling those three or four hundred yards. Several of them had to be beaten with sticks before they would face the stinging sleet.

But when the place, described by Bill and Sam, was reached, it proved a genuine haven, a great recess in the rocks, with an arching stone roof and a comparatively level floor. It was open on only one side, that toward the east, and the wind was blowing from the west.

The horses might not have been willing to enter such a place at any ordinary time, but now they went in willingly, and cowered against the stone wall for protection. The men felt an equal relief. They were no longer blinded by the driven snow, and the wind beat itself out against the stone wall.

But secure as they were for the present, Strong felt great apprehension lest the wind shift. If it turned about, and came out of the east, they would be protected only in part, and he was in a great hurry to fix the tents so firmly that they could not be blown away. They were tied to every available corner of stone, and then the edges were held down by other stones. Thus secured, it would take a mighty blast to tear them from their moorings. The horses were tethered also, lest they take fright and dash over a cliff.

A fire would have been cheerful, but no wood was to be found at that rocky height, and all of the men sought the shelter of the tents, where they sat wrapped in their heaviest clothing and blankets. But Louis Perolet, not daunted at all, brought forth a little alcohol lamp and lighted it. Then he cooked buffalo strips, made them hot coffee, and they were reasonably happy.

"Eet ees not so bad," said Perolet, cheerfully. "Eet ees like the great Napoleon, crossing the Alps to achieve the gran' victory of Marengo. Monsieur Strong ees Napoleon, an' we are the marshals."

The wind did not abate, but it still blew from the northwest, and shrieked over their heads. Although they heard' it well" they felt its force but little. Evans and Harris now and then went among the horses, and soothed them with a touch or a word.

"It's wonderful what a gift them two generals have with horses," said Sam Strong. "Some men are that way. I guess they know how to talk horse talk to a horse."

Dark came very early, and, while it was yet twilight, Bob and Sam stood at the edge of the alcove, looking out at what had been their trail.

The wind, loaded with snow, screamed past them, but Sam, who was looking up the sharp ascent, pressed his hand upon Bob's arm.

"Don't move or speak!" he whispered. "See who's coming."

A hundred yards above them, two Indians, wrapped in blankets and thick leggings, were staggering down the trail. Their heads were bent in the effort to secure firm footing, and they seemed to have neither eye nor thought for anything else.

"Unless they know of this place they won't see us," whispered Strong. "It's hid too much by the dark an' the snow. They're Utes from the other side of the mountains, an' they're no friends of ours."

Bob could not keep from asking one question.

"Suppose they do know of this place," he said, "and attempt to turn into it?"

"I don't like to think of it," replied the leader. But one hand in its buckskin gauntlet slipped down to the breech of his rifle. Bob's heart began to beat fast. He devoutly hoped that the Utes would go on. They were strong, determined men, and the; carried rifles, but they would have no chance if the turned aside into the fatal alcove.

Nearer they came. Now they were level with the white men, and it seemed impossible to Bob that the two warriors should not see the wide mouth of the stony alcove. But he forgot the dusk and the driving snow. The Utes passed on, and Bob's heart ceased its hard and painful beating. They were forty, fifty yards beyond the alcove, and then the snow and the darkness hid them. Bob gave a great sigh of relief and Sam Strong heard it.

"I guess I'm as glad as you are, Bob, that they went on," he said. "A fellow doesn't want to spill blood in a blizzard."

That night the storm became terrible in its strength and intensity. None of them slept, except at brief intervals, and Evans and Harris stayed almost all the time with the horses, which had to be soothed like frightened children. The screaming of the wind from the peaks and among the great clefts and canyons was almost like that of a human voice, although infinitely more powerful.

Both snow and wind ceased the next morning, but it was intensely cold. The surface of the snow was frozen, but Strong and Cole agreed that it would thereby afford a better footing for both men and animals and they resumed the march onward and upward. It was a cold, white world that Bob looked upon now, whether below or above. All the forests on the lower slopes were covered with snow and ice, and the plains were merely a white blur.

Far above them they again saw mountain sheep perched on jutting rocks, not one, this time, but a score, calmly regarding these curious two-legged creatures who were invading their domain. The sight of them and of their apparent confidence annoyed Louis Perolet. He shook his fist at an old ram and said:

"The great Napoleon when he was crossing the Alps to achieve the immortal victory of Marengo did not turn aside to shoot the chamois, an' I, Louis Perolet, started on the greatest fur hunt the world has ever known, will not stop an' waste my precious time to shoot an impudent old ram."

As they neared the summit of the pass, and the slope became steeper, the horses had fairly to be dragged along. Evans and Harris coaxed them as much as possible, but the stout stick had to come into play also. Their progress was so slow now that they scarcely seemed to move. Sometimes they started a snow-slide themselves, and they could hear it rolling away far below them.

Strong was anxious to reach the summit of the pass before night, but it still towered far above them, and there was no certainty that the blizzard might not begin again.

But, further on, the trail improved somewhat, leading between high ridges on either side, and the snow here was not so deep. Its effect was most beneficial upon the horses, which pricked up their heads, and nearly doubled their pace. Nature, too, seemed bent, for the moment, upon helping them, as the wind died entirely, and they made good speed, despite the rarefied air which was now trying.

"We will reach it," said Louis Perolet energetically.

"The new Napoleon an' his marshals will camp on the crest of the pass to-night. Eet ees so. I have said eet."

His prediction, or rather assertion, came true, and, just before sunset, they stood on the backbone of the pass, ten thousand feet or more above the sea. On either side of them, and, before them, towered other peaks nearly a mile higher, all white with snow.

It was to Bob a scene of indescribable majesty and solemnity. He was lifted far above the earth. Not only were the peaks white, but so was everything else, the ridges, the slopes and the far dim plains, except in the west, where a setting sun of supernatural brightness tinted half of the world with reddish gold. It was like some vast primeval planet, to which man had not yet been born.

The boy was awed, and, when he looked at his comrades, he knew that the same feeling was strong within them. They were not cultivated men in the ordinary sense, but the tremendous spectacle made a deep appeal to them. Sam Strong was the first to speak.

"I ain't a gushin' man" he said, "but I reckon it was worth the climb up here to see this. I've seen it twice before, but it's finest now."

Almost as he spoke, the sun dropped behind a vast range much further west, and the red gold of the sun, that fell across the snow, turned to a pale silver grey. Cold night came down swiftly, and all turned to the work of making a camp.

They could not find a place so suitable as that of the night before, but they were able to secure a fair degree of shelter behind some immense boulders, where they threw up a wall of smaller stones, facing towards the northwest, in case the wind that they dreaded most should begin to blow again. But the night passed, without trouble, although it was intensely cold, and, in the morning, they began the long descent, which would be extremely broken and irregular. In the valley they had cut grass for the horses which they brought on the packs, and, before starting, they served a liberal portion to them.

By the time they had been marching two hours, great masses of clouds floated in between them and the valley and the world was blotted out again. From the northwest came a mutter and then a whistle. The dreaded wind was blowing again. It was in their faces now, deadly cold, and they made many stops. Strong and Cole, as usual, led the way and they had to exercise extraordinary precaution lest the horses slip forward upon them.

Bob was put in the rear. He wished to be at the front with Strong and Cole, but he was assigned to his place, and he accepted it, without a protest. He was still resolute in his determination never to complain, always to do, as best he could, the duty assigned to him.

As the hours went on, the day steadily grew worse. They were now exposed to the full force of the wind, which never abated for a moment, and the cold was intense. The utmost precaution had to be taken against freezing or frost-bite. Bob began to think they never would succeed, but he put the thought away from him, calling up all his courage for the great work.

They struggled on bravely until night came again, and once more they found refuge in a corner of the cliff, aided a little by the fact that the wind had lulled somewhat. But it was still so strong that it required their united efforts to set the tents, and one of them was blown away before they could fasten it down. They put the horses, as usual, between the tents and the side of the cliff, and now they tethered them together, lest they be thrown into a panic and attempt flight.

They were all roused at dawn, but it was a misty yellowish day, the sun barely showing through great clouds, and before they could start again the snow began to fall heavily.

Bob went forward a little to look at the trail. Clothed thickly, and with his rifle over his shoulder, he made but little progress. Moreover the snow, coming straight into his face, blinded him, and he did not notice that he was stepping from the path, toward the edge of a precipice.

He heard a shout behind him, a shout of warning, uttered at once by Strong and Cole, and he uttered a cry himself, wrung from him by the suddenness of a great peril. He felt the snow yielding beneath his feet. He tried to step back, or to grasp at something. But he clutched only snow, and it slipped from his fingers.

He heard another cry from his comrades, and the roar of a mighty mass falling. He fell down, down with it, he knew not where, enveloped in a great white cloud, and his senses left him.

CHAPTER 7

In the Bearskin

When Bob recovered consciousness, he was coughing violently, and what caused him to cough was snow that insisted upon entering his mouth. But he cleared his mouth, and undertook to move. He found the operation difficult, but he only struggled the harder, whereupon he righted himself, and found that he was standing in snow to his chin. Moreover, it was still snowing, coming down in great flakes, and they were so thick that he could not see twenty yards from where he was. What he did see was snow, snow, only snow.

He remembered, although there was not much to remember, the sudden terrible sinking sensation, the warning shouts of the others, and then the white darkness. It was impossible to say how far he had fallen, but he had landed feet foremost in an immense drift, where it was well packed, a fact that kept him from going over his head. He had also been helped by the rifle, strapped on his back. It had crossed like a balancing pole, and impeded his sinking.

By cautiously treading the snow beneath him, Bob managed to raise his body up as far as his arm-pits. Then he felt himself, because he was quite sure at first that he was only a fragment of a boy who had fallen off a mountain two miles high. But he was whole, and even more, no bones were broken. There was a cut across his left arm, where his coat had pulled away from his buckskin glove, but the snow had stopped it from bleeding. He felt no especial pain, as he moved and hence there could be no internal bruise of importance.

He was sure that he could not have been in the snow long or he would have suffered frost-bite, and he was devoutly grateful that he had fared so well thus far, but he realized that he was still in a terrible plight. He looked up, and saw only the blank, white wall of a drift, for a hundred yards or so, and then the cloud of falling snow. The cliff was not perpendicular, but a steep slope. That doubtless had broken his fall and saved his life.

He raised his voice, and began to shout for his comrades:

"O Sam!"

"O Bill!"

Thunderous echoes came back, and he knew that he must be in a deep canyon, but nothing else came. There was not a reply either to the "Bill" or the "Sam." He called them over again. The same echo came back again and that alone. Then, moved by desperate fear, he called them all in turn:

"Sam!"

"Bill!"

"Obadiah!"

"Louis!"

"Porter!"

"Tom!"

Not one answered, and the boy's sense of desolation was so terrible, so overwhelming that, for a moment or two, he felt as one already dead. But he had great courage, fed by a strong body, and once more he took count of himself and his situation. He still had a chance, so long as his limbs were whole, and he had his weapons and ammunition.

He began to move forward slowly, finding the snow so well packed that he did not sink much above his knees. He did not know where he was going, but movement itself brought a new circulation of the blood, and fresh hope of life. He advanced about a rod, when instinct this time warned him. He felt a slight sliding of the snow, and he turned in abruptly, toward the face of the cliff. Ten yards to the right of him the white bank dropped away and he heard the familiar roar of the snow-slide.

The boy was appalled, but he drew inferences, nevertheless. He must be standing upon a shelf about twenty yards wide, and as long as he stood close to the cliff, he was in no imminent danger. But if he remained there, he might as well have dropped to death at once, and he continued, still hugging the side of the cliff.

He had no idea of the direction in which he was going, but, at intervals, he shouted again with all the might of a voice that was by no means weak. Still no answer but the echoes. Then another idea came to him. He took the rifle from his shoulder, and fired twice. The reports were sharp and clear, and the echoes rose far above the wind, but there was no answer.

He strapped the rifle upon his back again, and moved on. If only that blinding snow would cease he might discover where he was, and know what he ought to do. He had one advantage. He was more sheltered here from the wind than he had been before his fall, and he was fairly warm. He pulled himself along the edge of the cliff at least an hour, stopping at times to rest, and then the falling snow began to thin. He could still see nothing above him but white wall, but, below him, he saw the dim white floor of a chasm, apparently a thousand feet down. He was right in his surmise. He stood on a shelf which had broken his fall into the main canyon. He could only hope that the shelf would descend gradually, until he might reach the canyon, and, as he continued, there was evidence that the hope might come true. Another hour, and the valley was much nearer, a third and it was not two hundred yards away. Then the shelf ended in snowy rocks and a sheet of ice, which Bob thought must be a miniature glacier.

Further advance seemed impossible, but the resolute and resourceful boy did not yield. His hunting knife was always in its sheath at his belt, and he began to cut steps in the ice. It was slow work, and he had to be careful lest he break the blade, but sometimes there was a stretch of rough rock, not covered with ice, and then he descended more rapidly. It was a delicate task even then, and a slip might send him headlong. He was able to save himself, until he was within ten yards of the bottom. Then his feet flew from under him, and he shot downward into the deep snow.

The boy alighted on one shoulder, and again the rifle served partially as a sort of life belt. He did not sink far, and, when he righted himself, he found that he was unhurt. His first object was to see what kind of a place it was into which he had come. As far as he could make out, he was now standing in a valley, perhaps several hundred yards wide, maybe more, but containing only snow. He had not expected to find trees, as he knew that he was above the line of vegetation, but he did hope that the valley might contain a few shrubs, anything but that eternal snow.

Although the snow was still falling, he could see a faint yellowish sun, and, by taking observations from it, he knew in which direction the west lay. The great ravine led that way, and he moved along slowly, sinking into the snow above his knees, but in no fear of a fall over a precipice. At intervals of a half hour, he fired his rifle, hoping that his comrades would hear, but no reply ever came.

He was not especially cold, but a deadly weariness oppressed him. An increasing darkness in the pass showed him that night was now coming, and that he must rest and sleep. Fortunately, before beginning the ascent they provided for emergencies. Every man carried his blanket in a light roll on his back, food in his knapsack, and a little stimulant for dire need.

The boy found a place under a shelving rock that was free from snow. He pushed himself back into it, not caring for, or not noticing the animal odour that it exuded, and took the strips of dried buffalo meat from his knapsack. He ate them greedily, almost like an animal, and then he took a drink from the emergency stimulant. A pleasant warmth and drowsiness crept through every vein. The driving snow did not touch him here, and he must sleep. But he knew the treachery of the night that was coming, and he did not forget, in the luxury of the physical senses, to take every precaution. He wrapped the blanket about his body with the greatest care, enclosing the feet as usual, drew it up around his neck and face until it met the flaps of his cap, put the knapsack under his head, and then fell asleep as gently as a little child in its bed.

It was a vast cold world that looked down upon the lone boy, deep in a canyon of the Rocky Mountains, and lost to his comrades. His face was pale, and he showed signs of the terrible hours through which he had been, but his breathing was peaceful and regular, and his dreams were happy. Nothing disturbed him. The animal that had slept there before him had known enough to flee at the coming of the snows, and did not return. Bob slept all the night and far into the next day. He was so thoroughly exhausted that nature kept him in what was, perhaps, as much a stupor as sleep. When he awoke, half the forenoon was gone, the snow had ceased and the sun was shining. He was somewhat stiff, but he had not suffered any frost-bite, and he came out from the shelter of the ledge into the open space of the valley.

The valley or canyon was at least a quarter of a mile broad, but above it towered the cliffs to a great height, steep, white and apparently inaccessible. It was obvious that any attempt to climb them would fail, besides, in all likelihood, bringing down upon his head a snow-slide that would end his fur hunting expedition then and there. Nothing was left for him to do but to keep straight on for the west, and trust to happy chance.

The boy judged that he had fallen from the cliff at some point much lower than the present walls or he would have been killed, despite his plunge into the snow. The great heights above him made him shudder.

He inferred from the position of the sun that it was at least ten o'clock when he awoke, and feeling strong and much encouraged, he travelled at least four hours before stopping. He was hopeful that his comrades were marching along some fairly parallel path, but it might be only a hope.

His canyon turned somewhat to the right, and then he saw before him a vast valley, far beneath his feet, and shut in on the horizon rim by other mountains lower than those on which he stood, and probably a hundred miles away at least. He could tell nothing of the nature of this valley, whether plains or wooded, as it, like everything else, was deep in snow and presented only a white expanse.

As his view had widened greatly on every side, he was hopeful that he might see his comrades, but not a single black dot was in sight. He used another valuable cartridge with the usual result, and then, resolved not to repine, he resumed the descent, He saw great quantities of ice on the western side of the range, sometimes in vast sheets, and at other times in frozen torrents which would unlock when the summer was more advanced. He believed that he could now make out the tree range below him. There was a white tracery which must be the boughs of pines and cedars, and the sight filled him with gladness and courage. Trees mean life, not only living earth, but life for man as well.

Bob travelled all that day down a fairly easy slope, and at nightfall reached the first trees. He felt an immense sense of delight and victory when he was able to reach forward and touch the first scrub pine. He was like a shipwrecked sailor who had swum until his feet touched land, and, moreover, a single bush even was a relief from the everlasting snow.

Despite the danger from the snow-slides and precipices, he pushed on a little further in the half darkness until a place was found where the pines were larger and denser. Here, in the centre of a dense clump, he made a burrow like a rabbit. He scooped out the snow with his hands until it formed a little circular wall, buttressed by the trees, and, curling himself up in the hole, he lay down to sleep. He was hungry, but the last shred of food was gone, and he must make up his mind to do without it for the night at least, hoping to forget his pangs in slumber. He was warm enough when he lay in his blanket, and he would have been thoroughly comfortable if he could only have stopped that aching sensation in the pit of his stomach.

He did not go to sleep at once. His nerves, somewhat overstrained, would not let him, and he looked up at the sky from his burrow as from the bottom of a well. He saw, therefore, a circular expanse of cold blue, with cold, white stars dancing in it. It was so distant, and he was so alone, that he began to wonder vaguely whether he would ever see his comrades again.

But, while he was wondering, he fell asleep, and, when he awoke the next morning, he was assailed by a hunger so fierce that it could scarcely be endured. He made up his mind to abandon the descent of the range for the time and hunt. He might find a rabbit in the brush. He must find something if he would live.

The slope upon which he now stood was not very steep and it was forested well. It was extremely likely that in such a region, where man was practically unknown, game could be found, and Bob sought vigorously here and there in the snow, looking carefully under the pines and cedars, in the hope of stirring up a rabbit.

Thus passed over an hour without result, and he became very faint and weak. He was compelled to realize that he was reaching the end of his powers. Courage alone could not overcome starvation. He poked a stick that he had found into a clump of cedars, holding his rifle in the other hand, ready to shoot in case a rabbit jumped up.

A roar so thunderous followed that the boy leaped back five feet. It was well that his impulse carried him so far, as a great bear sprang up from the thicket, stood for a few moments on his hind legs and wheeled about, looking, with fiery little red eyes at the impudent creature who had dared to disturb him in his snug nest.

Bob was so terrified that his action was almost mechanical. He threw up his rifle and fired straight at the huge, hairy chest, then he turned and ran, doubling among the trees. The bear followed him a little distance and then stood, clutching at his chest. Bob, not hearing the tread behind him, stopped, saw that the bear was dazed, and, slipping another cartridge into his rifle, sent a bullet through the animal's brain. The bear fell over in the snow. He kicked a little, quivered once or twice and was dead.

Bob did not dare to approach for several minutes. He had heard so much about the vitality of grizzlies and silver tips that he was still apprehensive lest the huge beast jump up and make another dash for him, so he reloaded his rifle, and when it was quite certain that the bear was dead, came up and stood over him.

He did not realize at first the full meaning of his achievement. It was then merely a danger escaped and a trophy won, but later came the sudden and overwhelming thought that here was food, hundreds of pounds of it. The bear, probably ranging and feeding on the lower slopes, was in good condition, and Bob's mouth began to water. Probably no one ever regarded a slain bear with greater pleasure.

But the boy resolved to have his bear cooked. No savagery for him. He had plenty of matches with him. Sam Strong had urged upon everyone the necessity of carrying them always, and he looked around for a good place in which to kindle a fire. He found a spot behind some rocks, protected from the wind, and by stripping the bark from fallen wood, he managed to get at the dry inside from which he whittled shavings with his hunting knife. In a half hour's hard work, and after several failures, he had a good fire burning. He fed it and watched over it until there was no longer any danger of its extinction by wandering puffs of wind, and, before doing any further work, sat by it awhile, enjoying the glorious warmth. His whole being, after so much cold and snow and stiffness, seemed to glow and become flexible in the presence of flame and coal. The fire gave him new strength and courage for the second task, which was formidable enough for one who was not experienced.

But his hunting knife was large and sharp, and he set to work to skin the bear. It took him a full hour to remove the great pelt, but he succeeded in fairly good style, and hung it up in a tree. Then he cut strips from the tenderest part of the bear, and cooked them on the end of a stick over the fire.

That bear may not have been the finest in the world, but no steaks were ever more welcome. But Bob remembered both his manners and his stern wilderness training. It was not good to eat in too much haste after such a long fast, so he allowed a decent interval to elapse between each thin piece, and, as he luxuriated, he felt that a wonderful change had taken place in his life.

Bob had just finished toasting his eighth strip when his attention was drawn by a sound, half a growl and half a whine, but wholly unpleasant and menacing. He saw beneath a pine a pair of fiery red eyes and a long, lank grey body. It was a wolf, not the common creature of the plains, but the great mountain savage, almost as strong, and fully as fierce as a cougar.

The wolf had come to share in Bob's trophy, the bear, and the boy shuddered. This was an animal of unusual ferocity, and more might be behind him. He did not hesitate. He raised the loaded rifle that lay beside him, took quick aim at a point midway in the space between the eyes, and fired. The wolf bounded into the air and fell back in the snow.

Bob did not move, but presently he heard a snapping and snarling in the bushes and he knew that the slain wolf was being devoured by his comrades. He shuddered again, and, foreseeing the danger that might come, began at once to take precautions against it. The bear was too heavy to be dragged to his alcove in the rocks where the fire was burning, but he cut off as much of the flesh as he could possibly carry in his journey, put it in the rock and left the rest to the wolves. They cautiously approached it a little later, and as he did not fire upon them, they fell to work. They stripped it clean in an incredibly short space, and seeing their skill and speed in such a task, Bob was devoutly thankful that he had his rifle with him. The boy took the heavy bear-skin down from the tree, pounded the inside surface with stones, and rubbed it with snow. He worked so hard that the perspiration came, despite the great cold, and he was forced to rest his aching arms. But he wanted that bearskin, and he wanted it to be in shape for use. He had an idea that he would need it badly before he reached the valley and the warm country.

He spent all that day dressing the bearskin and dragging up wood for his fire. He knew by the feel of the wind and its sharp edge that the fiercest stage of the blizzard was coming, and he meant to see it through in his present camp. He cooked enough of the bear meat to last several days, built up the fire in front of the warmest and snuggest place in the alcove, and lay down there with the great bearskin around him, the inside turned outward. It was a magnificent robe, and the fur felt very soft and warm as he drew it around his face. He had not felt so warm, so splendidly comfortable in a week, and he lay there, watching the flames of his fire, which were dancing before the rising wind. By and by, he saw red eyes and shadowy, dark figures beyond the flames, and he knew that the wolves, not content with the larger part of a big silver tip bear, had come back for the bear's slayer. But he knew, too, that they would not dare to pass the fire, and that they were intelligent enough to have a healthy fear of his rifle.

He was really but little afraid of the wolves now, and soon they slunk away. All the time the wind was rising, and it had the edge of a knife. But the boy, wrapped to the eyes in the bear's robe, felt like a bear himself, gone into winter quarters. The great cold could not get at him. His food lay within reach of his gloved hand, and what more could he ask?

The day passed, night came and the wind whistled straight out of the northwest like a cannon ball. It brought with it now, not snow, but hail, which rattled among the trees like shot. It came at such an angle that the stone ledge, against which Bob lay, turned it like a shield, and by and by the regular rattling sound became pleasant and soothing. He was conscious that his fire was dying before the wind and hail, but he did not care. He did not believe that the wolves would seek him in such a storm, and, as for the storm itself, it might rise to any height, but it could never penetrate the great bearskin, in which he was enfolded as snugly as its original owner.

The boy, his rifle enclosed in the bearskin also, slept on, and all through the night the great blizzard raged and tore at the flanks of the immutable mountains. The fire was out long since and the charred sticks were covered with frozen snow. Once the mountain wolves, a dozen in number, gaunt, ferocious, and ready, in their fellowship, to attack anything, came back to the place where they had eaten so much good food. No red flame or glowing coal was left to frighten them, but the strange odour, that of a human being, came to their nostrils, and they knew its origin to be a rocky alcove that they could see.

They could have attacked and torn the boy to pieces before he had a chance to defend himself, but the wolves remembered. Their leader, the king of them all, had been slain at a distance by something in the hands of this boy. There had been a sharp crack, a gush of fire, and then the great mountain wolf was dead.

They were drawn by hunger, still unappeased, but shuddering fear, fear of the mysterious death, held them back. Hunger and fear fought, but fear conquered. They slunk away over the frozen snow, and the boy, wrapped in the bearskin in the rocky alcove, still slept, warm, and dreaming beautiful dreams.

After midnight the blizzard increased in violence and ferocity. It was the testimony of wandering Utes and Arapahos that not another such storm had been known on the mountains in a decade. Now the hail came like a vast rifle-fire, then it was only the wind itself, but with a breath that froze at its touch.

The mountain wolves gave up all thought of the human being who lay in the bearskin under the shelter of the rock. Hardy as they were, they were fleeing now to their own lairs to save their lives, and all the bears, up to the biggest and the strongest, sought their dens, unable to face the cutting sleet. The forest was full of wild creatures by day, but that night none stalked abroad.

The blizzard did not pass until daylight, and it was late when Bob awoke. It was a slight sense of suffocation that caused him to sit up, and he found that he moved with difficulty. Snow had packed in front of him, and, on either side, everywhere except at his back, where the rock thrust up, the surface of this snow was a sheet of packed hail. Only in front of him, where he had been breathing, it was moist around the edges. He was like a seal, with his blowhole in the ice.

Bob's first task was to make his den a little wider, to trample down the snow on all sides, and then to eat up his frozen bear steaks. He found his muscles somewhat stiff at first, but with exercise they soon recovered their elasticity. Again he was devoutly grateful to the bear which had saved him, first from starving and then from freezing.

The snow was not much deeper than on the day before, but the frozen crust of hail and ice made the travelling much harder. Nevertheless, he faced it with a bold heart. Heavy as was the bearskin, he rolled it up and packed it on his shoulders, adding the food to his burden, and then he set out.

Circumstances, which had been so long against the boy, now began to favour him. The slope became steep, though not dangerous, and he rapidly descended to a warmer air. The sun came out, bright and inspiring, and the temperature rose fast. The forest was thick, and he found many easy paths leading through it. At noon he stopped and managed to build another fire under some cedars. Here, while he warmed his body and ate, he took thought with himself and tried to plan the best way to reach his old comrades. They must be somewhere in the great valley before him, and they would follow the easiest trail to the next range of mountains, as he knew that they were yet far from their destination. He must also choose what he thought to be the easiest trail, and follow it as fast as he could.

He could see the valley now, and the greenish tint showed that no snow had fallen there. He surmised that it was much such a country as that which he had left behind him, on the other side of the range. He thought that he would reach the valley before dark, but it was further than it looked, and he was yet a long distance from it when night came. But he was below the snow line, and he had no difficulty in building a fire, by the side of which he slept well.

He deserted his beloved bearskin the next morning. He had come into a warmer zone, and it was too heavy to carry when not needed. But it had served him so well that he was unwilling to have it torn by wolves or other wild animals, and, making it into as small a package as he could, he tied it into the fork of a tree.

He now found clear, cold streams running down the side of the mountain, and he drank plentifully from them. He had used snow water so long that the streams were a relief, although they came from melting snows themselves.

The forest was thick all along the slopes, and as he descended, the trees, chiefly ash, oak and cedar, increased in size. There was beautiful springy turf here, and he knew from the nature of the country that game must be abundant. The sight was so exhilarating that he gave a shout of joy, and set off with renewed courage at an increased pace.

CHAPTER 8

The Midnight Meeting

The boy still had plenty of bear meat with him, and he decided not to seek game for the present. Instead, he luxuriated awhile under the trees and on the grass. The warmth was very generous and satisfying after so much snow and cold, and while Bob still admired the great white peaks and ranges, he felt that he had endured enough of them for the present.

He bathed in one of the streams, finding the water extremely cold, and then descended the last slope. As he was about to emerge upon the plain he saw many hoofprints in the soft earth, and his heart gave a great bound. He had experience enough to know that the tracks were made by shod animals, not by wild ponies, and surely good luck had brought him at once upon the path of his comrades.

The trail was broad and plain. A child could have followed it, and Bob hurried forward, his heart still leaping. He judged that the trail could not be more than an hour old, and it was likely that he could overtake them in two hours, at the furthest.

The footprints led straight away, through a fine forest of oak, without undergrowth, but with a soft turf in which the steel shoes sank deep. He came presently to a place at which they had evidently stopped. Fragments of food were scattered about, and the turf had been cropped close by the horses. Clearly they could be only a short distance ahead, and he increased his pace, eager to see them again.

In ten minutes he heard the neigh of a horse, and he began to run toward the sound. It was perhaps providence itself that caused him to trip on a vine. He did not fall, but it brought him up with a jerk, mentally as well as physically. Then, remembering Sam Strong's injunction that in the west caution, caution, caution was the quality upon which life most depended, he sank down among some bushes and approached more carefully.

The bushes ended and the ground dropped off into a sequestered little valley, in the centre of which men were resting and smoking, and horses were grazing. But they were not his comrades nor their horses. He beheld instead a band of at least a score, dressed like hunters, and with hardened, evil faces. As they talked they swore great oaths, and although they were white men, Bob felt instinctively that he had exercised caution none too soon. The Cheyennes had not inspired less aversion.

His eyes from his covert roamed over the men and alighted at last upon a face that he remembered. He could never forget that dark countenance, the black eyes set close together, and the cruel strength of the pointed chin. It was Juan Carver, trapper, free lance or representative of Hudson Bay, or something else still worse. Bob had listened well to Sam Strong and he never doubted that this band of men would try to rob his comrades of their furs, if they obtained them, or be ready to do any other deed of wickedness that was to their profit. They were men for him to avoid, and he thanked God for the kindly bush that had checked his headlong speed.

Bob surmised that they had found an easier pass over the range than the one chosen by Strong, as they did not show much trace of suffering. Luck seemed to have favoured them so far, and with a sigh of regret that it was so, he turned away.

He surmised that the Carver party would remain some time in their resting-place, and he wished to be so far out on the plain that they could not see him when they started. He felt apprehension when he left the cover of the last line of bushes, but it must be done.

The plain, as he had foreseen, was much like that on the other side of the range, waving, treeless, and with grass now turning to green. He did not think it probable that men had passed that way lately, as three bunches of antelope were grazing in the distance, and for a little while Bob was in great depression. It indicated that he was on the wrong trail, and could not overtake his comrades. But he dared not go back and hunt for the right trail. There were Carver and his men whom he must avoid.

He pressed forward all through the day, never stopping long at a time, but often looking back to see if he was followed. He did not see any moving dots on the plain behind him and he was greatly encouraged thereby. It was hot, and he suffered now from the sun, longing, as he thought he would never long again, for the snow of the high mountains,

He crossed one shallow brook from which he drank, and at nightfall came to another, fairly well wooded along its banks, by the side of which he decided to sleep.

He chose his place, well hidden in the bushes, lay down his blanket for softness, as the weather was too warm now to fold it about him, and fell asleep.

The boy was awakened in the middle of a dark night by the sound of voices and the tread of horses. All his faculties were alive on the instant.

Carver and his band had come, and he lay perfectly still under the bushes. The moonlight was so thin that he could not see anyone, although he heard them distinctly.

The sounds grew louder. They seemed to be coming straight towards him, and the boy, in spite of all his courage, had some minutes of nervous thinking. He decided to creep out of their path and deeper into the bushes. He made a yard or two silently, and then a twig snapped.

"Here! Hold up! What's that!" some one cried.

"A slinkin' coyote, I guess," replied another, and Bob Norton fairly leaped into the air at these two voices. It was Sam Strong who had asked the question, and it was Bill Cole who had replied.

"Sam! Bill!" shouted the boy, rushing through the bushes. "I'm here! and I've found you!"

The six men were all there on horseback, the pack horses following, and they had stopped short when he cried out. Now they sat motionless on their horses, staring at him, all except Louis Perolet who dropped his reins, crossed himself and began to patter out a prayer of his church.

Sam Strong at last uttered a great gasp, and exclaimed:

"Well, if it ain't the youngster, after all, riz right up from the dead."

"It must be him," said Bill Cole, still half in doubt. "He don't look like a ghost."

In another instant they were all off their horses, shaking hands with him, punching him in the shoulders and chest to see that he was real, and showing as much delight as frontiersmen ever permit to themselves. Bob himself was overflowing with exuberance, and shook every rough hand in return as hard as he could.

"I've always hoped for the best," said Sam. Strong, "but I never dared to hope that you'd come back to us, shakin' your grave clothes off, so to speak. If you hadn't hollered out loud I guess we'd all have rid on, takin' it for granted that you wuz a ghost ha'ntin' us."

"I could have believed it," said Tom Harris. "I remember a fellow killed at Chancellorsville when we was chasin' the rebels—"

"Why, you never chased us at Chancellorsville," exclaimed Porter Evans, indignantly. "That was our greatest victory, an'—"

"Well, you two generals shut up," said Sam Strong. "We ain't got time to fight the Civil War all over ag'in tonight. What we want to do is to camp here, an' hear the story of the youngster who has been right down into his grave, but who has come right out ag'in."

They had been making a night watch, but they tethered their horses and camped, lighting no fire, however. Then Bob told the story of his fight for life in detail, broken now and then by expressions of wonder from his comrades.

"I'll hope for the best more than ever after this," said Sam Strong. "You came through in great style. Tenderfoots, breakin' all rules, often do the right things, when the men that have seen an' done everything begin makin' mistakes right at the jump."

"It was not chance," said Louis Perolet, gravely, "eet ees because Bob is the bright, smart boy, Why did the great Napoleon, when he was not much more than a boy, whip all the Austrian generals in Italy who were so much older than himself an' with so much experience? Eet was because he had the great min', the genius, an' when he saw he remembered. Meester Bob be the genius, too, in his own way."

"Now you shut up," exclaimed Bob, blushing. "It was luck, just as Sam says."

But Louis would not be denied his assumption. He insisted that Bob was a genius; that he had proved it, and that he was destined to become the greatest of frontiersmen, the superior in time of the redoubtable Sam Strong himself.

Strong was somewhat apprehensive over the news of Carver's presence in the valley, but a careful examination showed that he and his band were not in the neighbourhood. Then Sam told their own story. They had thought Bob lost when he fell down the snowy cliff, but nevertheless they had descended into the valley and searched two days for him. The falling snow, of course, had covered his footprints. At last they had given him up as dead —certainly the chance of his escape was most remote— and they had gone sadly on. They had suffered much from cold, but they had managed to get themselves and their horses that far into the valley. Their long search for Bob had caused them to arrive later than he.

"But we found you,—or you found us," said Louis Perolet, triumphantly, "an' eet ees the good omen. To escape so great a danger proves that we will find all we seek an' more. Our fortune has been good, an' we'll push it."

"I reckon you're about right, Frenchy," said Sam Strong. "The best has happened an' we'll hope for it ag'in, though I don't like the presence of Carver here."

Strong did not fear an attack by Carver, as the man would have no object in making it now, but he did not like the way in which this band had hung upon his trail. It was the later days of the fur trade, and valleys, rich in furs, were hard to find. Battles often took place for their possession, and the powerful company north of the British line had poached more than once far down into the American mountains.

"We can fight Carver an' his crowd if we have to do it," said Strong, "but we don't want to waste ourselves that way. What we want to do is to get furs, an' we've got to hide ourselves from both the Indians an' land pirates."

"I move," said Bill Cole, "that we make double quick time to the next range of mountains an' then lay by in some thicket till Carver passes on. We can mark the course he takes, an' then choose another for ourselves."

The suggestion seemed good to them all, and they advanced rapidly for three days until they reached the second mass of mountains. There they found good refuge among dense pines and cedars, where they stayed two days, kindling no fire. On the second day Strong, Bob and Perolet, lying close in a covert, saw Carver and his band go by. They followed them until they saw them high up in a pass, going almost due west. Then they returned to camp, satisfied that Bill Cole's suggestion had been a happy one.

Sam Strong immediately turned his own expedition southward, marching along the flank of the mountain. Bob once more rode his own horse. He had suffered somewhat from fever, brought on by exposure and his great sufferings, and he had collapsed when they stopped to let Carver pass, but the rest had restored him entirely. Travelling now on one's own horse was a luxury, after his struggles in the snowy pass.

They kept a good watch for the Utes and Arapahos or wandering Apaches who sometimes strayed far northward, but saw none. The slopes, along which they were travelling, seemed to be wholly neglected by the tribes, as game was plentiful, and not especially wary.

After three days of the southern march at good speed they stopped to refresh their horses, and to renew their stock of provisions. They pitched a camp in one of the pleasantest places that the boy had yet seen, an open grove, with a clear little brook running through it. They stayed three days there, and killed several deer, including a splendid elk. Trout were caught in some deep pools of the stream, and proved to be of fine quality.

While they were resting, Strong revealed to Bob more of their plans. When they crossed the second range, a great mass of mountains tumbled together, they would advance south-westward, and enter once more the region of mountains, a huge system that extended with larger or smaller breaks almost to the Pacific. Hidden in these ranges were the beaver streams, some of which no white man had yet reached, and, along these, they expected to find a rich reward.

It was all one to the boy. He did not care where they went, as long as they retained him a member of this chosen band. His devotion to the six men, who had treated him so well, grew as the days passed, and he took fresh resolutions to repay them no matter what the cost.

It was now midsummer, but they did not hurry, as furs would not be in good condition until October. They frequently made stops of a day or two, and, in one wide valley, they chased a herd of mustangs. Sam Strong and Bill Cole succeeded in catching five with their lariats, and they were skilful enough to break them to their service.

"They'll come in handy," said Sam. "Each of 'em can carry back five hundred pounds of smooth, soft beaver skins."

"We'll get 'em," said Bob, with enthusiasm.

Sam smiled benevolently. The boy's freshness and enthusiasm had added new life to the little party.

"It will be a full two weeks yet," he said, "before we're at the beaver streams, an' then we've got to spend some time in locatin' an' makin' traps."

The maze of mountains deepened. Now and then they rode up great canyons, with cliffs a thousand feet high, on either side, and small streams trickling down the centre of the canyons over masses of rough boulders. The wilderness seemed to Bob so vast and so little peopled that he wondered how anybody could ever find anybody else in it. Apprehension in regard to Carver and his band disappeared from his mind, and apparently it was forgotten by the others also.

When the summer was well past, they came to a ravine, and deep valley, through which flowed a creek, emptying about ten miles further on into a river. The creek could be followed thirty or forty miles back into the mountains, and, for the full distance, it was thickly lined with trees and bushes. Many of the trees had been cut down as neatly as if it had been done with an axe, but Sam Strong explained to Bob that the weapon used was the teeth of the beaver.

"This is the best of the beaver streams that we had in mind," he said, "an' we're goin' to trap along here an' on others not far away, all through the winter."

They went up the creek about twenty miles further, until they came to a point where the valley widened out somewhat, and here Sam Strong chose the camp. He could not have found a more favourable spot. On either side of the creek, between the trees and the steep slope of the mountains, was a meadow, several acres in extent, covered with deep rich grass. The horses would find ample grazing here, and the trees and the mountains together would give them protection in winter. As for water, there was the creek.

On the northern side, the meadows made a little bay into the mountain, and here, in a smooth spot, with a clump of oaks circling about it, they selected their camp. They pitched their tents, and turned the horses loose in the meadow.

"It will be fine, here in the tents," said Bob.

Sam Strong smiled.

"It's fine now," he said, "but it won't be fine, when winter comes. No, Bob, we are goin' to build our house. Trappers, who expect to stay a long time in one place, must have a house."

They began the task with great energy the very next day. They were well supplied with axes, and seven pairs of strong arms soon felled the requisite number of trees. These were cut into even lengths, and squared at the ends. The bark was left on.

Then they built a large log cabin, with a lean-to in the rear. The space between the logs was chinked up with mud and chips. It was provided with a puncheon floor, a stone fireplace and a stick chimney. There were two windows, with swinging board shutters, and the roof was covered with shingles of their own splitting. All the men had had plenty of experience at this kind of building, and the work was done in a week.

"There she is," said Sam Strong, triumphantly. "Rain tight, wind tight, snow tight, an' cold tight."

They marked off on the inside seven spaces, one for every man. There he was to spread his bed of blankets, fur, or whatever he wished, and that space was to remain his own. But they slept, for a while, outside under the tents, and the cabin would remain without occupants, until the cold weather began.

They devoted nearly two weeks to the making of traps, embracing all the varieties known to the skilled hunters of furs. They had steel traps with them, but the new ones that they made of wood were far more numerous. Then they explored for miles around, seeking the best places in which to put them. Bob went on most of these expeditions, and invariably he was with Sam Strong. His sense of locality and his trapper's eye developed amazingly. In a very short time he became almost the equal of Strong in noticing the "runs" and other signs of wild life, and no matter how complicated the plexus of the mountains, it was almost impossible to lose him.

About thirty miles up the creek, which flowed almost due west, there was a rift in the mountains opening to the southward. Following it they came to another narrow creek which flowed, on a parallel line with this one, toward the river. This also proved to be stocked with beaver, and they set traps here as well, building another and a smaller log cabin on its banks, a necessity to them, as it could not be reached in a day's journey from their first house.

The foliage began to turn red and brown now with the first touch of October. Everything was ready and the trapping began.

CHAPTER 9

The Sunken River

The days that followed were full of activity and interest for Bob and all his comrades. The trapping was the best that any of them had ever found, and before the winter began, they were packing the beaver pelts in bales. They also took skins of the grizzly and silver tip, but they devoted themselves chiefly to the beaver.

"All kind of pelts are good," said Sam Strong, "but our big market is St. Louis, an' it's a long way from here to St. Louis. So we've got to consider the question of transportation an' carry the thing that weighs the least to the pound, an' that's beaver."

"It counts in more ways than in trapping" said Tom Harris. "If we hadn't had to take so many provisions into the south with us we'd have licked the rebels in one year, instead of taking four for the job."

They were sitting before the fire in their cabin, when Tom made this speech in a tone of finality. Porter Evans at once sprang to his feet.

"If you hadn't been lucky you never would have won!" he exclaimed. "Besides, you didn't really win. As I told you before we got tired an' reckoned that we ought to go home, an' look after our crops."

"Shut up," said Sam Strong, "I'm always hopin' for the best, an' I'm hopin' that some day you fellows will forget the war."

A few minutes later the two were industriously scraping the inside of a grizzly bearskin.

It was announced to Bob, late in November, that he would have a full share in the trapping, that there would be seven equal portions, one of which was to be his. He demurred, saying that he was entitled only to a half-share, but the others insisted. He had done his full part in every respect, and so he was compelled to acquiesce.

The year waned and cold gales began to roar up the valleys and canyons, although much red and brown foliage was yet left on the slopes. All the horses had grown fat on the grass of the meadows, and Harris and Evans now built them a shelter among the trees. They made, on three sides, a windbreak of thick, woven bushes, and carried it slightly overhead in the form of an arch. When completed it was a really admirable shelter for their hardy mustangs, both Harris and Evans being skilful at such work. It would protect entirely from the wind, and, in a great measure, from snow also. The ponies soon learned its advantages, and, as the nights increased in coldness, entered it, without being driven.

About ten days after the completion of the stable, as the two build-ers proudly called it, the party sat late by their cabin fire. The day had not been a hard one and Evans and Harris, who were in fine form, were telling stories, more or less highly coloured, generally highly, of the Civil War, with Sam Strong, as a discreet umpire, to prevent verbal encounters between them.

The fire was a good one. The dry logs crackled, and cast up merry flames. Genial warmth filled the cabin, and the roaring of the cold wind without made it all the more pleasant inside the log house. Bob was lying upon a grizzly bearskin, his chin upon his hand, listening, with all his soul, to the stories. It seemed wonderful to him that these two comrades of his should have been through such great battles. He ran over the names to himself, Chancellorsville, Gettysburg, Shiloh, Chick-amauga, The Wilderness, and the others.

"But though them was tre-men-jeous big battles," said Tom Harris, "you was safe after you was captured. Porter, here, knew that when I told him he wouldn't get hurt—that's right, Sam, make him keep still till I get through. As I was sayin', if you lived long enough to be cap-tured you was all right; so it's safer fightin' white men than it is Sioux or Cheyennes. When you're captured by them your troubles are just beginnin'. Why I—"

Every man of the seven leaped to his feet, as a scream of pain and terror, the like of which the boy had never heard before, rose above the roaring of the wind. Bob's blood ran chill in his veins. The scream was repeated, and Sam Strong exclaimed:

"It's one of our horses, an' like as not a grizzly bear is among 'em. Come quick with your rifles!"

Every man seized his weapon and rushed for the door, Sam Strong leading. The night was dark, but a terrible commotion came from the stable. The horses were plunging and rearing, and as they ran forward two, wild with terror, dashed past them. Bob kept just at the heels of Sam Strong, and as his eyes grew used to the darkness he saw a huge, dusky figure at the entrance to the stable, and then another.

"It's the grizzlies!" cried Sam Strong. "A whole tribe of 'em! Shoot as fast as you can, but look out for the horses!"

He fired at the first of the bears, and the huge brute, turning instantly, charged straight at him. That would have been the last night of Sam Strong, great hunter, trapper and Indian fighter, had not a boy, whom he had befriended, been just behind him, eager and ready with a loaded rifle.

Bob poked the muzzle of his weapon past Sam's shoulder, and fired point-blank into the eyes of the raging brute.

A grizzly bear has great vitality, but he cannot live with a bullet in his brain. Sam Strong felt the hot breath of his foe on his face, he saw those long, iron claws reached out to destroy him, and he may have felt, for a moment, that he was lost, but the great bear fell at his feet, stone dead. He turned and said only three words:

"Good boy, Bob!"

But they were the sweetest words that had ever sounded in Bob Norton's ears. He had saved the life of his chief, and that chief had given him praise. Meanwhile another huge, snarling form was charging, but Cole, Perolet and Obadiah Pirtle poured bullets into it, and it fell near the first. Two smaller ones ran, but the men followed and slew them at the banks of the creek.

"Now, Bob," said Sam Strong, "you run back to the cabin an' bring us a torch, an' we'll see jest what's been done here."

The boy, still trembling with excitement, obeyed, but by the time he returned with the light, the men had succeeded to some extent in quieting the horses, that is, all that were left in the stable, four being on the missing list. When Bob held up his torch he disclosed a genuine field of battle. Four grizzlies lay dead, two there and two at the creek, and one horse had deep parallel gashes along his shoulder. Sam Strong read all the signs with an unerring eye.

"It was a family of bears," he said, "father, mother, an' two boys. They smelled them horses, an' them horses smelled mighty good to 'em. They crept up an' old pa grizzly here made a jump. He meant to light on old Baldy, the strongest an' fightenest of the lot. He missed just what he was aimin' for, but he did give old Baldy a rake, an' then the flood turned loose. Mustangs, like ours, can kick fast an' powerful hard, but if we hadn't come so quick a lot of our best horses would have been chawed up."

It was indeed a providential rescue, as they relied upon the horses to get both themselves and their furs back to civilization, and it was a danger that might occur again.

"The care of the horses belongs mainly to Porter an' Tom," said Strong, "an' they've got to fix up somethin' that will keep any more bears away, long enough for us to come. Now, Bob, we'll help skin the lot, 'cause their hides are worth havin'. Besides, Louis, here, can get some pretty good steaks off the young ones."

They spent nearly the whole night skinning the grizzlies and cutting them up. Fierce mountain wolves, attracted by the odour, came down and prowled so near that they were forced to shoot several of them. The horses were continually uneasy, and the best efforts of Harris and Evans could not quiet them.

The two "generals" the next day entirely closed the fourth side of the "stable" with thorny brush which they removed every night and morning for the horses to pass in and out. They attached this brush rather strongly with bark, and Sam Strong gave his full approval.

"You've done well, boys," he said to Harris and Evans. "Not even a grizzly could butt through that without makin' a noise, an' by that time we could be on the spot."

Strong had said nothing more to Bob about the shot that saved him from the bear, but the boy noticed that the leader showed a great increase of confidence in him. He took him with him on nearly all his expeditions, and often these lasted several days. Strong did not work steadily at the details of trapping. He left the bulk of it to the others while he explored for new beaver streams, or for signs of other game wearing furs that would be of value in the great markets. He had a wonderful "scent" for beaver, and found many new dams along these unknown little mountain streams. Bob was now his comrade, and made two or three discoveries on his own account which elated him mightily, and increased his confidence.

Despite the growing cold, Strong and the boy, when on their expeditions, frequently slept in the bush along the slopes. They discarded their blankets, and made for themselves sleeping bags of fur, somewhat like the sleeping bag of the Arctic, and with these they practically defied cold.

On one of their journeys they went down the creek to its mouth. It was a clear mountain stream, emptying itself into a river, which also came from a mountain, and was clear. Strong sat down on a rock and looked meditatively at the larger stream.

"Bob," he said, "do you know what river this is?"

"No," replied the boy, "I don't. Perhaps not enough people have seen it to name it."

"Yes, they have," said Sam Strong. "This is one of the headwaters of the Colorado, an' we'll call it the Colorado. Maybe you never heard of the Colorado, Bob, but old Spaniards saw it more than three hundred years ago, an' Indians an' hunters say it's the funniest river on earth."

"How so?" asked Bob.

"It runs along for a spell as if it didn't mean more than any other river; specially these of the mountains, dodgin' roun' hills, dashin' thro' rock-cuts, foamin' over boulders, an' cuttin' up such didos. Lots of rivers do that, but with this river the hills keep gettin' higher, the rock-cuts deeper, an' the boulders bigger. Then the river itself runs faster an' faster. An' the faster it gets the deeper it sinks into the earth. Down, down it goes until you just see a ribbon of sky overhead, an' it goes on that way, they say, for hundreds of miles, rippin' an' roarin' an' dashin'."

The brown face of the trapper was illuminated as he spoke. The look there was not that of one who sought gain, it was the gaze of the explorer, gazing into vast, vague regions, and seeking by some power of the mind to penetrate their mystery. Some such look as this must have been in the eyes Columbus when he faced the Western Ocean.

"Does the river keep on that way forever!" asked Bob, catching his leader's spirit.

"Nobody knows," replied Strong. "It's one of the mysteries of the earth. This river goes right on, cuttin' right through mountains, not turnin' their flanks, but slashin' the solid stone right across, same as if God had done it with a sword-blade. I've heard tales that 'way off into the southwest it sinks down into the earth so far—well, so far it ain't worth while to tell it, 'cause you wouldn't believe it, an' then again I've heard that it runs clean underground, comes out maybe a thousand miles further on, an' goes into the Pacific."

"Which do you believe?" asked Bob.

"I don't know, but I do know that this is the riproarin'est, strangest river on top of this ball of ours, an' I want to know more about it. I want to satisfy my curiosity, an' I think there must be lots of beaver on the streams runnin' into it. We mean to stay 'roun' in these parts about two years, Bob, an' business an' pleasure can go together. Next year I mean to go down the Colorado, lookin' for beaver streams, an' if you want to go with me, Bob, all you've got to do is to say so."

"Of course I'll go, and thank you for taking me," exclaimed Bob, eagerly.

"Then it's settled, but don't say anything about it now to the boys. Jest put it in the back of your head, an' keep it there."

Strong made no further mention of the subject even then, but he sat long staring at the mysterious river, and the boy, whose eyes followed his, shared the spell. They were deep in the wilderness now, but this stream would carry them into regions yet wilder and grander.

The two slept that night within sight of the river, and in the morning the first snow came. They were back at the cabin by the next sundown, and found the rest of the party there. Strong hoped for an open winter, but no one could tell what was coming, and they made ample provision against every emergency, laying in great quantities of food and firewood. Despite the skim of snow, the grass was still fresh on the meadows, and the horses were fat and full of life. There had been a second alarm of bears, but the thorn fence served its purpose, and they fled in the darkness before the trappers could get a chance at them with their rifles.

The winter, to their great satisfaction, proved to be a mild one, and the trapping could be carried on with only a few breaks. Twice there were blizzards, but on each occasion they were present at the cabin, with the stout door shut and a big fire roaring on the hearth.

"Just think," said Louis Perolet, when the second blizzard was at its height, "it was in such weather as this that the great Napoleon an' hees French soldiers retreated from Moscow. Only French soldiers can stand such a wind an' such cold."

"As I've heard it, Frenchy," said Porter Evans, "not many of Napoleon's soldiers ever got back."

"That's what I've heard, too," said Tom Harris. "Now, we licked the rebels like thunder at Gettysburg, as Porter Evans there knows, though he won't admit it, but if Napoleon an' his French had been in their place we wouldn't have left a grease spot of 'em."

"Bah," said Perolet, "eef ze great Napoleon had been at Gettysburg he would have taken the Yankee army by one ear, an' the rebel army by the other ear; he would knock their heads together an' then he would say, 'go away an' play, leetle boys, mebbe when you grow up you can fight'."

Sam Strong laughed.

"He had you there, boys," he said, "an' what's more, he believes it."

But there was no animosity. Perolet, a few minutes later, was serving both "generals" with especially delicate pieces of beaver tail. The blizzard died down, passed, and they renewed their trapping. Christmas came, was celebrated duly, and then they went far into the New Year. Fortune was certainly good to them. All agreed that they had never known such trapping before. The furs were not only abundant, but of the highest quality, and if the second season proved as good as the first, they would return eastward with all their horses could carry.

But Sam Strong did not forget the Colorado. He was a man who looked far ahead. He knew that beaver streams were soon trapped out, and he wanted to have others in reserve. Partly for that reason, and partly because the mystery of the river called to him, he kept it continually in mind. When the winter began to break up he spoke of it to the entire party.

"We are goin' to stay here all of another year," he said, "an' not only that, after this trip's finished we're comin' back ag'in as long as the furs last. Now it is important for us to know where to find beaver, an' to know it before anybody else. Summer's no good for trappin', so it's my idea as soon as the spring is well opened out to go down the river on a boat, spyin' out the country. I want Bill, Obe an' Bob to go with me. T'other three can stay here, look after the horses an' furs, an' fight off Carver if he comes."

The agreement was soon made, and as soon as the weather admitted they began the task of building a strong boat. Trappers often carry their furs by boats, and they had provided iron spikes and other suitable materials for such a contingency. Seven pairs of strong and skilled hands built fast, and their craft was soon ready.

The boat was somewhat clumsy perhaps, but it was exceedingly strong. It was about twenty feet long, and a tarpaulin of skins was stretched tightly over the deck, as Sam Strong foresaw much rough water. It was shallow, and there were two pairs of heavy oars. All the provisions were packed under Sam Strong's direction in tightly closed skin bags. The ammunition and two extra rifles were protected in the same way, and a small supply of medicines was also placed aboard.

"There'll be a lot of rough goin'," said Sam Strong. "Falls an' currents an' eddies an' such like, an' mebbe, if our boat should turn over, we could get a lot of our things out, still dry an' useful."

The warm weather had fully come when they were ready for departure. The boat had been built at a point on the creek about four miles from its mouth, and the two "generals" and Louis Perolet were there to see the four adventurers leave upon their great trip. Strong and Bob were forward, and Cole and Obadiah were near the stern.

"Goodbye," said the three on the bank together, and reaching down they gave everyone in turn a hearty grip.

"I don't know how far we'll go an' I guess we'll have to walk back," said Strong, "but we'll be here again before the summer is over."

The signal was given, and all four pulled at the oars. Their boat, which they had aptly named the *Columbus* glided smoothly down the stream. Bob had been eager for the great adventure, but he could not help feeling a deep regret now as they left behind them their three comrades and their pleasant camp. They might never return. No one had allowed himself to speak of such a thought, but the possibility was there.

He gave the three who still stood on the bank a long look, and then, taking off his fur cap, waved it to them. They waved in reply, and a few moments later, trees and a curving bank hid them from view.

"Good fellers," said Sam Strong, in a tone of strong approval, "but some mighty battles will be fought back there at the camp while we're gone. Porter an' Tom will go through the whole Civil War, never agreein' on a thing, an' then Louis will step in with the great Napoleon an' show that both are always wrong."

Bob laughed, and homesickness did not then tug quite so hard at his heart. They reached the mouth of the creek, rowed into the middle of the river, and let the boat drift with the current, Bill Cole, with little effort, keeping it in the right course.

They drifted all that day, the strength of the current increasing perceptibly. Everyone of the four took his turn at steering, but they did not yet have any trouble. The water flowed smoothly on between shores not yet very high, although on either horizon were lofty mountains, dark with pines on the slopes, and white on the crests with snow. Towards night the river widened somewhat, and passed between cliffs about six hundred feet high. At the highest point on the right bank, a great silver tip bear stood looking down at the *Columbus*. Bob gazed straight up at the bear, and it was rather a singular fact that no one of the four, hunters and trappers though they were, wanted to shoot at him.

"I wonder what he thinks of us," said the boy.

"Mebbe he has seen white men before," said Bill Cole, "but it's the first time that he's ever seen 'em goin' down this river in a boat."

It was twilight when they passed the gorge, and running the boat into a little cove, they made it fast to some bushes for the night. All four were glad to step ashore, and stretch their cramped limbs, although the place was not particularly attractive, merely a sandy beach, clumps of dwarfed bushes, and back of them high and steep hills. The wind, blowing down the stream, was quite cold at the coming of the night, and Strong decided to build a fire. Plenty of dry driftwood, thrown up by floods, was scattered about, and in five minutes a big fire cast its welcome glow over the gloomy cove.

"We'll cook here," said Sam Strong, "but I think we'd better sleep in the boat. You can never tell in these regions when Indians will come, an' in that case we'd have no thin' to do but cut the rope an' get away. Still I'm hopin' for the best, an' I don't think they'll come."

Desolate howls came from the peaks, but the four only laughed. They knew the mountain wolves too well to pay any attention to their lament. They took watches of three hours apiece, and were off again the next morning at the first flush of dawn. Before noon they were further down the river than either Strong or Cole had ever been before, and the current was growing decidedly strong. They passed the mouth of another river, equal in size to their own, and the two streams united were now of great volume and power.

The second and third day passed, and they were now in regions incomparably wild and grand. The river, yellow with soil washed in its rapid flight, grew swift and turbulent. The four always sat with oars in their hands watching for rocks, whirlpools or falls. Often the spray and foam dashed all over them, but the skin tarpaulin kept their precious stores and ammunition dry.

It was tiring work. The sharp point of a rock might sink their boat at any time, or they might be dashed in pieces down a fall. The inattention of a single moment could prove fatal. But Bob, though his bones ached, felt all the wild thrill of their mysterious journey. None was readier at the oar than he. None had a quicker eye, and the blood raced through his veins as the river moved on in its steadily deepening channel.

They plunged sometimes between banks two thousand feet in height, again the banks sank to low hills, and black-tail deer scurried away at their approach. The cliffs were generally bare, but now and then early flowers bloomed brightly in the crannies. Evergreens were abundant on the crests, and on the beaches, where they camped, they always found an abundance of driftwood for fires. Then followed long nights of deep sleep, and in the morning Bob's aching bones would be well again.

The fourth camp was made at the mouth of a small creek, flowing in from the east between banks a thousand feet high, and as steep as the side of a church. Strong examined the creek carefully, and decided the next morning to go up it as far as they could in the boat.

"We're lookin' for beaver streams," he said, "an' this seems a likely one to me. Leastways I'm hopin' for the best."

Their boat was of shallow draught, and they were able to row it at least ten miles up the creek. On the way they found that it received two or three small tributaries and that the mountains were much lower here. Strong's surmise about beaver proved correct. They found fine colonies along all the streams. It seemed to be absolutely virgin territory, so far as trappers were concerned, but they touched nothing. They had no way to carry out the furs, as they could not row back against the stream, and after they had taken careful note of the country they returned to the river.

"We'll come here some day by land with plenty of horses and mules," said Sam Strong, "an' then them beaver had better look out."

CHAPTER 10

The Return by Land

All four enjoyed the rest on the beaver stream, as explorations even
were a relaxation after the rush and strain of the river, but they re-em-
barked with a willing spirit, first replenishing their supplies with a black-
tail deer that Bill Cole shot.

The *Columbus* swung once more into the yellow stream, and it seemed
to Bob, looking down a vast chasm, that they were going to enter the very
bowels of the earth. All around them now were great heights of black
lava, and back of these, snow-capped mountains. But nothing interrupted
the rush of the river. That very day it turned a vast mass of rock, at so
sharp an angle that, despite the promptness and exertions of the four, the
Columbus grazed it. Bob thought they were gone, but the blow was only
a glancing one. The boat tipped dangerously to one side, and foaming
water dashed over them all, but the stout wooden sides were not broken
in. the *Columbus* righted itself, and away they went with the white water
whirling about them. When they were fairly steady Obadiah Pirtle took
off his cap and said to the boy:

"Bob, has my hair turned grey in the last five minutes?"

They had smoother going the next day, and in the afternoon they
discovered another beaver stream, this time coming in from the west. Sam
Strong marked it carefully on a rude map that he was making.

"We'll be back here, too, some day," he said, "if nobody beats us to it.
I like to hope for the best, but I shouldn't be surprised if Carver an' his
band were down in these parts somewhere. Carver's a good trapper, an'
he's always ready, too, for any other business that's likely to pay. I believe
that he's hand in glove with the Indians."

"I hope we'll never see him again," said Bob.

Sam was silent. He knew better than the boy the dangers of mountain
and plain.

Occasionally when they tied up to the rocks, or in the coves, they
tried fishing in the muddy water. They caught a number of fish, but they

did not prove to be very good, and Bob greatly preferred the flesh of a second black-tail deer, which fell this time to the rifle of Obadiah Pirtle.

They had been on the river a week when the mountains sank down somewhat, and they floated between banks only three or four hundred feet high, covered with thin forest. The current was not so rapid, and they enjoyed a period of comparative ease, being released from the imminent fear of rocks and rapids.

Bob was sitting in the prow of the *Columbus*, leaning against the side. He had no particular duties just then, and he was in a half dreamy state, gazing upward at the blue sky which was soft with the breath of spring-time. His gaze wandered to the banks, crested with green, and suddenly he sat up a little straighter in the boat. He looked again, thinking that perhaps he had been tricked by the imagination. But he beheld the same figure, that of a man standing by a tree at the very brink. Then he saw two more, three more, a half dozen, and they were Indians.

"Look! Look!" he cried to the others. "There are warriors on the bank!" Sam Strong shot a swift glance upward.

"So there are," he said, "an' they're goin' to do us harm if they can. Bill, you an' Obe hold the boat steady, an' lay low everybody."

Bob lay almost flat in the boat, but he held his rifle ready. They could now see the Indians. They were about a dozen in number, and their intentions were plainly hostile.

Something whizzed in the air, there was a streak, and a long feathered arrow struck in the stream near the boat.

"Bows an' arrows!" said Sam Strong, cheerfully. "They'll have to use something better if they catch us."

Whiz! Whiz! went the arrows, striking in the stream, and some on the boat. One buried its barbed head deep in the wood, near Bob, and he shuddered when he saw it. He would rather have been struck by a bullet than by an arrow.

The boat was already moving rapidly, but Cole and Pirtle took the oars and increased the speed. The Indians could be seen running along the bank to keep pace. Part of them were now ahead of the boat, and were gathering at a place, where the cliffs lowered, and the river also narrowed. Here the boat would be in a much better range, but Sam Strong was watching closely.

"Bob, when we get to the pass there, shoot," he said, "an' aim at the best target. They've got to fire almost straight down at us while we fire nearly straight up at them. It's much the easier for us. Now, keep steady."

The sturdy *Columbus* shot toward the pass, and Bob, kneeling, aimed at the largest figure that he could see on the precipice. The rifle of Sam Strong was pointed at another warrior, standing at the very edge. The shouts of the Indians came to their ears, and then the whizzing of arrows and the crack of rifles.

Straight into the pass went the boat, and Bob and Strong pulled trigger. The warrior, at whom the boy aimed uttered a cry and fell back, but the one that Sam Strong had chosen, threw up his hands, and plunged straight down into the river. His body struck the water near the horrified boy, came up again further down, and then was swept away from sight forever.

The boat itself was moving forward with great speed, and, as it shot through the mouth of the pass, it took a foaming fall. Here was a second reason why the Indians had selected this place for their chief attack. the *Columbus* rocked mightily in the surge. Yellow water dashed over it, from either side, in such volume that the four occupants were drenched. Now its prow was buried in the rushing stream, and then the stern.

Nobly did Bill Cole and Obadiah Pirtle do their parts in these terrible moments. Theirs was a hard task, to pay attention only to the river and the boat, while the Indians fired upon them and their comrades fired back. But they never flinched. With their heavy oars they swung the boat around a jutting crag, then they dodged cruel rocks in the very middle of the stream, shot away from a whirlpool, and, with the most desperate efforts, kept the boat in the middle of the smoothest water.

Strong managed to send a second bullet at the warriors on the bank, but the task was too great for Bob. He was rocked about so violently that he could not do more than retain his rifle, and keep his seat in the boat. The Indians, meanwhile, shouted a great deal, and continued to discharge both arrows and bullets, but firing down from a perpendicular height accuracy was impossible. Only accident would send a missile true, and fortunately no such accident occurred. The boat was hit several times by both arrows and bullets, but its crew were untouched.

The *Columbus* gave one last terrifying lurch, portions of the Colorado swept entirely over Bob, and the fall was passed. They shot now through rapids, narrow and swift, but comparatively smooth, and the Indians were soon left far behind. But they did not try to check the speed of the boat, until they were at least ten miles away from the dangerous pinnacle. Then Strong gave a signal, and they steered the boat in toward a narrow beach at the foot of a cliff a thousand feet high. It was a somewhat difficult task, as the current still pulled, even at the shallow edge of the river, but, finally, they half-beached her on the sand, and tied her stoutly to some dwarf greasewood.

The four, when the task of securing the *Columbus* was finished, sat down on the sand, and drew deep, mighty breaths of relief.

"Hopin' for the best as I always try to do," said Sam Strong, "I was afraid of the worst when we came through that jug's mouth of a place, with all them Indians whoopin' an' yellin' an' fillin' the air with bullets an' arrows."

"I'd rather look back at it than forward to it," said Obadiah Pirtle, tersely.

"What kind of Indians were they?" asked Bob.

Sam Strong cut one of the arrows from the boat, and examined the sharp stone head critically.

"Utes, I should say," he replied, "an' it's lucky they couldn't get at us any better than they did. The river itself is mighty dangerous, but the banks are so high they mostly keep the Indians out of range."

They decided to remain where they were for the night, and they knew that they were absolutely safe from the Ute band. They were at the east edge of the river and the Utes were on the west bank. The Colorado now flowed between the cliffs high, steep and unbroken, and it was impossible for the warriors to cross it. They had so much faith in this protection that all four went to sleep at once on the boat, leaving no sentinel. Exhaustion gripped them so hard that none awoke until the sun was high the next day, and they decided to remain there until the following morning, especially as they wished to make a critical examination of the *Columbus*.

The good boat had passed the dangers wonderfully well. Her sides were scarred, where she had grazed the rocks more than once, but no cut was deep enough to require patching, and, the next morning, they set out again, with confidence in the boat and themselves increased.

Then followed a week of extreme danger and great wonders. Bob had scarcely credited to the full the tales of Sam Strong, but he found everything to be true. The river dropped down into a mighty chasm. All that they had seen before was merely the beginning. Now the cliffs, sometimes black basalt, and again red and yellow, rose far above them, so far that even if Indians had been standing on the bank they could not have been told from the shrubs that grew there. It might be a half mile or it might be a mile to the top. No one on the boat could tell.

Nor was the height of the cliffs the only wonder. The storms of the ages had carved them into strange and fantastic shapes. Bob's imaginative mind could make out towers and churches, vaster than any ever built by man, over which the light played in the most vivid fashion, now yellow, now red, now green, and all the blended shades.

All of them began to believe that the story of the subterranean river would prove true. The Colorado, sinking lower and lower, must finally plunge into the earth itself. Presently they might reach cliffs that had no break, no place where they could land, and carried on by the great torrent they must go underground with it. This thought was in the mind of every one of them, but none would speak it.

Their hardships increased also. One day they suffered five hours from a bitter storm of sleet and hail, from which they could not protect themselves, owing to the necessity of being always at the oars. The deep channel of the river, that immense slash in the mountains, seemed to serve as a sort of funnel down which the wind was drawn, shrieking with a power and ferocity that Bob had never heard before, and sending the hail and sleet like volleys from shotguns. Blood was actually drawn more than once from the hands and faces of the four. The river, too, was at its fiercest, demanding every exertion of eye and hand, and the time came when Bob tried to resign himself to death.

But resignation with the boy did not imply giving up. He still struggled at his oar, obeying all the signals of Strong, and after a long time the storm passed, leaving them cold, wet and stiff. Strong brought out a bottle from the stores and made everyone take a big drink, but they were still in such a state that they managed the *Columbus* with difficulty.

Strong grew very anxious. In such a condition they could not fight forever against this ferocious river, and unless they found anchorage they must perish through sheer exhaustion. He compelled Bob, although the boy was very unwilling, to ship his oars, and crawl under the tarpaulin, while he sought for any sign of a break in the cliffs that would afford anchorage.

It was after nightfall when Strong's keen eyes, piercing the dark, saw another canyon entering the mightier one down which the Colorado flowed.

"Hurrah, boys!" he cried. "We've hoped for the best, an' it's happened. All hands to the oars now, an' we'll row up the tributary!"

They swung the *Columbus* into the second canyon, and found themselves on the bosom of a stream quite different from the Colorado. It was shallow and slow-moving, and when Bob dipped down with a cup he found its waters bitter with salt and brine.

It comes from alkali plains somewhere," said Bill Cole. "A river ought to be ashamed of itself for bein' as dirty an' bitter as this is, but anyway it's doin' us a good turn, an' we oughtn't to complain."

They rowed far up the tributary in the moonlight, but it was nearly midnight before they came to low banks and a good stopping place. There they built two great fires, and sat between them.

"I want to roast myself till I can't stand it any longer," said Sam Strong. "I'd advise you fellows to do the same, an' in the mornin' we'll hold a council."

The question put to the council was very simple: should they go on or turn back? Sam Strong laid down the premises succinctly. They had come hundreds of miles, and they had passed through chasms which must be a mile deep. They had located several good beaver streams to which they could come on future trips. The river would probably grow wilder the further they went, and the *Columbus* was not adequate for increased risks. As it was, the return trip by land would consume many weeks.

All voted reluctantly to go back, and they began the task at once. They rowed ten or more miles further up the creek, stopping only when the water was too shallow for the boat, which they pushed into some dense shrubbery growing at the water's edge, where it was completely hidden from anyone, a yard away.

"We've got to leave the good old *Columbus*," said Sam Strong. "Maybe we'll find her jest as she is when we come down this way again three or four years from now, an' then she'll be of use."

They rolled up the skin tarpaulin and thrust it into the boat's little cabin. The oars were fastened aboard, and making of their ammunition and remaining supplies four packs, they bade the *Columbus* farewell.

"Good boat! Strong boat! She's served us well," said Obadiah Pirtle, sententiously.

"Yes, an' I'd like mighty well to go on a thousand miles further, if need be," said Sam Strong, the light of exploration shining in his eyes. "I'd like to be able to tell whether the Colorado goes into the earth or reaches the ocean above ground. Well, it can't be this time."

They now turned toward the northeast, every man carrying his pack, and they found the travelling over wild, rough ranges very slow and difficult. They had come at racing speed like a toboggan down an icy hill, but it was a heavy drag back, inch by inch. They were able, however, to examine the country, and Strong found further encouragement about beaver.

"We can find 'em in here for twenty years to come," he said.

They lived chiefly on the black-tail deer, which they found in abundance on the mountains, and now and then they killed a bear. As they advanced northward, Strong grew anxious about Indians. The country became more open, fit in many places for habitation, and he was sure that the tribes would not neglect such a region.

Strong was right. When they had been travelling about two weeks they saw a great cloud of smoke rising behind a hill to their left. They climbed the hill, and from the shelter of dense pines looked down upon an Indian village of forty or fifty skin *tepees*. Neither Strong nor Cole could tell to what tribe they belonged, and they did not stay to enquire into the matter.

"We'd better beat one of them masterly retreats Tom an' Porter are always talkin' about," he said. "We haven't got any river here to take us away from them warriors, if they should see us."

The Indians did not see them, and they continued their journey through country in which travelling was very slow. Often they did not make more than five miles a day, and it seemed to Bob that if he climbed one mountain ridge, he climbed a thousand.

They stopped sometimes for two or three days to hunt or rest, and they utilized one of these occasions to make for themselves new moccasins of deerskin, which they needed badly. Bob had now become quite skilful in all kinds of work. He could sew deerskin with neatness, and moreover he knew how to shape and fashion it. Nearly all the clothing with which he had started from Omaha had disappeared, and he was arrayed in deerskin, which set off his tall, well-knit, active figure. His stature had increased to a considerable degree, and his strength remarkably, during his year with the trappers.

Another week of steady climbing toward the northeast passed, and they came into a country less mountainous, but in the main bleak and sterile. Trees and grass were to be found along the rare little streams, but there were long stretches of country, burnt with lava and absolutely bare. They found game along the streams only, and were compelled to be very careful with their resources.

"Beaver country lies north of here," said Sam Strong one evening when they camped by the side of a brook, so weak that it was barely able to trickle over the sand, "an' we'll strike forests, too."

"I'm glad of it," said Bob. "I'd like to have a little shade."

It had been very hot all the day, and the glare of the sun off the black lava burnt into him. Now he lay against a boulder, seeking any coolness that the evening might bring.

"It's a country that's known to trappers to some extent," said Strong. "They've come here several times from some of the border posts, an' Hudson Bay poachers have been in here, too. As our own grounds are private, we don't want to meet any of 'em, an' I'm hopin' for the best."

"So say we all," said Obadiah Pirtle, and a little later Bob fell asleep through sheer exhaustion.

CHAPTER 11

The Coming of Carver

They entered the next day a more desolate country than any they had yet seen, a sea of lava without a trace of vegetation. As Strong remarked, they had to pass through the worst before they could get to the better. Bob glanced down at the hot, black slag that burned through his moccasins.

"This came from a volcano, somewhere," he said, looking at the rounded peaks far away.

"Volcano," said Bill Cole, incredulously. "I've been travellin' through the mountains most all my life an' I ain't ever heard of any belchin' out fire an' smoke and brimstone."

"It isn't that," said Bob, who had not studied his school-books in vain, "it never happened in your time, nor in your grandfather's time. That lava was probably thrown out a couple of million years ago."

Bill Cole laughed with the just scorn of a righteous man.

"You learned that from a book, Bob," he said. "What happened two million years ago has never happened at all for me. It's jest a part of creation."

All that day the sun burned and blazed, but the hottest part of it was its reflection. The lava seemed to shoot it back with double strength, and Bob, although he drew his cap as low down as he could, was unable to protect his face and eyes from the glare. The lava not only grew hotter, but sharper. Despite every precaution, it cut through their moccasins, and their feet were bleeding.

Bob suffered severely. The sun stole his strength, and his head ached. His feet, swollen and torn, gave him great pain. His eyes, made weak by the fiery glare and the dimness, magnified the heat waves before him, but he saw, nevertheless, far mountains which looked dim and cool.

The boy would not utter a word of complaint. He tried to hold himself erect, and to walk with as firm a step as the others, but his head did ache horribly, and his tongue lay like a coal in his mouth. Sam Strong had been watching him with a look sideways, but none the less inclusive, and the frontiersman was a shrewd reader of the human heart. For a long time he said nothing. At last he remarked in a tone apparently careless:

"Well, I'm gettin' my second wind. It comes to some fellows quicker than it does to others, but that don't mean that it will stay the longest. Bob, suppose I carry that pack of yours a spell while I'm so fresh an' gay."

Bob glanced at his chief, and Sam Strong, stalwart, sunburned, the man of a thousand perils, actually blushed right through his brown countenance. The boy understood him and showed that he knew.

"You said, Sam, that I was to be a full partner in the furs," Bob replied, "and I'm going to be a full partner here on the lava, too. You're just about as hot and tired as I am, and your feet are as much cut up, too."

Sam Strong looked down at his moccasins. A red streak ran across each. Then he smiled, and his smile was half kind, half grim.

"Bob," he said, "I'm glad you gave me that answer. You are, as you say, a full partner in everything, an' I won't try to fool you. Come on now, an' we'll see who can walk on the hottest an' sharpest lava without flinchin'."

But it was only a narrow stretch of the lava desert, a spit thrust out from the main body between the mountains, and towards the middle of the afternoon the green slope showed nearer. At twilight it seemed to Bob that he could reach out and touch it, and when the sun was quite gone they were there.

They had reached the foot of the first slope, and in the light night it was the most beautiful mountain that Bob had ever seen. It was cool, shadowy and protecting, a kindly father of mountains. There were only dwarf pines about him, but they appeared splendid after the glare of the lava. His eyes became clear again, and his tongue no longer burned in his mouth.

Just over the first slope they found a beautiful little clear brook, flowing down from snows far away somewhere above the clouds. Bob started to rush for it, but the hand of Sam Strong, falling upon his shoulder, held him back.

"We won't drink it all up right away, Bob," he said, "just a few drops apiece, an' then we'll look to our feet."

They drank moderately of the water which was very cold, and then stripping off their moccasins, buried their feet in it. Bob felt a deep sense of refreshment flowing from his toes to his head. He lifted up his feet, let the water run through his toes, and then, thrusting them back again, laughed like a happy child.

"I ain't as young as you, Bob, an' I ain't laughing" said Obadiah Pirtle, "but I enjoy it as much."

After a time they drank all the water they wanted and ate cold food from their packs. Then they lay on the ground, in their bare feet, and were happy. They repaired their moccasins by moonlight as best they could, and taking a night's sound sleep, went further into the mountains the next day. Coming to a likely valley, they agreed to separate and hunt for game, which they needed badly. A spring, bubbling up at the base of an old oak, was to be the point of return, and they started, all in different directions.

Bob bore towards the northwest and turned up a little canyon, well lined with oak and ash, pine and cedar. The coolness of the forest and the night's sleep had refreshed him greatly. Frequent bathing of his feet, both night and morning, in the cold water, had taken away the soreness, and he walked now with a strong and elastic tread.

It was a pleasant little canyon, two or three hundred yards wide, with frequent little pools of clear water, and a gentle slope to the enclosing ridges. Here one was almost sure to find game, and the boy's heart leaped with the desire of being the first to return to the camp with deer or wild turkey.

But the hunt led on. Search canyon and trees ever so well, he saw neither deer nor wild turkey. He was far from the camp now, three hours at least, and he neither saw nor heard anything. There was no wind, and the boughs of the trees hung motionless. The boy began to grow discouraged. He did not lose hope that in time he would find game, but his pride in being first would not be gratified.

The canyon turned suddenly almost at a right angle, and as Bob turned the angle, a thick clump of pines, he came face to face with a large man, dark of face and close-set of eyes. The man rushed out, seized Bob's shoulder in a powerful grasp, and began to laugh.

"Well, if it ain't the young sprout!" he exclaimed. "The boy that got away in Omaha with the others, when we lost the scent of the new fur country. What luck!"

Bob had recognized Carver in an instant, but he had hoped that the bully would not remember him. Now the hope was vain. What bad luck indeed! Carver showed his white teeth, while he still held a firm grip upon the boy's shoulder—he was a man of immense strength.

"It's quite sure," continued Carver, "that where you are the others are not far away. Now I knew that Sam Strong was headed for rich beaver streams, known to nobody else, and right there is where I want to go with my men. You will lead us, my boy. This is certainly my lucky day."

Bob was sure that the freebooter's band was not far away. He could see some distance up the canyon, but none of them was in view. He revolved rapidly in his mind some plan of escape. He must give a warning to his comrades, no matter how. But that fierce grip was still on his shoulder. The five fingers of Carver seemed to sink like iron into his flesh.

"Come, boy," said the man, "where are your friends and how far from here are those beautiful beaver streams? Not twenty miles, I'll wager, or I wouldn't find you wandering up this canyon."

"I will not answer either question," replied Bob with energy.

"You won't, won't you?" said Carver. "Well, I'll see that you do. There's an old saying that a bird that won't sing can be made to sing. Talk, I say!"

His fingers pressed right into the boy's shoulder, and pain shot all through him. A sudden passion of rage filled every vein of Bob's body. The passion and the pain together gave him a fierce impulse, backed by double his usual strength. He was held by the left shoulder, but doubling his right fist, he struck the man in the chest with great violence.

Powerful as he was, Carver's grip was torn loose, and despite himself he staggered back. The boy's anger was still at white heat, and now he swung his left fist also, this time full on the man's chin.

Carver staggered again, and fell upon his hands and knees. He remained there only a moment With the blood dripping from his chin, but lithe and strong as a panther, he sprang to his feet. His rifle, which had been held in his left hand, lay on the ground, but his right hand flew toward the pistol in his belt. It stopped there.

Bob, with every nerve and sense keyed to the highest tension, had sprung back as Carver fell, and now when the freebooter rose he found himself looking into the muzzle of the boy's rifle, not more than five feet away.

"I won't tell you where my comrades are, and I won't tell you where the beaver streams are," said Bob. "I'm a bird that can sing, but you can't make me sing. Take your hand from that pistol or I shoot."

Carver was not a common man. He knew by Bob's eyes, full of excitement and anger, that he meant what he said, and he was too clever to give way to his own passion. His hand came away from the pistol butt, and exercising his great power of self control, he laughed lightly.

"It was a jest," he said. "Of course I didn't mean you any harm, boy. But we are beaver trappers, just like your party, and we ought to join you. Two are stronger than one. I wanted you to lead us to Strong and the others."

Bob looked down the sights of his rifle into the swarthy face and the close-set, cunning eyes. As the man smiled he looked at the long, white teeth which seemed to him to be sharpened as if they had been pointed with a file, and he was not deceived for an instant. The face of Carver made upon his mind an impression exactly like that of a mountain wolf.

"A man's face often lies, and you can see it when it lies," he said. "Yours is lying now. Turn square around at once and walk, or I shoot!"

Carver's face as he heard the words was ugly to see. All his evil passions, to be dragooned thus by a boy, flared forth upon it, but he turned without delay and began to walk away in the other direction. He was hoping that some of his followers would appear. His camp was not more than a couple of miles up the canyon, and one of them might come within sight at any moment. Rarely had his heart been torn by so fierce an anger. It was not endurable to be marched away in this fashion' at the gun's muzzle. Black rage swelled the veins of his face. His hand stole again toward the pistol butt, but stopped halfway because he knew the boy with the rifle was watching.

A figure approached among the trees a hundred yards away. Carver, with savage joy, recognized it as that of one of his followers. The man saw his leader walking forward in seeming gravity and with measured step, and then he saw the figure now thirty yards behind him, covering him with levelled rifle. He was acute enough to know that the one with the rifle was a stranger and an enemy. He sprang forward, threw his weapon to his shoulder and fired.

Bob sent his own bullet at almost the same moment, but not at Carver. He could not fire into a man's back. He aimed instead at the man who had aimed at him. Neither bullet struck its target—the pulling of the trigger was too hasty—and Bob, whirling about, ran with all his speed toward the pool that had been chosen as the hub of their axis. He had no hesitation about flight, and two motives drove him on. He knew that he could not fight Carver and others, too, and he wished to warn his comrades as quickly as he might.

A shout arose behind him, another and then several more. Two more men had appeared at the sound of the shots, and Carver, whirling about, fired his own rifle at the fleeing boy. It would have been Bob's last moment had the freebooter not been so mad with rage that he was not cool enough to take good aim. As it was, Bob heard the bullet singing a little warning in his ear as it passed, and the lava cuts on his feet were forgotten. He flew over the ground with wonderful, light strides.

He slipped a fresh cartridge into his rifle almost without checking speed, and a little later looked back for the first time. Carver and three other men were in pursuit, but they were at least four hundred yards behind, and he believed that no running man could hit a running target at that distance. While he was taking his quick glance one of them fired, and he heard the bullet strike a stone ten yards away.

There was a strain of daring, a certain hardihood in the face of great peril, in Bob Norton's nature, and now by an impulse that he could not control this spirit found vent. He put two fingers of his free left hand across his mouth, about a quarter of an inch apart, and gave utterance to a long, shrill whistle that was defiant, even taunting. He knew that they would understand, and the verification came at once in the crack of a rifle-shot. But the bullet, like the other, struck twenty yards away, and Bob laughed to himself in scorn. Another shot did not come. Evidently Carver recognized the foolishness of the others, and restrained his men.

Bob did not glance back again for at least twenty minutes, and now he saw with a great surge of joy that the distance between him and his pursuers had widened at least fifty yards. His lightness gave him the advantage, and holding himself well in hand, with the rifle trailed on his right arm, he ran straight down the canyon. He gained another fifty and then a hundred. Now the freebooters, fearing that he would vanish quite from their sight, fired several shots, but they were all wasted. The speed of both pursuers and pursued slackened. They had been running nearly an hour, and now their pace was not much more than a walk, as they sought to pump fresh air into their lungs and rest tired muscles. Bob took the opportunity to try a shot of his own. He was not bloodthirsty, but when he saw one of the men jump he knew that he had inflicted a slight wound, and he was glad.

Carver shook his fist at him, but he did not fire. The pursuers increased their pace again. Bob did the same, and presently, as he ran along, looking mostly at the ground to keep from tripping, he heard a shout ahead. He looked up and there were Sam Strong and Bill Cole emerging from the woods, rifles held in their hands, and ready for instant action. It was wonderful to Bob how magnificent these two friends of his looked. He had never noticed before their great height and width, nor their fierce and terrible bearing. They were giants, well come to his rescue.

"It's Carver and his men!" he shouted, rushing toward them. "They want to raid our camp, and they tried to kill me."

Up flew the rifle of Sam Strong and a bullet struck one of the pursuing men in the shoulder. Carver and the three with him instantly fell back. It was one thing to pursue a single boy, but it was quite another to pursue him when two formidable frontiersmen stood by his side, ready to repel attack.

The two parties were now about five hundred yards apart, and stood for a moment or two looking at each other. Then Carver put a whistle to his lips and blew a long, shrill note.

"He's callin' to the rest of his people," said Sam Strong. "Well, we'll call to ours, an' hopin' for the best, I think he'll come, as there ain't but one of him."

He put his fingers to his lips and blew a note almost as loud as that of Carver's whistle. In three minutes they heard a rapid tread in the bush, and soon the lank figure of Obadiah Pirtle hove into view. His swift glance comprehended everything.

"Sorry I'm the last to get here," he said. "But I see that the real work ain't yet actually begun."

"No," said Strong, "nothin' much has been done yet, 'cept by Bob, here, though he ain't had time to tell me what that is, but I think we'll be busy soon. We'll drop back among the rocks."

The canyon was extremely rocky at that point and the four running in among the rocks, dropped down under shelter. Bob was still drawing long breaths, but they were growing shorter, and his lungs were refilling with fresh air. As he lay behind a high crag he briefly told the story of his encounter.

"They think that our beaver skins are stored close by," said Strong. "It's natural that they should think so, seein' that we're here. They expect to wipe out all but one or two of us, an' then make them that are left tell about the furs. Cur'us things, Bob, happen in these mountains, a thousand miles from nowhere, but hopin' for the best, I don't think they'll wipe us out."

"They're gatherin' in strong force," said Bill Cole. "See, the rest of his crowd have come."

It was evident that Cole was right, and that the shots had drawn all of Carver's force. More than twenty men were in the group that was now assembled about a thousand yards away, and in the clear, brilliant sunlight of the western mountains Bob saw them very distinctly, all strong, sunbrowned men, several of them half-breeds, and two obviously Indians, but of what tribe Bob could not tell.

Carver stood a little in front of the others, and Bob could surmise his feelings. He had seen enough of him to know very well that he was, at bottom, a man of ferocious temper, and he must be raging over his temporary defeat by a boy.

"They'll spread out directly in a half circle," said Sam Strong, "expectin' to get at us that way, but I don't think they'll be able to do it."

Sam was a good prophet, as the freebooters, after a short conference, began to trail off, some to the right and some to the left, excepting Carver and four or five, who remained where they were.

"The party that turned off to the left," said Strong, "will climb up on the mountainside an' try to get our range, but as you remember, Bob, when we were on the Colorado, it's hard to shoot down at a man an' hit him."

Strong spoke quietly, but with a stern certainty in his tone that boded ill for the skirmishers on the slope. Both the leader and Bill Cole were watching the mountainside attentively. The intense burning light threw every rock, tree and shrub into brilliant relief. It seemed to Bob that he could see the convolutions in bark, on trunks a thousand yards away. His heart was beating rather fast, but he had become inured to danger, and he did not tremble. He lay close behind his rock, and was content to wait, having an abiding faith in his leader.

Something moved on the mountainside and a rifle flashed. The bullet struck only the unoffending earth, but another bullet, fired in return at the flash, sped true, and one wilderness outlaw lay down forever in the bush. Sam Strong's face was stern and hard as he thrust another cartridge into his rifle.

"Good shot, Sam," said Bill Cole.

The leader nodded.

"It'll hold 'em a while," said Obadiah Pirtle.

Everything relapsed into quiet, and the rays of the sun came down hotter than ever. Bob saw Carver and the men who had remained with him lie down on the grass, as if they would take their ease just out of rifle-shot, and he began to grow impatient. "Waiting was getting upon his nerves. He wanted them to attack, if they were to do so, and have done with it. He moved a little from sheer restlessness.

"Careful, Bob," said Strong, "you're showin' yourself to them that are on the other side of the canyon."

Bob hastily drew back within the shelter of the rock, and not a moment too soon. A bullet, fired from the opposite side of the canyon, knocked up the earth where his knee had been. Both Cole and Pirtle fired in reply, but they did not hit their man. Nevertheless, he and his comrades were compelled to retreat swiftly.

"They won't try to get at us in that way again," said Sam Strong. "Too dangerous."

Strong was right again, and no other visible movement occurred for a long time. Then it came in a manner that they least expected. Carver walked deliberately down the canyon toward them, waving an old white handkerchief on the muzzle of his rifle. Strong expressed his frank astonishment.

"Now, I'd like to know what's at work in his brain," he exclaimed. "Comin' with a white flag. That means that he wants to talk to us. I'm hopin' for the best, but I hardly hope that he means to apologize. Anyhow, we'll let him say his say."

Strong came from cover and sat down on a rock in a comfortable position. Carver walked on boldly. Bob could not keep from admiring his easy bearing and air of confidence. It was quite evident that Carver was a man of quality, although the quality might be wicked. He came within about thirty paces, dropped his rifle stock to the ground, and leaned gracefully on the muzzle, old handkerchief and all.

"Hello, Strong," he said in quite a genial tone. "I've got a few things to say."

"You've got all the time there is to say 'em in," said Strong drily, "an' we're listenin', so go ahead."

"You're fur hunters and so are we," said Carver. "Good fur grounds and beaver streams ain't any too plenty now, as you know. But you and the fellows with you have made a big find somewhere in these parts. There ain't a doubt about it, and we want to be in on it. We're just bound to be in on it. Now, I lay it to you, fair and square. You take us in as partners, and we'll all divide even. You've just laid out one of my men, but I don't mind that. There'll be fewer to share. You need a strong party. Indians are troublesome, and are going to be more so. Few as you are you could never get back across the plains with your furs, even if you were so lucky as to reach the plains."

He paused as if he wished his words to sink in, but the face of the leader did not change a particle.

"That's our affair," said Sam tersely. "What's the other side?"

"The other won't be so pleasin' to you. It says that if you don't accept the first, we'll come an' take your furs. We're strong enough to do it, an' I don't know of any law in these parts that will keep us from it."

"No, there ain't no law," said Sam, "'cept that of our rifles, an' I want to say that I've listened to you, Juan Carver. Now, havin' considered the question for all of half a second, an' speakin' for my partners, whose feelin's I know without asking I've got to say that we choose rifles, hopin', at the same time, Juan Carver, that it won't hurt your feelin's."

Strong's tone was too decisive to admit of doubt, and Carver accepted it in a jaunty manner.

"A man always has his choice," he said, "an' you've made yours, though it's a bad one."

"I'm hopin' for the best," said Sam Strong.

CHAPTER 12

The Great Laugh

Carver walked back toward his men in the same graceful, careless manner. When he reached them he talked a moment with one, probably a lieutenant, and then disappeared further up the canyon, but the rest remained there on guard. Sam Strong removed himself from the rock where he had sat motionless throughout the negotiations, and laughed drily when he lay down upon the ground.

"Carver must have thought we were fools, when he made an offer like that," he said. "He knew that if we accepted it, we'd keep it an' that he wouldn't."

"What are we going to do now!" asked Bob.

"It depends a good deal on what they do. If the night comes on thick an' black we can slip away. Our packs are not more than two miles from here down the canyon. We can pick them up an' then light out for our real camp, where Louis and the two generals are."

Now came a long period of waiting and suspense that was very trying to Bob. Carver returned to the group in the canyon, but he made no movement, sitting down on the ground, apparently idling the time away. After two or three hours a little skirmishing was done, but it was at long range. The freebooters fired several shots, but they did not strike anywhere near, and Obadiah Pirtle fired one in return, which also found no target except the round earth. Then they relapsed into silence, and after a while Bob saw that the sun was setting. The dark haze spread slowly at first, and then so fast that the eastern mountains were gone, and the night was near. The four crept more closely together and held a council in whispers.

"It ain't our business to be fightin' a gang like that out there," said Sam Strong. "What we want to do is to be busy trappin' beaver. If we can slip away they'll spend all of a year roamin 'roun' through these parts lookin' for us an' our furs, while we're far away gettin' more."

They decided not to make the attempt until after midnight. Carver and his men would naturally expect it earlier, and after long and disappointed waiting their vigilance would be relaxed.

"An' if they undertake to move on us we'll be sure to hear 'em, even if we don't see 'em," said Sam Strong, confidently.

Bill Cole and Pirtle seemed to agree with him, as they stretched themselves at ease on the ground, although Bob observed that each kept an ear to the earth. He had so much confidence in them that he fell asleep. He was awakened by a rifle-shot. But when he sat up with sleep still heavy upon him, Sam Strong told him that the shot had been merely a warning.

"They undertook to creep near," he said, "an' I fired at the sound. I didn't hit anything, but it was enough to make 'em go back, which was all we wanted."

Bob fell asleep a second time, and when he was awakened again it was the hand of Sam Strong on his shoulder that did it.

"We're ready to go, boy," he said, "an' it's makin' no noise that will do it if we do it. I'm goin' to lead, you come right after me, Obe follows you, an' Bill brings up the rear. It would certainly be a great joke on 'em if we slipped right away, leavin' 'em here holdin' the basket an' knowin' no different. If we all hope for the best together maybe we can bring off the joke."

"I'm hoping with you," whispered Bob.

"I'm hopin', too," whispered Obadiah Pirtle.

"Me, too," came the whisper of Bill Cole.

Without further words they slipped away along the mountainside, everyone stepping so lightly that no sound arose as they passed. It was dark and the bush was thick, but Bob's pride was once more to the fore. If anyone stumbled, or broke a stick under his foot, or made the bushes rustle, he was resolved that it should not be he who stumbled or broke a stick under his foot or made the bushes rustle. He was clever enough now to see how it could be done. He was careful to step exactly in the tracks of Sam Strong, who was only a yard ahead of him, and as he did not look back he did not know that Obadiah Pirtle and Bill Cole followed this example, not from resolution, but from long training that had become habit and intuition.

When they had gone a hundred yards or so Sam Strong suddenly stopped. It was long a matter of pride with the boy that he did not run into the leader, but stopped noiselessly and in time, with a clear foot of space between them. The two behind him stopped automatically. Sam Strong turned slowly and looked in turn at Bob, Obadiah and Bill. The moonlight, faint though it was, was sufficient at that short range to disclose his face. Sam Strong, frontiersman, grim veteran of a thousand dangers, was laughing. No sound came from his lips, but he was laughing with every feature. The corners of his mouth turned up, his eyes were all mirth, and even the tip of his nose seemed to take a jocund tilt.

"The joke is comin' off," he said in the softest of whispers. "The greatest joke these mountains have ever known is about to be played. I felt it in all my bones that it was goin' to happen when we hoped together for the best. Raise up about four inches an' look down there to the right."

They rose to the ordered height and gazed over the tops of some bushes into a little ravine that evidently led into the canyon. Bob's pulses jumped when he saw half a score of men, Carver at their head and rifles in their hands, stealing forward.

"They're ambushin' the place where we ain't," said Strong in the same soft whisper, "an' as many more, comin' from other points, are doin' the same. Well, luck to you, boys. You'll get to that spot without bein' shot. But by the great horn spoon, the joke is on you all the same."

His face contracted again in a great spasm of silent laughter, and the infection passed down the line. The corners of Bob's mouth crinkled up, Obadiah Pirtle bent a little further forward and rubbed one hand appreciatively across his stomach, Bill Cole's eyes became like those of a child seeing his first clown at a circus.

Thus they stood motionless, while the attacking party filed by in the little canyon below them. Sam Strong cast a glance at the last man as he disappeared, and when the shadow was gone in the darkness, the leader dropped a heavy, sinewy hand over his own mouth. It was necessary. A great laugh struggling in his throat longed for vocal expression, and this was the only way in which he could keep it down. Not until he felt that he had acquired reasonable control did he take the hand away, and then he used it for making a signal to his comrades that they should move on.

Strong led a little higher up the slope of the mountain, crept another fifty yards, and the second time gave the signal to stop. Then he pointed through the bushes, and they saw another group of freebooters stealing upon the place that they had left. It was evident that the band of Carver were approaching it as the spokes of a wheel meet at the hub.

"The joke grows," whispered Strong. "By the great horn spoon, it is cert'nly the fanciest one that ever happened!"

The second detachment disappeared, stealing down upon the defenceless rocks, and when they were well out of sight the four sped swiftly along the mountain side. When they were a mile away they turned, descended into the canyon, passed by their camp, recovered their packs, and then leaving the canyon, entered the mountains again.

Now not a word was said. The marching was not so bad, as it was a fairly gentle slope, and their eyes had grown used to the darkness. Sam Strong led silently on one hour, two hours, three hours, until he came to a little hollow on the slope, where he stopped abruptly. The night had now lightened considerably, a good moon riding low in the heavens, and all the features of every face were visible to one another.

"Here we bust!" said Sam Strong.

"Let her rip!" said Bill Cole.

Sam Strong threw back his head, opened his mouth and shot forth a gigantic laugh, not a laugh of recent birth, a raw fledgling of a laugh, with only ordinary body and substance, but a laugh that had started four hours before, a laugh that had been nourished and vitalized every minute of that time, a laugh that was mighty, uncontrollable, that came rolling forth in wave after wave, everyone higher than its predecessor.

Bill Cole and Obadiah laughed, too, and in zest and volume and true spontaneity their laughs were but little inferior to that of the leader. Then the three laughs united, harmonious, and making one note, swept along the mountainside and came back in a musical echo. Tears gathered in the eyes of the men, but they were happy tears. The three bent forward, but it was not with the weight of years, it was with the weight of mirth.

Bob laughed, too. He was compelled to do so, but his was rather an under-note, a minor strain, as it were, in the grand diapason, and it was influenced somewhat by the laugh of the, others, while theirs was strictly original, having its cause in the scenes that they had witnessed four hours before.

The grand united laugh swelled to the zenith and then began to sink. Its waves rolled up less violently, the echoes became softer, and then died away. Then all ceased, as if by preconcerted action, and looked at one another.

"By the great horn spoon, it was cert'nly worth it!" said Sam Strong. "To think of Juan Carver and his men ambushin' some cold rocks, an' we a dozen miles away. I couldn't hold that laugh in another minute."

"Nor me," said Bill Cole.

"Nor me," said Obadiah Pirtle.

Bob gazed at his comrades in some curiosity. They were certainly men of the wilderness, and their jokes were those of the wilderness. But he said nothing. He was too happy to be asking questions.

"In case some wanderin' Indian, coyote or somethin' else that don't like us heard our laughin' we'll move on a couple of miles an' then rest," said Sam Strong.

They walked the appointed distance, and found a pleasant place in a clump of pines where they slept, the four by turns taking the watch until noon. Then they decided to pursue the journey to their mountain home, as if nothing had happened.

"Carver hasn't the least notion which way we've gone," said Strong, "an' he can't trail us over mountains. So we'll march an' wish 'em joy with their hunt down here."

They now passed days of marching and exertion, but they were pleasant to Bob. There was much climbing over rocks and mountain ridges, and often it was mercilessly hot, but they were rarely far from wood and water, and they found abundant game. They felt so safe, too, that several times they turned from their line of march to look for beaver streams. They were successful in locating two, and Sam Strong marked them carefully on the map of tanned deerskin that he carried inside his hunting shirt.

"May need 'em some day," he said, tersely.

The journey still led peacefully onward, and to Bob it was like a long ramble, the most interesting trip that anyone had ever undertaken. He had shot the rapids of the Colorado between mighty cliffs, more than a mile high—not knowing that others yet higher were below—and now he was returning through magnificent mountains, some of which no white man perhaps had ever seen before.

The boy's imagination was greatly stirred. Besides being a fur-hunter and man of arms, he was an explorer, too. He tried to surmise the height of the peaks, and he named the highest of them all Mt. Strong. A huge hog-back he called Cole Ridge, and the title Pirtle Crest was bestowed upon a singularly slender, but tall peak.

"It's good of you, Bob, ah' mighty flattering" said Sam Strong, "but them names won't stick. By an' by some feller from the east, wearin' big glasses an' carryin' measurin' instruments, will see our mountains, go back to the east, announce that he has discovered 'em, an' give 'em new names. Mt. Strong, Cole Ridge an' Pirtle Crest will fade right away like snow under the sun."

"That may be, but they will have been named right for a little while, at least," said Bob, loyally.

They crossed several rivers, mostly shallow and always cold, and on a beautiful golden day in late summer they reached their own creek and went up the little valley. It seemed to Bob that they had been away for ages, and he wondered if they would find the three comrades whom they had left behind alive and well. Some such thought was in the minds of the others, but they did not disclose it. Yet as they went up the valley they looked about very anxiously, lest they should see signs of a strange and hostile presence.

Everything was as they had left it, and as it should be. There was no smoke of an enemy on the horizon, no trail of a numerous band ran through the woods, there was no place where the camp of a war party had been. The very wind told of seclusion and peace, and at last they approached the good cabin that they had built the year before. The roof first came into the view of their knowing eyes, and then glimpses of the rough walls.

They saw no human being, but as they came nearer a most grateful odour assailed their nostrils.

"I've been hopin' for the best, an' it cert'nly has come to pass," said Sam Strong. "That's the smell of a deer steak, bein' cooked by Louis Perolet. I'll bet, too, that the 'generals' are in there with him, an' as the window is wide open, we'll slip up to it an' see what they are doin' before we have ourselves announced at the front door by the butler."

They trod very softly, and gaining the window, listened.

"Now, as I was tellin' to you, Louis, seem' that you're a Frenchman an' ain't informed, at the Battle of the Wilderness old Grant came hammerin' down with 'bout ten hundred thousand men, expectin' to smash us to flinders, blow us away, eat us up alive, an' do a lot of other things sudden an' unexpected, but General Bob Lee was there, a splendid, big man, ridin' at the front of our army on a grey horse, an' when he saw old Grant an' his million comin' he looked 'round at his army, Gen'ral Bob Lee did, an' he says in a loud voice: 'Is Porter Evans here?' an' someone answers also in a loud voice: 'He is.' Then says Gen'ral Bob Lee: 'Forward march; let the battle begin', an' then we gave 'em the most awful lickin' that was ever give to one army by another army."

"Don't you believe him, Louis. That Porter Evans ain't fit to write history. His fancy is so bright an' hot it burns facts right up. At the Battle of the Wilderness we didn't let more than ten thousand rebels get away. I remember takin' one general with my own hands, an' him all covered with gold lace, besides so many colonels an' captains that I forgot to count 'em."

"*Mon Dieu*, how you two fellows brag, you Yankee an' you rebel! What was your Grant, and what was your Lee to the great Napoleon? With his valiant Frenchmen, *grands soldats,* he conquered all Europe, every inch of it. He had kings and queens to do—what you call it? — eat breakfast out of his hand every morning. He frowns in Paris, an' the next minute the Czar in St. Petersburg an' the king in London shake all over with fear. He smiles, an' the next minute there is not a cloud in all Europe, not one so leetle as my hand. He is sitting at his grand council with his councillors an' secretaries an' one dozen kings an' queens sharpenin' the pens an' pencils for him, when a boy rush in with a telegram. He open it an' read an' say: 'Excuse me for two days, I have to go out an' whip the Emperor of Austria.'"

"But, Louis, there was no telegraph in those days."

"What, you think a poor, leetle man like you can get a telegram an' the great Napoleon not get one? You do not understan', Meester Tom Harris, that the great Napoleon was the greatest of all the great men the world has ever known."

"An' all three of you can lay down your arms an' surrender right here. Bless your ugly faces!" called out Sam Strong, suddenly thrusting his head in at the open window.

The three uttered cries of surprise, then of joy, and presently there was a mighty shaking of hands.

CHAPTER 13

The Departure

"I'm thinkin' that we arrived just in time," said Sam Strong, after the ferment had been stilled somewhat. "'Pears to me that the great Napoleon was jest about to wipe out all the rest of the world when we peeked in at the window."

"We'd have come back at him," said Porter Evans. "While me an' Tom here can't agree about the Civil War, Tom bein' so obstinate that he won't ever see the truth, we'd have united to down him. You did come just in time, just in time to save Frenchy."

Louis Perolet grinned. It was no ordinary grin. He had an expansive face, admirably adapted to grinning, large, white, even teeth, a wide mouth that stretched like rubber, and wonderful shining eyes. Now that expressive countenance was taxed to the utmost to show his joy. All his friends had come back sound and well, and the heart of Louis Perolet danced within him.

"Ah!" he exclaimed, "I am so glad to see you I go cook you more steak! I go cook you whole deer."

"Well," laughed Sam Strong, "we're just about hungry enough to eat one."

While Perolet prepared a grand banquet, they told of their adventures, and many long, deep breaths were drawn by the hearers as the narrative proceeded. Louis looked up from his fire in amazement when they told of rushing down the Colorado between cliffs of dizzy height.

"A river with banks a hundred miles high! What a wonder!" he exclaimed. "An' the great Napoleon never saw it."

Sam Strong laughed in unctuous delight. "No," he said, "that is one of the things the great Napoleon missed. The banks were somethin' stu-pen-je-ous, Louis, but I reckon they weren't all of a hundred miles high."

The three who had stayed at home made angry gestures when they heard of Carver and his attempts, but they laughed also when Sam Strong told how the four had stolen away.

"That was cert'nly a good trick, Sam," said Tom Harris. "I can hear Carver swearin' now, when he an' his gang bore down on that hidin' place of yours, an' it as empty as a last year's bird nest."

Not much had happened in the canyon during their absence; as it was the summer season the men did no trapping, but they took an occasional bearskin. They had drawn little from their stores, living almost wholly upon game, and the horses had grazed on the meadows. There could be no doubt, however, that the beaver were still plentiful, and another great season of fur-taking was assured. The party, now reunited, would pass the remainder of the warm weather waiting for it.

Bob had enjoyed the great adventure, the trip down the sunken river, and the return through the high mountains, but he was glad to be back again in their pleasant valley, down the centre of which ran the pleasant creek, with the pleasant meadows and woods on either shore. He renewed his acquaintance among the horses. Not one of them had died. All were as fat as butter, and Porter Evans and Tom Harris listened with deep content to his words of admiration.

"Yes," said Porter, "we've took good care of them. I'm a handy man among horses, an' by hard work an' stayin' reg'lar on the job, I've managed to teach Tom a little about 'em, too."

Tom Harris laughed scornfully.

"Port," he said, "you didn't know the difference between a horse an' an elephant till I showed you."

Not much of the summer was left, but they spent the remainder of it enlarging their cabin with another room, which they intended to devote wholly to the storing of furs. The completion of the task and the result gave them all great satisfaction.

"That's a fine, big house," said Obadiah Pirtle. "I ain't seen any other like it in these parts."

"Ah, eet ees the Versailles of the mountains," exclaimed Louis Perolet, triumphantly.

"Versy-y! What's that, Frenchy?" asked Bill Cole.

"Eet ees a grand palace, built a long time ago by Louis Quatorze, a great Frenchman, though not so great as the great Napoleon."

"We would say Versailles in this country, just as if that last syllable were spelled s-a-l-e-s," said Bob, "and we might as well name it Versailles, pronouncing it that way. Would you feel insulted, Louis, if we did so!"

"Not at all! Not at all!" replied Perolet, proudly. "Eet ees the preevelege of other nations to name their attempts after the grand achievements of France."

So it became Versailles with the pronunciation of the last syllable as if it were spelled s-a-l-e-s, and now the second autumn was at hand.

Again the forest reddened on the slopes; again a crisp sparkle came into the translucent air, and in the evening it was pleasant to hover somewhere near the glow of a fire. Now the trapping was resumed with great vigour and energy. They ranged further and further in pursuit of the beaver.

Heavy snows came later, and the winter was not so open as the preceding one had been, but they made snow-shoes for themselves, and still trapped with unfailing success. In such manner the cold months passed, filled with work, not untinged with danger because the mountain wolves were often numerous and always fierce, and when on long hunts the probability of snow-slides was always present. But success, continued success, infused everything with a rosy tint, and the time seemed short to them all when spring came.

The snows broke up with a mighty pouring of water down the slopes. Their pleasant, peaceful creek became a raging torrent, and it was many days before it subsided into its old channel. Then the snow being left only on the crests and upper ridges, an important question was laid before the Council of Seven, held in their Palace of Versailles in the spring of 1868.

The discovery of fine beaver streams, far down the Colorado, had turned in the minds of all the men throughout the winter. Some thought it might be better to cache the furs they now had in stock, go down to the new region, trap for another year, and then return to civilization, carrying at once the product of both territories. Others thought it might be the safer plan to go at once to the market with what they had, and then return direct to the new streams. Sam Strong inclined to the latter view, but he wished the whole party to be in agreement.

The session of the Council of Seven in their Palace of Versailles was long and arduous. Many astute arguments were produced on either side. The merits of the immediate return were shown, and so were those of the suggestion to go down the Colorado for another year. Shrewd trapping intellects were on either side, and so well did they debate that Sam Strong, president of the Council of Seven in their Palace of Versailles felt that the scales did not incline either way. With such a condition facing him he felt that he could not give any decision.

"We'll just wait a little while," he said. "Anyway it's too early to start. But we'll bale our furs, ready for the cache or the pony's back, whenever we do decide."

The work of packing took some time, and it was varied with an occasional hunt. One, by Bob and Louis Perolet, took them far down the creek to its mouth at the river.

It was the warmest day that they had yet felt, with a pleasant south-western wind and a sheer blue sky. The trees along the slopes and in the valley were bursting into green, and as they went along and the springtide rose high in their veins, Bob carolled lustily an old ditty that he had learned from Sam Strong:

"Railroad's too diggin'
"Gambling too low,
"If I go to stealin'
"To Frankfort I must go."

The mountain ridges gave back the fresh, young voice in pleasant echoes, and Louis Perolet looked approvingly at his young companion.

"Eet ees good to hear you sing, Meester Bob," he said, "you do not have the wonderful voice, you would not make your fortune at the opera in Paris, but you have youth an' you have happiness, an' when I hear you sing so I have youth an' I have happiness, too. Now, Meester Bob, I hear Meester Sam Strong sing that song before. What does he mean by 'to Frankfort I must go'?"

"Sam is from Kentucky, Louis, and the penitentiary is at Frankfort, the capital of the state. There's a lot of deep philosophy in that song. He can't work on a railroad, it's too hard; gambling is not respectable; if he steals, off to prison with him, so he comes out here and turns trapper."

"Meester Sam Strong one smart man, fit to be a soldier of the great Napoleon."

Bob threw back his head and laughed joyously, and Louis Perolet, because he too was joyous, also threw back his head and laughed.

They had not yet reached the river, while this talk was going on, but in fifteen minutes more they were in the thick woods, from which they could look down upon the larger stream, and the Frenchman, uttering a sharp little cry, put his hand upon the boy's shoulder.

"Look, Meester Bob," he said. "Look down the river!"

Bob looked, and, far down the stream, he saw four moving dots that he knew to be boats. As he looked they grew larger. Drops of water, glistening like silver in the brilliant sunshine, fell from moving oars, swung by strong arms. Figures grew into outline, and he saw that each boat contained eight or nine men. Nearer they came, and the boy saw that while some of the faces were red most of them were white. One of the figures in the boat he recognized by the set of the head and the swing of the shoulders. It was no less a personage than Juan Carver.

Louis Perolet felt the boy's shoulder quiver under his grasp.

"Eet ees the wicked Juan Carver, ees eet not?" he asked.

"Yes, it is he," replied Bob. "I'd know him a mile away. He has come with the band to take our furs."

"Eet ees so," said Louis Perolet, "but remember, Meester Bob that he has not yet found us. The mouth of our creek is narrow. Eet ees hid also by bushes an' reeds, an' tall grass. They do not know that eet ees here an' they may pass. We will wait an' see."

Kneeling down in a thicket, where they could not possibly be seen from the river, the two watched, with beating hearts. If they saw the mouth of the creek and turned into it, as was possible, because along such streams the beaver was found, there was nothing for them to do but hurry to the cabin, give the alarm and arrange for the defence. But if they passed on—then time would be left for many things.

It is not often that every sweep of an oar is watched so eagerly, but Bob believed afterward that he saw every blade as it flashed. He could now see Carver distinctly. The man sat upright in the prow, a cone-shaped, broad-brimmed Mexican hat crowning his head. But he seemed to be looking straight up the stream, and the other three boats, with their hard-faced crews, followed straight behind him.

Bob drew an imaginary line, extending from the mouth of the, creek to the other shore, and he measured the distance yet left between it and the leading boat. Allowing for the perspective of distance it was more than a hundred yards and alas! Carver could not but see!

Yet they went straight on up the stream, thirty yards more, forty, fifty, sixty, and then the boy's heart went down like a plummet in a pool. The leading boat checked its speed, and Bob was sure that it was going to turn, but one of the oarsmen had merely caught a crab. In an instant the full speed of the boat was resumed, and the others still came behind it in a straight line. Bob saw Carver turn his head, but he knew that he was rebuking the careless oarsman and was not drawn by the hidden mouth of the creek—at least not yet.

The sunlight seemed to grow more intense and brilliant. The bubbles that fell from the blades of the oars were now silver, now gold as the light fell upon them. Not twenty yards separated the boat of Carver from the imaginary line that Bob had drawn across the river. Now it was only ten, then the boat was upon it and passed on, the others still following in a straight line behind it.

A great sigh of relief burst from Bob, and Louis did not notice it because a sigh of about the same size burst from him also. The boats which had steadily been growing larger so long were now steadily becoming smaller at exactly the same pace, and to both Bob and Louis it was a beautiful sight to see—the gradual diminution of those boats.

"They didn't dream that we were here, that the beaver were here or that the creek was here," said Louis, "but that eesn't any sign that they won't come back tomorrow or a week from now. They are hunting all through this region an' we can't remain hidden. Een a great crisis the great Napoleon always did the best thing that was to be done, an' eemi-tating him we, too, will do the best thing that is to be done. We will rush back home an' warn Meester Sam an' the others."

They covered the long distance to their Palace of Versailles quicker than ever before, and found Sam Strong sitting before the door, scrap-ing some fresh skins. The leader looked up when he heard their hurried footsteps, and a single swift glance was sufficient to tell him that they had something important to say. But he went calmly on, scraping the inside of a skin.

"We've seen Carver," said Bob, panting.

Sam Strong's eyes flashed, but he did not stop his knife.

"Where!" he asked, casually.

"On the river; he had a large party in boats, thirty at least. We were near the mouth of the creek, and we saw them coming up the stream."

"Are they in our creek now!"

"No, they did not see it. They passed on."

Sam Strong shut up his clasp knife, thrust it into his pocket, and sat up quickly.

"They'll come back some time or other," he said, "an' if we stay here long enough they'll find us. Our question is settled. We've got to leave at once for the plains, and our market. We can get ready' and start tonight."

He put two fingers on his lips and emitted a shrill whistle. In a few minutes Bill Cole and Obadiah Pirtle came down through the woods, and presently Tom Harris and Porter Evans also approached, Sam Strong laid the case before them, and the decision was unanimous. They would go eastward, and their going would be immediate.

The horses were led from their corral or gathered from the meadows. Most of them, having led a life of idleness and luxury so long, fought against lariat and pack, but the two "generals" soon reduced them to submission. The bales of furs were so numerous now that they and the supplies made a load for every horse. The trappers themselves intended to walk, at least until they reached the plains.

Then they dismantled Versailles as far as they could, hiding some things under stones, where wolf or bear could not reach them, and just at the twilight were ready for departure. It was with real sorrow that Bob regarded their big, comfortable cabin, the doors and windows of which they had secured tightly in order to keep out prowling wild animals.

"It's been a genuine palace, a real Versailles to us," he said, "and I hate to leave it."

"We may find it again some day just as it is, the seven of us just as we are," said Sam Strong, "leastways, by hopin' for the best, I feel that we will."

"Goodbye to our home," said sentimental Louis Perolet. "It has sheltered us from many a storm. *Au revoir.*"

He took off his hat and waved it at the motionless building in the dusk. All the others did the same, and then turning their faces eastward, they trudged up the creek, the file of ponies, loaded with their riches, following close behind.

Bob glanced back once, but the stout log house was lost in the dusk. It was not until then that he realized fully the task upon which they had embarked. He was going back to fences, towns and many people. For the last two years this little world of the mountains was so sufficient to him that he never thought of the other, outside. He was returning with a sense of immense distance, not only in space, but in time and manners as well. But he resolved that he would not stay there. He had found companionship and satisfaction with these men. They, in a sense, had made him an equal, on the second and perhaps greater expedition far down the Colorado. He clutched his father's rifle more tightly, and with such brave comrades felt equal to any danger.

Their way led up the valley over the natural trail by which they had entered it, and for a long time they walked in silence save for the tread of the horses. The moon came out, the stars twinkled, and they saw clearly the ranges and peaks, and the slopes clothed with forest now turning green.

"There's one thing I hate about this," said Sam Strong, "an' that's to run away from a fellow like Juan Carver an' his crowd. By the great horn spoon, it would make my marrow jump to know that he was back there, sittin' in our palace, toastin' his feet on our hearthstone."

"Nevaire min'," said Louis Perolet, consolingly, "eet was the tactics of the great Napoleon to go away from a place when eet suited him, an' to come back again also when it suited him."

"I suppose you're right, Louis," grumbled Sam, "an' if we are followin' your Napoleon we are followin' the right kind of a leader. Some day I'll take a shot at that Juan Carver that will keep him from ever troublin' anybody else."

They left the creek valley after two hours of steady travelling, and entered a side cleft of the mountains, along which they led the horses for about two hours more, always rising. They encamped about midnight, finding it much colder than it had been in their valley, but for fear of a warning to possible enemies, they did not build any fire. The horses were all tethered, and the men rolled themselves in their blankets. The journey was resumed early the next morning, and for a week they went on without trouble or incident. Then they were compelled to stop a while to rest the loaded horses, some of which were growing footsore, Fortunately they found plenty of grass and water, and being in no hurry they took a rest of their own also.

They continued to follow in the main the trail by which they had come, and as they had an excellent sense of locality and direction, they were able to avoid difficulties that they had encountered before, For the last great range they chose the same pass that they had used on the outward trip. They knew now of one lower, but they avoided it, as Carver and his men, or others equally as dangerous, might be travelling that way.

"An' there's one thing I want to tell you, Bob," said Sam Strong, as they climbed towards the snow line, "if you see a nice, easy precipice to fall over don't you fall. There mayn't be enough soft snow at the bottom to break your fall, an' even if there was enough, you might never find us ag'in. Now, Bob, promise you won't do it ag'in, an' we'll all hope for the best."

Bob laughed at the banter which he knew was wholly good-natured.

"I give my faithful promise," he replied. "One exploit of that kind is enough for me."

There was plenty of snow in the heights of the pass, but they had a better knowledge of the way now. Here the loads of the horses became extremely heavy, and they moved at a very slow pace. Fortunately they encountered no blizzard, which was what they feared most, but everyone felt immense relief when they descended the last slope on the other side, and now had before them only the vast rolling plains which extended to their destination, but which, nevertheless, swarmed with great dangers as they were soon to learn. While they were in a pleasant valley, allowing the horses to recuperate after the great climb, a lone trapper wandered into their camp. He informed them that the war with the Cheyennes was still going on, that in fact it was at its height. Roman Nose and Black Kettle, their famous chiefs, had won some victories, and the passage of the plains was never more dangerous.

"An' it'll be all the harder for you because you carry such a load," added the trapper, glancing admiringly at the numerous bales of beaver fur.

"Yes, I s'pose so," said Sam Strong, "though I'm hopin' for the best."

"I know you won't tell me where you got 'em," said the trapper, "but you must have found some fine streams."

"You're right both ways," said Sam with a laugh.

"I think I'll go look for them creeks," said the trapper.

"All right," said Sam. "Creeks in the mountains are always free to them that can find 'em."

The trapper, an honest, open fellow, was as good as his word. He spent a night with them and departed the next morning on foot to look for the beaver streams.

"You just watch out for them Cheyennes," he called back. "They are buzzin' on the plains like hornets, an' they sting."

His words made an impression that stayed in Bob's mind.

CHAPTER 14

In Cheyenne Hands

They travelled many days, often at night in order to avoid the heat, as it was now midsummer, and their way led over the rolling swells with which Bob had become familiar two years before. They shot buffalo and antelope occasionally, but rarely turned aside to hunt, and never for more than a short distance. The grass turned quite brown under the strong sun, and the soil grew hard from the lack of rain. Nevertheless, they twice saw the clear trail of Indian ponies, and Strong and Cole reckoned that on each occasion at least one hundred warriors had passed. Obviously it was a time for anxiety, and all of them felt it.

Bob's lively imagination, impressed already by the trapper's warning, created a cloud before them, and this cloud was made of Indian warriors. It was not fear, it was merely his vivid brain that insisted upon making pictures. He had seen the Cheyennes once, and at close quarters, too, and he knew that they were formidable foes. He was continually searching the plains for a sight of the Dog Soldiers, rising under the horizon.

"These plains are so bright and they can see us so far," said Sam Strong, "that I'd like to ride through thick clouds all the way to the settlement. Still I'm hopin' for the best as much as ever."

They made several wide curves to avoid regions that seemed to be infested by the warriors, and the waning summer found them still on the plains in the Indian country, but down now towards the southeast. Barring the midday heat, the weather was good for travelling, as it had been very dry, and they were never forced to spread a tent. Game, previously so plentiful, now became scarce, and all of them pined for fresh buffalo or deer. There had been no sign of an Indian trail for more than ten days, and all agreed that it was safe to undertake a short hunt. Evans and Harris remained with the ponies, and the others went off in different directions. Since they had come upon the plains, and travelling had been easier for the ponies, they had been riding most of the time.

The country was rather more rolling than usual. Dip followed dip, and before they had gone five hundred yards Bob lost sight of the camp. Horses and men could remain concealed as long as they stayed in one dip, but when they moved on they could be seen every time they topped a swell. He saw the others in the hunt several times as they rose upon these crests, but as he rode further and further he lost sight of them entirely.

It looked like a game country, but he found nothing. There was not a sign of buffalo or deer or antelope. Not a jackrabbit scurried away before him, but Bob retained his great pride. He would not go back to the camp with hands empty when they needed game so badly. If one only persisted one would always win, and so he rode on and on, not realizing how many miles he had gone.

He noticed at length that the ground was rising, and that before him lay the sharpest and highest ridge he had seen in many days. He had an idea that beyond this ridge was a shallow valley, likely to contain grass and better game, and his spirits rose sharply. He urged his pony forward at a greater pace, and he was soon at the crest of the ridge. Then he saw that he had made the greatest mistake of his life.

But he was right, too, in his original surmise. A shallow valley lay beyond the dip, and it did contain better grass, but instead of the game that he wished to see, there was a numerous band of Indian warriors, some in camp, with their ponies cropping the turf, and others on horseback, just returning from some point and about to start for another.

Bob instantly turned his horse about, hoping that he had not been seen, but his hope was in vain. A dozen of the mounted warriors shouted, and at once urged their ponies into pursuit, guiding them by a pressure of the knee, their naked bodies glistening in the sun, rifles and lances shaken by uplifted hands, in anticipation of this prize which had literally ridden into their arms.

Bob struck his horse and shouted to him. The animal flew across the swell. If he could only outride his pursuers, and warn his comrades, they might get away in time. But before he had gone twenty rods a great thought was born in the boy's mind. It was a compound of idealism, chivalry and gratitude. The warriors were coming so fast that he could never leave them out of sight. He owed all to these men who had taken him, a friendless boy, into their band. He had resolved over and over again that if the time ever came he would repay them. The time had come now, and a wild thrill shot through every vein as he began to keep the resolve of many days. There was a strain of high poetry and exaltation in his nature, and when he took the step he never flinched.

Bob gradually turned his pony towards the northwest, and soon he was riding directly away from his own camp. He might not save himself, but he could save Sam and the others. The Cheyennes were not yet within rifle-shot, and the miles were dropping behind them. He rode a strong and true horse, and he would lead them a long chase. He might even get away.

The boy heard occasional shouts behind him, but for a long time he did not look back. When he did at last turn his gaze he saw that he was followed by about twenty warriors, who were spread out in a concave line, enclosing him, or at least his line of flight, between horns, as it were. So far as he could judge, they had neither gained nor lost Another mile and still they had not gained; a second and third mile and they had gained. There was not a doubt of it.

Now the boy bending somewhat in his saddle that the chance to escape trial shots might be better, prayed to kind providence that it would not withhold its favours that day. He prayed that his horse might last, that the horse's rider might keep up his courage, and that both horse and rider might escape all shots.

Before him stretched low, blue hills, far away, and almost buried in a faint haze. He kept a straight course towards them, hoping that he might reach them and find forests there where one might hide, or at least find a better chance of escape. If only his good horse had sinews of steel! But surely horse had never responded better, as the flight was now long, and he had not ever faltered.

He heard a sharp report, and a bullet flew past him; a second, and his horse's ear was nicked. The first report came from a point behind him, but towards the right; the second towards the left. He took a hasty glance. The horses of the pursuing crescent were closing on him, and presently he would be within fair range.

Now the boy knew that all his prayers to providence had been in vain. He would not escape. The low, blue hills had come much nearer, but they were not near enough. But whatever fate awaited him, he was sure that he had achieved his triumph. He had drawn the Cheyennes far away. Sam Strong and his comrades would escape. He had paid the great debt that he owed them. He felt anew that keen thrill of exultation. It was for a moment acute, penetrating and satisfying.

Crack! went another rifle, and then a second and a third. They did not touch him yet, but he saw the dust, flying from the dry plain ahead of him, where they struck. It was only a matter of time now when a bullet should reach him or his horse.

The Cheyennes knew it, too, and they set up a great shout of triumph which filled Bob with rage. He would make another desperate effort to escape from those enclosing horns, and he spoke persuasively to his good horse. He urged, he begged him to go faster. He entreated him to remember that he had no superior in strength and speed, and that it would be a disgrace to be overtaken by a lot of miserable Cheyenne ponies. It almost seemed to Bob that the horse understood. His head swayed a little from side to side, and his flanks heaved as he made a mighty effort.

They gained perhaps a yard, but another rifle cracked, and a great shiver ran through the horse. The next instant he pitched forward and fell. It was so sudden that Bob had no time to check himself and leap to one side. He shot over the horse's head, and ploughed along on his shoulder and side, although he managed to save himself from serious injury. But his rifle flew twelve or fifteen feet away, and when he sprang up again and stood erect, a Cheyenne, leaping from his horse, had already seized it and was waving it aloft in triumph. His belt also had broken as he scraped violently along, and with the pistol and knife in holster and sheath, it was lying out of his reach. Bob Norton stood erect, absolutely unarmed, with a chosen band of the Dog Soldiers of the Cheyennes in a circle around him.

The boy was bruised and his bones ached. The skin was torn off the back of one hand, and his shoulder and side were covered with the dry soil of the prairie, but he faced the silent circle with an undaunted eye. Another of the Cheyennes leaped down, secured the belt with pistol and knife, and in an instant was back on his horse.

The Cheyennes now gave no cry of triumph, nor did they address a word to the youth. They merely regarded him at a distance of eight or ten yards, motionless now on their horses, gazing intently as if he were some new and strange specimen of humankind who had come before them. Half of them carried long lances and shields. All were naked to the waist-cloth, and there was not one among them who was not a splendid specimen of a bold and savage race. Their black hair hung long, and the magnificent coronets of eagle feathers, their war-bonnets, waved lightly in the slight wind.

They were naked to the breech-cloth, and their lean, brown figures glowed with the tint of copper in the brilliant sunlight.

Bob's eyes were drawn at last by one warrior, as magnificent a figure of a man as he had ever seen. The warrior was of early middle age and of great stature. His face was large, and his mouth large, with thin, compressed lips. When these lips were opened they showed two rows of white teeth, as even and strong as those of a wolf. He had a great and splendidly shaped head, of which the most distinguishing feature was a long nose, hooked like that of an old Roman, and with fine nostrils. It gave him a look that was commanding to the last degree.

The chest and limbs of this magnificent savage were powerful and covered with woven muscle. He was naked except for moccasins, a scarlet breech-cloth adorned with little coloured beads, and a cloak looped back from his shoulders. But this cloak was made of the skin of that rarest of animals, a white buffalo, and it had been so finely tanned that it was as soft as velvet.

Bob felt in his heart that this was the great chief, Roman Nose, and despite himself, he could not keep from feeling deference. But he looked directly at him.

The chief's eyes met his own in a steady stare, and Bob plumbed their depths. He read there ambition, malice, hatred of himself and of the race to which he belonged, but with it all a certain largeness, as if he could appreciate a foe who was his match. Bob met his gaze unflinchingly. When he was discovered he made one resolution which he had carried out, and now that he was brought to earth like a fox, with the hounds about him, he took another. He expected to die, and he would die as became one of the white race. He would make no cry for mercy. He would not utter a word, but if it were decreed for him to die there on the prairie, far from his friends, he would meet the end in silence.

But it was hard to feel even then that he had to die. The sunlight was brilliant, the plains wild and free, and the world seemed beautiful. The chief presently said a word or two to the warriors, and turning their horses with a pressure of the knee, they rode in a slow and silent circle about him, every man keeping his eye upon the boy who stood in their centre. Bob's own eyes followed the commanding presence of the chief who seemed to dominate them all with a single glance, and unconsciously he began to wheel slowly with the wheeling circle.

Bob remembered afterwards that he suffered from a sort of spell, a kind of hypnotism. His fall and the strange action of the Cheyennes gave him a dizzy, vague feeling, as if he were in some mystic region of unreality. Around and around they rode, no one speaking, no sound whatever coming to the boy's ears but the light beat of the hoofs of the ponies, which presently became a monotonous rhythm, like the sound of the Hindu's flute when he charms the cobra.

Bob noticed soon that the circle was widening. The warriors were thirty, forty, fifty, sixty yards away, and a little later they stopped. His eyes, in all this turning, never ceased to follow the chief, and he saw him now take one of the long lances from a warrior and lean a little over his horse's neck.

Bob understood. He would be speared by the chief in full flight. A deep shiver ran over him from head to foot, and his heart turned cold within him. Again he saw that it was a beautiful world, and that he did not wish to leave it. But he once more summoned up his resolution. He would show these fierce Dog Soldiers that he was as brave as they. He would not, run, he would not try to dodge the inescapable lance, but he would stand up and face its point, praying to providence, which had been unkind hitherto, to finish it all quickly.

He was thankful now that a veil was drawn before his eyes. His dizziness and the terrible tensity of his situation caused him to see but dimly. But he never ceased to look straight towards the chief, and he saw him raise his lance, shake it twice, utter a single, sharp cry and then gallop directly at him.

It was almost an impossibility to stand still. Only the boy's bewildered state enabled him to do it. He did not fully understand just then what was occurring, but he heard the hoof-beats of the horse like thunder in his ears; he saw the shining point of the lance, and the large, coppery face of the warrior who held it. Then he was forced to shut his eyes, but something seemed to whistle by his cheek and the hoof-beats thundered past him.

He opened his eyes and beheld the chief now on the other side of the circle, shaking the long lance. A low hum, a hum of admiration, came from the warriors, but Bob did not know then that it was for him.

The chief pressed his horse with his knees again, uttered that sharp, little cry, and a second time galloped down upon the defenceless boy. Bob now did not close his eyes. He seemed to have lost all feeling, all sense of what was happening, and he himself seemed merely a spectator at this strange scene upon the prairie. On came the horse, the chief threw the lance, its point passed within six inches of Bob's face, and the horse galloped by, so close that its hoofs threw dust upon him.

And that hum of admiration rose again, and this time louder. The chief turned and came back to the boy, but he walked his horse, and when he reached Bob he sprang to the ground and uttered a word or two of approval. Bob looked at him with an anxious, uncomprehending glance, and then sitting down upon the prairie, laughed.

It was the laugh of hysteria, and for a moment or two the Cheyennes did not disturb him. Then the chief motioned to him to rise to his feet. Bob rose and they bound his hands behind him. Then they helped him upon a horse, behind a warrior, the chief gave the word, and the whole band, after one long, thrilling whoop, galloped away over the prairie.

Bob had only the pressure of his thighs to hold himself upon his horse, but he was trained to that method of riding, and he did it without thought or conscious exertion. He knew that he was weak, and his head was yet dizzy, but he was not going to fall, and the rapid motion was beginning to revive him somewhat.

He never had the remotest idea how long they galloped, but they stopped at last in a shallow valley that contained a campfire and other warriors. Whether it was the original valley in which he had found them he could never tell, as his first glimpse had been too brief, but it was an intense relief to him to know that the journey was ended.

The warrior, behind whom he was riding, jumped off his pony and then helped him to the ground. But Bob, with his bound arms, was unable to stand. He collapsed from weakness and excitement, and sank down in a heap. The chief strode forward, cut his bonds, raised him to his feet, and gave him a drink of water out of a calabash. The boy leaned against the stump of a fallen tree and revived slowly.

When his eyes were clear he looked fixedly at the chief and his opinion did not change, that this was the great Roman Nose of whom he had heard so much. His eyes wandered from the chief to the warriors, who stood near, in numbers, regarding him. They had high cheek bones, straight limbs, and high, ridged noses. The warriors were clad in breech-cloths only, and moccasins, as the weather was warm, and they wore but few ornaments, generally strings of bear claws around the neck. Their hair was cut straight across their foreheads, just above their eyes, and a small ornamented plait hung down in front of each shoulder. The remainder, twisted with horse or buffalo hair, was divided into two large plaits which flowed over the back.

Squaws too came up and gazed at Bob. The Cheyenne women were notably inferior in physique and looks to the men. They had wide mouths, ugly noses and, in fact, all their features were ugly. They wore skin tunics, fastened with straps over the shoulders, and falling almost to the knee. They had ornaments of beads, shells, elk tusks, and rings and bracelets of brass. Their hair was long and flowing, not braided.

Bob was in a large temporary village of the Cheyennes, led by their great chiefs, Roman Nose and Black Kettle. Around him were the ten principal divisions of the two branches of the Cheyenne nation, the northern and the southern. Their camp was a great circle, a mile in diameter, including at least six hundred *tepees*, or a fighting force of about twelve hundred warriors. The ten clans, or *gentes*, in their order of rank were:

1. Heviquesnipahis	2. Hevhaitaneo
3. Masikota	4. Omisis
5. Sutaio	6. Wotapio
7. Oivimana	8. Hisiometaneo
9. Oqutogona	10. Hownowa

The ten *gentes* were also re-divided into six warrior bands, every one with its own emblems and ritual. At the head of them stood the Hotamitaneo, or the famous Dog Soldiers, the ritual and instructions of whom had been given by a supernatural dog to their founder; hence their name.

Next came the Woksikitaneo, or Fox Men, who were called so because their leader carried ceremonial clubs, with the pendant skin of the fox.

They were followed by the Himoiyogis, or Those With Headed Lances, because they carried lances of a very peculiar make. Fourth were the Mahohivas, or Red Shield Owners, whose leaders bore shields painted red, with a pendant buffalo tail. Next to them were the Himatanohis, Those with the Bow String, who received their name because their leaders bore lances resembling a long bow in their shape. Last were the Hotaminasow, or Foolish Dogs, composed wholly of very young warriors, beginners in the art of war, who were not supposed to have much sense.

The tribes, or *gentes*, were ruled by forty-four chiefs, regularly elected at intervals of a few years. At each election forty new chiefs were chosen, while four older ones were selected from the retiring forty. These four were the head chiefs, and when they wished to call a council they sent around forty-four painted sticks to all the villages.

Such a council had been called recently, but Bob knew nothing of it, nor did he know anything then of the composition of the Cheyenne nation. He was destined to learn these things later. Now he was concerned about what was going to happen to him within the next few minutes.

"*Vehoc* (Little Chief)," said Roman Nose.

Bob shook his head. He did not have the faintest idea what *vehoc* meant.

"Strong boy. Brave boy," said the chief in English.

"Thanks," said Bob, who wished to deserve the Indian's praise. "I may be strong and I may be brave, but I'm willing to tell you, Mr. Roman Nose, that I'm just about played out."

"You go *tepee*," said Roman Nose. "We no hurt you—today."

Bob noticed the pause before "today," and he had to repress a tendency to shiver. But his life in the wilderness had taught him to make the best of the passing moment, and he went willingly with the two warriors, who guided him to a buffalo-skin *tepee*. It was a small place, with only a skin or two between him and the bare ground, but it was a haven of rest to one so tired and sore as he. He sank upon a wolf skin, and in some faint spirit of irony, waved a goodnight to the two warriors who had brought him there.

"You drink?" said one.

"You eat?" said the other.

Bob roused himself at these words.

"Yes, an emphatic *yes* to both of you," he said.

They did not understand his words, but the meaning of his tone was plain to them. They brought a calabash of good, cool water, and buffalo steaks freshly cooked. Bob drank thirstily and ate with a great appetite. Then he waved his hand to the warriors who had stood by, silent and impassive.

"It's really goodnight this time," he said, "I'm just bound to go to sleep."

126

He had no idea how long it was until night, and he did not care. His own fate, too, had glided into the background. He was exhausted, and rest was the only mortal affair that concerned him much.

The two Cheyennes went out and closed the skin doors of the *tepee*. It was dusky now within the lodge, and the boy felt a great peace. He had eaten, he had drunk, and he had found rest. His comrades were up and away with their furs. Let the future look to itself; it could not bother him.

He doubled a corner of the wolf skin under his head, making a pillow. Then he floated off on the pleasant sea of sleep.

CHAPTER 15

A Modern Mazeppa

Bob was awakened the next morning by the lifting of the flap of his tent. A flood of sunshine poured in, and his eyes opened. Then a figure bulked large in the opening, and the captive stared at it in great astonishment. Both figure and face were familiar, but for a while he could not believe that what he saw was true.

Yet it was true. There was the swarthy face, the close-set eyes, and the pointed chin of Juan Carver. Moreover, he showed his teeth in a malicious smile as he looked at the boy.

"Yes," he said, "it is I, Carver, whom you neither expect nor want to see. No, I am not a prisoner like you. I am on the best of terms with the great chiefs, Roman Nose and Black Kettle, whom you will see here beside me if you will deign to take your eyes off my face."

Bob rose to his feet. Long sleep had steadied his nerves, and he resolutely stilled every tremor. The very presence of Carver made him more determined than ever not to show fear, nor to ask for mercy. He stepped out of the *tepee*, no one opposing, and stood in the sunlight, which was warm and grateful.

Carver had spoken truly when he said that Roman Nose and Black Kettle were with him. Black Kettle was somewhat shorter and darker than Roman Nose, but he had all the bearing of a leader, and he, too, wore a fine robe made of light buffalo skin. Both chiefs carried shields of the stoutest buffalo hide, painted and decorated profusely with heraldic signs and a history of their exploits. In fact, nearly all the Cheyenne warriors whom Bob saw carried such shields. When Bob looked at them and bowed gravely he condescended to notice Carver.

"I should not be surprised to see you here," he said. "I know that you have all the qualities of a renegade."

As he thought of it, Bob saw that Carver's presence in the Cheyenne town was not at all extraordinary. He was a freebooter, and it would suit him to be hand in glove with the Cheyennes.

"Bad names don't hurt me," said Carver. "I am glad that the Cheyennes are my friends. Both Roman Nose and Black Kettle are old ones. I did not reach their village until last night, and when I found that you were here I gave them news worth knowing."

Bob's face fell. He knew that Carver had told the chief of his comrades and their treasure of furs. Carver, quick enough to make inferences, knew that Bob, when first seen, could not have been very far away from his comrades, and the fact that they were so well to the eastward proved that they were on their return to civilization, with a great taking of beaver.

Bob recovered his countenance, and said with an assumption of carelessness:

"I suppose that you are speaking of my friends. Well, I got lost from them, and I fancy that they are at least a couple of hundred miles further east by this time."

Carver looked at him closely, but Bob bore the scrutiny, without a change of feature.

"You may be telling the truth," said Carver. "We'd like mighty well to take that little train. I want the furs and the Cheyennes want the scalps, but I don't mind telling you that we have sent out scouts who have returned without them."

Bob felt a glow. His comrades had got clean away, and he had not made his great flight in vain. Carver, still watching him closely, saw him smile.

"We'll get them yet," said the freebooter.

"You'll never get them," said Bob.

"*Vehoc*," said Roman Nose, applying to Bob the word that he had used the afternoon before.

"What does he meant" asked Bob of Carver.

"*Vehoc* in Cheyenne means Little Chief," replied the man. "Roman Nose rather admires you. He tells me that you bore yourself well when he rode at you with the spear."

"I thank him for that much. I like him a good deal better than I do you," said the boy.

"Well, as to that," said Carver, grinning, "Roman Nose is not exactly growing wings. While he admires your courage under one test, he expects to put it to another soon."

Carver's tone was full of malice, but Bob again refused to show fear.

"It may be so," he said, "and if it is so I will do my best to stand it. But just now I'm hungry. Tell 'em I want something to eat."

Carver spoke to Roman Nose who seemed to have a sense of humour.

"*Vehoc* rather eat than have big talk," he said. "He eat here by *ohe*."

"*Ohe* means river," said Carver, "but ought rather to be *ohec*,' which is little river."

"So you have a river, have you?" said Bob.

"Yes, but as I said, it is a little one."

He pointed to a shallow stream, just beyond a fringe of cottonwoods, and Bob walked to its bank with his captors.

"*Ehona*," said Roman Nose.

Bob looked at him in doubt.

"*Ehona* means a stone," said Carver. "He wants you to sit on the flat rock you see there."

"Thanks for his courtesy," said Bob, and sat down.

There, good food, both buffalo and deer, and water were brought to him, and he ate and drank with satisfaction. Meanwhile the people came again to look at him, and there were many squaws among them.

Most of these women brought their work with them, and the work was of different kinds. The Cheyenne women, when they reached sufficient age, joined guilds like the labour unions of the white man, and when they became full members they were called *Moninico*, which meant women who have chosen. One union made the *tepees*, that is the bare walls, another adorned them, another tanned and decorated buffalo robes, another moccasins and leggings, and there were yet other guilds, the work for every one being different.

The warriors who came to see him were mostly in pairs. This was due to the Cheyenne custom of a young man taking a *howi*, or comrade, a friendship that endured through life, after marriage as well as before. Carver, who seemed to be much pleased with himself, told Bob more about the Indians as he ate.

"The Cheyennes are a great nation," he said. "The warriors are brave and skilful. They are organized, with their laws and their religion. The big *tepee* over there is their Council House. In it are the Four Sacred Arrows which are their holiest and most precious possession. Only the older men dare to mention them by name. On big public occasions they are brought out to be worshiped, but only by the warriors. No woman has ever been allowed to come near them, or to see them."

Bob was interested, despite himself.

"And these arrows are their guardian deities?" he asked.

"They are," replied Carver. "They used to carry them into battle to insure victory, but twenty-five or thirty years ago two of them were taken in a great conflict by the Pawnees, and have never been recovered. Two others were blessed and sanctified by the priests, and made to take their place, but the loss of the two original ones was the greatest blow that ever befell the Cheyenne nation."

Bob's interest continued, but he said to Carver:

"Why do you tell me these things?"

"I'm willing to make it as easy for you as I can," replied the freebooter, "until the time comes to apply the actual tests."

Bob thought that the man was trying to frighten him, and he turned scornfully away. Carver said no more, but left in a few minutes. Bob remained where he was, seated on the flat stone. The long, numbing process through which he had gone was now about finished, and he was fully awake to his situation. He was unbound, and his strength had returned, but there was no chance whatever of flight The Cheyenne warriors and waspish, old squaws were everywhere about him. The great circular village was on both sides of the shallow stream, and the prisoner was at least a quarter of a mile from the nearest point on its rim. Whatever it might be, he could not escape this test of which Carver spoke so maliciously.

Bob did not doubt that it meant death, and he rebelled fiercely against the thought. Here was a great village with perhaps three thousand people in it, and they were all happy as human life went. The squaws went about their work, children were playing, the warriors mended their weapons or lounged in the sun. He alone was doomed. He choked, but looked down again at the river lest anyone should see fear in his face.

After a while Roman Nose, Black Kettle, Carver and others came back to him. The two chiefs looked at him fixedly, and it seemed to Bob that there was a solitary gleam of pity in the gaze of Roman Nose.

"Come with us," said Carver, and Bob, rising without a word, went.

They led the way to the outskirts of the village, to a point on its rim facing the northwest, where the brown plains rolled away, swell after swell, to the horizon. A great crowd, silent, but watching intently, followed. When they stopped it was again Carver who spoke.

"We want to know from you," he said to Bob, "which way Strong and his party have gone. We expected our scouts to discover them last night, but they did not. Now you must tell us."

Roman Nose and Black Kettle nodded in affirmation.

Bob's figure stiffened. They must think him a child if he would help them, after the sacrifice he had made for his comrades.

"I do not know which way they have gone," he replied, "and if I knew I would not tell you."

"Perhaps you feel that way now," said Carver, "I've no doubt you do, but you may feel differently before many minutes. The bird that can sing will have to do it this time."

"I will not give you a particle of information that can help you," said Bob, quietly.

"There is the torture," said Carver in a tone of menace.

"Even so," said Bob, although he shuddered, "I still will not speak."

The two chiefs, who seemed to understand English, although they spoke it but little, at least to Bob, frowned. But Carver showed his sharp, white teeth, and smiled in his evil way.

"It will be the better for you if you tell," he said. "Put us on the track of Strong and the others, and you shall be spared. The chiefs promise it. You will not be released, at least not now, but you will be treated well. Look at this village; it is not a bad life for those who know the wilderness. Choose that or worse."

"I have nothing to say," replied Bob.

"Think again; think hard and you will find something."

"I have made up my mind," replied Bob, firmly.

Carver spoke rapidly to the chiefs in their own tongue, and they nodded their heads. Then he turned again to Bob. It seemed that the man had a sneering spirit, and some knowledge beyond that of an ordinary frontiersman.

"Indians are friends to their friends," he said, "but they are very bitter foes to their foes. Then, they have no use for milk and water. Now you are a foe, and since you will not speak they naturally turn to the torture, but by some chance a spark of mercy has lodged in the breast of Roman Nose. He has denied us the faggot and the stake, but he agrees to make a spectacle for his people."

Bob looked at him, but said nothing.

"The Cheyennes insist on amusement," said Carver, "and Roman Nose and Black Kettle, who are both statesmen, will give it to them. They are ready."

A warrior advanced, leading with a lariat a powerful mustang, one of the largest that Bob had ever seen, a wild and fiery animal, too, as the warrior, a strong man, was compelled to swing hard on the lariat. Four other warriors seized Bob and lifted him to the horse's back. Then they bound him, with his feet under the sides of the mustang, and his body bent forward on the neck and shoulders.

"Will you speak?" asked Carver.

"I know nothing to tell," replied the boy, "and if I knew I wouldn't tell you."

Carver said something to the warrior who held the horse. The man instantly slipped off the lariat and sprang away.

The mustang looked about for a few moments, and Bob could feel him trembling all over. Then he raced away towards the centre of the village, and with a wild shout, mounted Cheyennes started in pursuit, striking with switches at the frightened and angry mustang. Squaws and children threw sticks and clods of earth at horse and involuntary rider as they passed.

Bob was made almost breathless by the wild gallop of the mustang, but he understood. He was to be chased about the village, and be scourged with switches and missiles for the benefit of the whole Cheyenne population. When he was finally taken from the horse he would be so broken that he would be glad to tell anything he knew.

The boy, bent far down on the horse's neck, could not see very well, but as the mustang galloped about he was conscious of a mass of brown, excited faces, and he heard a continuous shouting. He was struck now and then by a missile, but he did not feel the bruise.

It was great sport for the Cheyennes. There were worse things to which a prisoner could be subjected, but since those were denied them, this was acceptable. They chased the frightened mustang around and around the village meadows. At least fifty horsemen were following him now, the riders leaning forward for a cut with a switch at either the horse or the burden on his back.

Bob struggled hard to keep his senses, and by mere impulse he pulled continually at the thongs that held his arms. He sought also to ease his position and stop the intolerable jolting.

The sport grew wilder. Warriors, squaws and children thrilled with the excitement of it. Roman Nose, Black Kettle and Carver stood grimly by as the excited mustang galloped about, driven around and around by the horde. The numbness and dizziness that Bob had felt after his flight from the Cheyennes, came over him again, but he made a continued effort to keep conscious and remain in the easiest position on the horse.

A boy, somewhere in the horde, shot an arrow, more of a toy than anything else, but it struck the mustang in the flank, and stung. The horse, now insane with fright and fear, suddenly made a bolt directly through the ring of Cheyennes. People rushed to one side to keep from being trampled down, and the masses kept back the pursuing horsemen who sought now to catch the mustang and the prisoner that he bore.

But a slip had occurred in the plans of Carver and the two chiefs. The mustang, freed for a moment from the goad of the switches and missiles, and seeing a clear space before him, made a rush for the plain. Two warriors on foot tried to seize him by the mane, but they were not quick enough and were compelled to leap back to avoid those trampling hoofs.

The mustang cleared the rim of the village and he saw freedom before him, the brown plain stretching away to the blue horizon, and nobody to torment him. He was in such a fever of rage, excitement and fear that his strength was the strength of three. He arched his back to make his burden lighter, laid back his ears a little, and ran with a speed worthy of the best mustang in all the Cheyenne village. The brown earth flew beneath his hoofs, and the gentle swells raced past.

Behind the mustang came a horde of mounted Cheyennes, eager now to repair the slip and to retake the prisoner. But they did not reckon with the full speed of the mustang. His involuntary rider, too, bent forward almost like a jockey, seemed to urge him to a faster pace.

Carver and the chiefs had mounted and pursued. Carver was raging, but a faint smile once or twice passed over the grim features of Roman Nose. Bob himself was dimly conscious of what had happened. The Indian village was behind him, but the knowledge brought him no great thrill. He was too much exhausted, too much numbed to feel it, but he was conscious that there was only space before him.

The Cheyennes shouted and sought to urge their horses to greater speed. The sound reached the mustang and increased his rage and fear. His strength, born of a great impulse, grew. His head was thrust out a little further, the sensitive ears quivered, and the long body, stretching itself for a faster flight, flew over the ground.

The mustang was gaining and the Cheyennes saw it. A little longer, and the gain was more decisive. There would be no chance for any warrior to throw his lariat, and Roman Nose gave the word to fire.

Rifles cracked and bullets sang by the mustang. One grazed his flank, drawing a little blood. It was like the touch of fire, and his indignant heart swelled to greater efforts. Right well that day did he prove himself a king of the prairie. He ran straight and true, there was no curving about which would enable his pursuers to gain upon him, but his head was always pointed to the blue horizon that hung over the northwest. The bullets still spattered around him now and then, but most of them fell short, and the sound of shots and shouts was further away.

The bullets yet came, but now all of them fell short. Nevertheless, the mustang did not decrease his speed. The burden on his back was quiet, not impeding him much, and he was as strong as ever. In his own horse heart he felt his triumph, and raising his head he neighed once. Then he sped on with renewed speed, and the Cheyennes and their horses sank into the prairie.

Bob came out of a period of unconsciousness and found that the mustang was walking. He heard no sound, but the steady hoof-beats. All his limbs and joints were aching, and the full weight of his body rested upon the horse. He pulled at one arm, and to his great amazement it came free from the thongs. It was cut, and he had probably been tugging at it for a long time without being conscious of the fact, but here it was free.

The surprising knowledge filled the boy with new life. The free hand and arm, at which he looked, were his own, and he could do great things with them. He began to pluck at the thongs holding the other arm. They, too, were loosened by and by. Then he remembered that he had carried a clasp knife in a small inside pocket of his coat. It was one that could easily have been overlooked by the Cheyennes, and when he felt tremblingly for it, he found it.

A few slashes released waist and legs, and then the boy, with a great and painful effort, sat up in the shape of a man on the bare back of the mustang. He was more like a bent, old man than a strong and active youth, but now he rode and was not merely carried.

He was very faint and weak, and he would have fallen to the ground, but the mustang's pace sank to the lowest and easiest walk, and he pulled himself together enough to take a comprehensive look about him.

The boy saw only the great plains, rolling away toward every point of the horizon, unbroken anywhere by a hill or a tree or a horseman. The Cheyennes were left far behind, and they would not be able to follow his trail on the hard, sun-baked prairie. He understood that he had escaped. By a miracle, as it were, he was out of the hands of his enemies. Their own trick, intended to torture and deride him, had turned upon them. He lifted his face to heaven and gave thanks. It was a face so dirty and begrimed that Sam Strong himself would not have known it, but for a few moments it was transfigured and glorified. Escaped and free! He raised his bruised hands and shook them in exultation.

Bob was so much occupied with the present that he took no thought of the future. He was proud of being able to keep his seat on the mustang, which now walked slowly on, his glossy, brown coat wet from head to heel with perspiration, his great eyes showing weariness, and a dim sort of inquiry as to what it all meant.

He was a noble mustang. He had been the largest, swiftest and wildest in all the Cheyenne village, and he had run a good race. But the victory won and the tormentors gone, he was very tired. He was conscious that his rider had straightened up, although he seemed to be more uncertain of his seat, but the mustang made no attempt to shake him off.

Bob leaned forward again and clutched the mustang's mane tightly. His weakness was coming back and the plains swam before him. But the long, coarse hair, grasped in his hands, sustained him and the mustang took no notice, merely walking on at a pace that did not seem to be much more than creeping.

The rider did not know how many hours passed. At times he saw clearly, and he knew that the country had not changed. At other times he seemed to be in a dream, and the faces of the Cheyennes came back to him. He awoke from one of these dreams with a shock, and saw that the mustang was standing still. The cessation from the slow walk had caused the shock, and the boy began to feel a great pity for the horse and himself.

They were together on the lone prairie, and he owed the mustang a mighty debt that he could not pay. The speed and strength of a dumb animal had brought him away from torture, and death to come. There was not an ungrateful fibre in him, and he leaned forward and patted the mustang on the neck.

"Good horse!" he said aloud. "Good old horse! The finest horse that ever was born!"

It may have been a mere coincidence, but the mustang stretched out his long neck and neighed. Bob felt at once that the relation of friends was established between them. He had spoken to the horse, and the horse had answered.

"Good horse!" he repeated. "I've ridden you long and hard, but it was from no choice of mine. Now you shall have the rest that you have so well earned."

He slipped from the horse's back to the ground, and he would have fallen on his face, but again he grasped the mane of the mustang and saved himself. The horse did not resent his fierce clutch, but turned his head a little and looked at him. Bob gazed into the great, dusky horse eyes, and it seemed to him that he read there a feeling akin to his own.

"You're lonely, partner," he said. "I'm sorry, but there's no other horse here, and it's just you and I. Come on, I don't know which way we're going, I don't know what we're going to, nor when we'll get there, but we're going."

He did not release the mane, and the mustang made no effort to pull away. So the two, now walking side by side, started again, the horse steady and upright, Bob staggering, but with one hand wound firmly in the long coarse hair that supported him.

But the boy could not last long. He had been through too much. The plains and the sky darkened before him, and he hung a dead weight on the mustang, which stopped.

"I've come to the end, comrade," said Bob, patting the horse's head with his free hand, "and I won't burden you any longer. Go on; you'll find other horses somewhere on the prairie. I stop here."

He released the horse entirely and now, unable to support his own weight, he sank to the ground. He was so far gone in collapse that he did not even care to make any further effort. His spirit, at that moment, was one of resignation. But he raised his head a little, made a weak gesture to the horse, and repeated:

"Go on! I stay here!"

The mustang did not go on. He turned and gazed from great dusky eyes at his fallen rider, and, unless Bob was dreaming, he saw pity there. They *were* friends! They *were* comrades. The mustang came closer, and touched the boy's face with his nose, as if in a spirit of compassion. Bob felt that there was one who would not desert him. He could not rise now, but he reached up and stroked the horse's face.

"Just you and I!" he murmured. "Here I stay and here you mean to stay with me."

The darkness of the plains and sky suddenly turned to complete blackness, and he sank into a stupor.

When Bob came to himself he was lying upon his back on the prairie, and the twilight was coming. The horse still stood by him. He may have nibbled for a while at the burnt grass, but the sound of the boy's movement had brought him back.

Bob, weakened by his great nervous strain, felt a throb of emotion. This was indeed a friend as true as steel. He staggered to his feet, but all his muscles were stiff, and his bones were sore. Once more, he took the mustang by the mane, and there was no resistance.

"You've had a rest, good old horse," he said, talking to his comrade, because the mustang was then, in nearly every sense, a human being to him, "and I'll ride again."

He dragged himself upon the horse's back, steadied himself there, and then bade him go on as he would. The mustang, fully refreshed and once more the strongest of his kind, started at a long easy walk toward the east. The wind may have brought pleasant odours to nostrils, far more acute than those of man, or it may have been instinct, but the mustang not only knew where he was going, he knew also when he would get there, and what he would find when he arrived.

The easy, swinging walk that ate up ground so fast continued a long time. The twilight merged into the night, the moon and the stars came out, and the sky was clear and cold after the hot day. The coolness was refreshing to Bob, and he seemed to gather a little strength. He saw, finally, a thin, dark line on the moonstruck horizon, and he knew that it was trees. Trees, extending away to right and left, in that manner, indicated water, and he felt now, for the first time, that his throat and mouth were burnt.

The horse neighed, and broke into a trot. In another minute he was through the trees, and at the sandy edge of the shallow stream of clear cold water, from which he drank eagerly. Bob slipped from his back, and, kneeling down, drank beside him. Life flowed back into him as he drank up the living water, and, when he and the horse were both satisfied and he had rested awhile on the bank, he took off his torn clothing and bathed. It was soothing to his scratches and bruises, and, when he had dried himself, and put on his clothing again, he sought the softest place that he could find in the grass, which grew in length and abundance along the stream.

He was terribly hungry, but he tried not to think of it, and soon forgot everything in a deep, dreamless sleep, the slumber of exhaustion. He lay so still in the long grass that a man, ten feet away, would not have noticed him. But the mustang, seeking the softest clumps for his teeth, looked at him now and then, and it may be that the sense of comradeship was as strong in the horse heart as it had been in the boy heart.

The mustang after a while, with a long sigh of content, lay down and rolled a little, then became quiet and motionless. An hour passed, and a long weird howl came from the open swells. It was the cry of the prairie wolf informing his brethren that the odour of pleasant food had come to his nostrils. It is possible that his instinct, as good as that of the horse, had told him that the boy who lay sleeping in the grass was unarmed.

Wolf answered wolf and soon the hungry line drew near. Fierce eyes looked down among the trees, and lips crinkled back from sharp teeth. They could not yet see the figure of the boy in the deep grass, but the odour of food was strong and it drew them on with the greatest temptation that a wolf can know. They crept into the belt of trees.

The mustang felt that something was wrong. He rose to his feet standing almost beside the boy, and saw the red eyes and sharp teeth of the advancing line. He had seen such brutes before and he hated them. He did not move now, but his own eyes began to gleam as they had done, when he was first beaten and pursued by the Cheyennes.

The mustang, standing there in the moonlight, was a formidable companion. The wolves, with their eyes of preternatural acuteness, could see how the great figure was tense and drawn, ready to lash out like lightning with those sharp, dreadful hoofs. They stopped, drew back, and then approached again, to find the mustang as ready and menacing as ever.

The drama of the night was played out slowly, and in complete silence. The wolves circled about, and drew near from another side. The horse still faced them. Then they circled slowly for another place of approach, but they could not escape the vigilance of the terrible horse, which only waited until one of them should come near enough, a thing that they were careful not to do.

The moonlight grew stronger, and flooded the cottonwoods with silver, enlarging the watchful mustang until he became gigantic. But the deep dreamless sleep of the boy was undisturbed. Nothing in the drama was known to him.

The wolf has infinite patience, else he would not live, and the drama was of the proper length, stretching on to an hour, two hours, three hours. Then the wolves gave up. They had made a thorough test, and they hew that the mustang was a champion whom they could not pass. Silently they fled away and, after a while, the mustang lay down in the grass again.

CHAPTER 16

The Island in the River

Two men, in buckskin, rode down the Arickaree, a shallow fork of the Republican River. It was early morning, and the glow of the great red sun illuminated the brown plains, but it did not hide the care in the faces of the two riders. One of them was quite young, without a beard, more boy than man, although his bronzed face showed a long life on the plains. The other, much older, was deeply seamed by weather, but like his younger comrade, he looked strong and active. Both rode warily, searching plains and cottonwoods alike for any sign of a strange presence.

"Cheyennes are somewhere in this region, Pete," said the younger man. "That's sure."

"Aye, it's sure as shootin' Jack," said the older, "but just whar, that's the question. We passed one trail yesterday, but ef we look long enough, I think we're likely to hit a bigger one, and I'm thinkin', Jack, that the major has got mighty few men fur the job that's cut out for him."

"Not a doubt of it, Pete," said Jack, "but we're here to find out things for him, an' we've got to find 'em out."

"That's so," said Pete, "an' unless I'm mightily mistook, thar's a horse yonder among them cottonwoods."

"I see him," said Jack, "a horse without a saddle or a bridle, but he don't look like a wild horse. Anyway, as the wind is blowin' toward him, he has scented us long ago, an' he'd have been up an' away, if he'd been a real live mustang."

"It means somethin', shore," said Pete, "an' it's one o' the things that we've got to find out."

They rode forward warily, not wishing to alarm the lone horse, but he showed no fear. As they came nearer, he raised his head and neighed, and the horse of Pete replied in kind to his friendly salute.

"He's used to people, some kind of people. That's shore," said Pete. "Now I call this right strange. Whar such a horse is some kind of human bein' ought to be."

"There he is," said the sharp-eyed Jack, "an' he's dead. See him stretched out in the grass! A white man, too."

"Yes, I do see him," said Pete, rising in his stirrups, "but how do you account for the horse havin' no saddle an' no bridle! Mebbe it's an ambush, an' that's only a stuffed figger in the grass."

"It's real," repeated Jack, "and there ain't any ambush. There ain't a chance for any."

They rode forward among the cottonwoods. The horse moved a yard or two away, but showed no fear of them.

"It's a boy!" exclaimed Jack, "an' he ain't dead, by thunder! He's asleep. If he sleeps like that out here in the Indian country, how would he sleep in town in his little trundle bed!"

"He's been manhandled," said Pete, whose experienced eye had run over the prostrate form, "an' it's stupor as well as sleep."

He sprang down, and seized Bob by the shoulders.

"Here, wake up, young feller," he exclaimed. "The sun's risin' high, and it's time for you to go milk the cows."

Bob opened his eyes, and rose to his feet in bewilderment. It was some time before he could see clearly, and understood who had come. Then his thankfulness was great.

"White men, thank God!" he exclaimed. "You're friends! You can't be anything else!"

"Of course we're friends," said Pete. "Here, young feller. Steady! Steady! Don't you go to tumblin' over again. You must have been through a lot. I can see it. Here, Jack, your flask, quick!"

Something hot and fiery was poured down Bob's throat, and he stood erect once more. His weakness had really been due to excitement at the coming of the two white men, as his long sleep had largely restored his nerves. But his wild ride had come to a happy end, and he knew that he was now with those who could help him. He looked longingly at a little knapsack that the older man carried.

"I haven't had anything to eat since yesterday morning," he said.

"Then you must be hungry," said Pete, taking from the knapsack some bread and strips of bacon. "Set down thar, an' see if these will make any sort o' an appeal to your palate."

Bob sat down on the grass, and quickly proved that they made a most powerful appeal. The two men looked at him, with curiosity, but they yet refrained from asking questions. The mustang came near, and touched his nose in friendly fashion to that of Pete's horse. Pete's eyes ran swiftly over the mustang, noting his long, easy lines and powerful build.

"Fine horse, that," he said. "I wonder ef he belongs to the boy, an' I wonder why he ain't got on any saddle and bridle?"

Bob looked up from his bread and bacon.

"I belong to him," he said.

"Now I'll be smoked if I know what you mean by that," said Pete.

Bob smiled, rather wearily.

"I ought to belong to him," he said, "since he took me out of the Cheyenne village yesterday, brought me clean away from Roman Nose, Black Kettle and their people, and, for all I know, may have watched over me while I was sleeping here."

Pete and Jack showed signs of the liveliest interest.

"Tell us all about it, if you're ready," said Pete.

Bob began his story, the two sitting down on the grass beside him, that they might listen at their ease. But very soon they straightened up, and their lips parted, as the tale went on. Every detail of that wild ride was vivid in Bob's memory, and he told it from a full heart. The picture was full of colour. It stood out complete, and like life itself, before the two listeners, who drew long breaths, when Bob finished.

"You're right'" said Pete. "It's the mustang that saved you. But that long ride broke him to the use of man, while it didn't break his spirit. See, how he hangs around you."

"Good horse," said Bob.

"Since you've told us who you are and where you come from," said Pete, "it's only right that you should know who we are. This worthless young feller here is Jack Stillwell an' I'm Pete Trudeau. We're scouts for the United States army, an' Colonel George Forsyth with fifty men, scouts an' skirmishers too, ain't far from here. We're detached by General Sheridan to look for the Cheyennes, an' Jack an' me are on a little scout o' our own this mornin'. It's lucky for you as well as us that we found you, 'cause we know now that Roman Nose an' a big force ain't far away."

"Maybe you can lend me a saddle and bridle, a rifle and some ammunition," said Bob, "and then I can look for my own party."

But Pete Trudeau sagely shook his head.

"We kin lend you them things," he said, "but it won't do for you to go roamin' around now in search of your friends. These plains are alive with Cheyennes, an' you'd shorely be killed and scalped inside o' twenty-four hours. It's pure luck that's saved you so far. Ef your friends are smart, they've made off to the hills somewhar."

Bob looked about him helplessly.

"What Pete tells you is true," said Jack. "There's nothing for you to do but mount that mustang, and ride with us to Colonel Forsyth. You can find your friends later, an' you've got to choose between life an' death. It's life to go with us."

Stillwell spoke with the greatest earnestness, and Bob was impressed.

141

But he meant to find his comrades some time or other, no matter how long it took him to do it.

"I choose life, of course, in preference to death," he said, smiling faintly. "If one of you can spare me a piece of rope or a rawhide, I'll catch my mustang and we can be off."

Trudeau had the rawhide, with which Bob made a rude kind of knot. He had no trouble in catching the mustang, which seemed to be tamed thoroughly, and he sprang upon his back.

"Now," he exclaimed, refreshed by the food, "I'll ride with you."

"We gallop at once to Forsyth," said Trudeau, "Your news about the Cheyennes is important."

They rode swiftly toward the north, the three of them, and they would have been stirrup to stirrup, but Bob had no stirrup. They kept close to the river, which broadened out considerably in places, but which was always shallow. Two hours, and they entered a little hollow among some cottonwoods. Bob saw soldiers walking back and forth, rifle on shoulder, and beyond them other soldiers. All were weather-beaten and in faded uniforms. A straight, active and alert man, an officer by his epaulets, came forward at the sound of the galloping hoofs, and Trudeau and Stillwell sprang to the ground. Bob, feeling that he was not as much at home as they, remained on the mustang.

The officer glanced at the boy, and then turned his attention to Trudeau and Stillwell, who had saluted respectfully.

"It appears that you found something," he said.

"Yes, Colonel," replied Trudeau, acting as spokesman by right of age. "We ran across this boy asleep in the grass. He escaped from the Cheyennes yesterday, and we know from what he said that Roman Nose an' his whole force ain't far away."

The officer's figure became more rigid and a spark leaped up in his eyes. Then his face fell a little as he looked at his force and saw the smallness of its numbers. But in an instant his face glowed again, with pride in his little band, and perhaps with the thrill of coming conflict.

"Then there may be a meeting, Pete," he said, "and if so, we'll try to bear our part in it. Meanwhile, come with me. You, too, my boy, and we'll hear further details."

They sat by a small fire, and Bob told it all again.

"We've got to find that village or the trail, or it's people, if they've gone, no matter what the odds," said Colonel Forsyth. "It's what we've come out for."

Trudeau and Stillwell nodded.

"Are you willing to go with us, my boy!" said the Colonel, kindly.

"I am, sir," replied Bob, with emphasis.

"Then you're enlisted, Bob," said Colonel Forsyth, calling him by his first name. "Pete, you and Jack find him a saddle, bridle, arms and ammunition, and we'll march at once."

Bob was soon provided with all that he needed, and the trumpet sounded *Boots and Saddles*. The little band of fifty mounted and rode out upon the prairie. Trudeau and Stillwell and Abner Grover, generally called Sharp Grover, a man of nearly fifty, acting as guides, were trying to make a reckoning of the direction in which the Cheyenne village lay. Bob confessed frankly that he did not know, but, by putting two and two together, they surmised that it was toward the southwest. So they left the Arickaree and rode over the plains.

Now Bob looked at his new comrades, and they filled his eye. Most of them were young, and most of them also had been soldiers in the Civil War, some on one side and some on the other, every animosity buried in the comradeship of the border. All were native born, except four, and one of these four, a young Irishman named Martin Burke who had served with the British army in India, soon attracted Bob's attention, showing all the proverbial wit and gayety of the Irishman. At least a half dozen of the men were graduates of eastern colleges, bearing their share in the dangerous work of the border.

The second in command was Lieutenant Fred Beecher, nephew of the famous minister, and, although but a young man, already a veteran. He had received a bullet through the knee at Gettysburg and he walked lame the rest of his days, which were not long now. By the side of Lieutenant Beecher rode First Sergeant William McCall, a man who had risen to the rank of general in the Civil War, had passed out of the army, when the great volunteer force was disbanded, and who now reappeared upon the plains in this humble rank, but faithful and devoted.

There were others with whom Bob was soon to become well acquainted. Louis and Hudson Farley, father and son, serving together, and considered the best shots on the plains, Mooers, the surgeon, and more.

Every man carried a repeating rifle, with six shots in the magazine and one in the barrel, a large revolver, 140 rounds of ammunition for the rifle, 30 for the revolver, and a large, strong hunter's knife. Everyone had rations for seven days, already cooked, in his haversack. Four pack mules bore picks, shovels, camp-kettles, four thousand rounds of ammunition, medical supplies, salt and coffee.

It was a gallant band. None finer could have been found anywhere, and, since Bob could not be with his own comrades, he was glad to be with these. The air rushed swiftly past as they rode onward and the tide of life rose high. He was by the side of Stillwell, who was scarcely older than himself, and the two were already fast friends. Martin Burke, a yard away, hummed Irish tunes under his breath, and the two Farleys, father and son, rode knee to knee.

"This is something like it, isn't it Bob?" said Jack Stillwell.

"It beats riding alone, tied on the back of a mustang," said Bob with so much sincerity, that Jack laughed.

"That's behind you," said the young scout "but we may have something that will keep us jumping, before us. Colonel Forsyth is not the man to turn back."

"No, I think not," said Bob, looking at the compact active figure of the leader, swinging easily in the saddle.

Bob soon became as much interested as his comrades in the quest, and he, too, scanned the brown soil for signs of a trail. He tried, also, but without success, to remember the direction in which he had come, examining every swell in the hope that he might remember some familiar sign. But it was too much like a dream, and a sleep without a dream for him to pick out landmarks from such obscurity.

"You're sure that none of it comes back to you?" said Colonel Forsyth.

"I wish I could bring it back," replied Bob, "but I can't. I'd know that village if I saw it, but whether it's north, east, south or west from here is more than I can tell."

Colonel Forsyth did not upbraid him because he could not answer. Instead, he regarded the boy more than once with sympathy. The commander, as Bob noticed, seemed to be regarded with great affection by his men.

The day was brilliant, and as it was the middle of September, there was a breath of coolness in the air. Bob drew deep breaths, and his happiness increased. He was naturally optimistic. He had been through so much, and he had been harried so much that it was like heaven to be free again, with fifty brave white men around him. He did not fear the whole Cheyenne nation now, and he had a firm belief, too, that Sam Strong and the others were somewhere in advance. The three scouts now led, Colonel Forsyth was just behind, with Bob by his side, and, after them, came the cavalrymen in a close group. The scouts suddenly reined in their horses, and the others automatically did the same.

"What is it, Sharp!" asked Colonel Forsyth eagerly.

"See, sir," said Sharp, pointing to the ground.

Bob looked down too, and there, imprinted across the plain was the broad trail of many unshod horsemen. The boy's heart throbbed when he saw it, and so did that of every man in the company.

In that expanse, vast and silent save for themselves, the trail was like a living thing. There it was, standing out on the brown soil, wide, vivid, and full of significance. It told Bob in words that must be understood that here the Cheyennes had passed, many warriors, hundreds and hundreds, hunters of men, with the fierce war chiefs, Roman Nose and Black Kettle at their head. This was the tale the trail told.

Colonel Forsyth examined it long and carefully, and his face was at once eager and anxious. He looked from the trail to his men, and he counted to himself the fearful odds. The trail led on before, but it was so wide that one had to go aside to see its farther edge. The commander rode a little apart, and beckoned to Grover and Stillwell.

"How many warriors would you say have passed here?" he asked.

"I reckon that countin' people of all kinds, about four thousand people have rid on this trail," replied Grover, "an', figurin' on the usual basis, that means about fifteen hundred warriors. What do you say, Jack?"

"That's about as near it as human calculation can come", replied young Stillwell, with emphasis.

"And we are only fifty," said Forsyth. "Well, General Sheridan sent us out to find the Cheyennes, and whether we're fifty or five thousand, we must find them. Isn't that so, boys!"

"It's so," replied the two scouts together.

"Do you think the men understand it?" asked Colonel Forsyth.

"Every one of them," replied Grover. "They read this trail like print."

"And they are not afraid," said Forsyth, looking at his troops with pride. He turned his horse and faced the little band, which drew up in a compact body, and saluted. Bob instinctively drew his mustang back until he rode in the first line. He now felt himself a member of this little force, as he had felt himself a member of Sam Strong's party, and he was accepted as such.

Colonel Forsyth raised his hand, and there was complete silence, save for the heavy breathing of the men.

"My lads," said the officer, in a firm, clear voice, "everyone of you has seen this trail and everyone of you knows what it means. Pretty nearly the whole of the Cheyenne nation has passed here, and their fighting men, if they should turn on us, would outnumber us twenty to one. But we follow! Do you understand that? What I wish to know is, do you follow with willing hearts!"

Fifty throats roared out, "We do!" and Bob shouted with them. He was carried away by excitement, and its impulse. He was as ready as any of them to gallop forward against twenty or thirty to one, or, if need be, against fifty to one.

"That is all, my lads," said the Colonel quietly. "Sharp, you and Jack and Pete lead on."

The three guides started up the trail at a trot, and the men, still in a close group, followed them, all looking closely as they rode to saddle and girth, rifle and pistol. The blindest novice could not mistake the trail. It stretched on, broad, obvious and menacing, mile after mile.

Moreover, other signs soon multiplied. Now they saw an abandoned tent pole lying by the trail, and then another. Farther on were fragments of buffalo meat, pieces of clothing, old moccasins, feathers from war-bonnets and other fragments, such as an army might leave behind on its march. It was evident that the Cheyennes were not seeking to hide their trail.

"It looks as if they were defying all the white forces, doesn't it?" said Stillwell to Bob, who had dropped back by his side again.

"Yes, they're telling us to come on if we dare," said Bob.

"The colonel dares," said Stillwell tersely and Bob felt a certain pride in it. He could see, too, a visible increase in his own importance and Pete and Jack accepted him as comrade.

The afternoon waxed and waned, and there was the trail yet before them, as broad, and as menacing as ever. It was impossible to tell how old it was, but the guides surmised that the Indians had a lead of ten or twelve hours. Sunset was at hand, and, to the great vexation of Colonel Forsyth, mists and vapours from the southwest promised a dark night. The promise was soon fulfilled, and in another hour they could not see fifty yards ahead of them.

It was impossible to continue the pursuit until morning, and they went into camp, if blankets and the bare prairie can be called a camp. But Bob did not think it so bad. He had the companionship of the men, and they found enough buffalo chips for a fire, over which they cooked bacon and made coffee.

The food and drink heartened them wonderfully and, although they put out the fire as soon as the cooking was over, the effect of its warmth lingered. Grover, Trudeau and Stillwell were off on the plain, scouting in the darkness. Bob would have gone with them, but Colonel Forsyth detained him, in order to ask further details about the Cheyennes. The younger officers also were allowed to sit by and listen.

Bob recounted again all that he had seen in the Cheyenne village, and he dwelt much on the figure of Roman Nose.

"A great chief," said Colonel Forsyth, "a dangerous and a worthy enemy. And the crafty Black Kettle is not much inferior to him. You have met him face to face, and maybe we will have the chance too."

The scouts came back, after a while, and reported that nothing could be found on the prairie. There was no danger of a night attack, and the men could sleep easily until the morning.

Colonel Forsyth uttered a sigh of satisfaction. He knew the value of peace of mind and a night's rest. He put a friendly hand on Bob's shoulder and said:

"Go to sleep as soon as you can, my boy, because we march early in the morning."

Bob drew his blanket closely about his body, pillowed his head upon the haversack which had been given to him as part of his outfit, and closed Ms eyes. Weariness had come back upon him. Some of the effects of the wild ride, bound upon the back of the mustang lingered, and he began to wish again for absolute rest.

He felt now, for the first time in days, the complete luxury of peace, the peace of both the body and the mind that rebuilds. Within this ring of brave men he took no thought of the Cheyennes, and the gentle wind that blew over the plains was as soothing as the sound of faint and distant music. He heard the tread of a horse now and then, the rustle of a trooper, seeking a better position for his body, and then he heard nothing. He was sound asleep and he did not wake again until the clear note of the bugle called to him to rise.

Food and coffee were served, and then the fifty remounted. Among all the horses there was none more tractable than the mustang. Bob raised himself in his stirrups, and searched the rolling plain with his strong, young eyes. He could see nothing. It was as bare as it had been the day before. Young Stillwell rode up by his side.

"You don't see anything, Bob," said Stillwell, "but that don't mean that you won't see anything. I'm thinking that the trail will grow pretty hot before the day is over."

"If it means a fight I hope to do my share," said Bob. "I've been in battle with the Cheyennes already."

"I've fired a lot of good metal at 'em," said Stillwell, "and they've fired a lot at me, but it's all in the job. Come on, Bob."

Bob spoke to his mustang, and the powerful horse leaped forward, his compact, muscular body taut like steel wire, and his spirit alight. Bob shared his eagerness. A second night's rest had driven away the last traces of his collapse and he was ready for anything. Jack Stillwell glanced at him approvingly.

The trail seemed broader than ever. It looked almost as if a buffalo herd had passed that way and Grover announced presently that two other parties had joined the great band.

"Never mind," said Colonel Forsyth, "we still follow."

He shut his lips tightly together and rode directly behind Bob and the three scouts, and, behind him, the troop rode as one, every man knowing to what he was riding, and no man flinching.

The trail veered after a while and once more they saw the Arickaree. Then it ran on for hours by the side of the river. They halted a little after noon, for a short rest and to water the horses, and when they resumed the pursuit Grover said to the commander that he did not think they would overtake the Cheyennes that day.

"They are movin' pretty fast," he said, "an' while the trail is growin' warmer it won't be warm enough by nightfall."

The hot sun began to cool, the afternoon passed its zenith, but the band rode on, now in silence. The trail wound along the south bank of the Arickaree, forty or fifty yards from the stream, among thickets of alder, willow and wild plum. Just as they had passed one of the densest parts of these thickets, the river made a bend, and, as they rode through a narrow gorge, they saw a pleasant valley, two miles wide, and a little longer, well grown in grass. On the south side, the land made a gentle incline down to the Arickaree. But on the north it stretched away in a level expanse for nearly a mile, the valley there ending abruptly against a line of bluffs, about fifty feet high.

Colonel Forsyth gave a signal, and the whole troop stopped, looking into the valley. He was troubled. He feared that he was going to face very great odds, and he was worried, too, by the scarcity of his provisions. Except the food in the haversacks everything was gone save a small quantity of coffee and salt. The horses had depended on grass, and the valley before him was full of it. Perhaps it would be best to camp here.

As he looked, his eyes fell upon an island in the middle of the stream, a peculiar little island, about a hundred yards long, and perhaps half as wide. It had been formed of sand, accumulating around a gravelly rift at its head. It was seventy or eighty yards from the shore on either side, but at this time of the year, most of the distance was sand. The water in either channel was not more than fifteen or twenty feet wide, and about half a foot deep.

Long sage grass covered the head of the island, in the centre grew a thicket of alders and willows to the height of about five feet, and at the foot stood a lone, young cottonwood. The colonel's eyes wandered away from the island and then he gave the command to ride into the valley and camp. Bob thought the colonel was going to have them camp on the island, but instead he chose a place opposite it on the mainland.

The colonel himself saw to the making of the camp and the posting of the sentries. Every man was directed to hobble his horse, and to see that his lariat was knotted right. He was ordered also to drive his picket pin firmly into the ground, and before lying down for the night he must see that it was still right. He also gave detailed instructions in case of surprise. Every man was to seize his horse's lariat with one hand and his rifle with the other. He was then to stand by his horse to prevent a stampede, a thing greatly to be feared in their situation.

Bob, after he had tethered the mustang, walked to the edge of the river and looked at the island. The sun had set but some of its last red rays lingered over the island tinting its sand and the alders and the willows and the lone young cottonwood as if with blood. A chill wind blew out of the west, and the water in the river looked dark and cold. A strange shiver, a premonition, as it were, of an event tremendous, ran through every nerve and vein of Bob's being, and he knew that it was the island, or something about it, something mysterious and uncanny. He looked so long at it that he seemed to see an ashy vapour rising from its sands, and, angry at himself, he dashed his hands before his eyes to drive it away.

"What's the matter, Bob?" asked Stillwell, who had seen the gesture.

"Nothing, at least not anything real. That island there was putting a spell on me, and I was seeing all sorts of things."

"I don't see anything but a spit of sand."

"And I don't now, either."

"Well, you'd better get to sleep."

"I want to stand my share of the watch."

"You don't have any share. The Colonel says that a fellow who has ridden a horse bare-backed, and at a gallop, two or three hundred miles without stopping, can't play sentinel, for at least a week afterward."

Bob was forced to acquiesce, and again wrapped in his blanket he sought sleep on the bare ground' It came quickly enough, but it was not so sound this second night. He awoke at some unknown hour, though the moon was shining, and, sitting up, looked over the camp. About him were the motionless figures of the men, deep in slumber. Further away were the figures of horses, and beyond them, the sentinels, with ready rifles, watching every point of the horizon.

But Bob's eyes came back to one point, drawn there by a sort of hypnotic spell. It was the island, the reach of sand, upon which the moon was shining. But the sand, instead of turning to silver in the moonlight, turned to ashen-grey. It was a cold and forbidding expanse and half-awake, half-asleep, Bob felt, for the second time, the premonition of something tremendous. But he shut his eyes and resolutely sought sleep again.

When he awoke it was only faint dawn, just three fingers of pale grey in the east, but he felt that he had sleep enough and he sat up, letting his blanket drop from him. He saw an erect figure just beyond the last row of figures and he recognized Colonel Forsyth. The leader of the little band was on guard. Beyond him stood another man, the young scout, Jack Stillwell.

It was Bob's first intention to join them, but he refrained. They might not want him. He sat a little longer, and the slim strip of grey in the east broadened to a band. The band turned from grey to silver and from silver to an edge of flaming red, the first herald of the sun. Bob was still looking at the colonel and the scout, and he saw both of them make a sudden movement, as if they had seen something unusual. They were staring at the crest of a low hill that lay some distance beyond the camp.

Bob, acting partly on impulse and partly on Sam Strong's training, leaned backward and put his ear to the earth. He heard distinctly a soft, regular sound and he knew it. It was the beat of horses' feet. He sprang erect, with a single motion, and he saw Stillwell bring his rifle forward with his finger on the trigger. Bob sprang to the colonel's side, and then, although erect, he could hear the soft thud of hoofs. He knew that the colonel heard it too, as he held in his hand his drawn revolver.

The dash of scarlet in the east turned to a blaze. Suddenly above the crest of the hill appeared the tips of waving eagle feathers, and then several mounted Cheyennes, phantom-like and gigantic against the first sunrise. He knew that they were the famous Dog Soldiers, and he knew too, that others must be near. Stillwell fired instantly at one of the warriors and sprang back shouting the alarm.

"Up, men! Up! The Cheyennes have come!" cried Colonel Forsyth, and instantly the fifty men were upon their feet, rifles in hand, the frightened horses held firmly by the lariats.

The mounted Indians appeared upon the brow of the hill, and the whole band galloped straight toward the group of white men, their robust bodies glistening in the morning light, and the long feathers in their hair streaming out defiantly. Some of them carried shields of buffalo hide, upon which they beat with a loud, rolling sound like that of drums.

"Steady, men! Steady!" said Colonel Forsyth. His men raised their rifles, and Bob, who was just in front, raised his also, but the Cheyennes suddenly veered, and charged around the flank of the whites, shouting the war-whoop with all the strength of their voices.

"Look out!" cried Trudeau, "they're trying to stampede our horses!"

The Cheyennes, bending low in their saddles, rushed the horses and pack-mules gathered behind the camp, intending to sweep them all away, and leave the little command on foot and practically helpless. But the soldiers ran forward and fired upon them rapidly. Grover, Trudeau and Stillwell, reckless of the return fire from the Indians, dashed forward to save the pack-mules and Bob followed them. A Cheyenne fired at him from under his pony's neck and missed. Bob did not fire back, because his hands were now occupied with his own struggling horse.

Then one of the Cheyennes uttered a short, sharp shout, and the band, turning about, galloped away at top speed. They had not created a stampede, but they carried with them two of the pack-mules loaded with stores and two horses that had not been picketed properly. Young Stillwell fired again at them, as they rode away, and a feathered warrior, throwing up his hands dropped backward from his pony to the plain where he lay still. There were other scattering shots, but the rest of the band galloped out of range with their prizes. Some of the soldiers started to follow, but the colonel ordered all to saddle and bridle their horses instantly, and stand fast.

The swift charge and the swift retreat passed in a minute or two, while the daylight was still showing in the east, and had not yet appeared in the west Bob was almost dazed by its rapidity. He stood, holding the bridle of the mustang, while a little cloud of dust, kicked up by the hoofs of the ponies, drifted over them.

He looked through the dust as through a mist, and an army of red horsemen seemed to rise out of the plain. The line stretched far to right and to left, and every man was bent forward a little over his horse's neck, like those who ride to the charge. The boy's heart gave a great jump, and then every nerve tingled and throbbed. The first band had been mere raiders. This was the Cheyenne army.

"Look! Look!" cried Grover, standing beside his commander. "All the Cheyennes have come!"

It was true. The great Cheyenne force had turned upon its own trail, and now it approached the little white band from all sides. Besides the horsemen in front, other Indians, some on foot and some mounted, were pressing forward along either bank of the river. Just in front of the red line, where the Indians were massed, a gigantic man sat on a great mustang. This man's appearance was ferocious and impressive to the last degree. Feathers and plumes, woven into a great gorgeous braid, swung from his hair. His face was covered with war-paint, red and black in many designs, even to the nose, which was large and curved. The head was crowned with the war-bonnet, a magnificent ornament of large coloured feathers, with two short, black buffalo horns projecting from it, at the temples. He was naked save for his moccasins and a broad scarf of blood-red about the waist.

The man sat perfectly still on his horse, and regarded the group of white men with a gaze that expressed hatred and triumph. He was like one who had long sought a foe, and who now held him in the hollow of his hand. Bob thought that he had never seen anything more impressive than this startling apparition. But he knew the man.

"Roman Nose!" he cried.

Every white eye was instantly turned upon the chief, but he yet sat motionless, gazing upon them with that look of malignant triumph, the certainty of victory to come.

CHAPTER 17

Little Thermopylae

Bob saw the great chief raise his hand, and then a wild cry burst from a thousand throats, a savage cry, so instinct with hatred, ferocity and triumph, that every man shuddered. Then the whole Indian army swept forward, horse and foot, more than twenty to one.

Bob felt himself recoiling as if an irresistible mass were rushing down upon him, but in a moment he checked himself. The white men stood now in a circle with their horses behind them in the centre. But the deadly muzzles of their rifles faced in every direction. Bob was between Trudeau and Stillwell and Colonel Forsyth was only a few yards away. The boy, although he stood motionless, was tremendously excited. The little pulses in his temple were beating furiously, and the charging horde came on in a red mist. Nevertheless he heard amid all the fierce yelling from hundreds of throats the low "steady! steady!" of the commander, an insistent undernote. All the time, the rising sun was pouring a flood of golden beams down upon this wild scene of the western plains.

Nearer came the red horsemen and the thousands of hoofs beat like thunder. It looked to Bob as if they must all be trodden under foot He saw through the clouds of dust, always tinted red, the wild faces of the warriors, their curved noses, and their white teeth, from which their thin, red lips were drawn back. He looked for Roman Nose. He did not see him, but he chose another, a large warrior who also wore a magnificent war-bonnet and who was in the very front of the charging red line. The trigger of his rifle fairly burned against his finger, but Colonel Forsyth had not yet given the command to fire, and he dared not pull it. Nearer they came, and it seemed that in another minute the Indians would be upon the troopers. Then the colonel shouted: "Fire!" the single sharp word rising above the roar like the crack of a pistol-shot.

Fifty eager fingers pulled trigger at once. The little circle of men was rimmed around with fire, and a cloud of smoke at once arose. But it was a deadly circle. From every point it emitted singing metal, as the men loaded and fired as fast as they could. Their bullets crashed into the masses of charging Cheyennes. Ponies and riders went down. Warriors fell as if smitten with a thunderbolt. Horses, screaming with pain, galloped about the plain. Dust and smoke mingled, and heavy with odours and vapours, floated over them all.

Bob aimed directly at the big warrior with the eagle beak, when he pulled the trigger. When the rifle flashed he saw the warrior no more. After that he fired at whatever was nearest. The little pulses in his head were beating more furiously than ever, and he was scarcely conscious of what he was doing, but he did not flinch. He remembered afterward that he could still feel Trudeau at his right and Stillwell at his left, while the commander stood as before only a few yards away.

The crash of the rifles was so steady now that it was like the roll of thunder. Mingled with it, the unbroken yelling of the Indians and the drum of hoofs beat upon the boy's ears, with such regularity that he became unconscious of sound at all. The troopers seldom shouted, but aiming low, sent their bullets straight to the mark. Bob saw the head of a pony almost in his face. He fired at it and the pony fell. Other ponies appeared through the clouds of dust and smoke but they too went down, and no wild horseman broke through the white ring.

Bullets struck in the ring also. Men were wounded but they hid it for the time, and kept their places in the defence. Bob felt something hot searing his side, but he knew that he was merely grazed and he forgot it the next moment. Then he became conscious of the great shouting and firing, but it was because both were decreasing and becoming irregular. The clouds of smoke and dust lifted, and showed the Cheyennes in retreat, the ground between the foes sprinkled with dead horses and fallen warriors.

The little band of fifty—though not fifty now—uttered a great shout of exultation. That invincible front of fire had beaten off the entire Cheyenne army—for an instant. The Cheyennes were sullenly withdrawing out of rifle range, but Colonel Forsyth knew well enough that the attack would soon come again, and that they could not beat it back a second time standing there in the open plain. His quick mind was at work and it was working well. He glanced toward the island, and he saw that the water would form a defence against a charge, or at least help.

"Come, my boys," he said, "we will fight from the island. Move toward it, as fast as you can, but do not break your ring."

The firing and the shouting had ceased, and in the silence his voice was like thunder to Bob. Then he heard Trudeau murmuring under his breath: "A good move; it's our only chance."

The ring, as even and orderly as a Macedonian phalanx, protected by the fire of their best marksmen, went swiftly toward the river, the frightened horses dragged with them by the lariats, the men carrying also their wounded and their dead. It was a perfect movement, which only the bravest of veterans could have executed at such a terrible moment. In an instant they had reached the shallow water, in another they were in it, and in a third they were on the sandy island.

The Cheyennes, when they saw the retreat, rushed forward and began to fire again from every point of vantage. They leaped from their horses, and took advantage of every inequality in the earth. They swarmed among the reeds and willows on either side of the river bed, and poured in a storm of bullets. More men were wounded. Several horses were killed and fell into the water, while the others were so terrified that it took half the time and strength of the men to hold them.

But the troopers were upon the island and Forsyth shouted to them to dig, dig for their lives. Bob understood when his heels sank in the soft sand. Half the men were at work already, while the other half, forming a ring about them, were returning the Indian fire.

The men were scooping up the sand, some with their hands, some with empty tin cans from the mess, but most with their hunting knives. Bob took out his own knife and he and Stillwell began to dig a hole.

"It will be a good place for us, dead or alive," said young Stillwell with grim humour.

Bob dug furiously and threw up the soft sand in a shower, while Stillwell arranged it all around the hole in the form of a breastwork. The sand seemed to go down to an unlimited depth, and it was so soft that the hole sank fast. Bob could not tell anything about time, but eight or ten minutes must have passed, when Stillwell shouted to him:

"Up with your rifle, Bob, the Cheyennes are about to charge again!"

All the men threw down the tools with which they had been digging and seized their weapons. Some of the horses had been tethered, but in the hurry the others were left to shift for themselves. But many holes had been dug, and many mounds of sand had been thrown up. The island, with its band of water on either side, and its sand protection, was a different place from the open plain. Stillwell sprang down by the side of Bob in the hole that they had dug, and the two on their knees were sheltered almost completely.

"Let 'em come, Bob, my boy," said Stillwell, the fire of battle flaming in his veins.

"Yes, let 'em come," said Bob, peering down the sights of his rifle, the barrel of which lay on the wall of sand.

The Cheyennes needed no invitation. They were coming fast enough, and from every side they swarmed toward the island, continuously shouting the war-whoop, and firing their rifles as they charged. The skirmishers in the beds of reeds also pressed closer and these were now the most dangerous. Picked sharpshooters, they sent the sand flying in little puffs. One puff struck Bob in the face, and it stung like small shot. He and Stillwell turned their attention to these wasps and their bullets sang among the reeds.

But the majority of the troopers, at the command of Colonel Forsyth, fired at the charging hordes of horsemen, and sheltered by their mounds and ridges of sand, they were able to break the lines, shooting down warriors and ponies alike. Now a great crowd of Indian women and children appeared on the bluffs, at the back of the valley, and added their shouts to the uproar.

The Indians charged to the very edge of the water, but they paused there in the face of the withering fire from the island, and then breaking, retreated rapidly out of rifle range, followed by the derisive cheering of the island's defenders.

"Twice we've licked 'em," exclaimed Jack Stillwell, joyfully, "but they'll come again. Hurt, Bob?"

"Not touched," replied the boy, "but I'm hot, and my heart has been pounding like a drum. Good Heavens! What's that?"

A wild scream of pain, more terrible than a man could utter, made them both jump. It came from a wounded horse, and presently two more joined in his shuddering cry. Several had torn loose and were running up and down the island. Others, mortally wounded had broken away, only to fall dead beyond the stream, and while the main attack had been repulsed, the skirmishers among the reeds turned their aim from the defenders to the horses which could not be protected from their bullets.

"It's all up with them," said Stillwell. "We can't save 'em. Our good horses have to go."

The rifles cracked fast among the reeds and horse after horse was struck.

"Turn them loose!" commanded the Colonel, and the men quickly obeyed, first securing their food and extra ammunition. Even then many of the horses were shot down as they galloped across the Arickaree. Bob approaching his mustang, and careless of a chance shot, took him by the mane.

The boy's heart was full of sadness. He had a genuine affection for this horse which had saved him, but he knew now that he must let him go, or see him slain almost at his feet. The mustang thrust out his head, and muzzled his hand. Bob's heart was rent again, but it was no time for waiting. A bullet struck in the sand at his feet. Another grazed his buckskin coat.

"Farewell, good horse!" he exclaimed. "Now go!"

He struck the mustang smartly on the side with his rifle-barrel, at the same moment slipping off the bridle. The horse galloped down the island, looked a few moments at the water, crossed it with a few bounds, and then stood upon the open plain.

Several of the withdrawing warriors fired at the mustang, but their bullets merely knocked up the dust about him. He stopped, and looked scornfully at them. Two more shots were fired at him, and then he broke into a run across the plain, which was encircled by the Indian line.

Bob jumped back into the pit with Stillwell and the two watched the mustang, whose fortunes had assumed a wholly human interest for them. The splendid beast galloped on toward the Indian line.

"They'll kill him," said Bob.

"Since they missed him first, it's more likely that they'll try to catch him now," said Stillwell. "They'll see that he's worth having."

Three or four of the best mounted Cheyennes galloped forward, and threw their lariats. But the rope missed his head every time, and slipped along his smooth side to fall fruitlessly on the ground.

"Good horse! Good horse!" repeated Bob. "They haven't got him yet."

The mustang went straight on, tore through the Indian line, the lariats whistling about him in vain, and then galloped at full speed toward the bluffs, the disappointed Cheyennes firing at him two or three shots that fell short. Presently he reached a crest out of range, looked back a moment, shook his long mane, and then with a final burst of speed, disappeared over the hill.

Bob laughed aloud in his pleasure.

"They could neither take nor kill him!" he exclaimed. "I was fond of that mustang, Jack. I ought to have been, as he saved my life."

"He may have been a wild horse once, and it's likely that he'll become one again," said Stillwell. "He's fit to be the head of a great herd."

"I hope so," said Bob, "and since he's got away, we'll take it as a good omen, and reckon it as a sure thing that we're going to get away too."

"Right enough," said Jack cheerfully. "Of course we'll get away. There ain't more than a million Cheyennes around us, but with our sand pits here, we could beat 'em off if they were two millions. Listen to that, Bob! We haven't been shooting for nothing."

From the bluffs back of the battlefield came a long, high-pitched wailing sound. It was the women and children mourning the dead warriors, most of whom had been carried away by their comrades and their horses. It was inexpressibly sad to Bob, and for the moment he felt sympathy for the Cheyennes.

"Fighting is hot business in more ways than one," said Stillwell, and one of the hot things that it does to you is to get up a thirst. The Arickaree is a cool, clear stream, and I'm bound to have some of it, right away."

"Don't you try it," said Bob. "It's too dangerous. Those fellows in the reeds would pick you off when you bent down for the water."

"I don't intend to do any bending down." said Stillwell "I'm going by underground, and you're going to help me."

All the men during the lull in the fighting were busily scooping their burrows deeper, and Stillwell, using a broad tin plate, set to work digging a shallow trench toward the river, which was only a few feet away. He lay almost on his side, and made the sand fly fast. Bob helped him with his hunting knife, and as they pulled forward eight or ten feet in the trench, the sand grew damp. Then the cool water oozed up and the two drank greedily, one from a can and the other from the plate. It was like nectar to their parched lips and throat, and they did not neglect to take a plentiful supply back to their comrades.

"Lucky thing for us," said Stillwell, "that we've been cooped up with a river full of good water all about us. We're likely to need it in our business before this thing is over. Look, there's Roman Nose!"

The great chief had ridden again to the brow of the low hill, and just out of rifle range, sat there looking down at the devoted band on the island, the blazing sun showing every bright feather in his magnificent war-bonnet.

"He's planning," said Stillwell, "as sure as shooting. I'll bet that he's as mad as a hornet, through and through, because we got upon this island, but he expects to get us out of it, all the same. Now I wonder what's turning in that cunning Indian brain of his?"

Colonel Forsyth was also wondering. He lay in a sand burrow by the side of his surgeon, Dr. Mooers, and closely watched his formidable antagonist. The dust had settled back to earth, the smoke had lifted, and everything could be seen clearly. The commander felt in his heart that an attack more determined and savage than either of the others was about to be made. He feared, too, that it would be accompanied by more craft, and he looked sorrowfully at his little band. The wounds were numerous, and several men lay dead in the sand. But there was no thought of surrender in his mind. Little mercy could be expected from the Cheyennes, and he would not have asked it, even had there been a chance. He and his band were resolved to die there, to the last man if need be.

"Look well to your rifles, boys," he said, "and see that all the cartridges are in."

Their rifles were the best of the time, and they knew that their lives depended upon them. Bob counted the cartridges in his to see that all

157

were in place, and also surveyed the pistol in his holster. The water had refreshed him greatly, and Stillwell gave him a strip of bacon to chew.

"You may not be able to taste it at all," he said, "but it will hearten you up and give you strength. I've saved another strip for myself."

Bob followed his advice, but as the young scout said, he could not taste the food. Meanwhile the Cheyennes were gathering for a greater effort than ever. The chiefs assembled for council on one of the low bluffs within sight of the island, and their great war-bonnets glowed in the sun. Roman Nose was there, so was Black Kettle, and so were chiefs from all the clans, the Dog Soldiers, the Fox Men, Those-with-Headed-Lances, The Bed-Shield-Owners, Those-with-the-Bow-String, and even the Foolish Dogs. There was with them, too, a white man, a freebooter, no less a person than Juan Carver; but Roman Nose was the great dominating personality. He had been successful for two years in his war with the whites, and he did not mean to fail, now that he held Forsyth in the hollow of his hand.

Bob could distinguish Roman Nose at the distance, and he felt that the coming charge would be far more formidable than either of the others. Roman Nose, not sparing his own men, would hurl the Cheyenne army directly upon them.

The little band finished its last preparation for defence. The saddles from the dead or injured horses were piled in rows on the mounds of sand. Everything that could serve as a shield against bullets was put in place, and then they waited.

The sun never ceased to shine with the utmost brilliancy. Only tiny white clouds dotted the blue of the heavens. In the transparent light it seemed almost possible to distinguish the features of the women and children on the bluffs, watching them to see the warriors destroy the white force to the last man.

The council of the chiefs was over. Bob could see them going away, and the Cheyenne skirmishers, advancing directly in their front, opened fire. It was not a headlong charge of horsemen now, but the slow and careful approach of sharpshooters who, lying almost flat on the plain, crawled forward and sent in a bullet whenever they caught sight of any portion of a trooper's body. The warriors, who had never left the cover of the reeds and willows, also resumed their fire, and the island, low, flat and bare, was swept by bullets.

Only their burrows in the sand saved the troopers, and raising themselves just enough to take aim they returned a careful and deadly fire. It was the order of Colonel Forsyth that no man was to pull trigger until he could draw a bead on his target, and despite the smoke, many a bullet struck true.

Stillwell was watching the advance intently, noting the white puffs of smoke on the plain wherever a Cheyenne fired, and he was puzzled.

"This can't be the main attack," he said to Bob. "Their riflemen may cut us up a lot, but I don't believe they mean to rush us in front. Look at that! Some of those fellows in the reeds have reached the end of the island. Keep close, Bob! Keep close!"

Several of the most daring of the Cheyennes had actually crawled through the reeds and water and effected a lodgement on the upper end of the island, where they hid in the sage, and from that ambush fired upon the troopers.

Colonel Forsyth was lying in one of the sand pits, within five feet of Bob and Stillwell. He was almost flat upon his side, firing with the others, but low as he lay, the bullets from the daring warriors on the island began to patter around him.

"We've got to clean those fellows out," said Stillwell. A Cheyenne rifle flashed, and the young scout instantly fired at the flash. A warrior, uttering a cry, sprang convulsively into the air, and fell back out of sight.

"One's gone," said Stillwell, "but more are left, and I tell you, Bob, they're mighty dangerous. Good God, why don't the colonel keep down?"

Colonel Forsyth had risen and was walking around among his men, encouraging them, telling them to stand fast, that they could yet beat off the Indians. Bob looked at him, the only upright figure on the island, and saw him stagger. Bob knew that he was hit, and his heart sank.

The colonel clapped his hand to his thigh where the blood was already running through the cloth of his trousers, and then sank down again in the sandy trench. The shot was seen by all the men, and they cried out, wishing to know if he were alive. Although suffering acute pain, as the bullet had ranged upward in his right thigh, he replied cheerfully that he was all right, and as the last word left his lips, another bullet struck his leg half way between knee and ankle, shattering the bone. But the indomitable man roused himself again and cried encouragement to the others. A third bullet passed through the crown of his felt hat, ploughed under the skin of his head and fractured his skull, a piece of the bone being taken out a month later. Surgeon Mooers was mortally wounded by his side.

But this dauntless commander did not lose either consciousness or courage. With these terrible wounds he propped himself up on his elbow, called to his men to fight on and, taking a rifle himself, fired at mounted Indians, who were now approaching from the front. With such an example no trooper could falter. Forsyth bleeding from his three great wounds, in spite of everything kept his faculties clear in this terrific moment, and directed the battle.

The Indian force steadily crept forward, wrapping themselves around three sides of the defenders, and sending in the bullets faster and faster. Man after man, despite the protection of the sand, was hit, and some were killed, usually dying without noise in the pits that they had dug, and the least exposure of an arm or a shoulder was sure to bring a bullet. Now the warriors redoubled their shouting, and from the bluffs a horde of women and children increased it with a great chorus.

It seemed to Bob that the final charge must come the next moment, and he did not see how it could be held back. Unconsciously he resigned himself, and he was glad that he was not to die in the darkness and alone.

"They'll rush upon us in a minute," he said to Stillwell.

"Not so," replied the experienced young scout. "They're not going to charge us in front. You don't see Roman Nose there. You don't see any of the big chiefs there. Now I wonder how they're coming at us. But they'll come sure."

Bob slipped new cartridges into his rifle, and peered again through the bank of smoke and dust. His eye swept entirely around the circle and rested upon one point from which no attack had come. There his gaze was fixed, and with a convulsive start he straightened up in the pit.

"Here they come now," exclaimed Stillwell. "Look, Roman Nose himself leads."

Five hundred red horsemen, Roman Nose at their head, rode up the bed of the river which was very low. Just behind Roman Nose were Black Kettle and all the chiefs, and on the flank an old medicine man, as brave as any of the chiefs, led. Every man in that wild army was stripped for battle, naked save for the breech-cloth, moccasins and war-bonnet. They held rifles and pistols in their hands, and they urged their horses forward with their heels. The sunlight, for here the air was clear of smoke and dust, floated down on them, and lighted up their features, the high cheek bones, the curved beaks, and the bare arms and shoulders, lean, sinewy and powerful.

The great mass of red horsemen halted for a few moments at the mouth of the narrow gorge through which the force of Forsyth had come the day before, and then the two forces looked at each other, the little white band half hidden in the sand on the island, and the chosen Indian warriors, more than ten to one.

It was a sight that Bob saw many a time afterwards in his dreams, so tense, so vivid, etched so strongly against the background of blazing sunlight, that it was real again.

There for an instant sat the gigantic figure of Roman Nose on his horse, general, warrior, worthy leader of a savage army. He turned a single glance toward the women and children who stood in thousands on the low line of bluffs. Then he raised his right arm and waved his hand to them, like a Roman gladiator saluting the multitude. When they saw the gesture they replied with a vast shout of joy that rolled in echoes up the valley and beyond. It was a cry so full of ferocity and the savour of triumph that the two youths lying together in the sandy hollow could not keep from shuddering.

Roman Nose turned his gaze back from the Cheyenne nation to the little white force on the island. He seemed fairly to rise upon his horse as he clenched one fist in the white man's fashion, and shook it fiercely at his foe. Then he threw back his head, clapped the palm of his hand across his mouth, and uttered the most tremendous war-cry that ever passed human lips. It pierced the air like a rifle shot, then swelled in volume and filled the whole valley. Before the terrible echoes died, the deep note of a bugle, captured from some trooper, sounded above all the battle that was raging elsewhere, and with one tremendous shout the five hundred rode for the island.

"Now, Bob," shouted Stillwell, "shoot as you never shot before! This is the real attack!"

Bob knew already that it was the crisis, and so did every man among the fifty who yet lived. They whirled about, ignoring for a moment the sharpshooters in front, and faced the charge, the indomitable commander himself, who could scarcely move, lying against the sand and raising a revolver.

A wind cleft still more the banks of smoke and dust, and the entire mass of horsemen was revealed, the sand flying in showers beneath the beating hoofs. By the power of will and the concentrated energy of the moment, Forsyth raised himself on the sand and gazed at the rushing host, Roman Nose still several paces in front.

There was a sudden lull in the firing from the plains, as if the sharpshooters had risen up to see. The women and children on the bluffs sank into silence. Forsyth watched for a few minutes longer, and no man fired. Then he uttered the single sharp syllable that everyone understood:

"Now!"

CHAPTER 18

The Charge of Roman Nose

When that single monosyllable, "Now!" shot forth, the men in the pits raised up a little and pulled trigger, so close together that there was only a single crash. But every rifle was aimed true, and a hole was torn in the Indian line, men and horses going down together. The Cheyennes, great warriors, did not falter, and the magnificent Roman Nose led as before.

The dismounted Indians on the flanks resumed their fire, but the defenders of the island took no notice of them. Their eyes were never turned from the horsemen. They were a dauntless band, sun-browned, nearly all wounded, but their hands were steady and their eyes alight with the flame of battle. Forsyth lay upon his back in the sand, unable to move, but despite it, sending bullets from his revolver. A second time they pulled the trigger and a third time, and always the bullets went low and to the mark. The air was full of whistling metal. Riders and horses struck down disappeared from the line, but others took their places, the mass closed up and never for an instant ceased its charge.

"Can we ever stop them!" exclaimed young Stillwell, and Bob echoed his words. The Cheyennes were rushing their horses now through the shallow water and would soon reach the island, carried on by their own courage and the fire of their daring leader. On the island more men were slain by the rifle fire of the Indians which now came from every point, and others received fresh wounds, but those who still lived pulled the trigger with fiercer energy. It was all a red whirl to the boy, a terrible medley of fire and sand and water and smoke, pierced by the mingled crash of shots and shouts. Despite his danger and the fierce excitement of the moment, he could not withhold admiration for the courage of the Cheyennes, and above all for the daring of their leaders.

The Cheyenne chief was still in the van. His powerful horse came on with great leaps, and Roman Nose riding without a saddle sat far forward on the bare back. His knees were under a horse-hair lariat, wound around the animal's body, and he held the bridle firmly in his left hand.

He grasped a heavy repeating rifle in his right hand, and now and then he whirled it aloft as he galloped down upon his enemy. Fearless of death, no more magnificent figure was ever seen upon the plains.

"Fire at Roman Nose!" Bob heard Stillwell shout. He raised his rifle in obedience to the impulse, and then he turned his muzzle upon someone else. He did not know why he shifted the rifle, but he was always glad of it. Others were not moved by the same feeling.

Roman Nose had already reached the island, riding at a gallop directly down upon the rifle pits. The medicine man who led the flank had been killed, but the other chiefs were close behind him.

"He will ride over us!" exclaimed Bob.

Stillwell's only reply was to pull the trigger of the rifle aimed directly at the chief. Several others fired upon him at the same time. Roman Nose leaped convulsively upward and then sank back on his horse. The rifle dropped from his outstretched hand to the ground. His great body swayed, darkness quenched the flame of his eyes, and he fell to the ground, dead, pierced by half a dozen bullets.

A cry of grief and rage rose from the Cheyennes when they saw the death of their best chief, but the charge did not stop. Swerving their horses to one side, or leaping them over his body, they rode to the very edge of the rifle pits, but the fire swept them away. More chiefs went down. Horses, riderless or wounded, galloped here and there and spread confusion among them. The thrice-wounded Forsyth, lying on the ground, never ceased to direct his men. The Indians were so close now that even an excited marksman could scarcely miss.

The charge, one of the bravest and most dramatic ever made, broke on the island. The fire from the rifle pits was so fast and so deadly that the Indians, their great leader gone, gave way at last and galloped back, carrying with them the bodies of most of their fallen chiefs. A great cry of grief rose from the multitude beyond, and then came a lull like that which had preceded the charge. It was broken for Bob by the exultant cry of Stillwell:

"We've won! We've won!"

The boy was gasping. He was so much excited by the charge, the conflict and the tremendous picture he had seen that he could not speak. He was conscious that the Cheyennes had been driven back, but he did not feel the full reality of it. His eyes, his ears and his throat were full of the mingled reek of smoke, dust, sweat and burnt gunpowder. He was about to choke, but at last he managed to say:

"Have we really fought them off?"

"Not a doubt of it," said Stillwell, joyfully, and then he added with emphatic admiration, "But that was a great charge. I never expect to see its like again. If Roman Nose hadn't been shot from his horse they might have ridden over us."

"Down, men! Down!" suddenly cried Forsyth with all his energy, and the troopers obeyed just in time, throwing themselves flat on their faces in the rifle pits. The swarm of Indians on foot among the reeds and alders and willows swept the island from side to side with a rain of bullets, volleys that had been withheld before for fear of hitting their own charging horsemen.

The fire was so fierce that the brave Lieutenant Beecher, despite the protection of the sand, was mortally wounded, and others received fresh hurts. But the best of the white riflemen began to pick off the Indians among the bushes, and gradually cleared out this deadly ambush. Then the shots ceased, the smoke lifted, and the battle stopped for a time.

Colonel Forsyth, white from the loss of blood, raised himself feebly on the sand and looked around at his men who now crawled again from the pits. A faint smile of mingled triumph and pity passed over his face. He was victorious so far, but the cost was great. His own dead were too numerous. Not more than six or seven in the whole command were without serious wounds. Heroic as had been the charge, the defence had been more so.

Stillwell and Bob seized the tin cans and began to bring water from the trench that they had made, giving it to the men who were hurt the worst Others, skilled from long experience, began to bind up hurts, while others brought forth fresh ammunition and looked to the rifles and re-volvers, knowing that there would still be full need of them.

Two of the troopers attended to the wounds of Colonel Forsyth, who was now extremely weak. But his intelligence and energy were as great as ever. He could not stand on his feet, but he had them remove him into an easier position, and while they were swathing him in numerous bandages, he was studying the Indian position.

Bob lay on the edge of his sand pit, gasping for breath, and scarcely yet understanding that it was all real. It had been like the passing of a terrible dream. Three or four Cheyenne warriors lay so close to him, shot dead from their horses, that he could have reached out and touched them with his rifle muzzle. Not far beyond were a dozen more, and for a distance of nearly half a mile, coming to the island and leaving it, was a broad trail of slain warriors and horses. Sometimes they were strewn along in single file, and then they lay in groups. Once more Bob paid his silent tribute to Cheyenne valour. As the boy looked he saw the body of Roman Nose. The great chief lay flat upon his back, his dead eyes staring up at the heavens, now blue again as the rifle smoke floated away. The splendid war-bonnet was still on his head, and the heavy repeating rifle lay by his side. He had died as he would have chosen, leading the fiercest charge red men ever made.

"Will they come again?" asked Colonel Forsyth of the oldest scout, Grover.

The veteran shook his head.

"Not that way," he replied. "I never saw its like before, an' I never expect to see it again, but they mean to get us yet."

The women and children, on the bluffs, within plain view of the island, maintained a wailing chant that rose and fell, but never ceased. It was a mingling of sorrow and anger, inexpressibly wild and savage, and it got upon Bob's nerves. He could see the figures upon the bluffs, leaping up and down, and he knew that he and his comrades could expect no more pity from them than from the warriors.

The warriors themselves were not noiseless. They rode around and around the island, but out of range, shaking their fists, brandishing rifles and lances, and uttering savage cries.

"They are telling us what they are going to do with us," said Stillwell, "and the things are so pleasant I won't repeat 'em to you, Bob."

"Let 'em shout," said Bob. "They haven't got us yet."

"That's the talk," said Stillwell. "There, they're drawing off! I guess they're going to have a big talk."

Although the dirge of the women and children still rose and fell, the shouts of the warriors gradually ceased, and they rode in a great body toward the gorge, whence they had issued for the charge. There they remained for a long time consulting, and the band on the island rested, although troubled, now and then, by sharpshooters.

The troopers ate a little food, and attended to the wounds of one another as best they could. They also threw up their banks of sand higher, but they suffered much from the sun, which poured fiery rays directly down upon their unprotected heads. It brought fever into their veins, but they were thankful now, for another reason, that they had been able to reach the island. Besides the defence that it gave them, plenty of good water was at hand for the taking, and they took freely. Bob and Jack bathed their faces, and all the others did likewise.

There was little sound on the island. Martin Burke hummed old Irish songs under his breath, but only the two youths heard him. In one rifle pit the elder Farley lay dying, and by the side of him, his son, hiding a severe wound of his own, held his hand, and listened to his last words. In the pit, with the triple-wounded leader, lay the dying lieutenant and the dying surgeon, one on either side. In every pit men eased their hurts. Upon all beat the pitiless sun, and great black birds began to wheel overhead.

Bob rested himself against the bank of sand, pulled the brim of his cap down over his eyes, shaded as much more of his face as he could with one arm, and remained motionless. Gradually his nerves sank into quiet. His eyelids drooped, although he had no desire to sleep. He merely sank into a strange sort of apathy, lulled now by the wild and weird wailing from the bluffs. Stillwell also did not move, although he continued to watch closely the mass of warriors at the head of the valley.

The sun shone in dazzling rays upon these warriors, showing their war-bonnets, their rifles, and their naked bodies, a savage group, stirred wholly by primitive emotions. A little wind sprang up, and blew away the last of the smoke and vapours that hung in the valley. Then Stillwell turned to Bob.

"I think they're coming again," he said.

The boy said nothing but raised up a little and pushed his rifle forward on the sand. Forsyth saw too, and called to all to be ready. The tremendous shout of the Cheyennes once more clove the air, and the valley thundered, as half a thousand horsemen, again galloped toward the island, the eagle and heron feathers in their war-bonnets trailing out behind them, their fierce brown faces bent forward over their horses.

At the same instant swarms of skirmishers in the bushes and reeds began to fire on the flanks of the island, but the defenders, as before, paid no attention to them. Their fingers burned on the triggers, but they waited until Forsyth should give the word. He cried "Fire!" long before the charge reached the island, and, once more, the hail of metal beat upon the wild horsemen. One volley followed another, so swift and deadly, that at a hundred yards the Cheyennes, lacking now the fire and passion of Roman Nose to lead them, broke and fled, leaving many more of their dead upon the ground.

Towards twilight they made a third attack that was beaten back in the same fashion, and then while the women still wailed, the warriors formed a great camp, in a ring about the island, but beyond the range of those rifles, which had cut down so many of their bravest warriors. Forsyth knew now that a close siege would be maintained and that, unless help came,—of which there seemed to be no chance —all the valour of his men would be as nothing.

Twilight was now at hand. The day was closing upon one of the most remarkable scenes of valour ever witnessed upon the American continent. Both white and red had done as much as man could expect The sun set in a sea of fire, throwing its last rays across the fatal plain. Here and there lay the bodies of fallen warriors. The mournful wailing came from the bluffs again. Then the sun vanished and after it came the grey of early night. A low wind rose and blew sadly.

The defenders came forth from the rifle pits and counted their wounds which were enough to supply two or three to every man, and they bound up their fresh hurts received in the last two attacks. The evening breeze was cool on Bob's forehead, but he walked in an unreal world. It seemed impossible that he could live after all the fire and tumult of the day. The island had been torn by thousands of bullets, and had it not been for the sand pits, not a man would have escaped.

The boy's heart throbbed. The roaring was still in his ears, and the night seemed weird and unearthly. He ate and drank with Stillwell, and then slowly came back to the earth. Trudeau and several of the best sharpshooters kept watch while the others rested, but the Cheyennes maintained their distance for the present. Lights by and by leaped up on the bluffs, but the mournful wailing still came. On the island they were wholly in the grey darkness, which did not hide the defenders from one another, but which rendered them invisible to the Indians on the plains.

The wind by and by rose a little and began to moan. But there was dampness in it as it touched Bob's face, and the fever left his veins. His temples, too, ceased to throb, and the sand no longer burned when his hand lay against it. The grey of the night turned to black, and the Indian fires on the bluffs shone through it like stars. The wind rose yet higher, and the dampness in its touch increased.

A low rumble came from the far southern horizon, inexpressibly solemn after the day's terrible strife. All the men heard it, but none spoke. It is likely that they felt the same awe that was in the breast of Bob. They were now but little more than the grains of sand beneath them, as they lay there on the tiny island in the vast wilderness.

The far rumble came again and was repeated, a little closer and a little louder. Lightning flared on the dim horizon, and the wind moaned without ceasing.

Drops of rain struck the men. They turned their faces upward to meet them, and were grateful for the cool touch. The rumble of the thunder ceased and became a crash. Then the lightning cut with such vivid strokes across the sky that the whole valley swam in its glare, disclosing the island, the shallow river, the grassy plain with the dark bodies of the dead lying thick upon it, and the hills beyond, crowned with the Indian fires. Then the darkness closed in again and the rushing rain came.

None of the white men cared how long the rain fell, but it ceased by and by and the moon and stars sprang out. Then troops of wolves, drawn by a hideous instinct, came down from the hills. But the same instinct would not let them come within range of the rifles, and they stood at a distance, howling in a terrible lupine chorus.

"How are you feeling now, Bob?" asked Stillwell at last.

"Better," sighed the boy. "Things are beginning to look real to me again. If only those wolves and women would stop howling."

"I've come back to earth myself," said Stillwell. "I've had a lot of Indian fighting, and I've been in some hot corners before, but I've never seen anything like this, and I hope never to see anything like it again. I don't understand how any of us ever came out of it alive."

Bob said nothing, but he felt a deep thankfulness. He was presently called with some others by the commander who thanked them for their bravery and tenacity, and encouraged them to endure still more. Forsyth lay against a mass of bandages with one blanket under him and another over him. Bob regarded him with wonder and an admiration that grew always. An ordinary man would have been dead already of his wounds, but Forsyth still lived and still commanded.

Bob volunteered to watch through the night with Trudeau, Stillwell and a half dozen more. He pointed to the fact that he was one of the five or six who had escaped without wounds, and the colonel consented. Then he and Stillwell, now close comrades who seemed to have known one another for years, went back to their sand pits where they talked in low tones as they watched.

The night darkened again, but their eyes became so well used to it that they could see the fallen horses and the plain, and the outline of the bluffs beyond. There the fires burned all through the night, and the mournful wailing did not cease until late.

After midnight some of the Cheyenne skirmishers crept along the plain and fired a few shots, but they flew wild, and the sentinels did not think it worth while to reply. Most of the others slept so heavily that the reports did not awaken them.

The two, wrapped in their blankets because the night was chill, ceased to whisper by and by, and sat almost motionless in the sand pits. The wind rose a little and came with a wailing sound up the bed of the river and among the reeds. But on the island scarcely anything stirred. Deep exhaustion reigned there. The cold moon looked down on an island which might well have been taken for an island of the dead. Colonel Forsyth, wrapped in his blankets, sank into a stupor, but he roused himself from it at dawn which came on crisp and cloudless, showing the Indians still in a circle about the island, but out of rifle range. The siege had begun.

Forsyth made preparations for a long and desperate defence. A circular breastwork of sand was thrown up entirely around this little camp. In the centre they dug a well, an easier task than it would seem as the cool waters rose in the sand when they had gone down a few feet. They also cut strips from the slain horses, not knowing to what straits they might arrive for food.

Their tasks occupied the whole morning, and the Cheyennes made no demonstration save an occasional distant rifle shot or a defiant whoop from a warrior well out of range. These things were the merest trifles to them now. The afternoon passed in the same way, the second night came, and then it was Bob's turn to sleep. His nerves were so well rested that he did not awake once during the night. While he slept the Cheyennes crept up and carried off most of their slain, including Roman Nose and the medicine man. The soldiers heard them, but did not seek to interfere.

The second day came and the horse meat could not longer be eaten. Other food was too scarce to withstand a long siege, and unless help was brought it became evident that sooner or later they must fall into the hands of the Cheyennes. Valour could avail nothing against starvation. But the dauntless soul of Forsyth, suffering from his terrible triple wounds, still would not despair.

"Somebody must get through tonight," he said, "and go to Fort Wallace for help. It is a desperate chance. Who will take it!"

"I! I! I!" shouted half a score, Bob among them. But Forsyth chose the two scouts, old Pete Trudeau and young Jack Stillwell.

"You have had the most experience outside of Grover whom I must keep with me," he said, "and you are the most likely to succeed. When do you think will be the best time to creep out, Pete?"

"Tonight along about midnight," replied the scout. "I think it is going to be dark. What do you say, Jack?"

"You're right," replied Stillwell. "If we can't get through then we never will, but we're going to get through."

They made their preparations in the afternoon, merely an increase of cartridges, a little more food in their wallets, and they were ready. Then the night came, cloudy and dark as Trudeau had predicted. All accepted it as a good omen. But the two men waited until midnight when, hearing no noise from the Cheyennes, they decided to start. Stillwell had selected what seemed to be the most dangerous plan. He intended to cross the river and go directly towards the bluffs where the main Indian encampment lay. It was his theory, and Colonel Forsyth approved of it, that the Indians would be less vigilant on that side. He and Trudeau would cross the plain, crawling on their stomachs, and then pass over the bluffs by the side of the Indian encampment.

It was Bob's night on the watch, and he was one of those who saw the daring scouts leave. His heart was filled with admiration for both, and he gave a strong farewell clasp to the hand of his good friend, Jack.

"We'll be back, Bob, and we'll bring the troopers with us," said Stillwell, confidently. "You can look for us."

He and Trudeau dropped silently over the earthworks and crawled along the sand. Bob followed their dark figures for a little distance as they crept on the edge of the island, and then he lost them in the further darkness. Listening intently he heard a faint splash or two in the water, but he neither saw nor heard anything more.

The boy was now beside the colonel, and the two waited a long time, dreading to hear the sound of shots or of exultant yells, telling that the two scouts were slain or taken. The minutes dragged, a slow chain.

"They are across the river now," whispered the colonel. "When I close my eyes I can see them lying almost flat, crawling across the plain."

Bob said nothing, but he never took his eyes off the campfires, shining through the darkness, which showed where the bluffs stood. Trudeau and Stillwell were going straight towards those lights.

"They must be at least three hundred yards away now," whispered the colonel. "Do you hear anything, Bob?"

"Not a thing, sir," replied Bob, "except those coyotes howling away off there to the north."

"Brave lads! Brave lads!" muttered the colonel. "They must have gone a quarter of a mile now. What do you think, Bob?"

"I should think so, sir," replied the boy.

"You are sure you don't hear anything—any sound of a struggle?"

"Nothing at all, sir, but if I have your consent I will creep a little way along the sand and listen."

"Do it."

Bob stepped over the earthworks, and then lying almost flat upon his face pushed himself along until he reached the river. There he lay with his ear to the sand, but heard nothing save the faint ripple of the water. He could now see objects on the opposite shore more distinctly. Presently his eyes made out the figure of a dead horse, and then that of a warrior huddled up, lying as he had fallen.

While he stared, trying to read in the darkness the whole story of the plain, he saw two moving shadows. Gazing at them long and intently, he saw that the shadows were men, and for the first time he felt despair. Trudeau and Stillwell, finding the way closed, were creeping back, and no help could ever come.

The figures advanced, and as they came closer they were outlined more clearly against the bank. Then the war-bonnets and naked shoulders showed that they were not the two scouts, but Cheyenne warriors creeping forward. Bob crouched closer and slipped his rifle in his hands until a finger rested on the trigger. Then he marked an imaginary spot. If they reached it he would fire.

The two warriors veered a little, and Bob let his rifle drop upon the sand again. He would not fire. The Cheyennes were now beside the dead warrior, lying in his cramped-up position. They suddenly straightened up, and when they did so they bore the body between them. Running swiftly, they carried it off for burial or the funeral pyre.

Bob waited a little longer, and still seeing and hearing nothing returned to the earthworks.

"The plain is quiet, sir," he said to Colonel Forsyth. "I can't detect a sign of a disturbance anywhere."

"It is good," said this man who could move but little, but who could command well. "I should judge that they are at least a half mile away. Watch those lights."

They watched them. A half hour—an hour passed, then a second hour and then a third. All the time the lights burned steadily and did not shift. It was after three o'clock in the morning when Colonel Forsyth moved slightly on his blanket.

"Now I can go to sleep," he said. "Trudeau and Stillwell are through, and we shall be saved."

CHAPTER 19

The Amazing Flight

While Colonel Forsyth and Bob watched and listened long at the bank of sand, Jack Stillwell and Pete Trudeau were creeping forward on a task so thickly bestrewed with dangers that the chance of ever achieving it seemed but slight. They had left the island, they had crossed the river, lying in its wide bed, and were now advancing toward the very bluffs on which the Indian camp lay.

The leader in this daring venture was the boy, Jack Stillwell. He was superior in intelligence to his older comrade, Pete Trudeau, and Colonel Forsyth recognizing it, had given him the instructions, and had told him that he must make Trudeau follow his judgment. But Trudeau himself willingly took second place, and followed the brave and handsome youth who was destined in later days to become a judge and man of large affairs in Oklahoma.

The two, after emerging from the sand bed of the river, lay for a few minutes flat upon the plain, their rifles close by their sides, listening intently and looking for enemies with eyes trained by the wild life of the border. They heard low sounds and then a pattering of light feet.

"That's coyotes, isn't it, Pete!" said Jack in the lowest of whispers.

"Coyotes and the big timber wolves, too," replied Trudeau in the same tone. "They've plenty of excuse for coming down here, Jack."

"That's so," said Stillwell, "but we don't mind them, Pete. They won't bother us. You just watch out for Cheyennes. Look, there are two now!"

About fifty yards ahead two dim figures walked noiselessly along the plain. The scouts faintly saw the outlines of their war-bonnets, but they would have known anyhow that they were Cheyennes. Neither Trudeau nor Stillwell moved now. They lay flat and extended upon the plain, and the keenest eyes, even at close range, might have missed the slightly darker blurs on the dark earth.

The Cheyennes saw nothing and passed on. The wolves howled again. The two scouts, the young and the old, rose to their hands and knees and resumed their slow, creeping advance. They could not see any Cheyenne figures now, but they knew that many alert sentinels watched the plain. They knew, too, that it was as much as their lives were worth to stand upright in the manner of men, and they hugged the earth like crawling wolves fearing fiercer beasts of prey.

A hundred yards from the river and they stopped again, lying as before flat upon the prairie for the sake of rest as well as to spy out the ground once more with eye and ear.

Jack, raising a little on one shoulder, looked back toward the island. It and everything on it were lost in the darkness, save the faint outline of the lone young cottonwood at its foot. Forsyth and his gallant band had disappeared as completely as if they had never been. Jack Stillwell passed his hands before his eyes as if he would sweep away a mist or veil. Used as he was to the wilderness, he was oppressed by its ominous loneliness, and their own position on a narrow strip, between life and death. But he could shut his eyes and see the faces of his comrades, especially that of the gallant youth, Bob Norton, who had become such a good comrade of his. He and Trudeau must get through! They must save the heroic little band that had made such a tremendous fight against more than twenty to one.

Jack turned his eyes away from the island and toward the bluffs, where lights burned and where even after the third day the wailing of the women for their dead still arose. It was a singular weird chant, and it contained a threat as well as grief. It got upon the nerves of the older man.

"Jack," whispered Trudeau, "don't you think we'd better turn back and try to escape up or down the bed of the river!"

"No," replied Jack. "They'll be keeping a double watch there, and we could never get by. If we make it, Pete, and we're going to make it, we must take a road they won't expect us to choose."

He resumed the slow crawling on hands and knees, and Trudeau, obeying the superior will, followed. Jack led straight toward the lights and now, both to right and left, they saw the figures of Cheyennes passing. Never did men need a dark night more, and fortunately the early promise held good. There was a little moon, but heavy clouds were continually floating before it, and the whole surface of the plain was in deep obscurity. They hoped that as long as they lay so close to the earth they might pass. Both were in great fear lest Indian dogs should scent them and betray their presence, but this danger did not yet develop itself. The two heard the stamp of the Indian ponies, and an occasional neigh, and they saw squaws bringing fuel for the fires, and the dark outlines of skin *tepees* that the Indians had pitched on the bluffs. Then they rested once more and tried to pick out the place for their passage.

Jack noticed at last a dark spot in the bluffs, and he was convinced that a dip or depression between the hills lay there. The fires burned both to right and left, and he could account for the hiatus on no other ground. He felt sure that it was the road by which they must pass, and he touched Trudeau's arm lightly.

"Don't you think that's our path, Pete?" he said, pointing to the dark space.

"If we are to find any, that's it," Trudeau whispered in reply.

Both now remained flat and still, longer than usual. Their knees and elbows were sore from so much creeping, and since they were upon the Indian camp they must choose the way well. If the chance failed there would be no other.

"Now, Pete," Jack whispered at length, "well make the try."

They scarcely crawled; they lay almost flat on the ground, dragging themselves forward by a series of muscular contortions like a snake, and making no noise. They heard voices, the crackling of dry wood in the fires, and the death chant of the squaws.

There was a sudden growl, and an Indian cur, shooting out of the darkness, leaped like a wolf straight at Jack. But Trudeau, reaching straight up, grasped the dog by the throat and compressed it between two powerful brown hands. Another growl had arisen into the cur's mouth, but it died behind his teeth, and then the fierce human grip permitted no more to come.

A warrior heard the growl and stopped, but not hearing it a second time, walked on. A cur snapping at a bone and yelping at another cur was common in an Indian camp, and the warrior, dismissing the incident from his mind, looked with vengeful glance toward the island where the white foe lay hidden in the sand. He did not know that the greatest of all opportunities was almost within reach of his hand.

Jack saw the warrior, and his fingers slipped forward to the trigger of his rifle. But he made no movement, and his glance turned back to Trudeau and the dog. Pete lay flat upon his side, and his great brown fingers were sunk deep in the hairy throat. The powerful muscles in his arms rose under his sleeves as he poured all his strength into them. The dog kicked, tore at the earth with his hind paws, shuddered and then was still. Trudeau loosed his grip and laid him upon the ground. The dog was quite dead.

"You did that in great style, Pete," whispered Jack, "and it saved us. Come on."

They were a long time in making the short distance that separated them from the dark space between the bluffs, and both rejoiced when they saw that their guess was correct. The bluff dipped down there, making a sort of sunken ridge, covered with short bushes and too rough for a camp.

Although low fires burned on either side not many yards away, they believed that they could pass through the depression. At least they must try. Stillwell still led, and they entered the little pass, moving scarcely more than a yard a minute. When they reached the shelter of the bushes they paused at least five minutes. From where they lay they saw the fires quite well, and the Indians sitting ox standing beside them. They even heard words, some of which they understood. The warriors were speaking of their losses, and of their confidence that they would yet secure the foe whom they encircled. Savage and implacable, they had no thought of giving up.

Stillwell slowly led the way again. The bushes were at once a help and a danger. They covered their bodies, but a rustling among them might draw the Indian's gaze. Now the two scouts exercised every precaution known to the most skilful of borderers. Neither put down hand or foot until he saw that it would rest in a place that gave forth no noise. It was painfully slow, it was hard to be so patient, with warriors all about them not twenty yards away, but they held their nerves under control, and never sought to increase speed. They even dared to rest more than once, lying still for five minutes at a time, and from the cover of the bushes, surveying the Indian camp about them. It was a full hour before they traversed the length of the little ravine between the bluffs. Then they found themselves on the far side of the Indian camp, and outside the circle. But they did not stop until they had gone several hundred yards beyond the lights, where they lay among some bushes and held a brief and whispered conference.

"I think we'd better get out now and make a break for it," said Trudeau. "Let's trust to our speed."

"Don't think of it," Jack replied, earnestly. "The main camp's behind us I know, but the country for miles is bound to be swarming with their scouts and skirmishers, and we've got to be all the more careful now because it won't be long till dawn."

Trudeau, as usual, gave up to his younger comrade, and they continued to crawl on hands and knees, soon finding that their action was fully justified, as Cheyennes, both on foot and horseback, passed them, and they saw one fire in a little grove where several Indians slept and two others watched.

The country here, luckily for them, had a considerable growth of bushes, and as long as they remained on hands and knees they were not likely to be seen, unless the enemy came very close. But the crawling was horribly monotonous, and was growing quite painful. Their knees were bruised, and every joint was stiff and sore. They were compelled to take a long rest among some willows, and there they ate scraps of food that they carried in their haversacks.

While they ate they saw the east lighten, and the aspens and willows began to whiten and quiver. Then, as the world turned slowly, the great sun swung into view, the white lights turned to red, and the wild plains were suffused with its glow. In six hours of crawling they had come three miles, and the day showed more clearly than ever that they still had need of the utmost caution. A half dozen bands of Indians were in sight, and the smoke of campfires rose straight in front of them.

"It's crawling again for us," said Stillwell.

"It looks like it," said Pete, ruefully. "I guess, Jack, that if we ever get through with this it'll be hard for us to rise up and walk like men."

"That isn't our worst trouble," said Jack. "Practice will bring it back. Come on, Pete, and we'll see which of us is the better crawler."

The grim competition lasted all the morning. Again and again the temptation to stand up and walk like men was almost overpowering, indeed it would have been overpowering for Trudeau, but Stillwell resisted for both. Twice he pulled the older man down and encouraged him continually, justifying the confidence that Forsyth had put in him, despite his youth. Throughout the long, terrible hours they were never out of sight of Indians. They saw them on foot and on horseback, in little parties and alone, and at intervals they heard the distant sound of rifle-shots coming from the island through the thin, clear air.

The Indians were so numerous, even beyond the bluffs, that it seemed now as if they could never pass. Trudeau spoke despondently, but Stillwell, despite the sinking of his heart, would not let a word of discouragement escape him.

"We've just got to do it! We've just got to do it, Pete!" he said with energy.

The sun was brilliant and intensely clear, making all objects conspicuous, and they could not relax caution for a moment. Their soreness and stiffness increased. Their knees now were cut and bleeding, and their backs ached. The sun, too, beat down upon them. In the afternoon they came to the divide that separates the Arickaree from the Republican River, and here Stillwell saw a wash-out around which sunflowers and tall grass clustered thickly, forming a dense screen. He was so tired that he could scarcely move, and he saw that Trudeau was almost in a state of collapse.

"Pete," he said, "let's creep in here and rest the remainder of the day."

"I don't have to be asked twice," said Trudeau.

They slipped in through the grass and sunflowers, rearranging the latter behind them so carefully that no sign of a trail would be shown, and then lay down panting, but thankful, in the little sandy washout.

It was a close, snug place, and they remained in it all the afternoon, hearing at intervals rifle shots about the island, and now and then when they peeped through the tall grass, seeing Indians riding about the prairie.

Stillwell grew very anxious. He knew that time was precious as diamonds, but he did not dare to move from the wash-out until night had fully come. Both he and Trudeau awaited eagerly the advance of the twilight, and then the heavier darkness of the night. Before the moon could come up they slipped from the protection of the grass and sunflowers, and started erect like men.

"I can walk again, Jack," whispered Trudeau, "and I'm a man, not a monkey."

The youth laughed softly in the darkness.

"It does feel good to stand on one's own feet," he whispered back. "Come on now, Pete. We've got to make the most of the night-time. I hope it will stay dark as it did last night."

His hopes were fulfilled. When the moon came out it was veiled in vapours and shed but little light although enough for them to see the way, which led through bushes and now and then across a ravine. It was also sufficient to disclose to their watchful eyes numerous Indian trails, and they knew that the time had not yet come when they could relax their caution a particle.

Before midnight clouds began to gather and the moon was hidden. A wind, damp to the touch, blew with a sad, sighing sound out of the southwest. Low thunder rolled, and now and then the lightning flared across the prairie.

"I hope we won't have any storm," said Stillwell "It would hold us back."

"There won't be much rain," said Trudeau, weather-wise with the experience of many years.

The wind presently blew a little harder, and a slant of rain came, but it soon ceased. Then the low thunder rolled again, and the lightning flared fitfully, but neither lasted long, and the two scouts, messengers now, went on as swiftly as they could. They were going toward the south, and about an hour after the rain passed the two, by the same impulse and at the same moment, sank softly down among the bushes where they lay flat against the earth.

A war party of Cheyennes, at least fifty in number and mounted, was passing. There was enough light now to disclose their painted faces, their war-bonnets, and their naked bodies. They rode in single file, and not one spoke. The unshod hoofs of their ponies made a low measured beat as they passed.

"They're going to the island to take part in the siege," whispered Jack. "Bob and all those fellows will surely need help as soon as we can bring it."

Two hours later they passed another Indian band of about the same size, and again they lay hidden among the bushes while it passed.

Dawn came a second time, and to their alarm they found that they were on the outskirts of a great Indian village, probably the one which furnished the warriors who were attacking Forsyth. They had come so close to it in the darkness that they could not retreat in the day. They saw many lodges, and warriors, women and children were everywhere.

Jack and Trudeau thought themselves lost, but the eyes of the boy, always extremely quick, alighted upon a small swamp, that is, a patch of tall grass growing out of water.

"Come, Pete," he exclaimed, "we've got to hide in there. It's great luck that we haven't been seen already."

They slipped into the swamp and went to its very centre where they sat down to their waists in the grass and water. Here they could not be seen from the edge of the swamp, but they could hear the many noises of the village, the squaws talking, the barking of dogs, the whistling of boys to the ponies, and even the tread of warriors passing the little marsh. About ten o'clock a party of mounted Indians stopped and watered their horses at its edge. The two hidden scouts could hear the horses as they swallowed.

Jack and Trudeau scarcely breathed until the horses finished drinking and the men rode on. Then they looked at each other, two strange creatures with their heads and shoulders projecting above the water, but hidden in the grass.

"Do you think we'll ever get through, Jack? Do you think we'll ever get through!" asked Trudeau, something weak and plaintive appearing in his voice.

"Of course we will," replied Jack, showing a confidence that he scarcely felt. "Think what a fine rest we can get, Pete, while we're here with nothing to do but sit in the water."

The day was warm, but they were so long in the water that they began to grow cold. Jack felt the chill creeping up his body, but he did not dare move. The slightest noise might attract the dogs, and Pete could not choke them all to death before they gave the alarm. At noon they ate scraps of food again, and then they waited for the long afternoon to pass.

The chill and the tension became so great that they were forced at last to take the chances and move a little. They even dared to straighten up in the grass and stand erect for a minute or two. When they sank down again they felt much better.

Their third night came, and cold and stiff they crept out of the swamp. It was some time before they could stand erect with ease, and men less resolute than they would have given up. It was now a pain to exert the mind as well as the body, but they rubbed their wrists and legs until the circulation was restored, and then, haggard and wan, their wet clothing streaked with mud and their eyes red from watching and loss of sleep, they took up once more their flight toward help.

They passed around the village without being seen, and with a new strength that came from hope, fled onward at a pace that would not have seemed possible in men who had endured so much. They were not able to travel the entire night, as the strength of both, particularly Trudeau's, began to wane again. Feeling that they must take the chances, both lay down after midnight, and at once sank into a deep slumber.

Jack was the first to awake, and it was dawn. He sprang to his feet, but saw nothing alarming, and then he awakened Trudeau. Before them lay open plains, and as they believed that they had now left the Indians behind, they resolved to travel by day. Time, be it repeated, was more precious than diamonds, and the lives of their friends might turn on a single hour. They agreed to risk it, and set off at a good pace across the plain.

The sun rose, flooding the land with the usual sharp, clear light. They had been walking more than an hour, and just as they were about to top a swell Jack seized Trudeau and pulled him down in the grass, falling himself at the same time by his side. A party of at least a dozen warriors were coming straight toward them, but had not yet seen them. Yet, it seemed that they were now surely lost

But Jack Stillwell was one who never gave up hope. A few yards to the right he saw a patch of weeds, and he and Trudeau at once crept into it. Then they made a discovery. In the centre of this patch lay the skeleton of a big buffalo, long since dead, but with some of the skin hanging upon it, and all the bones intact and upright. Men in desperate case often do desperate things, and do them quickly. Jack Stillwell and Pete Trudeau at once crawled inside the ribs of the buffalo, and lay, side by side, in that extraordinary hiding-place. They did not dare move, but they peeped between the ribs and pieces of skin, and saw the Indian party go on. They rejoiced, but too soon. Other Indians, mounted and apparently scouts, appeared. This seemed to be a post for sentinels, and they were constantly coming and going. The singular hiding place of Jack and Trudeau became an equally singular trap, and there they lay.

The Indians often came as near as twenty yards. One came within fifteen yards and sat there on his horse a full hour, examining the country in all directions. He was a fine warrior, entirely naked save for moccasins and war-bonnet, and he carried a magnificent lance. While the Indian's side was turned toward the buffalo, Trudeau softly pressed Jack's shoulder with his hand.

"What is it, Pete?" whispered Jack.

"Somethin' else is in here with us."

Jack listened and heard a faint, soft sound that made the blood grow cold in every vein. A rattlesnake, before them, had taken up its abode in the skeleton of the buffalo. They did not know why it had remained quiescent so long, but now it was moving.

It is probable that no men have ever been in a more terrible position, one so dangerous, and at the same time so full of horror. They could see but little, a chance blow would not do, and the slightest noise would attract the attention of the Indian warrior.

They lay still for a while—how long they could not tell—in a sort of paralysis, and then it was Trudeau, the weaker of the two, who saved them. The lives of many people may turn upon absurd things, and now the fortune of a campaign was to be decided by a chew of tobacco. It would be doubly ridiculous, if it were not true.

Trudeau was of the old type, and he always carried tobacco with him. Now he had a quid in his mouth, and he was chewing vigorously for consolation and strength. Lying upon his side and one shoulder, he faintly saw the snake near his feet, coiling, and raising his head to strike. Perhaps it was impulse, an inspiration of the moment, but old Pete Trudeau spat a stream of bitter brown tobacco juice straight at the venomous head. It struck full and true. Blinded and dazed the rattlesnake uncoiled and slid swiftly out of the skeleton.

Pete lay back exhausted, and Jack, himself, was dizzy with the relapse after such tension. The Indian, on his horse, never moved. Trudeau, by and by, raised up a little and began to talk to himself. Jack tried to quiet him, and presently he understood what had happened. Trudeau's mind had become affected for the time, by one tremendous ordeal after another. He was tired now, he said, of crawling and hiding. He wanted to fight, and he meant to fight. He would not stay where he was forever, even if all the Indians that ever lived were out there. Rage steadily rose and grew in his breast, and he meant to take vengeance.

This was the most terrible moment of all for Jack. In the lowest of voices he tried to soothe Trudeau and make him see reason. It was a sort of mental struggle between them while the Indians rode outside, but the valiant youth conquered. Under his soothing words the rage of Trudeau began to abate. He ceased by and by to mutter, and lay still for a long time.

They did not move until dark. Then they came forth, a sorry sight, but still uncaptured, and still zealous for their mission. They found a pool of cool water near, and when Trudeau drank from it and bathed his face, his mind regained its balance.

They travelled all night without meeting any more Indian parties, and with their experience of the day before fresh in their minds, they meant to hide the next day, but a pale, yellowish sun rose in a fog, so dense that one could see but a little distance. The sun did not dispel the fog, and they pressed on through it. About an hour before noon, they saw through the haze, two mounted figures near them on the prairie. The eyes of Jack Stillwell, yet strong and alert, recognized the uniforms of the United States Army.

"Soldiers!" he cried.

Then he and Trudeau rushed forward.

CHAPTER 20

A Light in the Dark

The morning of the third day came, and although little was said in the island camp, the spirits of the men were better. All felt sure that Trudeau and Stillwell had got through the Indian lines, and that some time or other, help would arrive. It was now their task to hold out as long as food and life lasted'Another reduction was made in the rations, and they found it necessary to bury the bodies of the horses in the sand.

Bob, that afternoon, fell into a fever caused by the excitement and the great strain. For a little while he was unconscious, and he babbled of Sam Strong and his old comrades, of trapping beaver, and of shooting down a great river between cliffs a mile high. In the cool of the night he revived, and was much ashamed of himself, but the others laughed at his apologies. Almost everyone in his turn, suffered from some sort of delirium or other, but they were so hardy that nearly all of them began to recover fast, although their wounds were sufficient to kill ordinary men. Colonel Forsyth was one of the worst hurt of them all, but his courage never flinched for a moment. In fact, he cut the bullet from his thigh himself with his own razor which was in his haversack, and with its removal, began to improve fast.

That night they sent out two more messengers— Donovan and Pliley—for help, in case the first two should fail, and Forsyth dispatched by them a letter to the commanding officer at Fort Wallace, written with a pencil on a leaf from his memorandum book. He gave details of the battle and said that he could hold out six days longer. Donovan and Pliley slipped away in the darkness and the rest settled back to waiting again.

The Cheyennes maintained a continual stalking of the island. Their sharpshooters, by night and by day, crept forward and sent bullets at the breastworks. The men were compelled to be very watchful, but they did not often fire in return, reserving their strength and ammunition for another charge, if one should be made. But as the time passed and the Indians did nothing but skirmish, Colonel Forsyth became convinced that a grand attack would not be made again.

"They think starvation will do the work," he said, "and it would if our messengers had not slipped through their lines."

He did not waver in his belief that the scouts had succeeded and Bob shared his faith. If they had been taken it would have been the Indian nature to have exulted over it and to have shown some sign, but none came from the bluffs. The lights still shone there at night and often by day they could see the Indians moving about on the plain out of rifle range, but nothing occurred to indicate any change in the siege.

The fourth day, the fifth and the sixth passed with the same constant sniping of the skirmishers and the same incessant watchfulness on the island. It was so tense a life, so singular in all its aspects, that Bob fell again into a state of unreality. It seemed to him that he had been there forever. His range was limited to a circle of sand ten yards across. The people with whom he lived, and the only ones whom he knew, were a few men. brown as leather, carrying many gun-shot wounds in tight bandages. Their sentences were few and short Conversation was as restricted as their home on the island.

The spell was deepest at night. Then he would sit long with his rifle across his knees and look at the river. It was a shallow stream at low water, not more than a foot deep now, but it hemmed them in like an ocean. No one sought to pass beyond it Under the moonlight it took on aspects of death which it had not. Then its surface was dark, breaking into little crinkly waves here and there, and his attentive ear magnified the sighing of the wind among the reeds into a gale. Then he would grow lonesome, longing for Stillwell, and above all for Sam Strong and his old comrades.

The Cheyennes, despite all their losses, seemed to regard the troopers as their sure prey. Sometimes they came out on the plain and derided the defenders. One morning, a large and very fat Cheyenne appeared beyond what seemed to be safe rifle range, and began to make derisive gestures. He was entirely naked, and his actions continued so long that the troopers, whose nerves were not in a good state, began to grow angry. They did not wish to be ridiculed by an unclothed savage.

Colonel Forsyth shared in the annoyance. After carefully surveying the distance, he called the best three shots in the band and gave to them three rifles which would carry about four hundred yards further than the others. These rifles had sights for 1200 yards, but he directed them to aim well over the sights at the dancing Cheyenne and fire together, at his signal. It was a long chance, and Bob watched eagerly for the result.

"Fire!" shouted Forsyth.

The three rifles cracked together. The fat savage leaped into the air, fell upon his face and lay there stone dead. But no one of the three marksmen ever knew which slew him. After that the Cheyennes kept further away and taunted less.

The seventh day passed and the rations were reduced in size again. Men spoke less than ever. They were lean and wasted with hunger and disease, wounds and watching. But there was still no thought of surrender. The little island was yet ready to spout fire at any moment, should the Cheyennes rush forward to attack, and knowing it, they refrained. The long list of great warriors, Roman Nose at their head, gone to the happy hunting grounds, told them too well that waiting was their only road to success. Yet the snipers never ceased to worry the island, by day and by night.

The eighth day was at hand and Bob felt that unless help came soon it would come in vain. He was reduced greatly in weight, and his strength was declining, but all the others were in the same condition. The food, with the utmost possible saving, could not last more than two or three days longer, and that would be the end.

The eighth day passed, and Bob sat much of that night with Colonel Forsyth, who trusted him and treated him like a young cadet. He did not seek to hide from the boy the full gravity of their situation.

"Trudeau and Stillwell will make for Fort Wallace, which is about a hundred miles from here," he said. "It would not take them so long to do that distance, even on foot, but as the country is swarming with Indians they will have to travel by night I think we can expect the troops in three more days."

Bob was not so sure now. When he thought over the immense difficulties, it scarcely seemed possible that the two scouts could get to Fort Wallace. But he said nothing and he had grown so used to danger and death that his feelings were blunted. His decreasing confidence did not make his heart throb any faster. Then the colonel himself fell into silence. He lay upon a blanket with a little heaped-up sand for a pillow, as he was not yet able to stand. His figure was wasted almost to a skeleton, and his face was as white as death. His head was swathed in wrapping after wrapping, and his legs, lying useless, were also clothed in bandages. But his eyes, deep and fiery, shone out from the white and sunken face. Bob looked at him with admiration, wonder and affection. He had not believed that any man could endure so much, and yet, shot to pieces, he still lived and led.

The colonel by and by fell asleep, and a soldier, himself wounded, softly spread a blanket over him. Bob rose, walked over the noiseless sand, and softly dropped outside the earthwork. There he lay down on the sand, and looked up at the moon and the great stars dancing in the blue. It was a silent and peaceful moment. The Indian snipers were at rest, for the time, and as the boy lay there, the spirit of hope crept once more into his mind. It could not be that they, who had endured so much, that they who had done deeds, seemingly impossible to mortal man, should fail and die obscurely on that little island of sand in the western wilderness.

After a while, he crept to the edge of the river. It did not now look dark and menacing, but flowed slowly, with the faintest of soft, singing sounds. The bubbles that broke on its surface were tinted silver in the moonlight. He looked toward the bluffs where the light from the Indian camp had never gone out, and then his eyes passed on to another point on the horizon, hitherto always dark. But it was not dark now. A light like that of a torch twinkled there for a few moments, and then went out. It reappeared again presently, but for not more than a minute. In a quarter of an hour it showed for a third time and then no more, although he watched a long while.

Bob did not know what the brief and fitful light meant, but he accepted it as a good omen, and when he crept back inside the earthwork, hope was stronger within him than it had been at any time since the first day. He slept well and saw the dawn of the ninth day, brilliant with sunshine, and cool with the touch of early autumn. Then the morning moved on, with the usual slow procession of hours, and the fitful shots of the snipers.

Bob sat at the earthwork, gazing at the bluffs and the far circle of the horizon. He was very still. He had learned in the last few days the Indian virtues of patience and of rest, when work was not needed. He was so much at ease that he let his eyelids droop, and soon a soft, sweet sound came to his ears. The wind among the reeds! No, it was not that, because no wind was blowing, and the sound came from another quarter.

He shut his eyes again, because he had an impression that he could hear better with them shut, and the soft, penetrating note came again. He knew it now. It was the far call of a bugle and he sat up as suddenly as if an electric shock had shot through him. He opened his eyes and looked off toward the point where he had seen the fitful light of the night before. Something was moving on the brown slopes, indistinct figures that came forward in the sunlight, until they looked like horses and men.

Others saw, at the same time, and a deep cheer came from all left of the fifty. The troops, in strong force, were advancing. Already they were marching upon the plain, and the Cheyennes, breaking up their camp with great speed, were preparing to retreat.

After his share in the great cheer Bob became dizzy. The relief coming after that long and tremendous strain was so great that the earth reeled. He steadied himself against a mound of sand, and as his eyes cleared, looked again at the glorious sight, the troopers galloping across the plain toward the island, waving their hats and shouting now, and the Indians sullenly withdrawing.

Then came an extraordinary spectacle. Living skeletons crawled out from the holes in the sand. Bandaged heads, arms and shoulders showed over the earthwork. All were pale or white of face, ghastly and sunken, from which looked eyes preternaturally enlarged. The graves had literally given up their dead.

The rescuers, with a shout, galloped through the stream and then stopped, gazing in amazement at the few gaunt figures that had so long held off the Cheyenne nation. But Jack Stillwell threw himself from his horse, rushed forward and grasped Bob by the hand.

"We've come, Bob, my boy! We've come!" he cried. "This is the command of Colonel Carpenter that we found at Lake Slater, and you're saved!"

The troopers were off their horses now, bringing both food and medicines, and hearing the wonderful tale of Forsyth's great defence. While their horses drank from the stream they looked curiously at the little island fortress, the burrows in the sand, the shallow well, and all the desperate shifts and expedients to which the defenders had resorted.

For the first time in nine days Forsyth's men walked freely about the plain. Some scattering shots had been fired by skirmishers as the relief came up, but the Cheyennes seemed to have enough, and now, with their women and children, were far away, waiting to fight again at some other time and place. Over the good food that the troopers brought, Jack told Bob of the thrilling passage of Trudeau and himself through the Cheyenne lines.

Bob listened breathlessly to the extraordinary narrative, one of the most remarkable in the history of the plains. He followed all their adventures as they crawled night and day, as they hid in the washout, in the marsh, and at last in the skeleton of the buffalo, and he uttered a laugh, half of relief, half of amusement, when Trudeau once more put to flight the terrible rattlesnake with a stream of tobacco juice.

"The two mounted soldiers we met," concluded Stillwell, "were carrying despatches from Colonel Carpenter's command, which was then at Lake Slater, only fifty miles from our sand island in the Arickaree. That was tall luck, as I don't think we could ever have got to Fort Wallace in time. The two soldiers galloped to Colonel Carpenter, he came as fast as he could, and here we are."

Such was the extraordinary and truthful story of the rescue, and it kept Bob's eyes sparkling with excitement and amazement. The wonderful defence of the island had been crowned by an equally wonderful escape of the two men through the Indian lines in search of rescue, and young Stillwell did not seem to be much the worse for his extraordinary adventures. Donovan and Pliley also, had made their way through the lines, and they returned later.

Bob revived rapidly. His youth, great strength and elasticity served him well. In a day or two he was as well as ever in all respects. On the second day he and Stillwell rode on borrowed horses to examine the country in a wide circle about the island. The Cheyennes had disappeared completely, evidently in search of easier victims elsewhere, and they had no fear of ambush or other attack.

As they rode they came to a small valley, not far from the field of battle, and the eye of Bob was attracted by an object among some small trees. They hastened forward to investigate, and they saw a wigwam, constructed with great care from freshly tanned buffalo skins of the finest quality. The two dismounted, opened the door of the *tepee*, and then they started, awed by what they beheld.

In the centre of the *tepee* on a heap of brush lay the body of a magnificent savage, the body of a man six feet three inches high, with mighty shoulders and chest, and the features of a great Roman in bronze. The body was wrapped in buffalo robes, and by the side of it lay a beautiful repeating rifle, revolver, tomahawk and knife.

Bob, in the faint light, looked down upon the features of the great chief, Roman Nose, whom he knew so well, and his feeling of awe was succeeded by one of respect and admiration. The Cheyenne had fallen fighting for his people and their hunting grounds, and he had fallen like a hero, leading the warriors to the charge.

"We'll leave him here, Jack, just as he is," he said to Stillwell.

"We'll fasten the door tight so the wolves can't get at him," said Stillwell. "The Indians have embalmed him in their own way and the body will rest here."

They made the lodge secure, and then reported what they had found. Others went to see it, but the body of the great Roman Nose was not disturbed, being left in all honour as the Cheyennes themselves had placed it.

The little army was now ready to move again and Bob was confronted by an important problem. Sam Strong and his comrades had never left his mind, and he must find them. But it was the most difficult of all things to do in the vast expanse of the west Diligent inquiry among the soldiers indicated that no party of trappers had passed to the eastward along any of the known lines of travel. Cheyennes, Sioux and Arapahos were so thick everywhere that in all probability they were still hiding in the hills awaiting a chance.

"You can't go alone hunting them, Bob," said Stillwell. "Why, if your scalp were nailed down and riveted with copper it wouldn't stay on your head more than forty-eight hours. From north to south thirty or forty thousand warriors are wandering about, eager to snap up any stray white."

"I'm afraid you're right," said Bob. "It's hard to decide what to do."

"Why don't you enlist with Custer? This war is going to be pushed, and he's the man who will push it. With him you'll have more chance to find your friends, because they'll naturally make for a strong force of soldiers as soon as they hear that it's near."

The suggestion appealed to Bob, and he decided to offer his services to Custer as soon as they reached him. Meanwhile he bade farewell to Forsyth, destined, despite his terrible wounds, to live many years more and become a general. Then he and some others rode into Custer's camp not long after the Battle of the Arickaree, and Bob frankly stated why he had come. Custer looked at him with interest.

"And so you are one of that little band who made the great defence on the island in the Arickaree?" he said. "It was a marvellous achievement."

Bob blushed at the high praise.

"I was there by chance," he said. "I did not really belong to Colonel Forsyth's command."

"I have heard all about it. You were a hero with the others. I shall be glad to take you. We need lads of strength and courage like you, and since you are riding a borrowed horse, the United States will quickly furnish you with another."

Bob's heart warmed within him. He liked the commander, who himself was a very young man, under thirty, and an hour later was enrolled in the service for the campaign that Custer intended.

CHAPTER 21

A-Horse with Custer

Bob now spent several weeks riding about the plains with Custer and his men in search of the Cheyennes who were still raiding everywhere, causing great loss of life, cutting off emigrant trains, hunters, and detachments of all kinds. Now and then they overtook and defeated small bands, but the great force kept out of their way. It was known definitely that since the death of Roman Nose, Black Kettle was head chief, and he was proving himself a general of ability. It was also rumoured that he was helped by a white man, and Bob had no doubt that it was Carver.

Bob never failed to enquire of everyone whom they met of news of Sam Strong and his friends. Nobody had heard anything. It became a certainty that they had not reached civilization, but that was all. So the boy, as he rode with Custer, continued his quest, and he could not have carried it on in any other way. The life itself was not without its compensations. He was well treated, and the companionship was good.

The autumn advanced. The brown grass was dead to its roots. Then fierce winds blew out of the northwest, and often they had an edge of hail or snow. But the country, through which they now rode, was wooded in part, and they nearly always encamped at night in groves where they could find plenty of fuel. There the troopers built fires high, and gathered in a circle about them, while their brethren, the horses, stood in another circle just behind the men. Often the snow would blow about them, and the horses would come still closer, reaching over and touching the men with their noses. The friendship between man and horse was exceedingly strong, the result of close association, and of the service that each did for the other. Bob remembered with feeling the splendid mustang that had carried him out of danger, but he did not wish to have him with him now. He was glad that the great horse had gone to take his true place at the head of some wild herd.

They came one evening in a light snowfall to a dense wood along a shallow stream, and Bob, who was in advance with the scouts, pointed to the trees on the branches of which roosted a great throng of splendid, bronze turkeys. The hunters at once became busy, and shot all that they could possibly eat. That night they had a feast. The fires were built higher than ever, the men congregated about them, and as it was known that no enemy was near, Custer allowed them to sing and talk as much as they pleased, while the turkeys were roasted or broiled, and the savoury odours penetrated every corner of the dark woods.

It was a night that Bob will never forget, the roaring fires showing the tree trunks, filing away in the distance, the hundreds of soldiers with their brown or ruddy faces, and the feelings of courage and friendship that pervaded everything. It reminded him of evenings with his old comrades, only this was on a much greater scale.

They had been short of rations, and he ate turkey as heartily as any of them. Afterwards he sat a while, listening to the laughter and the songs, and then, wrapping himself in his blanket, he lay down under an oak tree. He dozed for a while most pleasantly, body and mind relaxed into a soothing and peaceful state. The soldiers and the fires wavered before him, and beyond both he could just see the backs of the horses, basking also in the genial glow. He thought vaguely of the many things that he had seen, and he wondered with equal vagueness to what end all this marching would come. Then he dropped into a sleep that was deep and without dreams. Others presently wrapped themselves in their blankets, and they, too, were soon in a sleep as sound as Bob's.

The next day the whole force, encouraged and refreshed, resumed the march, travelling here and there among the hills and on the plains in search of the Cheyennes, Bob also seeking for some trace of his lost comrades of whom he never despaired, although it was now weeks since his capture by the Indians. His confidence in Sam Strong, Bill Cole and the others was so great that their taking or destruction by the Cheyennes seemed impossible to him.

Bob's earnestness and efficiency, his willingness at all times to help gave him a high place in the regard of the young commander, Custer, who attached him to his personal staff, and because of merit, favoured him in many ways. The fact that Bob's father had fallen in the great Civil War also caused Custer's heart to warm towards him, and he sometimes talked to the boy of the long struggle, particularly of the mighty battle of Gettysburg, where Custer, then scarcely more than a boy, had proved himself a brilliant cavalry leader.

"Two of my friends, Porter Evans and Tom Harris, were there," said Bob. "One was on one side, and one on the other, but that fact seems to make them like each other all the better, though they never agree about the result of that or any other battle."

"It's a way the boys have," Custer said, "but it does no harm. Out here on the plains we have veterans of either army, and they are all fighting well under the old flag."

"I've found my best friends here in this wild country," said Bob.

"The wilderness breeds friendship," said Custer. "Men are compelled to rely upon one another."

The weather now increased in coldness. All the signs betokened an extremely severe winter. Snow and hail were frequent, but the fierce winds, coming off the vast reaches of plain, were the worst. They cut to the bone, and many of the men made skin masks to protect their faces. An ordinary leader would have gone into winter quarters, but Custer resolved to defy winter itself, no matter how terrible it became. The ravages of the Cheyennes had been so severe, so many people had been killed in the last two years, and there had been so much devastation of all kinds that he was not willing to give them another chance. With his regiment, the Seventh Cavalry, he pressed the hunt anew.

It was now the last week of November, and winter was in full blast. The regiment, led by friendly Osage Indian guides, hit upon a trail so large that they believed it to be that of the main Cheyenne band under Black Kettle. All the men woke to new life at the news, and they pressed forward, hoping that they would now find their elusive foe, and compel a battle.

But their bad luck pursued them. About noon the skies became overcast. Heavy, solemn clouds marched in battalions, fused into one great mass, and then began to pour forth snow. To make it still worse, the wind arose and the storm was blinding. The trail, of course, was quickly lost, and then it was as much as the men could do to keep in touch with one another.

As the afternoon waned the storm increased in violence. The regiment rode forward, a little army of white phantoms. Men and horses were robed in snow from head to foot. It was impossible for any man to keep clear of it. As fast as they shook off one white coat it was replaced by another, and they soon gave up the effort.

As time passed the storm only deepened. The air was filled with whirling, white flakes, driven fiercely by the wind, and they could not see more than two or three hundred yards ahead. But they did not complain. It was only one such incident in the long story of the American army on the border, fighting for generations in the lonely wastes against a brave and crafty foe, obscure battles of which the world heard but little, but which were marked by courage and devotion equal to any shown on great fields like Gettysburg or Chickamauga.

Bob was near the head of the army, just behind General Custer, who closely followed two Osage Indian guides, Little Beaver and Hard Rope, and several times he turned to look back at one of the most remarkable sights that he ever beheld, nearly a thousand figures wrapped in snow, riding silently on, not a man speaking, not a horse neighing, every soldier bent well forward to protect his face from the storm, while all the time the shriek of the wind across the plain was full of menace. They rode, too, through a country of which they knew nothing, wholly uninhabited, except by a savage foe who might at any time lay a well-planned ambush for them. It was a time and situation when even the stoutest heart could find abundant excuse for going into winter quarters and awaiting a milder season to make war.

But Custer had no thought of turning back. It was his intention now to reach a point on Wolf Creek, about thirteen miles from his fortified camp, which he had called Camp Supply, and he still hoped to make it before dark, but the two Indian scouts suddenly stopped and looked at the general. Custer read bad news in his eye and he half guessed its nature but he asked of the nearer:

"What is it, Little Beaver?"

"The snow took the Cheyenne trail from us," replied the Indian, a fine tall warrior, "and now it has done more. We have lost the way to Wolf Creek. Hard Rope and I have talked it over and we tell you the truth. We do not now know which way Wolf Creek lies. What does the yellow-haired chief wish to do with us!"

The Indian spoke with resignation, but Bob who heard the words knew that the pride of both Little Beaver and Hard Rope was deeply hurt. Custer, although his disappointment must have been great, did not rebuke them. He had now the hearts of the friendly Osages, and he knew how to keep them.

"The storm hides all the country from us," he said, "and where you, Little Beaver and Hard Rope, have failed, all other men would fail too. It is no fault of yours."

The eyes of the two Osages flashed with gratitude, and they bent their heads in a sort of proud salute, although they said nothing.

"But," resumed Custer, cheerfully, "where man's own senses have failed, maybe something that man has made will help us."

He drew from his pocket a little compass, studied it carefully, and then announced that Wolf Creek lay not many miles almost directly ahead. Little Beaver and Hard Rope, who looked curiously at the singular little instrument, bowed their heads in submission. It was not for them to question the white man's magic or to feel hurt because it knew more than they.

The soldiers, who had been sitting silently on their horses, letting the snow beat upon them, raised their heads and silently resumed the march. Bob kept near Custer, and now two white scouts rode with him, one on either side. They were California Joe, a famous veteran, and a brave young

Mexican, named Romero, but whom the troops always called Romeo. Bob, in the easy fashion of the border already called him Romeo too.

"Romeo," he asked, "did you ever hear of a man called Juan Carver? He is half of your race."

Young Romeo's eyes darkened.

"I've heard of him," he replied, "and I have seen him too, Senor Bob. He is half American, half Mexican and all bad. He has led a band to raid the beaver grounds either for himself or the Hudson Bay Company, and he will do any evil thing that he can if he may gain by it. I know that he is with the Cheyennes now."

"I knew that he was," said Bob. "He's an able man, and he's probably helping Black Kettle."

Late in the afternoon they came to Wolf Creek, Custer's pocket compass leading them aright, and made camp in some thick woods along the stream. They managed to clear away a good deal of the snow, and to build fires, but the night was trying in the extreme. It snowed hard, for a long time, and then turned bitterly cold. Had they not been able to reach the firewood along the creek, many of them would certainly have frozen to death. None slept long and they were careful also to see that their horses shared in the heat of the fire.

Morning came, the skies were clear and the snow ceased to fall, but it lay on the ground nearly two feet deep, and a bitter wind blew out of the north. The trumpet sang *Boots and Saddles*, and the men mounted, casting, despite themselves, reluctant looks at the fires that they were leaving behind.

"Where are we going now!" asked Bob of California Joe.

"I don't know," replied Joe, "but I know where we ain't goin'. We ain't goin' to no warm house; we ain't goin' to crawl in on top o' a feather bed under a pile of covers; we ain't goin' to any nice, little town, where you can hear the girls play the pianners, we ain't goin' to do none o' them soft, sweet things; we're jest goin' to march, poundin' two feet o' snow an' mebbe runnin' across a crowd o' howlin' Cheyennes that will give us the picnic of our lives."

Bob laughed. In the company of hundreds of brave men, he felt cheerful, despite every hardship.

"Isn't that the kind of a picnic that we're looking for?" he asked.

"So it is; so it is," said California Joe, "but I never before had to look so hard for a scrap, through snow up to your neck, with the mercury a hundred degrees below zero, an' the wind blowin' a thousand miles an hour."

Bob laughed, feeling sure that California Joe, despite his much grumbling, would be in the thick of the fray when they found it.

But they did not yet find it. Several days passed, and they were still ploughing around in the snow and cold, sometimes on the plains and sometimes through forests, crossing shallow creeks and rivers that were frozen fast in the ice. The Osage scouts and trackers, in particular, Little Beaver and Hard Rope, showed the greatest courage and devotion, but the deep snow seemed to have covered up all trails, and their skill and energy availed nothing. Custer still refused to go into winter quarters, and continued the hunt. Game was abundant. Buffalo and deer were everywhere, from which fact the scouts drew the inference that the Cheyennes were resting in a hidden camp, with plentiful stores of food.

Various bodies of scouts were sent out, including one under Major Elliott that went toward the south, and the main body of the army, moving on, came to the wide and shallow stream of the Canadian River, the crossing of which was long, difficult and dangerous. The heavy wagons containing the supplies broke through the ice, and the teamsters, in order to keep the horses to their duty, were compelled to leap down in the freezing flood, and pull on the lines, or put their shoulders to the wheels. Many of the cavalrymen helped them, standing waist deep amid the water and the floating ice. It was an extraordinary scene, typical of the great American wilderness and the heroism with which it was won.

Nature could not have provided a sterner aspect, the leafless trees, coated with ice, the bleak desolation of the rolling plains under that great pall of snow, the wide sullen river, filled now with broken ice, and the grim, silent men whom Custer ever drove on and who were always willing to go. Custer himself rode back and forth amid the ice, encouraging and helping.

It took nearly the whole day to get all the wagons across the dangerous flood. Just as the last of them was drawn upon the further bank, they heard the soft crunch, crunch of swift hoofs in the snow and Major Elliott and his scouting party galloped up. Bob knew from the look on their faces that they had news, and he heard the major's words when he saluted and addressed Custer.

"We have struck an Indian trail, sir," said Major Elliott. "At least one hundred and fifty warriors and their ponies have passed since the last snow fall. I suspect that it is a returning party of hunters."

"If so, it will go straight to the big Cheyenne camp, wherever it is, and we follow," said Custer.

Custer, full of youthful fire and enthusiasm, organized the pursuit with amazing rapidity. The soldiers, who had been wading in the water, exchanged their wet clothing for dry from the wagons, and eighty men, with the poorest horses, were detailed as a guard for the wagons, which must advance with relative slowness. The rest, eager, all their toils and privations forgotten, galloped off, Bob as usual with his friends, California Joe and Romeo. They had started twenty minutes after receiving the news.

"It makes me feel young again," said California Joe. "I don't know that I'm fond o' fightin' as a reg'lar diet, but when I'm lookin' for a fight I'd just as soon find it as keep on lookin' for it till I froze to death."

Bob was serious. He had a sensitive, impressionable nature, and in Forsyth's great defence of the island in the Arickaree, he had seen what war could be. Still, he was relieved to know that they had found the Indians and that in all likelihood the campaign would come to an issue. He looked to his rifle, and felt of the pistol in its holster.

Custer, in his eagerness, was at the very head, with Major Elliott and the two Osages, Little Beaver and Hard Rope. The Major had left a party of his troops on the trail that he had discovered, and Custer, turning to the southwest, galloped toward that point as fast as the deep snow would allow. It was now late in the afternoon, and the sun cast a glowing red tint over the white wilderness. It was weird, like a portent of great events and Bob felt, in every bone of him, that the time had come.

California Joe and Romeo, who had been exchanging low comments, sank into silence. The snow flew in showers beneath the rapid hoofs of the command, which left a broad, deep trail behind it, but the speed was not diminished. The sun, with a last blaze of red sank into the prairie, and then they struck the path of the Indian band. They found that the troops left there by Major Elliott had gone on, and they followed.

The night was at hand, but it was not dark, and the white gleam of the snow helped also. Even had it been dark they could not have missed a road, broken through snow nearly two feet deep. Evidently the Cheyennes did not suspect the nearness of the white army, and California Joe and Romeo began to talk about surprising them.

"The watchfulest men in the world are caught off guard sometime or other," said Joe, "an' it may be our chance."

About 9 o'clock in the evening they overtook the detachment, left by Major Elliott, and now the whole force was united, 800 strong, experienced, brave, on fire with zeal, and led by a great captain. But Custer, eager as he was to strike his evasive enemy, now became watchful and cautious. They had already come long and far, and he ordered his men to take a rest of an hour.

"The general is right," said California Joe to Bob, who was now burning with impatience. "Of course, I know how it is. When you think you've got your game in range you want to shoot, but our horses are nigh pumped out, and we need to steady ourselves."

"It is surely so," said Romeo, twisting up the ends of his curly, black moustache. "It is well to have the nerves before you fight, and then to fight like a Cortez or a Pizarro."

The young Mexican, brave and courteous, a master of the craft of wood and plain, was a general favourite with the army, and now Bob watched him with interest and admiration, as he prepared for battle. After curling up his moustache in a satisfactory manner, Romeo carefully arranged the red silk handkerchief around his neck, and smoothed down his beautifully tanned buckskin hunting shirt and leggings. He caught Bob's eye and said earnestly:

"If I fall, I wish to fall like a gentleman, clad properly and with everything in order. It will be a great comfort to me."

California Joe laughed softly.

"Mighty little you'll know about it, Romeo," he said, "but I ain't criticisin' you, though, by gum, you're the finest dandy I ever saw on these plains."

Romeo smiled in supreme satisfaction.

"Ah, California Joe," he said, "you pay me the great compliment. Some day when I am rich I shall go far down to the City of Mexico. I shall wear the magnificent suit of red velvet, with a broad and flowing red silk sash around my waist. I shall have the broad-brimmed black hat, with a single immense red plume. Great jewels, diamond, ruby, sapphire, emerald, will glitter all over me like stars. The king of the bull fighters will be but a shadow beside me, and all the beautiful *senoritas* will be at my feet."

"They'll be struck plum' blind by your splendour," said California Joe, grinning in admiration at the vivid picture that Romeo had drawn.

The two relapsed into silence, and Bob was silent with them. In fact, the whole army was silent, save for the occasional low words of a trooper, and the soft crunch of horses' feet in the deep snow. The men were dismounted now, that their horses might rest too, but they stood beside them and held the reins.

The night was very cold, although Bob, in his excitement and anticipation, did not notice it. But on the eve of battle the feeling of unreality came over him again. It was a phantom army standing there in the icy moonlight on the vast, unpeopled plains, and he was a phantom himself. The cold increased, and the wind that came now and then, cut like a knife. An icy crust was forming on the snow.

Custer gave the word to advance at ten o'clock, and a deep sigh ran through the whole army. But it was a sigh of relief; it was like the unleashing of a hound, eager to move forward. The troopers sprang into the saddle and the stern command of silence was passed all along the line. No one knew how near the enemy might be.

The two Osage scouts, Little Beaver and Hard Rope, led the way on foot, fully four hundred yards in advance, their moccasins making no sound on the snow, their brown figures flitting forward like ghosts. Then in a little group, came about a dozen more Osages, California Joe, Romeo, the rest of the white scouts and Bob. About a third of a mile behind them, in order to keep the noise' of so many hoofs from being heard by the Indians, rode the army, Custer at its head, with Major Elliott, Captain Whittaker and other important officers beside him.

They did not move very fast. The surface of the snow on the trail had frozen after the Indians had passed, and now it broke with a crackling sound, faint when one horse made it, but steady and insistent when eight hundred made it together. It was impossible to avoid it, and as the alert ears of the Cheyennes might hear it some distance, Custer did not dare to go faster than a walk.

This crackling sound, at times almost a tinkle, was not unmusical, and it was soothing to Bob's excited senses. He was not apprehensive. He had full confidence in Custer and his army, and he was proud to be riding there in this group of brave and loyal scouts.

They rode on, hour after hour, mile after mile, in the snowy desolation of the wilderness. The moonlight faded, brightened and faded again. little Beaver and Hard Rope still led with sureness and precision, keeping their distance of four hundred yards ahead of the others. At times, when the moon darkened, their figures seemed to fade away, and only the keen and accustomed eyes of the scouts saw them. But they were always there.

"It's a long trail," whispered California Joe to Bob, "but I think these Osages will take us to the end of it."

It was now far past midnight, and Bob responded in an excited whisper:

"Look! Little Beaver and Hard Rope have stopped!"

The two Osages were standing motionless in the trail, but were looking back toward the little group of scouts, who rode forward quickly.

"What is it?" asked California Joe.

"Me don't know," replied Little Beaver in a soft tone, "but me smell smoke."

Hard Rope nodded in confirmation. Bob sniffed, but could not smell anything. Neither could California Joe, nor Romeo, nor any of the scouts. Custer, Wittaker, Elliott and other officers came up, and they could not detect an odour, either. But they did not lose confidence in the two Osages; the wonderful keenness of their senses had been tested too often. When Custer himself questioned them the Osages still remained absolutely sure.

"Me smell smoke," repeated Little Beaver, and Hard Rope nodded again in confirmation.

"If they say they smell it, they smell it," said Custer, "and the Cheyennes are somewhere near. Now, Little Beaver, you and Hard Rope go on again, but Whittaker, you and Elliott caution the troop to be quieter than ever. Maybe we can strike the Cheyennes before they see us. The snow and the great cold will keep them close to their lodges."

The slow advance was resumed, the two Osages once more becoming shadows that led silently on. Bob's heart began to beat a little livelier tune. He was quite as confident as Custer that the Osages had made no mistake, and that the great moment was at hand. His own little group did not say a word, and Romeo, satisfied that his costume was correct in every detail for battle, ceased to preen.

Little Beaver and Hard Rope decreased speed again. Bob saw the two shadows moving slowly, and yet more slowly, over the white snow, and soon they stopped, remaining upright, motionless, waiting for the group of scouts, which Custer and several of his officers had now joined, to come up. They were no longer shadows, but were now two bronze statues, silhouetted against the gleaming snow. The second stop was about a half mile from the first When Custer reached them, Little Beaver looking up said quietly and without any change of countenance:

"Me told you so!"

He pointed, with a long brown forefinger, to a small, dark spot beside the trail, but well inside a patch of timber. Custer, his officers and Bob followed the pointing forefinger, and saw the embers of a small fire. It had never thrown out more than a faint smoke, but in the cold, absolutely pure air of the night, the two Osage trackers had smelt it at a distance of half a mile, and had identified it, without the shadow of a doubt in their own minds.

"Isn't it wonderful?" whispered Bob to California Joe.

"It's wonderful, an' it's true," California Joe whispered back.

"What does this little fire mean!" asked Custer of the Osages.

Little Beaver and Hard Rope looked around in the timber a while, before answering. Then they told Custer that they had reached the edge of ground used by the Cheyennes for herding their ponies. Beyond lay a considerable open space, a fine, large meadow when not covered by the snow, thickly surrounded on all sides by timber, hence making it easy for the boys to hold the ponies there. Some of the boys undoubtedly had built the fire for warmth, and the great Cheyenne village could not be more than two or three miles away.

Custer drew a long, deep breath when Little Beaver told the terse tale, and the others also felt their blood leap.

CHAPTER 22

The Battle of the Washita

Custer, always quick and decisive, instantly arranged his plan. He would go forward himself with the two Osage trackers and see, for the sake of absolute certainty, if the Cheyenne village was at hand. The others would follow very slowly. When he announced his plan, the general glanced at the group about him and caught Bob's appealing eyes. He knew very well what it meant, and Bob's youth and the great efficiency that he had shown moved him.

"Well, come along," he said. "You have proved yourself a good boy and a useful one, and you may be of help now."

Bob instantly rode forward by the general's side, and California Joe and Romeo cast envious, but not jealous looks at him. Romeo gave his moustache another and more ferocious twist, and then waved his hand to Bob, in a gesture of brief farewell and many good wishes.

The two Osages on foot, moved forward for the third time, the young general and the boy on horseback following close behind, none of them speaking, and the footfalls of the horses making very little sound. They went forward about two miles, the road dipping down between ridges, and at the top of every ridge they stopped, both to look and listen. When they came to one a little higher than the others, Little Beaver, who was in advance, suddenly crouched down on the snow, and Hard Rope, who was just behind him, at once did the same. The general and Bob stopped their horses.

"What is it?" asked Custer in a whisper.

"Heaps Injuns down there," replied Little Beaver, pointing toward a valley, which lay to their right, partly shut in by timber. Bob, whose eyes naturally keen, were trained now by experience, saw, through the timber, a great dark group of large animals. They were at least a half mile away, and he took them to be buffaloes. Custer, looking intently at them, was of the same opinion, and he turned again to Little Beaver.

"Why do you think Indians are down there?" he asked.

"We heard dog bark," replied Little Beaver.

Neither the general nor the boy had heard anything, but they already had ample proof of the wonderful acuteness of the Osage senses, and Custer knew that Little Beaver and Hard Rope were to be trusted absolutely.

"Suppose we go forward a little further," whispered the general.

They advanced about a rod, and then stopped to listen. Presently both the general and the boy heard the faint sound of a dog's bark in the heavy timber to the right of the herd. "Ah!" uttered Custer softly, and then, following the bark, came a sound, singular for the time and place. It was a low tinkle, very soft and sweet, but penetrating in the still night.

"That little bell on a pony," said Little Beaver, "and down there you see the great herd of Cheyenne horses."

So that was what the general and the boy had mistaken for buffaloes! Not the slightest doubt could exist any longer. There were the Cheyenne ponies, and the Cheyenne village was bound to be close by.

"Come Bob," said the general, "we'll go back now for the others. Little Beaver, you and Hard Rope stay here and watch."

The two Osages, without a word, crouched down, remaining silent and motionless, while Custer and Bob rode back to the group that contained the other scouts and principal officers. The whole army had halted a few hundred yards back of this group. The officers took off their sabres and laid them on the snow that their rattling might not be heard, and rode back to the crest of the hill, where Little Beaver and Hard Rope had been left. Thence, they looked long at the herd, and also saw a few lights twinkling among the trees beyond. There the Osages located the Cheyenne village.

All were convinced, and they rode back to the point where they had left their sabres, which they regained. Then they held a council, to which Bob and the scouts were admitted, a council between midnight and morning, in the snow and ice of a vast wilderness. Custer decided to surround the village and attack at daylight. He divided his army into four detachments. Two moved off at once, making a circuit of several miles, in order to gain the far side of the village, where they were to attack at different points. An hour before dawn the third should move up toward the right, where it was to charge at the signal. The fourth, under Custer himself, remained on the hill, from which the discovery of the village had been made, and would attack from that point. Little Beaver, Hard Rope, Bob, California Joe and Romeo remained with Custer.

Theirs was the hardest part, as they were compelled to sit absolutely quiet and wait. Bob had never felt such hours as these before, sitting on his horse in the darkness and in the cold, which was growing more intense, fearing at any moment that their presence would be discovered, and the alarm given, before the circle of steel was complete. The boy's hands grew stiff in his buckskin gauntlets, and the men, who were dismounted and standing beside their horses, were not permitted to stamp their feet to keep them warm, or to walk back and forth for the sake of circulation. Some of the officers, wrapped in huge overcoats, lay softly down on the snow and slept. But Bob had neither the ability, nor the wish to sleep. He looked steadily down into the valley, where the dark figures of the ponies were growing plainer, and several times he heard the sweet, penetrating tinkle of the bell, taken, doubtless, from the horse of some slaughtered emigrant.

The Osages, under Little Beaver and Hard Rope, who were chiefs as well as incomparable trailers, collected in a little group on one side, under the low branches of a tree, and presently Bob learned from California Joe that they had become uneasy. Now that the Cheyennes were found the Osages feared that, with their great force, they would be more than a match for Custer's army. Custer learned of it and he did not upbraid them, but he whispered to California Joe:

"Will the Cheyennes put up a big fight?"

Bob saw the weather-beaten face of the scout become very serious.

"Yes," replied the veteran, "they will. You can depend on that, general. Mebbe we've bit off more'n we can chaw."

"We'll see about that," said General Custer, firmly.

"I'm with you to the end, general," said California Joe quietly.

Very little was said after that, and the icy hours trailed slowly away. Bob saw afar in the east a faint, greyish tinge. The dawn was coming, and with it the attack. His heart gave a great leap. Custer awakened the officers who lay wrapped in their overcoats on the snow. They sprang to their feet, and all thought that they had been discovered by the Cheyennes, because they saw a sudden, beautiful light, as if from a great fire.

"What on earth is it!" asked Bob in a whisper of California Joe.

"Look! a star!" said Joe.

It was a brilliant morning star, fleeing before the dawn, and, seen intensified and magnified through the atmosphere of the plains. In a moment it faded, and all understood. The Cheyenne village was still in ignorance.

"Forward!" said Custer, and the stiffened figures of the men became elastic once more, as the blood bounded through their veins. They rode down the slope, and reached the outskirts of the great herd of ponies, which was stretched out, hundreds and hundreds. The dawn was growing stronger.

Custer, Bob, California Joe and Romeo were now in the lead. Just behind them, at Custer's command, came the mounted regimental band, the leader holding the cornet to his lips.

201

The tops of many tall white *tepees* rose out of the morning mists, and from many of these tops plumes of smoke shot up. But the presence of the army was still unknown to the Cheyennes. For once the cunning and craft of the white man, had outwitted the cunning and craft of the red. Bob could scarcely believe it. Every pulse in him was leaping wildly.

Custer was turning in his saddle to give the leader of the band the word to play *Garryowen*, which was to be the signal for attack, when a single rifle shot came from the village. The Cheyennes, not dreaming of attack in such terrible weather, were lying close in their *tepees*, but one warrior now saw the coming foe, and fired.

But the signal was given. Forth from the band came the famous, old air, loud, clear and sweet, singing over the whole village. Up sprang a sun of uncommon splendour, filling the valley with winter gold, gleaming across the skin lodges and on the tawny stream of the Washita which ran through the Cheyenne town.

The men uttered a tremendous cheer, and from three points in the ring about the town came the answering cry. The other three detachments had come up at the exact time, and the circle of steel was complete. High above the band rose the fierce pealing note of a bugle, and then, with Custer waving his sword aloft, and his long, yellow hair floating out under his hat, they charged the village, the great winter camp of the Cheyennes, containing fifteen hundred or two thousand warriors.

But surprised, though they were, at the dawn of a winter morning, the Cheyennes, Dog Soldiers and all, fought with a courage worthy of their brave and powerful nation. The men rushed from the *tepees*, rifle in hand. Many of them sprang into the river, breaking the ice, and, standing in the water waist deep under the shelter of the banks, poured a deadly fire upon the advancing army, replying to the cheers of the cavalry with defiant shouts of their own.

A small body, seventeen in number, leaped into a rocky depression, where they lay down, protected from the white fire, and sent in bullets rapidly. A formidable force reached a deep ravine, within the limits of the village, and the hail from their rifles was deadly. The women and children, perhaps having confidence that the white troops would not fire upon them, remained in the lodges and began singing the death song, a wild, wailing chant from hundreds of throats, that never ceased during all the fury and tumult of the battle, rising over everything like the solemn despair of a Greek chorus.

Despite all the advantages of the surprise, the army of Custer was faced by a powerful and formidable foe. The alert Cheyennes, trained by lives of incessant danger, now took advantage of every opportunity. In addition to those already in shelter, they hid behind trees, rocks and bushes, which were thick in the village, and added to the defensive fire which was now fast increasing in volume. At intervals they sent forth their defiant war-whoop.

Bob, carried away by the excitement of the moment and the intensity of feelings so long held in leash, was shouting with the shouting cavalrymen, and urging his horse to a gallop. But a line of fire seemed to blaze directly into his face, as a thousand Cheyenne warriors pulled the trigger. He heard the whistle of bullets, the low cry of men, and the wild scream of horses as they were struck. He saw men plunge suddenly from the saddle and fall into the snow where they lay still. He saw horses without riders break from the line and gallop away in the smoke that was now rising fast, but he saw also the yellow hair and waving blade of Custer just in front of him, and he followed where the leader led.

The first charge of nearly a thousand cavalry was irresistible, and the Cheyennes were driven in toward a common centre. The circle of steel wrapped the village around, and closed tighter and tighter. Custer seized the lodges, and the women and children, who still kept up the terrible death chant, were prisoners, but the warriors were not. They were in great force, wherever cover could be found, and the troopers were falling under the bullets of the red marksmen. The huge cloud of smoke rising from so many rifles helped them. They knew every inch of the ground and the soldiers knew none of it. Their yells of defiance became yells of triumph because many of them now began to believe that they would not only drive off the white foe, but destroy him.

"We've bit off a lot," Bob heard California Joe say, but the veteran showed no signs of discouragement, firing slowly and only when he had picked his target. Bob also fired, but he was confused by the great volume of sound, the shouting, the crash of the rifles, and the dense smoke that was now enveloping the whole village and making all things obscure. The snow was trodden into slush under the horses' feet, and particles of it kicked into his face stung like shot. More than once he thought that he had been hit by a bullet, only to find that it was a ball of snow or a piece of ice.

He did not know, in all the confusion and obscurity, that the advance had ceased. The ring of steel seemed to have tightened as far as it would go. It had now met a body that would not yield. Bob felt a sinking sensation. Were they to be beaten, after having executed so complete a surprise? Then he heard Custer give an order to dismount, and he leaped from his saddle. Some of the men dropped to the rear, holding the reins of the horses, but Bob was not designated as one of them. He remained in the front line, on foot now, feeling that he was better able thus to continue in the battle.

"Sharpshooters!" cried Custer, and he rapidly detailed men to pick off the small body of Cheyennes who had taken refuge in the rocky depression, and were doing deadly execution. As long as these Indian marksmen stung their flank no battle could be won.

Bob, California Joe and Romeo were in this force, and Bob noted with surprise that the brave, young Mexican was still a dandy. His clothing seemed to have escaped all the snow and slush, and the pointed black moustache still curved up beautifully at either end.

"Down flat!" cried California Joe, and every man threw himself face forward in the snow which almost buried them. Then they began to creep toward the Cheyennes, holding their fire, while the battle whistled and thundered on either side of them. Bob was humane, but the odour of the smoke and burnt gunpowder entered his nostrils and he felt all the passion of the hunter. For the time he was as eager as any of them to get at the Cheyennes in the rocky hollow.

California Joe looked back at his creeping band.

"Don't any of you dare to pull trigger till I say the word," he called, commandingly.

Bob glanced along the line. All the faces were fierce and eager. The snow and the cold were forgotten. The rifles were held well forward, ready for a shot when the time came. The rest of the battle, which was always increasing in volume and ferocity, was wholly forgotten by everyone of them.

They reached the side of a little knoll, and crawling cautiously to its crest, they could see the heads of the Indians in the smoky hollow. Bob detected, through the film of smoke and vapour, the feathers of warbonnets, and black eyes, as hot with the fire of battle as any of those in California Joe's band.

"Now," said California Joe, "lay low an' pick your men."

Bullets struck among the Indians in the hollow, so long immune hitherto. Several of their best warriors were slain before they knew whence the fire came, and then they turned their attention from the main army to this new danger. A deadly duel ensued, but the sharpshooters of California Joe were too much for the Cheyenne marksmen. Although two or three of the whites were slain and several wounded, they never ceased to send bullets, aimed with a sure eye and firm hand, into the hollow. The Cheyennes at last looked around for flight, but they knew that the moment they rose from the hollow they would be swept away by the fire from the main army, so they stayed there, fighting the sharpshooters of California Joe, and died where they lay to the last man. Their bodies, seventeen in number, were found among the rocks after the battle. Then California Joe and his band, Bob with them, turned to other work.

The main body of the troops, relieved of the terrible fire on their flanks, pressed farther in. The white sharpshooters from all sides poured a perfect storm of bullets into the ravine, where the big Indian force lay. The Cheyennes there stood it long, but broke at last. They leaped to their feet and ran up the ravine, leaving half a hundred dead behind them. They renewed their fire from other points, while that of the warriors hidden under the banks of the river had never ceased for a moment, and the doubtful battle still surged to and fro.

It was now ten o'clock, and the combat was three hours old. The brilliant sun now and then made its way through the clouds of smoke and mist rising from the snow, and in one of these rifts Bob saw Indians collecting on a knoll below the village. He instantly pointed them out to General Custer, who viewed them with great alarm, although he did not let his face show it. If a second strong force was coming up, could his men withstand them?

At that moment Romeo ran up and explained the presence of the warriors on the knoll. He knew a dozen Indian languages, and he had learned from a squaw in a lodge that only two or three miles below them was another great Indian village occupied by Arapahos under their head chief, Little Raven, Kiowas, under their head chief Satanta, and some Comanches and Apaches who would undoubtedly come to the relief of their hard-pressed brethren, the Cheyennes.

Bob, who now remained close to Custer, as an aide, heard the words, and he knew their full import. The combat with one Indian army had been fierce enough, what would it be with two? But he did not feel any deep depression. The excitement of the moment would not permit. He merely watched the General to see what he would do.

Custer knew the value of time. Once more the bugle sounded the charge, and the circle of steel pressed in with a force that was irresistible. The riflemen leaped down into the river and cleared out the Indians lurking under the bank. The four detachments, charging with the greatest fire, met in the centre of the village, and the Cheyennes were beaten before their kinsmen had made up their minds to attack.

At this critical moment, Major Bell, the quartermaster, cutting his way through the Indian lines, arrived with a great supply of fresh ammunition. A tremendous cheer greeted him, and, with replenished belts the army wheeled to meet the second Indian force.

Custer was thorough. Two hundred of his men were detailed to tear down the lodges and set them on fire, first having brought out the women and children. The task was quickly done, and a vast column of smoke and fire shot up where the Cheyenne village had been. Outside, the squaws and children kept up the terrible wailing death chant, that had never been broken for an instant.

But the battle itself sank for a few moments, while the white army faced the new foe, who was gathering his forces for the attack. California Joe brought word that the head chief, Black Kettle, had been found among the slain. Though not as great as Roman Nose, he had been an able chief and a valiant warrior, and he had died fighting for the hunting grounds of his people. Bob had caught two glimpses of a white man who he was sure was Carver, but the wily freebooter disappeared each time in the confusion.

When the great fire from the burning *tepees* rose, the rage of the Indians rose with it. Those Cheyennes, who had broken through the lines and the Kiowas, Arapahoes and others outside, rushed forward to a new attack. The deep snow in the village was trampled into a slush, red for wide spaces. The smoke hung in heavy banks, which a stray wind now and then lifted, and revealed the two armies, white and red, firing along a long, curving line, creeping rather than standing, but always coming closer.

Bob was thoroughly possessed by the fury of the conflict. He had abandoned his horse, long since, to the little body of troopers detailed for this service, and keeping with California Joe and Romeo, he was at the point in the line, where the Indian attack was fiercest. But Custer was not waiting for the Indians. He also was attacking, pressing forward his men who now fought on foot, taking advantage, in Indian fashion, of every shelter afforded by rock or bush or swell of the ground. Meanwhile, he held many of the Cheyenne warriors prisoners, all their women and children, and a herd of fifteen hundred ponies.

Noon came, and despite the cold, the men felt parched and burnt from the long struggle which was yet far from a decision. Another hour passed, and then another, and both sides stood firm, neither able to advance further. Custer now was consumed with anxiety for his wagon train, with its escort of eighty men, which he knew must be coming up, and which was likely to come straight into ambush. His own losses, moreover, were heavy. The gallant Major Elliott and nineteen men had been ambushed and all killed. Many more were killed elsewhere, and there was a great swarm of the wounded, although all of the latter, who could stand, yet fought.

"Will we beat 'em, Joe? Will we beat 'em?" gasped Bob, who was covered from head to foot with snow and mud.

The old scout paused a half minute before replying, and then he said very gravely:

"I said we'd bit off a lot, mebbe more'n we could chaw. We've got iron jaws an' we've been chawin' hard an' long, but I don't know yet. By the great horn spoon, Bob, them Injuns fight well, as they gen'ally do! We don't know what would have happened if old Roman Nose had been alive an' kickin'."

California Joe was right. The North American Indian, always a formidable foe, full of courage, skill and tenacity, was fully justifying on that day his title as a great fighter. The warriors, although surprised in their *tepees*, had held a powerful white force, led by a great captain, at bay for more than eight hours.

But Custer was now preparing for a supreme effort. The mellow notes of the bugle sang over the desperate field, and the whole army was quickly formed into a hollow square with the prisoners in the centre. It was no longer necessary to hold the Cheyenne village, because there was no Cheyenne village to hold. As soon as the square was complete the bugle sang again, and then the army rushed with its full weight upon the second Indian force, many of the remounted cavalry charging, sabre in hand.

The Indians fired one volley, two volleys, three volleys, and then, as the troop still came on, they could stand no more. They broke and fled in all directions, leaving their dead behind them. Custer, waving his sword, did not permit his men to stop, but continued the chase, pursuing the Indians to the second village, taking that also, and scattering Cheyennes, Arapahoes, Kiowas, and all the rest in one wild rout.

The Cheyenne nation was practically destroyed, but it went down to ruin fighting with a valour worthy of any race. The great battle of the Washita was over, and the Indians had suffered the greatest defeat in their history beyond the Mississippi, but the white army was exhausted. The men threw themselves down among the *tepees* in the second village, and some of them sank into a stupor. The surgeons were busy with many others, and the rest still stood to their arms.

Bob also felt this great temptation to sink down and lapse into forgetfulness, but he resisted it, and looked with a sort of dim wonder back over the great trail by which they had come. He saw the smoke still rising from the Cheyenne village, and here and there in the trodden slush dark spots that he knew to be bodies. On the distant hills stood brown figures, those of the defeated Indians, but they no longer fought. They were merely looking sadly at the scene of desolation and ruin.

Not a shot was fired now, and the silence, after such a continuous crash, was heavy and oppressive. The huge bank of smoke, made by so much firing, lifted, but coils and eddies of vapour still rose from the ground. The sun in all the brilliancy of mid-afternoon, presently scattered the smoke entirely, and poured down a torrent of vivid, golden light that disclosed all the terrible field, the trodden snow, the fallen men, white and red, the slain horses, and the columns of smoke that still rose from the burning ruins of the first village.

"Well, we've won, boy," said the voice of California Joe in Bob's ear, "but, by the great horn spoon, we know we've had a fight. It was a case of pitch and toss for about eight hours, an' I don't min' tellin' you now, Bob, that I thought more than once we'd be singin' our last little death songs. Even Romeo here has lost all the gilt off his clothes."

It was true. The attire of the young Mexican was stained in many places with snow and mud, and in one with red. He took a look of dismay at himself, blushed through the olive of his cheeks, and hastily began to make repairs.

Bob turned away from the scene up the river, the great trail of battle that they had made. He did not know which way he was going, but he was tired of looking upon the marks of combat, and the fallen. He was weak, and he saw dimly. His eyes were stinging with the smoke, and the lodges, the soldiers and the wintry landscape wavered before him. Suddenly he fell to trembling, and California Joe, who was watching him, clapped a strong hand on his shoulder.

"Hold up, Bob, my boy!" he cried. "Here, come in this lodge and sit down a bit!"

They entered a lodge of buffalo skin. Everything showed signs of a hasty flight. There were two couches of buffalo robes undisturbed. Dried herbs hung from the skin walls, and in one corner was a heap of jerked meat. In another lay an old musket.

"Just you spread yourself out here for a few minutes," said Joe, indicating one of the couches or pallets, and the boy, without protest, stretched himself on the buffalo skins. Then the dimness passed away from his eyes, and his nerves ceased to tremble. Oh, the deep, intense luxury of rest at such a time! Moreover, the battle and its ruin were hidden from him. He saw only the walls of the *tepee* and California Joe, sitting on the other pallet and hugging his knees in pleasure.

"This ain't the finest house in the world," said California Joe, "but I'm glad to be here, come safe through what I reckon was the terriblest Injun battle ever fought."

Bob was fully restored in fifteen minutes, and then he sprang up from the pallet. California Joe joined him, and they went outside. The sun had already passed the zenith of the quick winter day, and far off the twilight was darkening, while the cold deepened. The soldiers had lighted fires, and were beginning to cook their scanty supplies of food. Romeo was already helping them, and Bob and California Joe joined in the task.

The fires brought warmth, comfort and cheer, and the steadily darkening twilight hid the sanguine field that they had left behind them. To the right the women and children and the captured warriors were gathered in a dark mass with troopers, rifle on thigh, riding incessantly about them.

Bob, now that his strength and spirits were back, was assailed by a fierce, ravening hunger, and when the time came he ate like one who had not tasted food in a week. Then he drank cupful after cupful of black coffee. He was ashamed of himself presently, but when he saw that the others were doing the same, he resumed his congenial task.

Night came, clothing the valley, but not obscuring the circle of red light where the fires burned. Custer was still extremely anxious about his wagon train, and at ten o'clock he took up the march again, despite the darkness. But before going he set fire to the second village also, and it burned for a long time, a pillar of light behind them.

The march was kept up for four hours, when they encamped again in the valley of the Washita, and Bob, wrapped in a coat, slept on the snow till dawn. He rose to see another brilliant day, and shortly after they resumed the march a dark line appeared on the hills. Custer was the first to see it, through his glasses, and he gave a little cry of joy.

It was the wagon train, coming up through the deep snow, and its very slowness had saved it. Had it been able to move faster the Indians about Custer would certainly have destroyed it.

The whole army advanced swiftly, met the train, and there was great rejoicing and congratulation. Ample supplies of food, ammunition, medicines and fresh clothing were at hand, and the spirits of the men rose to the zenith.

CHAPTER 23

The Lone Search

The army, still holding its captives, moved slowly and encamped again the second day on the banks of the Washita. Despite the slain and the large number of wounded, it was in excellent condition, and since the wagon train had come, it would have been in condition to fight another battle had there been need of it. But there was no need. The power of the Cheyennes was shattered, and they would not be able to raise their heads again for years. They would never be able to raise them as high as they had once held them.

But for lone, white wanderers, or those in small numbers, the plains would be more dangerous than ever throughout the winter, because the scattered Cheyennes, Arapahoes and Kiowas, without villages now, would be wandering everywhere, eager for revenge. Yet, the knowledge of these facts did not keep down a resolution which was forming in Bob's breast.

He must find Sam Strong and his old comrades. Two buffalo hunters who came in that morning reported rumours of a little band of troopers, hidden somewhere among the hills to the southwest. Bob believed from the first that these were his friends, and he was quite sure now that if he had not come with Custer he would never have obtained this news. He was encouraged, too, by what he considered a good omen. Among the spoil of arms, picked up in the Cheyenne village, was the rifle that he had inherited from his father. Bob happened to see it in the hands of a trooper, who readily exchanged it for the weapon that the boy carried. Such omens as this decided him. He would brave all dangers, and start at once.

He went to General Custer and told him of his plan. The young commander looked around at the vast wilderness, deep in snow, and infested with wandering warriors burning with hate of the white man. Then he looked at the brave youth for whom he felt a real affection.

"Don't do it, Bob, lad," he said. "This may be a false rumour. Besides, if your friends are in hiding somewhere, it is likely that they will come out safe in the spring. I'm afraid that inside of a week your scalp would be hanging at the belt of some vengeful Cheyenne. Stay with me. You have the making of a good soldier, and you shall be an officer on my staff."

Bob flushed with pleasure, but his resolution wag not shaken.

"I thank you, General, I thank you from my heart," he said, "but I belong with these men whom I wish to seek. I'm used to the wilderness now, and I know its ways. I must find them."

Custer glanced at him and read his spirit in Ids firm eyes and chin.

"If you feel that way then you must go," lie said "Remember that the horse on which you ride is your own, and take all the ammunition and other supplies you can carry. The United States Government owes you at least that much."

Bob thanked him. The general gave his hand the warm clasp of sincere friendship, and turned away to his tent. Bob speedily made ready, and dozens of the men, who had fought with him in battle, came to tell him goodbye. Many believed that it would be a goodbye forever.

Most notable among these were California Joe and Romeo. The young Mexican was again the perfect Spanish dandy, fit to thrum on the guitar under the window of some *senorita*, far down in the warm valleys of Mexico. Never had he ruffled it more bravely. The plume in his hat had taken a fresh curve, the red sash around his waist was looped in jauntier folds, and not a speck of mud or snow disfigured his velvet costume.

"Goodbye, Senor Bob," he said, "I am sorry to see you go. You have fought with Senor Joe and me in the great battle of the Washita. You would do better to stay and be a soldier. Ah, Senor Bob, you lose your life alone on the great plains, and it is not good."

Genuine tears stood in the eyes of the emotional, but brave, Romeo. Bob was grateful to him.

"I shall never forget the time when we fought side by side, Romeo," he said, "and I hope that you won't either."

"What you want to do, Bob," said California Joe gruffly to hide his Anglo-Saxon feelings, "is to keep a mighty good lookout, an' if you see any human bein' that acts suspicious, shoot first. Then, after you've put a bullet through his head, ask him whether he's a friend or not."

Bob laughed, partly to hide his own feelings, and then took the reins of his horse in hand. At that moment, two men rode up and greeted him joyously. One was old and the other young. They were Pete Trudeau and Jack Stillwell. Bob was full of delight to see them again and he took their coming as a second good omen.

"And so, Bob, boy, you've been distinguishing yourself again," said Stillwell. "Not satisfied with being with Forsyth, in the great fight at the island, you've come with Custer and licked the whole Cheyenne nation."

"I did just the same, Jack, that a thousand others did," said Bob. "We had to fight for all we were worth, or be wiped out. There wasn't any choice."

"I believe you, from what I've heard," said Stillwell admiringly. "You're having your young life, Bob, crowded with about as much action as it can hold."

But both he and Trudeau looked very grave when they heard of Bob's expedition. They did not believe that he could ever succeed, and tried to dissuade him, but, as before, he was unshakable in his resolution. Nevertheless, he waited an hour or two, as they were the bearers of dispatches, and returning, would ride with him some miles. Bob was glad of their companionship even for a short distance.

When they were ready the three rode away, the boy in the centre, and the soldiers knowing why he went, gave three great cheers for the brave youth. He looked back, lifted his cap in reply and let his eyes linger for a few moments on the scene outspread before him, the line of wagons, the files of soldiers, the dark mass of captives, and encircling all, the white world of untouched snow, which seemed to stretch away into infinity. He had found many good friends among these soldiers. He knew the great work that they were doing in the obscurity of the west, and he hoped to meet them again.

The three glanced back several times from the crest of the swells, and it was some time before they completely lost sight of the army, but it sank into the plain at last, and they were alone with the snow. After that they rode on more than an hour in silence. Then Stillwell asked:

"What are your plans, Bob?"

"I'm going to ride straight for the range of big hills down there, and I believe that I'll find Sam and the boys among them. I've food enough for two weeks, and I've got two big blankets rolled up here on my saddle."

"The blankets will do against the cold," said Trudeau, "an' I don't think you'll lack for food. You're sure to run against buffalo long before the two weeks are up. I'm hopin' you won't run against Cheyennes too."

"I'm willing to take the chances," said Bob bravely, and they rode on another hour in silence. Then the time for parting came, as they must go toward the east, while he went southward. They shook hands, said a few words only, although these were very real and very earnest, and then a single horseman rode through the snow into the south. The other two stopped presently, and sitting motionless, watched him until he was out of sight.

Bob, at the first parting from these good friends, felt an overwhelming loneliness. That was why he did not look back, but as he crossed swell after swell, and became used to the desolation, his spirits returned. He was strong and enduring. He had passed through great dangers. He had come wholly unharmed from the thick of two long and desperate battles, and one who had been so fortunate might hope for much. He had a good horse under him, a good rifle at his back, and he knew wild life. What more could he ask?

The boy's spirits rose fast, coming up from reserves of great strength in his nature. He whistled a tune, the gay lilt of which was heard only by himself, and his horse, sharing his high courage, raised his head and neighed once. The cold had moderated somewhat, and the snow was no longer covered with a crust of ice. The going was fairly easy, but Bob did not urge the horse beyond a walk, knowing that he must husband his strength, as without him, he would be lost on the great snowy plains.

He maintained his course throughout the day, always scanning the horizon with great care, for wandering bands of the defeated Indians. But his great safeguard lay in the fact that the sunlight was intense and brilliant, and he could see a horseman miles away. Despite his vigilance, no black speck appeared upon the horizon, and he rode all through the brilliant afternoon without interruption. Towards night he began to think of a place for a camp, and marked a dark line, on his left, which his skilful eye told him was trees.

He turned his horse toward the timber and approached cautiously. While the trees would afford shelter for him, they would afford shelter for the Indians also, and one must choose his bed well before sleeping in it. Bob relied to a certain extent upon his horse, a trained army campaigner, likely to shy at the presence of Indians, but the horse gave no sign of alarm, and just at the coming of the twilight, he entered a fine grove of oak, ash and cotton-wood, which stretched for an indefinite distance along both sides of a broad but shallow creek. The plains could offer no more inviting place for a camp, and to one as hardy as he, it seemed good. The creek was frozen over to the depth of several inches, but he broke the ice and drank and his horse drank after him. The snow among the trees was not deep, and Bob scraped away large places, revealing grass yet alive, of which the horse ate eagerly, then pushed his nose through the snow on his own account for more.

Having provided first for the faithful animal that carried him, the young horseman then provided for his own comfort. He found a little secluded arbour, as it were, in the thickest clump of trees and cleared away all the snow. By this time the sun was gone and it was quite dark, with the cold increasing fast. Satisfied that a little smoke would not be seen in the night, he gathered a heap of dead wood and lighted it with matches. He never suffered the blaze to rise much, but it threw out a great heat which warmed him through and through, and gave him a feeling of comfort, even luxury.

The grass around the fire thawed and then dried. The boy drew pemmican and army biscuits from his stores, and sitting on one of the blankets, with the other wrapped around him, he ate and felt a great content. The horse satisfied after his grazing, also came over and stood by the fire, basking in the heat. His great, mild eyes like those of the boy expressed content.

Bob knew that he was taking a certain risk by sleeping there without a sentinel, but it must be taken if he would preserve the strength to continue his long search. By and by he put out the fire, smothering it in snow, and then searched the woods for some distance, in either direction. There was no sign of an enemy, and coming back to the dry place in the thick shadow of the clump, he rolled himself from head to foot in the two blankets. He stretched himself at full length on the ground, and luxuriously contemplated the stars for a few minutes. Then he dropped into one of the deepest and pleasantest sleeps of his life, never stirring until the daylight came.

He rode all that day slowly, but without a break, eating his brief noonday meal from the saddle. It turned somewhat warmer and the snow began to melt, making it more difficult for his horse on account of the deep slush. He camped the second night on the open prairie, and only his blankets saved him from the raw, wet cold. Toward the middle of the third morning he saw a dark, blue line which one less experienced might have taken for a low cloud, but which he knew to be the foot-hills. Once again his pulses took a great leap. His comrades, these men who had done so much for him, would surely be there.

He was anxious to urge his horse to greater speed, but he knew that he must spare him, in all that snow and slush, and they went on at the same slow, steady walk. The air was so thin and so intensely bright that the blue line did not seem to grow any stronger or more distinct. But Bob was not discouraged. He knew that the hills were yet far off, and that he could not possibly reach them until late the next day.

In the afternoon he saw dark, moving specks which came nearer, and which proved to be buffaloes, nosing through the snow for the short grass which winter had not killed. They were uncommonly tame, indicating that they had been hunted but little, from which Bob drew a cheerful omen, feeling sure that very few Indians, perhaps none, had passed that way. It was pleasant also to see his dinner on the hoof, if the supplies he carried should become exhausted.

He was fortunate enough to find another creek, and more thick covert of trees for his third night, but he did not build a fire. He had an idea that, as he approached the hills, he was more likely to be in the vicinity of wandering Indians in search of shelter and refuge.

He fastened the horse to a bush in the very darkest' shadow, and lay down himself, under another bush, where in the night he was not visible to the best eye ten yards away. It was not very cold now, and with one blanket beneath him, and the other wrapped around his body, he was warm enough. He did not fall asleep for at least an hour and he woke again about midnight. The night had now cleared and a full silver moon and many bright stars were shining. The horse was standing peacefully by his bush, and for all Bob knew, was asleep on his feet.

The boy would have gone back to sleep also, but his roving eye caught a pin-point of light far down the stream. He remembered the brilliant morning star that they had seen just before the dawn at the Battle of the Washita, and he believed at first that he was now deceived in the same way, but a longer look convinced him that it was a real earthly light, probably the flame from a fire.

It might be Sam and the others, and for a moment his heart beat high at the thought, but the next moment, cold reason told him he must be wrong. It was not at all likely that they would yet come down into the plain.

The boy, knowing that a fire at such a time and place must have some great significance, resolved to investigate it. He saddled the horse in case he should have to take a sudden flight, rolled up the blankets tightly, and tied them to the saddle. He patted the intelligent animal on the nose and said in a whisper that he would soon be back; the horse might not understand the words, but he would the stroke of the hand. Then, with his finger on the trigger of his rifle, he stole down among the trees toward the light.

It was a windless, quiet night. The restless airs of the plains were still for once, and the leafless boughs of the trees did riot move. The creek broadened as he advanced, and seemed to have a fair depth. It was filled everywhere with ice, broken up by the thaw, and moving slowly. The forest seemed to extend back at least a quarter of a mile, on either side.

Bob kept his eyes fixed on the light, which burned steadily and grew larger as he advanced. He was quite sure now that it was the flame from a fire. He had gone about a half mile, when he stopped suddenly, and despite all his experience and self control shuddered violently.

The boughs of the trees above his head contained many long, dark objects, and he knew what they were. He had come to an ancient Indian burying ground. Perhaps the mummies swinging from the boughs were the very ancestors of the warriors who had fallen on the Arickaree and the Washita, and this most certainly was *not* a good omen.

He steadied his nerves and continued his advance toward the light, coming near enough now to know absolutely that it was the flame from a campfire. It was obscured, at moments, by dark figures passing before it, and these figures must be men. Many would have turned back now, but Bob's resolve to see who these men were increased in strength. There was the barest of chances that they might be Sam Strong and his comrades, and every probability that they were hostile Indians. In either case he wished to know.

Bob stalked the campfire. The snow was so soft now that it gave back no sound at all, and there were bushes in plenty. He was soon near enough to see that the campfire was large, surrounded by perhaps thirty men, and as he lay down in the snow and drew his body yet closer, he perceived that three or four of these men were white, the rest being Indians, mostly of the Cheyenne nation, but with four or five Arapahoes and Kiowas.

The boy, lying in the dark, and with his body almost covered by the snow, saw that the principal figure among the white men was that of Juan Carver. He sat where the full light of the fire fell upon his sombre face, and in the luminous glow, he looked very cruel and very powerful. Evidently he had come out of the battles without a wound.

The three other white men belonged to the band with which Carver had expected to take the beaver skins from Sam Strong and his comrades. The rest, Bob supposed, had either been killed or had wandered away. The fire threw out much heat, and Indians and white men were grouped about it, enjoying the warmth. Bob surmised that they had made a night march, and that the fire had just been built. Carver was talking to one of the white men, and judging from the deference paid to him by both white and red, he was the leader of the party.

Bob, feeling secure in his snowy ambush was extremely anxious to hear what was being said, and he gradually crept closer. All the horses were on the far side of the flames and there was no danger from them. He was soon within fifteen or twenty yards of the fire, lying among the thick bushes. There he had the reward of skill and daring. Carver and another of the white men finally rose, walked toward an open space in which their blankets were spread, but did not cease their talk.

Bob did not catch all the words, but he caught enough to make a connected story. Carver and the Indians, refugees from the Washita, also had heard the rumours that a party of trappers were hiding in the hills, with a rich store of furs, waiting a chance to get through to civilization. Bob heard Carver twice say the word "Strong" and he could not doubt that his comrades were beyond the low, blue line that marked the beginning of the hills. Carver and this strong band were seeking them also, and now his obligation to reach them was all the greater.

He remained quite still, while Carver and most all the others lay down to sleep, in a circle about the fire, leaving three Indians and one white man to keep the watch. Then he began his slow retreat. He was so careful about it, that it was twenty minutes before he was well beyond the circle of the firelight, and could safely rise to his feet. But after that he sped back to his horse, mounted, rode out upon the plain, and making a wide curve around the hostile camp, advanced as swiftly as the snow would allow, toward the hills.

CHAPTER 24

A Miracle

Bob turned back into the timber towards morning. He deemed it wiser to risk a chance of encounter with Indians there than to remain in the bright sunlight on the open plain, where anyone could see him for miles. Besides a wary man, alone in the timber, would be likely to see an enemy first and there would always be a chance to hide.

He took his breakfast in the saddle and as he advanced, the snow became thinner, melting rapidly under the rays of a fairly warm sun. None of it was left on the boughs, and the creek was beginning to rise, under the influence of the innumerable streams that poured into it from the thaw. Bob surmised that this creek entered the hills, passed through into the mountains, and probably flowed into some river on the other side. Its valley offered a path, easy for his horse, and all the more likely to take him to his comrades, who would surely seek some warm valley, containing flowing water.

The dim, blue line of the day before now became high and dark, a ridge of hills, shaggy with pine and cedar, and beyond them were white summits and crests, which showed where the ridges sloped up into mountains. Bob was sure that he could reach them before dark, and he was equally sure that Carver and the Cheyenne band were far behind him. That night's start of six or seven hours was a great thing, and might prove the salvation of more than one man.

At noon he gave his horse a rest of more than an hour, bathed his face and hands in the icy creek, and walked vigorously up and down, in order to take the stiffness from his limbs, caused by so much riding. When he sprang into the saddle again it was with renewed vigour. Throughout the afternoon he saw great quantities of game, buffalo and deer, which had sought the shelter of the forest, and many wolves lurking about, in the hope of pulling down the weak. The wolves often were so bold, or were so hard driven by hunger, that he was tempted to take a shot at some particularly ferocious haunter of the timber, but he did not dare, because of those whom he knew to be behind him.

At dusk he reached the first slopes, and he was glad to see that the plains and cedars were very dense, but with a fairly good trail leading into the hills by the side of the creek, which was now a foaming torrent. He continued as long as the light made travel safe, and then turned aside into a narrow valley like a cleft, which cut through the hills. He did not know how far it went or to what it would lead him, but he could not afford to camp beside the creek, because the Cheyennes would certainly come that way. He went fully two miles, and then he was somewhat surprised to find the trail leading into a wide valley which, as nearly as he could make out in the moonlight, seemed to be two or three miles square.

It was now about midnight and thoroughly exhausted with twenty-four hours of riding, watching and supremest tension, he stopped among the trees that fringed the valley, tethered his horse, leaving him saddled, took the usual refuge among his blankets, and in five minutes was asleep.

Bob's awakening was sudden and alarming. He heard a terrified neigh and sprang to his feet just in time to see his horse break the lariat, and gallop off wildly down the valley. All this he saw through a great, white veil, because the snow was pouring down as if the bottom of the very heavens had dropped out. He also saw rushing directly upon him a great dark, heaving mass, a herd of buffaloes in a panic.

Bob's action was partly due to quickness of mind and partly to impulse. He had slept with his rifle, rolled in the blankets beside him, and when he sprang to his feet it was still in his hands. Now, with the blankets still hanging about his shoulders, he ran swiftly to one side, endeavouring to secure the slope on the right. It was fortunate for him that he was strong and active, as the need of speed was heavy upon him. It seemed to him that he felt the breath of the leading bulls on the back of his neck, and the thunder of their hoofs was a deafening roar in his ears. He slipped once on the first slope, but remembering at the same time to cling to his rifle and blankets, regained his feet and ran, with all his might, reaching the crest, as the black herd thundered over the place where he had been.

The buffaloes seemed to be frantic with terror, either of the storm or some force behind them, and they plunged, with irresistible force, down the narrow ravine into the valley. The weaker members of the herd, driven to the outside, were pushed up the slopes, and Bob found them coming dangerously near to him. For further protection he climbed a huge oak tree and sat down in a low fork. There he was in no danger of being trampled, although he might freeze to death.

He made himself as easy as he could in the fork, drew the blankets as closely as possible around his body, and watched the buffaloes go by. The buffalo is subject to panic, and he believed now that they had been attacked somewhere else by Indians, possibly by the warriors who were with Carver, and that the sudden coming of so great a snowstorm had added to their terror.

It was not a large herd, two or three thousand, perhaps, and they were not long in passing. Bob watched the last big, black form disappear in the driving veil of snow, and then he took thought of himself. He was in a serious case, perched in an oak, in the wild hills, his horse lost, his friends far, his foes near, and the snow coming down so fast that it seemed to crowd the air.

He dropped to the ground and tried to get his bearings. But he knew nothing, except that before him lay a large valley into which the buffaloes had gone. The great trail that they made was quickly covered by the falling snow. In the east was a yellowish blur, which told that the sun was rising, but the sun itself was invisible through the mass of sullen clouds.

Bob was in great doubt. He might stay among the trees and find some sort of shelter there, but it would lead to nothing. On the other hand, it might be that his friends had taken refuge in some such valley as this, and he decided at last to enter it, and cross it if possible. When he fell down the cliff in crossing the pass, he had taken the boldest course and won. He might succeed again. At least, if he needed food the buffaloes would be there, and he had his rifle.

He left the trees and entered the plain, plunging forward over rough ground, through the snow, and unable to tell much about the region into which he was coming. The falling snow was so dense that when he looked back he could no longer see the trees. He kept manfully on, trying to maintain the direction in which he had started, but not at all certain about it. Fortunately the cold was not great, and the exercise made his blood circulate freely.

He expected to cross the valley in an hour or two, but he did not come to any trees, and he thought that he might be walking in a circle. There was no way in which to tell, and he stuck to his task, going forward without stopping, until he thought it must be noon. Then he stopped, crouched down in a little hollow and drew the blankets over his head. Most of his food supplies were gone with the horse, but with a hunter's precaution, he had put some pemmican in his belt, and now he ate eagerly. Then he rested a while, but he was afraid to stay long, and transferring the blankets from his head to his body he started again.

Bob fought the snow all that afternoon without coming to a forest. He passed several clumps of bushes and every time he was tempted to seek some sort of shelter among them, but always he successfully resisted the temptation, knowing that it would not do to yield. The afternoon passed in such struggles, and then, the yellowish, pale sunlight showing dimly through the veil of snow, began to fade. In its place came a whitish darkness that filled the boy's soul with apprehension. One could not live forever, unsheltered in such a storm. The night was at hand, the snow was not abating, and he was becoming so weak from his long exertions that he could not keep his feet another hour.

He stood still for four or five minutes, trying to choose a course, like a mariner in a storm. Then his weakness grew great upon him, but he thought that he saw off to the left a dark line which might be trees. At least hope put trees there, and summoning his last reserve of strength he walked toward the dark line. As he came nearer, he was quite sure that he could discern the outline of boughs, and then he became aware of peculiar noises, something like groanings or gruntings, and he dimly saw darker figures under the dark trees. He could not tell what they were because he was staggering now with weakness, and besides he did not care. He was so weary of the eternal snow that he was ready to walk straight into an Indian camp, if it was there.

He reached the trees, and saw what had made the noises. Many of the buffaloes were lying under them, evidently having sought such shelter from the storm, and near the edge of it, some of the biggest were lying in a group, surrounded by the deep snow, but keeping one another warm.

The buffaloes continued their groanings and heavings, but did not stir from their places, when Bob came near. They shook the snow from their manes and looked at him with great, red, incurious eyes. Perhaps some instinct told them that he was harmless, that he too merely sought shelter.

The boy, the blanket drawn around his shoulders and falling down around him like the folds of a tunic, stood regarding the group of big bulls, at a distance of less than a dozen feet. He was in a haze, and the animals, that he would have hunted so zealously another time, were now like tame cattle to him. They were more. They were sympathetic friends, friends in need. He could see it in their mild, incurious eyes. Man and beast had come together at last in a common brotherhood.

The boy was wholly without fear. Some of his reasoning faculties were atrophied for the time, but primitive instincts were strong within him. He walked boldly forward, and touched one of the big bulls, lying well under the trees, and close to some bushes. The animal, apparently, made an effort to rise, but sank back in his bed of snow and lay quite still.

Bob surmised that the buffalo was hurt, that in the mad rush into the valley a leg perhaps had been sprained too severely for him to move after he had lain down and it had become stiff.

He was sorry for the bull. He had gone through so much himself that he could understand the sufferings of another, even though it was only a four footed animal.

He stroked the big bull's side, and the fur was warm to his fingers. The buffalo, hurt and weak, no longer tried to move, Beyond a question, his instinct told him that it was a friend, one who would help him if he could. He uttered a low sound, like a pleased sigh, and Bob, more from weakness than intent, leaned against him. Still the buffalo made no effort to move, and his great body was very warm. The boy sought to rise, but his full weakness was upon him now, and he sank lower against the huge, warm, furry side of the buffalo. He remembered to draw the blankets all about him, even to enveloping his feet, and the faithful rifle was again enclosed in their folds by his side. Then his eyes closed, and he dropped into warm forgetfulness.

The snow did not cease. It was driven by the wind now, but the big bodies of the buffaloes intercepted most of it and the sleeping boy, lying close against the sheltered furry side of the biggest of them all, caught but little, even upon his blanket. All through the night the snow fell, but neither the boy nor the big buffalo moved. Both were at peace, and all around them the other buffaloes stirred little. There was an occasional groan or sigh, and at the edge of the forest the timber wolves howled their sorrow because the game was too big and strong for them to attack. But Bob never heard groan of buffalo or howl of timber wolf. While he slept glorious warmth permeated his being, enriching the blood in every vein and soothing every tired and strained nerve.

The boy was awakened at dawn by the sound of heavy, shuffling feet, and sprang up in alarm. Several of the buffaloes were moving about, but the big bull, who had furnished the furnace by the side of which he had slept so well, lay still. Then Bob remembered everything, and his alarm left him. He was filled with awe that morning, and this seemed to him a miracle, a miracle sent to save his life. He could never again fire upon a buffalo without almost feeling that he was slaying a fellow creature.

He touched the furry side of the great bull and said, as if he were speaking to a human being:

"I hope that your hurt will soon heal and that no hunter, white or red, will ever find you with bullet or arrow."

Then he looked about in order to observe his situation anew. The snow had ceased, although it lay more than two feet deep on the ground, and a bright sun was casting a golden glow over a white world. Before him was the valley, across which he had come, and he knew now that he had travelled long in a circle because it was not more than two miles in diameter. Yet he could easily have perished there had not chance guided him to a warm bed in the buffalo-fold. Once more he gave thanks for the miracle. Three times had his life been saved by animals, although one of them was dead, once by the skin of the grizzly bear that he had shot, once by a wild horse that had become tame, and now by a crippled buffalo. Since a miracle had intervened on his behalf, he must succeed. Bob was not superstitious, but all these circumstances seemed to him an omen, powerful and propitious. As they had intervened in his favour at the most critical moments of his life he must succeed. Hope leaped up with mighty impulse.

CHAPTER 25

The Final Settlement

Back of Bob was forest, extending for an indefinite distance along the slopes of hills and mountains, and he was quite sure that Sam Strong and the others were in this maze. It would be his wisest procedure to find some small stream and follow it That course might also lead him to his lost horse.

After a breakfast of pemmican, he went down through the edge of the forest to what seemed to be its lowest point, making his way with difficulty through the deep snow, but he was rewarded with the discovery of a brook that he had no doubt ran into the creek. He undertook to follow this to its source, and he found that it led upward through an extremely narrow ravine. He went against the stream four or five hours, making perhaps ten miles, and then came upon a little plateau clothed in forest Here he was so much exhausted that he sank down on a fallen log, ready for a long rest The long rest did not come because a voice powerful and penetrating hailed him with these words:

"Hold up your hands! Tell who you are! And be quick about it!"

Bob knew that voice. Its tones filled him with delight, and he felt moreover an overwhelming sense of triumph, because he had succeeded in the face of such tremendous obstacles. He threw both hands as high above his head as they would go, and shouted:

"My name is Robert Norton! I come from many places, and I'm looking for six rascals, Samuel Strong, William Cole, Obadiah Pirtle, Louis Perolet, Thomas Harris and Porter Evans. Have you seen them?"

"By all the stars! And the sun! And the moon, too! If it ain't the youngster, alive an' kickin'!"

Sam Strong made a rush through the snow, seized Bob by the hand, and nearly wrung it off in the violence of his joy.

"Is it you, Bob? Is it really you?" he exclaimed. "An' did you come on the edge of the storm! Are you sure you ain't no ghost, slippin' aroun' to ha'nt us?"

"No," replied Bob, exuberantly, "I'm no ghost, but I did come in on the edge of the storm. Where are the others? Are they alive? Are they well?"

"They're alive, an' if they ain't well I don't want to see 'em when they are well. They're eatin' their heads off in the stall at a rate that's somethin· tre-men-jeous. I s'pose if they was real well they'd eat up a whole buffalo herd, hoof an' horns. Now, Bob, boy, I've always been hopin' for the best, but I sca'cely hoped for this."

He wrung Bob's hand again, and then the boy said:

"I believe, Sam, it was a miracle that saved me last night, and maybe it was another miracle that sent me here. I'll tell about it after I've seen the fellows. Where are they?"

"Back in our shack in the woods. We hunted for you, days an' days, an' at last had to give you up. Then we started ag'in for the east, but the Cheyennes were so thick on the plains that we had to come here in the hills, an' hole up for the winter."

"The Cheyennes are in these hills, too," said Bob, "but I've come ahead of 'em an' I think I'm in time. I'll tell that, too, as soon as I reach the others."

Sam Strong repressed a start.

"Come on," he said, and led the way to the thickest part of the woods, in which Bob presently saw the outlines of a rude cabin.

"We didn't build as well as we did back there near the Colorado," said Sam, apologetically, "because we wasn't expectin' to stay as long. All we needed was a shanty. But all the boys are inside, an' the horses are in the woods back of us."

He pushed open the rude door and said simply:

"Boys, here's Bob; he's come back ag'in!"

Bill Cole dropped the rifle that he was polishing. Louis Perolet dropped the fish that he was cooking. Obadiah Pirtle dropped a moccasin that he was repairing, and an elaborate discussion on the Civil War, conducted with some heat by Tom Harris and Porter Evans, was dropped in the middle of a sentence. The five sprang to their feet and made a rush at the boy. They overwhelmed him with handshakings, and then pushed him to the fire where he might thaw out.

Bob's joy, like that of the others, was exuberant and bubbling, but he did not spend more than fifteen minutes in impulsive question and answer. In that time he told briefly of the two great battles through which he had passed, and listened to their expressions of wonder. Then he said:

"A band of Cheyennes, with Carver and two or three other white men like him, are in these hills, not far away, looking for us. I have seen them myself, and they may come up the valley as I did."

"Tell us all you know about it, Bob," said Sam Strong, instantly becoming the quiet, resolute and resourceful leader.

Bob told everything. His imaginative mind painted all the details vividly, and they understood clearly what they must expect. Sam Strong quickly made his decision.

"Ef they come," he said, "they'll come up the ravine that you followed, Bob. It's the only possible way in here, through such deep snow, an' they'll have to come slow. 'Stead o' waitin' for them to attack us, we'll go meet 'em. like as not, they'll come along tonight, ploghin' through the snow, an' what with an ambush an' a surprise, it'll be plum' funny ef we don't beat 'em. Does my plan seem proper to you, boys!"

"General Lee hisself couldn't have arranged better," said Porter Evans.

"It's exactly what General Grant would have done," said Tom Harris.

"Since you two mighty captains agree with me," said Sam Strong, "I reckon there ain't nothin' more to be said. Bill, you an' Obe take your rifles, go straight to the mouth of that pass an' watch. The rest of us will be there at sunset, ef you don't bring us an alarm before then."

Bill and the Maine man went forth at once, and the others began to prepare fresh ammunition, all except Bob, who was compelled to rest on a pallet of skins. Strong would not let him work, and he became reconciled to his enforced rest when told that he must recover his strength for battle.

They had abundant cartridges, as they had used very few in the winter, and when the long shadows began to fall across the snow in the west, they went forth, resolved, in the words of Sam Strong, to make an end of it.

"We're tired of bein' chased aroun' by Cheyennes an' fellers like Carver," he said, "an' want to go about our business, which is trappin' an' sellin' the proceeds."

As they had the sunset light to guide them, it did not take them long to cross the plain, and when the twilight was fully come they were signalled by Bill Cole and the Maine man. The two were hidden behind some big trees, where they had a view of the pass for a long distance. The narrow way was now filled with deep snow, and no one could come through it except slowly. The steep sides were impossible, as any attempt to climb them now would bring down an avalanche of snow. Sam Strong surveyed the position with delight.

"It was jest made for us," he said. "Why, Bill, standin' here, we could drive back an army."

"Certain," said Bill Cole. "We could drive back two of 'em. Do you think, Sam, we ought to put our own army on both sides of the pass?"

"No," replied Strong. "It'll be better fur us to stick together. Then, whatever happens to one of us will happen to all, an' there won't be no divisions of any kind."

"Reckon you're right, Sam," said Bill.

They settled down in a close group and waited, speaking rarely, and then only in whispers. They had brought their blankets along in order that they might be warm and their sinews elastic when the time came for battle. These blankets were wrapped closely about them, and each huddled figure looked shapeless in the darkness.

Bob had seen so much now of Indian combat that his imagination was not lively, as he sat there with his friends in the pass, awaiting the advance of the Cheyennes and Carver. The joy that he felt at the reunion carried over, as it were, and the coming event cast no shadow.

There was a yellow half moon and it tinted the snow. The pass itself seemed to have a sort of golden glow. A timber wolf howled at the crest of a hill, but the huddled figures behind the trees filled him with terror, and he would go no further. He howled again, and fled to the higher hills. The huddled figures paid no attention.

It was half way between twilight and midnight, and the moon was fading, but the seven could still see clearly anything that might move in the pass. They saw nothing, but Sam Strong held up a warning finger.

"Listen!" he said.

They heard a faint crushing sound.

"Their footsteps in the snow," said Sam. "They're comin'."

Bob strained his eyes down the pass, and a dark face emerged into the moonlight, then another and another, until the whole band of the Indians, with Carver and his friends appeared, laboriously toiling through the snow, in which they sank to their knees at every step. The moon at that moment seemed to shine at a new angle and its rays fell full upon them. As they drew near Bob saw that their faces were eager and hideous with the passion for blood and revenge. Whatever compunctions he might have had about firing upon them from ambush, were dissipated now. He and his friends, for the sake of their own lives, must use the advantage they held.

"When they come opposite that fallen tree, fire," whispered Sam Strong. "I'll count, but I'll count only one."

Bob drew an imaginary line across the snow, and pushed his rifle forward a little. He saw that all the Indians carried their rifles well in advance, and that they were looking eagerly up the pass. He had no doubt that they had obtained information from some wandering warrior of the presence of the band.

"One!" said Sam Strong in a sharp, tense whisper.

Seven rifles were fired so close together that they made but a single report, and all the leaders of the Indian band went down in the snow, while the others gave forth a shout of consternation and rage. Before they could recover, the seven poured in another volley.

Overwhelmed by the surprise, which had in it also a strong element of superstitious terror, since the attack seemed to come like a thunderbolt from heaven, the Indians rushed back down the pass.

"After 'em!" cried Sam Strong, "but keep behind the trees where they can't see us. We must hit 'em as they run, an' they'll never come back!"

He led along the slope, and they shot rapidly at the running Indians who were now in a state of absolute panic. Bob and Sam were in advance, firing as fast as they could reload and pull the trigger. Neither, in the excitement of the pursuit, noticed that a dark figure detached itself from the mass and climbed the slope.

Bob was farthest down the incline, and he had just emptied his rifle when the dark figure, pistol in hand, came face to face with him.

"You don't escape this time!" said Juan Carver, raising his pistol and aiming at the boy.

Bob, paralyzed at the sudden appearance of the freebooter, was unable to move. The face of Carver blazed with triumph. He, at least, would find revenge. But as his finger moved toward the trigger, Sam Strong hurled himself upon him. The pistol was fired, but the bullet went upward, and the two men writhed in a powerful embrace.

Bob, recovering his power over himself, drew his own pistol and ran forward. But he could not use it. The two men, almost equal in strength, went down in the snow, and whirled over and over. He heard hard breathing, muttered cries, and the crunching of snow. Then they rolled toward the last edge of the slope, and Bob himself uttered a cry. The snow gave way and the two, still locked fast in each other's arms, shot down in a white avalanche into the pass. The sliding snow moved for a minute, and then the boy, looking down, could neither see nor hear anything.

"They're both killed!" exclaimed Bob in horror.

"We'll see," said Bill Cole.

All the surviving Indians had disappeared, fleeing in such terror that they would never return again, and Bill did not consider it worth while to bother about them any longer. He and the others carefully climbed down the slope, and stood in the deep snow at the bottom of the pass. But they saw nothing.

"Now, I wonder where Sam is," said Bill Cole in much alarm.

"Here!" replied a voice, weak but confident, and a white figure, rising out of the depths, stood erect

"Sam!" they exclaimed joyfully and together.

Then they added:

"Where's Carver!"

"There," replied Sam, pointing to the place in the snow from which he had arisen, his voice very solemn. "He's dead. I think that, as we rolled down, his head hit a rock which mine didn't."

It was true. Carver's skull was fractured, and he was quite dead.

"Providence must have been watchin' over me as it was watchin' over you last night, Bob," said Sam Strong, and his tone was devout and grateful. "I'm always hopin' for the best, and often I get better than I deserve."

They took the body of Carver from the snow the next day and gave it Christian burial.

* * * * * * * *

Bob and his comrades remained in the hills until the winter broke up. His lost horse, driven by the instinct of companionship, joined the others, saddle, blanket and supplies still strapped on him, and Bob soon reduced him to order.

The snow melted, the trail became good, and they went down into the plains, taking a straight course to the northeast. Fortune was with them, and they met no more Indian bands, but they passed many troops, and Bob saw again all his old friends, Jack Stillwell, Pete Trudeau, California Joe, and the young Mexican, Romeo.

When their furs were sold and the money was put where it would be safe, Sam Strong asked the question:

"What is to become of this band!"

"It's goin' to the new beaver streams you an' Bob an' Obe an' me found away down the Colorado," said Bill Cole.

"Is that so!" said Sam Strong to the Maine man.

"I reckon it is," replied Obadiah Pirtle.

"I know eet ees," said Louis Perolet. "The great Napoleon, after making one brilliant campaign, would make another."

Tom Harris and Porter Evans joined in the general approval.

"An' you, Bob!" said the leader.

The boy's eyes were shining.

"We're bound to go to those new beaver streams," he said.

That was where they went.

The Last of the Chiefs

CHAPTER 1

The Train

The boy in the third wagon was suffering from exhaustion. The days and days of walking over the rolling prairie, under a brassy sun, the hard food of the train, and the short hours of rest, had put too severe a trial upon his delicate frame. Now, as he lay against the sacks and boxes that had been drawn up to form a sort of couch for him, his breath came in short gasps, and his face was very pale. His brother, older, and stronger by far, who walked at the wheel, regarded him with a look in which affection and intense anxiety were mingled. It was not a time and place in which one could afford to be ill.

Richard and Albert Howard were bound together by the strongest of brotherly ties. Richard had inherited his father's bigness and powerful constitution, Albert his mother's slenderness and fragility. But it was the mother who lived the longer, although even she did not attain middle age, and her last words to her older son were: "Richard, take care of Albert." He had promised, and now was thinking how he could keep the promise.

It was a terrible problem that confronted Richard Howard. He felt no fear on his own account. A boy in years, he was a man in the ability to care for himself, wherever he might be. In a boyhood spent on an Illinois farm, where the prairies slope up to the forest, he had learned the ways of wood and field, and was full of courage, strength, and resource.

But Albert was different. He had not thrived in the moist air of the great valley. Tall enough he was, but the width of chest and thickness of bone were lacking. Noticing this, the idea of going to California had come to the older brother. The great gold days had passed years since, but it was still a land of enchantment to the youth of the older states, and the long journey in the high, dry air of the plains would be good for Albert. There was nothing to keep them back. They had no property save a little money—enough for their equipment, and a few dollars over to live on in California until they could get work.

233

To decide was to start, and here they were in the middle of the vast country that rolled away west of the Missouri, known but little, and full of dangers. The journey had been much harder than the older boy had expected. The days stretched out, the weeks trailed away, and still the plains rolled before them. The summer had been of the hottest, and the heated earth gave back the glare until the air quivered in torrid waves. Richard had drawn back the cover of the wagon that his brother might breathe the air, but he replaced it now to protect him from the overpowering beams. Once more he anxiously studied the country, but it gave him little hope. The green of the grass was gone, and most of the grass with it. The brown undulations swept away from horizon to horizon, treeless, waterless, and bare. In all that vast desolation there was nothing save the tired and dusty train at the very centre of it.

"Anything in sight, Dick?" asked Albert, who had followed his brother's questioning look.

Dick shook his head.

"Nothing, Al," he replied.

"I wish we'd come to a grove," said the sick boy.

He longed, as do all those who are born in the hills, for the sight of trees and clear, running water.

"I was thinking, Dick," he resumed in short, gasping tones, "that it would be well for us, just as the evening was coming on, to go over a swell and ride right into a forest of big oaks and maples, with the finest little creek that you ever saw running through the middle of it. It would be pleasant and shady there. Leaves would be lying about, the water would be cold, and maybe we'd see elk coming down to drink."

"Perhaps we'll have such luck, Al," said Dick, although his tone showed no such hope. But he added, assuming a cheerful manner: "This can't go on forever; we'll be reaching the mountains soon, and then you'll get well."

"How's that brother of yours? No better, I see, and he's got to ride all the time now, making more load for the animals."

It was Sam Conway, the leader of the train, who spoke, a rough man of middle age, for whom both Dick and Albert had acquired a deep dislike. Dick flushed through his tan at the hard words.

"If he's sick he had the right to ride," he replied sharply. "We've paid our share for this trip and maybe a little more. You know that."

Conway gave him an ugly look, but Dick stood up straight and strong, and met him eye for eye. He was aware of their rights and he meant to defend them. Conway, confronted by a dauntless spirit, turned away, muttering in a surly fashion:

"We didn't bargain to take corpses across the plains."

Fortunately, the boy in the wagon did not hear him, and, though his eyes flashed ominously, Dick said nothing. It was not a time for quarrelling, but it was often hard to restrain one's temper. He had realized, soon after the start, when it was too late to withdraw, that the train was not a good one. It was made up mostly of men. There were no children, and the few women, like the men, were coarse and rough. Turbulent scenes had occurred, but Dick and Albert kept aloof, steadily minding their own business.

"What did Conway say?" asked Albert, after the man had gone.

"Nothing of any importance. He was merely growling as usual. He likes to make himself disagreeable. I never saw another man who got as much enjoyment out of that sort of thing."

Albert said nothing more, but closed his eyes. The canvas cover protected him from the glare of the sun, but seemed to hold the heat within it. Drops of perspiration stood on his face, and Dick longed for the mountains, for his brother's sake.

All the train fell into a sullen silence, and no sound was heard but the unsteady rumble of the wheels, the creak of an ungreased axle, and the occasional crack of a whip. Clouds of dust arose and were whipped by the stray winds into the faces of the travellers, the fine particles burning like hot ashes. The train moved slowly and heavily, as if it dragged a wounded length over the hard ground.

Dick Howard kept his position by the side of the wagon in which his brother lay. He did not intend that Albert should hear bitter words levelled at his weakness, and he knew that his own presence was a deterrent. The strong figures and dauntless port of the older youth inspired respect. Moreover, he carried over his shoulder a repeating rifle of the latest pattern, and his belt was full of cartridges. He and Albert had been particular about their arms. It was a necessity. The plains and the mountains were subject to all the dangers of Indian warfare, and they had taken a natural youthful pride in buying the finest of weapons.

The hot dust burned Dick Howard's face and crept into his eyes and throat. His tongue lay dry in his mouth. He might have ridden in one of the wagons, too, had he chosen. As he truly said, he and Albert had paid their full share, and in the labour of the trail, he was more efficient than anybody else in the train. But his pride had been touched by Conway's words. He would not ride, nor would he show any signs of weakness. He strode on by the side of the wagon, head erect, his step firm and springy.

The sun crept slowly down the brassy arch of the heavens, and the glare grew less blinding. The heat abated, but Albert Howard, who had fallen asleep, slept on. His brother drew a blanket over him, knowing that he could not afford to catch cold, and breathed the cooler air himself, with thankfulness. Conway came back again, and was scarcely less gruff than before, although he said nothing about Albert.

"Bright Sun says than in another day or two we'll be seeing the mountains," he vouchsafed; "and I'll be glad of it, because then we'll be coming to water and game."

"I'd like to be seeing them now," responded Dick; "but do you believe everything that Bright Sun says?"

"Of course I do. Hasn't he brought us along all right? What are you driving at?"

His voice rose to a challenging tone, in full accordance with the nature of the man, whenever anyone disagreed with him, but Dick Howard took not the least fear.

"I don't altogether like Bright Sun," he replied. "Just why, I can't say, but the fact remains that I don't like him. It doesn't seem natural for an Indian to be so fond of white people, and to prefer another race to his own."

Conway laughed harshly.

"That shows how much you know," he said. "Bright Sun is smart, smarter than a steel trap. He knows that the day of the red is passing, and he's going to train with the white. What's the use of being on the losing side? It's what I say, and it's what Bright Sun thinks."

The man's manner was gross and materialistic, so repellent that Dick would have turned away, but at that moment Bright Sun himself approached. Dick regarded him, as always, with the keenest interest and curiosity mixed with some suspicion. Yet almost anyone would have been reassured by the appearance of Bright Sun. He was a splendid specimen of the Indian, although in white garb, even to the soft felt hat shading his face. But he could never have been taken for a white man. His hair was thick, black, and coarse, his skin of the red man's typical coppery tint, and his cheek bones high and sharp. His lean but sinewy and powerful figure rose two inches above six feet. There was an air about him, too, that told of strength other than that of the body. Guide he was, but leader he looked.

"Say, Bright Sun," exclaimed Conway coarsely, "Dick Howard here thinks you're too friendly with the whites. It don't seem natural to him that one of your colour should consort so freely with us."

Dick's face flushed through the brown, and he shot an angry glance at Conway, but Bright Sun did not seem to be offended.

"Why not?" he asked in perfect English. "I was educated in a mission school. I have been with white people most of my life, I have read your books, I know your civilization, and I like it."

"There now!" exclaimed Conway triumphantly. "Ain't that an answer for you? I tell you what, Bright Sun, I'm for you, I believe in you, and if anybody can take us through all right to California, you're the man."

"It is my task and I will accomplish it," said Bright Sun in the precise English he had learned at the mission school.

His eyes met Dick's for a moment, and the boy saw there a flash that might mean many things—defiance, primeval force, and the quality that plans and does. But the flash was gone in an instant, like a dying spark, and Bright Sun turned away. Conway also left, but Dick's gaze followed the Indian.

He did not know Bright Sun's tribe. He had heard that he was a Sioux, also that he was a Crow, and a third report credited him with being a Cheyenne. As he never painted his face, dressed like a white man, and did not talk of himself and his people, the curious were free to surmise as they chose. But Dick was sure of one thing: Bright Sun was a man of power. It was not a matter of surmise, he felt it instinctively.

The tall figure of the Indian was lost among the wagons, and Dick turned his attention to the trail. The cooling waves continued to roll up, as the west reddened into a brilliant sunset. Great bars of crimson, then of gold, and the shades in between, piled above one another on the horizon. The plains lost their brown, and gleamed in wonderful shimmering tints. The great desolate world became beautiful.

The train stopped with a rumble, a creak, and a lurch, and the men began to unharness the animals. Albert awoke with a start and sat up in the wagon.

"Night and the camp, Al," said Dick cheerfully; "feel better, don't you?

"Yes, I do," replied Albert, as a faint colour came into his face.

"Thought the rest and the coolness would brace you up," continued Dick in the same cheerful tone.

Albert, a tall, emaciated boy with a face of great refinement and delicacy, climbed out of the wagon and looked about. Dick busied himself with the work of making camp, letting Albert give what help he could.

But Dick always undertook to do enough for two—his brother and himself—and he really did enough for three. No other was so swift and skilful at taking the gear off horse or mule, nor was there a stronger or readier arm at the wheel when it was necessary to complete the circle of wagons that they nightly made. When this was done, he went out on the prairie in search of buffalo chips for the fire, which he was fortunate enough to find without any trouble.

Before returning with his burden, Dick stood a few moments looking back at the camp. The dusk had fully come, but the fires were not yet lighted, and he saw only the shadowy forms of the wagons and flitting figures about them. But much talked reached his ears, most of it coarse and rough, with a liberal sprinkling of oaths. Dick sighed. His regret was keener than ever that Albert and he were in such company. Then he looked the other way out upon the fathomless plains, where the night had gathered, and the wind was moaning among the swells. The air was now chill enough to make him shiver, and he gazed with certain awe into the black depths. The camp, even with all its coarseness and roughness, was better, and he walked swiftly back with his load of fuel.

They built a dozen fires within the circle of the wagons, and again Dick was the most active and industrious of them all, doing his share, Albert's, and something besides. When the fires were lighted they burned rapidly and merrily, sending up great tongues of red or yellow flame, which shed a flickering light over wagons, animals, and men. A pleasant heat was suffused and Dick began to cook supper for Albert and himself, bringing it from the wagon in which his brother and he had a share. He fried bacon and strips of dried beef, boiled coffee, and warmed slices of bread over the coals. He saw with intense pleasure that Albert ate with a better appetite than he had shown for days. As for himself, he was as hungry as a horse—he always was on this great journey—and since there was plenty, he ate long, and was happy. Dick went to the wagon, and returned with a heavy cloak, which he threw over Albert's shoulders.

"The night's getting colder," he said, "and you mustn't take any risks, Al. There's one trouble about a camp fire in the open—your face can burn while your back freezes."

Content fell over the camp. Even rough men of savage instincts are willing to lie quiet when they are warm and well fed. Jokes, coarse but invariably in good humour, were exchanged. The fires still burned brightly, and the camp formed a core of light and warmth in the dark, cold wilderness.

Albert, wrapped in the cloak, lay upon his side and elbow gazing dreamily into the flames. Dick sat near him, frying a piece of bacon on the end of a stick. Neither heard the step behind them because it was noiseless, but both saw the tall figure of Bright Sun, as he came up to their fire.

"Have a piece of bacon, Bright Sun," said Dick hospitably, holding out the slice to him, and at the same time wondering whether the Indian would take it. Bright Sun shook his head.

"I thank you," he replied, "but I have eaten enough. How is Mr. Albert Howard now?"

Dick appreciated the inquiry, whether or not it was prompted by sympathy.

"Good," he replied. "Al's picking up. Haven't seen him eat as he did tonight for months. If he keeps on this way, he'll devour a whole buffalo as soon as he's able to kill one."

Bright Sun smiled, and sat down on the ground near them. It seemed to the boy, a keen observer of his kind, that he wished to talk. Dick was willing.

"Do you know," asked Bright Sun, "that reports of gold in the region to the north, called by you the Black Hills, have come to us?"

"I heard some one speak of it two or three days ago," replied Dick, "but I paid no attention to it."

Bright Sun looked thoughtfully into the fire, the glow of which fell full upon his face, revealing every feature like carving. His nose was hooked slightly, and to Dick it now looked like the beak of an eagle. The sombre eyes, too, expressed brooding and mastery alike.

Despite himself, Dick felt again that he was in the presence of power, and he was oppressed by a sense of foreboding.

"It was worth attention," said Bright Sun in the slow, precise tones of one who speaks a language not his own, but who speaks it perfectly. "The white man's gold is calling to him loudly. It calls all through the day and night. Do these men with whom you travel go to anything certain far over on the coast of the western ocean? No, they are leaves blown by the wind. The wind now blows in the direction of the Black Hills, where the gold is said to be, and tomorrow the wagon train turns its head that way."

Dick sat up straight, and Albert, wrapped in his blanket, leaned forward to listen.

"But the engagement with us all," said Dick, "was to go to the Pacific. Albert and I paid our share for that purpose. Conway knows it."

The Indian looked at Dick. The boy thought he saw a flickering smile of amusement in his eyes, but it was faint, and gone in a moment.

"Conway does not care for that," said the Indian. "Your contracts are nothing to him. This is the wilderness, and it stretches away for many hundreds of miles in every direction. The white man's law does not come here. Moreover, nearly all wish him to turn to the north and the gold."

Albert suddenly spoke, and his tone, though thin from physical weakness, was quick, intense, and eager.

"Why couldn't we go on with them, Dick?" he said. "We have nothing definite on the Pacific coast. We are merely taking chances, and if the Black Hills are full of gold, we might get our share!"

Dick's eyes glistened. If one had to go, one might make the best of it. The spirit of romance was alive within him. He was only a boy.

"Of course we'll go, Al," he said lightly, "and you and I will have a tone of gold inside a year."

Bright Sun looked at the two boys, first one and then the other, stalwart Dick and weak Albert. It seemed to Dick that he saw a new expression in the Indian's eyes, one that indicated the shadow of regret. He resented it. Did Bright Sun think that Albert and he were not equal to the task?

"I am strong," he said; "I can lift and dig enough for two; but Albert will also be strong, after we have been a little while in the mountains."

"You might have strength enough. I do not doubt it," said Bright Sun softly, "but the Black Hills are claimed by the Sioux. They do not wish the white men to come there, and the Sioux are a great and powerful tribe, or rather a nation of several allied and kindred tribes, the most powerful Indian nation west of the Mississippi."

Bright Sun's voice rose a little toward the last, and the slight upward tendency gave emphasis and significance to his words. The brooding eyes suddenly shot forth a challenging light.

"Are you a Sioux?" asked Dick involuntarily.

Bright Sun bent upon him a look of gentle reproof.

"Since I have taken the ways of your race I have no tribe," he replied. "But, as I have said, the Sioux claim the Black Hills, and they have many thousands of warriors, brave, warlike, and resolved to keep the country."

"The government will see that there is no war," said Dick.

"Governments can do little in a wilderness," replied Bright Sun.

Dick might have made a rejoinder, but at that moment a burly figure came into the light of the fire. It was Sam Conway, and he glanced suspiciously at the Indian and the two boys.

"Are you telling 'em, Bright Sun, when we'll reach California?" he asked.

Bright Sun gave him an oblique glance. The Indian seldom looks the white man in the face, but it was obvious that Bright Sun was not afraid of the leader. Conway, as well as the others, knew it. "No," he replied briefly.

"It's just as well that you haven't," said Conway briskly, "'cause we're not going to California at all—at least not this year. It's the wish and general consensus of this here train that we turn to the north, go into the Black Hills, and fill our wagons with gold."

"So it's decided, then, is it?" asked Dick.

"Yes, it's decided," replied Conway, his tone now becoming positively brutal, "and if you and your brother don't like it, you know what you can do."

"Keep on alone for the coast, I suppose," said Dick, looking him steadily in the face.

"If you put it that way."

"But we don't choose," said Dick, "Al and I have an interest in one wagon and team, and we're going to hold on to it. Besides, we're quite willing to try our luck in the Black Hills, too. We're going with you."

Conway frowned, but Dick also was not afraid of him, and knew that he could not turn the two boys out on the prairie. They had a full right to go with the train.

"That settles it," he said, turning away. "You can do as you please, but what happens after we get into the Black Hills is another thing. Likely, we'll scatter."

The sound of his retreating footsteps quickly died away in the darkness, and Bright Sun, too, slid among the shadows. He was gone so quickly and quietly that it gave Dick an uncanny feeling.

"What do you make of it, Al?" he asked his brother. "What does Bright Sun mean by what he said to us?"

The glow of the flame fell across Albert's pale face, and, by the light of it, Dick saw that he was very thoughtful. He seemed to be looking over and beyond the fire and the dark prairie, into time rather than space.

"I think it was a warning, Dick," replied Albert at last. "Maybe Bright Sun intended it for only you and me. But I want to go up there in the Black Hills, Dick."

"And so do I. It'll be easier for you, Al, than the trip across the continent. When you are a mile and a half or two miles above the sea, you'll begin to take on flesh like a bear in summer. Besides, the gold, Al! think of the gold!"

Albert smiled. He, too, was having happy thoughts. The warm glow of the fire clothed him and he was breathing easily and peacefully. By and by he sank down in his blanket and fell into a sound sleep. Dick himself did not yet have any thought of slumber. Wide-awake visions were pursuing one another through his brain. He saw the mountains, dark and shaggy with pine forests, the thin, healing air over them, and the beds of gold in their bosom, with Albert and himself discovering and triumphant.

The fire died down, and glowed a mass of red embers. The talk sank. Most of the men were asleep, either in their blankets or in the wagons. The darkness thickened and deepened and came close up to the fires, a circling rim of blackness. But Dick was still wakeful, dreaming with wide-open eyes his golden dreams.

As the visions followed one after another, a shadow which was not a part of any of them seemed to Dick to melt into the uttermost darkness beyond the fires. A trace of something familiar in the figure impressed him, and, rising, he followed swiftly.

The figure, still nebulous and noiseless, went on in the darkness, and another like it seemed to rise from the plain and join it. Then they were lost to the sight of the pursuer, seeming to melt into and become a part of the surrounding darkness. Dick, perplexed and uneasy, returned to the fire. The second shadow must certainly have been that of a stranger. What did it mean?

He resumed his seat before the red glow, clasping his arms around his knees, a splendid, resourceful youth whom nature and a hardy life had combined to make what he was. His brother still slept soundly and peacefully, but the procession of golden visions did not pass again through Dick's brain; instead, it was a long trail of clouds, dark and threatening. He sought again and again to conjure the clouds away and bring back the golden dreams, but he could not.

The fire fell to nothing, the triumphant darkness swept up and blotted out the last core of light, the wind, edged with ice, blew in from the plains. Dick shivered, drew a heavy blanket around his own shoulders, and moved a little, as he saw the dim figure of Bright Sun passing at the far edge of the wagons, but quickly relapsed into stillness.

Sleep at last pulled down his troubled lids. His figure sank, and, head on arms, he slumbered soundly.

CHAPTER 2

King Bison

"Up! Up, everybody!" was the shout that reached Dick's sleeping ears. He sprang to his feet and found that the gorgeous sun was flooding the prairie with light. Already the high, brilliant skies of the great west were arching over him. Men were cooking breakfast. Teamsters were cracking their whips and the whole camp was alive with a gay and cheerful spirit. Everybody seemed to know now that they were going for the gold, and, like Dick, they had found it in fancy already.

Breakfast over, the train took up its march, turning at a right angle from its old course and now advancing almost due north. But this start was made with uncommon alacrity and zeal. There were no sluggards now. They, too, had golden visions, and, as if to encourage them, the aspect of the country soon began to change, and rapidly to grow better. The clouds of dust that they raised were thinner. The bunch grass grew thicker. Off on the crest of a swell a moving figure was seen now and then. "Antelope," said the hunters. Once they passed a slow creek. The water was muddy, but it contained no alkali, and animals and men drank eagerly. Cottonwoods, the first trees they had seen in days, grew on either side of the stream, and they rested there awhile in the shade, because the sun was now out in full splendour, and the vast plains shimmered in the heat.

Albert resumed his place in the wagon. Dick had a horse which, on becoming foot-sore, had been allowed to rest for a few days, and was now well. He mounted it and galloped on ahead. The clouds were all gone away and the golden visions had come back. He felt so strong, so young, and the wonderful air of the plains was such a tonic that he urged his horse to a gallop, and it was hard for him to keep from shouting aloud in joy. He looked eagerly into the north, striving already for a sight of the dark mountains that men called the Black Hills. The blue gave back nothing but its own blue.

His horse seemed to share his spirits, and swung along with swift and easy stride. Dick looked back presently, and saw that the train which had been winding like a serpent over the plains was lost to sight behind the swells. The surface of the earth had become more rolling as they advanced northward, and he knew that the train, though out of sight, was nor far away.

He enjoyed for the moment the complete absence of all human beings save himself. To be alone then meant anything but loneliness. He galloped to the crest of a higher swell than usual, and then stopped short. Far off on the plain he saw tiny moving figures, a dozen or so, and he was sure that they were antelope. They had seen antelope before at a great distance, but had not bothered about them. Now the instincts of the hunter rose in Dick, and he resolved to make a trial of his skill.

He found in one of the depressions between the swells a stunted cottonwood, to which he hitched his horse, knowing it would be well hidden there from the observation of the herd. He then advanced on foot. He had heard that the antelope was a slave to its own curiosity, and through that weakness he intended to secure his game.

When he had gone about half the distance he sank down on his hands and knees and began to crawl, a laborious and sometimes painful operation, burdened as he was with his rifle, and unused to such methods of locomotion. Presently he noticed a flutter among the antelope, a raising of timid heads, an alarmed looking in his direction. But Dick was prepared. He lay flat upon his face, and dug the point of the long hunting knife that he carried into the ground, while the wind blew out the folds of the red handkerchief which he had tied to the handle.

Mr. Big Buck Antelope, the chief of the herd and a wary veteran, saw the waving red spot on the horizon and his interest was aroused, despite his caution. What a singular thing! It must be investigated! It might be some new kind of food very good for Mr. Big Buck's palate and stomach, and no provident antelope could afford to let such an opportunity pass.

He was trembling all over with curiosity, and perhaps his excitement kept him from seeing the dark shape that blurred with the earth just beyond the red something, or he may have taken it for a shadow. At any event, his curiosity kept him from paying heed to it, and he began to approach. His steps were hesitating, and now and then he drew away a little, but that singular red object lured him on, and yard by yard he drew nearer.

He suddenly saw the black shadow beyond the fluttering red object detach itself from the ground, and resolve into a terrible shape. His heart sprang up in his bosom, and he was about to rush madly away, but it was too late. A stream of fire shot forth from the dark object and the buck fell, a bullet through him.

Dick prepared the animal for dressing, thinking of the tender, juicy steaks that Albert would enjoy, and then throwing the body across the horse, behind him, rode back to the train, proud of his success.

Conway frowned and said grudging words. He did not like, he said, for anybody to leave the train without his permission, and it was foolish, anyhow, for a boy to be galloping about as he pleased over the prairie; he might get lost, and there would be nobody to take care of the other boy, the sick one. Dick made an easy diplomatic reply. He knew that Conway merely wished to be unpleasant, but Dick was of a very good nature, and he was particularly averse just then to quarrelling with anybody. He was too full of the glory of living. Instead, he offered some of the antelope steaks to Conway, who churlishly accepted them, and that night he broiled others for Albert and himself, dividing the rest among the men.

Albert found antelope steak tender and juicy, and he ate with an increasing appetite. Dick noted the increase with pleasure.

"I wish I could go out and kill antelope," said Albert.

Dick laughed cheerfully.

"Kill antelope," he said. "Why, Al, in six months you'll be taking a grizzly bear by the neck and choking him to death with your two hands."

"Wish I could believe it," said Albert.

But Dick went to sleep early that night, and slept peacefully without dreams or visions, and the next morning the train resumed its sanguine march. They were still ascending, and the character of the country continued to improve. Bunch grass steadily grew thicker and buffalo chips were numerous. The heat in the middle of the day was still great, but the air was so dry and pure that it was not oppressive. Albert dismounted from the wagon, and walked for several miles by the side of his brother.

"Shouldn't be surprised if we saw buffalo," said Dick. "Heard 'em talking about it in the train. Bright Sun says these are favourite grazing grounds, and there's still a lot of buffalo scattered about the plains."

Albert showed excitement.

"A buffalo herd!" he exclaimed. "Do you think it can really happen, Dick? I never thought I'd see such a thing! I hope it'll come true!"

It came true much sooner than Albert hoped.

Scarcely a half hour after he spoke, Bright Sun, who was at the head of the column, stopped his pony and pointed to indistinct tiny shadows just under the horizon.

"Buffalo!" he said tersely, and after a moment's pause he added: "A great herd comes!"

Dick and Albert were on foot then, but they heard his words and followed his pointing finger with the deepest interest. The tiny black shadows seemed to come out of the horizon as if they stepped from a wall. They grew in size and number, and all the west was filled with their forms.

The train resumed its march, bending off under the guidance of Bright Sun a little toward the west, and it was obvious that the herd would pass near. Dick and Albert rejoiced, because they wished to see the buffaloes at close quarters, and Dick was hoping also for a shot. Others, too, in the train, although their minds were set on gold, began to turn their attention now to the herd. The sport and the fresh meat alike would be welcome. It was Dick's impulse to mount his horse and gallop away again, gun in hand, but he made a supreme conquest over self and remained. He remembered Albert's longing words about the antelope, his wish that he, too, tireless, might be able to pursue the game. Dick remained quietly by his brother's side.

The whole train stopped presently at Conway's order on the crest of a swell, and drew itself up in a circle. Many of the men were now mounted and armed for an attack upon the herd, but at the suggestion of Bright Sun they waited a little, until the opportunity should become more convenient.

"It is a big herd," said Bright Sun; "perhaps the biggest that one can ever see now."

It certainly seemed immense to Dick and Albert. The great animals came on in an endless stream from the blue wall of the horizon. The vast procession steadily broadened and lengthened and it moved with unceasing step toward the south. The body of it was solid black, with figures which at the distance blended into one mass, but on the flanks hung stragglers, lawless old bulls or weaklings, and outside there was a fringe of hungry wolves, snapping and snarling, and waiting a chance to drag down some failing straggler.

Far over the plain spread the herd, thousands and tens of thousands, and the earth shook with their tread. Confused, bellowings and snortings arose, and the dust hung thick.

Dick and Albert stared with intent eyes at the wonderful scene. The herd was drawing nearer and nearer. It would pass only a few hundred yards from the crest on which the train stood. Already the hunters were shouting to one another and galloping away, but Dick did not stir from Albert's side. Albert's eyes were expanded, and the new colour in his face deepened. His breath cam in the short, quick fashion of one who is excited. He suddenly turned to his brother.

"The men are off! Why aren't you with them Dick?" he exclaimed.

"I thought I wouldn't go," replied Dick evasively. "There'll be enough without me."

Albert stared. Not hunt buffalo when one could. It was unbelievable. Then he comprehended. But he would not have it that way! It was noble of Dick, but it should not be so for a moment. He cried out, a note of anxiety in this voice:

"No, Dick, you shall not say here with me! My time will come later on! Jump on your horse, Dick, and join 'em! I won't forgive you if you don't!"

Dick saw that Albert was in earnest, and he knew that it would be better for them both now if he should go.

"All right, Al!" he cried, "I'll pick out a good fat one." He jumped on his horse and in a moment was galloping at full speed over the plain toward the great herd which now rushed on, black and thundering.

Dick heard shots already from those who had preceded him, and the exultant shouts of the men mingled with the roar of mighty tramplings. But it was not all triumph for the men, few of whom were experienced. Two or three had been thrown by shying horses, and with difficulty escaped being trodden to death under the feet of the herd. The herd itself was so immense that it did not notice these few wasps on a distant flank, and thundered steadily on southward.

Dick's own horse, frightened by such a tremendous sight, shied and jumped, but the boy had a sure seat and brought him around again. Dick himself was somewhat daunted by the aspect of the herd. If he and his hose got in the way, they would go down forever, as surely as if engulfed by an avalanche.

The horse shied again and made a mighty jump, as a huge bull, red-eyed and puffing, charged by. Dick, who was holding his rifle in one hand, slipped far over, and with great difficulty regained his balance on the horse's back. When he was secure again, he turned his mount and galloped along for some distance on the flank of the herd, seeking a suitable target for his bullet. The effect was dizzying. So many thousands were rushing beside him that the shifting panorama made him wink his eyes rapidly. Vast clouds of dust floated about, now and then enveloping him, and that made him wink his eyes, too. But he continued, nevertheless, to seek for his target a fat cow. Somehow he didn't seem to see anything just then but old bulls. They were thick on the flanks of the herd either as stragglers or protectors, and Dick was afraid to press in among them in his search for the cow.

His opportunity came at last. A young cow, as fat as one could wish, was thrown on the outside by some movement of the herd, caught, as it were, like a piece of driftwood in an eddy, and Dick instantly fired at her. She staggered and went down, but at the same instant a huge, shaggy bull careened against Dick and his horse. It was not so much a charge as an accident, the chance of Dick's getting in the bull's way, and the boy's escape was exceedingly narrow.

His horse staggered and fell to his knees. The violence of the shock wrested Dick's rifle from his hand, and he was barely quick enough to grasp it as it was sliding across the saddle. But he did save it, and the horse, trembling and frightened, recovered his feet. By that time the old bull and his comrades were gone.

Dick glanced around and was relieved to see that nobody had noticed his plight. They were all too much absorbed in their own efforts to pay any heed to him. The body took a deep, long breath. He had killed a buffalo, despite his inexperience. There was the cow to show for it.

The herd thundered off to the southward, the clouds of dust and the fringe of wolves following it. About a dozen of their number had fallen before the rifles, but Dick had secured the fattest and the tenderest. Albert, as proud as Dick himself of his triumph, came down on the plain and helped as much as he could in skinning and cutting up the cow. Dick wished to preserve the robe, and they spread it out on the wagon to dry.

The train made no further attempt to advance that day, but devoted the afternoon to a great feast. Bright Sun showed them how to cook the tenderest part of the hump in the coals, and far into the night the fires blazed.

"We will see no more buffaloes for a while," said Bright Sun. "Tomorrow we reach another little river coming down from the hills, and the ground becomes rough."

Bright Sun told the truth. They reached the river about noon of the next day, and, as it flowed between steep banks, the crossing was difficult. It took many hours to get on the other side, and two or three axles were broken by the heavy jolts. Conway raged and swore, calling them a clumsy lot, and some of the men refused to take his abuse, replying to his hard words with others equally as hard. Pistols were drawn and there was promise of trouble, but it was finally stopped, partly by the persuasion of others, and partly of its own accord. The men were still feeling the desire for gold too strongly to fight while on the way to it. Dick and Albert kept aloof from these contentions, steadily minding their own business, and they found, as others do, that it paid.

They came presently into a better country, and the way led for a day or two through a typical part of the great plains, not a flat region, but one of low, monotonous swells. Now and then they crossed a shallow little creek, and occasionally they came to pools, some of which were tinged with alkali. There were numerous small depressions, two or three feet deep, and Dick knew that they were "buffalo wallows." He and Albert examined them with interest.

"This is buffalo country again," said Dick. "Everything proves it. The grass here is the best that we have seen in a long time, and I imagine that it's just the sort of place they would love."

The grass was, indeed, good, as Dick had said, not merely clumps of it, but often wide, carpeted spaces. It was somewhat dry, and turning brown, but so big and strong an animal as the buffalo would not mind it. In fact, they saw several small groups of buffaloes grazing at a distance, usually on the crest of one of the low swells. As they already had plenty of buffalo meat, the men of the train did not trouble them, and the great animals would continue to crop the grass undisturbed.

About a week after the buffalo hunt they camped in a great plain somewhat flatter than any that they had encountered hitherto, and drew up the wagons in a loose circle.

The day had been very hot, but, as usual on the plains, the night brought coolness. The fire which Dick made of buffalo chips was not only useful, but it felt pleasant, too, as they sat beside it, ate their supper, and watched the great inclosing circle of darkness creep up closer and closer to the camp. There was not much noise about them. The men were tired, and as soon as they ate their food they fell asleep in the wagons or on the ground. The tethered horses and mules stirred a little for a while, but they, too, soon rested in peace.

"You take the wagon, Al," said Dick, "but I think I'll sleep on the ground."

Albert said good night and disappeared in the wagon. Dick stood up and looked over the camp. Only two or three fires were yet burning, and not a dozen men were awake. He saw dark figures here and there on the ground, and knew that they were those of sleepers. Three sentinels had been posted, but Dick was quite sure from the general character of the train that later on they would sleep like the others. All his instincts of order and fitness rebelled against the management of this camp.

Dick rolled himself in his blanket and lay down by the little fire that he had built. The dry, clean earth made a good bed, and with his left elbow under his head he gazed into the fire, which, like all fires of buffalo chips, was now rapidly dying, leaving little behind but light ashes that the first breeze would scatter through space.

He watched the last blaze sink and go out, he saw the last coal die, then, when a few sparks flew upward, there was blank darkness where the fire had been. All the other fires were out, too, and only the dim figures of the wagons showed. He felt, for a little while, as if he were alone in the wilderness, but he was not afraid. All was darkness below, and the wind was moaning, but overhead was a blue sky filled with friendly stars.

Dick could not go to sleep for a long time. From the point where he lay he could now see two of the sentinels walking back and forth, rifle on shoulder. He did not believe that they would continue to do so many hours, and he had a vague sort of desire to prove that he was right. Having nothing else to do he watched them.

The nearer sentinel grew lazier in his walk, and his beat became shorter. At last he dropped his rifle to the ground, leaned his folded arms on its muzzle, and gazed toward the camp, where, so far as he could see, there was nothing but darkness and sleep. The other presently did the same. Then they began short walks back and forth, but soon both sat down on the ground, with their rifles between their knees, and after that they did not stir. Watching as closely as he could Dick could not observe the slightest movement on the part of either, and he knew that they were asleep. He laughed to himself, pleased, in a way, to know that he had been right, although it was only another evidence of the carelessness and indifference general throughout the train.

He fell asleep himself in another half hour, but he awoke about midnight, and he was conscious at once that he had been awakened not by a troubled mind, but by something external and unusual. He was lying with his right ear to the ground, and it seemed to him that a slight trembling motion ran through the solid earth. He did not so much hear it as feel it, and tried to persuade himself that it was mere fancy, but failed. He sat up, and he no longer observed the trembling, but when he put his ear to the ground again it was stronger.

It could not be fancy. It was something real and extraordinary. He glanced at the sentinels, but they were sound asleep. He felt a desire to rouse somebody, but if it proved to be nothing they would laugh at him, or more likely call him hard names. He tried ear to earth once more. The trembling was still growing in strength, and mixed with it was a low, groaning sound, like the swell of the sea on the shore. The sound came with the wind from the north.

Dick sprang to his feet. There, in the north was a faint light which grew with amazing rapidity. In a minutes almost it seemed to redden the whole northern heavens, and the groaning sound became a roll, like that of approaching thunder.

A shadow flitted by Dick.

"What is it, Bright Sun?? What is it?" exclaimed the boy.

"The dry grass burns, and a mighty buffalo herd flees before it."

Then Bright Sun was gone, and the full sense of their danger burst upon Dick in overwhelming tide. The flames came on, as fast as a horse's gallop, and the buffaloes, in thousands and tens of thousands, were their vanguard. The camp lay directly in the path of fire and buffalo. The awakened sentinels were on their feet now, and half-clad men were springing from the wagons.

Dick stood perfectly still for perhaps a minute, while the fire grew brighter and the thunder of a myriad hoofs grew louder. Then he remembered what he had so often read and heard, and the crisis stirred him to swift action. While the whole camp was a scene of confusion, of shouts, of oaths, and of running men, he sped to its south side, to a point twenty or thirty yards from the nearest wagon. There he knelt in the dry grass and drew his box of matches from his pocket. It happened that Conway saw.

"What are you doing, you boy?" he cried, threateningly.

But Dick did not care for Conway just then.

"Back fire! Back fire!" he shouted, and struck a match. It went out, but he quickly struck another, shielded it with one hand and touched the tiny flame to the grass. A flame equally tiny answered, but in an instant it leaped into the size and strength of a giant. The blaze rose higher than Dick's head, ran swiftly to right and left, and then roared away to the south, eating up everything in its path.

"Well done," said a voice at Dick's elbow. "It is the only thing that could save the train."

It was Bright Sun who spoke, and he had come so silently that Dick did not see him until then.

Conway understood now, but without a word of approval he turned away and began to give orders, mixed with much swearing. He had a rough sort of efficiency, and spurred by his tongue and their own dreadful necessity, the men worked fast. The horses and mules, except three or four which had broken loose and were lost, were hitched to the wagons in half the usual time. There were no sluggards now.

Dick helped, and Albert, too, but to both it seemed that the work would never be done. The back fire was already a half mile away, gathering volume and speed as it went, but the other was coming on at an equal pace. Deer and antelope were darting past them, and the horses and mules were rearing in terror.

"Into the burned ground," shouted Conway, "an' keep the wagons close together!"

No need to urge the animals. They galloped southward over earth which was still hot and smoking, but they knew that something was behind them, far more terrible than sparks and smoke.

Dick made Albert jump into their own wagon, while he ran beside it. As he ran, he looked back, and saw a sight that might well fill the bravest soul with dread. A great black line, crested with tossing horns, was bearing down on them. The thunder of hoofs was like the roar of a hurricane, but behind the herd was a vast wall of light, which seemed to reach from the earth to the heavens and which gave forth sparks in myriads. Dick knew that they had been just in time.

They did not stop until they had gone a full quarter of a mile, and then the wagons were hastily drawn up in a rude circle, with the animals facing the centre, that is, the inside, and still rearing and neighing in terror. Then the men, rifle in hand, and sitting in the rear of the wagons, faced the buffalo herd.

Dick was with the riflemen, and, like the others, he began to fire as soon as the vanguard of the buffaloes was near enough. The wagons were a solid obstacle which not even King Bison could easily run over, but Dick and Albert thought the herd would never split, although the bullets were poured into it at a central point like a driven wedge.

But the falling buffaloes were an obstacle to those behind them, and despite their mad panic, the living became conscious of the danger in front. The herd split at last, the cleft widened to right and left, and then the tide, in two great streams, flowed past the wagon train.

Dick ceased firing and sat with Albert on the tail of the wagon. The wall of fire, coming to the burned ground, went out in the centre, but the right and left ends of it, swinging around, still roared to the southward, passing at a distance of a quarter of a mile on either side.

Dick and Albert watched until all the herd was gone, and when only smoke and sparks were left, helped to get the camp into trim again. Conway knew that the boy had saved them, but he gave him no thanks.

It took the ground a long time to cool, and they advanced all the next day over a burned area. They travelled northward ten days, always ascending, and they were coming now to a wooded country. They crossed several creeks, flowing down from the higher mountains, and along the beds of these they found cottonwood, ash, box elder, elm, and birch. On the steeper slops were numerous cedar brakes and also groves of yellow pine. There was very little undergrowth, but the grass grew in abundance. Although it was now somewhat dry, the horses and mules ate it eagerly. The buffaloes did not appear here, but they saw many signs of bear, mule deer, panther or mountain lion, and other game.

They camped one night in a pine grove by the side of a brook that came rushing and foaming down from the mountains, and the next morning Albert, who walked some distance from the water, saw a silver-tip bear lapping the water of the stream. The bear raised his head and looked at Albert, and Albert stopped and looked at the bear. The boy was unarmed, but he was not afraid. The bear showed no hostility, only curiosity. He gazed a few moments, stretched his nose as if he would sniff the air, then turned and lumbered away among the pines. Albert returned to camp, but he said nothing of the bear to anybody except Dick.

"He was such a jolly, friendly looking fellow, Dick," he said, "that I didn't want any of these men to go hunting him."

Dick laughed.

"Don't you worry about that, Al," he said. "They are hunting gold, not bears."

On the twelfth day they came out on a comparatively level plateau, where antelope were grazing and prairie chickens whirring. It looked like a fertile country, and they were glad of easy travelling for the wagons. Just at the edge of the pine woods that they were leaving was a beautiful little lake of clear, blue water, by which they stayed half a day, refreshing themselves, and catching some excellent fish, the names of which they did not know.

"How much long, Bright Sun, will it take us to reach the gold country?" asked Conway of the Indian, in Dick's hearing.

"About a week," replied Bright Sun. "The way presently will be very rough and steep, up! up! up! and we can go only a few miles a day, but the mountains are already before us. See!"

He pointed northward and upward, and there before them was the misty blue loom that Dick knew was the high mountains. In those dark ridges lay the gold that they were going to seek, and his heart throbbed. Albert and he could do such wonderful things with it.

They were so high already that the nights were crisp with cold; but at the edge of the forest, running down to the little lake, fallen wood was abundant, and they built that night a great fire of fallen boughs that crackled and roared merrily. Yet they hovered closely, because the wind, sharp with ice, was whistling down from the mountains, and the night air, even in the little valley, was heavy with frost. Dick's buffalo robe was dry now, and he threw it around Albert, as he sat before the fire. It enveloped the boy like a great blanket, but far warmer, the soft, smooth fur caressing his cheeks, and as Albert drew it closer, he felt very snug indeed.

"We cross this valley tomorrow," said Dick, "and then we begin a steeper climb."

"Then it will be mountains, only mountains," said Bright Sun. "We go into regions which no white men except the fur hunters, have ever trod."

Dick started. He had not known that the Indian was near. Certainly he was not there a moment ago. There was something uncanny in the way in which Bright Sun would appear on noiseless footstep, like a wraith rising from the earth.

"I shall be glad of it, Bright Sun," said Albert. "I'm tired of the plains, and they say that the mountains are good for many ills."

Bright Sun's enigmatic glance rested upon Albert a moment.

"Yes," he said, "the mountains will cure many ills."

Dick glanced at him, and once more he received the impression of thought and power. The Indian's nose curved like an eagle's beak, and the firelight perhaps exaggerated both the curve and its effect. The whole impression of thought and force was heightened by the wide brow and the strong chin.

Dick looked back into the fire, and when he glanced around a few moments again, Bright Sun was not there. He had gone as silently as he had come.

"That Indian gives me the shivers sometimes," he said to Albert. "What do you make of him?"

"I don't know," replied the boy. "Sometimes I like him and sometimes I don't."

Albert was soon asleep, wrapped in the buffalo robe, and Dick by and by followed him to the same pleasant land. The wind, whistling as it blew down from the mountains, grew stronger and colder, and its tone was hostile, as if it resented the first presence of white men in the little valley by the lake.

CHAPTER 3

The Pass

They resumed the journey early the next day, Bright Sun telling Conway that they could reach the range before sunset, and that they would find there an easy pass leading a mile or two farther on to a protected and warm glen.

"That's the place for our camp," said Conway, and he urged the train forward.

The travelling was smooth and easy, and they soon left the little blue lake well behind, passing through a pleasant country well wooded with elm, ash, birch, cottonwood, and box elder, and the grass growing high everywhere. They crossed more than one clear little stream, a pleasant contrast to the sluggish, muddy creeks of the prairies.

The range, toward which the head of the train was pointing, now came nearer. The boys saw its slopes, shaggy with dark pine, and they knew that beyond it lay other and higher slopes, also dark with pine. The air was of a wonderful clearness, showing in the east and beyond the zenith a clear silver tint, while the west was pure red gold with the setting sun.

Nearer and nearer came the range. The great pines blurred at first into an unbroken mass, now stood out singly, showing their giant stems. Afar a flash of foamy white appeared, where a brook fell in a foamy cascade. Presently they were within a quarter of a mile of the range, and its shadow fell over the train. In the west the sun was low.

"The pass is there, straight ahead," said Bright Sun, pointing to the steep range.

"I don't see any opening," said Conway.

"It is so narrow and the pines hide it," rejoined Bright Sun, "but it is smooth and easy."

Albert was at the rear of the train. He had chosen to walk in the later hours of the afternoon. He had become very tired, but, unwilling to confess it even to himself, he did not resume his place in the wagon. His weariness made him lag behind.

255

Albert was deeply sensitive to the impressions of time and place. The twilight seemed to him to fall suddenly like a great black robe. The pines once more blurred into a dark, unbroken mass. The low sun in the west dipped behind the hills, and the rays of red and gold that it left were chill and cold.

"Your brother wishes to see you. He is at the foot of the creek that we crossed fifteen minutes ago."

It was Bright Sun who spoke.

"Dick wants to see me at the crossing of the creek! Why, I thought he was ahead of me with the train!" exclaimed Albert.

"No, he is waiting for you. He said that it was important," repeated Bright Sun.

Albert turned in the darkening twilight and went back on the trail of the train toward the crossing of the creek. Bright Sun went to the head of the train, and saw Dick walking there alone and looking at the hills.

"Your brother is behind at the creek," said Bright Sun. "He is ill and wishes you. Hurry! I think it is important!"

"Albert at the creek, ill?" exclaimed Dick in surprise and alarm. "Why, I thought he was here with the train!"

But Bright Sun had gone on ahead. Dick turned back hastily, and ran along the trail through the twilight that was now fast merging into the night.

"Al, ill and left behind!" he exclaimed again and again. "He must have overexerted himself!"

His alarm deepened when he saw how fast the darkness was increasing. The chill bars of red and gold were gone from the west. When he looked back he could see the train no more, and heard only the faint sound of the cracking of whips. The train was fast disappearing in the pass.

But Dick had become a good woodsman and plainsman. His sense of direction was rarely wrong, and he went straight upon the trail for the creek. Night had now come but it was not very dark, and presently he saw the flash of water. It was the creek, and a few more steps took him there. A figure rose out of the shadows.

"Al!" he cried. "Have you broken down? Why didn't you get into the wagon?"

"Dick," replied Albert in a puzzled tone, "there's nothing the matter with me, except that I'm tired. Bright Sun told me that you were here waiting for me, and that you had something important to tell me. I couldn't find you, and now you come running."

Dick stopped in amazement.

"Bright Sun said I was waiting here for you, and had something important to tell you?" exclaimed Dick. "Why, he told me that you were ill, and had been left unnoticed at the crossing!"

The two boys stared at each other.

"What does it mean?" they exclaimed together.

From the dark pass before them came a sound which in the distance resembled the report of a firecracker, followed quickly by two or three other sounds, and then by many, as if the whole pack had been ignited at once. But both boys knew it was not firecrackers. It was something far more deadly and terrible—a hail of rifle bullets. They looked toward the pass and saw there pink and red flashes appearing and reappearing. Shouts, and mingled with them a continuous long, whining cry, a dreadful overnote, came to their ears.

"The train has been attacked!" cried Dick. "It has marched straight into an ambush!"

"Indians?" exclaimed Albert, who was trembling violently from sheer physical and mental excitement.

"It couldn't be anything else!" replied Dick. "This is their country! And they must be in great force, too! Listen how the fight grows!"

The volume of the firing increased rapidly, but above it always rose that terrible whining note. The red and pink flashes in the pass danced and multiplied, and the wind brought the faint odour of smoke.

"We must help!" exclaimed Dick. "One can't stand here and see them all cut down!"

He forgot in his generous heart, at that moment, that he disliked Conway and all his men, and that he and Albert had scarcely a friend in the train. He thought only of doing what he could to beat back the Indian attack, and Albert felt the same impulse. Both had their rifles—fine, breech-loading, repeating weapons, and with these the two might do much. No one ever parted with his arms after entering the Indian country.

"Come on, Albert!" exclaimed Dick, and the two ran toward the pass. But before they had gone a hundred yards they stopped as if by the same impulse. That terrible whining note was now rising higher and higher. It was not merely a war whoop, it had become also a song of triumph. There was a certain silvery quality in the night air, a quality that made for illumination, and Dick thought he saw dusky forms flitting here and there in the mouth of the pass behind the train. It was only fancy, because he was too far away for such perception, but in this case fancy and truth were the same.

"Hurry, Dick! Let's hurry!" exclaimed the impulsive and generous Albert. "If we don't, we'll be too late to do anything!"

They started again, running as fast as they could toward that space in the dark well where the flashes of red and blue came and went. Dick was so intent that he did not hear the short, quick gasps of Albert, but he did hear a sudden fall beside him and stopped short. Albert was lying on his back unconscious. A faint tinge of abnormal red showed on his lips.

"Oh, I forgot! I forgot!" groaned Dick.

Such sudden and violent exertion, allied with the excitement of the terrible moment, had overpowered the weak boy. Dick bent down in grief. At first he thought his brother was dead, but the breath still came.

Dick did not know what to do. In the pass, under the shadow of night, the pines, and the mountain wall, the battle still flared and crackled, but its volume was dying. Louder rose the fierce, whining yell, and its note was full of ferocity and triumph, while the hoarser cries of the white men became fewer and lower. Now Dick really saw dusky figures leaping about between him and the train. Something uttering a shrill, unearthly cry of pain crashed heavily through the bushes near him and quickly passed on. It was a wounded horse, running away.

Dick shuddered. Then he lifted Albert in his arms, and he had the forethought, even in that moment of excitement and danger, to pick up Albert's rifle also. Strong as he naturally was, he had then the strength of four, and, turning off at a sharp angle, he ran with Albert toward a dense thicket which clustered at the foot of the mountain wall.

He went a full three hundred yards before he was conscious of weariness, and he was then at the edge of the thicket, which spread over a wide space. He laid Albert down on some of last year's old leaves, and then his quick eyes caught the sight of a little pool among some rocks. He dipped up the water in his felt hat, and after carefully wiping the red stain from his brother's lips, poured the cold fluid upon his face.

Albert revived, sat up, and tried to speak, but Dick pressed his hand upon his mouth.

"Nothing above a whisper, Al," he said softly. "The fight is not yet wholly over, and the Sioux are all about."

"I fainted," said Albert in a whisper. "O Dick, what a miserable, useless fellow I am! But it was the excitement and the run!"

"It was doubtless a lucky thing that you fainted," Dick whispered back. "If you hadn't, both of us would probably be dead now."

"It's not all over yet," said Albert.

"No, but it soon will be. Thank God, we've got our rifles. Do you feel strong enough to walk now, Al? The deeper we get into the thicket the better it will be for us."

Albert rose slowly to his feet, rocked a little, and then stood straight.

Only a few flashes were appearing now in the pass. Dick knew too well who had been victorious. The battle over, the Sioux would presently be ranging for stragglers and for plunder. He put one arm under Albert, while he carried both of the rifles himself. They walked on through the thicket and the night gradually darkened. The silvery quality was gone from the air, and the two boys were glad. It would not be easy to find them now. In the pass both the firing and the long, whining whoop ceased entirely. The flashes of red or blue appeared no more. Silence reigned there and in the valley. Dick shivered despite himself. For the moment the silence was more terrible than the noise of battle had been. Black, ominous shadows seemed to float down from the mountains, clothing all the valley. A chill wind came up, moaning among the pines. The valley, so warm and beautiful in the day, now inspired Dick with a sudden and violent repulsion. It was a hateful place, the abode of horror and dread. He wished to escape from it.

They crossed the thicket and came up against the mountain wall. But it was not quite so steep as it had looked in the distance, and in the faint light Dick saw the trace of a trail leading up the slope among the pines. It was not the trail of human beings, merely a faint path indicating that wild animals, perhaps cougars, had passed that way.

"How are you feeling, Al?" he asked, repeating his anxious query.

"Better. My strength has come back," replied his brother.

"Then we'll go up the mountain. We must get as far away as we can from those fiends, the Sioux. Thank God, Al, we're spared together!"

Each boy felt a moment of devout thankfulness. They had not fallen, and they were there together! Each also thought of the singular message that Bright Sun had given to them, but neither spoke of it.

They climbed for more than half an hour in silence, save for an occasional whisper. The bushes helped Albert greatly. He pulled himself along by means of them, and now and then the two boys stopped that he might rest. He was still excited under the influence of the night, the distant battle, and their peril, and he breathed in short gasps, but did not faint again. Dick thrust his arm at intervals under his brother's and helped him in the ascent.

After climbing a quarter of an hour, they stopped longer than usual and looked down at the pass, which Dick reckoned should be almost beneath them. They heard the faint sound of a shot, saw a tiny beam of red appear, then disappear, and after that there was only silence and blank darkness.

"It's all over now," whispered Albert, and it was a whisper not of caution, but of awe.

"Yes, it's all over," Dick said in the same tone. "It's likely, Al, that you and I alone out of all that train are alive. Conway and all the others are gone."

"Except Bright Sun," said Albert.

The two boys looked at each other again, but said nothing. They then resumed their climbing, finding it easier this time. They reached a height at which the undergrowth ceased, but the pines, growing almost in ordered rows, stretched onward and upward.

Dick sent occasional glances toward the pass, but the darkness there remained unbroken. Every time he turned his eyes that way he seemed to be looking into a black well of terror.

Both Dick and Albert, after the first hour of ascent, had a feeling of complete safety. The Sioux, occupied with their great ambush and victory, would not know there had been two stragglers behind the train, and even had they known, to search for them among the dense forests of distant mountain slopes would be a futile task. Dick's mind turned instead to the needs of their situation, and he began to appreciate the full danger and hardship of it.

Albert and he were right in feeling thankful that they were spared together, although they were alone in the wilderness in every sense of the word. It was hundreds of miles north, east, south, and west to the habitations of white men. Before them, fold on fold, lay unknown mountains, over which only hostile savages roamed. Both he and Albert had good rifles and belts full of cartridges, but that was all. It was a situation to daunt the most fearless heart, and the shiver that suddenly ran over Dick did not come from the cold of the night.

They took a long rest in a little clump of high pines and saw a cold, clear moon come out in the pale sky. They felt the awful sense of desolation and loneliness, for it seemed to them that the moon was looking down on an uninhabited world in which only they were left. They heard presently little rustlings in the grass, and thought at first it was another ambush, though they knew upon second thought that it was wild creatures moving on the mountain side.

"Come, Al," said Dick. "Another half hour will put us on top of the ridge, and then I think it will be safe for us to stop."

"I hope they'll be keeping a good room for us at the hotel up there," said Albert wanly.

Dick tried to laugh, but it was a poor imitation and he gave it up.

"We may find some sort of a sheltered nook," he said hopefully.

Dick had become conscious that it was cold, since the fever in his blood was dying down. Whenever they stopped and their bodies relaxed, they suffered from chill. He was deeply worried about Albert, who was in no condition to endure exposure on a bleak mountain, and wished now for the buffalo robe they had regarded as such a fine trophy.

They reached the crest of the ridge in a half hour, as Dick had expected, and looking northward in the moonlight saw the dim outlines of other ridges and peaks in a vast, intricate maze. A narrow, wooded valley seemed to occupy the space between the ridge on which they stood and the next one parallel to it to the northward.

"It ought to be a good place down there to hide and rest," said Albert.

"I think you're right," said Dick, "and we'll go down the slope part of the way before we camp for the night."

They found the descent easy. It was still open forest, mostly pine with a sprinkling of ash and oak, and it was warmer on the northern side, the winds having but little sweep there.

The moon became brighter, but it remained cold and pitiless, recking nothing of the tragedy in the pass. It gave Dick a chill to look at it. But he spent most of the time watching among the trees for some sheltered spot that nature had made. It was over an hour before he found it, a hollow among rocks, with dwarf pines clustering thickly at the sides and in front. It was so well hidden that he would have missed it had he not been looking for just such a happy alcove, and at first he was quite sure that some wild animal must be using it as a den.

He poked in the barrel of his rifle, but nothing flew out, and then, pulling back the pine boughs, he saw no signs of a previous occupation.

"It's just waiting for us, Al, old fellow," he said gaily, "but nothing of this kind is so good that it can't be made better. Look at all those dead leaves over there under the oaks. Been drying ever since last year and full of warmth."

They raked the dead leaves into the nook, covering the floor of it thickly, and piling them up on the sides as high as they would stay, and then they lay down inside, letting the pine boughs in front fall back into place. It was really warm and cosy in there for two boys who had been living out of doors for weeks, and Dick drew a deep, long breath of content.

"Suppose a panther should come snooping along," said Albert, "and think this the proper place for his bed and board?"

"He'd never come in, don't you fear. He'd smell us long before he got here, and then strike out in the other direction."

Albert was silent quite a while, and as he made no noise, Dick thought he was asleep. But Albert spoke at last, though he spoke low and his tone was very solemn.

"Dick," he said, "we've really got a lot to be thankful for. You know that."

"I certainly do," said Dick with emphasis. "Now you go to sleep, Al."

Albert was silent again, and presently his breathing became very steady and regular. Dick touched him and saw that he was fast asleep. Then the older boy took off his coat and carefully spread it on the younger, after which he raked a great lot of the dry leaves over himself, and soon he, too, was sound asleep.

Dick awoke far in the night and stirred in his bed of leaves. But the movement caused him a little pain, and he wondered dimly, because he had not yet fully come through the gates of sleep, and he did not remember where he was or what had happened. A tiny shaft of pale light fell on his forehead, and he looked up through pine branches. It was the moon that sent the beam down upon him, but he could see nothing else. He stirred again and the little pain returned. Then all of it came back to him.

Dick reached out his hand and touched Albert. His brother was sleeping soundly, and he was still warm, the coat having protected him. But Dick was cold, despite the pines, the rocks, and the leaves. It was the cold that had caused the slight pain in his joints when he moved, but he rose softly lest he wake Albert, and slipped outside, standing in a clear space between the pines.

The late moon was of uncommon brilliancy. It seemed a molten mass of burnished silver, and its light fell over forest and valley, range and peak. The trees on the slopes stood out like lacework, but far down in the valley the light seemed to shimmer like waves on a sea of silver mist. It was all inexpressibly cold, and of a loneliness that was uncanny. Nothing stirred, not a twig, not a blade of grass. It seemed to Dick that if even a leaf fell on the far side of the mountain he could hear it. It was a great, primeval world, voiceless and unpeopled, brooding in a dread and mystic silence.

Dick shivered. He had shivered often that night, but now the chill went to the marrow. It was the chill the first man must have felt when he was driven from the garden and faced the globe-girdling forest. He came back to the rock covert and leaned over until he could hear his brother breathing beneath the pine boughs. Then he felt the surge of relief, of companionship—after all, he was not alone in the wilderness!—and returned to the clear space between the pines. There he walked up and down briskly, swinging his arms, exercising all his limbs, until the circulation was fully restored and he was warm again.

Dick felt the immensity of the problem that lay before him—one that he alone must solve if it were to be solved at all. He and Albert had escaped the massacre, but how were they to live in that wilderness of mountains? It was not alone the question of food. How were they to save themselves from death by exposure? Those twinges in his knees had been warning signs. Oddly enough, his mind now fastened upon one thing. He was longing for the lost buffalo robe, his first great prize. It had been so large and so warm, and the fur was so soft. It would cover both Albert and himself, and keep them warm on the coldest night. If they only had it now! He thought more of that robe just then than he did of the food that they would need in the morning. Cast forth upon a primeval world, this first want occupied his mind to the exclusion of all others.

He returned to the rocky alcove presently, and lay down again. He was too young and too healthy to remain awake long, despite the full measure of their situation, and soon he slept soundly once more. He was first to awake in the morning, and the beam that struck upon his forehead was golden instead of silver. It was warm, too, and cheerful, and as Dick parted the branches and looked out, he saw that the sun was riding high. It had been daylight a full three hours at least, but it did not matter. Time was perhaps the only commodity of which he and Albert now had enough and to spare.

He took his coat off Albert and put it on himself, lest Albert might suspect, and then began to sing purposely, with loudness and levity, an old farm rhyme that had been familiar to the boys of his vicinity:

"Wake up, Jake, the day is breaking.
"The old cow died, her tail shaking."

Albert sat up, rubbed his eyes, and stared at Dick and the wilderness.

"Now look at him!" cried Dick. "He thinks he's been called too early. He thinks he'd like to sleep eight or ten hours longer! Get up, little boy! Yes, it's Christmas morning! Come and see what good old Santa has put in your stocking!"

Albert yawned again and laughed. Really, Dick was such a cheerful, funny fellow that he always kept one in good spirits. Good old Dick!

"Old Santa filled our stockings, all right," continued Dick, "but he was so busy cramming 'em full of great forests and magnificent scenery that he forgot to leave any breakfast for us, and I'm afraid we'll have to hustle for it."

They started down the mountain slope, and presently they came to a swift little brook, in which they bathed their faces, removing, at the same time, fragments of twigs and dried leaves from their hair.

"That was fine and refreshing," said Dick, "but it doesn't fill my stomach. Al, I could bite a tenpenny nail in half and digest both pieces, too."

"I don't care for nails," said Albert, "but I think I could gnaw down a good-sized sapling. Hold me, Dick, or I'll be devouring a pine tree."

Both laughed, and put as good a face on it as they could, but they were frightfully hungry, nevertheless. But they had grown up on farms, and they knew that the woods must contain food of some kind or other. They began a search, and after a while they found wild plums, now ripe, which they ate freely. They then felt stronger and better, but, after all, it was a light diet and they must obtain food of more sustenance.

"There are deer, of course, in this valley," said Dick, fingering his rifle, "and sooner or later we'll get a shot at one of them, but it may be days, and—Al—I've got another plan."

"What is it?"

"You know, Al, that I can travel pretty fast anywhere. Now those Sioux, after cutting down the train and wiping out all the people, would naturally go away. They'd load themselves up with spoil and scoot. But a lot, scattered here and there, would be left behind. Some of the teams would run away in all the shooting and shouting. And, Al, you and I need those things! We must have them if we are going to live, and we both want to live!"

"Do you mean, Dick, that you're going back down there in that awful pass?"

"That's just about what I had on my mind," replied Dick cheerfully; "and now I've got it off, I feel better." "But you can never get back alive, Dick!" exclaimed Albert, his eyes widening in horror at the memory of what they had seen and heard the night before.

"Get back alive? Why, of course I will," responded Dick. "And I'll do more than that, too. You'll see me come galloping up the mountain, bearing hogsheads and barrels of provisions. But, seriously, Al, it must be done. If I don't go, we'll starve to death."

"Then I'm going, too."

"No, Al, old boy, you're not strong enough just yet, though you will be soon. There are certainly no Sioux in this little valley, and it would be well if you were to go back up the slope and stay in the pine shelter. It's likely that I'll be gone nearly all day, but don't be worried. You'll have one of the rifles with you, and you know how to use it."

Albert had a clear and penetrating mind, and he saw the truth of Dick's words. They went back up the slope, where he crept within the pine shelter and lay down on the leaves, while Dick went alone on his mission.

Chapter 4

Treasure-Trove

When Dick passed the crest of the ridge and began the descent toward the fatal pass, his heart beat heavily. The terror and shock of the night before, those distant shots and shouts, returned to him, and it was many minutes before he could shake off a dread that was almost superstitious in its nature. But youth, health, and the sunlight conquered. The day was uncommonly brilliant. The mountains rolled back, green on the slopes, blue at the crests, and below him, like a brown robe, lay the wavering plain across which they had come.

Dick could see no sign of human life down there. No rejoicing Sioux warrior galloped over the swells, no echo of a triumphant war whoop came to his ear. Over mountain and plain alike the silence of the desert brooded. But high above the pass great black birds wheeled on lazy pinions.

Dick believed more strongly than ever that the Sioux had gone away. Savage tribes do not linger over a battlefield that is finished; yet as he reached the bottom of the slope his heart began to beat heavily again, and he was loath to leave the protecting shadow of the pines. He fingered his rifle, passing his hand gently over the barrel and the trigger. It was a fine weapon, a beautiful weapon, and just at this moment it was a wonderful weapon. He felt in its full force, for the first time in his life, what the rifle meant to the pioneer.

The boy, after much hesitation and a great searching of eye and ear, entered the pass. At once the sunlight dimmed. Walls as straight as the side of a house rose above him three of four hundred feet, while the distance between was not more than thirty feet. Dwarf pines grew here and there in the crannies of the cliffs, but mostly the black rock showed. Dwarf pines also grew at the bottom of the pass close to either cliff, and Dick kept among them, bending far down and advancing very slowly.

Fifty yards were passed, and still there was no sound save a slight moaning through the pass, which Dick knew was the sigh of the wind drawn into the narrow cleft. It made him shudder, and had he not been of uncommon courage he would have turned back.

He looked up. The great black birds, wheeling on lazy pinions, seemed to have sunk lower. That made him shudder, too, but it was another confirmation of his belief that all the Sioux had gone. He went eight or ten yards farther and then stopped short. Before him lay two dead horses and an overturned wagon. Both horses had been shot, and were still in their gear attached to the wagon.

Dick examined the wagon carefully, and as he yet heard and saw no signs of a human being save himself, his courage grew. It was a big wagon of the kind used for crossing the plains, with boxes around the inside like lockers. Almost everything of value had been taken by the Sioux, but in one of the lockers Dick was lucky enough to find a large, heavy, gray blanket. He rolled it up at once, and with a strap cut from the horse's gear tied it on his back, after the fashion of a soldier on the march.

"The first great treasure!" he murmured exultantly. "Now for the next!"

He found in the same wagon, jammed under the driver's seat and hidden from hasty view, about the half of a side of bacon—ten pounds, perhaps. Dick fairly laughed when he got his hands upon it, and he clasped it lovingly, as if it were a ten-pound nugget of pure gold. But it was far better than gold just then. He wrapped it in a piece of canvas which he cut from the cover of the wagon, and tied it on his back above the blanket.

Finding nothing more of value in the wagon, he resumed his progress up the pass. It was well for Dick that he was stout-hearted, and well for him, too, that he was driven by great need, else he would surely have gone back.

He was now come into the thick of it. Around him everywhere lay the fallen, and the deeds done in Indian warfare were not lacking. Sam Conway lay upon his side, and brutal as the man had been, Dick felt grief when he saw him. Here were others, too, that he knew, and he counted the bodies of the few women who had been with the train. They had died probably in the battle like the rest. They, like the men, had been hardened, rough, and coarse of speech and act, but Dick felt grief, too, when he saw them. Nearly all the animals had been slain also in the fury of the attack, and they were scattered far up the pass.

Dick resolutely turned his face away from the dead and began to glean among the wagons for what the Sioux might have left. All these wagons were built like the first that he had searched, and he was confident that he would find much of value. Nor was he disappointed. He found three more blankets, and in their own wagon the buffalo robe that he had lamented. Doubtless, its presence there was accounted for by the fact that the Sioux did not consider a buffalo robe a trophy of their victory over white men.

Other treasures were several boxes of crackers, about twenty boxes of sardines, three flasks of brandy, suitable for illness, a heavy riding cloak, a Virginia ham, two boxes of matches, a small iron skillet, and an empty tin canteen. He might have searched further, but he realized that time was passing, and that Albert must be on the verge of starvation. He had forgotten his own hunger in the excitement of seek and find, but it came back now and gnawed at him fiercely. Yet he would not touch any of the food. No matter how great the temptation he would not take a single bite until Albert had the same chance.

He now made all his treasures into one great package, except the buffalo robe. That was too heavy to add to the others, and he tied it among the boughs of a pine, where the wolves could not reach it. Then, with the big pack on his back, he began the return. It was more weight than he would have liked to carry at an ordinary time, but now in his elation he scarcely felt it. He went rapidly up the slope and by the middle of the afternoon was going down the other side.

As he approached the pine alcove he whistled a familiar tune, popular at the time—*Silver Threads Among the Gold*. He knew that Albert, if he were there—and he surely must be there—would recognize his whistle and come forth. He stopped, and his heart hammered for a moment, but Albert's whistle took up the second line of the air and Albert himself came forth jauntily.

"We win, Al, old boy!" called Dick. "Just look at this pack!"

"I can't look at anything else," replied Albert in the same joyful tones. "It's so big that I don't see you under it. Dick, have you robbed a treasure ship?"

"No, Al," replied Dick, very soberly. "I haven't robbed a treasure ship, but I've been prowling with success over a lost battlefield—a ghoul I believe they call such a person, but it had to be done. I've enough food here to last a week at least, and we may find more."

He put down his pack and took out the bacon. As Albert looked at it he began unconsciously to clinch and unclinch his teeth. Dick saw his face, and, knowing that the same eager look was in his own, he laughed a little.

"Al," he said, "you and I know now how wolves often feel, but we're not going to behave like wolves. We're going to light a fire and cook this bacon. We'll take the risk of the flame or smoke being seen by Sioux. In so vast a country the chances are all in our favour."

They gathered up pine cones and other fallen wood, and with the help of the matches soon had a fire. Then they cut strips of bacon and fried them on the ends of sharpened sticks, the sputter making the finest music in their ears.

Never before had either tasted food so delicious, and they ate strip after strip. Dick noticed with pleasure how the colour came into Albert's cheeks, and how his eyes began to sparkle. Sleeping under the pines seemed to have benefited instead of injuring him, and certainly there was a wonderful healing balm in the air of that pine-clad mountain slope. Dick could feel it himself. How strong he was after eating! He shook his big shoulders.

"What are you bristling up about?" asked Albert.

"Merely getting ready to start again," replied Dick. "You know the old saying, Al, 'you've got to hit while the iron's hot.' More treasure is down there in the pass, but if we wait it won't stay there. Everything that we get now is worth more to us than diamonds."

"It's so," said Albert, and then he sighed sadly as he added, "How I wish I were strong enough to go with you and help!"

"Just you wait," said Dick. "You'll be as strong as a horse in a month, and then you'll have to do all the work and bring me my breakfast in the morning as I lie in bed. Besides, you'd have to stay here and guard the treasure that we already have. Better get into the pine den. Bears and wolves may be drawn by the scent of the food, and they might think of attacking you."

They put out the fire, and while Albert withdrew into the pine shelter, Dick started again over the mountain. The sun was setting blood red in the west, and in the east the shadows of twilight were advancing. It required a new kind of courage to enter the pass in the night, and Dick's shudders returned. At certain times there is something in the dark that frightens the bravest and those most used to it.

Dick hurried. He knew the way down the mountain now, and after the food and rest he was completely refreshed. But as fast as he went the shadows of twilight came faster, and when he reached the bottom of the mountain it was quite dark. The plain before him was invisible, and the forest on the slope behind him was a solid robe of black.

Dick set foot in the pass and then stopped. It was not dread but awe that thrilled him in every vein. He saw nothing before him but the well of darkness that was the great slash in the mountains. The wind, caught between the walls, moaned as in the day, and he knew perfectly well what if was, but it had all the nature of a dirge, nevertheless. Overhead a few dim stars wavered in a dusky sky.

Dick forced himself to go on. It required now moral, as well as physical, courage to approach that lost battlefield lying under its pall of night. Never was the boy a greater hero than at that moment. He advanced slowly. A bush caught him by the coat and held him an instant. He felt as if he had been seized in a man's grasp. He reached the first wagon, and it seemed to him, broken and rifled, an emblem of desolation. As he passed it a strange, low, whining cry made his backbone turn to ice. But he recovered and forced an uneasy little laugh at himself. It was only a wolf, the mean coyote of the prairies!

He came now into the space where the mass of the wagons and the fallen lay. Dark figures, low and skulking, darted away. More wolves! But one, a huge timber wolf, with a powerful body and long fangs, stood up boldly and stared at him with red eyes. Dick's own eyes were used to the darkness now, and he stared back at the wolf, which seemed to be giving him a challenge. He half raised his rifle, but the monster did not move. It was a stranger to guns, and this wilderness was its own.

It was Dick's first impulse to fire at the space between the red eyes, but he restrained it. He had not come there to fight with wolves, nor to send the report of a shot through the mountains. He picked up a stone and threw it at the wolf, striking him on the flank. The monster turned and stalked sullenly away, showing but little sign of fear. Dick pursued his task, and as he advanced something rose and, flapping heavily, sailed away. The shiver came again, but his will stopped it.

He was now in the centre of the wreckage, which in the darkness looked as if it had all happened long ago. Nearly every wagon had been turned over, and now and then dark forms lay between the wheels. The wind moaned incessantly down the pass and over the ruin.

Overcoming his repulsion, Dick went to work. The moon was now coming out and he could see well enough for his task. There was still much gleaning left by the quick raiders, and everything would be of use to Albert and himself, even to the very gear on the fallen animals. He cut off a great quantity of this at once and put it in a heap at the foot of the cliff. Then he invaded the wagons and again brought forth treasures better than gold.

He found in one side box some bottles of medicine, the simple remedies of the border, which he packed very carefully, and in another he discovered half a sack of flour—fifty pounds, perhaps. A third rewarded him with a canister of tea and a twenty-pound bag of ground coffee. He clutched these treasures eagerly. They would be invaluable to Albert.

Continuing his search, he was rewarded with two pairs of heavy shoes, an axe, a hatchet, some packages of pins, needles, and thread, and a number of cooking utensils—pots, kettles, pans, and skillets. Just as he was about to quit for the purpose of making up his pack, he noticed in one of the wagons a long, narrow locker made into the side and fastened with a stout padlock. The wagon had been plundered, but evidently the Sioux had balked at the time this stout box would take for opening, and had passed on. Dick, feeling sure that it must contain something of value, broke the padlock with the head of the axe. When he looked in he uttered a cry of delight at his reward.

He brought forth from the box a beautiful double-barrelled breech-loading shotgun, and the bounty of chance did not stop with the gun, for in the locker were over a thousand cartridges to fit it. Dick foresaw at once that it would be invaluable to Albert and himself in the pursuit of wild ducks, wild geese, and other feathered game. He removed some of the articles from his pack, which was already heavy enough, and put the shotgun and cartridges in their place. Then he set forth on the return journey.

As he left the wagons and went toward the mouth of the pass, he heard soft, padding sounds behind him, and knew that the wolves were returning, almost on his heels. He looked back once, and saw a pair of fiery red eyes which he felt must belong to the monster, the timber wolf, but Dick was no longer under the uncanny spell of the night and the place; he was rejoicing too much in his new treasures, like a miser who has just added a great sum to his hoard, to feel further awe of the wolves, the darkness, and a new battlefield.

Dick's second pack was heavier than his first, but as before, he trod lightly. He took a different path when he left the pass, and here in the moonlight, which was now much brighter, he saw the trace of wheels on the earth. The trace ran off irregularly through the short bushes and veered violently to and fro like the path of a drunken man. Dick inferred at once that it had been made, not by a wagon entering the pass, but by one leaving it, and in great haste. No doubt the horses or mules had been running away in fright at the firing.

Dick's curiosity was excited. He wished to see what had become of that wagon. The trail continued to lead through the short bushes that covered the plain just before entering the pass, and then turned off sharply to the right, where it led to an abrupt little canyon or gully about ten feet deep. The gully also was lined with bushes, and at first Dick could see nothing else, but presently he made out a wagon lying on its side. No horses or mules were there; undoubtedly, they had torn themselves loose from the gear in time to escape the fall.

Dick laid down his pack and descended to the wagon. He believed that in such a place it had escaped the plundering hands of the hasty Sioux, and his belief was correct. The wagon, a large one, was loaded with all the articles necessary for the passage of the plains. Although much tossed about by the fall, nothing was hurt.

Here was a treasure-trove, indeed! Dick's sudden sense of wealth was so overpowering that he felt a great embarrassment. How was he to take care of such riches? He longed at that moment for the strength of twenty men, that he might take it all at once and go over the mountain to Albert.

It was quite a quarter of an hour before he was able to compose himself thoroughly. Then he made a hasty examination of the wagon, so far as its position allowed. He found in it a rifle of the same pattern as that used by Albert and himself, a sixteen-shot repeater, the most advanced weapon of the time, and a great quantity of cartridges to fit. There was also two of the new revolvers, with sufficient cartridges, another axe, hatchets, saws, hammers, chisels, and a lot of mining tools. The remaining space in the wagon was occupied by clothing, bedding, provisions, and medicines.

Dick judged that the wolves could not get at the wagon as it lay, and leaving it he began his third ascent of the slope. He found Albert sound asleep in the pine alcove with his rifle beside him. He looked so peaceful that Dick was careful not to awaken him. He stored the second load of treasure in the alcove, and, wrapping one of the heavy blankets around himself, slept heavily.

He told Albert the next day of the wagon in the gully, and nothing could keep him from returning in the morning for salvage. He worked there two or three days, carrying heavy loads up the mountain, and finally, when it was all in their den, he and Albert felt equipped for anything. Nor had the buffalo robe been neglected. It was spread over much of the treasure. Albert, meanwhile, had assumed the functions of cook, and he discharged them with considerable ability. His strength was quite sufficient to permit of his collecting firewood, and he could fry bacon and make coffee and tea beautifully. But they were very sparing of the coffee and tea, as they also were of the flour, although their supplies of all three of these were greatly increased by the wagon in the gully. In fact, the very last thing that Dick had brought over the mountain was a hundred-pound sack of flour, and after accomplishing this feat he had rested a long time.

Both boys felt that they had been remarkably fortunate while this work was going on. One circumstance, apparently simple in itself, had been a piece of great luck, and that was the absence of rain. It was not a particularly rainy country, but a shower could have made them thoroughly miserable, and, moreover, would have been extremely dangerous for Albert. But nights and days alike remained dry and cool, and as Albert breathed the marvellous balsamic air he could almost feel himself transfused with its healing property. Meanwhile, the colour in his cheeks was steadily deepening.

"We've certainly had good fortune," said Dick.

"Aided by your courage and strength," said Albert. "It took a lot of nerve to go down there in that pass and hunt for what the Sioux might have left behind."

Dick disclaimed any superior merit, but he said nothing of the many tremors that he felt while performing the great task.

An hour or two later, Albert, who was hunting through their belongings, uttered a cry of joy on finding a little package of fishhooks. String they had among their stores, and it was easy enough to cut a slim rod for a pole.

"Now I can be useful for something besides cooking," he said. "It doesn't require any great strength to be a fisherman, and I'm much mistaken if I don't soon have our table supplied with trout."

There was a swift creek farther down the slope, and, angling with much patience, Albert succeeded in catching several mountain trout and a larger number of fish of an unknown species, but which, like the trout, were very good to eat.

Albert's exploit caused him intense satisfaction, and Dick rejoiced with him, not alone because of the fish, but also because of his brother's triumph.

CHAPTER 5

The Lost Valley

They spent a week on the slope, sleeping securely and warmly under their blankets in the pine alcove, and fortune favoured them throughout that time. It did not rain once, and there was not a sign of the Sioux. Dick did not revisit the pass after the first three days, and he knew that the wolves and buzzards had been busy there. But he stripped quite clean the wagon which had fallen in the gully, even carrying away the canvas cover, which was rainproof. Albert wondered that the Sioux had not returned, but Dick had a very plausible theory to account for it.

"The Sioux are making war upon our people," he said, "and why should they stay around here? They have cut off what is doubtless the first party entering this region in a long time, and now they have gone eastward to meet our troops. Beside, the Sioux are mostly plains Indians, and they won't bother much about these mountains. Other Indians, through fear of the Sioux, will not come and live here, which accounts for this region being uninhabited."

"Still a wandering band of Sioux might come through at any time and see us," said Albert.

"That's so, and for other reasons, too, we must move. It's mighty fine, Al, sleeping out in the open when the weather's dry and not too cold, but I've read that the winter in the north-western mountains is something terrible, and we've got to prepare for it."

It was Dick's idea to go deeper into the mountains. He knew very well that the chance of their getting out before spring were too slender to be considered, and he believed that they could find better shelter and a more secure hiding place farther in. So he resolved upon a journey of exploration, and though Albert was now stronger, he must go alone. It was his brother's duty to remain and guard their precious stores. Already bears and mountain lions, drawn by the odours of the food, had come snuffing about the alcove, but they always retreated from the presence of either of the brothers. One huge silver tip had come rather alarmingly close, but when Dick shouted at him he, too, turned and lumbered off among the pines.

"What you want to guard against, Al," said Dick, "is thieves rather than robbers. Look out for the sneaks. We'll fill the canteen and all our iron vessels with water so that you won't have to go even to the brook. Then you stay right here by the fire in the daytime, and in the den at night. You can keep a bed of coals before the den when you're asleep, and no wild animal will ever come past it."

"All right, Dick," said Albert courageously; "but don't you get lost over there among those ranges and peaks."

"I couldn't do it if I tried," replied Dick in the same cheerful tone. "You don't know what a woodsman and mountaineer I've become, Al, old boy!"

Albert smiled. Yet each boy felt the full gravity of the occasion when the time for Dick's departure came, at dawn of a cool morning, gleams of silver frost showing here and there on the slopes. Both knew the necessity of the journey, however, and hid their feelings.

"Be back tomorrow night, Al," said Dick.

"Be ready for you, Dick," said Albert.

Then they waved their hands to each other, and Dick strode away toward the higher mountains. He was well armed, carrying his repeating rifle and the large hunting knife which was useful for so many purposes. He had also thrust one of the revolvers into his belt.

Flushed with youth and strength, and equipped with such good weapons, he felt able to take care of himself in any company into which he might be thrown.

He reached the bottom of the slope, and looking back, saw Albert standing on a fallen log. His brother was watching him and waved his hand. Dick waved his in reply, and then, crossing the creek, began the ascent of the farther slope. There the pines and the distance rendered the brothers invisible to each other, and Dick pressed on with vigour. His recent trips over the lower slopes for supplies had greatly increased his skill in mountain climbing, and he did not suffer from weariness. Up, up, he went, and the pines grew shorter and scrubbier. But the thin, crisp air was a sheer delight, and he felt an extraordinary pleasure in mere living.

Dick looked back once more from the heights toward the spot where their camp lay and saw lying against the blue a thin gray thread that only the keenest eye would notice. He knew it to be the smoke from Albert's fire and felt sure that all was well.

While the slope which he was ascending was fairly steep, it was easy enough to find a good trail among the pines. There was little undergrowth and the ascent was not rocky. When Dick stood at last on the crest of the ridge he uttered a cry of delight and amazement.

The slope on which he stood was merely a sort of gate to the higher mountains, or rather it was a curtain hiding the view.

Before him, range on range and peak on peak, lay mighty mountains, some of them shooting up almost three miles above the sea, their crests and heads hid in eternal snow. Far away to northward and westward stretched the tremendous maze, and it seemed to Dick to have no end. A cold, dazzling sunlight poured in floods over the snowy summits, and he felt a great sense of awe. It was all so grand, so silent, and so near to the Infinite. He saw the full majesty of the world and of the Power that had created it. For a little while his mission and all human passions and emotions floated away from him; he was content merely to stand there, without thinking, but to feel the immensity and majesty of it all.

Dick presently recovered himself and with a little laugh came back to earth. But he was glad to have had those moments. He began the descent, which was rougher and rockier than the ascent had been, but the prospect was encouraging. The valley between the ridge on the slope of which he stood and the higher one beyond it seemed narrow, but he believed that he would find in it the shelter and hiding that he and Albert wished.

As he went down the slope became steeper, but once more the pines, sheltered from the snows and cruel winds, grew to a great size. There was also so much outcropping of rock that Dick was hopeful of finding another alcove deep enough to be converted into a house.

When nearly down, he caught a gleam among the trees that he knew was water, and again he was encouraged. Here was a certainty of one thing that was an absolute necessity. Soon he was in the valley, which he found exceedingly narrow and almost choked with a growth of pine, ash, and aspen, a tiny brook flowing down its centre. He was tired and warm from the long descent and knelt down and drank from the brook. Its waters were as cold as ice, flowing down from the crest of one of the great peaks clad, winter and summer, in snow.

Dick followed the brook for fully a mile, seeking everywhere a suitable place in which he and his brother might make a home, but he found none. The valley resembled in most of its aspects a great canyon, and all the fertile earth on either side of the brook was set closely with pine, ash, and aspen. These would form a shelter from winds, but they would not protect from rain and the great colds and snows of the high Rockies.

Dick noticed many footprints of animals at the margin of the stream, some of great size, which he had no doubt were made by grizzlies or silver tips. He also believed that the beaver might be found farther down along this cold and secluded water, but he was not interested greatly just then in animals; he was seeking for that most necessary of all things—something that must be had—a home.

It seemed to him at the end of his estimated mile that the brook was going to flow directly into the mountain which rose before him many hundreds of feet; but when he came to the rocky wall he found that the valley turned off at a sharp angle to the left, and the stream, of course, followed it, although it now descended more rapidly, breaking three times into little foamy falls five or six feet in height. Then another brook came from a deep cleft between the mountains on the eastern side and swelled with its volume the main stream, which now became a creek.

The new valley widened out to a width of perhaps a quarter of a mile, although the rocky walls on either side rose to a great height and were almost precipitous. Springs flowed from these walls and joined the creek. Some of them came down the face of the cliffs in little cascades of foam and vapour, but others spouted from the base of the rock. Dick knelt down to drink from one of the latter, but as his face approached the water he jumped away. He dipped up a little of it in his soft hat and tasted it. It was brackish and almost boiling hot.

Dick was rather pleased at the discovery. A bitter and hot spring might be very useful. He had imbibed—like many others—from the teaching of his childhood that any bitter liquid was good for you. As he advanced farther the valley continued to spread out. It was now perhaps a half mile in width, and well wooded. The creek became less turbulent, flowing with a depth of several feet in a narrow channel.

The whole aspect of the valley so far had been that of a wilderness uninhabited and unvisited. A mule deer looked curiously at Dick, then walked away a few paces and stood there. When Dick glanced back his deership was still curious and gazing. A bear crashed through a thicket, stared at the boy with red eyes, then rolled languidly away. Dick was quick to interpret these signs. They were unfamiliar with human presence, and he was cheered by the evidence. Yet at the end of another hundred yards of progress he sank down suddenly among some bushes and remained perfectly silent, but intently watchful.

He had seen a column of smoke rising above the pines and aspens. Smoke meant fire, fire meant human beings, and human beings, in that region, meant enemies. He had no doubt that Sioux were at the foot of that column of smoke. It was a tragic discovery. He was looking for a home for Albert and himself somewhere in this valley, but there could be no home anywhere near the Sioux. He and his brother must turn in another direction, and with painful effort lug their stores over the ridges. But Dick was resolved to see. There were great springs of courage and tenacity in his nature, and he wished, moreover, to prove his new craft as a woodsman and mountaineer. He remained awhile in the bushes, watching the spire, and presently, to his amazement, it thinned quickly and was gone. It had disappeared swiftly, while the smoke from a fire usually dies down. It was Dick's surmise that the Sioux had put out their fire by artificial means and then had moved on. Such an act would indicate a fear of observation, and his curiosity increased greatly.

But Dick did not forget his caution. He crouched in the bushes for quite a while yet, watching the place where the smoke had been, but the sky remained clear and undefiled. He heard nothing and saw nothing but the lonely valley. At last he crept forward slowly, and with the greatest care, keeping among bushes and treading very softly. He advanced in this manner three or four hundred yards, to the very point which must have been the base of the spire of smoke—he had marked it so well that he could not be mistaken—and from his leafy covert saw a large open space entirely destitute of vegetation. He expected to see there also the remains of a camp fire, but none was visible, not a single charred stick, nor a coal.

Dick was astonished. A new and smoking camp fire must leave some trace. One could not wipe it away absolutely. He remained a comparatively long time, watching in the edge of the bushes beside the wide and open space.

He still saw and heard nothing. Never before had a camp fire vanished so mysteriously and completely, and with it those who had built it. At last, his curiosity overcoming his caution, he advanced into the open space, and now saw that it fell away toward the centre. Advancing more boldly, he found himself near the edge of a deep pit.

The pit was almost perfectly round and had a diameter of about ten feet. So far as Dick could judge, it was about forty feet deep and entirely empty. It looked like a huge well dug by the hand of man.

While Dick was gazing at the pit, an extraordinary and terrifying thing happened. The earth under his feet began to shake. At first he could not believe it, but when he steadied himself and watched closely, the oscillating motion was undoubtedly there. It was accompanied, too, by a rumble, dull and low, but which steadily grew louder. It seemed to Dick that the round pit was the centre of this sound.

Despite the quaking of the earth, he ventured again into the open space and saw that the pit had filled with water. Moreover, this water was boiling, as he could see it seething and bubbling. As he looked, clouds of steam shot up to a height of two or three hundred feet, and Dick, in alarm, ran back to the bushes. He knew that this was the column of vapour he had first seen from a distance, but he was not prepared for what followed.

There was an explosion so loud that it made Dick jump. Then a great column of water shot up from the boiling pit to a height of perhaps fifty feet, and remained there rising and falling. From the apex of this column several great jets rose, perhaps, three times as high.

The column of hot water glittered and shimmered in the sun, and Dick gazed in wonder and delight. He had read enough to recognize the phenomenon that he now saw. It was a geyser, a column of hot water shooting up, at regular intervals and with great force, from the unknown deeps of the earth.

As he gazed, the column gradually sank, the boiling water in the pit sank, too, and there was no longer any rumble or quaking of the earth. Dick cautiously approached the pit again. It was as empty as a dry well, but he knew that in due time the phenomenon would be repeated. He was vastly interested, but he did not wait to see the recurrence of the marvel, continuing his way down the valley over heaps of crinkly black slag and stone, which were age-old lava, although he did not know it, and through groves of pine and ash, aspen, and cedar. He saw other round pits and watched a second geyser in eruption. He saw, too, numerous hot springs, and much steamy vapour floating about. There were also mineral springs and springs of the clearest and purest cold water. It seemed to Dick that every minute of his wanderings revealed to him some new and interesting sight, while on all sides of the little valley rose the mighty mountains, their summits in eternal snow.

A great relief was mingled with the intense interest that Dick felt. He had been sure at first that he saw the camp fires of the Sioux, but after the revulsion it seemed as if it were a place never visited by man, either savage or civilized. As he continued down the valley, he noticed narrow clefts in the mountains opening into them from either side, but he felt sure from the nature of the country that they could not go back far. The clefts were four in number, and down two of them came considerable streams of clear, cold water emptying into the main creek.

The valley now narrowed again and Dick heard ahead a slight humming sound which presently grew into a roar. He was puzzled at first, but soon divined the cause. The creek, or rather little river, much increased in volume by the tributary brooks, made a great increase of speed in its current. Dick saw before him a rising column of vapour and foam, and in another minute or two stood beside a fine fall, where the little river took a sheer drop of forty feet, then rushed foaming and boiling through a narrow chasm, to empty about a mile farther on into a beautiful blue lake.

Dick, standing on a high rock beside the fall, could see the lake easily. Its blue was of a deep, splendid tint, and on every side pines and cedars thickly clothed the narrow belt of ground between it and the mountains. The far end seemed to back up abruptly against a mighty range crowned with snow, but Dick felt sure that an outlet must be there through some cleft in the range. The lake itself was of an almost perfect crescent shape, and Dick reckoned its length at seven miles, with a greatest breadth, that is, at the centre, of about two miles. He judged, too, from its colour and its position in a fissure that its depth must be very great.

The surface of the lake lay two or three hundred feet lower than the rock on which Dick was standing, and he could see its entire expanse, rippling gently under the wind and telling only of peace and rest. Flocks of wild fowl flew here and there, showing white or black against the blue of its waters, and at the nearer shore Dick thought he saw an animal like a deer drinking, but the distance was too great to tell certainly.

He left the rock and pursued his way through dwarf pines and cedars along the edge of the chasm in which the torrent boiled and foamed, intending to go down to the lake. Halfway he stopped, startled by a long, shrill, whistling sound that bore some resemblance to the shriek of a distant locomotive. The wilderness had been so silent before that the sound seemed to fill all the valley, the ridges taking it up and giving it back in one echo after another until it died away among the peaks. In a minute or so the whistling shriek was repeated and then two or three times more.

Dick was not apprehensive. It was merely a new wonder in that valley of wonders, and none of these wonders seemed to have anything to do with man. The sound apparently came from a point two or three hundred yards to his left at the base of the mountain, and turning, Dick went toward it, walking very slowly and carefully through the undergrowth. He had gone almost the whole distance seeing nothing but the mountain and the forest, when the whistling shriek was suddenly repeated so close to him that he jumped. He sank down behind a dwarf pine, and then he saw not thirty feet away the cause of the sound.

A gigantic deer, a great greyish animal, stood in a little open space, and at intervals emitted that tremendous whistle. It stood as high as a horse, and Dick estimated its weight at more than a thousand pounds. He was looking at a magnificent specimen of the Rocky Mountain elk, by far the largest member of the deer tribe that he had ever seen. The animal, the wind blowing from him toward Dick, was entirely unsuspicious of danger, and the boy could easily have put a bullet into his heart, but he had no desire to do so. Whether the elk was whistling to his mate or sending a challenge to a rival bull he did not know, and after watching and admiring him for a little while he crept away.

But Dick was not wholly swayed by sentiment. He said to himself

279

as he went away among the pines: "Don't you feel too safe, Mr. Elk, we'll have to take you or some of your brethren later on. I've heard that elk meat is good."

He resumed his journey and was soon at the edge of the lake, which at this point had a narrow sandy margin. Its waters were fresh and cold, and wold duck, fearless of Dick, swam within a few yards of him. The view here was not less majestic and beautiful than it had been from the rock, and Dick, sensitive to nature, was steeped in all its wonder and charm. He was glad to be there, he was glad that chance or providence had led him to this lovely valley. He felt no loneliness, no fear for the future, he was content merely to breathe and feel the glory of it permeate his being.

He picked up a pebble presently and threw it into the lake. It sank with the sullen plunk that told unmistakably to the boy's ears of great depths below. Once or twice he saw a fish leap up, and it occurred to him that here was another food supply.

He suddenly pulled himself together with a jerk. He could not sit there all day dreaming. He had come to find a winter home for Albert and himself, and he had not yet found it. But he had a plan from which he had been turned aside for a while by the sight of the lake, and now he went back to carry it out.

There were two clefts opening into the mountains from his side of the river, and he went into the first on the return path. It was choked with pine and cedars and quickly ended against a mountain wall, proving to be nothing but a very short canyon. There was much outcropping of rock here, but nothing that would help toward a shelter, and Dick went on to the second cleft.

This cleft, wider than the other, was the one down which the considerable brook flowed, and the few yards or so of fertile ground on either side of the stream produced a rank growth of trees. They were so thick that the boy could see only a little distance ahead, but he believed that this slip of a tributary valley ran far back in the mountains, perhaps a dozen miles.

He picked his way about a mile and then came suddenly upon a house. It stood in an alcove protected by rocks and trees, but safe from snow slide. It was only a log hut of one room, with the roof broken in and the door fallen from its hinges, but Dick knew well enough the handiwork of the white man. As he approached, some wild animal darted out of the open door and crashed away among the undergrowth, but Dick knew that white men had once lived there. It was equally evident that they had long been gone.

It was a cabin of stout build, its thick logs fitted nicely together, and the boards of the roof had been strong and well laid. Many years must have passed to have caused so much decay. Dick entered and was saluted by a strong, catlike odour. Doubtless a mountain lion had been sleeping there, and this was the tenant that he had heard crashing away among the undergrowth. On one side was a window closed by a sagging oaken shutter, which Dick threw open. The open door and window established a draught, and as the clean sweet air blew through the cabin the odour of the cat began to disappear.

Dick examined everything with the greatest interest and curiosity. There was a floor of puncheons fairly smooth, a stone fireplace, a chimney of mud and sticks, dusty wooden hooks, and rests nailed into the wall, a rude table overturned in a corner, and something that looked like a trap. It was the last that told the tale to Dick. When he examined it more critically, he had no doubt that it was a beaver trap.

Nor did he have any doubt but that this hut had been built by beaver trappers long ago, either by independent hunters, or by those belonging to one of the great fur companies. The beaver, he believed, had been found on this very brook, and when they were all taken the trappers had gone away, leaving the cabin forever, as they had left many another one. It might be at least forty years old.

Dick laughed aloud in his pleasure at this good luck. The cabin was dusty, dirty, disreputable, and odorous, but that draught would take away all the odours and his stout arm could soon repair the holes in the roof, put the door back on its hinges, and straighten the sagging window shutter. Here was their home, a house built by white men as a home, and now about to be used as such again. Dick did not feel like a tenant moving in, but like an owner. It would be a long, hard task to bring their supplies over the range but Albert and he had all the time in the world. It was one of the effects of their isolation to make Dick feel that there was no such thing as time.

He took another survey of the cabin. It was really a splendid place, a palace in its contrast with the surrounding wilderness, and he laughed with pure delight. When it was swept and cleaned, and a fire blazing on the flat stone that served for a hearth, while the cold winds roared without, it would be the snuggest home west of the Missouri. He was so pleased that he undertook at once some primary steps in the process of purification. He cut a number of small, straight boughs, tied them together with a piece of bark, the leaves at the head thus forming a kind of broom, and went to work.

He raised a great dust, which the draught blew into his eyes, ears, and nose, and he retreated from the place, willing to let the wind take it away. He would finish the task some other day. Then the clear waters of the brook tempted him. Just above the cabin was a deep pool which may have been the home of the beaver in an older time. Now it was undisturbed, and the waters were so pure that he could see the sand and rock on the bottom.

Still tingling from the dust, he took off his clothes and dived head foremost into the pool. He came up shivering and sputtering. It was certainly the coldest water into which he had ever leaped! After such a dash one might lie on a slab of ice to warm. Dick forgot that every drop in the brook had come from melting snows far up on the peaks, but, once in, he resolved to fight the element. He dived again, jumped up and down, and kicked and thrashed those waters as no beaver had ever done. Gradually he grew warm, and a wonderful exhilaration shot through every vein. Then he swam around and around and across and across the pool, disporting like a young white water god.

Dick was thoroughly enjoying himself, but when he began to feel cold again in seven or eight minutes he sprang out, ran up and down the bank, and rubbed himself with bunches of leaves until he was dry. After he had dressed, he felt that he had actually grown in size and strength in the last half hour.

He was now ravenously hungry. His absorption in his explorations and discoveries had kept him from thinking of such a thing as food until this moment, but when nature finally got in her claim she made it strong and urgent. He had brought cold supplies with him, upon which he feasted, sitting in the doorway of the cabin. Then he noticed the lateness of the hour. Shadows were falling across the snow on the western peaks and ridges. The golden light of the sun was turning red, and in the valley the air was growing misty with the coming twilight.

He resolved to pass the night in the cabin. He secured the window shutter again, tied up the fallen door on rude bark hinges, and fastened it on the inside with a stick—hasps for the bar were there yet—but before retiring he took a long look in the direction in which Albert and their camp lay.

A great range of mountains lay between, but Dick felt that he could almost see his brother, his camp fire, and the pine alcove. He was Albert's protector, and this would be the first entire night in the mountains in which the weaker boy had been left alone, but Dick was not apprehensive about him. He believed that their good fortune would still endure, and secure in that belief he rolled himself up in the blanket which he had brought in a little pack on his back, and laid himself down in the corner of the cabin.

The place was not yet free from dust and odour, but Dick's hardy life was teaching him to take as trifles things that civilization usually regarded as onerous, and he felt quite comfortable where he lay. He knew that it was growing cold in the gorge, and the shelter of the cabin was acceptable. He saw a little strip of wan twilight through a crack in the window, but it soon faded and pitchy darkness filled the narrow valley.

Dick fell into a sound sleep, from which he awoke only once in the night, and then it was a noise of something as of claws scratching at the door which stirred him. The scratch was repeated only once or twice, and with it came the sound of heavy, gasping puffs, like a big animal breathing. Then the creature went away, and Dick, half asleep, murmured: "I've put you out of your house, my fine friend, bear or panther, whichever you may be." In another minute he was wholly asleep again and did not waken until an edge of glittering sunlight, like a sword blade, came through the crack in the window and struck him across the eyes.

He bathed a second time in the pool, ate what was left of the food, and started on the return journey, moving at a brisk pace. He made many calculations on the way. It would take a week to move all their goods over the range to the cabin, but, once there, he believed that they would be safe for a long time; indeed, they might spend years in the valley, if they wished, and never see a stranger.

It was afternoon when he approached the pine alcove, but the familiar spire of smoke against the blue had assured him already that Albert was there and safe. In fact, Albert saw him first. He had just returned from the creek, and, standing on a rock, a fish in his hand, hailed his brother, who was coming up the slope.

"Halloo, Dick!" he shouted. "Decided to come home, have you? Hope you've had a pleasant visit."

"Fine trip, Al, old man," Dick replied. "Great place over there. Think we'd better move to it."

"That so? Tell us about it."

Dick, ever sensitive to Albert's manner and appearance, noticed that the boy's voice was fuller, and he believed that the dry, piny air of the mountains was still at its healing work. He joined Albert, who was waiting for him, and who, after giving his hand a hearty grasp, told him what he had found.

CHAPTER 6

Castle Howard

Albert agreed with Dick that they should begin to more at once, and his imagination was greatly stirred by Dick's narrative. "Why, it's an enchanted valley!" he exclaimed. "And a house is there waiting for us, too! Dick, I want to see it right away!"

Dick smiled.

"Sorry, but you'll have to wait a little, Al, old man," he said. "You're not strong enough yet to carry stores over the big range, though you will be very soon, and we can't leave our precious things here unguarded. So you'll have to stay and act as quartermaster while I make myself pack mule. When we have all the things over there, we can fasten them up in our house, where bears, panthers, and wolves can't get at them."

Albert made a wry face, but he knew that he must yield to necessity. Dick began the task the next morning, and it was long, tedious, and most wearing. More than once he felt like abandoning some of their goods, but he hardened his resolution with the reflection that all were precious, and not a single thing was abandoned.

It was more than a week before it was all done, and it was not until the last trip that Albert went with him, carrying besides his gun a small pack. The weather was still propitious. Once there had been a light shower in the night, but Albert was protected from it by the tarpaulin which they had made of the wagon cover, and nothing occurred to check his progress. He ate with an appetite that he had never known before, and he breathed by night as well as by day the crisp air of the mountains tingling with the balsam of the pines. It occurred to Dick that to be marooned in these mountains was perhaps the best of all things that could have happened to Albert.

They went slowly over the range toward the enchanted valley, stopping now and then because Albert, despite his improvement, was not yet equal to the task of strenuous climbing, but all things continued auspicious. There was a touch of autumn on the foliage, and the shades of red and yellow were appearing on the leaves of all the trees except the evergreens, but everything told of vigorous life. As they passed the crest of the range and began the descent of the slope toward the enchanted valley, a mule deer crashed from the covert and fled away with great bounds. Flocks of birds rose with whirrings from the bushes. From some point far away came the long, whistling sound that made Albert cry out in wonder. But Dick laughed.

"It's the elk," he said. "I saw one when I first came into the valley. I think they are thick hereabout, and I suspect that they will furnish us with some good winter food."

Albert found the valley all that Dick had represented it to be, and more. He watched the regular eruptions of the geysers with amazement and delight; he insisted on sampling the mineral springs, and intended to learn in time their various properties. The lake, in all its shimmering aspects, appealed to his love of the grand and beautiful, and he promptly named it "The Howard Sea, after its discoverer, you know," he said to Dick. Finally, the cabin itself filled him with delight, because he foresaw even more thoroughly than Dick how suitable it would be for a home in the long winter months. He installed himself as housekeeper and set to work at once.

The little cabin was almost choked with their supplies, which Dick had been afraid to leave outside for fear that the provisions would be eaten and the other things injured by the wild animals, and now they began the task of assorting and putting them into place.

The full equipment of the wagon that Dick had found in the gully, particularly the tools, proved to be a godsend. They made more racks on the walls—boring holes with the augers and then driving in pegs—on which they laid their axes and extra rifles. In the same manner they made high shelves, on which their food would be safe from prowling wild beasts, even should they succeed in breaking in the door. But Dick soon made the latter impossible by putting the door on strong hinges of leather which he made from the gear that he had cut from the horses. He also split a new bar from one of the young ash trees and strengthened the hasps on the inside. He felt now that when the bar was in place not even the heaviest grizzly could force the door.

The task of mending the roof was more difficult. He knew how to split rude boards with his axe, but he had only a few nails with which to hold them in place. He solved the problem by boring auger holes, into which he drove pegs made from strong twigs. The roof looked water-tight, and he intended to reinforce it later on with the skins of wild animals that he expected to kill—there had been no time yet for hunting.

Throughout these operations, which took about a week, they slept in the open in a rude tent which they made of the wagon cover and set beside the cabin, for two reasons: because Dick believed the open air at all times to be good for Albert, and because he was averse to using the cabin as a dormitory until it was thoroughly cleansed and aired.

Albert made himself extremely useful in the task of refurbishing the cabin. He brushed out all the dust, brought water from the brook and scrubbed the floor, and to dry the latter built their first fire on the hearth with pine cones and other fallen wood. As he touched the match to it, he did not conceal his anxiety.

"The big thing to us," he said, "is whether or not this chimney will draw. That's vital, I tell you, Dick, to a housekeeper. If it puffs out smoke and fills the cabin with it, we're to have a hard time and be miserable. If it draws like a porous plaster and takes all the smoke up it, then we're to have an easy time of it and be happy."

Both watched anxiously as Albert touched the match to some pine shavings which were to form the kindling wood. The shavings caught, a light blaze leaped up, there came a warning crackle, and smoke, too, arose. Which way would it go? The little column wavered a moment and then shot straight up the chimney. It grew larger, but still shot straight up the chimney. The flames roared and were drawn in the same direction.

Albert laughed and clapped his hands.

"It's to be an easy time and a happy life!" he exclaimed. "Those old beaver hunters knew what they were about when they built this chimney!"

"You can cook in here, Al," said Dick; "but I suggest that we sleep in the tent until the weather grows bad."

Dick had more than one thing in mind in making this suggestion about the tent and sleeping. The air of the cabin could be close at night even with the window open, but in the tent with the flap thrown back— they never closed it—they breathed only a fresh balsamic odour, crisp with the coolness of autumn. He had watched Albert all the time. Now and then when he had exerted himself more than usual, the younger boy would cough, and at times he was very tired, but Dick, however sharply he watched, did not see again the crimson stain on the lips that he had noticed the night of the flight from the massacre.

But the older brother, two years older only, in fact, but ten years older, at least, in feeling, did notice a great change in Albert, mental as well as physical. The younger boy ceased to have periods of despondency. While he could not do the things that Dick did, he was improving, and he never lamented his lack of strength. It seemed to him a matter of course, so far as Dick could judge, that in due time he should be the equal of the older and bigger boy in muscle and skill.

Albert, moreover, had no regrets for the world without. Their life with the wagon train had been far from pleasant, and he had only Dick, and Dick had only him. Now the life in the enchanted valley, which was a real valley of enchantments, was sufficient for him. Each day brought forth some new wonder, some fresh and interesting detail. He was a capable fisherman, and he caught trout in both the brook and the river, while the lake yielded to his line other and larger fish, the names of which neither boy knew, but which proved to be of delicate flavour when broiled over the coals. Just above them was a boiling hot spring, and Albert used the water from this for cooking purposes. "Hot and cold water whenever you please," he said to Dick. "Nothing to do but to turn the tap."

Dick smiled; he, too, was happy. He enjoyed life in the enchanted valley, where everything seemed to have conspired in their favour. When they had been there about a week, and their home was ready for any emergency, Dick took his gun and went forth, the hunting spirit strong within him. They had heard the elk whistling on the mountain side nearly every day, and he believed that elk meat would prove tender and good. Anyway he would see.

Dick did not feel much concern about their food supply. He believed that vast quantities of big game would come into this valley in the winter to seek protection from the mighty snows of the northern Rockies, but it was just as well to begin the task of filling the larder.

He came out into the main valley and turned toward the lake. Autumn was now well advanced, but in the cool sunshine the lake seemed more beautiful than ever. Its waters were golden today, but with a silver tint at the edges where the pine-clad banks overhung it. Dick did not linger, however. He turned away toward the slopes, whence the whistling call had come the oftenest, and was soon among the pines and cedars. He searched here an hour or more, and at last he found two feeding, a male and a female.

Dick had the instinct of the hunter, and already he had acquired great skill. Creeping through the undergrowth, he came within easy shot of the animals, and he looked at them a little before shooting. The bull was magnificent, and he, if any, seemed a fit subject for the bullet, but Dick chose the cow, knowing that she would be the tenderer. Only a single shot was needed, and then he had a great task to carry the hide and the body in sections to the cabin. They ate elk steaks and then hung the rest in the trees for drying and jerking. Dick, according to his previous plan, used the skin to cover the newly mended places in the roof, fastening it down tightly with small wooden pegs. His forethought was vindicated two days later when a great storm came. Both he and Albert had noticed throughout the afternoon an unusual warmth in the air. It affected Albert particularly, as it made his respiration difficult. Over

the mountains in the west they saw small dark clouds which soon began to grow and unite. Dick thought he knew what it portended, and
he and his brother quickly taking down the tent, carried it and all its
equipment inside the cabin. Then making fast the door and leaving the
window open, they waited.

The heat endured, but all the clouds became one that overspread the
entire heavens. Despite the lateness of the season, the thunder, inexpressibly solemn and majestic, rumbled among the gorges, and there was a
quiver of lightening. It was as dark as twilight.

The rain came, roaring down the clefts and driving against the cabin
with such force that they were compelled to close the window. How
thankful Dick was now for Albert's sake that they had such a secure shelter! Nor did he despise it for his own.

The rain, driven by a west wind, poured heavily, and the air rapidly
grew colder. Albert piled dry firewood on the hearth and lighted it. The
flames leaped up, and warmth, dryness, and cheer filled all the little cabin.
Dick had been anxiously regarding the roof, but the new boards and the
elk skin were water-tight. Not a drop came through. Higher leaped the
flames and the rosy shadows fell upon the floor.

"It's well we took the tent down and came in here," said Albert. "Listen to that!"

The steady, driving sweep changed to a rattle and a crackle. The rain
had turned to hail, and it was like the patter of rifle fire on the stout
little cabin.

"It may rain or hail or snow, or do whatever it pleases, but it can't get
at us," said Albert exultingly.

"No, it can't," said Dick. "I wonder, Al, what Bright Sun is doing now?"

"A peculiar Indian," said Albert thoughtfully, "but it's safe to say that
wherever he is he's planning and acting."

"At any rate," said Dick, "we're not likely to know it, whatever it is, for
a long time, and we won't bother trying to guess about it."

It hailed for an hour and then changed to rain again, pouring down in
great steadiness and volume. Dick opened the window a little way once,
but the night was far advanced, and it was pitchy black outside. They let
the coals die down to a glowing bed, and then, wrapping themselves in
their blankets, they slept soundly all through the night and the driving rain,
their little cabin as precious to them as any palace was ever to a king.

Albert, contrary to custom, was the first to awake the next morning. A
few coals from the fire were yet alive on the hearth, and the atmosphere
of the room, breathed over and over again throughout the night, was
close and heavy. He threw back the window shutter, and the great rush
of pure cold air into the opening made his body thrill with delight. This

was a physical pleasure, but the sight outside gave him a mental rapture even greater. Nothing was falling now, but the rain had turned back to hail before it ceased, and all the earth was in glittering white. The trees in the valley, clothed in ice, were like lace work, and above them towered the shining white mountains.

Albert looked back at Dick. His brother, wrapped in his blanket, still slept, with his arm under his head and his face toward the hearth. He looked so strong, so enduring, as he lay there sleeping soundly, and Albert knew that he was both. But a curious feeling was in the younger boy's mind that morning. He was glad that he had awakened first. Hitherto he had always opened his eyes to find Dick up and doing. It was Dick who had done everything. It was Dick who had saved him from the Sioux; it was Dick who had practically carried him over the first range; Dick had found their shelter in the pine alcove; Dick had laboured day and night, day after day, and night after night, bringing the stores over the mountain from the lost train, then he had found their new home in the enchanted valley, which Albert persisted in calling it, and he had done nearly all the hard work of repairing and furnishing the cabin.

It should not always be so. Albert's heart was full of gratitude to this brother of his who was so brave and resourceful, but he wanted to do his share. The feeling was based partly on pride and partly on a new increase of physical strength. He took a deep inhalation of the cold mountain air and held it long in his lungs. Then he emitted it slowly. There was no pain, no feeling of soreness, and it was the first time he could remember that it had been so. A new thrill of pleasure, keener and more powerful than any other, shook him for a moment. It was a belief, nay, a certainty, or at least a conviction, that he was going to be whole and sound. The mountains were doing their kindly healing. He could have shouted aloud with pleasure, but instead he restrained himself and went outside, softly shutting the door behind him.

Autumn had gone and winter had come in a night. The trees were stripped of every leaf and in their place was the sheathing of ice. The brook roared past, swollen for the time to a little river. The air, though very cold, was dry despite the heavy rain of the night before. Albert shivered more than once, but it was not the shiver of weakness. It did not bite to the very marrow of him. Instead, when he exercised legs and arms vigorously, warmth came back. He was not a crushed and shrivelled thing. Now he laughed aloud in sheer delight. He had subjected himself to another test, and he had passed it in triumph.

He built up the fire, and when Dick awoke, the pleasant aroma of cooking filled the room.

"Why, what's this, Al?" exclaimed the big youth, rubbing his eyes.

"Oh, I've been up pretty near an hour," replied Albert airily. "Saw that you were having a fine sleep, so I thought I wouldn't disturb you."

Dick looked inquiringly at him. He thought he detected a new note in his brother's voice, a note, too, that he liked.

"I see," he said; "and you've been at work sometime, Do you feel fully equal to the task?"

Albert turned and faced his brother squarely.

"I've been thinking a lot, and feeling a lot more this morning," he replied. "I've been trying myself out, as they say, and if I'm not well I'm travelling fast in that direction. Hereafter I share the work as well as the rewards."

Albert spoke almost defiantly, but Dick liked his tone and manner better than ever. He would not, on any account, have said anything in opposition at this moment.

"All right, Al, old fellow. That's agreed," he said.

CHAPTER 7

An Animal Progression

The thin sheath of ice did not last long. On the second day the sun came out and melted it in an hour. Then a warm wind blew and in a few more hours the earth was dry. On the third day Albert took his repeating rifle from the hooks on the wall and calmly announced that he was going hunting.

"All right," said Dick; "and as I feel lazy I'll keep house until you come back. Don't get chewed up by a grizzly bear."

Dick sat down in the doorway of the cabin and watched his brother striding off down the valley, gun on shoulder, figure very erect. Dick smiled; but it was a smile of pride, not derision.

"Good old Al! He'll do!" he murmured.

Albert followed the brook into the larger valley and then went down by the side of the lake. Though a skilful shot, he was not yet a good hunter, but he knew that one must make a beginning and he wanted to learn through his own mistakes.

He had an idea that game could be found most easily in the forest that ran down the mountain side to the lake, and he was thinking most particularly just then of elk. He had become familiar with the loud, whistling sound, and he listened for it now but did not hear it.

He passed the spot at which Dick had killed the big cow elk and continued northward among the trees that covered the slopes and flat land between the mountain and the lake. This area broadened as he proceeded, and, although the forest was leafless now, it was so dense and there was such a large proportion of evergreens, cedars, and pines that Albert could not see very far ahead. He crossed several brooks pouring down from the peaks. All were in flood, and once or twice it was all that he could do with a flying leap to clear them, but he went on, undiscouraged, keeping a sharp watch for that which he was hunting.

Albert did not know much about big game, but he remembered hearing Dick say that elk and mule deer would be likely to come into the valley for shelter at the approach of winter, and he was hopeful that he might have the luck to encounter a whole herd of the big elk. Then, indeed, he would prove that he was an equal partner with Dick in the work as well as the reward. He wished to give the proof at once.

He had not been so far up the north end of the valley before, and he noticed that here was quite an expanse of flat country on either side of the lake. But the mountains all around the valley were so high that it seemed to Albert that deer and other wild animals might find food as well as shelter throughout the winter. Hence he was quite confident, despite his poor luck so far, that he should find big game soon, and his hunting fever increased. He had never shot anything bigger than a rabbit, but Albert was an impressionable boy, and his imagination at once leaped over the gulf from a rabbit to a grizzly bear.

He had the lake, an immense and beautiful blue mirror, on his right and the mountains on his left, but the space between was now nearly two miles in width, sown thickly in spots with pine and cedar, ash and aspen, and in other places quite open. In the latter the grass was green despite the lateness of the season, and Albert surmised that good grazing could be found there all through the winter, even under the snow. Game must be plentiful there, too.

The way dropped down a little into a sheltered depression, and Albert heard a grunt and a great puffing breath. A huge dark animal that had been lying among some dwarf pines shuffled to its feet and Albert's heart slipped right up into his throat. Here was his grizzly, and he certainly was a monster! Every nerve in Albert was tingling, and instinct bade him run. Will had a hard time of it for a few moments, struggling with instinct, but will conquered, and, standing his ground, Albert fired a bullet from his repeater at the great dark mass.

The animal emitted his puffing roar again and rushed, head down, but blindly. Then Albert saw that he had roused not a grizzly bear but an enormous bull buffalo, a shaggy, fierce old fellow who would not eat him, but who might gore or trample him to death. His aspect was so terrible that will again came near going down before instinct, but Albert did not run. Instead, he leaped aside, and, as the buffalo rushed past, he fired another bullet from his repeater into his body just back of the fore legs.

The animal staggered, and Albert staggered, too, from excitement and nervousness, but he remembered to take aim and fire again and again with his heavy repeater. In his heat and haste he did not hear a shout behind him, but he did see the great bull stagger, then reel and fall on his side, after which he lay quite still.

Albert stood, rifle in hand, trembling and incredulous. Could it be he who had slain the mightiest buffalo that ever trod the earth? The bull seemed to his distended eyes and flushed brain to weigh ten tons at least, and to dwarf the biggest elephant. He raised his hand to his forehead and then sat down beside his trophy, overcome with weakness.

"Well, now, you have done it, young one! I thought I'd get a finger in this pie, but I came up too late! Say, young fellow, what's your name? Is it Daniel Boone or Davy Crockett?"

It was Dick who had followed in an apparently casual manner. He had rushed to his brother's rescue when he saw the bull charging, but he had arrived too late—and he was glad of it; the triumph was wholly Albert's.

Albert, recovering from his weakness, looked at Dick, looked at the buffalo, and then looked back at Dick. All three looks were as full of triumph, glory, and pride as any boy's look could be.

"He's as big as a mountain, isn't he, Dick?" he said.

"Well, not quite that," replied Dick gravely. "A good-sized hill would be a better comparison."

The buffalo certainly was a monster, and the two boys examined him critically. Dick was of the opinion that he belonged to the species known as the wood bison, which is not numerous among the mountains, but which is larger than the ordinary buffalo of the plains. The divergence of type, however, is very slight.

"He must have been an outlaw," said Dick; "a vicious old bull compelled to wander alone because of his bad manners. Still, it's likely that he's not the only buffalo in our valley."

"Can we eat him?" asked Albert.

"That's a question. He's sure to be tough, but I remember how we used to make steak tender at home by beating it before it was cooked. We might serve a thousand pounds or two of this bull in that manner. Besides, we want that robe."

The robe was magnificent, and both boys felt that it would prove useful. Dick had gained some experience from his own buffalo hunt on the plains, and they began work at once with their sharp hunting knives. It was no light task to take the skin, and the beast was so heavy that they could not get it entirely free until they partly chopped up the body with an axe that Dick brought from the cabin. Then it made a roll of great weight, but Dick spread it on the roof of their home to cure. They also cut out great sections of the buffalo, which they put in the same place for drying and jerking.

While they were engaged at this task, Albert saw a pair of fiery eyes regarding them from the undergrowth.

"See, Dick," he said, "what is that?"

Dick saw the eyes, the lean ugly body behind it, and he shuddered. He knew. It was the timber wolf, largest and fiercest of the species, brother to him whom he had seen prowling about the ruined wagon train. The brute called up painful memories, and, seizing his rifle, he fired at a spot midway between the red eyes. The wolf uttered a howl, leaped high in the air, and fell dead, lying without motion, stretched on his side.

"I didn't like the way he looked at us," explained Dick.

A horrible growling and snapping came from the bushes presently.

"What's that?" asked Albert.

"It's only Mr. Timber Wolf's brethren eating up Mr. Timber Wolf, now that he is no longer of any use to himself."

Albert shuddered, too.

It was nightfall when they took away the last of the buffalo for which they cared, and as they departed they heard in the twilight the patter of light feet.

"It's the timber wolves rushing for what we've left," said Dick. "Those are big and fierce brutes, and you and I, Al, must never go out without a rifle or a revolver. You can't tell what they'll try, especially in the winter."

The entire roof of the cabin was covered the next day with the buffalo robe and the drying meat, and birds of prey began to hover above it. Albert constituted himself watchman, and, armed with a long stick, took his place on the roof, where he spent the day.

Dick shouldered one of the shotguns and went down to the lake. There he shot several fine teal, and in one of the grassy glades near it he roused up prairie hen. Being a fine shot, he secured four of these, and returned to the cabin with his acceptable spoil.

They had now such a great supply of stores and equipment that their place was crowded and they scarcely had room for sleeping on the floor.

"What we need," said Dick, "is an annex, a place that can be used for a storehouse only, and this valley, which has been so kind to us, ought to continue being kind and furnish it."

The valley did furnish the annex, and it was Albert who found it. He discovered a little further up the cleft an enormous oak, old and decayed. The tree was at lease seven feet through, and the hollow itself was fully five feet in diameter, with a height of perhaps fourteen feet. It was very rough inside with sharp projections in every direction which had kept any large animal from making his den there, but Albert knew at once that the needed place had been found. Full of enthusiasm he ran for Dick, who came instantly to see.

"Fine," said Dick approvingly. "We'll call it the 'annex,' sure enough, and we'll get to work right away with our axes."

They cut out all the splinters and other projections, smoothing off the round walls and the floor, and they also extended the hollow overhead somewhat.

"This is to be a two-story annex," said Dick. "We need lots of room."

High up they ran small poles across, fixing them firmly in the tree on either side, and lower down they planted many wooden pegs and hooks on which they might hang various articles.

"Everything will keep dry in here," said Albert. "I would not mind sleeping in the annex, but when the door is closed there won't be a particle of air."

It was the "door" that gave them the greatest trouble. The opening by which they entered the hollow was about four feet high and a foot and a half across, and both boys looked at it a long time before they could see a way to solve the puzzle.

"That door has to be strong enough to keep everything out," said Dick. "We mean to keep most of our meat supply in there, and that, of course, will draw wild animals, little and big; it's the big ones we've got to guard against."

After strenuous thinking, they smoothed off all the sides of the opening in order that a flat surface might fit perfectly against them. Then Dick cut down a small oak, and split out several boards—not a difficult task for him, as he had often helped to make boards in Illinois. The boards were laid together the width of the opening and were held in place by cross pieces fastened with wooden pegs. Among their stores were two augers and two gimlets, and they were veritable godsends; they enabled the boys to make use of pegs and to save the few nails that they had for other and greater emergencies.

The door was made, and now came the task to "hang" it. "Hang" was merely a metaphorical word, as they fitted it into place instead. The wood all around the opening was about a foot thick, and they cut it out somewhat after the fashion of the lintels of a doorway. Then they fitted in the door, which rested securely in its grooves, but they knew that the claws of a grizzly bear or mountain lion might scratch it out, and they intended to make it secure against any such mischance.

With the aid of hatchet and auger they put three wooden hooks on either side of the doorway, exactly like those that defend the door of a frontier cabin, and into these they dropped three stout bars. It was true that the bars were on the outside, but no wild animal would have the intelligence enough to pry up those three bars and scratch the door out of place. Moreover, it could not happen by accident. It took them three laborious days to make and fit this door, but when the task was done they contemplated it with just pride.

"I call that about the finest piece of carpenter's work ever done in these mountains," said Albert in tones suffused with satisfaction.

"Of course," said Dick. "Why shouldn't it be, when the best carpenters in the world did the job?"

The two laughed, but their pride was real and no jest. It was late in the afternoon when they finished this task, and on the way to the cabin Albert suddenly turned white and reeled. Dick caught him, but he remained faint for sometime. He had over-tasked himself, and when they reached the cabin Dick made him lie down on the great buffalo robe while he cooked supper. But, contrary to his former habit, Albert revived rapidly. The colour returned to his face and he sprang up presently, saying that he was hungry enough to eat a whole elk. Dick felt a might sense of relief. Albert in his zeal had merely overexerted himself. It was not any relapse. "Here's the elk steak and you can eat ten pounds of it if you want it," he said.

They began early the next morning to move supplies to the annex. High up in the hollow they hung great quantities of dried meat of buffalo, elk, and mule deer. They also stored there several elk and mule deer skins, two wolf skins, and other supplies that they thought they would not need for a while. But in the main it was what they called a smokehouse, as it was universally known in the Mississippi Valley, their former home— that is, a place for keeping meat cured or to be cured.

This task filled the entire day, and when the door was securely fastened in place they returned to the cabin. After supper Dick opened the window, from which they could see the annex, as they had cut away a quantity of the intervening bushes. Albert meanwhile put out the last coals of the fire. Then he joined Dick at the window. Both had an idea that they were going to see something interesting.

The valley filled with darkness, but the moon came out, and, growing used to the darkness, they could see the annex fairly well.

Dick wet his finger and held it up.

"The wind is blowing from the annex toward us," he said.

"That's good," said Albert, nodding.

They watched for a long time, hearing only the dry rustling of the light wind among the bare boughs, but at last Dick softly pushed his shoulder against Albert's. Albert nodded again, with comprehension. A small dark animal came into the open space around the annex. The boys had difficulty in tracing his outlines at first, but once they had them fixed, they followed his movements with ease. He advanced furtively, stopping at intervals evidently both to listen and look. Some other of his kind, or not of his kind, might be on the same quest and it was his business to know.

"Is it a fox?" whispered Albert.

"I think not," replied Dick in the same tone. "It must be a wolverine. He scents the good things in the annex and he wants, oh, how he wants, the taste of them!"

The little dark animal, after delicate manoeuvring, came close up to the tree, and they saw him push his nose against the cold bark.

"I know just how he feels," whispered Albert with some sympathy. "It's all there, but he must know the quest is hopeless."

The little animal went all around the tree nosing the cold bark, and then stopped again at the side of the door.

"No use, sir," whispered Albert. "That door won't open just because you're hungry."

The little animal suddenly cocked up his head and darted swiftly away into the shadows. But another and somewhat larger beast came creeping into the open, advancing with caution toward the annex.

"Aha!" whispered Dick. "Little fellow displaced by a bigger one. That must be a wild cat."

The wild cat went through the same performance. He nosed eagerly at the door, circled the tree two or three times, but always came back to the place where that tempting, well-nigh irresistible odour assailed him. The boys heard a low growl and the scratching of sharp claws on the door.

"Now he's swearing and fighting," whispered Albert, "but it will do him no good. Save your throat and your claws, old fellow."

"Look, he's gone!" whispered Dick.

The wild cat suddenly tucked his tail between his legs and fled from the opening so swiftly that they could scarcely see him go.

"And here comes his successor," whispered Albert. "I suppose, Dick, we might call this an arithmetical or geometrical progression."

An enormous timber wolf stalked into the clear space. He bore no resemblance to the mean, sneaking little coyote of the prairie. As he stood upright his white teeth could be seen, and there was the slaver of hunger on his lips. He, too, was restive, watchful, and suspicious, but it did not seem to either Dick or Albert that his movements betokened fear. There was strength in his long, lean body, and ferocity in his little red eyes.

"What a hideous brute!" whispered Albert, shuddering.

"And as wicked as he is ugly," replied Dick. "I hate the sight of these timber wolves. I don't wonder that the wild cat made himself scarce so quickly."

"And he's surely hungry!" said Albert. "See how he stretches out his head toward our annex, as if he would devour everything inside it!"

Albert was right. The big wolf was hungry, hungry through and through, and the odour that came from the tree was exquisite and permeating; it was a mingled odour of many things and everything was good. He had never before known a tree to give forth such a delightful aroma and he thrilled in every wolfish fibre as it tickled his nostrils.

He approached the tree with all the caution of his cautious and crafty race, and, as he laid his nose upon the bark, that mingled aroma of many things good grew so keen and powerful that he came as near as a big wolf can to fainting with delight. He pushed at the places where the door fitted into the tree, but nothing yielded. Those keen and powerful odours that penetrated delightfully to every marrow of him were still there, but he could not reach their source. A certain disappointment, a vague fear of failure mingled with his anticipation, and as the wolverine and the wild cat had done, he moved uneasily around the tree, scratching at the bark, and now and then biting it with teeth that were very long and cruel.

His troubled circuit brought him back to the door, where the aroma was finest and strongest. There he tore at the lowest bar with tooth and claw, but it did not move. He had the aroma and nothing more, and no big, strong wolf can live on odours only. The vague disappointment grew into a positive rage. He felt instinctively that he could not reach the good things that the wonderful tree held within itself, but he persisted. He bent his back, uttered a growl of wrath just as a man swears, and fell to again with tooth and claw.

"If I didn't know that door was so very strong, I'd be afraid he'd get it," whispered Albert.

"Never fear," Dick whispered back with confidence.

The big wolf suddenly paused in his effort. Tooth and claw were still, and he crouched hard against the tree, as if he would have his body to blend with its shadow. A new odour had come to his nostrils. It did not come from the tree. Nor was it pleasant. Instead, it told him of something hostile and powerful. He was big and strong himself, but this that came was bigger and stronger. The growl that had risen in his throat stopped at his teeth. A chill ran down his backbone and the hair upon it stood up. The great wolf was afraid, and he knew he was afraid.

"Look!" whispered Albert in rising excitement. "The wolf, too, is stealing away! He is scared by something!"

"And good cause he has to be scared," said Dick. "See what's coming!"

A great tawny beast stood for a moment at the edge of the clearing. He was crouched low against the ground, but his body was long and powerful, with massive shoulders and fore arms. His eyes were yellow in the moonlight, and they stared straight at the annex. The big wolf took one hasty frightened look and then fled silently in the other direction. He knew now that the treasures of the annex were not for him.

"It's a cougar," whispered Dick, "and it must be the king of them all. Did you ever see such a whopper?"

The cougar came farther into the clearing. He was of great size, but he was a cat—a huge cat, but a cat, nevertheless—and like a cat he acted. He dragged his body along the earth, and his eyes, now yellow, now green, in the moonlight, were swung suspiciously from side to side. He felt all that the wolf had felt, but he was even more cunning and his approach was slower. It was his habit to spring when close enough, but he saw nothing to spring at except a tree trunk, and so he still crept forward on noiseless pads.

"Now, what will Mr. Cougar do?" asked Albert.

"Just what the others have done," replied Dick. "He will scratch and bite harder because he is bigger and stronger, but we've fixed our annex for just such attacks. It will keep him out."

Dick was right. The cougar or mountain lion behaved exactly as the others had done. He tore at the door, then he circled the tree two or three times, hunting in vain for an opening. Every vein in him was swollen with rage, and the yellowish-green eyes flared with anger.

"He'd be an ugly creature to meet just now," whispered Dick. "He's so mad that I believe he'd attack an elephant."

"He's certainly in no good humour," replied Dick. "But look, Al! See his tail drop between his legs! Now what under the moon is about to happen?"

Albert, surcharged with interest and excitement, stared as Dick was staring. The mighty cat seemed suddenly to crumple up. His frame shrank, his head was drawn in, he sank lower to the earth, as if he would burrow into it, but he uttered no sound whatever. He was to both the boys a symbol of fear.

"What a change! What does it mean?" whispered Albert.

"It must mean," replied Dick, "that he, too, has a master and that master is coming."

The cougar suddenly bunched himself up and there was a flash of tawny fur as he shot through the air. A second leap and the trees closed over his frightened figure. Albert believed that he would not stop running for an hour. Into the opening, mighty and fearless, shambled a monstrous beast. He had a square head, a long, immense body, and the claws of his great feet were hooked, many inches in length, and as sharp and hard as if made of steel. The figure of the beast stood for power and unbounded strength, and his movements indicated overwhelming confidence. There was nothing for him to fear. He had never seen any living creature that could do him harm. It was a gigantic grizzly bear.

Albert, despite himself, as he looked at the terrible brute, felt fear. It was there, unconfined, and a single blow of its paw could sweep the strongest man out of existence.

"I'm glad I'm in this cabin and that this cabin is strong," he whispered tremulously.

"So am I," said Dick, and his own whisper was a little shaky. "It's one thing to see a grizzly in a cage, and another to see him out here in the dark in these wild mountains. And that fellow must weigh at least a thousand pounds."

King Bruin shambled boldly across the opening to the annex. Why should he be careful? There might be other animals among the bushes and trees watching him, but they were weak, timid things, and they would run from his shadow. In the wan moonlight, which distorted and exaggerated, his huge bulk seemed to the two boys to grow to twice its size. When he reached the tree he reared up against it, growled in a manner that made the blood of the boys run cold, and began to tear with teeth and claws of hooked steel. The bark and splinters flew, and, for a moment, Dick was fearful lest he should force the door to their treasure. But it was only for a moment; not even a grizzly could break or tear his way through such a thickness of oak.

"Nothing can displace him," whispered Albert. "He's the real king."

"He's not the king," replied Dick, "and something can displace him."

"What do you mean?" asked Albert with incredulity.

"No beast is king. It's man, and man is here. I'm going to have a shot at that monster who is trying to rob us. We can reach him from here with a bullet. You take aim, too, Al."

They opened the window a little wider, being careful to make no noise, and aimed their rifles at the bear, who was still tearing at the tree in his rage.

"Try to hit him in the heart, Al," whispered Dick, "and I'll try to do the same. I'll count three in a whisper, and at the 'three' we'll fire together."

The hands of both boys as they levelled their weapons were trembling, not with fear, but from sheer nervousness. The bear, meanwhile, had taken no notice and was still striving to reach the hidden treasures. Like the others, he had made the circuit of the annex more than once, but now he was reared up again at the door, pulling at it with mighty tooth and claw. It seemed to both as they looked down the barrels of their rifles and chose the vulnerable spot that, monstrous and misshapen, he was constantly growing in size, so powerful was the effect of the moonlight and their imagination. But it was terrible fact to them.

They could see him with great distinctness, and so silent was the valley otherwise that they could hear the sound of his claws ripping across the bark. He was like some gigantic survival of another age. Dick waited until both his brother and himself grew steadier.

"Now don't miss, Albert," he said.

He counted "One, two, three," slowly, and at the "three!" the report of the two rifles came as one. They saw the great bear drop down from the tree, they heard an indescribable roar of pain and rage, and then they saw his huge bulk rushing down upon them. Dick fired three times and Albert twice, but the bear still came, and then Dick slammed the window shut and fastened it just as the full weight of the bear was hurled against the cabin.

Neither boy ever concealed from himself the fact that he was in a panic for a few moments. Their bullets seemed to have had no effect upon the huge grizzly, who was growling ferociously and tearing at the logs of the cabin. Glad they were that those logs were so stout and thick, and they stood there a little while in the darkness, their blood chilling at the sounds outside. Presently the roaring and tearing ceased and there was the sound of a fall. It was so dark in the cabin that the brothers could not see the faces of each other, but Dick whispered:

"Albert, I believe we've killed him, after all."

Albert said nothing and they waited a full ten minutes. No sound whatever came to their ears. Then Dick opened the window an inch or two and peeped out. The great bear lay upon his side quite still, and Dick uttered a cry of joy.

"We've killed him, Al! we've killed him!" he cried.

"Are you sure?" asked Albert.

"Quite sure. He does not stir in the slightest."

They opened the door and went out. The great grizzly was really dead. Their bullets had gone true, but his vitality was so enormous that he had been able to rush upon the cabin and tear at it in his rage until he fell dead. Both boys looked at him with admiration and awe; even dead, he was terrifying in every respect.

"I don't wonder that the cougar, big and strong as he was, slunk away in terror when he saw old Ephraim coming," said Dick.

"We must have his skin to put with our two buffalo robes," said Albert.

"And we must take it tonight," said Dick, "or the wolves will be here while we sleep."

They had acquired some skill in the art of removing furs and pelts, but it took them hours to strip the coat from the big grizzly. Then, as in the case of the buffalo, they cut away some portions of the meat that they thought might prove tender. They put the hide upon the roof to dry, and, their work over, they went to sleep behind a door securely fastened.

Dick was awakened once by what he thought was a sound of growling and fighting outside, but he was so sleepy that it made no impression upon him. They did not awake fully until nearly noon, and when they went forth they found that nothing was left of the great bear but his skeleton.

"The timber wolves have been busy," said Dick.

CHAPTER 8

The Trap Makers

The hide of the bear, which they cured in good style, was a magnificent trophy; the fur was soft and long, and when spread out came near covering the floor of their cabin. It was a fit match for the robe of the buffalo. They did not know much about grizzlies, but they believed that no larger bear would ever be killed in the Rocky Mountains.

A few days later Dick shot another buffalo in one of the defiles, but this was a young cow and her flesh was tender. They lived on a portion of it from day to day and the rest they cured and put in the annex. They added the robe to their store of furs.

"I'm thinking," said Dick, "that you and I, Al, might turn fur hunters." This seems to be an isolated corner of the mountains. It may have been tapped out long ago, but when man goes away the game comes back. We've got a comfortable house, and, with this as a basis, we might do better hunting furs here than if we were hunting gold in California, where the chances are always against you.

The idea appealed to Albert, but for the present they contented themselves with improving their house and surroundings. Other bears, cougars, and wolves came at night and prowled around the annex, but it was secure against them all, and Dick and Albert never troubled themselves again to keep awake and watch for such intruders.

Winter now advanced and it was very cold, but, to Dick's great relief, no snow came. It was on Albert's account that he wished air and earth to remain dry, and it seemed as if nature were doing her best to help the boy's recovery. The cough did not come again, he had no more spells of great exhaustion, the physical uplift became mental also, and his spirits, because of the rebound, fairly bubbled. He was full of ideas, continually making experiments, and had great plans in regard to the valley and Castle Howard, as he sometimes playfully called their cabin.

One of the things that pleased Albert most was his diversion of water from a hot spring about fifty yards from the cabin and higher up the

302

ravine. He dug a trench all the way from the pool to the house, and the hot water came bubbling down to their very door. It cooled, of course, a little on the way, but it was still warm enough for cooking purposes, and Albert was hugely delighted.

"Hot water! Cold water! Whatever you wish, Dick," he said; "just turn on the tap. If my inventive faculty keeps on growing, I'll soon have a shower bath, hot and cold, rigged up here."

"It won't grow enough for that," said Dick; "but I want to tell you, Al, that the big game in the valley is increasing at a remarkable rate. Although cold, it's been a very open winter so far, but I suppose the instinct of these animals warns them to seek a sheltered place in time."

"Instinct or the habit of endless generations," said Albert.

"Which may be the same thing," rejoined Dick.

"There's a whole herd of elk beyond the far end of the lake, I've noticed on the cliffs what I take to be mountain sheep, and thirty or forty buffalos at least must be ranging about in here."

"Then," said Albert, "let's have a try at the buffaloes. Their robes will be worth a lot when we go back to civilization, and there is more room left in the annex."

They took their repeaters and soon proved Dick's words to be true. In a sheltered meadow three or more miles up the valley they found about twenty buffaloes grazing. Each shot down a fat cow, and they could have secured more had not the minds of both boys rebelled at the idea of slaughter.

"It's true we'd like to have the robes," said Dick, "but we'd have to leave most of the carcasses rotting here. Even with the wonderful appetites that we've developed, we couldn't eat a whole buffalo herd in one winter."

But after they had eaten the tongue, brisket, and tenderloin of the two cows, while fresh, these being the tenderest and best parts of the buffalo, they added the rest of the meat to their stores in the annex. As they had done already in several cases, they jerked it, a most useful operation that observant Dick had learned when they were with the wagon train.

It took a lot of labour and time to jerk the buffaloes, but neither boy had a lazy bone in him, and time seemed to stretch away into eternity before them. They cut the flesh into long, thin strips, taking it all from the bones. Then all these pieces were thoroughly mixed with salt—fortunately, they could obtain an unlimited supply of salt by boiling out the water from the numerous salt springs in the valley—chiefly by pounding and rubbing. They let these strips remain inside the hides about three hours, then all was ready for the main process of jerking.

Albert had been doing the salting and Dick meanwhile had been getting ready the frame for the jerking. He drove four forked poles into the ground, in the form of a square and about seven feet apart. The forks were between four and five feet above the ground. On opposite sides of the square, from fork to fork, he laid two stout young poles of fresh, green wood. Then from pole to pole he laid many other and smaller poles, generally about an inch apart. They laid the strips of buffalo meat, taken from their salt bath, upon the network of small poles, and beneath they built a good fire of birch, ash, and oak.

"Why, it makes me think of a smokehouse at home," said Albert.

"Same principle," said Dick, "but if you let that fire under there go out, Al, I'll take one of those birch rods and give you the biggest whaling you ever had in your life. You're strong enough now to stand a good licking."

Albert laughed. He thought his big brother Dick about the greatest fellow on earth. But he paid assiduous attention to the fire, and Dick did so, too. They kept it chiefly a great bed of coals, never allowing the flames to rise as high as the buffalo meat, and they watched over it twenty-four hours. In order to keep this watch, they deserted the cabin for a night, sleeping by turns before the fire under the frame of poles, which was no hardship to them.

The fierce timber wolves came again in the night, attracted by the savoury odour of buffalo meat; and once they crept near and were so threatening that Albert, whose turn it was at the watch, became alarmed. He awakened Dick, and, in order to teach these dangerous marauders a lesson, they shot two of them. Then the shrewd animals, perceiving that the two-legged beasts by the fire carried something very deadly with which they slew at a distance, kept for a while to the forest and out of sight.

After the twenty-four hours of fire drying, the buffalo meat was greatly reduced in weight and bulk, though it was packed as full as ever with sustenance. It was now cured, that is, jerked, and would keep any length of time. While the frame was ready they jerked an elk, two mule deer, a big silver-tip bear that Dick shot on the mountain side, and many fish that they caught in the lake and the little river. They would scale the fish, cut them open down the back, and then remove the bone. After that the flesh was jerked on the scaffold in the same way that the meat of the buffalo and deer was treated.

Before these operations were finished, the big timber wolves began to be troublesome again. Neither boy dared to be anywhere near the jerking stage without a rifle or revolver, and Dick finally invented a spring pole upon which they could put the fresh meat that was waiting its turn to be prepared—they did not want to carry the heavy weight to the house for safety, and then have to bring it back again.

While Dick's spring pole was his own invention, as far as he was concerned, it was the same as that used by thousands of other trappers and hunters. He chose a big strong sapling which Albert and he with a great effort bent down. Then he cut off a number of the boughs high up, and in each crotch fastened a big piece of meat. The sapling was then allowed to spring back into place and the meat was beyond the reach of wolf.

But the wolves tried for it, nevertheless. Dick awakened Albert the first night after this invention was tried and asked him if he wished to see a ghost dance. Albert, wrapped to his eyes in the great buffalo robe, promptly sat up and looked.

They had filled four neighbouring saplings with meat, and at least twenty wolves were gathered under them, looking skyward, but not at the sky—it was the flesh of elk and buffalo that they gazed at so longingly, and delicious odours that they knew assailed their nostrils.

But the wolf is an enterprising animal. He does not merely sit and look at what he wants, expecting it to come to him. Every wolf in the band knew that no matter how hard and long he might look that splendid food in the tree would not drop down into his waiting mouth. So they began to jump for it, and it was this midnight and wilderness ballet that Albert opened his eyes to watch.

One wolf, the biggest of the lot, leaped. It was a fine leap, and might have won him a championship among his kind, but he did not reach the prize. His teeth snapped together, touching only one another, and he fell. Albert imagined that he could hear a disappointed growl. Another wolf leaped, the chief leaped again, a third, a fourth, and a fifth leaped, and then all began to leap together.

The air was full of flying wolfish forms, going up or coming down. They went up, hearts full of hope, and came down, mouths empty of everything but disappointed foam. Teeth savagely hit teeth, and growls of wrath were abundant. Albert felt a ridiculous inclination to laugh. The whole affair presented its ludicrous aspect to him.

"Did you ever see so much jumping for so little reward?" he whispered to Dick.

"No, not unless they're taking exercise to keep themselves thin, although I never heard of a fat wolf."

But a wolf does not give up easily. They continued to leap faster and faster, and now and then a little higher than before, although empty tooth still struck empty tooth. Now and then a wolf more prone to complaint than the others lifted up his voice and howled his rage and chagrin to the moon. It was a genuine moan, a long, whining cry that echoed far through the forest and along the slopes, and whenever Albert heard it he felt more strongly than ever the inclination to laugh.

"I suppose that a wolf's woes are as real as our own," he whispered, "but they do look funny and act funny."

"Strikes me the same way," replied Dick with a grin. "But they're robbers, or would be if they could. That meat's ours, and they're trying to get it."

It was in truth a hard case for the wolves. They were very big and very strong. Doubtless, the selfsame wolf that had been driven away from the annex by the mountain lion was among them, and all of them were atrociously hungry. It was not merely an odour now, they could also see the splendid food hanging just above their heads. Never before had they leaped so persistently, so ardently, and so high, but there was no reward, absolutely none. Not a tooth felt the touch of flesh. The wolves looked around at one another jealously, but the record was as clean as their teeth. There had been no surreptitious captures.

"Will they keep it up all night?" whispered Albert.

"Can't say," replied Dick. "We'll just watch."

All the wolves presently stopped leaping and crouched on the earth, staring straight up at the prizes which hung, as ever, most tantalizingly out of reach. The moonlight fell full upon them, a score or more, and Albert fancied that he could see their hungry, disappointed eyes. The spectacle was at once weird and ludicrous. Albert felt again that temptation to laugh, but he restrained it.

Suddenly the wolves, as if it were a preconcerted matter, uttered one long, simultaneous howl, full, alike in its rising and falling note, of pain, anguish, and despair, then they were gone in such swiftness and silence that it was like the instant melting of ghosts into thin air. It took a little effort of will to persuade Albert that they had really been there.

"They've given it up," he said. "The demon dancers have gone."

"Demon dancers fits them," said Dick. "It's a good name. Yes, they've gone, and I don't think they'll come back. Wolves are smart, they know when they're wasting time."

When they finished jerking their buffalo meat and venison, Dick took the fine double-barrelled shotgun which they had used but little hitherto, and went down to the lake in search of succulent waterfowl. The far shore of the lake was generally very high, but on the side of the cabin there were low places, little shallow bays, the bottoms covered with grass, which were much frequented by wild geese and wild ducks, many of which, owing to the open character of the winter, had not yet gone southward. The ducks, in particular, Muscovy, mallard, teal, widgeon, and other kinds, the names of which Dick did not know, were numerous. They had been molested so little that they were quite tame, and it was so easy to kill them in quantities that the element of sport was entirely lacking.

Dick did not fancy shooting at a range of a dozen yards or so into a dense flock of wild ducks that would not go away, and he wished also to save as many as he could of their shot cartridges, for he had an idea that he and his brother would remain in the valley a long time. But both he and Albert wanted good supplies of duck and geese, which were certainly toothsome and succulent, and they were taking a pride, too, in filling the annex with the best things that the mountains could afford. Hence Dick did some deep thinking and finally evolved a plan, being aided in his thoughts by earlier experience in Illinois marshes.

He would trap the ducks and geese instead of shooting them, and he and Albert at once set about the task of making the trap. This idea was not original with Dick. As so many others have been, he was, in part, and unconscious imitator. He planted in the shallow water a series of hoops, graded in height, the largest being in the deepest water, while they diminished steadily in size as they came nearer to the land. They made the hoops of split saplings, and planted them about four feet apart.

Then the covered all these hoops with a netting, the total length of which was about twenty-five feet. They also faced each hoop with a netting, leaving an aperture large enough for the ducts to enter. It was long and tedious work to make the netting, as this was done by cutting the hide of an elk and the hide of a mule deer into strips and plaiting the strips on the hoops. They then had a network tunnel, at the smaller end of which they constructed an enclosure five or six feet square by means of stout poles which they thrust into the mud, and the same network covering which they used on the tunnel.

"It's like going in at the big end of a horn and coming out at the little one into a cell," said Albert. "Will it work?"

"Work?" replied Dick. "Of course, it will. You just wait and you'll see."

Albert looked out upon the lake, where many ducks were swimming about placidly, and he raised his hand.

"Oh, foolish birds!" he apostrophized. "Here is your enemy, man, making before your very eyes the snare that will lead you to destruction, and you go on taking no notice, thinking that the sunshine will last forever for you."

"Shut up, Al," said Dick, "you'll make me feel sorry for those ducks. Besides, you're not much of a poet, anyway."

When the trap was finished they put around the mouth and all along the tunnel quantities of the grass and herbs that the ducks seemed to like, and then Dick announced that the enterprise was finished.

"We have nothing further to do about it," he said, "but to take out our ducks."

It was toward twilight when they finished the trap, and both had been in the cold water up to their knees. Dick had long since become hardened to such things, but he looked at Albert rather anxiously. The younger boy, however, did not begin to cough. He merely hurried back to the fire, took off his wet leggings, and toasted his feet and legs. Then he ate voraciously and slept like a log the night through. But both he and Dick went down to the lake the next morning with much eagerness to see what the trap contained, if anything.

It was a fresh winter morning, not cold enough to freeze the surface of the lake, but extremely crisp. The air contained the extraordinary exhilarating quality which Dick had noticed when they first came into the mountains, but which he had never breathed anywhere else. It seemed to him to make everything sparkle, even his blood, and suddenly he leaped up, cracked his heels together, and shouted.

"Why, Dick," exclaimed Albert, "what on earth is the matter with you?"

"Nothing is the matter with me. Instead, all's right. I'm so glad I'm alive, Al, old man, that I wanted to shout out the fact to all creation."

"Feel that way myself," said Albert, "and since you've given such a good example, think I'll do as you did."

He leaped up, cracked his heels together, and let out a yell that the mountains sent back in twenty echoes. Then both boys laughed with sheer pleasure in life, the golden morning, and their happy valley. So engrossed were they in the many things that they were doing that they did not yet find time to miss human faces.

As they approached the trap, they heard a great squawking and cackling and found that the cell, as Albert called the square enclosure, contained ten ducks and two geese swimming about in a great state of trepidation. They had come down the winding tunnel and through the apertures in the hoops, but they did not have sense enough to go back the same way. Instead they merely swam around the square and squawked.

"Now, aren't they silly?" exclaimed Albert. "With the door to freedom open, they won't take it."

"I wonder," said Dick philosophically, "if we human beings are not just the same. Perhaps there are easy paths out of our troubles lying right before us and superior creatures up in the air somewhere are always wondering why we are such fools that we don't see them."

"Shut up, Dick," said Albert, "your getting too deep. I've no doubt that in our net are some ducks that are rated as uncommonly intelligent ducks as ducks go."

They forgot all about philosophy a few moments later when they began to dispose of their capture. They took them out, one by one, through a hole that they made in the cell and cut off their heads. The net was soon full up again, and they caught all the ducks and geese they wanted with such ridiculous ease that at the end of a week they took it down and stored it in the cabin.

They jerked the ducks and geese that they did not need for immediate use, and used the feathers to stuff beds and pillows for themselves. The coverings of these beds were furs which they stitched together with the tendons of the deer.

They began to be annoyed about this time by the depredations of mountain lions, which, attracted by the pleasant odours, came down from the slopes to the number of at least half a dozen, Dick surmised, and prowled incessantly about the cabin and annex, taking the place of the timber wolves, and proving more troublesome and dangerous alike. One of them managed at night to seize the edge of an elk skin that hung on the roof of the cabin, and the next morning the skin was half chewed up and wholly ruined.

Both boys were full of rage, and they watched for the lions, but failed to get a shot at them. But Dick, out of the stores of his memory, either some suggestion from reading, or trappers' and hunters' tales, devised a gun trap. He put a large piece of fresh deer meat in the woods about a quarter of a mile from the cabin. It was gone the next morning, and the tracks about showed that the lions had been present.

Then Dick drove two stout forked sticks into the ground, the forks being about a yard above the earth. Upon these he lashed one of their rifles. Then he cut a two-foot section of a very small sapling, one end of which he inserted carefully between the ground that the trigger of the rifle. The other end was supported upon a small fork somewhat higher than those supporting the rifle. Then he procured another slender but long section of sapling that reached from the end of the short piece in the crotch some distance beyond the muzzle of the rifle. The end beyond the muzzle had the stub of a bough on it, but the end in the crotch was tied there with a strip of hide. Now, if anything should pull on the end of this stick, it would cause the shorter stick to spring the trigger of the rifle and discharge it. Dick tested everything, saw that all was firmly and properly in place, and the next thing to do was to bait the trap.

He selected a piece of most tempting deer meat and fastened it tightly on the hooked end of the long stick. It was obvious that any animal pulling at this bait would cause the short stick tied at the other end of it to press against the trigger of the rifle, and the rifle would be fired as certainly as if the trigger had been pulled by the hand of man. Moreover, the barrel of the rifle was parallel with the long stick, and the bullet would certainly be discharged into the animal pulling at the bait.

After the bait had been put on Dick put the cartridge in the rifle. He was careful to do this last, as he did not wish to take any chances with the trap while he was testing it. But he and Albert ran a little wall of brush off on either side in order that the cougar, if cougar it were, should be induced to approach the muzzle directly in front. When all the work was finished, the two boys inspected it critically.

"I believe that our timber wolves would be too smart to come up to that trap," said Albert.

"Perhaps," said Dick; "but the wolf has a fine intellect, and I've never heard that the cougar or puma was particularly noted for brain power. Anyhow, I know that traps are built for him in this manner, and we shall see whether it will work."

"Are we going to hide somewhere near by and watch during the night?"

"There's no need to make ourselves uncomfortable. If the gun gets him, it'll get him whether we are or are not here."

"That's so," said Albert. "Well, I'm willing enough to take to the cabin. These nights are growing pretty cold, I can tell you."

Taking a last look at the gun trap and assuring themselves that it was all right, they hurried away to Castle Howard. The night was coming on much colder than any that they had yet had, and both were glad to get inside. Albert stirred the coals from beneath the ashes, put on fresh wood, and soon they had a fine blaze. The light flickered over a cabin greatly improved in appearance and wonderfully snug.

The floor, except directly in front of the hearth, where sparks and coals would pop out, was covered with the well-tanned skins of buffalo, elk, mule deer, bear, and wolf. The walls were also thickly hung with furs, while their extra weapons, tools, and clothing hung there on hooks. It was warm, homelike, and showed all the tokens of prosperity. Dick looked around at it with an approving eye. It was not only a house, and a good house at that, but it was a place that one might make a base for a plan that he had in mind. Yes, circumstance had certainly favoured them. Their own courage, skill, and energy had done the rest.

Albert soon fell asleep after supper, but Dick was more wakeful, although he did not wish to be so. It was the gun trap that kept his eyes open. He took a pride in doing things well, and he wanted the trap to work right. A fear that it might not do so worried him, but in turn he fell into a sound sleep from which he was awakened by a report. He thought at first that something had struck the house, but when his confused senses were gathered into a focus he knew that it was a rifle shot.

"Up, Al, up!" he cried, "I think a cougar has been fooling with our trap!"

Albert jumped up. They threw on their coats and went out into a dark and bitterly cold night. If they had not been so eager to see what had happened, they would have fled back to the refuge of the warm cabin, but they hurried on toward the snug little hollow in which the gun trap had been placed. At fifty yards they stopped and went much more slowly, as a terrific growling and snarling smote their ears.

"It's the cougar, and we've got him," said Dick. "He's hit bad or he wouldn't be making such a terrible fuss."

They approached cautiously and saw on the ground, almost in front of the gun, a large yellowish animal writhing about and tearing the earth. His snarls and rage increased as he scented the two boys drawing near.

"I think his shoulder is broken and his backbone injured," said Dick. "That's probably the reason he can't get away. I don't like to see him suffer and I'll finish him now."

He sent a bullet through the cougar's head and that was the end of him. In order to save it from the wolves, they took his hide from him where he lay, and spread it the next day on the roof of the cabin.

The gun trap was so successful that they baited it again and again, securing three more cougars, until the animals became too wary to try for the bait. The fourth cougar did not sustain a severe wound and fled up the mountain side, but Dick tracked him by the trail of blood that he left, overtook him far up the slope, and slew him with single shot. All these skins were added to their collection, and when the last was spread out to dry, Dick spoke of the plan that he had in mind.

"Al," he said, "these mountains, or at least this corner of them, seem to be left to us. The Sioux, I suppose, are on the warpath elsewhere, and they don't like mountains much, anyhow. Our wonderful valley, the slopes, and all the ravines and canyons are full of game. The beaver must be abundant farther in, and I propose that we use our opportunity and turn fur hunters. There's wealth around us for the taking, and we were never sure of it in California. We've got enough ammunition to last us two years if we want to stay that long. Besides, Al, old boy, the valley has been the remaking of you. You know that."

Albert laughed from sheer delight.

"Dick," he said, "you won't have to get a gun and threaten me with death unless I stay. I'll be glad to be a fur hunter, and, Dick, I tell you, I'm in love with this valley. As you say, it's made me over again, and oh, it's fine to be well and strong, to do what you please, and not always to be thinking, 'how can I stand this? Will it hurt me?'"

"Then," said Dick, "it's settled. We'll not think for a long time of getting back to civilization, but devote ourselves to gathering up furs and skins."

Chapter 9

The Timber Wolves

The cold increased, although snow fell but little, which Dick considered good luck, chiefly on Albert's account. He wanted the hardening process to continue and not to be checked by thaws and permeating dampness. Meanwhile, they plunged with all the energy and fire of youth into the task of fur hunting. They had already done much in that respect, but now it was undertaken as a vocation. They became less scrupulous about sparing the buffaloes, and they shot more than twenty in the defiles of the mountains, gathering a fine lot of robes. Several more skins of the bear, grizzly, and silver tip were added to their collection, and the elk also furnished an additional store. Many wolverines were taken in dead falls and snares, and their skins were added to the rapidly growing heap.

They baited the trap gun once more, hoping that a fifth cougar might prove rash enough to dare it. No cougar came, but on the third night a scornful grizzly swallowed the deer meat as a titbit, and got a bullet in the neck for his carelessness. In his rage, he tore the trap to pieces and tossed the rifle to one side, but, fortunately, he did not injure the valuable weapon, his attention turning instantly to something else. Later on the boys dispatched him as he lay wounded upon the ground.

Their old clothing was now about worn out and it also became necessary to provide garments of another kind in order to guard against the great cold. Here their furs became invaluable; they made moccasins, leggings, caps, and coats alike of them, often crude in construction, but always warm.

They found the beaver father in the mountains, as Dick had surmised, and trapped them in great abundance. This was by far their most valuable discovery, and they soon had a pack of sixty skins, which Dick said would be worth more than a thousand dollars in any good market. They also made destructive inroads upon the timber wolves, the hides of which were more valuable than those of any other wolf. In fact, they made such havoc that the shrewd timber wolf deserted the valley almost entirely.

As the boys now made their fur hunting a business, they attended to every detail with the greatest care. They always removed the skin immediately after the death of the animal, or, if taken in a trap, as soon after as possible. Every particle of fat or flesh was removed from the inside of the skin, and they were careful at the same time never to cut into the skin itself, as they knew that the piercing of a fur with a knife would injure its value greatly. Then the skin was put to dry in a cold, airy place, free alike from the rays of the sun or the heat of a fire. They built near the cabin a high scaffold for such purposes, too high and strong for any wild beast to tear down or to reach the furs upon it. Then they built above this on additional poles a strongly thatched bark roof that would protect the skins from rain, and there they cured them in security.

"I've heard," said Dick, "that some trappers put preparations or compounds on the skins in order to cure them, but since we don't have any preparations or compounds we won't use them. Besides, our furs seem to cure up well enough without them."

Dick was right. The cold, dry air of the mountains cured them admirably. Two or three times they thought to help along the process by rubbing salt upon the inner sides. They could always get plenty of salt by boiling out water from the salt springs, but as they seemed to do as well without it, they ceased to take the trouble.

The boys were so absorbed now in their interesting and profitable tasks that they lost all count of the days. They knew they were far advanced into a splendid open winter, but it is probably that they could not have guessed within a week of the exact day. However, that was a question of which they thought little. Albert's health and strength continued to improve, and with the mental stimulus added to the physical, the tide of life was flowing very high for both.

They now undertook a new work in order to facilitate their trapping operations. The beaver stream, and another that they found a little later, ran far back into the mountains, and the best trapping place was about ten miles away. After a day's work around the beaver pond, they had to choose between a long journey in the night to the cabin or sleeping in the open, the latter not a pleasant thing since the nights had become so cold. Hence, they began the erection of a bark shanty in a well-sheltered cove near the most important of the beaver localities. This was a work of much labour, but, as in all other cases, they persisted until the result was achieved triumphantly.

They drove two stout, forked poles deep into the ground, leaving a projection of about eight feet above the earth. The poles themselves were about eight feet apart. From fork to fork they placed a strong ridgepole. Then they rested against the ridgepole from either side other and smaller poles at an angle of forty or fifty degrees. The sloping poles were about a foot and a half apart. These poles were like the scantling or inside framework of a wooden house and they covered it all with spruce and birch bark, beginning at the bottom and allowing each piece to overlap the one beneath it, after the fashion of a shingled roof. They secured pieces partly with wooden pegs and partly with other and heavier wooden poles leaned against them. One end of the shelter was closed up with bark wholly, secured with wooden pegs, and the other end was left open in order that its tenants might face the fire which would be built three or four feet in front of it. They packed the floor with dead leaves, and put on the top of the leaves a layer of thick bark with the smooth side upward.

The bark shanty was within a clump of trees, and its open side was not fifteen feet from the face of an abrupt cliff. Hence there was never any wind to drive the smoke from the fire back into their faces, and, wrapped in their furs, they slept as snugly in the shanty as if they had been in the cabin itself. But they were too wise to leave anything there in their absence, knowing that it was not sufficient protection against the larger wild animals. In fact, a big grizzly, one night when they were at the cabin, thrust his nose into the shanty and, lumbering about in an awkward and perhaps frightened manner, knocked off half of one of the bark sides. It took nearly a day's work to repair the damage, and it put Dick in an ill humour.

"I'd like to get a shot at that bear!" he exclaimed. "He had no business trying to come into a house when he was not invited."

"But he is an older settler than we are," said Albert, in a whimsical tone.

Dick did get a shot at a bear a few days later, and it was a grizzly, at that. The wound was not fatal, and the animal came on with great courage and ferocity. A second shot from Dick did not stop him and the boy was in great danger. But Albert, who was near, sent two heavy bullets, one after the other, into the beast, and he toppled over, dying. It was characteristic of the hardy life they were leading and its tendency toward the repression of words and emotion that Dick merely uttered a brief, "Thanks, Al, you were just in time," and Albert nodded in reply.

The skin of old Ephraim went to join that of his brother who had been taken sometime before, and Dick himself shot a little later a third, which contributed a fine skin.

The boys did not know how hard they were really working, but their appetites would have been a fine gauge. Toiling incessantly in a crisp, cold air, as pure as any that the world affords, they were nearly always hungry. Fortunately, the happy valley, their own skill and courage, and the supplies that Dick had brought from the last wagon train furnished them an unlimited larder. Game of great variety was their staple, but they had both flour and meal, from which, though they were sparing of their use, they made cakes now and then. They had several ways of preparing the Indian meal that Dick had taken from the wagon. They would boil it for about an hour, then, after it cooled, would mix it with the fat of game and fry it, after which the compound was eaten in slices. They also made meal cakes, johnnycakes and hoecakes.

Albert was fond of fish, especially of the fine trout that they caught in the little river, and soon he invented or discovered a way of cooking them that provided an uncommon delicacy for their table. He would slit the trout open, clean it, and the season it with salt and also with pepper, which they had among their stores. Then he would lay the fish in the hot ashes of a fire that had burned down to embers, cover it up thoroughly with the hot ashes and embers, and let it cook thirty or forty minutes—thirty minutes for the little fellows and forty minutes for the big ones. When he thought the fish was done to the proper turn, he would take it from the ashes, clean it, and then remove the skin, which would almost peel off of its own accord.

The fish was then ready for the eating, and neither Dick nor Albert could ever bear to wait. The flesh looked so tempting and the odour was so savoury that hunger instantly became acute.

"They are so good," said Albert, "because my method of cooking preserves all the juices and flavours of the fish. Nothing escapes."

"Thanks, professor," said Dick. "You must be right, so kindly pass me another of those trout, and be quick about it."

It is a truth that both boys became epicures. Their valley furnished so much, and they had a seasoning of hard work and open mountain air that was beyond compare. They even imitated Indian and trapper ways of cooking geese, ducks, quail, sage hens, and other wild fowl that the region afforded. They could cook these in the ashes as they did the trout, and they also had other methods. Albert would take a duck, cut it open and clean it, but leave the feathers on. Then he would put it in water, until the feathers were soaked thoroughly, after which he would cover it up with ashes, and put hot coals on top of the ashes. When the bird was properly cooked and drawn from the ashes, the skin could be pulled off easily, taking the feathers, of course, with it. Then a duck, sweet, tender, and delicate, such as no restaurant could furnish, was ready for the hardy youngsters. At rare intervals they improve on this by stuffing the duck with seasoning and Indian meal. Now and then they served a fat goose the same way and found it equally good.

They cooked the smaller birds in a simpler manner, especially when they were at the bark shanty, which they nicknamed the "Suburban Villa." The bird was plucked of its feathers, drawn and washed, and then they cut it down the back in order to spread it out. Nothing was left but to put the bird on the end of a sharp stick, hold it over the coals, and turn it around until it was thoroughly broiled or roasted. They also roasted slices of big game in the same way.

As Albert was cooking a partridge in this manner one evening at the Suburban Villa, Dick, who was sitting on his buffalo-robe blanket in the doorway, watched him and began to make comparisons. He recalled the boy who had left Omaha with the wagon train six or eight months before, a thin, spiritless fellow with a slender, weak neck, hollow, white cheeks, pale lips, and listless eyes. That boy drew coughs incessantly from a hollow chest, and the backs of his hands were ridged when the flesh had gone away, leaving the bones standing up. This boy whom Dick contemplated was quite a different being. His face was no longer white, it was instead a mixture of red and brown, and both tints were vivid. Across one cheek were some brier scratches which he had acquired the day before, but which he had never noticed. The red-brown cheeks were filled out with the effects of large quantities of good food digested well. As he bent over the fire, a chest of good width seemed to puff out with muscle and wind expansion. Despite the extreme cold, his sleeves were rolled up to the elbow, and the red wrists and hands were well covered with tough, seasoned flesh. The eyes that watched the roasting bird were intent, alert, keenly interested in that particular task, and in due course, in any other that might present itself.

Dick drew a long breath of satisfaction. Providence had treated them well. Then he called loudly for his share of the bird, saying that he was starving, and in a few moments both fell to work.

Their fur operations continued to extend. They had really found a pocket, and isolated corner in the high Rockies where the fur-bearing animals, not only abundant, were also increasing. It was, too, the dead of winter, the very best time for trapping, and so, as far as their own goings and comings were concerned, they were favoured further by the lucky and unusual absence of snow. They increased the number of their traps—dead falls, box traps, snares, and other kinds, and most of them were successful.

They knew instinctively the quality of the furs that they obtained. They could tell at a glance whether they were prime, that is, thick and full, and as they cured them and baled them, they classified them.

Constant application bred new ideas. In their pursuit of furs, they found that they were not quite so sparing of the game as they had been at first. Some of their scruples melted away. Albert now recalled a device of trappers of which he had read. This was the use of a substance generally called barkstone, which they found to be of great help to them in the capture of that animal.

The barkstone or *castoreum*, as it is commercially known, was obtained principally from the beaver himself. The basis of it was an acrid secretion with a musky odour of great power, found in two glands just under the root of the beaver's tail. Each gland was from one and one half to two inches in length. The boys cut out these glands and squeezed the contents into an empty tin can. This at first was of a yellowish-red colour, but after a while, when it dried, it became a light brown.

This substance formed the main ingredient of barkstone, and in their medicine chest they found a part of the remainder. The secretion was transferred to a bottle and the mixed with it essence of peppermint and ground cinnamon. As Albert remembered it, ground nutmeg also was needed, but as they had no nutmeg they were compelled to take their chances without it. Then they poured whisky on the compound until it looked like a paste.

Then the bottle was stopped up with the greatest care, and in about a week, when they stole a sniff or two at it, they found that the odour had increased ten or a dozen times in power.

They put eight or ten drops of the barkstone upon the bait for the beaver, or somewhere near the trap, and, despite some defects in the composition, it proved an extraordinary success. The wariest beaver of all would be drawn by it, and their beaver bales grew faster than any other.

Dick calculated one day that they had at least five thousand dollars worth of furs, which seemed a great sum to both boys. It certainly meant, at that time and in that region, a competence, and it could be increased greatly.

"Of course," said Dick, "we'll have to think some day of the way in which we must get these furs out, and for that we will need horses or mules, but we won't bother our heads about it yet."

After the long period of clear, open weather, the delayed snow came. It began to fall one evening at twilight, when both boys were snug in the cabin, and it came in a very gentle, soothing way, as if it meant no harm whatever. Big, soft flakes fell as softly as the touch of down, but every time the boys looked out they were still coming in the same gentle but persistent way. The next morning the big flakes still came down and all that day and all the next night. When the snow stopped it lay five feet deep on the level, and uncounted feet deep in the gullies and canyons.

"We're snowed in," said Albert in some dismay, "and we can't go to our traps. Why, this is likely to last a month!"

"We can't walk through it," said Dick meditatively, "but we can walk on it. We've got to make snowshoes. They're what we need."

"Good!" said Albert with enthusiasm. "Let's get to work at once."

Deep snows fall in Illinois, and both, in their earlier boyhood, had experimented for the sake of sport with a crude form of snowshoe. Now they were to build upon this slender knowledge, for the sake of an immediate necessity, and it was the hardest task that they had yet set for themselves. Nevertheless, it was achieved, like the others.

They made a framework of elastic stripes of ash bent in the well-known shape of the snowshoe, which bears some resemblance to the shape of the ordinary shoe, only many times larger and sharply pointed at the rear end. Its length was between five and six feet, and the ends were tightly wound with strips of hide. This frame was bent into the shoe shape after it had been soaked in boiling water.

Then they put two very strong strips of hide across the front part of the framework, and in addition passed at least a half dozen stout bands of hide from strip to strip.

Then came the hard task of attaching the shoe to the foot of the boy who was to wear it. The ball of the foot was set on the second cross-piece and the foot was then tied there with a broad strip of hide which passed over the instep and was secured behind the ankle. It required a good deal of practice to fasten the foot so it would not slip up and down; and also in such a manner that the weight of the shoe would be proportioned to it properly.

They had to exercise infinite patience before two pairs of snowshoes were finished. There was much hunting in deep snow for proper wood, many strips and some good hide were spoiled, but the shoes were made and then another equally as great confronted the two boys—to learn how to use them.

Each boy put on his pair at the same time and went forth on the snow, which was now packed and hard. Albert promptly caught one of his shoes on the other, toppled over, and went down through the crust of the snow, head first. Dick, although in an extremely awkward situation himself, managed to pull his brother out and put him in the proper position, with his head pointing toward the sky instead of the earth. Albert brushed the snow out of his eyes and ears, and laughed.

"Good start, bad ending," he said. "This is certainly the biggest pair of shoes that I ever had on, Dick. They feel at least a mile long to me."

"I know that mine are a mile long," said Dick, as he, too, brought the toe of one shoe down upon the heel of the other, staggered, fell over sideways, but managed to right himself in time.

"It seems to me," said Albert, "that the proper thing to do is to step very high and very far, so you won't tangle up one shoe with the other."

"That seems reasonable," said Dick, "and we'll try it."

They practiced this step for an hour, making their ankles ache badly. After a good rest they tried it for another hour, and then they began to make progress. They found that they got along over the snow at a fair rate of speed, although it remained an awkward and tiring gait. Nevertheless, one could travel an indefinite distance, when it was impossible to break one's way far through five or six feet of packed snow, and the shoes met a need.

"They'll do," said Albert; "but it will never be like walking on the solid earth in common shoes."

Albert was right. Their chief use for these objects, so laboriously constructed, was for the purpose of visiting their traps, some of which were set at least a dozen miles away. They wished also to go back to the shanty and see that it was all right. They found a number of valuable furs in the traps, but the bark shanty had been almost crushed in by the weight of the snow, and they spent sometime strengthening and repairing it.

In the course of these excursions their skill with the snowshoes increased and they were also able to improve upon the construction, correcting little errors in measurement and balance. The snow showed no signs of melting, but they made good progress, nevertheless, with their trapping, and all the furs taken were of the highest quality.

It would have been easy for them to kill enough game to feed a small army, as the valley now fairly swarmed with it, although nearly all of it was of large species, chiefly buffalo, elk, and bear. There was one immense herd of elk congregated in a great sheltered space at the northern end of the valley, where they fed chiefly upon twigs and lichens.

Hanging always upon the flanks of this herd was a band of timber wolves of great size and ferocity, which never neglected an opportunity to pull down a cripple or a straying yearling.

"I thought we had killed off all these timber wolves," said Albert when he first caught sight of the band.

"We did kill off most of those that were here when we came," said Dick, "but others, I suppose, have followed the game from the mountains into the valley."

Albert went alone a few days later to one of their traps up the valley, walking at a good pace on his snowshoes. A small colony of beavers had been discovered on a stream that came down between two high cliffs, and the trap contained a beaver of unusually fine fur. Albert removed the skin, put it on his shoulder, and, tightening his snowshoes, started back to Castle Howard.

The snow had melted a little recently, and in many places among the trees it was not deep, but Albert and Dick had made it a point to wear their snowshoes whenever they could, for the sake of the skill resulting from practice.

Albert was in a very happy frame of mind. He felt always now a physical elation, which, of course, became mental also. It is likely, too, that the rebound from long and despairing ill health still made itself felt. None so well as those who have been ill and are cured! He drew great draughts of the frosty air into his strong, sound lungs, and the emitted it slowly and with ease. It was a fine mechanism, complex, but working beautifully. Moreover, he had an uncommonly large and rich beaver fur over his shoulder. Such a skin as that would bring twenty-five dollars in any decent market.

Albert kept to the deep snow on account of his shoes, and was making pretty good time, when he heard a long howl, varied by a kind of snappy, growling bark.

"One of those timber wolves," said Albert to himself, "and he has scented the blood of the beaver."

He thought no more about the wolf until two or three minutes later when he heard another howl and then two or three more. Moreover, they were much nearer.

"Now, I wonder what they're after?" thought Albert.

But he went on, maintaining his good pace, and then he heard behind him a cry that was a long, ferocious whine rather than a howl. Albert looked back and saw under the trees, where the snow was lighter, a dozen leaping forms. He recognized at once the old pests, the timber wolves.

"Now, I wonder what they're after?" he repeated, and then as the whole pack suddenly gave tongue in a fierce, murderous howl, he saw that it was himself. Albert, armed though he was—neither boy ever went forth without gun or revolver—felt the blood grow cold in every vein. These were not the common wolves of the prairie, nor yet the ordinary wolf of the east and middle west, but the great timber wolf of the northwest, the largest and fiercest of the dog tribe. He had grown used to the presence of timber wolves hovering somewhere near, but now they presented themselves in a new aspect, bearing down straight upon him, and pushed by hunger. He understood why they were about to attack him. They had been able to secure but little of the large game in the valley, and they were drawn on by starvation.

He looked again and looked fearfully. They seemed to him monstrous in size for wolves, and their long, yellowish-gray bodies were instinct with power. Teeth and eyes alike were gleaming. Albert scarcely knew what to do first. Should he run, taking to the deepest snow, where the wolves might sink to their bodies and thus fail to overtake him? But in his own haste he might trip himself with the long, ungainly snowshoes, and then everything would quickly be over. Yet it must be tried. He could see no other way.

Albert, almost unconsciously prayed for coolness and judgment, and it was well for him that his life in recent months had taught him hardihood and resource. He turned at once into the open space, away from the trees, where the snow lay several feet deep, and he took long, flying leaps on his snowshoes. Behind him came the pack of great, fierce brutes, snapping and snarling, howling and whining, a horrible chorus that made shivers chase one another up and down the boy's spine. But as he reckoned, the deep snow made them flounder, and checked their speed.

Before him the open ground and the deep snow stretched straight away beside the lake until it reached the opening between the mountains in which stood Castle Howard. As Albert saw the good track lie before him, his hopes rose, but presently, when he looked back again, they fell with cruel speed. The wolves, despite the depth of the snow, had gained upon him. Sometimes, perhaps, it proved hard enough to sustain the weight of their bodies, and then they more than made up lost ground.

Albert noted a wolf which he took at once to be the leader, not only because he led all the others, but because also of his monstrous size. Even in that moment of danger he wondered that a wolf could grow so large, and that he should have such long teeth. But the boy, despite his great danger, retained his presence of mind. If the wolves were gaining, then he must inflict a check upon them. He whirled about, steadied himself a moment on his snowshoes, and fired directly at the huge leader. The wolf had swung aside when he saw the barrel of the rifle raised, but the bullet struck down another just behind him. Instantly, some of the rest fell upon the wounded brute and began to devour him, while the remainder, after a little hesitation, continued to pursue Albert.

But the boy had gained, and he felt that the repeating rifle would be for a while like a circle of steel to him. He could hold them back for a time with bullet after bullet, although it would not suffice to stop the final rush when it came, if it came.

Albert looked longingly ahead. He saw a feather of blue smoke against the dazzling white and silver of the sky, and he knew that it came from their cabin. If he were only there behind those stout log walls! A hundred wolves, bigger than the big leader, might tear at them in vain! And perhaps Dick, too, would come! He felt that the two together would have little to fear.

The wolves set up their fierce, whining howl again, and once more it showed that they had gained upon the fleeing boy. He turned and fired once, twice, three times, four times, as fast as he could pull the trigger, directly into the mass of the pack. He could not tell what he had slain and what he had wounded, but there was a hideous snapping and snarling, and the sight of wolf teeth flashing into wolf flesh.

Albert ran on and that feather of blue smoke was larger and nearer.

But was it near enough? He could hear the wolves behind him again. All these diversions were only temporary. No matter how many of their number were slain or wounded, no matter how many paused to devour the dead and hurt, enough were always left to follow him. The pursuit, too, had brought reinforcements from the lurking coverts of the woods and bushes.

Albert saw that none of his bullets had struck the leader. The yellowish-gray monster still hung close upon him, and he was to Albert like a demon wolf, one that could not be slain. He would try again. He wheeled and fired. The leader, as before, swerved to one side and a less fortunate wolf behind him received the bullet. Albert fired two more bullets, and then he turned to continue his flight. But the long run, the excitement, and his weakened nerves caused the fatal misstep. The toe of one snowshoe caught on the heel of the other, and as a shout pierced the air, he went down.

The huge gray leader leaped at the fallen boy, and as his body paused a fleeting moment in midair before it began the descent, a rifle cracked, a bullet struck him in the throat, cutting the jugular vein and coming out behind. His body fell lifeless on the snow, and he who had fired the shot came on swiftly, shouting and firing again.

It was well that Dick, sometime after Albert's departure, had concluded to go forth for a little hunt, and it was well also that in addition to his rifle he had taken the double-barrelled shotgun thinking that he might find some winter wild fowl flying over the snow and ice-covered surface of the lake. His first shot slew the master wolf, his second struck down another, his third was as fortunate, his fourth likewise, and then, still running forward, he bethought himself of the shotgun that was strapped over his shoulder. He levelled it in an instant and fairly sprayed the pack of wolves with stinging shot. Before that it had been each bullet for a wolf and the rest untouched, but now there was a perfect shower of those hot little pellets. It was more than they could stand, big, fierce, and hungry timber wolves though they were. They turned and fled with beaten howls into the woods.

Albert was painfully righting himself, when Dick gave him his hand and sped the task. Albert had thought himself lost, and it was yet hard to realize that he had not disappeared down the throat of the master wolf. His nerves were overtaxed, and he was near collapse.

"Thank you, Dick, old boy," he said. "If you hadn't come when you did, I shouldn't be here."

"No, you wouldn't," replied Dick grimly. "Those wolves eat fast. But look, Al, what a monster this fellow is! Did you ever see such a wolf?"

The great leader lay on his side upon the snow, and a full seven feet he

322

stretched from the tip of his nose to the root of his stumpy tail. No such wolf as he had ever been put inside a cage, and it was rare, indeed, to find one so large, even in the mountains south of the very far north.

"That's a skin that will be worth something," said Dick, "and here are more, but before we begin the work of taking them off, you'll have to be braced up, Al. You need a stimulant."

He hurried back to Castle Howard and brought one of the bottles of whisky, a little store that they had never touched except in the compounding of the barkstone for the capture of beaver. He gave Albert a good stiff drink of it, after which the boy felt better, well enough, in fact, to help Dick skin the monster wolf.

"It gives me pleasure to do this," said Albert, as he wielded the knife. "You thought, Mr. Wolf, that I was going to adorn your inside; instead, your outside will be used as an adornment trodden on by the foot of my kind."

They secured four other fine and unimpaired skins among the slain, and after dressing and curing, they were sent to join the stores in the annex.

CHAPTER 10

Dick Goes Scouting

Dick did not believe that the timber wolves, after suffering so much in the pursuit of Albert, would venture again to attack either his brother or himself. He knew that the wolf was one of the shrewdest of all animals, and that, unless the circumstances were very unusual indeed, the sight of a gun would be sufficient to warn them off. Nevertheless, he decided to begin a campaign against them, though he had to wait a day or two until Albert's shaken nerves were restored.

They wished to save their ammunition as much as possible, and they built three large dead falls, in which they caught six or seven great wolves, despite their cunning. In addition they hunted them with rifles with great patience and care, never risking a shot until they felt quite sure that it would find a vital spot. In this manner they slew about fifteen more, and by that time the wolves were thoroughly terrified. The scent of the beings carrying sticks which poured forth death and destruction at almost any distance, was sufficient to send the boldest band of timber wolves scurrying into the shadows of the deepest forest in search of hiding and safety.

The snow melted and poured in a thousand streams from the mountains. The river and all the creeks and brooks roared in torrents, the earth soaked in water, and the two boys spent much of the time indoors making new clothing, repairing traps and nets, and fashioning all kinds of little implements that were of use in their daily life. They could realize, only because they now had to make them, how numerous such implements were. Yet they made toasting sticks of hard wood, carved out wooden platters, constructed a rude but serviceable dining table, added to their supply of traps of various kinds, and finally made two large baskets of split willow. The last task was not as difficult as some others, as both had seen and taken a part in basket making in Illinois. The cabin was now crowded to inconvenience. Over their beds, from side to side, and up under the sloping roof, they had fastened poles, and from all of these hung furs and skins, buffalo, deer, wolf, wild cat, beaver, wolverine, and others, and also stores of jerked game. The annex was in the same crowded condition. The boys had carried the hollow somewhat higher up with their axes, but the extension gave them far less room than they needed.

"It's just this, Dick," said Albert, "we getting so rich that we don't know what to do with all our property. I used to think it a joke that the rich were unhappy, but now I see where their trouble comes in."

"I know that the trappers cache their furs, that is, bury them or hide them until they can take them away," said Dick, "but we don't know how to bury furs so they'll keep all right. Still, we've got to find a new place of some kind. Besides, it would be better to have them hidden where only you and I could find them, Al. Maybe we can find such a place."

Albert agreed, and they began a search along the cliffs. Dick knew that extensive rocky formations must mean a cave or an opening of some kind, if they only looked long enough for it, at last they found in the side of a slope a place that he thought could be made to suit. It was a rocky hollow running back about fifteen feet, and with a height and width of perhaps ten feet. It was approached by an opening about four feet in height and two feet in width. Dick wondered at first that it had not been used as a den by some wild animal, but surmised that the steepness of the ascent and the extreme roughness of the rocky floor had kept them out.

But these very qualities recommended the hollow to the boys for the use that they intended it. Its position in the side of the cliff made it a hard place to find, and the solid rock of its floor, walls, and roof insured the dryness that was necessary for the storage of their furs.

"We'll call this the Cliff House," said Albert, "and we'll take possession at once."

They broke off the sharper of the stone projections with their axe heads, and then began the transfer of the furs. It was no light task to carry them up the step slope to the Cliff House, but, forced to do all things for themselves, they had learned perseverance, and they carried all their stock of beaver furs and all the buffalo robes and bearskins, except those in actual use, together with a goodly portion of the wolf-skins, elk hides, and others.

Dick made a rude but heavy door which fitted well enough into the opening to keep out any wild animal, no matter how small, and in front of it, in a little patch of soft soil, they set out two transplanted pine bushes which seemed to take root, and which Dick was sure would grow in the spring.

When the boys looked up from the bottom of the slope, they saw no trace of the Cliff House, only an expanse of rock, save a little patch of earth where two tiny pines were growing.

"Nobody but ourselves will ever find our furs!" exclaimed Dick exultingly. "The most cunning Indian would not dream that anything was hidden up there behind those little pines, and the furs will keep as well inside as if they were in the best storehouse ever built."

The discovery and use of the rock cache was a great relief to both. Their cabin had become so crowded with furs and stores, that the air was often thick and heavy, and they did not have what Dick called elbow room. Now they used the cabin almost exclusively for living purposes. Most of the stores were in the annex, while the dry and solid Cliff House held the furs.

"Have you thought, Dick, what you and I are?" asked Albert.

"I don't catch your meaning."

"We're aristocrats of the first water, Mr. Richard Howard and Mr. Albert Howard, the Mountain Kings. We can't get along with less than four residences. We live in Castle Howard, the main mansion, superior to anything of its kind in a vast region; then we have the annex, a tower used chiefly as a supply room and treasure chest; then the Suburban Villa, a light, airy place of graceful architecture, very suitable as a summer residence, and now we have the Cliff House, in a lofty and commanding position noted for its wonderful view. We are really a fortunate pair, Dick."

"I've been thinking that for sometime," replied Dick rather gravely.

Hitherto they had confined their operations chiefly to their own side of the lake, but as they ranged farther and farther in search of furs they began to prowl among the canyons and narrow valleys in the mountains on the other side. They made, rather far up the northern side, some valuable catches of beaver, but in order to return with them, they were compelled to come around either the northern or southern end of the lake, and the round trip was tremendously long and tiring.

"It's part of a man's business to economize time and strength," said Dick, "and we must do it. You and I, Al, are going to make a canoe."

"How?"

"I don't know just yet, but I'm studying it out. The idea will jump out of my head in two or three days."

It was four days before it jumped, but when it did, it jumped to some purpose.

"First, we'll make a dugout," he said. "We've got the tools—axes, knives, saws, and augers—and we'd better start with that."

They cut down a big and perfectly straight pine and chose a length of about twelve feet from the largest part of the trunk. Both boys had seen dugouts, and they knew, in a general way, how to proceed. Their native intelligence supplied the rest.

They cut off one side of the log until it was flat, thus making the bottom for the future canoe. They cut the opposite side away in the well-known curve that a boat makes, low in the middle and high at each end. This part of the work was done with great caution, but Dick had an artistic eye, and they made a fairly good curve. Next they began the tedious and laborious work of digging out, using axes, hatchets, and chisel.

This was a genuine test of Albert's new strength, but he stood it nobly. They chipped away for a long time, until the wood on the sides and bottom was thin but strong enough to stand any pressure. Then they made the proper angle and curve of bow and stern, cut and made two stout broad paddles, and their dugout was ready—a long canoe with a fairly good width, as the original log had been more than two feet in diameter. It was both light and strong, and, raising it on their shoulders, they carried it down to the lake where they put it in the water.

Albert, full of enthusiasm, sprang into the canoe and made a mighty sweep with his paddle. The light dugout shot away, tipped on one side, and as Albert made another sweep with his paddle to right it, it turned over, bottom side up, casting the rash young paddler into ten feet of pure cold water. Albert came up with a mighty splash and sputter. He was a good swimmer, and he had also retained hold of the paddle unconsciously, perhaps. Dick regarded him contemplatively from the land. He had no idea of jumping in. One wet and cold boy was enough. Beside, rashness deserved its punishment.

"Get the canoe before it floats farther away," he called out, "and tow it to land. It has cost us too much work to be lost out on the lake."

Albert swam to the canoe, which was now a dozen yards away, and quickly towed it and the paddle to land. There, shivering, the water running from him in streams, he stepped upon the solid earth.

"Run to the cabin as fast as you can," said Dick. "Take off those wet things, rub yourself down before the fire; then put on dry clothes and come back here and help me."

Albert needed no urging, but it seemed to him that he would freeze before he reached the cabin, short as the distance was. Fortunately, there was a good fire on the hearth, and, after he had rubbed down and put on his dry, warm suit of deerskin, he never felt finer in his life. He returned to the lake, but he felt sheepish on the way. That had been a rash movement of his, overenthusiastic, but he had been properly punished. His chagrin was increased when he saw Dick a considerable distance out on the lake in the canoe, driving it about in graceful curves with long sweeps of his paddle.

"This is the way it ought to be done," called out Dick cheerily. "Behold me, Richard Howard, the king of canoe men!"

"You've been practicing while I was gone!" exclaimed Albert.

"No doubt of it, my young friend, and that is why you see me showing such skill, grace, and knowledge. I give you the same recipe without charge: Look before you leap, especially if you're going to leap into a canoe. Now we'll try it together."

He brought the canoe back to land, Albert got in cautiously, and for the rest of the day they practiced paddling, both together and alone. Albert got another ducking, and Dick, in a moment of overconfidence, got one, too, somewhat to Albert's pleasure and relief, as it has been truly said that misery loves company, but in two or three days they learned to use the canoe with ease. Then, either together or alone, they would paddle boldly the full length of the lake, and soon acquired dexterity enough to use it for freight, too; that is, they would bring back in it across the lake anything that they had shot or trapped on the other side.

So completely had they lost count of time that Dick had an idea spring was coming, but winter suddenly shut down upon them again. It did not arrive with wind and snow this time, but in the night a wave of cold came down from the north so intense that the sheltered valley even did not repel it.

Dick and Albert did not appreciate how really cold it was until they went from the cabin into the clear morning air, when they were warned by the numbing sensation that assailed their ears and noses. They hurried into the house and thawed out their faces, which stung greatly as they were exposed to the fire. Remembering the experiences of their early boyhood, they applied cold water freely, which allayed the stinging. After that they were very careful to wrap up fingers, ears, and noses when they went forth.

Now, the channel that Albert had made from the water of the hot spring proved of great use. The water that came boiling from the earth cooled off rapidly, but it was not yet frozen when it reached the side of Castle Howard, and they could make use of it.

The very first morning they found their new boat, of which they were so proud, hard and fast with ten inches of solid ice all around it. Albert suggested leaving it there.

"We have no need of it so long as the lake is covered with ice," he said, "and when the ice melts it will be released."

But Dick looked a little farther. The ice might press in on it and crush it, and hence Albert and he cut it out with axes, after which they put it in the lee of the cabin. Meanwhile, when they wished to reach the traps on the farther side of the lake, they crossed it on the ice, and, presuming that the cold might last long, they easily made a rude sledge which they used in place of the canoe.

"If we can't go through the water, we can at least go over it," said Albert.

While the great cold lasted, a period of about two weeks, the boys went on no errands except to their traps. The cold was so intense that often they could hear the logs of Castle Howard contracting with a sound like pistol shots. Then they would build the fire high and sit comfortably before it. Fortunately, the valley afforded plenty of fuel. Both boys wished now that they had a few books, but books were out of the question, and they sought always to keep themselves busy with the tasks that their life in the valley entailed upon them. Both knew that this was best.

The cold was so great that even the wild animals suffered from it. The timber wolves, despite their terrible lessons, were driven by it down the valley, and at night a stray one now and then would howl mournfully near the cabin.

"He's a robber and would like to be a murderer," Albert would say, "but he probably smells this jerked buffalo meat that I'm cooking and I'm sorry for him."

But the wolves were careful to keep out of rifle shot.

Dick made one trip up the valley and found about fifty buffaloes sheltered in a deep ravine and clustering close together for warmth. They were quite thin, as the grass, although it had been protected by the snow, was very scanty at that period of the year. Dick could have obtained a number of good robes, but he spared them.

"Maybe I won't be so soft-hearted when the spring comes and you are fatter," he said.

The two, about this time, took stock of their ammunition, which was the most vital of all things to them. For sometime they had used both the shot and ball cartridges only in cases of necessity, and they were relying more and more on traps, continually devising new kinds, their skill and ingenuity increasing with practice.

Dick had brought a great store of cartridges from the last train, especially from the unrifled wagon in the gully, and both boys were surprised to see how many they had left. They had enough to last a long time, according to their present mode of life.

"If you are willing, that settles it," said Dick.

"If I am willing for what?" asked Albert.

"Willing to stay over another year. You see, Al, we've wandered into a happy hunting ground. There are more furs, by the hundreds, for the taking, and it seems that this is a lost valley. Nobody else comes here. Besides, you are doing wonderfully. All that old trouble is gone, and we want it to stay gone. If we stay here another year, and you continue to eat the way you do and grow the way you do, you'll be able to take a buffalo by the horns and wring its neck."

Albert grinned pleasantly at his brother.

"You don't have to beg me to stay," he said. "I like this valley. It has given me life and what is to be our fortune, our furs. Why not do all we can while we can? I'm in favour of the extra year, Dick."

"Then no more need be said about it. The Cliff House isn't half full of furs yet, but in another year we can fill it."

The great cold began to break up, the ice on the lake grew thinner and thinner and then disappeared, much of the big game left the valley, the winds from the north ceased to blow, and in their stead came breezes from the south, tipped with warmth. Dick knew that spring was near. It was no guess, he could feel it in every bone of him, and he rejoiced. He had had enough of winter, and it gave him the keenest pleasure when he saw tiny blades of new grass peeping up in sheltered places here and there.

Dick, although he was not conscious of it, had changed almost as much as Albert in the last eight or nine months. He had had no weak chest and throat to cure, but his vigorous young frame had responded nobly to the stimulus of self-reliant life. The physical experience, as well as the mental, of those eight or nine months, had been equal to five times their number spent under ordinary conditions, and he had grown greatly in every respect. Few men were as strong, as agile, and as alert as he.

He and Albert, throughout that long winter, had been sufficient unto each other. They had a great sense of ownership, the valley and all its manifold treasurers belonged to them—a feeling that was true, as no one else came to claim it—and they believed that in their furs they were acquiring and ample provision for a start in life.

When the first tender shades of green began to appear in the valley and on the slopes, Dick decided upon a journey.

"Do you know, Al, how long we have been in this valley?" he asked.

"Eight or ten months, I suppose," replied Albert.

"It must be something like that, and we've been entirely away from our race. If we had anybody to think about us—although we haven't—they'd be sure that we are dead. We're just as ignorant of what is happening in the world, and I want to go on a skirmishing trip over the mountains. You keep house while I'm gone."

Albert offered mild objections, which he soon withdrew, as at heart he thought his brother right, and the next day, early in the morning, Dick started on his journey. He carried jerked buffalo meat in a deerskin pouch that he had made for himself, his customary repeating rifle, revolver, and a serviceable hatchet.

"Look after things closely, Al," said Dick, "and don't bother about setting the traps. Furs are not good in the spring."

"All right," responded Albert. "How long do you think you'll be gone?"

"Can't say, precisely. Three or four days, I presume, but don't you worry unless it's a full week."

It was characteristic of the strength and self-restraint acquired by the two that they parted with these words and a hand clasp only, yet both had deep feeling. Dick looked back from the mouth of the cleft toward Castle Howard and saw a boy in front of it waving a cap. He waved his own in reply and then went forward more swiftly down the valley.

It did not take him long to reach the first slope, and, when he had ascended a little, he paused for rest and inspection. Spring had really made considerable progress. All the trees except the evergreens had put forth young leaves and, as he looked toward the north, the mountains unrolled like a vast green blanket that swept away in ascending folds until it ended, and then the peaks and ridges, white with snow, began.

Dick climbed father, and their valley was wholly lost to sight. It was not so wonderful after all that nobody came to it. Trappers who knew of it long ago never returned, believing that the beaver were all gone forever, and it was too near to the warlike Sioux of the plains for mountain Indians to make a home there.

Dick did not stop long for the look backward—he was too intent upon his mission—but resumed the ascent with light foot and light heart. He remembered very well the way in which he and Albert had come, and he followed it on the return. All night, with his buffalo robe about him, he slept in the pine alcove that had been the temporary home of Albert and himself. He could see no change in it in all the months, except traces to show that some wild animal had slept there.

"Maybe you'll come tonight, Mr. Bear or Mr. Mountain Lion, to sleep in your little bed." said Dick as he lay down in his buffalo robe, "but you'll find me here before you."

He was wise enough to know that neither bear nor mountain lion would ever molest him, and he slept soundly. He descended the last slopes and came in sight of the plains on the afternoon of the next day. Everything seemed familiar. The events of that fatal time had made too deep an impression upon him and Albert ever to be forgotten. He knew the very rocks and trees and so went straight to the valley in which he had found the wagon filled with supplies. It lay there yet, crumpled somewhat by time and the weight of snow that had fallen upon it during the winter, but a strong man with good tools might put it in shape for future service.

"Now, if Al and I only had horses, we might get it out and take away our furs in it," said Dick, "but I suppose I might as well wish for a railroad as for horses."

He descended into the gully and found the tracks of wolves and other wild beasts about the wagon. In their hunger, they had chewed up every fragment of leather or cloth, and had clawed and scratched among the lockers. Dick had searched those pretty well before, but now he looked for gleanings. He found little of value until he discovered, jammed down in a corner, an old history and geography of the United States combined in one volume with many maps and illustrations. It was a big octavo book, and Dick seized it with the same delight with which a miner snatches up his nugget of gold. He opened it, took a rapid look through flying pages, murmured, "Just the thing," closed it again, and buttoned it securely inside his deerskin coat. He had not expected anything; nevertheless, he had gleaned to some purpose.

Dick left the wagon and went into the pass where the massacre had occurred. Time had not dimmed the horror of the place for him and he shuddered as he approached the scene of ambush, but he forced himself to go on.

The wagons were scattered about, but little changed, although, as in the case of the one in the gully, all the remaining cloth and leather had been chewed by wild animals. Here and there were the skeletons of the fallen, and Dick knew that the wild beasts had not been content with leather and cloth alone. He went through the wagons one by one, but found nothing of value left except a paper of needles, some spools of thread, and a large pair of scissors, all of which he put in the package with the history.

It was nightfall when he finished the task, and retiring to the slope, he made his bed among some pines. He heard wolves howling twice in the night, but he merely settled himself more easily in his warm buffalo robe and went to sleep again. Replenishing his canteen with water the next morning, he started out upon the plains, intending to make some explorations.

Dick had thought at first that they were in the Black Hills, but he concluded later that they were further west. The mountains about them were altogether too high for the Black Hills, and he wished to gain some idea of their position upon the map. The thought reminded him that he had a book with maps in his pocket, and he took out the precious volume.

He found a map of the Rocky Mountain territory, but most of the space upon it was vague, often blank, and he could not exactly locate himself and Albert, although he knew that they were very far west of any settled country.

"I can learn from that book all about the world except ourselves," he said, as he put it back in his pocket. But he was not sulky over it. His was a bold and adventurous spirit and he was not afraid, nor was his present trip merely to satisfy curiosity. He and Albert must leave the valley some day, and it was well to know the best way in which it could be done.

He started across the plain in a general south-westerly direction, intending to travel for about a day perhaps, camp for the night, and return on the following day to his mountains. He walked along with a bold, swinging step and did not look back for an hour, but when he turned at last he felt as if he had ventured upon the open ocean in a treacherous canoe. There were the mountains, high, sheltered, and friendly, while off to the south and west the plains rolled away in swell after swell as long and desolate as an untraveled sea, and as hopeless.

Dick saw toward noon some antelope grazing on the horizon, but he was not a hunter now, and he did not trouble himself to seek a shot. An hour or two later he saw a considerable herd of buffaloes scattered about over the plain, nibbling the short bunch grass that had lived under the snow. They were rather an inspiring sight, and Dick felt as if, in a sense, they were furnishing him company. They drove away the desolation and loneliness of the plains, and his inclinations toward them were those of genuine friendliness. They were in danger of no bullet from him.

While he was looking at them, he saw new figures coming over the distant swell. At first he thought they were antelope, but when they reached the crest of the swell and their figures were thrown into relief against the brilliant sky, he saw that they were horsemen.

They came on with such regularity and precision, that, for a moment or two, Dick believed them to be a troop of cavalry, but he learned better when they scattered with a shout and began to chase the buffaloes. Then he knew that they were a band of Sioux Indians hunting.

The full extent of his danger dawned upon him instantly. He was alone and on foot. The hunt might bring them down upon him in five minutes. He was about to run, but his figure would certainly be exposed upon the crest of one of the swells, as theirs had been, and he dropped instead into one of a number of little gullies that intersected the plain.

It was an abrupt little gully, and Dick was well hidden from any eyes not within ten yards of him. He lay at first so he could not see, but soon he began to hear shots and the trampling of mighty hoofs. He knew now that the Sioux were in among the buffaloes, dealing out death, and he began to have a fear of being trodden upon either by horsemen or huge hoofs. He could not bear to lie there and he warned only by sound, so he turned a little further on one side and peeped over the edge of the gully.

The hunters and hunter were not as near as he thought; he had been deceived by sound, the earth being such a good conductor. Yet they were near enough for him to see that he was in great danger and should remain well hidden. He could observe, however, that the hunt was attended with great success. Over a dozen buffaloes had fallen and the others were running about singly or in little groups, closely pursued by the exultant Sioux. Some were on one side of him and some on the other. There was no chance for him, no matter how careful he might be, to rise from the gully and sneak away over the plain. Instead, he crouched more closely and contracted himself into the narrowest possible space, while the hunt wheeled and thundered about him.

It is not to be denied that Dick felt many tremors. He had seen what the Sioux could do. He knew that they were the most merciless of all the north-western Indians, and he expected only torture and death if he fell into their hands, and there was his brother alone now in the valley. Once the hunt swung away to the westward and the sounds of it grew faint. Dick hoped it would continue in that direction, but by and by it came back again and he crouched down anew in his narrow quarters. He felt that every bone in him was stiffening with cramp and needlelike pains shot through his nerves. Yet he dared not move. And upon top of his painful position came the knowledge that the Sioux would stay there to cut up the slain buffaloes. He was tempted more than once to jump up, run for it and take his chances.

He noticed presently a gray quality in the air, and as he glanced off toward the west, he saw that the red sun was burning very low. Dick's heart sprang up in gladness; it was the twilight, and the blessed darkness would bring chance of escape. Seldom has anyone watched the coming of night with keener pleasure. The sun dropped down behind the swells, the gray twilight passed over all the sky, and after it came the night, on black wings.

Fires sprang up on the plain, fires of buffalo chips lighted by the Sioux, who were now busy skinning and cutting up the slain buffaloes. Dick saw the fires all about him, but none was nearer than a hundred yards, and, despite them, he decided that now was his best time to attempt escape before the moon should come out and lighten up the night.

He pulled himself painfully from the kind gully. He had lain there hours, and he tested every joint as he crept a few feet on the plain. They creaked for a while, but presently the circulation was restored, and, rising to a stooping position, with his rifle ready, he slipped off toward the westward.

Dick knew that great caution was necessary, but he had confidence in the veiling darkness. Off to the eastward he could see one fire, around which a half dozen warriors were gathered, busy with a slain buffalo, working and feasting. He fancied that he could trace their savage features against the red firelight, but he himself was in the darkness. Another fire rose up, and this was straight before him. Like the others, warriors were around it, and Dick turned off abruptly to the south. Then he heard ponies stamping and he shifted his course again. When he had gone about a dozen yards he lay flat upon the plain and listened. He was hardy and bold, but, for a little while, he was almost in despair. It seemed to him that he was ringed around by a circle of savage warriors and that he could not break through it.

His courage returned, and, rising to his knees, he resumed his slow progress. His course was now south-westerly, and soon he heard again the stamping of hoofs. It was then that a daring idea came into Dick's head.

That stamping of hoofs was obviously made by the ponies of the Sioux. Either the ponies were tethered to short sticks, or they had only a small guard, perhaps a single man. But as they were with the buffaloes, and unsuspecting of a strange presence, they would not detail more than one man to watch their horses. It was wisdom for him to slip away one of the horses, mount it when at a safe distance, and then gallop toward the mountains.

Dick sank down a little lower and crept very slowly toward the point from which the stamping of hoofs proceeded. When he had gone about a dozen yards he heard another stamping of hoofs to his right and then a faint whinny. This encouraged him. It showed him that the ponies were tethered in groups, and the group toward which he was going might be without a guard. He continued his progress another dozen yards, and then lay flat upon the plain. He had seen two vague forms in the darkness, and he wished to make himself a blur with the earth. They were warriors passing from one camp fire to another, and Dick saw them plainly, tall men with blankets folded about them like togas, long hair in which eagle feathers were braided after the Sioux style, and strong aquiline features. They looked like chiefs, men of courage, dignity, and mind, and Dick contrasted them with the ruffians of the wagon train. The contrast was not favourable to the white faces that he remembered so well.

But the boy saw nothing of mercy or pity in these red countenances. Bold and able they might be, but it was no part of theirs to spare their enemies. He fairly crowded himself against the earth, but they went on, absorbed in their own talk, and he was not seen. He raised up again and began to crawl. The group of ponies came into view, and he saw with delight that they had no watchman. A half dozen in number and well hobbled, they cropped the buffalo grass. They were bare of back, but they wore their Indian bridles, which hung from their heads.

Dick knew a good deal about horses, and he was aware that the approach would be critical. The Indian ponies might take alarm or they might not, but the venture must be made. He did not believe that he could get beyond the ring of the Sioux fires without being discovered, and only a dash was left.

Dick marked the pony nearest to him. It seemed a strong animal, somewhat larger than the others, and, pulling up a handful of bunch grass, he approached it, whistling very softly. He held the grass in his left hand and his hunting knife in the right, his rifle being fastened to his back. The pony raised his head, looked at him in a friendly manner, then seemed to change his mind and backed away. But Dick came on, still holding out the grass and emitting that soft, almost inaudible whistle. The pony stopped and wavered between belief and suspicion. Dick was not more than a dozen feet away now, and he began to calculate when he might make a leap and seize the bridle.

The boy and the pony were intently watching the eyes of each other. Dick, in that extreme moment, was gifted with preternatural acuteness of mind and vision, and he saw that the pony still wavered. He took another step forward, and the eyes of the pony inclined distinctly from belief to suspicion; another short and cautious step, and they were all suspicion. But it was too late for the pony. The agile youth sprang, and dropping the grass, seized him with his left hand by the bridle. A sweep or two of the hunting knife and the hobbles were cut through.

The pony reared and gave forth an alarmed neigh, but Dick, quickly replacing the knife in his belt, now held the bridle with both hands, and those two hands were very strong. He pulled the pony back to its four feet and sprang, with one bound, upon his back. Then kicking him vigorously in the side, he dashed away, with rifle shots spattering behind him.

CHAPTER 11

The Terrible Pursuit

Dick knew enough to bend low down on the neck of the flying mustang, and he was untouched, although he heard the bullets whistling about him. The neigh of the pony had betrayed him, but he was aided by his quickness and the friendly darkness, and he felt a surge of exultation that he could not control, boy that he was. The Sioux, jumping upon their ponies, sent forth a savage war whoop that the desolate prairie returned in moaning echoes, and Dick could not refrain from a reply. He uttered one shout, swung his rifle defiantly over his head, then bending down again, urged his pony to increased speed.

Dick heard the hoofs of his pursuers thundering behind him, and more rifle shots came, but they ceased quickly. He knew that the Sioux would not fire again soon, because of the distance and the uncertain darkness. It was his object to increase that distance, trusting that the darkness would continue free from moonlight. He took one swift look backward and saw the Sioux, a dozen or more, following steadily after. He knew that they would hang on as long as any chance of capturing him remained, and he resolved to make use of the next swell that he crossed. He would swerve when he passed the crest, and while it was yet between him and his pursuers, perhaps he could find some friendly covert that would hide him. Meanwhile he clung tightly to his rifle, something that one always needed in this wild and dangerous region.

He crossed a swell, but there was no friendly increase of the darkness and he was afraid to swerve, knowing that the Sioux would thereby gain upon him, since he would make himself the curve of the bow, while they remained the string.

In fact, the hasty glance back showed that the Sioux had gained, and Dick felt tremors. He was tempted for a moment to fire upon his pursuers, but it would certainly cause a loss of speed, and he did not believe that he could hit anything under such circumstances. No, he would save his bullets for a last stand, if they ran him to earth.

The Sioux raised their war whoop again and fired three or four shots. Dick felt a slight jarring movement run through his pony, and then the animal swerved. He was afraid that he had trodden in a prairie-dog hole or perhaps a little gully, but in an instant or two he was running steadily again, and Dick forgot the incident in the excitement of the flight.

He was in constant fear lest the coming out of the moon should lighten up the prairie and make him a good target for the Sioux bullets, but he noted instead, and with great joy, that it was growing darker. Heavy clouds drifted across the sky, and a cold wind arose and began to whistle out of the northwest. It was a friendly black robe that was settling down over the earth. It had never before seemed to him that thick night could be so welcome.

Dick's pony rose again on a swell higher than the others, and was poised there for the fraction of a second, a dark silhouette against the darker sky. Several of the Sioux fired. Dick felt once more that momentary jar of his horse's mechanism, but it disappeared quickly and his hopes rose, because he saw that the darkness lay thickly between this swell and the next, and he believed that he now could lose his pursuers.

He urged his horse vigorously. He had made no mistake when he chose this pony as strong and true. The response was instant and emphatic. He flew down the slope, but instead of ascending the next swell he turned at an angle and went down the depression that lay between them. There the darkness was thickest, and the burst of speed by the pony was so great that the shapes of his pursuers became vague and then were lost. Nevertheless, he heard the thudding of their hoofs and knew that they could also hear the beat of his. That would guide them for a while yet. He thought he might turn again and cross the next swell, thus throwing them entirely off his track, but he was afraid that he would be cast into relief again when he reached the crest, and so continued down the depression.

He heard shouts behind him, and it seemed to him that they were not now the shouts of triumph, but the shouts of chagrin. Clearly, he was gaining because after the cries ceased, the sound of hoof beats came but faintly. He urged his horse to the last ounce of his speed and soon the sound of the pursuing hoofs ceased entirely.

The depression ended and he was on the flat plain. It was still cloudy, with no moon, but his eyes were used enough to the dark to tell him that the appearance of the country had changed. It now lay before him almost as smooth as the surface of a table, and never relaxing the swift gallop, he turned at another angle.

He was confident now that the Sioux could not overtake or find him. A lone object in the vast darkness, there was not a chance in a hundred for them to blunder upon him. But the farther away the better, and he went on for an hour. He would not have stopped then, but the good pony suddenly began to quiver, and then halted so abruptly that Dick, rifle and all, shot over his shoulder. He felt a stunning blow, a beautiful set of stars flashed before his eyes, and he was gone, for the time, to another land.

When Dick awoke he felt very cold and his head ached. He was lying flat upon his back, and, with involuntary motion, he put his hand to his head. He felt a bump there and the hand came back damp and stained. He could see that the fingers were red—there was light enough for that ominous sight, although the night had no yet passed.

Then the flight, the danger, and his fall all came back in a rush to Dick. He leaped to his feet, and the act gave him pain, but not enough to show that any bone was broken. His rifle, the plainsman's staff and defence, lay at his feet. He quickly picked it up and found that it, too, was unbroken. In fact, it was not bent in the slightest, and here his luck had stood him well. But ten feet away lay a horse, the pony that had been a good friend to him in need.

Dick walked over to the pony. It was dead and cold. It must have been dead two to three hours at least, and he had lain that long unconscious. There was a bullet hole in its side and Dick understood now the cause of those two shivers, like the momentary stopping of a clock's mechanism. The gallant horse had galloped on until he was stopped only by death. Dick felt sadness and pity.

"I hope you've gone to the horse heaven," he murmured.

Then he turned to thoughts of his own position. Alone and afoot upon the prairie, with hostile and mounted Sioux somewhere about, he was still in bad case. He longed now for his mountains, the lost valley, the warm cabin, and his brother.

It was quite dark and a wind, sharp with cold, was blowing. It came over vast wastes, and as it swept across the swells kept up a bitter moaning sound. Dick shivered and fastened his deerskin tunic a little tighter. He looked up at the sky. Not a star was there, and sullen black clouds rolled very near to the earth. The cold had a raw damp in it, and Dick feared those clouds.

Had it been day he could have seen his mountains, and he would have made for them at once, but now his eyes did not reach a hundred yards, and that bitter, moaning wind told him nothing save that he must fight hard against many things if he would keep the life that was in him. He had lost all idea of direction. North and south, east and west were the same to him, but one must go even if one went wrong.

He tried all his limbs again and found that they were sound. The wound on his head had ceased to bleed and the ache was easier. He put his rifle on his shoulder, waved, almost unconsciously, a farewell to the horse, as one leaves the grave of a friend, and walked swiftly away, in what course he knew not.

He felt much better with motion. The blood began to circulate more warmly, and hope sprang up. If only that bitter, moaning wind would cease. It was inexpressibly weird and dismal. It seemed to Dick a song of desolation, it seemed to tell him at times that it was not worth while to try, that, struggle as he would, his doom was only waiting.

Dick looked up. The black clouds had sunk lower and they must open before long. If only day were near at hand, then he might choose the right course. Hark! Did he not hear hoof beats? He paused in doubt, and then lay down with his ear to the earth. Then he distinctly heard the sound, the regular tread of a horse, urged forward in a straight course, and he knew that it could be made only by the Sioux. But the sound indicated only one horse, or not more than two or three at the most.

Dick's courage sprang up. Here was a real danger and not the mysterious chill that the moaning of the wind brought to him. If the Sioux had found him, they had divided, and it was only a few of their number that he would have to face. He hugged his repeating rifle. It was a fine weapon, and just then he was in love with it. There was no ferocity in Dick's nature, but the Sioux were seeking the life that he wished to keep.

He rose from the earth and walked slowly on in his original course. He had no doubt that the Sioux, guided by some demon instinct, would overtake him. He looked around for a good place of defence, but saw none. Just the same low swells, just the same bare earth, and not even a gully like that in which he had lain while the hunt of the buffalo wheeled about him.

He heard the hoof beats distinctly now, and he became quite sure that they were made by only a single horseman. His own senses had become preternaturally acute, and, with the conviction that he was followed by but one, came a rush of shame. Why should he, strong and armed, seek to evade a lone pursuer? He stopped, holding his rifle ready, and waited, a vague, shadowy figure, black on the black prairie.

Dick saw the phantom horseman rise on a swell, the faint figure of an Indian and his pony, and there was no other. He was glad now that he had waited. The horse, trained for such work as this, gave the Sioux warrior a great advantage, but he would fight it out with him.

Dick sank down on one knee in order to offer a smaller target, and thrust his rifle forward for an instant shot. But the Sioux had stopped and was looking intently at the boy. For fully two minutes neither he nor his horse moved, and Dick almost began to believe that he was the victim of an illusion, the creation of the desolate plains, the night, the floating black vapours, his tense nerves, and heated imagination. He was tempted to try a shot to see if it were real, but the distance and the darkness were too great. He strengthened his will and remained crouched and still, his finger ready for the trigger of his rifle.

The Sioux and his horse moved at last, but they did not come forward; they rode slowly toward the right, curving in a circle about the kneeling boy, but coming no nearer. They were still vague and indistinct, but they seemed blended into one, and the supernatural aspect of the misty form of horse and rider increased. The horse trod lightly now, and Dick no longer heard the sound of footsteps, only the bitter moaning of the wind over the vast dark spaces.

The rider rode silently on his circle about the boy, and Dick turned slowly with him, always facing the eyes that faced him. He could dimly make out the shape of a rifle at the saddlebow, but the Sioux did not raise it, he merely rode on in that ceaseless treadmill tramp, and Dick wondered what he meant to do. Was he waiting for the others to come up?

Time passed and there was no sign of a second horseman. The single warrior still rode around him, and Dick still turned with him. He might be coming nearer in his ceaseless curves, but Dick could not tell. Although he was the hub of the circle, he began to have a dizzy sensation, as if the world were swimming about him. He became benumbed, as if his head were that of a whirling dervish.

Dick became quite sure now that the warrior and his horse were unreal, a creation of the vapours and the mists, and that he himself was dreaming. He saw, too, at last that they were coming nearer, and he felt horror, as if something demonic were about to seize him and drag him down. He crouched so long that he felt pain in his knees, and all things were becoming a blur before his eyes. Yet there had not been a sound but that of the bitter, moaning wind.

There was a flash, a shot, the sigh of a bullet rushing past, and Dick came out of his dream. The Sioux had raised the rifle from his saddlebow and fired. But he had been too soon. The shifting and deceptive quality of the darkness caused him to miss. Dick promptly raised his own rifle and fired in return. He also missed, but a second bullet from the warrior cut a lock from his temple.

Dick was now alert in every nerve. He had not wanted the life of this savage, but the savage wanted his; it seemed also that everything was in favour of the savage getting it, but his own spirit rose to meet the emergency; he, too, became the hunter.

He sank a little lower and saved his fire until the warrior galloped nearer. Then he sent a bullet so close that he saw one of the long eagle feathers drop from the hair of the warrior. The sight gave him a savage exultation that he would have believed a few hours before impossible to him. The next bullet might not merely clip a feather!

The Sioux, contrary to the custom of the Indian, did not utter a sound, nor did Dick say a word. The combat, save for the reports of the rifle shots, went on in absolute silence. It lasted a full ten minutes, when the Indian urged his horse to a gallop, threw himself behind the body and began firing under the neck. A bullet struck Dick in the left arm and wounded him slightly, but it did not take any of his strength and spirit.

Dick sought in vain for a sight of the face of his fleeting foe. He could catch only a glimpse of long, trailing hair beneath the horse's mane, and then would come the flash of a rifle shot. Another bullet clipped his side, but only cut the skin. Nevertheless, it stung, and while it stung the body it stung Dick's wits also into keener action. He knew that the Sioux warrior was steadily coming closer and closer in his deadly circle, and in time one of his bullets must strike a vital spot, despite the clouds and darkness.

Dick steadied himself, calming every nerve and muscle. Then he lay down on his stomach on the plain, resting slightly on his elbow, and took careful aim at the flying pony. He felt some regret as he looked down the sights. This horse might be as faithful and true as the one that had carried him to temporary safety, but he must do the deed. He marked the brown patch of hair that lay over the heart and pulled the trigger.

Dick's aim was true—the vapours and clouds had not disturbed it— and when the rifle flashed, the pony bounded into the and fell dead. But the agile Sioux leaped clear and darted away. Dick marked his brown body, and then was his opportunity to send a mortal bullet, but a feeling of which he was almost ashamed held his hand. His foe was running, and he was no longer hunted. The feeling lasted but a moment, and when it passed, the Sioux was out of range. A moment later and his misty foe had become a part of the solid darkness.

Dick stood upright once more. He had been the victor in a combat that still had for him all the elements of the ghostly. He had triumphed, but just in time. His nerves were relaxed and unstrung, and his hands were damp. He carefully reloaded all the empty chambers of his repeating rifle, and without looking at the falling horse, which he felt had suffered for the wickedness of another, strode away again over the plain, abandoning the rifle of the fallen Sioux as a useless burden.

It took Dick sometime after his fight with the phantom horseman to come back to real earth. Then he noticed that both the clouds and the dampness had increased, and presently something cold and wet settled upon his face. It was a flake of snow, and a troop came at its heels, gentle but insistent, chilling his hands and gradually whitening the earth, until it was a gleaming floor under a pall of darkness.

Dick was in dismay. Here was a foe that he could not fight with rifle balls. He knew that the heavy clouds would continue to pour forth snow, and the day, which he thought was not far away, would disclose as little as the night. The white pall would hide the mountains as well as the black pall had done, and he might be going farther and father from his valley.

He felt that he had been released from one danger and then another, only to encounter a third. It seemed to him, in his minute of despair, that Fate had resolved to defeat all his efforts, but, the minute over, he renewed his courage and trudged bravely on, he knew not whither. It was fortunate for him that he wore a pair of the heavy shoes saved from the wagon, and put on for just such a journey as this. The wet from the snow would have soon soaked though his moccasins, but, as his thick deerskin leggings fitted well over his shoes, he kept dry, and that was a comfort.

The snow came down without wind and fuss, but more heavily than ever, persistent, unceasing, and sure of victory. It was not particularly cold, and the walking kept up a warm and pleasant circulation in Dick's veins. But he knew that he must not stop. Whether he was going on in a straight line he had no way to determine. He had often heard that men, lost on the plains, soon begin to travel in a circle, and he watched awhile for his own tracks; but if they were there, they were covered up by snow too soon for him to see, and, after all, what did it matter?

He saw after a while a pallid yellowish light showing dimly through the snow, and he knew that it was the sunrise. But it illuminated nothing. The white gloom began to replace the black one. It was soon full day, but the snow was so thick that he could not see more than two or three hundred yards in any direction. He longed now for shelter, some kind of hollow, or perhaps a lone tree. The incessant fall of the snow upon his head and its incessant clogging under his feet were tiring him, but he only trod a plain, naked save for its blanket of snow.

Dick had been careful to keep his rifle dry, putting the barrel of it under his long deerskin coat. Once as he shifted it, he felt a lump over his chest, and for an instant or two did not know what caused it. Then he remember the history and geography of the United States. He laughed with grim humour.

"I am lost to history," he murmured, "and geography will not tell me where I am."

He crossed a swell—he knew them now more by feeling than by sight—and before beginning the slight assent of the next one he stopped to eat. He had been enough of a frontiersman, before starting upon such a trip, to store jerked buffalo in the skin knapsack that he had saved for himself. The jerked meat offered the largest possible amount of sustenance in the smallest possible space, and Dick ate eagerly. Then he felt a great renewal of courage and strength. He also drank of the snow water, that is, he dissolved the snow in his mouth, but he did not like it much.

He stood there for a while resting, and resolved only to walk enough to keep himself warm. Certainly, nothing was to be gained by exhausting himself and the snow which was now a foot deep showed no signs of abating. The white gloom hung all about him and he could not see the sky overhead.

Just as he took this resolution, Dick saw a shadow in the circling white. The shadow was like that of a man, but before he could see farther there was a little flash of red, a sharp, stinging report, and a bullet clipped the skin of his cheek, burning like fire. Dick was startled, and for full cause—but he recognized the Sioux warrior who had fought him on horseback. He had stared too long at that man and at a time too deadly not to know that head and face and the set of his figure. He had followed Dick through all the hours and falling snow, bent upon taking his life. A second shot, quickly following the first, showed that he meant to miss no chance.

The second bullet, like the first, just grazed Dick, and mild of temper though he habitually was, he was instantly seized with the fiercest rage. He could not understand such hatred, such ferocity, such an eagerness to take human life. And this was the man whom he had spared, whom he could easily have slain when he was running! The Sioux was raising his rifle for a third bullet, when Dick shot him through the chest. There was no doubt about his aim now. It was not disturbed by the whitish mist and the falling snow.

The Sioux fell full length, without noise and without struggle, and his gun flew from his hand. His body lay half buried in the snow, some of the long eagle feathers in his hair thrusting up like the wing of a slain bird. Dick looked at him with shuddering horror. All the anger was gone from him now, and it is true that in his heart he felt pity for this man, who had striven so hard and without cause to take his life. He would have been glad to go away now, but forced himself to approach and look down at the Indian.

The warrior lay partly on his side with one arm beneath his body. The blood from the bullet hole in his chest dyed the snow, and Dick believed that he had been killed instantly. But Dick would not touch him. He could not bring himself to do that. Nor would he take any of his arms. Instead, he turned away, after the single look, and, bending his head a little to the snow, walked rapidly toward the yellowish glare that told where the sun was rising. He did not know just why he went in that direction, but it seemed to him the proper thing to walk toward the morning.

Two hours, perhaps, passed and the fall of snow began to lighten. The flakes still came down steadily, but not in such a torrent. The area of vision widened. He saw dimly, as through a mist, three or four hundred yards, perhaps, but beyond was only the white blur, and there was nothing yet to tell him whether he was going toward the mountains or away from them.

He rested and ate again. Then he recovered somewhat, mentally as well as physically. Part of the horror of the Indian, his deadly pursuit, and the deadly ending passed. He ached with weariness and his nerves were quite unstrung, but the snow would cease, the skies would clear, and then he could tell which way lay the mountains and his brother.

He rested here longer than usual and studied the plain as far as he could see it. He concluded that its character had changed somewhat, that the swells were high than they had been, and he was hopeful that he might find shelter soon, a deep gully, perhaps, or a shallow prairie stream with sheltering cottonwoods along its course.

Another hour passed, but he did not make much progress. The snow was now up to his knees, and it became an effort to walk. The area of vision had widened, but no mountains yet showed through the white mist. He was becoming tired with a tiredness that was scarcely to be born. If he stood still long enough to rest he became cold, a deadly chill that he knew to be the precursor of death's benumbing sleep would creep over him, and then he would force himself to resume the monotonous, aching walk.

Dick's strength waned. His eyesight, affected by the glare of the snow, became short and unsteady, and he felt a dizziness of the brain. Things seemed to dance about, but his will was so strong that he could still reason clearly, and he knew that he was in desperate case. It was his will that resisted the impulse of his flesh to throw his rifle away as a useless burden, but he laughed aloud when he thought of the map of the United States in the inside pocket of his coat.

"They'll find me, if they ever find me, with that upon me," he said aloud, "and they, too, will laugh."

He stumbled against something and doubled his fist angrily as if he would strike a man who had maliciously got in his way. It was the solid bark of a big cottonwood that had stopped him, and his anger vanished in joy. Where one cottonwood was, others were likely to be, and their presence betokened a stream, a valley, and a shelter of some kind.

He was still dazed, suffering partially from snow blindness, but now he saw a line of sturdy cottonwoods and beyond it another line. The stream, he knew, flowed between. He went down the line a few hundred yards and came, as he had hoped, into more broken ground.

The creek ran between banks six or seven feet high, with a margin between stream and bank, and the cottonwoods on these banks were reinforced by some thick clumps of willows. Between the largest clump and the line of cottonwoods, with the bank as a shelter for the third side, was a comparatively clear space. The snow was only a few inches deep there, and Dick believed that he could make a shelter. He had, of course, brought his blanket with him in a tight roll on his back, and he was hopeful enough to have some thought of building a fire.

He stooped down to feel in the snow at a likely spot, and the act saved his life. A bullet, intended for his head, was buried in the snow beyond him, and a body falling down the bank lay quite still at his feet. It was the long Sioux. Wounded mortally, he had followed Dick, nevertheless, with mortal intent, crawling, perhaps most of the time, and with his last breath he had fired what he intended to be the fatal shot.

He was quite dead now, his power for evil gone forever. There could be no doubt about it. Dick at length forced himself to touch the face. It had grown cold and the pulse in the wrist was still. It yet gave him a feeling of horror to touch the Sioux, but his own struggle for life would be bitter and he could spare nothing. The dead warrior wore a good blanket, which Dick now took, together with his rifle and ammunition, but he left all the rest. Then he dragged the warrior from the sheltered space to a deep snow bank, where he sank him out of sight. He even took the trouble to heap more snow upon him in the form of a burial, and he felt a great relief when he could no longer see the savage brown features.

He went back to his sheltered space, and, upon the single unprotected side threw up a high wall of snow, so high that it would serve as a wind-break. Then he began to search for fallen brushwood. Meanwhile, it was turning colder, and a bitter wind began to moan across the plain.

CHAPTER 12

The Fight With Nature

Dick realized suddenly that he was very cold. The terrible pursuit was over, ending mortally for the pursuer, but he was menaced by a new danger. Sheltered though his little valley was, he could, nevertheless, freeze to death in it with great ease. In fact, he had begun already to shiver, and he noticed that while his feet were dry, the snow at last had soaked through his deerskin leggings and he was wet from knee to ankle. The snow had ceased, although a white mist hovered in a great circle and the chill of the wind was increasing steadily. He must have a fire or die.

He resumed his search, plunging into the snow banks under the cottonwoods and other trees, and at last he brought out dead boughs, which he broke into short pieces and piled in a heap in the centre of the open space. The wood was damp on the outside, of course, but he expected nothing better and was not discouraged. Selecting a large, well-seasoned piece, he carefully cut away all the wet outside with his strong hunting knife. Then he whittled off large quantities of dry shavings, put them under the heap of boughs, and took from his inside a pocket a small package of lucifer matches.

Dick struck one of the matches across the heel of his shoe. No spark leaped up. Instead, his heart sank down, sank further, perhaps, than it had ever done before in his life. The match was wet. He took another from the pocket; it, too, was wet, and the next and the next and all. The damp from the snow, melted by the heat of his body, had penetrated his buckskin coat, although in the excitement of pursuit and combat he had not noticed it.

Dick was in despair. He turned to the snow a face no less white. Had he escaped all the dangers of the Sioux for this? To freeze to death merely because he did not have a dry lucifer match? The wind was still rising and it cut to his very marrow. Reality and imagination were allied, and Dick was almost overpowered. He angrily thrust the wet little package of matches back into the inside pocket of his coat—his border training

347

in economy had become so strong that even in the moment of despair he would throw away nothing—and his hand in the pocket came into contact with something else, small, hard, and polished. Dick instantly felt a violent revulsion from despair to hope.

The small object was a sunglass. That wagon train was well equipped. Dick had made salvage of two sunglasses, and in a moment of forethought had given one to Albert, keeping the other for himself, each agreeing then and there to carry his always for the moment of need that might come.

Dick drew out the sunglass and fingered it as one would a diamond of great size. Then he looked up. A brilliant sun was shining beyond white, misty clouds, but its rays came through them dim and weak. The mists or, rather, cloudy vapour might lift or thin, and in that chance lay the result of his fight for life. While he waited a little, he stamped up and down violently, and threw his arms about with energy. It did not have much effect. The wet, cold, the raw kind that goes through, was in him and, despite all the power of his will, he shivered almost continually. But he persisted for a half hour and then became conscious of an increasing brightness about him. The white mist was not gone, but it was thinning greatly, and the rays of the sun fell on the snow brilliant and strong.

Dick took the dry stick again and scraped off particles of wood so fine that they were almost a power. He did not stop until he had a little heap more than an inch high. Meanwhile, the sun's rays, pouring through the whitish mist, continued to grow fuller and stronger.

Dick carefully polished the glass and held it at the right angle between the touchwood, that is, the scrapings, and the sun. The rays passing through the glass increased many times in power and struck directly upon the touchwood. Dick crouched over the wood in order to protect it from the wind, and watched, his breath constricted, while his life waited on the chance.

A minute, two minutes, three minutes, five passed and then a spark appeared in the touchwood, and following it came a tiny flame. Dick shouted with joy and shifted his body a little to put shavings on the touchwood. An ill wind struck the feeble blaze, which was not yet strong enough to stand fanning into greater life, and it went out, leaving a little black ash to mark where the touchwood had been.

Dick's nerves were so much overwrought that he cried aloud again, and now it was a cry of despair, not of joy. He looked at the little black ash as if his last chance were gone, but his despair did not last long. He seized the dry stick again and scraped off another little pile of touchwood. Once more the sunglass and once more the dreadful waiting, now longer than five minutes and nearer ten, while Dick waited in terrible fear, lest the sun itself should fail him, and go behind impenetrable clouds.

But the second spark came and after it, as before, followed the little flame. No turning aside now to allow a cruel chance to an ill wind. Instead, he bent down his body more closely than ever to protect the vital blaze, and, reaching out one cautious arm, fed it first with the smallest of the splinters, and then with the larger in an ascending scale.

Up leaped the flames, red and strong. Dick's body could not wholly protect them now, but they fought for themselves. When the wind shrieked and whipped against them, they waved back defiance, and the more the wind whipped them, the higher and stronger they grew.

The victory was with the flames, and Dick fed them with wood, almost with his body and soul, and all the time as the wind bent them over they crackled and ate deeper and deeper into the wood. He could put on damp wood now. The flames merely leaped out, licked up the melted snow with a hiss and a sputter, and developed the stick in a mass of glowing red.

Dick fed his fire a full half hour, hunting continually in the snow under the trees for brushwood and finding much of it, enough to start a second fire at the far end of the sheltered place, with more left in reserve. He spent another half hour heaping up the snow as a bulwark about his den, and then sat down between the two fires to dry and warm, almost to roast himself.

It was the first time that Dick understood how much pleasure could be drawn from a fire alone. What beautiful red and yellow flames! What magnificent glowing coals! What a glorious thing to be there, while the wind above was howling over the snowy and forlorn plain! His clothes dried rapidly. He no longer shivered. The grateful warmth penetrated every fibre of him and it seemed strange now that he should have been in despair only an hour ago. Life was a wonderful and brilliant thing. There was no ache in his bones, and the first tingling of his hands, ears, and nose he had relieved with the application of wet snow. Now he felt only comfort.

After a while Dick ate again of his jerked buffalo meat, and with the food, warmth, and rest, he began to feel sleepy. He plunged into the snow, hunted out more wood to add to his reserve, and then, with the two blankets, the Indian's and his own, wrapped about him, sat down where the heat of the two fires could reach him from either side, and with a heap of the wood as a rest for his back.

Dick did not really intend to go to sleep, but he had been through great labours and dangers and had been awake long. He drew up one of the blankets until it covered all of his head and most of his face, and began to gaze into the coals of the larger fire. The wind—and it was now so cold that the surface of the snow was freezing—still whis-

349

tled over him, but the blanket protected his head from its touch. The whistle instead increased his comfort like the patter of rain on a roof to him who is dry inside.

The fire had now burned down considerable and the beds of coals were large and beautiful. They enveloped Dick in their warmth and cheer and began to pain splendid words of hope for him. He could read what they said in glowing letters, but the singular feeling of peace and rest deepened all the while. He wondered vaguely that one could be so happy.

The white snow became less white, the red fire less red, and a great gray mist came floating down over Dick's eyes. Up rose a shadowy world in which all things were vague and wavering. Then the tired lids dropped down, the gray mist gave way to a soft blackness, and Dick sank peacefully into the valley of sleep.

The boy slept heavily hour after hour, with his hooded head sunk upon his knees, and his rifle lying across his lap, while over him shrieked the coldest wind of the great north-western plains. The surface of the frozen ground presented a gleaming sheet like ice, over which the wind acquired new strength and a sharper edge, but the boy in his alcove remained safe and warm. Now and then a drift of fine snowy particles that would have stung like small shot was blown over the barrier, but they only stuck upon the thick folds of the blankets and the boy slept on. The white mist dissolved. The sun poured down beams brilliantly cold and hard, and over them was the loom of the mountains, but the boy knew nothing of them, nor cared.

The fires ceased to flame and became great masses of glowing coals that would endure long. The alcove was filled with the grateful warmth, and when the sun was in the zenith, Dick still slept, drawing long, regular breaths from a deep strong chest. The afternoon grew and waned, twilight came over the desolate snow fields, the loom of the mountains was gone, and the twilight gave way to an icy night.

When Dick awoke it was quite dark, save for the heaps of coals which still glowed and threw out warmth. He felt at first a little wonderment that he had slept so long, but he was not alarmed. His forethought and energy had provided plenty of wood and he threw on fresh billets. Once more the flames leaped up to brighten and to cheer, and Dick, walking to the edge of his snow bank, looked over. The wind had piled up the snow there somewhat higher before the surface froze, and across the barrier he gazed upon some such scene as one might behold near the North Pole. He seemed to be looking over ice fields that stretched away to infinity, and the wind certainly had a voice that was a compound of chill and desolation.

It was so solemn and weird that Dick was glad to duck down again into his den, and resume the seat where he had slept so long. He ate a little and then tried to slumber again, but he had already slept so much that he remained wide awake. He opened his eyes and let them stay open, after several vain efforts.

The moonlight now came out with uncommon brilliancy and the plain glittered. But it was the coldest moon that Dick had ever seen. He began to feel desolate and lonely again, and, since he could not sleep, he longed for something to do. Then the knowledge came to him. He put on fresh wood, and between firelight and moonlight he could see everything clearly.

Satisfied with his light, Dick took from his pocket the *History of the United States* that was accompanying him so strangely in his adventures, and began to study it. He looked once more at the map of the Rocky Mountain territories, and judged that he was in Southern Montana. Although his curiosity as to the exact spot in which he lay haunted him, there was no way to tell, and turning the leaves away from the map, he began to read.

It was chance, perhaps, that made him open at the story that never grows old to American youth—Valley Forge. It was not a great history, it had no brilliant and vivid style, but the simple facts were enough for Dick. He read once more of the last hope of the great man, never greater than then, praying in the snow, and his own soul leaped at the sting of example. He was only a boy, obscure, unknown, and the fate of but two rested with him, yet he, too, would persevere, and in the end his triumph also would be complete. He read no further, but closed the book and returned it carefully to his pocket. Then he stared into the fire, which he built up higher that the cheerful light might shine before him.

Dick did not hide from himself even now the dangers of his position. He was warm and sheltered for the present, he had enough of the jerked buffalo to last several days, but sooner or later he must leave his den and invade the snowy plain with its top crust of ice. This snow might last two or three weeks or a month. It was true that spring had come, but it was equally true, as so often happens in the great north-west, that spring had refused to stay.

Dick tried now to see the mountains. The night was full of brilliant moonlight, but the horizon was too limited; it ended everywhere, a black wall against the snow, and still speculating and pondering, Dick at last fell asleep again.

When the boy awoke it was another clear, cold day, with the wind still blowing, and there in the northwest he joyously saw the white line of the mountains. He believed that he could recognize the shape of certain peaks and ridges, and he fixed on a spot in the blue sky which he was sure overhung Castle Howard.

351

Dick saw now that he had been going away from the mountains. He was certainly farther than he had been when he first met the Sioux, and it was probable that he had been wandering then in an irregular course, with its general drift toward the southwest. The mountains in the thin, high air looked near, but his experience of the west told him that they were far, forty miles perhaps, and the tramp that lay before him was a mighty undertaking. He prepared for it at once.

He cut a stout stick that would serve as a cane, looked carefully to the security of his precious sun glass, and bidding his little den, which already had begun to wear some of the aspects of a home, a regretful farewell, started through the deep snow.

He had wrapped his head in the Indian's blanket, covering everything but eyes, nose, and mouth, and he did not suffer greatly from the bitter wind. But it was weary work breaking the way through the snow, rendered all the more difficult by the icy crust on top. The snow rose to his waist and he broke it at first with his body, but by and by he used the stick, and thus he plodded on, not making much more than a mile an hour. Dick longed now for the shelter of the warm den. The cold wind, despite the protection of the blanket, began to seek out the crannies in it and sting his face. He knew that he was wet again from ankle to knee, but he struggled resolutely on, alike for the sake of keeping warm and for the sake of shortening the distance. Yet there were other difficulties than those of the snow. The ground became rough. Now and then he would go suddenly through the treacherous snow into an old buffalo wallow or a deep gully, and no agility could keep him from falling on his face or side. This not only made him weary and sore, but it was a great trial to his temper also, and the climax came when he went through the snow into a prairie brook and came out with his shoes full of water.

Dick shivered, stamped his feet violently, and went on painfully breaking his way through the snow. He began to have that dull stupor of mind and body again. He could see nothing on the surface of the white plain save himself. The world was entirely desolate. But if the Sioux were coming a second time he did not care. He was amused at the thought of the Sioux coming. There were hidden away somewhere in some snug valley, and were too sensible to venture upon the plain.

Late in the afternoon the wind became so fierce, and Dick was so tired, that he dug a hole in the deepest snow bank he could find, wrapped the blankets tightly around him, and crouched there for warmth and shelter. Then, when the muscles were at rest, he began to feel the cold all through his wet feet and legs. He took off his shoes and leggings inside the shelter of his blankets, and chafed feet and legs with vigorous hands. This restored warmth and circulation, but he was compelled after a while to put on his wet garments again. He had gained a rest, however, and as he did not fear the damp so much while he was moving, he resumed the painful march.

The mountains seemed as far away as ever, but Dick knew that he had come five or six miles. He could look back and see his own path through the deep snow, winding and zigzagging toward the northwest. It would wind and zigzag no matter how hard he tried to go in a straight line, and finally he refused to look back any more at the disclosure of his weakness.

He sought more trees before the sun went down, as his glass could no longer be of use without them, but found none. There could be no fire for him that night, and digging another deep hole in the snow he slept the darkness through, nevertheless, warmly and comfortably, like an Eskimo in his ice hut. He did not suffer as much as he had thought he would from his wet shoes and leggings, and in the night, wrapped within the blankets they dried on him.

Dick spent the second day in alternate tramps of an hour and rests of half an hour. He was conscious that he was growing weaker from this prodigious exertion, but he was not willing to acknowledge it. In the afternoon he came upon a grove of cottonwoods and some undergrowth and he tried to kindle a fire, but the sun was not strong enough for his glass, and, after an hour's wasted effort, he gave it up, discouraged greatly. Before night the wind, which had been from the northwest, shifted to the southwest and became much warmer. By and by it snowed again heavily and Dick, who could no longer see his mountains, being afraid that he would wander in the wrong direction, dug another burrow and went to sleep.

He was awakened by the patter of something warm upon his face, and found that the day and rain had come together. Dick once more was struck to the heart with dismay. How could he stand this and the snow together? The plain would now run rivers of water and he must trudge through a terrible mire, worse even than the snow.

He imagined that he could see his mountains through the rain sheets, and he resumed his march, making no effort now to keep anything but his rifle and ammunition dry. He crossed more than one brook, either permanent or made by the rain and melting snow, and sloshed though the water, ankle deep, but paid no attention to it. He walked with intervals of rest all through the day and the night, and the warm rain never ceased. The snow melted at a prodigious rate, and Dick thought several times in the night that he heard the sound of plunging waters. These must be cataracts from the snow and rain, and he was convinced that he was near the mountains.

The day came again, the rain ceased, the sun sprang out, the warm winds blew, and there were the mountains. Perhaps the snow had not been so heavy on them as on the plain, but most of it was gone from the peaks and slopes and they stood up, sheltering and beautiful, with a shade of green that the snow had not been able to take away.

The sight put fresh courage in Dick's heart, but he was very weak. He staggered as he ploughed through the mixed snow and mud, and plains and mountains alike were rocking about in a most uncertain fashion.

In a ravine at the foot of the mountains he saw a herd of about twenty buffaloes which had probably taken refuge there from the snowstorm, but he did not molest them. Instead, he shook his rifle at them and called out:

"I'm too glad to escape with my own life to take any of yours."

Dick's brain was in a feverish state and he was not wholly responsible for what he said or did, but he began the ascent with a fairly good supply of strength and toiled on all the day. He never knew where he slept that night, but he thinks it was in a clump of pines, and the next morning when he continued, he felt that he had made a wonderful improvement. His feet were light and so was his head, but he had never before seen slopes and peaks and pines and ash doing a daylight dance. They whirled about in the most eccentric manner, yet it was all exhilarating, in thorough accord with his own spirits, and Dick laughed aloud with glee. What a merry, funny world it was! Feet and head both grew lighter. He shouted aloud and began to sing. Then he felt so strong and exuberant that he ran down one of the slopes, waving his cap. An elk sprang out of a pine thicket, stared a moment or two with startled eyes at the boy, and then dashed away over the mountain.

Dick continued to sing, and waved his fur cap at the fleeing elk. It was the funniest thing he had ever seen in his life. The whirling dance of mountain and forest became bewildering in its speed and violence. He was unable to keep his feet, and plunged forward into the arms of his brother, Albert. Then everything sank away from him.

Chapter 13

Albert's Victory

When Dick opened his eyes again he raised his hand once more to wave it at the fleeing elk and then he stopped in astonishment. The hand was singularly weak. He had made a great effort, but it did not go up very far. Nor did his eyes, which had opened slowly and heavily, see any elk. They saw instead rows and rows of furs and then other rows hanging above one another. His eyes travelled downward and they saw log walls almost covered with furs and skins, but with rifles, axes, and other weapons and implements on hooks between. A heavy oaken window shutter was thrown back and a glorious golden sunlight poured into the room.

The sunlight happened to fall upon Dick's own hand, and that was the next object at which he looked. His amazement increased. Could such a thin white hand as that belong to him who had lately owned such a big red one? He surveyed it critically, in particular, the bones showing so prominently in the back of it, and then he was interrupted by a full, cheerful voice which called out:

"Enough of that stargazing and hand examination! Here, drink this soup, and while you're doing it, I'll tell you how glad I am to see you back in your right mind! I tell you you've been whooping out some tall yarns about an Indian following you for a year or two through snow a mile or so deep! How you fought him for a month without stopping! And how you then waded for another year through snow two or three times as deep as the first!"

It was his brother Albert, and he lay on his own bed of furs and skins in their own cabin, commonly called by them Castle Howard, snugly situated in the lost or enchanted valley. And here was Albert, healthy, strong, and dictatorial, while he, stretched weakly upon a bed, held our a hand through which the sun could almost shine. Truly, there had been great changes!

He raised his head as commanded by Albert—the thin, pallid, drooping Albert of last summer, the lusty, red-faced Albert of today—and drank the soup, which tasted very good indeed. He felt stronger and held up the thin, white hand to see if it had not grown fatter and redder in the last ten seconds. Albert laughed, and it seemed to Dick such a full, loud laugh, as if it were drawn up from a deep, iron-walled chest, inclosing lungs made of leather, with an uncommon expansion. It jarred upon Dick. It seemed too loud for so small a room.

"I see you enjoyed that soup, Dick, old fellow," continued Albert in the same thundering tones. "Well, you ought to like it. It was chicken soup, and it was made by an artist—myself. I shot a fat and tender prairie hen down the valley, and here she is in soup. It's only a step from grass to pot and I did it all myself. Have another."

"Think I will," said Dick.

He drank a second tin plate of the soup, and he could feel life and strength flowing into every vein.

"How did I get here, Al?" he asked.

"That's a pretty hard question to answer," replied Albert, smiling and still filling the room with his big voice. "You were partly brought, partly led, partly pushed, you partly walked, partly jumped, and partly crawled, and there were even little stretches of the march when you were carried on somebody's shoulder, big and heavy as you are. Dick, I don't know any name for such a mixed gait. Words fail me."

Dick smiled, too.

"Well, no matter how I got here, it's certain that I'm here," he said, looking around contentedly.

"Absolutely sure, and it's equally as sure that you've been here five days. I, the nurse, I, the doctor, and I, the spectator, can vouch for that. There were times when I had to hold you in your bed, there were times when you were so hot with fever that I expected to see you burst into a mass of red and yellow flames, and most all the while you talked with a vividness and imagination that I've never known before outside of the Arabian Nights. Dick, where did you get the idea about a Sioux Indian following you all the way from the Atlantic to the Pacific, with stops every half hour for you and him to fight?"

"It's true," said Dick, and then he told the eager boy the story of his escape from the Sioux band, the terrible pursuit, the storm, and his dreadful wandering.

"It was wonderful luck that I met you, Al, old fellow," he said devoutly.

"Not luck exactly," said Albert. "You were coming back to the valley on our old trail, and, as I had grown very anxious about you, I was out on the same path to see if I could see any sign of you. It was natural that we should meet, but I think that, after all, Dick, providence had the biggest hand in it."

"No doubt," said Dick, and after a moment's pause he added, "Did it snow much up here?"

"But lightly. The clouds seem to have avoided these mountains. It was only from your delirium that I gathered the news of the great storm on the plains. Now, I think you've talked enough for an invalid. Drop you head back on that buffalo robe and go to sleep again."

It seemed so amazing to Dick ever to receive orders from Albert that he obeyed promptly, closed his eyes, and in five minutes was in sound slumber.

Albert hovered about the room, until he saw that Dick was asleep and breathing strongly and regularly. Then he put his hand on Dick's brow, and when he felt the temperature his own eyes were lighted up by a fine smile. That forehead, hot so long, was cool now, and it would be only a matter of a few days until Dick was his old, strong and buoyant self again. Albert never told his brother how he had gone two days and nights without sleep, watching every moment by the delirious bedside, how, taking the chances, he had dosed him with quinine from their medical stores, and how, later, he had cooked for him the tenderest and most delicate food. Nor did he speak of those awful hours—so many of them—when Dick's life might go at any time.

Albert knew now that the great crisis was over, and rejoicing, he went forth from Castle Howard. It was his intention to kill another prairie chicken and make more of the soup that Dick liked so much. As he walked, his manner was expansive, indicating a deep satisfaction. Dick had saved his life and he had saved Dick's. But Dick was still an invalid and it was his duty, meanwhile to carry on the business of the valley. He was sole workman, watchman, and defender, and his spirit rose to meet the responsibility. He would certainly look after his brother as well as anyone could do it.

Albert whistled as he went along, and swung his gun in debonair fashion. It would not take him, an expert borderer and woodsman, long to get that prairie chicken, and after that, as he had said before, it was only a step from grass to pot.

It was perhaps the greatest hour of Albert Howard's life. He, the helped, was now the helper; he, the defended, was now the defender. His chest could scarcely contain the mighty surge of exultation that heart and lungs together accomplished. He was far from having any rejoicings over Dick's prostration; he rejoiced instead that he was able, since the prostration had come, to care for both. He had had the forethought and courage to go forth and seek for Dick, and the strength to save him when found.

Albert broke into a rollicking whistle and he still swung his shotgun somewhat carelessly for a hunter and marksman. He passed by one of the geysers just as it was sending up its high column of hot water and its high column of steam. "That's the way I feel, old fellow," he said. "I could erupt with just as much force."

He resumed his caution farther on and shot two fine, fat prairie hens, returning with them to Castle Howard before Dick awoke. When Dick did awake, the second instalment of the soup was ready for him and he ate it hungrily. He was naturally so strong and vigorous and had lived such a wholesome life that he recovered, now that the crisis was past, with astonishing rapidity. But Albert played the benevolent tyrant for a few days yet, insisting that Dick should sleep a great number of hours out of every twenty-four, and making him eat four times a day of the tenderest and most succulent things. He allowed him to walk but a little at first, and, though the walks were extended from day to day, made him keep inside when the weather was bad.

Dick took it all, this alternate spoiling and overlordship, with amazing mildness. He had some dim perception of the true state of affairs, and was willing that his brother should enjoy his triumph to the full. But in a week he was entirely well again, thin and pale yet, but with a pulsing tide in his veins as strong as ever. Then he and Albert took counsel with each other. All trace of snow was gone, even far up on the highest slope, and the valley was a wonderful symphony in green and gold, gold on the lake and green on the new grass and the new leaves of the trees.

"It's quite settled," said Albert, "that we're to stay another year in the valley."

"Oh, yes," said Dick, "we had already resolved on that, and my excursion on the plains shows that we were wise in doing so. But you know, Al, we can't do fur hunting in the spring and summer. Furs are not in good condition now."

"No," said Albert, "but we can get ready for the fall and winter, and I propose that we undertake right away a birch-bark canoe. The dugout is a little bit heavy and awkward, hard to control in a high wind, and we'll really need the birch bark."

"Good enough," said Dick. "We'll do it."

With the habits of promptness and precision they had learned from old Mother Necessity, they went to work at once, planning and toiling on equal terms, a full half-and-half partnership. Both were in great spirits.

In this task they fell back partly on talk that they had heard from some of the men with whom they had started across the plains, and partly on old reading, and it took quite a lot of time. They looked first for large specimens of the white birch, and finally found several on one of the lower slopes. This was the first and, in fact, the absolutely vital requisite. Without it they could do nothing, but, having located their bark supply, they left the trees and began at the lake edge the upper framework of their canoe, consisting of four strips of cedar, two for either side of the boat, every one of the four having a length of about fifteen feet. These strips had a width of about an inch, with a thickness a third as great.

The strips were tied together in pairs at the ends, and the two pairs were joined together at the same place after the general fashion in use for the construction of such canoes.

The frame being ready, they went to their white birch trees for the bark. They marked off the utmost possible length on the largest and finest tree, made a straight cut through the bark at either end, and triumphantly peeled off a splendid piece, large enough for the entire canoe. Then they laid it on the ground in a nice smooth place and marked off a distance two feet less than their framework or gunwales. They drove into the ground at each end of this space two tall stakes, three inches apart. The bark was then laid upon the ground inside up and folded evenly throughout its entire length. After that it was lifted and set between the stakes with the edges up. The foot of bark projecting beyond each stake was covered in each case with another piece of bark folded firmly over it and sewed to the sides by means of an awl and deer tendon.

This sewing done, they put a large stone under each end of the bark construction, causing it to sag from the middle in either direction into the curve suitable for a canoe. The gunwale which they had constructed previously was now fitted into the bark, and the bark was stitched tightly to it, both at top and bottom, with a further use of awl and tendon, the winding stitch being used.

They now had the outside of the canoe, but they had drawn many a long breath and perspired many a big drop before it was done. They felt, however, that the most serious part of the task was over, and after a short rest they began on the inside, which they lined with long strips of cedar running the full length of the boat. The pieces were about an inch and a half in width and about a third of an inch in thickness and were fitted very closely together. Over these they put the ribs of touch ash, which was very abundant in the valley and on the slopes. Strips two inches wide and a half inch thick were bent crosswise across the interior of the curve, close together, and were firmly fastened under the gunwales with a loop stitch of the strong tendon through the bark.

To make their canoe firm and steady, they securely lashed three string pieces across it and then smeared deeply all the seams with pitch, which they were fortunate enough to secure from one of the many strange springs and exudations in the valley. They now had a strong, light canoe, fifteen feet long and a little over two feet wide at the centre. They had been compelled to exercise great patience and endurance in this task, particularly in the work with the awl and tendons. Skilful as they had become with their hands, they acquired several sore fingers in the task, but their pride was great when it was done. They launched the canoe, tried it several times near the shore in order to detect invisible seams, and then, when all such were stopped up tightly with pitch, they paddled boldly out into deep and far waters.

The practice they had acquired already with the dugout helped them greatly with the birch bark, and after one or two duckings they handled it with great ease. As amateurs sometimes do, they had achieved either by plan or accident a perfect design and found that they had a splendid canoe. This was demonstrated when the two boys rowed a race, after Dick had recovered his full strength—Dick in the dugout and Albert in the birch bark. The race was the full length of the lake, and the younger and smaller boy won an easy triumph.

"Well paddled, Al!" said Dick.

"It wasn't the paddling, Dick," replied Albert, "it was light bark against heavy wood that did it."

They were very proud of their two canoes and made a little landing for them in a convenient cove. Here, tied to trees with skin lariats, they were safe from wind and wave.

An evening or two after the landing was made secure, Dick, who had been out alone, came home in the dark and found Albert reading a book by the firelight.

"What's this?" he exclaimed.

"I took it out of the inside pocket of your coat, when I help you here in the snow," replied Albert. "I put it on a shelf and in the strain of your illness forgot all about it until today."

"That's my *History and Map of the United States*," said Dick, smiling. "I took it from the wagon which yielded up so much to us. It wouldn't tell me where I was in the storm; but, do you know, Al, it helped me when I read in there about that greatest of all men praying in the snow."

"I know who it is whom you mean," said Albert earnestly, "and I intend to read about him and all the others. It's likely, Dick, before another year is past, that you and I will become about the finest historians of our country to be found anywhere between the Atlantic and Pacific. Maybe this is the greatest treasure of all that the wagon has yielded up to us."

Albert was right. A single volume, where no other could be obtained, was a precious treasure to them, and it made many an evening pass pleasantly that would otherwise have been dull. They liked especially to linger over the hardships of the borderers and of their countrymen in war, because they found so many parallels to their own case, and the reading always brought them new courage and energy.

They spent the next month after the completion of the canoe in making all kinds of traps, including some huge dead falls for grizzly bear and silver tip.

They intended as soon as the autumn opened to begin their fur operations on a much larger scale than those of the year before. Numerous excursions into the surrounding mountains showed abundant signs of game and no signs of an invader, and they calculated that if all went well they would have stored safely by next spring at least twenty thousand dollars' worth of furs.

The summer passed pleasantly for both, being filled with work in which they took a great interest, and hence a great pleasure. They found another rock cavity, which they fitted up like the first in anticipation of an auspicious trapping season.

"They say, 'don't put all your eggs in one basket,'" said Albert, "and so we won't put all our furs in one cave. The Sioux may come sometime or other, and even if they should get our three residences, Castle Howard, the annex, and the Suburban Villa, and all that is in them, they are pretty sure to miss our caves and our furs."

"Of course some Indians must know of this valley," said Dick, "and most likely it's the Sioux. Perhaps none ever wander in here now, because they're at war with our people and are using all their forces on the plains."

Albert thought it likely, and both Dick and he had moments when they wondered greatly what was occurring in the world without. But, on the whole, they were not troubled much by the affairs of the rest of the universe.

Traps, house building, and curing food occupied them throughout the summer. Once the days were very hot in the valley, which served as a focus for the rays of the sun, but it was invariably cool, often cold, at night. They slept usually under a tent, or sometimes, on their longer expeditions in that direction, at the bark hut. Dick made a point of this, as he resolved that Albert should have no relapse. He could not see any danger of such a catastrophe, but he felt that another year of absolutely fresh and pure mountain air, breathed both night and day, would put his brother beyond all possible danger.

The life that both led even in the summer was thoroughly hardening. They bathed every morning, if in the tent by Castle Howard, in the torrent, the waters of which were always icy, flowing as they did from melting snows on the highest peaks. They swam often in the lake, which was also cold always, and at one of the hot springs they hollowed out a pool, where they could take a hot bath whenever they needed it.

The game increased in the valley as usual toward autumn, and they replenished their stores of jerked meat. They had spared their ammunition entirely throughout the summer and now they used it only on buffalo, elk, and mule deer. They were fortunate enough to catch several big bears in their huge dead falls, and, with very little expenditure of cartridges, they felt that they could open their second winter as well equipped with food as they had been when they began the first. They also put a new bark thatching on the roof of Castle Howard, and then felt ready for anything that might come.

"Rain, hail, sleet, snow, and ice, it's all the same to us," said Dick.

They did not resume their trapping until October came, as they knew that the furs would not be in good condition until then. They merely made a good guess that it was October. They had long since lost all count of days and months, and took their reckoning from the change of the foliage into beautiful reds and yellows and the increasing coldness of the air.

It proved to be a cold but not rainy autumn, a circumstance that favoured greatly their trapping operations. They had learned much in the preceding winter from observation and experience, and now they put it to practice. They knew many of the runways or paths frequented by the animals, and now they would place their traps in these, concealing them as carefully as possible, and, acting on an idea of Albert's, they made buckskin gloves for themselves, with which they handled the traps, in order to leave, if possible, no human odour to warn the wary game. Such devices as this and the more skilful making of their traps caused the second season to be a greater success than the first, good as the latter had been. They shot an additional number of buffaloes and elk, but what they sought in particular was the beaver, and they were lucky enough to find two or three new and secluded little streams, on which he had built his dams.

The valuable furs now accumulated rapidly, and it was wise forethought that had made them fit up the second cave or hollow. They were glad to have two places for them, in case one was discovered by an enemy stronger than themselves.

Autumn turned into winter, with snow, slush, and ice-cold rain. The preceding winter had been mild, but this bade fair to break some records for severe and variegated weather. Now came the true test for Albert. To trudge all day long in snow, icy rain or deep slush, to paddle across the lake in a nipping wind, with the chilly spray all over him, to go for hours soaking wet on every inch of his skin—these were the things that would have surely tried the dwellers in the houses of men, even those with healthy bodies.

Albert coughed a little after his first big soaking, but after a hot bath, a big supper, and a long night's sleep, it left, not to return. He became so thoroughly inured now to exposure that nothing seemed to affect him. Late in December—so they reckoned the time—when, going farther than usual into a long crevice of the mountains, they were overtaken by a heavy snowstorm. They might have reached the Suburban Villa by night, or they might not, but in any event the going would have been full of danger, and they decided to camp in the broadest part of the canyon in which they now were, not far from the little brook that flowed down it.

They had matches with them—they were always careful to keep them dry now—and after securing their dry shavings they lighted a good fire. Then they are their food, and looked up without fear at the dark mountains and the thick, driving snow. They were partially sheltered by the bank and some great ash trees, and, for further protection, they wrapped about themselves the blankets, without which they never went on any long journey.

Having each other for company, the adventure was like a picnic to both. It was no such desperate affair as that of Dick's when he was alone on the plain. They further increased their shelter from the snow by an artful contrivance of brush and fallen boughs, and although enough still fell upon them to make miserable the house-bred, they did not care. Both fell asleep after a while, with flurries of snow still striking upon their faces, and were awakened far in the night by the roar of an avalanche farther up the canyon; but they soon went to sleep again and arose the next day with injury.

Thus the winter passed, one of storm and cold, but the trapping was wonderful, and each boy grew in a remarkable manner in strength, endurance, and skill. When signs of spring appeared again, they decided that it was time for them to go. Had it not been for Dick's misadventure on the plain, and their belief that a great war was now in progress between the Sioux and the white people, one might have gone out to return with horses and mules for furs, while the other remained behind to guard them. But in view of all the dangers, they resolved to keep together. The furs would be secreted and the rest of their property must take its chances.

So they made ready.

CHAPTER 14

Prisoners

It gave both Dick and Albert a severe wrench to leave their beautiful valley. They had lived in it now nearly two years, and it had brought strength and abounding life to Albert, infinite variety, content, and gratitude to Dick, and what seemed a fortune—their furs—to both. It was a beautiful valley, in which nature had done for them many strange and wonderful things, and they loved it, the splendid lake, the grassy levels, the rushing streams, the noble groves, and the great mountains all about.

"I'd like to live here, Dick," said Albert, "for some years, anyway. After we take out our furs and sell 'em, we can come back and use it as a base for more trapping."

"If the Indians will let up," said Dick.

"Do you think we'll meet 'em?"

"I don't know, but I believe the plains are alive with hostile Sioux."

But Albert could not foresee any trouble. He was too young, to sanguine, too full now of the joy of life to think of difficulties.

They chose their weapons for the march with great care, each taking a repeating rifle, a revolver, a hunting knife, and a hatchet, the latter chiefly for camping purposes. They also divided equally among themselves what was left of the ball cartridges, and each took his sunglass and half of the remaining matches. The extra weapons, including the shotguns and shot cartridges, they hid with their furs. They also put in the caves many more of their most valuable possessions, especially the tools and remnants of medical supplies. They left everything else in the houses, just as they were when they were using them, except the bark hut, from which they took away all furnishings, as it was too light to resist the invasion of a large wild beast like a grizzly bear. But they fastened up Castle Howard and the annex so securely that no wandering beast could possibly break in. They sunk their canoes in shallow water among reeds, and then, when each had provided himself with a large supply of jerked buffalo and deer meat and a skin water bag, they were ready to depart.

"We may find our houses and what is in them all right when we come back, or we may not," said Dick.

"But we take the chance," said Albert cheerfully.

Early on a spring morning they started down the valley by the same way in which they had first entered it. They walked along in silence for some minutes, and then, as if by the same impulse, the two turned and looked back. There was their house, which had sheltered them so snugly and so safely for so long, almost hidden now in the foliage of the new spring. There was a bit of moisture in the eyes of Albert, the younger and more sentimental.

"Goodbye," he said, waving his hand. "I've found life here."

Dick said nothing, and they turned into the main valley. They walked with long and springy steps, left the valley behind them, and began to climb the slopes. Presently the valley itself became invisible, the mountains seeming to close in and blot it out.

"A stranger would have to blunder on it to find it," said Dick.

"I hope no one will make any such blunder," said Albert.

The passage over the mountains was easy, the weather continuing favourable, and on another sunshiny morning they reached the plains, which flowed out boundlessly before them. These, too, were touched with green, but the boys were perplexed. The space was so vast, and it was all so much alike, that it did not look as if they could ever arrive anywhere.

"I think we'd better make for Cheyenne in Wyoming Territory," said Dick.

"But we don't know how far away it is, nor in what direction," said Albert.

"No; but if we keep on going we're bound to get somewhere. We've got lots of time before us, and we'll take it easy."

They had filled their skin water bags, made in the winter, at the last spring, and they set out at a moderate pace over the plain. Dick had thought once of visiting again the scene of the train's destruction in the pass, but Albert opposed it.

"No," he said, "I don't want to see that place."

This journey, they knew not whither, continued easy and pleasant throughout the day. The grass was growing fast on the plains, and all the little steams that wound now and then between the swells were full of water, and, although they still carried the filled water bags, Dick inferred that they were not likely to suffer from thirst. Late in the afternoon they saw a small herd of antelope and a lone buffalo grazing at a considerable distance, and Dick drew the second and comforting inference that game would prove to be abundant. He was so pleased with these inferences that he stated them to Albert, who promptly drew a third.

"Wouldn't the presence of buffalo and antelope indicate that there are not many Indians hereabouts?" he asked.

"It looks likely," replied Dick.

They continued southward until twilight came, when they built in a hollow a fire of buffalo chips, which were abundant all over the plain, and watched their friendly mountains sink away in the dark.

"Gives me a sort of homesick feeling," said Albert. "They've been good mountains to us. Shelter and home are there, but out here I feel as if I were stripped to the wind."

"That describes it," said Dick.

They did not keep any watch, but put out their fire and slept snugly in their blankets. They were awakened in the morning by the whine of a coyote that did not dare to come too near, and resumed their leisurely march, to continue in this manner for several days, meeting no human being either white or red. They saw the mountains sink behind the sky line and then they felt entirely without a rudder. There was nothing to go by now except the sun, but they kept to their southern course. They were not greatly troubled. They found plenty of game, as Dick had surmised, and killed an antelope and a fat young buffalo cow.

"We may travel a long journey, Al," said Dick with some satisfaction, "but it's not hard on us. It's more like loafing along on an easy holiday."

On the fifth day they ran into a large buffalo herd, but did not molest any of its members, as they did not need fresh meat.

"Seems to me," said Dick, "that Sioux would be after this herd if they weren't busy elsewhere. It looks like more proof that the Sioux are on the warpath and are to the eastward of us, fighting our own people."

"The Sioux are a great and warlike tribe, are they not?" asked Albert.

"The greatest and most warlike west of the Mississippi," replied Dick. "I understand that they are really a group of closely related tribes and can put thousands of warriors in the field."

"Bright Sun, I suppose, is with them?"

"Yes, I suppose so. He is an Indian, a Sioux, no matter if he was at white schools and for years with white people. He must feel for his own, just as you and I, Al, feel for our own race."

They wandered three or four more days across the plains, and were still without sign of white man or red. They experienced no hardship. Water was plentiful. Game was to be had for the stalking and life, had they been hunting or exploring, would have been pleasant; but both felt a sense of disappointment—they never came to anything. The expanse of plains was boundless, the loneliness became overpowering. They had not the remotest idea whether they were travelling toward any white settlement. Human life seemed to shun them.

"Dick," said Albert one day, "do you remember the story of the Flying Dutchman, how he kept trying for years to round the Cape of Storms, and couldn't do it? I wonder if some such penalty is put on us, and if so, what for?"

The thought lodged in the minds of both. Oppressed by long and fruitless wanderings, they began to have a superstition that they were to continue them forever. They knew that it was unreasonable, but it clung, nevertheless. There were the rolling plains, the high, brassy sky, and the clear line of the horizon on all sides, with nothing that savoured of human life between.

They had hoped for an emigrant train, or a wandering band of hunters, or possibly a troop of cavalry, but days passed and they met none. Still the same high, brassy sky, still the same unbroken horizons. The plains increased in beauty. There was a fine, delicate shade of green on the buffalo grass, and wonderful little flowers peeped shy heads just above the earth, but Dick and Albert took little notice of either. They had sunk into an uncommon depression. The terrible superstition that they were to wander forever was strengthening its hold upon them, despite every effort of will and reason. In the hope of better success they changed their course two or three times, continuing in each case several days in that direction before the next change was made.

"We've travelled around so much now," said Albert despondently, "that we couldn't go back to our mountains if we wanted to do it. We don't know any longer in what direction they lie."

"That's so," said Dick, with equal despondency showing in his tone.

His comment was brief, because they talked but little now, and every day were talking less. Their spirits were affected too much to permit any excess of words. But they came finally to rougher, much more broken country, and they saw a line of trees on the crest of hills just under the sunset horizon. The sight, the break in the monotony, the cheerful trees made them lift up their drooping heads.

"Well, at any rate, here's something new," said Dick. "Let's consider it an omen of good luck, Al."

They reached the slope, a long one, with many depressions and hollows, containing thick groves of large trees, the heights beyond being crowned with trees of much taller growth. They would have gone to the summit, but they were tired with a long day's tramp and they had not yet fully aroused themselves from the lethargy that had overtaken them in their weary wanderings.

"Night's coming," said Albert, "so let's take to that hollow over there with the scrub ash in it."

"All right," said Dick. "Suits me."

It was a cosy little hollow, deeply shaded by the ash trees, but too rocky to be damp, and they did not take the trouble to light a fire. They had been living for some time on fresh buffalo and antelope, and had saved their jerked meat, on which they now drew for supper.

It was now quite dark, and each, throwing his blanket lightly around his shoulders, propped himself in a comfortable position. Then, for the first time in days, they began to talk in the easy, idle fashion of those who feel some degree of contentment, a change made merely by the difference in scene, the presence of hills, trees, and rocks after the monotonous world of the plains.

"We'll explore that country tomorrow," said Dick, nodding his head toward the crest of the hills. "Must be something over there, a river, a lake, and maybe trappers."

"Hope it won't make me homesick again for our valley," said Albert sleepily. "I've been thinking too much of it, anyway, in the last few days. Dick, wasn't that the most beautiful lake of ours that you ever saw? Did you ever see another house as snug as Castle Howard? And how about the annex and the Suburban Villa? And all those beautiful streams that came jumping down between the mountains?"

"If you don't shut up, Al," said Dick, "I'll thrash you with this good handy stick that I've found here."

"All right," replied Albert, laughing; "I didn't mean to harrow up your feelings any more than I did my own."

Albert was tired, and the measure of content that he now felt was soothing. Hence, his drowsiness increased, and in ten minutes he went comfortably to sleep. Dick's eyes were yet open, and he felt within himself such new supplies of energy and strength that he resolved to explore a little. The task that had seemed so hard two or three hours before was quite easy now. Albert would remain sleeping safely where he was, and, acting promptly, Dick left the hollow, rifle on shoulder.

It was an easy slope, but a long one. As he ascended, the trees grew more thickly and near the ascent were comparatively free from undergrowth. Just over the hill shone a magnificent full moon, touching the crest with a line of molten silver.

Dick soon reached the summit and looked down the far slope into a valley three or four hundred yards deep. The moon shed its full glory into the valley and filled it with rays of light.

The valley was at least two miles wide, and down its centre flowed a fine young river, which Dick could see here and there in stretches, while the rest was hidden by forest. In fact, the whole valley seemed to be well clothed with mountain forest, except in one wide space where Dick's gaze remained after it had alighted once.

Here was human life, and plenty of it. He looked down upon a circle of at least two hundred lodges, tent-shaped structures of saplings covered with bark, and he had heard quite enough about such things to know these were the winter homes of the Sioux. The moonlight was so clear and his position so good that he was able to see figures moving about the lodges.

The sight thrilled Dick. Here he had truly come upon human life, but not the kind he wished to see. But it was vastly interesting, and he sought a closer look. His daring told him to go down the slope toward them, and he obeyed. The descent was not difficult, and there was cover in abundance—pines, ash, and oak.

As he was very careful, taking time not to break a twig or set a stone rolling, and stopping at intervals to look and listen, he was a half hour in reaching the valley, where, through the trees, he saw the Indian village. He felt that he was rash, but wishing to see, he crept closer, the cover still holding good. He was, in a way, fascinated by what he saw. It had the quality of a dream, and its very unreality made him think less of the danger. But he really did not know how expert he had become as a woodsman and trailer through his long training as a trapper, where delicacy of movement and craft were required.

He believed that the Indians, in such a secure location, would not be stirring beyond the village at this late hour, and he had little fear of anything except the sharp-nosed dogs that are always prowling about an Indian village. He was within three hundred yards of the lodges when he heard the faint sound of voices and footsteps. He instantly lay down among the bushes, but raised himself a little on his elbow in order to see.

Three Indians were walking slowly along a woodland path toward the village, and the presence of the path indicated the village had been here for many months, perhaps was permanent. The Indians were talking very earnestly and they made gestures. One raised his voice a little and turned toward one of his companions, as if he would emphasize his words. Then Dick saw his face clearly, and drew a long breath of surprise.

It was Bright Sun, but a Bright Sun greatly changed. He was wholly in native attire—moccasins, leggings, and a beautiful blue blanket draped about his shoulders. A row of eagle feathers adorned his long black hair, but it was the look and manner of the man that had so much significance. He towered above the other Indians, who were men of no mean height; but it was not his height either, it was his face, the fire of his eyes, the proud eagle beak which the Sioux had not less than the Roman, and the swift glance of command that could not be denied. Here was a great chief, a leader of men, and Dick was ready to admit it.

He could easily have shot Bright Sun dead as he passed, but he did not dream of doing such a thing. Yet Bright Sun, while seeming to play the part of a friend, had deliberately led the wagon train into a fatal ambush—of that Dick had no doubt. He felt, moreover, that Bright Sun was destined to cause great woe to the white people, his own people, but he could not fire; nor would he have fired even if the deed had been without danger to himself.

Dick, instead, gave Bright Sun a reluctant admiration. He looked well enough as the guide in white men's clothes, but in his own native dress he looked like one to be served, not to serve. The three paused for a full two minutes exactly opposite Dick, and he could have reached out and touched them with the barrel of his rifle; but they were thinking little of the presence of an enemy. Dick judged by the emphasis of their talk that it was on a matter of some great moment, and he saw all three of them point at times toward the east.

"It's surely war," he thought, "and our army if somewhere off there in the east."

Dick saw that Bright Sun remained the dominating figure throughout the discussion. Its whole effect was that of Bright Sun talking and the others listening. He seemed to communicate his fire and enthusiasm to his comrades, and soon they nodded a vigorous assent. Then the three walked silently away toward the village.

Dick rose from his covert, cast a single glance at the direction in which the three chiefs had disappeared, and then began to retrace his own steps. It was his purpose to arouse Albert and flee at once to a less dangerous region. But the fate of Dick and his brother rested at that moment with a mean, mangy, mongrel cur, such as have always been a part of Indian villages, a cur that had wandered farther from the village than usual that night upon some unknown errand.

Dick had gone about thirty yards when he became conscious of a light, almost faint, pattering sound behind him. He stepped swiftly into the heaviest shadow of trees and sought to see what pursued. He thought at first it was some base-born wolf of the humblest tribe, but, when he looked longer, he knew that it was one of the meanest of mean curs, a hideous, little yellowish animal, sneaking in his movements, a dog that one would gladly kick out of his way.

Dick felt considerable contempt for himself because he had been alarmed over such a miserable little beast, and resumed his swift walk. Thirty yards farther he threw a glance over his shoulder, and there was the wretched cur still following. Dick did not like it, considering it an insult to himself to be trailed by anything so ugly and insignificant. He picked up a stone, but hesitated a moment, and then put it down again.

If he threw the stone the dog might bark or howl, and that was the last thing that he wanted. Already the cur, mean and miserable as he looked, had won a victory over him.

Dick turned into a course that he would not have taken otherwise, thinking to shake off his pursuer, but at the next open space he saw him still following, his malignant red eyes fixed upon the boy. The cur would not have weighed twenty cowardly pounds, but he became a horrible obsession to Dick. He picked up a stone again, put it down again, and for a mad instant seriously considered the question of shooting him.

The cur seemed to become alarmed at the second threat, and broke suddenly into a sharp, snarling, yapping bark, much like that of a coyote. It was terribly loud in the still night, and cold dread assailed Dick in every nerve. He picked up the stone that he had dropped, and this time he threw it.

"You brute!" he exclaimed, as the stone whizzed by the cur's ear.

The cur returned the compliment of names with compounded many times over. His snarling bark became almost continuous, and although he did not come any nearer, he showed sharp white teeth. Dick paused in doubt, but when, from a point nearer the village, he heard a bark in reply, then another, and then a dozen, he ran with all speed up the slope. He knew without looking back that the cur was following, and it made him feel cold again.

Certainly Dick had good cause to run. All the world was up and listening now, and most of it was making a noise, too. He heard a tumult of barking, growling, and snapping toward the village, and then above it a long, mournful cry that ended in an ominous note. Dick knew that it was a Sioux war whoop, and that the mean, miserable little cur had done his work. The village would be at his heels. Seized with an unreasoning passion, he whirled about and shot the cur dead. It was a mad act, and he instantly repented it. Never had there been another rifle shot so loud. It crashed like the report of a cannon. Mountain and valley gave it back in a multitude of echoes, and on the last dying echo came, not a single war whoop, but the shout of many, the fierce, insistent, falsetto yell that has sounded the doom of many a borderer.

Dick shuddered. He had been pursued once before by a single man, but he was not afraid of a lone warrior. Now a score would be at his heels. He might shake them off in the dark, but the dogs would keep the scent, and his chief object was to go fast. He ran up the slope at his utmost speed for a hundred yards or more, and then remembering in time to nurse his strength, he slackened his footsteps.

He had thought of turning the pursuit away from the hollow in which Albert lay, but now that the alarm was out they would find him, anyway, and it was best for the two to stand or fall together. Hence, he went straight for the hollow.

It was bitter work running up a slope, but his two years of life in the open were a great help to him now. The strong heart and the powerful lungs responded nobly to the call. He ran lightly, holding his rifle in the hollow of his arm, ready for use if need be, and he watch warily lest he make an incautious footstep and fall. The moonlight was still full and clear, but when he took an occasional hurried glance backward he could not yet see his pursuers. He heard, now and then, however, the barking of a dog or the cry of a warrior.

Dick reached the crest of the hill, and there for an instant or two his figure stood, under the pines, a black silhouette against the moonlight. Four or five shots were fired at the living target. One bullet whizzed so near that it seemed to Dick to scorch his face.

He had gathered fresh strength, and that hot bullet gave a new impetus also. He ran down the slope at a great speed now, and he had calculated craftily. He could descend nearly twice as fast as they could ascend, and while they were reaching the crest he would put a wide gap between them.

He kept well in the shadow now as he made with long leaps straight toward the hollow, and he hoped with every heart beat that Albert, aroused by the shots, would be awake and ready. "Albert!" he cried, when he was within twenty feet of their camp, and his hope was rewarded. Albert was up, rifle in hand, crying:

"What is it, Dick?"

"The Sioux!" exclaimed Dick. "They're not far away! You heard the shots! Come!"

He turned off at an angle and ran in a parallel line along the slope, Albert by his side. He wished to keep to the forests and thickets, knowing they would have little chance of escape on the plain. As they ran he told Albert, in short, choppy sentences, what had happened.

"I don't hear anything," said Albert, after ten minutes. "Maybe they've lost us."

"No such good luck! Those curs of theirs would lead them. No, Al, we've got to keep straight on as long as we can!"

Albert stumbled on a rock, but, quickly recovering himself, put greater speed in every jump, when he heard the Indian shout behind him.

"We've got to shoot their dogs," said Dick. "We'll have no other chance to shake them off."

"If we get a chance," replied Albert.

But they did not see any chance just yet. They heard the occasional howl of a cur, but both curs and Indians remained invisible. Yet Dick felt that the pursuers were gaining. They were numerous, and they could spread. Every time he and Albert diverged from a straight line—and they could not help doing so now and then—some portion of the pursuing body came nearer. It was the advantage that the many had over the few.

Dick prayed for darkness, a shading of the moon, but it did not come, and five minutes later he saw the yellow form of a cur emerge into an open space. He took a shot at it and heard a howl. He did not know whether he had killed the dog or not, but he hoped he had succeeded. The shot brought forth a cry to their right, and then another to the left. It was obvious that the Sioux, besides being behind them, were also on either side of them. They were gasping, too, from their long run, and knew that they could not continue much farther.

"We can't shake them off, Al," said Dick, "and we'll have to fight. This is as good a place as any other."

They dropped down into a rocky hollow, a depression not more than a foot deep, and lay on their faces, gasping for breath. Despite the deadly danger Dick felt a certain relief that he did not have to run any more—there comes a time when a moment's physical rest will overweigh any amount of mortal peril.

"If they've surrounded us, they're very quiet about it," said Albert, when the fresh air had flowed back into his lungs. "I don't see or hear anything at all."

"At least we don't hear those confounded dogs any more," said Dick. "Maybe there was only one pursuing us, and that shot of mine got him. The howls of the cur upset my nerves more than the shouts of the Sioux."

"Maybe so," said Albert.

Then they were both quite still. The moonlight was silvery clear, and they could see pines, oaks, and cedars waving in a gentle wind, but they saw nothing else. Yet Dick was well aware that the Sioux had not abandoned the chase; they knew well where the boys lay, and were all about them in the woods.

"Keep close, Albert," he said. "Indians are sly, and the Sioux are the slyest of them all. They're only waiting until one of us pops up his head, thinking they're gone."

Albert took Dick's advice, but so long a time passed without sign from the Sioux that he began to believe that, in some mysterious manner, they had evaded the savages. The belief had grown almost into a certainty, when there was a flash and a report from a point higher up the slope. Albert felt something hot and stinging in his face. But it was only a tiny fragment of rock chipped off by the bullet as it passed.

Both Dick and Albert lay closer, as if they would press themselves into the earth, and soon two or three more shots were fired. All came from points higher up the slope, and none hit a living target, though they struck unpleasantly close.

"I wish I could see something," exclaimed Albert impatiently. "It's not pleasant to be shot at and to get no shot in return."

Dick did not answer. He was watching a point among some scrub pines higher up the slope, where the boughs seemed to him to be waving too much for the slight wind. Looking intently, he thought he saw a patch of brown through the evergreen, and he fired at it. A faint cry followed the shot, and Dick felt a strange satisfaction; they were hunting him— well, he had given a blow in return.

Silence settled down again after Dick's shot. The boys lay perfectly still, although they could hear each other's breathing. The silvery moonlight seemed to grow fuller and clearer all the time. It flooded the whole slope. Boughs and twigs were sheathed in it. Apparently, the moon looked down upon a scene that was all peace and without the presence of a human being.

"Do you think they'll rush us?" whispered Albert.

"No," replied Dick. "I've always heard that the Indian takes as little risk as he possibly can."

They waited a little longer, and then came a flare of rifle shots from a point farther up the slope. Brown forms appeared faintly, and Dick and Albert, intent and eager, began to fire in reply. Bullets sang by their ears and clipped the stones around them, but their blood rose the higher and they fired faster and faster.

"We'll drive 'em back!" exclaimed Dick.

They did not hear the rapid patter of soft, light footsteps coming from another direction, until a half dozen Sioux were upon them. Then the firing in front ceased abruptly, and Dick and Albert whirled to meet their new foes.

It was too late. Dick saw Albert struggling in the grasp of two big warriors, and then saw and heard nothing more. He had received a heavy blow on the head from the butt of a rifle and became unconscious.

CHAPTER 15

The Indian Village

When Dick awoke from his second period of unconsciousness it was to awake, as he did from the first, under a roof, but not, as in the case of the first, under his own roof. He saw above him an immense sloping thatch of bark on poles, and his eyes, wandering lower, saw walls of bark, also fastened to poles. He himself was lying on a large rush mat, and beside the door of the great *tepee* sat two Sioux warriors cleaning their rifles.

Dick's gaze rested upon the warriors. Curiously, he felt at that time neither hostility nor apprehension. He rather admired them. They were fine, tall men, and their bare arms and legs were sinewy and powerful. Then he thought of Albert. He was nowhere to be seen, but from the shadow of the wall on his right came a tall figure, full of dignity and majesty. It was Bright Sun, who looked down at Dick with a gaze that expressed inquiry rather than anger.

"Why have you come here?" he asked.

Although Dick's head ached and he was a captive, the question made a faint appeal to his sense of humour.

"I didn't come," he replied; "I was brought."

Bright Sun smiled.

"That is true," he said, speaking the precise English of the schools, with every word enunciated distinctly. "You were brought, and by my warriors; but why were you upon these hills?"

"I give you the best answer I can, Bright Sun," replied Dick frankly; "I don't know. My brother and I were lost upon the plains, and we wandered here. Nor have I the remotest idea now where I am."

"You are in a village of the tribe of the Mendewahkanton Sioux, of the clan Queyata-oto-we," replied Bright Sun gravely, "the clan and tribe to which I belong. The Mendewahkantons are one of the first tribes of the Seven Fireplaces, or the Great Sioux Nation. But all are great—Mendewahkanton, Wahpeton, Sisseton, Yankton, Teton, Ogalala, and Hunkpapa—down to the last clan of every tribe."

He began with gravity and an even intonation, but his voice rose with pride at the last. Nothing of the white man's training was left to him but the slow, precise English. It was the Indian, the pride of his Indian race, that spoke. Dick recognized it and respected it.

"And this?" said Dick, looking around at the great house of bark and poles in which he lay.

"This," replied Bright Sun, pride again showing in this tone, "is the house of the Akitcita, our soldiers and policemen, the men between twenty and forty, the warriors of the first rank, who live here in common, and into whose house women and children may not enter. I have read in the books at your schools how the Spartan young men lived together as soldiers in a common house, eating rough food and doing the severest duty, and the whole world has long applauded. The Sioux, who never heard of the Spartans, have been doing the same far back into the shadowy time. We, too, are a race of warriors."

Dick looked with renewed interest at the extraordinary man before him, and an amazing suggestion found lodgement in his mind. Perhaps the Sioux chief thought himself not merely as good as the white man, but better, better than any other man except those of his own race. It was so surprising that Dick forgot for a moment the question that he was eagerly awaiting a chance to ask—where was his brother Albert?

"I've always heard that the Sioux were brave," said Dick vaguely, "and I know they are powerful."

"We are the Seven Fireplaces. What the Six Nations once were in the East, we now are in the West, save that we are far more numerous and powerful, and we will not be divided. We have leaders who see the truth and who know what to do."

The pride in his tone was tinged now with defiance, and Dick could but look at him in wonder. But his mind now came back to the anxious question: "Where is my brother Albert, who was taken with me? You have not killed him?"

"He has not been hurt, although we are at war with your people," replied Bright Sun. "He is here in the village, and he, like you, is safe for the present. Some of the warriors wished to kill both you and him, but I have learned wisdom in these matters from your people. Why throw away pawns that we hold? I keep your brother and you as hostages."

Dick, who had raised himself up in his eagerness, sank back again, relieved. He could feel that Bright Sun told the truth, and he had faith, too, in the man's power as well as his word. Yet there was another question that he wished to ask.

"Bright Sun," he said, "it was you, our guide, who led the train into the pass that all might be killed?"

Bright Sun shrugged his shoulders, but a spark leaped from his eyes.

"What would you ask of me?" he replied. "In your code it was cunning, but the few and small must fight with cunning. The little man, to confront the big man, needs the advantage of weapons. The Sioux make the last stand for the Indian race, and we strike when and where we can."

The conscience of the chief was clear, so far as Dick could see, and there was nothing that he could say in reply. It was Bright Sun himself who resumed:

"But I spared you and your brother. I did that which caused you to be absent when the others were slain."

"Why?"

"Because you were different. You were not like the others. It may be that I pitied you, and it may be also that I like you—a little—and—you were young."

The man's face bore no more expression than carven oak, but Dick was grateful.

"I thank you, Bright Sun," he said, "and I know that Albert thanks you, too."

Bright sun nodded, and then fixed an intent gaze upon Dick.

"You and your brother escaped," he said. "That was nearly two years ago, and you have not gone back to your people. Where have you been?"

Dick saw a deep curiosity lurking behind the intent gaze, but whatever he might owe to Bright Sun, he had no intention of gratifying it.

"Would you tell me where you have been in the last two years and all that you have done?" the chief asked.

"I cannot answer; but you see that we have lived, Albert and I," Dick replied.

"And that you have learned the virtues of silence," said Bright Sun. "I ask you no more about it today. Give me your word for the present that you will not try to escape, and your life and that of your brother will be the easier. It would be useless, anyhow, for you to make such an attempt. When you feel that you have a chance, you can withdraw your promise."

Dick laughed, and the laugh was one of genuine good humour.

"That's certainly fair," he said. "Since I can't escape, I might as well give my promise not to try it for the time being. Well, I give it."

Bright Sun nodded gravely.

"Your brother will come in soon," he said. "He has already given his promise, that is, a conditional one, good until he can confer with you."

"I'll confirm it," said Dick.

Bright Sun saluted and left the great lodge. Some warriors near the door moved aside with the greatest deference to let him pass. Dick lay on his rush mat, gazing after him, and deeply impressed.

When Bright Sun was gone he examined the lodge again. It was obvious that it was a great common hall or barracks for warriors, and Bright Sun's simile of the Spartans was correct. More warriors came in, all splendid, athletic young men of a high and confident bearing. A few were dressed in the white man's costume, but most of them were in blankets, leggings, and moccasins, and had magnificent rows of feathers in their hair. Every man carried a carbine, and most of them had revolvers also. Such were the Akitcita or chosen band, and in this village of about two hundred lodges they numbered sixty men. Dick did not know then that in times of peace all guests, whether white or red, were entertained in the lodge of the Akitcita.

Impressed as he had been by Bright Sun, he was impressed also by these warriors. Not one of them spoke to him or annoyed him in any manner. They went about their tasks, cleaning and polishing their weapons, or sitting on rough wooden benches, smoking pipes with a certain dignity that belonged to men of strength and courage. All around the lodge were rush mats, on which they slept, and near the door was a carved totem pole.

A form darkened the doorway, and Albert came in. He rushed to Dick when he saw that he was conscious again, and shook his hand with great fervour. The warriors went on with their tasks or their smoking, and still took no notice.

"This is a most wonderful place, Dick," exclaimed the impressionable Albert, "and Bright Sun has treated us well. We can go about the village if we give a promise, for the time, that we'll not try to escape."

"He's been here," said Dick, "and I've given it."

"Then, if you feel strong enough, let's go on and take a look."

"Wait until I see if this head of mine swims around," said Dick.

He rose slowly to his feet, and his bandaged head was dizzy at first, but as he steadied himself it became normal. Albert thrust out his hand to support him. It delighted him that he could be again of help to his older and bigger brother, and Dick, divining Albert's feeling, let it lie for a minute. Then they went to the door, Dick walking quite easily, as his strength came back fast.

The warriors of the Akitcita, of whom fully a dozen were now present in the great lodge, still paid no attention to the two youths, and Dick surmised that it was the orders of Bright Sun. But this absolute ignoring of their existence was uncanny, nevertheless. Dick studies some of the faces as he passed. Bold and fearless they were, and not without a certain nobility, but there was little touch of gentleness or pity, it was rather the strength of the wild animal, the flesh-eater, that seeks its prey. Sioux they were, and Sioux they would remain in heart, no matter what happened, wild warriors of the northwest. Dick perceived this fact in a lightening flash, but it was the lightening flash of conviction.

Outside the fresh air saluted Dick, mouth and nostrils, and the ache in his head went quite away. He had seen the valley by moonlight, when it was beautiful, but not as beautiful as their own valley, the one of which they would not tell to anybody. But it was full of interest. The village life, the life of the wild, was in progress all about him, and in the sunshine, amidst such picturesque surroundings, it had much that was attractive to the strong and brave.

Dick judged correctly that the village contained about two hundred winter lodges of bark and poles, and could therefore furnish about four hundred warriors. It was evident, too, that it was the scene of prosperity. The flesh of buffalo, elk, and deer was drying in the sun, hanging from trees or on little platforms of poles. Children played with the dogs or practiced with small bows and arrows. In the shadow of a tepee six old women sat gambling, and the two boys stopped to watch them.

The Indians are more inveterate gamblers than the whites, and the old women, wrinkled, hideous hags of vast age, played their games with an intent, almost breathless, interest.

They were playing *Woskate Tanpan*, or the game of dice, as it is known to the Sioux. Three women were on each side, and they played it with *tanpan* (the basket), *kansu* (the dice), and *canyiwawa* (the counting sticks). The *tanpan*, made of willow twigs, was a tiny basket, about three inches in diameter at the bottom, but broader at the top, and about two inches deep. Into this one woman would put the *kansu* or dice, a set of six plum stones, some carved and some not carved. She would put her hand over the *tanpan*, shake the *kansu* just as the white dice player does, and then throw them out. The value of the throw would be according to the kind and number of carvings that were turned up when the *kansu* fell.

The opposing sides, three each, sat facing each other, and the stakes for which they played—*canyiwawa* (the counting sticks)—lay between them. These were little round sticks about the thickness of a lead pencil, and the size of each heap went up or down, as fortune shifted back or forth. They could make the counting sticks represent whatever value they chose, this being agreed upon beforehand, and the old Sioux women had been known to play *Woskate Tanpan* two days and nights without ever rising from their seats.

"What old harpies they are!" said Dick. "Did you ever see anybody so eager over anything?"

"They are no worse than the men," replied Albert. "A lot of warriors are gambling, too."

A group of the men were gathered on a little green farther on, and the brothers joined them, beginning to share at once the interest that the spectators showed in several warriors who were playing *Woskate Pain-yankapi*, or the game of the Wands and the Hoop.

The warriors used in the sport *canyleska* (the hoop) and *cansakala* (the wands). The hoops were of ash, two or three feet in diameter, the ash itself being about an inch in diameter. Every hoop was carefully marked off into spaces, something like the face of a watch.

Cansakala (the wands) were of chokecherry, four feet long and three fourths of an inch in diameter. One end of every wand was squared for a distance of about a foot. The wands were in pairs, the two being fastened together with buckskin thongs about nine inches in length, and fastened at a point about one third of the length of the wands from the rounded ends. A warrior would roll the hoop, and he was required to roll it straight and correctly. If he did not do so, the umpire made him roll it over, as in the white man's game of baseball the pitcher cannot get a strike until he pitches the ball right.

When the hoop was rolled correctly, the opposing player dropped his pair of wands somewhere in front of it. It was his object so to calculate the speed and course of the hoop when it fell it would lie upon his wands. If he succeeded, he secured his points according to the spaces on each wand within which the hoop lay—an exceedingly difficult game, requiring great skill of hand and judgment of eye. That if was absorbing was shown by the great interest with which all the spectators followed it and by their eager betting.

"I don't believe I could learn to do that in ten years," said Albert; "you've got to combine too many things and to combine them fast."

"They must begin on it while they're young," said Dick; "but the Indian has a mind, and don't you forget it."

"But they're not as we are," rejoined Albert. "Nothing can ever make them so."

Here, as in the house of the Akitcita, nobody paid any attention to the two boys, but Dick began to have a feeling that he was watched, not watched openly as man watches man, but in the furtive dangerous way of the great wild beasts, the man-eaters. The feeling grew into a conviction that, despite what they were doing, everybody in the camp—warrior, squaw, and child—was watching Albert and him. He knew that half of this was fancy, but he was sure that the other half was real.

"Albert," he said, "I wouldn't make any break for liberty now, even if I hadn't given my promise."

"Nor I," said Albert. "By the time we had gone ten feet the whole village would be on top of us. Dick, while I'm here I'm going to make the best of it I can."

In pursuance of this worthy intention Albert pressed forward and almost took the *cansakala* from the hands of a stalwart warrior. The man, amazed at first, yielded up the pair of wands with a grin. Albert signalled imperiously to the warrior with the hoop, and he, too, grinning, sent *canyleska* whirling.

Albert cast the wands, and the hoop fell many feet from them. A shout of laughter arose. The white youth was showing himself a poor match for the Sioux, and the women and children came running to see this proof of the superiority of their race.

The warrior from whom he had taken them gravely picked up the *cansakala* and handed them back to Albert, the other warrior again sent *canyleska* rolling, and again Albert threw the wands with the same ill fortune. A third and fourth time he tried, with but slight improvement, and the crowd, well pleased to see him fail, thickened all the time, until nearly the whole village was present.

"It's just as hard as we thought it was, Dick, and harder," said Albert ruefully. "Here, you take it and see what you can do."

He handed *cansakala* to Dick, who also tried in vain, while the crowd enjoyed the sport, laughing and chatting to one another, as they will in their own villages. Dick made a little more progress than Albert had achieved, but not enough to score any points worth mentioning, and he, too, retired discomfited, while the Sioux, especially the women, continued to laugh.

"I don't like to be beaten that way," said Albert in a nettled tone.

"Never mind, Al, old fellow," said Dick soothingly. "Remember it's their game, not ours, and as it makes them feel good, it's all the better for us. Since they've beaten us, they're apt to like us and treat us better."

It was hard for Albert to take the more philosophical view, which was also the truthful one, but he did his best to reconcile himself, and he and Dick moved on to other sights.

Dick noticed that the village had been located with great judgment. On one side was the river, narrow but swift and deep; on the other, a broad open space that would not permit an enemy to approach through ambush, and beyond that the forest.

The *tepees* stood in a great circle, and, although Dick did not know it, their camps were always pitched according to rule, each gens or clan having its regular place in the circle. The tribe of the Mendewahkantons—a leading one of the Seven Fireplaces or Council Fires of the great Sioux nation—was subdivided into seven *gentes* or clans; the *Kiyukas*, or Breakers, so called because they disregarded the general marriage law and married outside their own clan; the Que-mini-tea, or Mountain Wood and Water people; the Kap'oja, or Light Travellers; the Maxa-yuta-cui, the

People who Eat no Grease; the Queyata-oto-we, or the People of the Village Back from the River; the Oyata Citca, the Bad Nation, and the Tita-otowe, the People of the Village on the Prairie.

Each clan was composed of related families, and all this great tribe, as the boys learned later, had once dwelled around Spirit Lake, Minnesota, their name meaning Mysterious Lake Dwellers, but had been pushed westward years before by the advancing wave of white settlement. This was now a composite village, including parts of every gens of the Mendewahkantons, but there were other villages of the same tribe scattered over a large area.

When Dick and Albert reached the northern end of the village they saw a great number of Indian ponies, six or seven hundred perhaps, grazing in a wide grassy space and guarded by half-grown Indian boys.

"Dick," said Albert, "if we only had a dozen of those we could go back and get our furs."

"Yes," said Dick, "if we had the ponies, if we knew where we are now, if we were free of the Sioux village, and if we could find the way to our valley, we might do what you say."

"Yes, it does take a pile of 'ifs,'" said Albert, laughing, "and so I won't expect it. I'll try to be resigned."

So free were they from any immediate restriction that it almost seemed to them that they could walk away as they chose, up the valley and over the hills and across the plains. How were the Sioux to know that these two would keep their promised word? But both became conscious again of those watchful eyes, ferocious, like the eyes of man-eating wild beasts, and both shivered a little as they turned back into the great circle of bark *teepees*.

CHAPTER 16

The Gathering of the Sioux

Dick and Albert abode nearly two weeks in the great lodge of the Akitcita, that is, as guests, although they were prisoners, whose lives might be taken at any time, and they had splendid opportunities for observing what a genuine Spartan band the Akitcita were. Everyone had his appointed place for arms and his rush or fur mat for sleeping. There was no quarrelling, no unseemly chatter, always a grave and dignified order and the sense of stern discipline. Not all the Akitcita were ever present in the daytime, but some always were. All tribal business was transacted here. The women had to bring wood and water to it daily, and the entire village supplied it every day with regular rations of tobacco, almost the only luxury of the Akitcita.

Both Dick and Albert were keenly observant, and they did not hesitate also to ask questions of Bright Sun whenever they had the chance. They learned from him that the different tribes of the Sioux had general councils at irregular intervals, that there was no hereditary rank among the chiefs, it being usually a question of energy and merit, although the rank was sometimes obtained by gifts, and ambitious man giving away all that he had for the prize. There were no women chiefs, and women were not admitted to the great council.

The boys perceived, too, that much in the life of the Sioux was governed by ancient ritual; nearly everything had its religious meaning, and both boys having an inherent respect for religion of any kind, were in constant fear lest they should violate unwillingly some honoured law.

The two made friendly advances to the members of the Akitcita but they were received with a grave courtesy that did not invite a continuance. They felt daily a deepening sense of racial difference. They appreciated the humane treatment they had received, but they and the Sioux did not seem to come into touch anywhere. And this difference was accentuated in the case of Bright Sun. The very fact that he had been educated in their schools, that he spoke their language so well, and that he knew their customs seemed to widen the gulf between them into a sea. They felt that he had tasted of their life, and liked it not.

The two, although they could not like Bright Sun, began to have a certain deference for him. The old sense of power he had created in their minds increased greatly, and now it was not merely a matter of mind and manner; all the outward signs, the obvious respect in which he was held by everybody and the way in which the eyes of the warriors, as well as those of women and children, followed him, showed that he was a great leader.

After ten days or so in the great lodge of the Akitcita, Dick and Albert were removed to a small bark *tepee* of their own, to which they were content to go. They had no arms, not even a knife, but they were already used to their captivity, and however great their ultimate danger might be, it was far away for them to think much about it.

They observed, soon after their removal, that the life of the village changed greatly. The old women were not often to be found in the shadow of the lodges playing *Woskate Tanpan*, the men gave up wholly *Woskate Painyankapi*, and throughout the village, no matter how stoical the Sioux might be, there was a perceptible air of excitement and suspense. Often at night the boys heard the rolling of the Sioux war drums, and the medicine men made medicine incessantly inside their *tepees*. Dick chafed greatly.

"Big things are afoot," he would say to Albert. "We know that the Sioux and our people are at war, but you and I, Al, don't know a single thing that has occurred. I wish we could get away from here. Our people are our own people, and I'd like to tell them to look out."

"I feel just as you do, Dick," Albert would reply; "but we might recall our promise to Bright Sun. Besides, we wouldn't have the ghost of a chance to escape. I feel that a hundred eyes are looking at me all the time."

"I feel that two hundred are looking at me," said Dick, with a grim little laugh. "No, Al, you're right. We haven't a chance on earth to escape."

Five days after their removal to the small lodge there was a sudden and great increase in the excitement in the village. In truth, it burst into a wild elation, and all the women and children, running toward the northern side of the village, began to shout cries of welcome. The warriors followed more sedately, and Dick and Albert, no one detaining them, joined in the throng.

"Somebody's coming, Al, that's sure," said Dick.

"Yes, and that somebody's a lot of men," said Albert. "Look!"

Three or four hundred warriors, a long line of them, were coming down the valley, tall, strong, silent men, with brilliant headdresses of feathers and bright blankets. Everyone carried a carbine or rifle, and they looked what they were—a truly formidable band, resolved upon some great attempt.

Dick and Albert inferred the character of the arrivals from the shouts that they heard the squaws and children utter: "Sisseton!"

"Wahpeton!"

"Ogalala!"

"Yankton!"

"Teton!"

"Hunkpapa!"

The arriving warriors, many of whom were undoubtedly chiefs, gravely nodded to their welcome, and came silently on as the admiring crowd opened to receive them.

"It's my opinion," said Dick, "that the Seven Fireplaces are about to hold a grand council in the lodge of the Akitcita."

"I don't think there's any doubt about it," replied Albert.

They also heard, amidst the names of the tribes, the names of great warriors or medicine men, names which they were destined to hear many times again, both in Indian and English—Sitting Bull, Rain-in-the-Face, Little Big Man, and others. Then they meant nothing to either Dick or Albert.

All the chiefs, led by Bright Sun, went directly to the lodge of the Akitcita, and the other warriors were taken into the lodges of their friends, the Mendewahkantons. Then the women ran to the lodges and returned with the best food that the village could furnish. It was given to the guests, and also many pounds of choice tobacco.

Dick and Albert had made no mistake in their surmise. The great council of the Seven Fireplaces of the Sioux was in session. All that day the chiefs remained in the lodge of the Akitcita, and when night was far advanced they were still there.

Dick and Albert shared the excitement of the village, although knowing far less of its nature, but they knew that a grand council of the Seven Fireplaces would not be held without great cause, and they feared much for their people. It was a warm, close night, with a thin moon and flashes of heat lightening on the hilly horizon. Through the heavy air came the monotonous rolling of a war drum, and the chant of a medicine man making medicine in a *tepee* near by went on without ceasing.

The boys did not try to sleep, and unable to stifle curiosity, they came from the little bark lodge. One or two Sioux warriors glanced at them, but none spoke. The Sioux knew that the village was guarded so closely by a ring of sentinels that a cat could not have crept through without being seen. The boys walked on undisturbed until they came near the great council lodge, where they stopped to look at the armed warriors standing by the door.

The dim light and the excited imaginations of the boys made the lodge grow in size and assume fantastic shapes. So many great chiefs had come together for a mighty purpose, and Dick was sure that Bright Sun, sitting in the ring of his equals, urged on the project, whatever it might be, and would be the dominating figure through all.

Although they saw nothing, they were fascinated by what they wished to see. The great lodge held them with a spell that they did not seek to break. Although it was past midnight, they stayed there, staring at the blank walls. Warriors passed and gave them sharp glances, but nothing was said to them. The air remained close and heavy. Heat lightening continued to flare on the distant hills, but no rain fell.

The chiefs finally came forth from the great council. There was no light for them save the cloudy skies and one smoking torch that a warrior held aloft, but the active imagination of the two boys were again impressed. Every chief seemed to show in his face and manner his pride of race and the savage strength that well became such a time and place. Some bore themselves more haughtily and were more brilliantly adorned than Bright Sun, but he was still the magnet from which power and influence streamed. Dick and Albert did not know why they knew it, but they knew it.

The chiefs did not go away to friendly lodges, but after they came forth remained in a group, talking. Dick surmised that they had come to an agreement upon whatever question they debated; now they were outside for fresh air, and soon would return to the lodge of the Akitcita, which, according to custom, would shelter them as guests.

Bright Sun noticed the brothers standing in the shadow of the lodge, and, leaving the group, he walked over to them. His manner did not express hostility, but he made upon both boys that old impression of power and confidence, tinged now with a certain exultation.

"You would know what we have been doing?" he said, speaking directly to Dick, the older.

"We don't ask," replied Dick, "but I will say this, Bright Sun: we believe that the thing done was the thing you wished."

Bright Sun permitted himself a little smile.

"You have learned to flatter," he said.

"It was not meant as flattery," said Dick; "but there is something more I have to say. We wish to withdraw our pledge not to attempt to escape. You remember it was in the agreement we could withdraw whenever we chose."

"That is true," said Bright Sun, giving Dick a penetrating look. "And so you think that it is time for you to go?"

"We will go, if we can," said Dick boldly.

386

Bright Sun, who had permitted himself a smile a little while ago, now permitted himself a soft laugh.

"You put it well," he said in his precise English, "'if we can.' But the understanding is clear. The agreement is at an end. However, you will not escape. We need you as hostages, and I will tell you, too, that we leave this village and valley tomorrow. We begin a great march."

"I am not surprised," said Dick.

Bright Sun rejoined the other chiefs, and all of them went back into the lodge of the Akitcita, while Dick and Albert returned to their own little *tepee*. There, as each lay on his rush mat, they talked in whispers.

"What meaning do you give to it, Dick?" asked Albert.

"That all the Sioux tribes are going to make a mighty effort against our people, and they're going to make it soon. Why else are they holding this great council of the Seven Fireplaces? I tell you, Al, big things are afoot. Oh, if we could only find a chance to get away!"

Albert rolled over to the door of the lodge and peeped out. Several warriors were pacing up and down in front of the rows of *tepees*. He rolled back to his rush mat.

"They've got inside as well as outside guards now," he whispered.

"I thought it likely," Dick whispered back. "Al, the best thing that you and I can do now is to go to sleep."

They finally achieved slumber, but were up early the next morning and saw Bright Sun's words come true. The village was dismantled with extraordinary rapidity. Most of the lighter lodges were taken down, but how much of the place was left, and what people were left with it, the boys did not know, because they departed with the warriors, each riding a bridleless pony. Although mounted, their chance of escape was not increased. Warriors were all about them, they were unarmed, and their ponies, uncontrolled by bridles, could not be made to leave their comrades.

Dick and Albert, nevertheless, found an interest in this journey, wondering to what mysterious destination it would lead them. They heard behind them the chant of the old women driving the ponies that drew the baggage on poles, but the warriors around them were silent. Bright Sun was not visible. Dick surmised that he was at the head of the column.

The clouds of the preceding night had gone away, and the day was cooler, although it was now summer, and both Dick and Albert found a certain pleasure in the journey. In their present of suspense any change was welcome.

They rode straight up the valley, a long and formidable procession, and as they went northward the depression became both shallower and narrower. Finally, they crossed the river at a rather deep ford and rode directly ahead. Soon the hills and the forest that clothed them sank out of sight, and Dick and Albert were once again in the midst of the rolling immensity of the plains. They could judge the point of the compass by the sun, but they knew nothing else of the country over which they travelled. They tried two or three times to open conversation with the warriors about them, trusting that the latter knew English, but they received no reply and gave up the attempt.

"At any rate, I can talk to you, Al," said Dick after the last futile attempt.

"Yes, but you can't get any information out of me," replied Albert with a laugh.

The procession moved on, straight as an arrow, over the swells, turning aside for nothing. Some buffaloes were seen on the horizon, but they were permitted to crop the bunch grass undisturbed. No Indian hunter left the ranks.

They camped that night on the open prairie, Dick and Albert sleeping in their blankets in the centre of the savage group. It might have seemed to the ordinary observer that there was looseness and disorder about the camp, but Dick was experienced enough to know that all the Mendewahkantons were posted in the circle according to their clans, and that the delegates were distributed with them in places of honour.

Dick noticed, also, that no fires were built, and that the warriors had scrutinized the entire circle of the horizon with uncommon care. It could signify but one thing to him—white people, and perhaps white troops, were near. If so, he prayed that they were in sufficient force. He was awakened in the night by voices, and raising himself on his elbow he saw a group of men, at least a hundred in number, riding into the camp.

The latest arrivals were Sioux warriors, but of what tribe he could not tell. Yet it was always the Sioux who were coming, and it would have been obvious to the least observant that Dick's foreboding about a mighty movement was right. They were joined the next day by another detachment coming from the southwest, and rode on, full seven hundred warriors, every man armed with the white man's weapons, carbine or rifle and revolver.

"I pity any poor emigrants whom they may meet," thought Dick; but, fortunately, they met none. The swelling host continued its march a second day, a third, and a fourth through sunshiny weather, increasing in warmth, and over country that changed but little. Dick and Albert saw Bright Sun only once or twice, but he had nothing to say to them. The others, too, maintained their impenetrable silence, although they never offered any ill treatment.

They were joined every day by bands of warriors, sometimes not more than two or three at a time, and again as many as twenty. They came from all points of the compass, but, so far as Dick and Albert could see, little was said on their arrival. Everything was understood. They came as if in answer to a call, took their places without ado in the savage army, and rode silently on. Dick saw a great will at work, and with it a great discipline. A master mind had provided for all things.

"Al," he said to his brother, "you and I are not in the plan at all. We've been out of the world two years, and we're just that many years behind."

"I know it's 1876," said Albert, with some confidence, but he added in confession: "I've no idea what month it is, although it must be somewhere near summer."

"About the beginning of June, I should think," said Dick.

An hour after this little talk the country became more hilly, and presently they saw trees and high bluffs to their right. Both boys understood the signs. They were approaching a river, and possibly their destination.

"I've a feeling," said Dick, "that we're going to stop now. The warriors look as if they were getting ready for a rest."

He was quickly confirmed in his opinion by the appearance of mounted Indians galloping to meet them. These warriors showed no signs of fatigue or a long march, and it was now obvious that a village was near.

The new band greeted the force of Bright Sun with joy, and the stern silence was relaxed. There was much chattering and laughing, much asking and answering of questions, and soon Indian women and Indian boys, with little bows and arrows, came over the bluffs, and joining the great mounted force, followed on its flanks.

Dick and Albert were on ponies near the head of the column, and their troubles and dangers were forgotten in their eager interest in what they were about to see. The feeling that a first step in a great plan was accomplished was in the air. They could see it in the cessation of the Sioux reserve and in the joyous manner of the warriors, as well as the women. Even the ponies picked up their heads, as if they, too, saw rest.

The procession wound round the base of a hill, and then each boy uttered a little gasp. Before them lay a valley, about a mile wide, down the centre of which flowed a shallow yellow river fringed with trees and also with undergrowth, very dense in places. But it was neither the river nor trees that had drawn the little gasps from the two boys, it was an Indian village, or rather a great town, extending as far as they could see—and they saw far—on either side of the stream. There were hundreds and hundreds of lodges, and a vast scene of animated and varied life. Warriors, squaws, children, and dogs moved about; smoke rose from scores and scores of fires, and on grassy meadows grazed ponies, thousands in number.

"Why, I didn't think there was so big an Indian town in all the west!" exclaimed Albert.

389

"Nor did I," said Dick gravely, "and I'm thinking, Al, that it's gathered here for a purpose. It must be made up of all the Sioux tribes."

Albert nodded. He knew the thought in Dick's mind, and he believed it to be correct.

Chance so had it that Bright Sun at this moment rode near them and heard their words. Dick of late had surmised shrewdly that Bright Sun treated them well, not alone for the sake of their value as hostages, but for a reason personal to himself. He had been associated long with white people in their schools, but he was at heart and in fact a great Sioux chief; he had felt the white man's assumption of racial superiority, and he would have these two with the white faces witness some great triumph that he intended to achieve over these same white people. This belief was growing on Dick, and it received more confirmation when Bright Sun said:

"You see that the Sioux nation has many warriors and is mighty."

"I see that it is so, Bright Sun," replied Dick frankly. "I did not know you were so numerous and so powerful; but bear in mind, Bright Sun, that no matter how many the Sioux may be, the white men are like the leaves of the tree—thousands, tens of thousands may fall, and yet only their own kin miss them."

But Bright Sun shook his head.

"What you say is true," he said, "because I have seen and I know; but they are not here. The mountains, the plains, the wilderness keep them back."

Dick forbore a retort, because he felt that he owed Bright Sun something, and the chief seemed to take it for granted that he was silenced by logic.

"This is the Little Big Horn River," Bright Sun said, "and you behold now in this village, which extends five miles on either side of it, the Seven Fireplaces of the Sioux. All tribes are gathered here."

"And it is you who have gathered them," said Dick. He was looking straight into Bright Sun's eyes as he spoke, and he saw the pupils of the Sioux expand, in fact dilate, with a sudden overwhelming sense of power and triumph. Dick knew he had guessed aright, but the Sioux replied with restraint:

"If I have had some small part in the doing of it, I feel proud."

With that he left them, and Dick and Albert rode on into the valley of the river, in whatsoever direction their bridleless horses might carry them, although that direction was bound to be the one in which rode the group surrounding them.

Some of the squaws and boys, who caught sight of Dick and Albert among the warriors, began to shout and jeer, but a chief sternly bade them to be silent, and they slunk away, to the great relief of the two lads, who had little relish for such attention.

They were full in the valley now, and on one side of them was thick undergrowth that spread to the edge of the river. A few hundred yards father the undergrowth ceased, sand taking its place. All the warriors turned their ponies abruptly away from one particular stretch of sand, and Dick understood.

"It's a quicksand, Al," he said; "it would suck up pony, rider, and all."

They left the quicksand behind and entered the village, passing among the groups of lodges. Here they realized more fully than on the hills the great extent of the Indian town. Its inhabitants seemed a myriad to Dick and Albert, so long used to silence and the lack of numbers.

"How many warriors do you suppose this place could turn out, Dick?" asked Albert.

"Five thousand, but that's only a guess. It doesn't look much like our own valley, does it, Al?"

"No, it doesn't," replied Albert with emphasis; "and I can tell you, Dick, I wish I was back there right now. I believe that's the finest valley the sun ever shone on."

"But we had to leave sometime or other," said Dick, "and how could we tell that we were going to run into anything like this? But it's surely a big change for us."

"The biggest in the world."

The group in which they rode continued along the river about two miles, and then stopped at a point where both valley and village were widest. A young warrior, speaking crude English, roughly bade them dismount, and gladly they sprang from the ponies. Albert fell over when he struck the ground, his legs were cramped so much by the long ride, but the circulation was soon restored, and he and Dick went without resistance to the lodge that was pointed out to them as their temporary home and prison.

It was a small lodge of poles leaning toward a common centre at the top, there lashed together firmly with rawhide, and the whole covered with skins. It contained only two rude mats, two bowls of Sioux pottery, and a drinking gourd, but it was welcome to Dick and Albert, who wanted rest and at the same time security from the fierce old squaws and the equally fierce young boys. They were glad enough to lie a while on the rush mats and rub their tired limbs. When they were fully rested they became very hungry.

"I wonder if they mean to starve us to death?" said Albert.

A negative answer was given in about ten minutes by two old squaws who appeared, bearing food, some venison, and more particularly *wa-nsa*, a favourite dish with the Sioux, a compound made of buffalo meat and wild cherries, which, after being dried, are pounded separately until they are very fine; then the two are pounded together for quite a while, after which the whole is stored in bladders, somewhat after the fashion of the white man's sausage.

"This isn't bad at all," said Albert when he bit into his portion. "Now, if we only had something good to drink."

Neither of the old squaws understood his words, but one of them answered his wish, nevertheless. She brought cherry-bark tea in abundance, which both found greatly to their liking and they ate and drank with deep content. A mental cheer was added also to their physical good feeling.

"Thanks, madam," said Albert, when one of the old squaws refilled the little earthen bowl from which he drank the cherry-bark tea. "You are indeed kind. I did not expect to meet with such hospitality."

The Indian woman did not understand his words, but anybody could understand the boy's ingratiating smile. She smiled back at him.

"Be careful, Al, old man," said Dick with the utmost gravity. "These old Indian women adopt children sometimes, or perhaps she will want to marry you. In fact, I think the latter is more likely, and you can't help yourself."

"Don't, Dick, don't!" said Albert imploringly. "I am willing to pay a high price for hospitality, but not that."

The women withdrew, and after a while, when the boys felt fully rested, they stepped outside the lodge, to find two tall young Sioux warriors on guard. Dick looked at them inquiringly, and one of them said in fair English:

"I am Lone Wolf, and this is Tall Pine. You can go in the village, but we go with you. Bright Sun has said so, and we obey."

"All right, Mr. Lone Wolf," said Dick cheerfully. "Four are company, two are none. We couldn't escape if we tried; but Bright Sun says that you and your friend Mr. Pine Tree are to be our comrades on our travels, well and good. I don't know any other couple in this camp that I'd choose before you two."

Lone Wolf and Pine Tree were young, and maybe their youth caused them to smile slightly at Dick's pleasantry. Nor did they annoy the boys with excessive vigilance, and they answered many questions. It was, indeed, they said, the greatest village in the West that was now gathered on the banks of the Little Big Horn. Sioux from all tribes had come including those on reservations. All the clans of the Mendewahkantons, for instance, were represented on the reservations, but all of them were represented here, too.

It was a great war that was now going on, they said, and they had taken many white scalps, but they intimated that those they had taken were few in comparison with the number they would take. Dick asked them of their present purpose, but here they grew wary. The white soldiers might be near or they might be far, but the god of the Sioux was Wakantaka, the good spirit, and the god of the white man was Wakansica, the bad spirit.

Dick did not consider it worth while to argue with them. Indeed, he was in no position to do so. The history of the world in the last two years was a blank to him and Albert. But he observed throughout the vast encampment the same air of expectancy and excitement that had been noticeable in the smaller village. He also saw a group of warriors arrive, their ponies loaded with repeating rifles, carbines and revolvers. He surmised that they had been obtained from French-Canadian traders, and he knew well for what they were meant. Once again he made his silent prayer that if the white soldiers came they could come in great force.

Dick observed in the huge village all the signs of an abundant and easy life, according to Sioux standards. Throughout its confines kettles gave forth the odours pleasing to an Indian's nostrils. Boys broiled strips of venison on twigs before the fires. Squaws were jerking buffalo and deer meat in a hundred places, and strings of fish ready for the cooking hung before the lodges. Plenty showed everywhere.

Dick understood that if one were really a wild man, with all instincts of a wild man inherited through untold centuries of wild life, he could find no more pleasing sight than this great encampment abounding in the good things for wild men that the plains, hills, and water furnished. He saw it readily from the point of view of the Sioux and could appreciate their confidence.

Albert, who was a little ahead of Dick, peered between two lodges, and suddenly turned away with a ghastly face.

"What's the trouble, Al?" asked Dick.

"I saw a warrior passing on the other side of those lodges," replied Albert, "and he had something at his belt—the yellow hair of a white man, and there was blood on it."

"We have taken many scalps already," interrupted the young Sioux, Lone Wolf, some pride showing in his tone.

Both Dick and Albert shuddered and were silent. The gulf between these men and themselves widened again into quite a sea. Their thoughts could not touch those of the Sioux at any point.

"I think we'd better go back to our own lodge," said Dick.

"No," said Lone Wolf. "The great chief, Bright Sun, has commanded us when we return to bring you into his presence, and it is time for us to go to him."

"What does he want with us?" asked Albert.

"He knows, but I do not," replied Lone Wolf sententiously.

"Lead on," said Dick lightly. "Here, we go wherever we are invited."

They walked back a full mile, and Lone Wolf and Pine Tree led the way to a great lodge, evidently one used by the Akitcita, although Dick judged that in so great a village as this, which was certainly a fusion of many villages, there must be at least a dozen lodges of the Akitcita.

Lone Wolf and Pine Tree showed Dick and Albert into the door, but they themselves remained outside. The two boys paused just inside the door until their eyes became used to the half gloom of the place. Before them stood a dozen men, all great chiefs, and in the centre was Bright Sun, the dominating presence.

Despite their natural courage and hardihood and the wild life to which they had grown used, Dick and Albert were somewhat awed by the appearance of these men, every one of whom was of stern presence, looking every inch a warrior. They had discarded the last particle of white man's attire, keeping only the white man's weapons, the repeating rifle and revolver. Every one wore, more or less loosely folded about him, a robe of the buffalo, and in all cases the inner side of this robe was painted throughout in the most vivid manner with scenes from the hunt or warpath, chiefly those that had occurred in the life of the wearer. Many colours were used in these paintings, but mostly those of cardinal dyes, red and blue being favourites.

"These," said Bright Sun, speaking more directly to Dick, "are mighty chiefs of the Sioux Nation. This is Ta Sun Ke Ka-Kipapi-Hok'silan (Young-Man-Afraid-of-His-Horses)."

He nodded toward a tall warrior, who made a slight and grave inclination.

"I'd cut out at least half of that name," said Dick under his breath.

"And this," continued Bright Sun in his measured, precise English, "is Ite-Mogu'Ju (Rain-in-the-Face), and this Kun-Sun'ka (Crow Dog), and this Pizi (Gall), and this Peji (Grass)".

Thus he continued introducing them, giving to every one his long Indian appellation until all were named. The famous Sitting Bull (Tatanka Yotanka) was not present. Dick learned afterwards that he was at that very moment in his own *tepee* making medicine.

"What we wish to know," said Bright Sun—"and we have ways to make you tell us—is whether you saw the white troops before we took you?"

Dick shivered a little. He knew what Bright Sun meant by the phrase "we have ways to make you tell," and he knew also that Bright Sun would be merciless if mercy stood in the way of getting what he wished. No shred of the white man's training was now left about the Indian chief save the white man's speech.

"I have not seen a white man in two years," replied Dick, "nor has my brother. We told you the truth when you took us."

Bright Sun was silent for a space, regarding him with black eyes seeking to read every throb of his heart. Dick was conscious, too, that the similar gaze of all the others was upon him. But he did not flinch. Why should he? He had told the truth.

"Then I ask you again," said Bright Sun, "where have you been all this time?"

"I cannot tell you," replied Dick. "It is a place that we wish to keep secret. It is hidden far from here. But it is one to which no one else goes. I can say that much."

Rain-in-the-Face made an impatient movement, and said some words in the Sioux tongue. Dick feared it was a suggestion that he be put to the torture, and he was glad when Bright Sun shook his head.

"There are such places," said Bright Sun, "because the mountains are high and vast and but few people travel among them. It may be that he tells the truth."

"It is the truth. I swear it!" said Dick earnestly.

"Then why do you refuse to tell of this place?" asked Bright Sun.

"Because we wish to keep it for ourselves," replied Dick frankly.

The faintest trace of a smile was visible in Bright Sun's eyes.

"Wherever it may be it belongs to us," said the chief; "but I believe that you are telling the truth. Nor do I hesitate to tell you that we have asked these questions because we wish to learn all that we can. The soldiers of your people are advancing under the yellow-haired general, Custer, Terry, Gibbon, and others. They come in great force, but the Sioux, in greater force and more cunning will destroy them."

Dick was silent. He knew too little to make any reply to the statements of Bright Sun. Rain-in-the-Face and Crazy Horse spoke to Bright Sun, and they seemed to be urging something. But the chief again shook his head, and they, too, became silent. It was obvious to both boys that his influence was enormous.

"You can go," he said to Dick and Albert, and they gladly left the lodge. Outside, Lone Wolf and Pine Tree fell in on either side of them and escorted them to their own *tepee*, in front of which they stood guard while the boys slept that night.

CHAPTER 17

The Great Sun Dance

Dick and Albert remained in their *tepee* throughout the next morning, but in the afternoon they were allowed to go in the village a second time. Lone Wolf and Pine Tree, who had slept in the morning, were again their guards. Both saw at once that some great event was at hand. The excitement in the village had increased visibly, and a multitude was pouring toward a certain point, a wide, grassy plain beside the Little Big Horn. Lone Wolf and Pine Tree willingly took the captives with the crowd, and the two boys looked upon a sight which few white men have beheld in all its savage convulsions.

The wide, grassy space before them had been carefully chosen by the great medicine men of the nation, Sitting Bull at their head. Then the squaws had put up a great circular awning, like a circus tent, with part of the top cut out. This awning was over one hundred and fifty feet in diameter. After this, the medicine men had selected a small tree, which was cut down by a young, unmarried squaw. Then the tree, after it had been trimmed of all its branches and consecrated and prayed over by the medicine men, was erected in the centre of the enclosed space, rising from the ground to a height of about twenty feet.

To the top of the pole were fastened many long thongs of rawhide reaching nearly to the ground, and as Dick and Albert looked a swarm of young men in strange array, or rather lack of array, came forth from among the lodges and entered the enclosed space. Dick had some dim perception of what was about to occur, but Lone Wolf informed him definitely.

"The sun dance," he said. "Many youths are about to become great warriors."

The greatest of sun dances, a sun dance of the mighty allied Sioux tribes, was about to begin. Forward went the neophytes, every one clad only in a breechclout ornamented with beads, coloured horsehair and eagle feathers, and with horse tails attached to it, falling to the ground. But every square inch of the neophyte's skin was painted in vivid and fantastic colours. Even the nails on his fingers and toes were painted. Moreover, everyone had pushed two small sticks of tough wood under the skin on each side of the breast, and to those two sticks was fastened a rawhide cord, making a loop about ten inches long.

"What under the sun are those sticks and cords for?" asked Albert, shuddering.

"Wait and we'll see," replied Dick, who guessed too well their purpose, although he could not help but look.

The neophytes advanced, and every one tied one of the long rawhide thongs depending from the top of the pole to the loop of cord that hung from his breast. When all were ready they formed a great circle, somewhat after the fashion of the dancers around a Maypole, and outside of those formed another and greater circle of those already initiated.

A medicine man began to blow a small whistle made from the wing bone of an eagle, the sacred bird of the Sioux, and he never stopped blowing it for an instant. It gave forth a shrill, penetrating sound, that began after a while to work upon the nerves in a way that was almost unendurable to Dick and Albert.

At the first sound of the whistle the warriors began to dance around the pole, keeping time to the weird music. It was a hideous and frightful dance, like some cruel rite of a far-off time. The object was to tear the peg from the body, breaking by violence through the skin and flesh that held it, and this proved that the neophyte by his endurance of excessive pain was fit to become a great warrior.

But the pegs held fast for a long time, while the terrible, wailing cry of the whistle went on and on. Dick and Albert wanted to turn away—in fact, they had a violent impulse more than once to run from it—but the eyes of the Sioux were upon them, and they knew that they would consider them cowards if they could not bear to look upon that which others no older than themselves endured. There was also the incessant, terrible wailing of the whistle, which seemed to charm them and hold them.

The youths by and by began to pull loose from the thongs, and in some cases where it was evident that they would not be able to do so a medicine man would seize them by the shoulders and help pull. In no case did a dancer give up, although they often fell in a faint when loosed. Then they were carried away to be revived, but for three days and three nights not a single neophyte could touch food, water, or any other kind of drink. They were also compelled, as soon as they recovered a measurable degree of strength, to join the larger group and dance three days and nights around the neophytes, who successively took their places.

The whole sight, with the wailing of the whistle, the shouts of the dancers, the beat of their feet, and the hard, excited breathing of the thousands about them, became weird and uncanny. Dick felt as if some strange, deadly odour had mounted to his brain, and while he struggled between going and staying a new shout arose.

A fresh group of neophytes sprang into the enclosed place. Every one of these had the little sticks thrust through the upper point of the shoulder blade instead of the breast, while from the loop dangled a buffalo head. They danced violently until the weight of the head pulled the sticks loose, and then, like their brethren of the pole, joined the great ring of outside dancers when they were able.

The crowd of neophytes increased, as they gave way in turn to one another, and the thong about them thickened. Hundreds and hundreds of dancers whirled and jumped to the shrill, incessant blowing of the eagle-bone whistle. It seemed at times to the excited imaginations of Dick and Albert that the earth rocked to the mighty tread of the greatest of all sun dances. Indian stoicism was gone, perspiration streamed from dark faces, eyes became bloodshot as their owners danced with feverish vigour, savage shouts burst forth, and the demon dance grew wilder and wilder.

The tread of thousands of feet caused a fine, impalpable dust to rise from the earth beneath the grass and to permeate all the air, filling the eyes and nostrils of the dancers, heating their brains and causing them to see through a red mist. Some fell exhausted. If they were in the way, they were dragged to one side; if not, they lay where they fell, but in either case others took their places and the whirling multitude always increased in numbers.

As far as Dick and Albert could see the Sioux were dancing. There was a sea of tossing heads and a multitude of brown bodies shining with perspiration. Never for a moment did the shrill, monotonous, unceasing rhythm of the whistle cease to dominate the dance. It always rose above the beat of the dancers, it penetrated everything, ruled everything—this single, shrill note, like the chant of a snake charmer. It even showed its power over Dick and Albert. They felt their nerves throbbing to it in an unwilling response, and the dust and the vivid electric excitement of the dancers began to heat their own brains.

"Don't forget that we're white, Al! Don't forget it!" cried Dick.

"I'm trying not to forget it!" gasped Albert.

The sun, a lurid, red sun, went down behind the hills, and a twilight that seemed to Dick and Albert phantasmagorial and shot with red crept over the earth. But the dance did not abate in either vigour or excitement; rather it increased. In the twilight and the darkness that followed it assumed new aspects of the weird and uncanny. Despite the torches that flared up, the darkness was mainly in control. Now the dancers, whirling about the pole and straining on the cords, were seen plainly, and now they were only shadows, phantoms in the dusk.

Dick and Albert had moved but little for a long time; the wailing of the demon whistle held them; and they felt that there was a singular attraction, too, in this sight, which was barbarism and superstition pure and simple, yet not without its power. They were still standing there when the moon came out, throwing a veil of silver gauze over the dancers, the lodges, the surface of the river, and the hills, but it took nothing away from the ferocious aspect of the dance; it was still savagery, the custom of a remote, fierce, old world. Dick and Albert at last recovered somewhat; they threw off the power of the flute and the excited air that they breathed and began to assume again the position of mere spectators.

It was then that Bright Sun came upon them, and they noticed with astonishment that he, the product of the white schools and of years of white civilization, had been dancing, too. There was perspiration on his face, his breath was short and quick, and his eyes were red with excitement. He marked their surprise, and said:

"You think it strange that I, too, dance. You think all this barbarism and superstition, but it is not. It is the custom of my people, a custom that has the sanction of many centuries, and that is bred into our bone and blood. Therefore it is of use to us, and it is more fit than anything else to arouse us for the great crisis that we are to meet."

Neither Dick nor Albert made any reply. Both saw that the great deep of the Sioux chief's stoicism was for the moment broken up. He might never be so stirred again, but there was no doubt of it now, and they could see his side of it, too. It was his people and their customs against the white man, the stranger. The blood of a thousand years was speaking in him.

When he saw that they had no answer for him, Bright Sun left them and became engrossed once more with the dance, continually urging it forward, bringing on more neophytes, and increasing the excitement. Dick and Albert remained a while longer, looking on. Their guards, Lone Wolf and Pine Tree, still stood beside them. The two young warriors, true to their orders, had made no effort to join the dancers, but their nostrils were twitching and their eyes bloodshot. The revel called to them incessantly, but they could not go.

Dick felt at last that he had seen enough of so wild a scene. One could not longer endure the surcharged air, the wailing of the whistle, the shouts, the chants, and the beat of thousands of feet.

"Al," he said, "let's go back to our lodge, if our guards will let us, and try to sleep."

"The sooner the better," said Albert.

Lone Wolf and Pine Tree were willing enough, and Dick suspected that they would join the dance later. After Albert had gone in, he stood a moment at the door of the lodge and looked again upon this, the wildest and most extraordinary scene that he had yet beheld. It was late in the night and the centre of the sun dance was some distance from the lodge, but the shrill wailing of the whistle still reached him and the heavy tread of the dancers came in monotonous rhythm. "It's the greatest of all nightmares," he said to himself.

It was a long time before either Dick or Albert could sleep, and when Dick awoke at some vague hour between midnight and morning he was troubled by a shrill, wailing note that the drum of his ear. Then he remembered. The whistle! And after it came the rhythmic, monotonous beat of many feet, as steady and persistent as ever. The sun dance had never ceased for a moment, and he fell asleep again with the sounds of it still in his ear.

The dance, which was begun at the ripening of the wild sage, continued three days and nights without the stop of an instant. No food and no drink passed the lips of the neophytes, who danced throughout that time—if they fell they rose to dance again. Then at the appointed hour it all ceased, although every warrior's brain was at white heat and he was ready to go forth at once against a myriad enemies. It was as if everyone had drunk of some powerful and exciting Eastern drug.

The dance ended, they began to eat, and neither Dick nor Albert had ever before seen such eating. The cooking fires of the squaws rose throughout the entire five miles of the village. They had buffalo, deer, bear, antelope, and smaller game in abundance, and the warriors ate until they fell upon the ground, where the lay in a long stupor. The boys thought that many of them would surely die, but they came from their stupor unharmed and were ready for instant battle. There were many new warriors, too, because none had failed at the test, and all were eager to show their valour.

"It's like baiting a wild beast," said Dick. "There are five thousand ravening savages here, ready to fight anything, and tonight I'm going to try to escape."

"If you try, I try, too," said Albert.

"Of course," said Dick.

The village was resting from its emotional orgy, and the guard upon the two boys was relaxed somewhat. In fact, it seemed wholly unnecessary, as they were rimmed around by the vigilance of many thousand eyes. But, spurred by the cruel need, Dick resolved that they should try. Fortunately, the very next night was quite dark, and only a single Indian, Pine Tree, was on guard.

"It's tonight or never," whispered Dick to Albert within the shelter of the lodge. "They've never taken the trouble to bind us, and that gives us at least a fighting chance."

"When shall we slip out?"

"Not before about three in the morning. That is the most nearly silent hour, and if the heathenish curs let us alone we may get away."

Fortune seemed to favour the two. The moon did not come out, and the promise of a dark night was fulfilled. An unusual stillness was over the village. It seemed that everybody slept. Dick and Albert waited through long, long hours. Dick had nothing by which to reckon time, but he believed that he could calculate fairly well by guess, and once, when he thought it was fully midnight, he peeped out at the door of the lodge. Pine Tree was there, leasing against a sapling, but his attitude showed laziness and a lack of vigilance. It might be that, feeling little need of watching, he slept on his feet. Dick devoutly hoped so. He waited at least two hours longer, and again peeped out. The attitude of Pine Tree had not changed. It must certainly be sleep that held him, and Dick and Albert prepared to go forth. They had no arms, and could trust only to silence and speed.

Dick was the first outside, and stood in the shadow of the lodge until Albert joined him. There they paused to choose a way among the lodges and to make a further inspection of sleeping Pine Tree.

The quiet of the village was not broken. The lodges stretched away in dusky rows and then were lost in darkness. This promised well, and their eyes came back to Pine Tree, who was still sleeping. Then Dick became conscious of a beam of light, or rather two beams. These beams shot straight from the open eyes of Pine Tree, who was not asleep at all. The next instant Pine Tree opened his mouth, uttered a yell that was amazingly loud and piercing, and leaped straight for the two boys.

As neither Dick nor Albert had arms, they could do nothing but run, and they fled between the lodges at great speed, Pine Tree hot upon their heels. It amazed Dick to find that the whole population of a big town could awake so quickly. Warriors, squaws, and children swarmed from the lodges and fell upon him and Albert in a mass. He could only see in the darkness that Albert had been seized and dragged away, but he knew that two uncommonly strong old squaws had him by the hair, three half-grown boys were clinging to his legs, and a powerful warrior laid hold of his right shoulder. He deemed it wisest in such a position to yield as quickly and gracefully as he could, in the hope that the two wiry old women would be detached speedily from his hair. This object was achieved as soon as the Sioux saw that he did not resist, and the vigilant Pine Tree stood before him, watching with an expression that Dick feared could be called a grin.

"The honours are yours," said Dick as politely as he could, "but tell me what has become of my brother."

"He is being taken to the other side of the river," said the voice of Bright Sun over Pine Tree's shoulder, "and he and you will be kept apart until we decide what to do with you. It was foolish in you to attempt to escape. I had warned you."

"I admit it," said Dick, "but you in my place would have done the same. One can only try."

He tried to speak with philosophy, but he was sorely troubled over being separated from his brother. Their comradeship in captivity had been a support to each other.

There was no sympathy in the voice of Bright Sun. He spoke coldly, sternly, like a great war chief. Dick understood, and was too proud to make any appeal. Bright Sun said a few words to the warriors, and walked away.

Dick was taken to another and larger lodge, in which several warriors slept. There, after his arms were securely bound, he was allowed to lie down on a rush mat, with warriors on rush mats on either side of him. Dick was not certain whether the warriors slept, but he knew that he did not close his eyes again that night.

Although strong and courageous, Dick Howard suffered much mental torture. Bright Sun was a Sioux, wholly an Indian (he had seen that at the sun dance), and if Albert and he were no longer of any possible use as hostages, Bright Sun would not trouble himself to protect them. He deeply regretted their wild attempt at escape, which he had felt from the first was almost hopeless. Yet he believed, on second thought, that they had been justified in making the trial. The great sun dance, the immense gathering of warriors keyed for battle, showed the imminent need for warning to the white commanders, who would not dream that the Sioux were in such mighty force. Between this anxiety and that other one for Albert, thinking little of himself meanwhile, Dick writhed in his bonds. But he could do nothing else.

The warriors rose from their rush mats at dawn and ate flesh of the buffalo and deer and their favourite *wa-nsa*. Dick's arms were unbound, and he, too, was allowed to eat; but he had little appetite, and when the warriors saw that he had finished they bound him again.

"What are you going to do to me?" asked Dick in a kind of vague curiosity.

No one gave any answer. They did not seem to hear him. Dick fancied that some of them understood English, but chose to leave him in ignorance. He resolved to imitate their own stoicism and wait. When they bound his arms again, and his feet also, he made no resistance, but lay down quietly on the rush mat and gazed with an air of indifference at the skin wall of the lodge. All warriors went out, except one, who sat in the doorway with his rifle on his knee.

"They flatter me," thought Dick. "They must think me of some importance or that I'm dangerous, since they bind and guard me so well."

His thongs of soft deerskin, while secure, were not galling. They neither chafed nor prevented the circulation, and when he grew tired of lying in one position he could turn into another. But it was terribly hard waiting. He did not know what was before him. Torture or death? Both, most likely. He tried to be resigned, but how could one be resigned when one was so young and so strong? The hum of the village life came to him, the sound of voices, the tread of feet, the twang of a boyish bowstring, but the guard in the doorway never stirred. It seemed to Dick that the Sioux, who wore very little clothing, was carved out of reddish-brown stone. Dick wondered if he would ever move, and lying on his back he managed to raise his head a little on the doubled corner of the rush mat, and watch that he might see.

Bound, helpless, and shut off from the rest of the world, this question suddenly became vital to him: Would that Indian ever move, or would he not? He must have been sitting in that position at least two hours. Always he stared straight before him, the muscles on his bare arms never quivered in the slightest, and the rifle lay immovable across knees which also were bare. How could he do it? How could he have such control over his nerves and body? Dick's mind slowly filled with wonder, and then he began to have a suspicion that the Sioux was not real, merely some phantom of the fancy, or that he himself was dreaming. It made him angry—angry at himself, angry at the Sioux, angry at everything. He closed his eyes, held them tightly shut for five minutes, and then opened them again. The Sioux was still there. Dick was about to break through his assumed stoicism and shout at the warrior, but he checked himself, and with a great effort took control again of his wandering nerves.

He knew now that the warrior was real, and that he must have moved some time or other, but he did not find rest of spirit. A shaft of sunshine by and by entered the narrow door of the lodge and fell across Dick himself. He knew that it must be a fair day, but he was sorry for it. The sun ought not to shine when he was at such a pass.

Another interminable period passed, and an old squaw entered with a bowl of wa-nsa, and behind her came Lone Wolf, who unbound Dick.

"What's up now, Mr. Lone Wolf?" asked Dick with an attempt at levity. "Is it a fight or a foot race?"

"Eat," replied Lone Wolf sententiously, pointing of the bowl wa-nsa. "You will need your strength."

Dick's heart fell at these words despite all his self-command. "My time's come," he thought. He tried to eat—in fact, he forced himself to eat—that Lone Wolf might not think that he quailed, and when he had eaten as much as his honour seemed to demand he stretched his muscles and said to Lone Wolf, with a good attempt at indifference:

"Lead on, my wolfish friend. I don't know what kind of a welcome mine is going to be, but I suppose it is just as well to find out now."

The face of Lone Wolf did not relax. He seemed to have a full appreciation of what was to come and no time for idle jests. He merely pointed to the doorway, and Dick stepped into the sunshine. Lying so long in the dusky lodge, he was dazzled at first by the brilliancy of the day, but when his sight grew stronger he beheld a multitude about him. The women and children began to chatter, but the warriors were silent. Dick saw that he was the centre of interest, and was quite sure that he was looking upon his last sun. "O Lord, let me die bravely!" was his silent prayer.

He resolved to imitate as nearly as he could the bearing of an Indian warrior in his position, and made no resistance as Lone Wolf led him on, with the great thong following. He glanced around once for Bright Sun, but did not see him. The fierce chief whom they called Ite-Moga' Ju (Rain-in-the-Face) seemed to be in charge of Dick's fate, and he directed the proceedings.

But stoicism could not prevail entirely, and Dick looked about him again. He saw the yellow waters of the river with the sunlight playing upon them; the great village stretching away on either shore until it was hidden by the trees and undergrowth; the pleasant hills and all the pleasant world, so hard to leave. His eyes dwelt particularly upon the hill, a high one, overlooking the whole valley of the Little Big Horn, and the light was so clear that he could see every bush and shrub waving there.

His eyes came back from the hill to the throng about him. He had felt at times a sympathy for the Sioux because the white man was pressing upon them, driving them from their ancient hunting grounds that they loved; but they were now wholly savage and cruel—men, women, and children alike. He hated them all.

Dick was taken to the summit of one of the lower hills, on which he could be seen by everybody and from which he could see in a vast circle. He was tied in a peculiar manner. His hands remained bound behind him, but his feet were free. One end of a stout rawhide was secured around his waist and the other around a sapling, leaving him a play of about a half yard. He could not divine the purpose of this, but he was soon to learn.

Six half-grown boys, with bows and arrows, then seldom used by grown Sioux, formed a line at a little distance from him, and at a word from Rain-in-the-Face levelled their bows and fitted arrow to the string. Dick thought at first they were going to slay him at once, but he remembered that the Indian did not do things that way. He knew it was some kind of torture and although he shivered he steadied his mind to face it.

Rain-in-the-Face spoke again, and six bowstrings twanged. Six arrows whizzed by Dick, three on one side and three on the other, but all so close that, despite every effort of will, he shrank back against the sapling. A roar of laughter came from the crowd, and Dick flushed through all the tan of two years in the open air. Now he understood why the rawhide allowed him so much play. It was a torture of the nerves and of the mind. They would shoot their arrows by him, graze him perhaps if he stood steady, but if he sought to evade through fear, if he sprang either to one side or the other, they might strike in a vital spot.

He summoned up the last ounce of his courage, put his back against the sapling and resolved that he would not move, even if an arrow carried some of his skin with it. The bowstrings twanged again, and again six arrows whistled by. Dick quivered, but he did not move, and some applause came from the crowd. Although it was the applause of enemies, of barbarians, who wished to see him suffer, it encouraged Dick. He would endure everything and he would not look at these cruel faces; so he fixed his eyes on the high hill and did not look away when the bowstrings twanged a third time. As before, he heard the arrows whistle by him, and the shiver came into his blood, but his will did not let it extend to his body. He kept his eyes fixed upon the hill, and suddenly a speck appeared before them. No, it was not a speck, and, incredible as it seemed, Dick was sure that he saw a horseman come around the base of the hill and stop there, gazing into the valley upon the great village and the people thronging about the bound boy.

A second and third horseman appeared, and Dick could doubt no longer. They were white cavalrymen in the army uniform, scouts or the vanguard, he knew not what. Dick held his breath, and again that shiver came into his blood. Then he heard and saw an extraordinary thing. A singular deep, long-drawn cry came from the multitude in unison, a note of surprise and mingled threat. Then all whirled about at the same moment and gazed at the horsemen at the base of the hill.

The cavalrymen quickly turned back, rode around the hill and out of sight. Dozens of warriors rushed forward, hundreds ran to the lodges for more weapons and ammunition, the women poured in a stream down toward the river and away, the boys with the bows and arrows disappeared, and in a few minutes Dick was left alone.

Unnoticed, but bound and helpless, the boy stood there on the little hill, while the feverish life, bursting now into a turbulent stream, whirled and eddied around him.

CHAPTER 18

The Circle of Death

The quiver in Dick's blood did not cease now. He forgot for the time being that he was bound, and stood there staring at the hill where three horsemen had been for a few vivid moments. These men must be proof that a white army was near; but would this army know what an immense Sioux force was waiting for it in the valley of the Little Big Horn?

He tried to take his eyes away from the hill, but he could not. He seemed to know every tree and shrub on it. There at the base, in that slight depression, the three horsemen had stood, but none came to take their place. In the Indian village an immense activity was going on, both on Dick's side of the river and the other. A multitude of warriors plunged into the undergrowth on the far bank of the stream, where they lay hidden, while another multitude was gathering on this side in front of the lodges. The gullies and ravines were lined with hordes. The time was about two in the afternoon.

A chief appeared on the slope not far from Dick. It was Bright Sun in all the glory of battle array, and he glanced at the tethered youth. Dick's glance met his, and he saw the shadow of a faint, superior smile on the face of the chief. Bright Sun started to say something to a warrior, but checked himself. He seemed to think that Dick was secured well enough, and he did not look at him again. Instead, he gazed at the base of the hill where the horsemen had been, and while he stood there he was joined by the chiefs Rain-in-the-Face and Young-Man-Afraid-of-His-Horses.

Dick never knew how long a time passed while they all waited. The rattle of arms, the shouts, and the tread of feet in the village ceased. There was an intense, ominous silence broken only, whether in fact or fancy Dick could not tell, by the heavy breathing of thousands. The sun came out more brightly and poured its light over the town and the river, but it did not reveal the army of the Sioux swallowed up in the undergrowth on the far bank. So well were they hidden that their arms gave back no gleam.

Dick forgot where he was, forgot that he was bound, so tense were the moments and so eagerly did he watch the base of the hill. When a long time—at least, Dick thought it so—had passed, a murmur came from the village below. The men were but scouts and had gone away, and no white army was near. That was Dick's own thought, too.

As the murmur sank, Dick suddenly straightened up. The black speck appeared again before his eyes. New horsemen stood where the three had been, and behind them was a moving mass, black in the sun. The white army had come!

Bright Sun suddenly turned upon Dick a glance so full of malignant triumph that the boy shuddered. Then, clear and full over the valley rose the battle cry of the trumpets, a joyous inspiring sound calling men on to glory or death. Out from the hill came the moving mass of white horsemen, rank after rank, and Dick saw one in front, a man with long yellow hair, snatch off his hat, wave it around his head, and come on at a gallop. Behind him thundered the whole army, stirrup to stirrup.

Bright Sun, Rain-in-the-Face, and Young-Man-Afraid-of-His-Horses darted away, and then Dick thought of the freedom that he wanted so much. They were his people coming so gallantly down the valley, and he should be there. He pulled at the rawhide, but it would not break; he tried to slip his wrists loose, but they would not come; and, although unnoticed now, he was compelled to stand there, still a prisoner, and merely see.

The horsemen came on swiftly, a splendid force riding well—trained soldiers, compact of body and ready of hand. The slope thundered with their hoofbeats as they came straight toward the river. Dick drew one long, deep breath of admiration, and then a terrible fear assailed him. Did these men who rode so well know unto what they were riding?

The stillness prevailed yet a little longer in the Indian village. The women and children were again running up the river, but they were too far away for Dick to hear them, and he was watching his own army. Straight on toward the river rode the horsemen, with the yellow-haired general at their head, still waving his hat. Strong and mellow, the song of the trumpet again sang over the valley, but the terrible fear at Dick's heard grew.

It was obvious to the boy that the army of Custer intended to cross the river, here not more than two feet deep, but on their flank was the deadly quicksand and on the opposite shore facing them the hidden warriors lay in the hundreds. Dick pulled again at his bonds and began to shout: "Not there! Not there! Turn away!" But his voice was lost in the pealing of the trumpets and the hoof beats of many horses.

They were nearing the river and the warriors were swarming on their flank, still held in leash by Bright Sun, while the great medicine man, Sitting Bull, the sweat pouring from his face, was making the most powerful medicine of his life. Nearer and nearer they rode, the undergrowth still waving gently and harmlessly in the light wind.

Dick stopped shouting. All at once he was conscious of its futility. Nobody heard him. Nobody heeded him. He was only an unnoticed spectator of a great event. He stood still now, back to the tree, gazing toward the river and the advancing force. Something wet dropped into his eye and he winked it away. It was the sweat from his own brow.

The mellow notes of the trumpet sang once more, echoing far over the valley, and the hoofs beat with rhythmic tread. The splendid array of blue-clad men was still unbroken. They still rode heel to heel and toe to toe, and across the river the dense undergrowth moved a little in the gentle wind, but disclosed nothing.

A few yards more and they would be at the water. Then Dick saw a long line of flame burst from the bushes, so vivid, so intense that it was like a blazing bar of lightening, and a thousand rifles seemed to crash as one. Hard on the echo of the great volley came the fierce war cry of the ambushed Sioux, taken up in turn by the larger force on the flank and swelled by the multitude of women and children farther back. It was to Dick like the howl of wolves about to leap on their prey, but many times stronger and fiercer.

The white army shivered under the impact of the blow, when a thousand unexpected bullets were sent into its ranks. All the front line was blown away, the men were shot from their saddles, and many of the horses went down with them. Others, riderless, galloped about screaming with pain and fright.

Although the little army shivered and reeled for a moment, it closed up again and went on toward the water. Once more the deadly rifle fire burst from the undergrowth, not a single volley now, but continuous, rising and falling a little perhaps, but always heavy, filling the air with singing metal and littering the ground with the wounded and the dead. The far side of the river was a sheet of fire, and in the red blaze the Sioux could be seen plainly springing about in the undergrowth.

The cavalrymen began to fire also, sending their bullets across the river as fast as they could pull the trigger, but they were attacked on the flank, too, by the vast horde of warriors, directed by the bravest of the Sioux chiefs, the famous Pizi (Gall), one of the most skilful and daring fighters the red race ever produced, a man of uncommon appearance, of great height, and with the legendary head of a Caesar. He now led on the horde with voice and gesture, and hurled it against Custer's force, which was reeling again under the deadly fire from the other shore of the Little Big Horn.

The shouting of the warriors and of the thousands of women and children who watched the battle was soon lost to Dick in the steady crash of the rifle fire which filled the whole valley—sharp, incessant, like the drum of thunder in the ear. A great cloud of smoke arose and drifted over the combatants, white and red, but this smoke was pierced by innumerable flashes of fire as the red swarms pressed closer and the white replied.

Some flaw in the wind lifted the smoke and sent it high over the heads of all. Dick saw Custer, the general with the yellow hair, still on horseback and apparently unwounded, but the little army had stopped. It had been riddled already by the rifle fire from the undergrowth and could not cross the river. The dead and wounded on the ground had increased greatly in numbers, and the riderless horses galloped everywhere. Some of them rushed blindly into the Indian ranks, where they were seized.

Three or four troopers had fallen or plunged into the terrible quicksand on the other flank, and as Dick looked they were slowly swallowed up. He shut his eyes, unable to bear the sight, and when he opened them he did not see the men any more.

The smoke flowed in again and then was driven away once more. Dick saw that all of Custer's front ranks were now dismounted, and were replying to the fire from the other side of the river. Undaunted by the terrible trap into which they had ridden they came so near to the bank that many of them were slain there, and their bodies fell into the water, where they floated.

Dick saw the yellow-haired leader wave his hat again, and the front troopers turned back from the bank. The whole force turned with them. All who yet lived or could ride now sprang from their horses, firing at the same time into the horde about them. Their ranks were terribly thinned, but they still formed a compact body, despite the rearing and kicking of the horses, many of which were wounded also.

Dick was soldier enough to know what they wished to do. They were trying to reach the higher ground, the hills, where they could make a better defence, and he prayed mutely that they might do it.

The Sioux saw, too, what was intended, and they gave forth a yell so full of ferocity and exultation that Dick shuddered from head to foot. The yell was taken up by the fierce squaws and boys who hovered in the rear, until it echoed far up and down the banks of the Little Big Horn.

The white force, still presenting a steady front and firing fast, made way. The warriors between them and the hill which they seemed to be seeking were driven back, but the attack on their rear, and now on both flanks, grew heavier and almost unbearable. The outer rim of Custer's army was continually being cut off, and when new men took the places of the others they, too, were shot down. His numbers and the space on which they stood were reduced steadily, yet they did not cease to go on, although the pace became slower. It was like a wounded beast creeping along and fighting with tooth and claw, while the hunters swarmed about him in numbers always increasing.

Custer bore diagonally to the left, going, in the main, downstream, but a fresh force was now thrown against him. The great body of warriors who had been hidden in the undergrowth on the other side of the Little Big Horn crossed the stream when he fell back and flung themselves upon his flank and front. He was compelled now to stop, although he had not gone more than four hundred yards, and Dick, from his hill, saw the actions of the troops.

They stood there for perhaps five minutes firing into the Sioux, who were now on every side. They formed a kind of hollow square with some of the men in the centre holding the horses, which were kicking and struggling and adding to the terrible confusion. The leader with the yellow hair was yet alive. Dick saw him plainly, and knew by his gestures that he was still cheering on his men.

A movement now took place. Dick saw the white force divided. A portion of it deployed in a circular manner to the left, and the remainder turned in a similar fashion to the right, although they did not lose touch. The square was now turned into a rude circle with the horses still in the centre. They stood on a low hill, and so far as Dick could see they would not try to go any farther. The fire of the defenders had sunk somewhat, but he saw the men rushing to the horses for the extra ammunition— that was why they hung to the horses—and then the fire rose again in intensity and volume.

Confident in their numbers and the success that they had already won, the Sioux pressed forward from every side in overwhelming masses. All the great chiefs led them—Gall, Crazy Horse, Young-Man-Afraid-of-His-Horses, Grass, and the others. Bright Sun continually passed like a flame, inciting the hordes to renewed attacks, while the redoubtable Sitting Bull never ceased to make triumphant medicine. But it was Gall, of the magnificent head and figure, the very model of a great savage warrior, who led at the battle front. Reckless of death, but always unwounded, he led the Sioux up to the very muzzles of the white rifles, and when they were driven back he would lead them up again. Dick had heard all his life that Indians would not charge white troops in the open field, but here they did it, not one time, but many.

Dick believed that if he were to die that moment the picture of that terrible scene would be found photographed upon his eyeballs. It had now but little form or feature for him. All he could see was the ring of his own blue-clad people in the centre and everywhere around them the howling thousands, men mostly naked to the breechclout, their bodies wet with the sweat of their toiling, and their eyes filled with the fury of the savage in victorious battle—details that he could not see, although they were there. Alike over the small circle and the vast one inclosing it the smoke drifted in great clouds, but beneath it the field was lit up by the continuous red flash of the rifles. Dick wondered that anybody could live where so many bullets were flying in the air; yet there was Custer's force, cut down much more, but the core of it still alive and fighting, while the Sioux were so numerous that they did not miss their own warriors who had fallen, although there were many.

The unbroken crash of the rifle fire had gone on so long now that Dick scarcely noticed it, nor did he heed the great howling of the squaws farther up the stream. He was held by what his eyes saw, and he did not take them from the field for an instant. He saw one charge, a second and third hurled back, and although he was not conscious of it he shouted aloud in joy.

"They'll drive them off! They'll drive them off for good!" he exclaimed, although in his heart he never believed it.

The wind after a while took another change, and the dense clouds of smoke hung low over the field, hiding for the time the little white army that yet fought. Although Dick could see nothing now, he still gazed into the heart of the smoke bank. He did not know then that a second battle was in progress on the other side of the town. Custer before advancing had divided his force, giving a little more than half of it to Reno, who, unconscious of Custer's deadly peril, was now being beaten off. Dick had no thought for anything but Custer, not even of his own fate. Would they drive the Sioux away? He ran his tongue over his parched lips and tugged at the bonds that held his wrists.

The wind rose again and blew the smoke to one side. The battlefield came back into the light, and Dick saw that the white force still fought. But many of the men were on their knees now, using their revolvers, and Dick feared the terrible event that really happened—their ammunition was giving out, and the savage horde, rimming them on all sides, was very near.

He did not know how long the battle had lasted, but it seemed many hours to him. The sun was far down in the west, gilding the plains and hills with tawny gold, but the fire and smoke of conflict filled the whole valley of the Little Big Horn. "Perhaps night will save those who yet live," thought Dick. But the fire of the savages rose. Fresh ammunition was brought to them, and after every repulse they returned to the attack, pressing closer at every renewal.

Dick saw the leader at the edge of the circle almost facing his hill. His hat was gone, and his long yellow hair flew wildly, but he still made gestures to his men and bade them fight on. Then Dick lost him in the turmoil, but he saw some of the horses pull loose from the detaining hands, burst through the circle, and plunge among the Sioux.

Now came a pause in the firing, a sudden sinking, as if by command, and the smoke thinned. The circle which had been sprouting flame on every side also grew silent for a moment, whether because the enemy had ceased or the cartridges were all gone Dick never knew. But it was the silence of only an instant. There was a tremendous shout, a burst of firing greater than any that had gone before, and the whole Sioux horde poured forward.

The warriors, charging in irresistible masses from side to side, met in the centre, and when the smoke lifted from the last great struggle Dick saw only Sioux.

Of all the gallant little army that had charged into the valley not a soul was now living, save a Crow Indian scout, who, when all was lost, let down his hair after the fashion of a Sioux, and escaped in the turmoil as one of their own people.

CHAPTER 19

A Happy Meeting

When Dick Howard saw that the raging Sioux covered the field and that the little army was destroyed wholly he could bear the sight no longer, and, reeling back against the tree, closed his eyes. For a little while, even with eyes shut, he still beheld the red ruin, and then darkness came over him.

He never knew whether he really fainted or whether it was merely a kind of stupor brought on by so many hours of battle and fierce excitement, but when he opened his eyes again much time had passed. The sun was far down in the west and the dusky shadows were advancing. Over the low hill where Custer had made his last stand the Sioux swarmed, scalping until they could scalp no more. Behind them came thousands of women and boys, shouting from excitement and the drunkenness of victory.

It was all incredible, unreal to Dick, some hideous nightmare that would soon pass away when he awoke. Such a thing as this could not be! Yet it was real, it was credible, he was awake and he had seen it—he had seen it all from the moment that the first trooper appeared in the valley until the last fell under the overwhelming charge of the Sioux. He still heard, in the waning afternoon, their joyous cries over their great victory, and he saw their dusky forms as they rushed here and there over the field in search of some new trophy.

Dick was not conscious of any physical feeling at all—neither weariness, nor fear, nor thought of the future. It seemed to him that the world had come to an end with the ending of the day.

The shadows thickened and advanced. The west was a sea of dusk. The distant lodges of the village passed out of sight. The battlefield itself became dim and it was only phantom figures that roamed over it. All the while Dick was unnoticed, forgotten in the great event, and as the night approached the desire for freedom returned to him. He was again a physical being, feeling pain, and from habit rather than hope he pulled once more at the rawhide cords that held his wrists—he did not know that he had been tugging at them nearly all afternoon.

He wrenched hard and the unbelievable happened. The rawhide, strained upon so long, parted, and his hands fell to his side. Dick slowly raised his right wrist to the level of his eyes and looked at it, as if it belonged to another man. There was a red and bleeding ring around it where the rawhide had cut deep, making a scar that took a year in the fading, but his numbed nerves still felt no pain.

He let the right wrist sink back and raised the left one. It had the same red ring around it, and he looked at it curiously, wonderingly. Then he let the left also drop to his side, while he stood, back against the tree, looking vaguely at the dim figures of the Sioux who roamed about in the late twilight still in that hideous search for trophies.

It was while he was looking at the Sioux that an abrupt thought came to Dick. Those were his own wrists at which he had been looking. His hands were free! Why not escape in all this turmoil and excitement, with the friendly and covering night also at hand. It was like the touch of electricity. He was instantly alive, body and mind. He knew who he was and what had happened, and he wanted to get away. Now was the time!

The rawhide around Dick's waist was strong and it had been secured with many knots. He picked at it slowly and with greatest care, and all the time he was in fear lest the Sioux should remember him. But the sun was now quite down, the last bars of red and gold were gone, and the east as well as the west was in darkness. The field of battle was hidden and only voices came up from it. Two warriors passed on the slope of the hill and Dick, ceasing his work, shrank against the trunk of the tree, but they went on, and when they were out of sight he began again to pick at the knots.

One knot after another was unloosed, and at last the rawhide fell from his waist. He was free, but he staggered as he walked a little way down the slope of the hill and his fingers were numb. Yet his mind was wholly clear. It had recovered from the great paralytic shock caused by the sight of the lost battle, and he intended to take every precaution needed for escape.

He sat down in a little clump of bushes, where he was quite lost to view, and rubbed his limbs long and hard until the circulation was active. His wrists had stopped bleeding, and he bound about them little strips that he tore from his clothing. Then he threw away his cap—the Sioux did not wear caps, and he meant to look as much like a Sioux as he could. That was not such a difficult matter, as he was dressed in tanned skins, and wind and weather had made him almost as brown as an Indian.

Midway of the slope he stopped and looked down. The night had come, but the stars were not yet out. He could see only the near lodges, but many torches flared now over the battle field and in the village. He started again, bearing away from the hill on which Custer had fallen, but pursuing a course that led chiefly downstream. Once he saw dusky figures, but they took no notice of him. Once a hideous old squaw, carrying some terrible trophy in her hand, passed near, and Dick thought that all was lost. He was really more afraid at this time of the sharp eyes of the old squaws than those of the warriors. But she passed on, and Dick dropped down into a little ravine that ran from the field. His feet touched a tiny stream that trickled at the bottom of the ravine, and he leaped away in shuddering horror. The soles of his moccasins were now red.

But he made progress. He was leaving the village farther behind, and the hum of voices was not so loud. One of his greatest wishes now was to find arms. He did not intend to be recaptured, and if the Sioux came upon him he wanted at least to make a fight.

A dark shape among some short bushes attracted his attention. It looked like the form of a man, and when he went closer he saw that it was the body of a Sioux warrior, slain by a distant bullet from Custer's circle. His carbine lay beside him and he wore an ammunition belt full of cartridges. Dick, without hesitation, took both, and felt immensely strengthened. The touch of the rifle gave him new courage. He was a man now ready to meet men.

He reached another low hill and stood there a little while, listening. He heard an occasional whoop, and may lights flared here and there in the village, but no warrior was near. He saw on one side of him the high hill, at the base of which the first cavalrymen had appeared, and around which the army had ridden a little later to its fate. Dick was seized with a sudden unreasoning hatred of the hill itself, standing there black and lowering in the darkness. He shook his fist at it, and then, ashamed of his own folly, hurried his flight.

Everything was aiding him now. If any chance befell, that chance was in his favour. Swiftly he left behind the field of battle, the great Indian village, and all the sights and sounds of that fatal day, which would remain stamped on his brain as long as he lived. He did not stop until he was beyond the hills inclosing the valley, and then he bent back again toward the Little Big Horn. He intended to cross the river and return toward the village on the other side, having some dim idea that he might find and rescue Albert.

Dick was now in total silence. The moon and the stars were not yet out, but he had grown used to the darkness and he could see the low hills, the straggling trees, and the clumps of undergrowth. He was absolutely alone again, but when he closed his eyes he saw once more with all the vividness of reality that terrible battle field, the closing in of the circle of death, the last great rush of the Sioux horde, and the blotting out of the white force. He still heard the unbroken crash of the rifle fire that had continued for hours, and the yelling of the Sioux that rose and fell.

But when he opened his eyes the silence became painful, it was so heavy and oppressive. He felt lonely and afraid, more afraid than he had even been for himself while the battle was in progress. It seemed to him that he was pursued by the ghosts of the fallen, and he longed for the company of his own race.

Dick was not conscious of hunger or fatigue. His nerves were still keyed too high to remember such things, and now he turned down to the Little Big Horn. Remembering the terrible quicksand, he tried the bank very gingerly before he stepped into the water. It was sandy, but it held him, and then he waded in boldly, holding his rifle and belt of cartridges above his head. He knew that the river was not deep, but it came to his waist here, and once he stepped into a hole to his armpits, but he kept the rifle and cartridges dry. The waters were extremely cold, but Dick did not know it, and when he reached the desired shore he shook himself like a dog until the drops flew and then began the perilous task of returning to the village on the side farthest from Custer's battle.

He went carefully along the low, wooded shores, keeping well in the undergrowth, which was dense, and for an hour he heard and saw nothing of the Sioux. He knew why. They were still rejoicing over their great victory, and although he knew little of Indian customs he believed that the scalp dance must be in progress.

The moon and stars came out. A dark-blue sky, troubled by occasional light clouds, bent over him. He began at last to feel the effects of the long strain, mental and physical. His clothes were nearly dry on him, but for the first time he felt cold and weak. He went on, nevertheless; he had no idea of stopping even if he were forced to crawl.

He reached the crest of a low hill and looked down again on the Indian village, but from a point far from the hill on which he had stood during the battle. He saw many lights, torches and camp fires, and now and then dusky figures moving against the background of the flames, and then a great despair overtook him. To rescue Albert would be in itself difficult enough, but how was he ever to find him in that huge village, five miles long?

He did not permit his despair to last long. He would make the trial in some manner, how he did not yet know, but he must make it. He descended the low hill and entered a clump of bushes about fifty yards from the banks of the Little Big Horn. Here he stopped and quickly sank down. He had heard a rustling at the far edge of the clump, and he was sure, too, that he had seen a shadowy figure. The figure had disappeared instantly, but Dick was confident that a Sioux warrior was hidden in the bushes not ten yards away.

It was his first impulse to retreat as silently as he could, but the impulse swiftly gave way to a fierce anger. He remembered that he carried a rifle and plenty of cartridges, and he was seized with a sudden vague belief that he might strike a blow in revenge for the terrible loss of the day. It could be but a little blow, he could strike down only one, but he was resolved to do it—he had been through what few boys are ever compelled to see and endure, and his mind was not in its normal state.

He turned himself now into an Indian, crawling and creeping with deadly caution through the bushes, exercising an infinite patience that he might make no leaf or twig rustle, and now and then looking carefully over the tops of the bushes to see that his enemy had not fled. As he advanced he held his rifle well forward, that he might take instant aim when the time came.

Dick was a full ten minutes in travelling ten yards, and then he saw the dark figure of the warrior crouched low in the bushes. The Sioux had not seen him and was watching for his approach from some other point. The figure was dim, but Dick slowly raised his rifle and took careful aim at the head. His finger reached the trigger, but when it got there it refused to obey his will. He was not a savage; he was white, with the civilized blood of many generations, and he could not shoot down an enemy whose back was turned to him. But he maintained his aim, and using some old expression that he had heard he cried, "Throw up your hands!"

The crouching figure sprang to its feet, and a remembered voice exclaimed in overwhelming surprise and delight:

"Dick! Dick! Is that you, Dick?"

Dick dropped the muzzle of his rifle and stared. He could not take it in for the moment. It was Albert—a ragged, dirty, pale, and tired Albert, but a real live Albert just the same.

The brothers stared at each other by the same impulse, and then by the same impulse rushed forward, grasped each other's hands, wringing them and shouting aloud for joy.

"Is it you, Al? How on earth did you ever get here?"

"Is it you, Dick? Where on earth did you come from?"

They sat down in the bushes, both still trembling with excitement and the relief from suspense, and Dick told of the fatal day, how he had been bound to the tree on the hill, and how he had seen all the battle, from its beginning to the end, when no white soldier was left alive.

"Do you mean that they were all killed, Dick?" asked Albert in awed tones.

"Every one," replied Dick. "There was a ring of fire and steel around them through which no man could break. But they were brave, Al, they were brave! They beat off the thousands of that awful horde for hours and hours."

"Who led them?"

"I don't know. I had no way of knowing, but it was a gallant man with long yellow hair. I saw him with his hat off, waving it to encourage his men. Now tell me, Al, how you got here."

"When they seized us," replied Albert, "they carried me, kicking and fighting as best I could, up the river. I made up my mind that I'd never see you again, Dick, as I was sure that they'd kill you right away. I expected them to finish me up, too, soon, but they didn't. I suppose it was because they were busy with bigger things.

"They pushed me along for at least two miles. Then they crossed the river, shoved me into a bark lodge, and fastened the door on me. They didn't take the trouble to bind me, feeling sure, I suppose, that I couldn't get out of the lodge and the village, too; and I certainly wouldn't have had any chance to do it if a battle hadn't begun after I had been there a long time in the darkness of the lodge. I thought at first that it was the Sioux firing at targets, but then it became too heavy and there was too much shouting.

"The firing went on a long time, and I pulled and kicked for an hour at the lodge door. Because no one came, no matter how much noise I made, I knew that something big was going on, and I worked all the harder. When I looked out at last, I saw many warriors running up and down and great clouds of smoke. I sneaked out, got into a smoke bank just as a Sioux shot at me, lay down in a little ravine, after a while jumped up and ran again through the smoke, and reached the bushes, where I lay hidden flat on my face until the night came. While I was there I heard the firing die down and saw our men driven off after being cut up badly."

"It's awful! awful!" groaned Dick. "I didn't know there were so many Sioux in the world, and maybe our generals didn't, either. That must have been the trouble."

"When the darkness set in good," resumed Albert. "I started to run. I knew that no Sioux were bothering about me then, but I tell you that I made tracks, Dick. I had no arms, and I didn't know where I was going; but I meant to leave those Sioux some good miles behind. After a while I got back part of my courage, and then I came back here to look around for you, thinking you might have just such a chance as I did."

"Brave old Al," said Dick.

"You came, too."

"I was armed and you were not."

"It comes to the same thing, and you did have the chance."

"Yes, and we're together again. We've been saved once more, Al, when the others have fallen. Now the thing for us to do is to get away from here as fast as we can. Which way do you think those troops on your side of the village retreated?"

Albert extended his finger toward a point on the dusky horizon.

"Off there somewhere," he replied.

"Then we'll follow them. Come on."

The two left the bushes and entered the hills.

CHAPTER 20

Bright Sun's Goodbye

Dick and Albert had not gone far before they saw lights on the bluffs of the Little Big Horn. Dick had uncommonly keen eyes, and when he saw a figure pass between him and the firelight he was confident that it was not that of a Sioux. The clothing was too much like a trooper's.

"Stop, Al," he said, putting his hand on his brother's shoulder. "I believe some of our soldiers are here."

The two crept as near as they dared and watched until they saw another figure pause momentarily against the background of the firelight.

"It's a trooper, sure," said Dick, "and we've come to our own people at last. Come, Al, we'll join them."

They started forward on a run. There was a flash of flame, a report, and a bullet whistled between them.

"We're friends, not Sioux!" shouted Dick. "We're escaping from the savages! Don't fire!"

They ran forward again, coming boldly into the light, and no more shots were fired at them. They ran up the slope to the crest of the bluff, leaped over a fresh earthwork, and fell among a crowd of soldiers in blue. Dick quickly raised himself to his feet, and saw soldiers about him, many of them wounded, all of them weary and drawn. Others were hard at work with pick and spade, and from a distant point of the earthwork came the sharp report of rifle shots. These were the first white men that Dick and Albert had seen in nearly two years, and their hearts rose in their throats.

"Who are you?" asked a lieutenant, holding up a lantern and looking curiously at the two bare-headed, brown, and half-wild youths who stood before him in their rough attire of tanned skins. They might readily have passed in the darkness for young Sioux warriors.

"I am Dick Howard," replied Dick, standing up as straight as his weakness would let him, "and this is my brother Albert. We were with an emigrant trail, all the rest of which was massacred two years ago by the Sioux. Since then we have been in the mountains, hunting and trapping."

The lieutenant looked at him suspiciously. Dick still stood erect and returned his gaze, but Albert, overpowered by fatigue, was leaning against the earthwork. A half dozen soldiers stood near, watching them curiously. From the woods toward the river came the sound of more rifle shots.

"Where have you come from tonight? And how?" asked the lieutenant sharply.

"We escaped from the Sioux village," replied Dick. "I was in one part of it and my brother in another. We met by chance or luck in the night, but in the afternoon I saw all the battle in which the army was destroyed."

"Army destroyed! What do you mean?" exclaimed the officer. "We were repulsed, but we are here. We are not destroyed."

The suspicion in his look deepened, but Dick met him with unwavering eye.

"It was on the other side of the town," he replied. "Another army was there. It was surrounded by thousands of Sioux, but it perished to the last man. I saw them gallop into the valley, led by a general with long yellow hair."

"Custer!" exclaimed some one, and a deep groan came from the men in the dusk.

"What nonsense is this!" exclaimed the officer. "Do you dare tell me that Custer and his entire command have perished?"

Dick felt his resentment rising.

"I tell you only the truth," he said. "There was a great battle, and our troops, led by a general with long yellow hair, perished utterly. The last one of them is dead. I saw it all with my own eyes."

Again that deep groan came from the men in the dusk.

"I can't believe it!" exclaimed the lieutenant. "Custer and whole force dead! Where were you? How did you see all this?"

"The Sioux had tied me to a tree in order that the Indian boys might amuse themselves by grazing me with arrows—my brother and I had been captured when we were on the plains—but they were interrupted by the appearance of troops in the valley. Then the battle began. It lasted a long time, and I was forgotten. About twilight I managed to break loose, and I escaped by hiding in the undergrowth. My brother, who was on the other side of town, escaped in much the same way."

"Sounds improbable, very improbable!" muttered the lieutenant.

Suddenly an old sergeant, who had been standing near, listening attentively, exclaimed:

"Look at the boy's wrists, lieutenant! They've got just the marks than an Indian rawhide would make!"

Dick impulsively held up his wrists, from which the bandages had fallen without his notice. A deep red ring encircled each, and it was obvious from their faces that others believed, even if the lieutenant did not. But he, too, dropped at least a part of his disbelief.

"I cannot deny your story of being captives among the Sioux," he said, "because you are white and the look of your eyes is honest. But you must be mistaken about Custer. They cannot all have fallen; it was your excitement that made you think it."

Dick did not insist. He was the bearer of bad news, but he would not seek to make others believe it if they did not wish to do so. The dreadful confirmation would come soon enough.

"Take them away, Williams," said the lieutenant to the sergeant, "and give them food and drink. They look as if they needed it."

The sergeant was kindly, and he asked Dick and Albert many questions as he led them to a point farther back on the bluff beyond the rifle shots of the Sioux, who were now firing heavily in the darkness upon Reno's command, the troops driven off from the far side of the town, and the commands of Benteen and McDougall, which had formed a junction with Reno. It was evident that he believed all Dick told him, and his eyes became heavy with sorrow.

"Poor lads!" he murmured. "And so many of them gone!"

He took them to a fire, and here both of them collapsed completely. But with stimulants, good food, and water they recovered in an hour, and then Dick was asked to tell again what he had seen to the chief officers. They listened attentively, but Dick knew that they, too, went away incredulous.

Throughout the talk Dick and Albert heard the sound of pick and spade as the men continued to throw up the earthworks, and there was an incessant patter of rifle fire as the Sioux crept forward in the darkness, firing from every tree, or rock, or hillock, and keeping up a frightful yelling, half of menace and half of triumph. But their bullets whistled mostly overhead, and once, when they made a great rush, they were quickly driven back with great loss. Troops on a bluff behind earthworks were a hard nut even for an overwhelming force to crack.

Dick and Albert fell asleep on the ground from sheer exhaustion, but Dick did not sleep long. He was awakened by a fresh burst of firing, and saw that it was still dark. He did not sleep again that night, although Albert failed to awake, and, asking for a rifle, bore a part in the defence.

The troops, having made a forced march with scant supplies, suffered greatly from thirst, but volunteers, taking buckets, slipped down to the river, at the imminent risk of torture and death, and brought them back filled for their comrades. It was done more than a dozen times, and Dick himself was one of the heroes, which pleased Sergeant Williams greatly.

"You're the right stuff, my boy," he said, clapping him on the shoulder, "though you ought to be asleep and resting."

"I couldn't sleep long," replied Dick. "I think my nerves have been upset so much that I won't feel just right again for months."

Nevertheless he bore a valiant part in the defence, besides risking his life to obtain the water, and won high praise from many besides his stanch friend, Sergeant Williams. It was well that the troops had thrown up the earthwork, as the Sioux, flushed with their great victory in the afternoon, hung on the flanks of the bluffs and kept up a continuous rifle fire. There was light enough for sharpshooting, and more than one soldier who incautiously raised his head above the earthwork was slain.

Toward morning the Sioux made another great rush. There had been a lull in the firing just when the night was darker than usual and many little black clouds were floating up from the southwest. Dick was oppressed by the silence. He remembered the phases of the battle in the afternoon, and he felt that it portended some great effort by the Sioux. He peeped carefully over the earthwork and studied the trees, bushes, and hillocks below. He saw nothing there, but it seemed to him that he could actually feel the presence of the Sioux.

"Look out for 'em," he said to Sergeant Williams. "I think they're going to make a rush."

"I think it, too," replied the veteran. "I've learnt something of their cunnin' since I've been out here on the plains."

Five minutes later the Sioux sprang from their ambush and rushed forward, hoping to surprise enemies who had grown careless. But they were met by a withering fire that drove them headlong to cover again. Nevertheless they kept up the siege throughout all the following day and night, firing incessantly from ambush, and at times giving forth whoops full of taunt and menace. Dick was able to sleep a little during the day, and gradually his nerves became more steady. Albert also took a part in the defence, and, like Dick, he won many friends.

The day was a long and heavy one. The fortified camp was filled with the gloomiest apprehensions. The officers still refused to believe all of Dick's story, that Custer and every man of his command had perished at the hands of the Sioux. They were yet hopeful that his eyes had deceived him, a thing which could happen amid so much fire, and smoke, and excitement, and that only a part of Custer's force had fallen. Yet neither Custer nor any of his men returned; there was no sign of them anywhere, and below the bluffs the Sioux gave forth taunting shouts and flaunted terrible trophies.

Dick and Albert sat together about twilight before one of the camp fires, and Dick's face showed that he shared the gloom of those around him.

"What are you expecting, Dick?" asked Albert, who read his countenance.

"Nothing in particular," replied Dick; "but I'm hoping that help will come soon. I've heard from the men that General Gibbon is out on the plain with a strong force, and we need him bad. We're short of both water and food, and we'll soon be short of ammunition. Custer fell, I think, because his ammunition gave out, and if ours gives out the same thing will happen to us. It's no use trying to conceal it."

"Then we'll pray for Gibbon," said Albert.

The second night passed like the first, to the accompaniment of shouts and shots, the incessant sharpshooting of the Sioux, and an occasional rush that was always driven back. But it was terribly exhausting. The men were growing irritable and nervous under such a siege, and the anxiety in the camp increased.

Dick, after a good sleep, was up early on the morning of the second day, and, like others, he looked out over the plain in the hope that he might see Gibbon coming. He looked all around the circle of the horizon and saw only distant lodges in the valley and Sioux warriors. But Dick had uncommonly good ears, trained further by two years of wild life, and he heard something, a new note in the common life of the morning. He listened with the utmost attention, and heard it again. He had heard the same sound on the terrible day when Custer galloped into the valley— the mellow, pealing note of a trumpet, but now very faint and far.

"They're coming!" he said to Sergeant Williams joyfully. "I hear the sound of a trumpet out on the plain!"

"I don't," said the sergeant. "It's your hopes that are deceivin' you. No, by Jove, I think I do hear it! Yes, there it is! They're comin'! They're comin'!"

The whole camp burst into a joyous cheer, and although they did not hear the trumpet again for some time, the belief that help was at hand became a certainty when they saw hurried movements among the Sioux in the valley and the sudden upspringing of flames at many points.

"They're goin' to retreat," said the veteran Sergeant Williams, "an' they're burnin' their village behind 'em."

A little later the army of Gibbon, with infantry and artillery, showed over the plain, and was welcomed with cheers that came from the heart. Uniting with the commands on the fortified bluff, Gibbon now had a powerful force, and he advanced cautiously into the valley of the Little Big Horn and directly upon the Indian village. But the Sioux were gone northward, taking with them their arms, ammunition, and all movable equipment, and the lodges that they left behind were burning.

Dick led the force to the field of battle, and all his terrible story was confirmed. There were hundreds of brave men, Custer and every one of his officers among them, lay, most of them mutilated, but all with their backs to the earth.

The army spent the day burying the dead, and then began the pursuit of the Sioux. Dick and Albert went with them, fighting as scouts and skirmishers. They were willing, for the present, to let their furs remain hidden in their lost valley until they could gain a more definite idea of its location, and until the dangerous Sioux were driven far to the northward.

As the armies grew larger the Sioux forces, despite the skill and courage of their leaders, were continually beaten. Their great victory on the Little Big Horn availed them nothing. It became evident that the last of the chiefs—and to Dick and Albert this was Bright Sun—had made the last stand for his race, and had failed.

"They were doomed the day the first white man landed in America," said Dick to Albert, "and nothing could save them."

"I suppose it's so," said Albert; "but I feel sorry for Bright Sun, all the same."

"So do I," said Dick.

The Sioux were finally crowded against the Canadian line, and Sitting Bull and most of the warriors fled across it for safety. But just before the crossing Dick and Albert bore a gallant part in a severe skirmish that began before daylight. A small Sioux band, fighting in a forest with great courage and tenacity, was gradually driven back by dismounted white troopers. Dick, a skirmisher on the right flank, became separated from his comrades during the fighting. He was aware that the Sioux had been defeated, but, like the others, he followed in eager pursuit, wishing to drive the blow home.

Dick lost sight of both troopers and Sioux, but he became aware of a figure in the undergrowth ahead of him, and he stalked it. The warrior, for such he was sure the man to be, was unable to continue his flight without entering an open space where he would be exposed to Dick's bullet, and he stayed to meet his antagonist.

There was much delicate manoeuvring of the kind that must occur when lives are known to be at stake, but at last the two came within reach of each other. The Sioux fired first and missed, and then Dick held his enemy at the muzzle of his rifle. He was about to fire in his turn, when he saw that it was Bright Sun.

The chief, worn and depressed, recognized Dick at the same moment.

"Fire," he said. "I have lost and I might as well die by your hand as another."

Dick lowered his weapon.

"I can't do it, Bright Sun," he said. "My brother and I owe you our lives, and I've got to give you yours. Goodbye."

"But I am an Indian," said Bright Sun. "I will never surrender to your people."

"It is for you to say," replied Dick.

Bright Sun waved his hand in a grave and sad farewell salute and went northward. Dick heard from a trapper some time later of a small band of Sioux Indians far up near the Great Slave Lake, led by a chief of uncommon qualities. He was sure, from the description of this chief given by the trapper, that it was Bright Sun.

Their part in the war ended, Dick and Albert took for their pay a number of captured Indian ponies, and turning southward found the old trail of the train that had been slaughtered. Then, with the ponies, they entered their beloved valley again.

No one had come in their absence. Castle Howard, the Annex, the Suburban Villa, the Cliff House and all their treasures were undisturbed. They carried their furs to Helena, in Montana, where the entire lot was sold for thirty-two thousand dollars—a great sum for two youths.

"Now what shall we do?" said Albert when the money was paid to them.

"I vote we buy United States Government bonds," replied Dick, "register 'em in our names, and go back to the valley to hunt and trap. Of course people will find it after a while, but we may get another lot of the furs before anyone comes."

"Just what I'd have proposed myself," said Albert.

They started the next day on their ponies, with the pack ponies following, and reached their destination in due time. It was just about sunset when they descended the last slope and once more beheld their valley, stretching before them in all its beauty and splendour, still untrodden by any human footsteps save their own.

"What a fine place!" exclaimed Albert.

"The finest in the world!" said Dick.

LEONAUR

ALSO FROM LEONAUR
AVAILABLE IN SOFTCOVER OR HARDCOVER WITH DUST JACKET

THE COLLECTED SCIENCE FICTION AND FANTASY OF STANLEY G. WEINBAUM 1—INTERPLANETARY ODYSSEYS *by Stanley G. Weinbaum*—Classic Tales of Interplanetary Adventure Including: A Martian Odyssey, its Sequel Valley of Dreams, the Complete 'Ham' Hammond Stories and Others.

THE COLLECTED SCIENCE FICTION AND FANTASY OF STANLEY G. WEINBAUM 2—OTHER EARTHS *by Stanley G. Weinbaum*—Classic Futuristic Tales Including: *Dawn of Flame* & its Sequel The Black Flame, plus The Revolution of 1960 & Others.

THE COLLECTED SCIENCE FICTION AND FANTASY OF STANLEY G. WEINBAUM 3—STRANGE GENIUS *by Stanley G. Weinbaum*—Classic Tales of the Human Mind at Work Including the Complete Novel The New Adam, the 'van Manderpootz' Stories and Others.

THE COLLECTED SCIENCE FICTION AND FANTASY OF STANLEY G. WEINBAUM 4—THE BLACK HEART *by Stanley G. Weinbaum*—Classic Strange Tales Including: the Complete Novel The Dark Other, Plus Proteus Island and Others.

THE COLLECTED SCIENCE FICTION & FANTASY OF JACK LONDON 1—BEFORE ADAM & OTHER STORIES *by Jack London*—included in this Volume Before Adam The Scarlet Plague A Relic of the Pliocene When the World Was Young The Red One Planchette A Thousand Deaths Goliah A Curious Fragment The Rejuvenation of Major Rathbone.

THE COLLECTED SCIENCE FICTION & FANTASY OF JACK LONDON 2—THE IRON HEEL & OTHER STORIES *by Jack London*—included in this Volume The Iron Heel The Enemy of All the World The Shadow and the Flash The Strength of the Strong The Unparalleled Invasion The Dream of Debs.

THE COLLECTED SCIENCE FICTION & FANTASY OF JACK LONDON 3—THE STAR ROVER & OTHER STORIES *by Jack London*—included in this Volume The Star Rover The Minions of Midas The Eternity of Forms The Man With the Gash.

THE CRETAN TEAT *by Brian Aldiss*—The Cretan Teat is a wry and comic novel that interweaves its own fiction with an inner fiction about the discovery of a Byzantine painting of the Mother of the Blessed Virgin Mary suckling the infant Jesus and a fake ikon that becomes an instrument of Nemesis.

THE FIRST BOOK OF AYESHA *by H. Rider Haggard*—Contains *She & Ayesha: the Return of She.*

THE SECOND BOOK OF AYESHA *by H. Rider Haggard*—Contains *She and Allan & Wisdom's Daughter.*

QUATERMAIN: THE COMPLETE ADVENTURES—1 *by H. Rider Haggard*—Contains *King Solomon's Mines & Allan Quatermain.*

QUATERMAIN: THE COMPLETE ADVENTURES—2 *by H. Rider Haggard*—Contains *Allan's Wife, Maiwa's Revenge & Marie.*

QUATERMAIN: THE COMPLETE ADVENTURES—3 *by H. Rider Haggard*—Contains *Child of Storm & Allan and the Holy Flower.*

QUATERMAIN: THE COMPLETE ADVENTURES—4 *by H. Rider Haggard*—Contains *Finished & The Ivory Child.*

QUATERMAIN: THE COMPLETE ADVENTURES—5 *by H. Rider Haggard*—Contains *The Ancient Allan & She and Allan.*

QUATERMAIN: THE COMPLETE ADVENTURES—6 *by H. Rider Haggard*—Contains *Heu-Heu or, the Monster & The Treasure of the Lake.*

QUATERMAIN: THE COMPLETE ADVENTURES—7 *by H. Rider Haggard*—Contains *Allan and the Ice Gods, Four Short Adventures & Nada the Lily.*

TROS OF SAMOTHRACE 1: WOLVES OF THE TIBER *by Talbot Mundy*—55 B.C.--an adventurer set during the Roman invasion of Britain.

TROS OF SAMOTHRACE 2: DRAGONS OF THE NORTH *by Talbot Mundy*—55 B.C. —Caesar plots, Britons war among themselves and the Vikings are coming.

TROS OF SAMOTHRACE 3: SERPENT OF THE WAVES *by Talbot Mundy*—55 B.C.--Caesar is poised to invade Britain—only a grand strategy can foil him!.

TROS OF SAMOTHRACE 4: CITY OF THE EAGLES *by Talbot Mundy*—54 B.C.—Rome—Tros treads in the streets of his sworn enemies!.

TROS OF SAMOTHRACE 5: CLEOPATRA *by Talbot Mundy*—Tros and the Roman Empire turn to the Egypt of the Pharaohs.

TROS OF SAMOTHRACE 6: THE PURPLE PIRATE *by Talbot Mundy*—The epic saga of the ancient world—Tros of Samothrace—draws to a conclusion in this sixth—and final—volume.

www.ingramcontent.com/pod-product-compliance
Lightning Source LLC
Chambersburg PA
CBHW030349030726
47497CB00002B/245